The Greek Key

The Power

Colin Forbes writes a novel every year. For the past twenty-seven years he has earned his living solely as a full-time writer.

He visits all the locations which will appear in a new novel. Forbes says, 'It is essential for me to see for myself where the book will take place. Only in this way can I conjure up the unique atmosphere of the chosen locales.'

He has explored most of Western Europe, the East and West coasts of America, and has made excursions to Africa and Asia. Each new book appears on all major bestseller lists. He is translated into thirty languages.

Surveys have shown his readership is divided equally between women and men.

Colin Forbes 'Has no equal'
Sunday Mirror

COLIN FORBES

The Greek Key

The Power

PAN BOOKS

The Greek Key first published 1989 by William Collins Sons & Co. Ltd
First published by Pan Books 2000
The Power first published 1994 by Pan Books

This omnibus edition published 2004 by Pan Books
an imprint of Pan Macmillan Ltd
Pan Macmillan, 20 New Wharf Road, London N1 9RR
Basingstoke and Oxford
Associated companies throughout the world
www.panmacmillan.com

ISBN 0 330 43915 4

1 3 5 7 9 8 6 4 2

A CIP catalogue record for this book is available from
the British Library

Printed and bound in Great Britain by
Mackays of Chatham plc, Chatham, Kent

The Greek Key

The Greek Key

For Jane

AUTHOR'S NOTE

This novel is based on facts told to me about a strange and grim murder committed over forty years ago. *That murder remains unsolved to this day.*

It happened in Cairo in 1944 – inside a weird triangular-shaped building near the banks of the River Nile. Not only the building was weird: it housed a mix of army, naval and air force personnel, and secret units whose missions were unknown to the other inhabitants.

The story moves to the present day and all the facts are provided for the reader to identify who was responsible – but I emphasize that the characters portrayed are creatures of the author's imagination and bear no relationship to any living person. Also, the island of Siros – as described – does not exist.

CONTENTS

Prologue

Cairo, February 1944. Staff-Sergeant Higgins – 'Higgy' to his friends – had no warning this would be the last time he would ascend in the creaking lift climbing slowly to the fourth floor of the Antikhana Building.

At ten in the evening it was silent as a tomb within the walls of the three-sided building. The only sound was the ghostly creak of the old lift as it crawled upwards past deserted landings. Through the iron grille of the cage he could see the stone staircase which rose round the central lift shaft. It felt as though no one else was in the place – no one except the Sudanese receptionist behind his desk on the ground floor.

Not surprising if he was the first to get back, thought Higgy. The few military men who slept there occupied small bedrooms on the rooftop. And they rarely arrived back from drinking and eating in Cairo before eleven. Personally, he liked an early night . . .

He frowned as he slid the door of the cage shut when it had wobbled to a stop. They switched off the lights in the corridors running round the three sides of the building at seven. So where was the glow of light beyond the entrance to the corridor coming from?

He hesitated, listening. Normally he would head straight for one of the three spiral staircases at each corner of the building – the enclosed staircases which led to the rooftop. The light was gleaming from under the closed door at the end of the corridor. The Greek Unit's quarters.

He had no idea what Ionides, who had escaped from

11

German-occupied Greece, did. Something connected with propaganda, they said. He must have forgotten to turn off the light before leaving for his billet. Or he could just still be working.

Hitching up his khaki drill trousers, he walked quietly along the tiled passage. The first twinge of unease ruffled him when he thought he heard a noise from the room next to the last one. Also part of the Greek Unit's quarters, the two rooms were linked by an inner door. But no light glowed from under this second door. Who would be moving about in the dark?

He paused, grasped the handle, turned it slowly, pushed. The door wouldn't budge, was locked. He stiffened. He'd never known that door to be locked before when one of the Greek Unit was working.

Higgy walked a few paces further and stopped at the second door. Beyond, at the corridor's end, the black hole leading to the spiral staircase gaped. He took a grip on the handle of the door, turned it, entered. He froze.

At the last moment, it occurred to him it might be Ionides' colleague, Gavalas, who was working late. But it was Ionides all right. Except he wasn't all right.

Higgy had his share of battle-hardened courage. An ex-tank commander, he'd seen friends in the desert scorched to death in what they cynically called a 'brew-up'. Not the normal brew-up of tea – the fearsome sight of another tank, hit by a German shell, going up in flames. Locked inside their steel box, few escaped alive.

The office, with barred windows facing the native quarter across the street, looked as though a hurricane had struck it. Drawers were pulled out, contents scattered across the floor. Filing cabinets had been overturned. Crimson splashes smeared the white walls.

The black-haired young Ionides lay amid the carnage,

12

sprawled on the floor on top of a mess of papers. He was drenched with blood, his dark eyes stared sightless at the ceiling, his head had been almost severed from his neck, his face was slashed brutally, the weathered skin coated with more blood. Blood was everywhere – spattered across the desk where presumably he had been working. The splashes on the walls were more blood.

Higgy shivered. He closed the outer door. Six feet tall, well-built, twenty-eight years old, he stood motionless, gazing at the horror lying a few feet away. Then he remembered the noise he'd heard from the locked room. He stared at the communicating door. God! The maniac who had done this must be inside.

Panic gripped him. His first instinct was to haul open the outer door and run like hell for the roof up the spiral staircase. His throat felt parched. His hands trembled. The silence from the room beyond the communicating door was insidious, made him want to yell.

The silence went on: not a hint of a sound from behind that closed door. Higgy sucked in a deep breath. Had it been imagination, nerves tingling from the empty building? Had he, in fact, really heard anything? He glanced down and saw again the dreadful corpse which had recently been a living man. A black foot-long circular ruler of ebony lay on the floor. He picked it up, took a firmer hold of himself, walked towards the closed communicating door. Still no sound.

He was scared shitless. He was growing more convinced the next room was empty, but if the murderer was still there he wasn't going to let the bastard escape. Ionides was a nice chap, always liked a chat and a joke. Higgy held the ruler like a baton, reached for the door handle with his left hand.

If the killer was inside he was probably holding the knife used to inflict the terrible mutilations Ionides had suffered. The state of the office showed the Greek had fought for

13

his life. No, Higgy thought, should the assassin still be here I'm damned if I'm letting the swine get away.

He opened the door a few inches. The room beyond was dark. He reached his left hand inside, found the light switch, turned it on. Light flooded the second office and he pushed the door wide open, flat against the wall. His right foot tangled with something. A screwed-up bundle, a whole mess of it, and all the sheets were stained a darkish red. Blood.

He took a step inside the office often used by Gavalas. He had heard a rumour that Gavalas had gone on leave. There were no signs of disturbance in this room as far as he was able to see. He gripped the ruler tightly and walked in.

He walked across the empty office which showed no evidence of the ghastly death struggle behind him. He must report this at once. In his dazed state he tried to open the door leading to the corridor without turning the key. *It opened*.

The significance of this hit him like a second shock wave. The door had been locked when he had tried to open it from the corridor. The confirmation that the assassin had been hiding inside the darkened room minutes – moments – after completing his hideous act was too much for Higgy.

He felt his bowels loosening. Throwing open the door, he ran for the nearest toilet, locked the door. Afterwards he was never sure how long he sat on the lavatory.

He went back down through the deserted building by the stone staircase. The lift cage was a potential death-trap. The Sudanese receptionist stifled a yawn as he appeared at the foot of the stairs, gazing at the black ruler Higgy was still holding, sat up straight and adjusted his red fez.

'Who has left the building since I came in here?' Higgy demanded.

14

'No one, sir. I would have seen them. They have to pass my desk . . .'

'I know that. Who came into the building?'

'No one, sir,' the Sudanese replied in perfect English again. 'You are the only person here at the moment.'

'Selim. You fell asleep,' Higgy accused.

'No, sir,' Selim protested. 'The night shift is my usual duty. I sleep in the day.'

'Then call the SIB. Now! Urgently.'

'SIB?'

'Special Investigation Branch, idiot.' Higgy regretted the insult the second he had spoken. 'Just call them,' he repeated. 'Someone has been killed. I'll talk to them when you get them on the line.'

He sat on the stone steps while the Sudanese used the telephone. He felt washed out, drained. To stop his hands trembling in front of Selim he gripped the ebony ruler like a vice. And while he waited he kept asking himself the question. How could anyone have got into the building unnoticed when the only way in was the two huge double doors beyond Selim's desk?

Second Lieutenant Samuel Partridge of the SIB sat beside his chief, Captain Orde Humble, who drove the jeep slowly as they came close to the dirty grey Antikhana Building. It was the morning after the late night call from Sergeant Higgins and it was going to be another glorious sunny day.

'Seems we were here only five minutes ago,' Partridge remarked as a horse-drawn gharry with an Arab driver pulled up at the entrance to the building.

'Precisely three hours,' growled Humble and parked the jeep by the kerb.

Partridge, a one-pipper, twenty years old, wished once again he'd kept his mouth shut. Humble was fifty-six, ex-Scotland Yard, long-faced and pessimistic. He never

15

missed a chance to put Partridge in his place. The lowest of the low – one-pippers. Not that it was Partridge's fault he had been posted to the SIB at his youthful age. You didn't create fallen arches under your feet. Hauled out of his regiment by a medical officer who had spotted this physical defect. 'Feet like that. You can't wear Army boots, my lad . . .'

An attractive fair-haired girl in her late twenties, wearing a wide-brimmed straw hat, a blue frock, high-heeled shoes, paid off the gharry driver and started up the wide steps leading to the huge closed double doors. Partridge felt the adrenalin start to pump as he studied her snow-white skin.

Humble leapt out of the jeep and intercepted her. She stared arrogantly at him, reaching for the doorbell. A wrinkled face stared back from under the peaked military cap, his eyes cynical, the thin mouth of a man who has learned over the years to choose his words.

'Don't press that bell. You're not going in there. Who are you, anyway?'

'Flying Officer Malloy's wife. His unit is based here. And may I enquire your authority to order me about? Incidentally, who is that young boy getting out of your jeep?'

With appraising interest she watched Partridge alighting from the vehicle. A gaggle of Arab street urchins appearing from nowhere surrounded the jeep.

'This is my authority. SIB.' Humble waved his ID card in her face. 'A particularly unpleasant murder took place inside this building yesterday.'

'Not really? Some wog got in, I suppose. I tried to phone my husband and the operator refused to put me through. Such damned sauce.'

'Acting under orders, madam. No communication is permitted for the present. I suggest you go straight back to your married quarters.' He put two fingers in his mouth

16

and whistled down a passing gharry. 'There's your transport home.'

'You've a bloody nerve. I shall complain . . .'

As she strolled back down the steps Partridge was handing a few piastres to the leading urchin. 'Watch this jeep until we get back. If it's OK you get the same again.'

It was a necessary precaution. They could have returned to find the wheels missing. He had heard every word of the conversation between Humble and Mrs Malloy. He passed her on the way up the steps. She gave him a direct look with half-closed eyes and was gone.

'Barmy outfit, this one,' Humble complained as he thumbed the bell. 'Allowing women like that to visit the place. Our first stop is Colonel Grogan. Right tartar from what I hear. Runs this pansy bunch of propagandists.'

'That attractive girl you were talking to . . .' Partridge began.

'Married to some RAF type. Flying Officer Malloy. And she had her eye on you. If you know what I mean.' Humble made a crude gesture with his fingers which Partridge found distasteful.

'I was going to say,' Partridge persisted as Humble pressed the bell again, 'it was odd. She never asked who had been murdered.'

'Who knows what goes through a woman's mind?'

The door was opened by a private in the SIB. 'They're still examining the murder room,' he informed Humble. 'Haven't found anything that helps much yet, sir,' he continued as he escorted them into the lift. 'The body was removed hours ago.'

'I know. You needn't come up with us. Colonel Grogan's on the third floor? We'll find him.'

'Anything from the pathologist yet?' Partridge enquired as the lift began its rheumatic ascent.

'He's been up all night working on the *corpus delicti*. All he'll say so far is that the weapon which carved up Ionides

17

could be a commando-type knife. *Could* be.' he snorted. 'I have yet to get a straight answer from any of those buggers.'

Colonel Grogan's door faced the lift beyond the entrance to the corridor running round the building. Humble knocked on the top panel, a voice rapped out, 'Come in, close the door, you're two minutes late.'

'Accounted for, sir, by the two minutes we had to wait outside to gain admittance to this place.'

'Sit down. This place, as you call it, is one of the most sensitive propaganda centres in Mid-East Command. And who am I talking to?'

Humble introduced himself and his companion, produced his identification, which Grogan glanced at and settled back in his chair. Humble had him weighed up at a glance. A regular soldier, contemptuous of all those 'in for the duration', which appeared to include his visitors.

Grogan, he estimated, would be in his late fifties. His thatch of white hair was trimmed close to his bony skull, his clean-shaven face was craggy, his expression bleak. He sat erect as a poker in his hard-backed chair.

'What do you want?' he demanded.

'Well, sir, we are investigating a particularly horrific murder which took place on these premises . . .'

'Get to the point. I haven't all day.'

'Up to this moment we have interviewed Sergeant Higgins who found the body. Nothing much he could tell us. But I understand that among the units you oversee . . .'

'Command!' Grogan snapped.

'As you say, sir. I understand there is a secret unit led by a Colonel Maurice Barrymore . . .'

'Half-colonel. Temporary appointment. Lieutenant-Colonel Barrymore you must be referring to.'

Oh, my God, Humble thought, no wonder they gave him a desk job a thousand miles behind the lines. A World

18

War One type. Up boys, and at 'em. Never mind the casualties – take that machine-gun post. He changed tactics.

'I need to interview this Lieutenant-Colonel Barrymore – and his men. I understand they've just returned from some training course. That they've only been back here in Cairo for two days . . .'

'Good luck to you.' Grogan stood up. 'They're waiting for you. Can't imagine why you're interested in them.'

'I don't have to explain my reasons. Sir.'

'Can't imagine why they call you Humble.' Grogan glared. 'Follow me.'

Stiff in his walk, he led the way down the corridor, back straight, the veteran of a thousand inspection parades. Turning along a fresh corridor, he stopped in front of a closed door, opened it and walked in. He made a dismissive gesture towards Humble and Partridge.

'SIB. Over to you.'

Without a glance at them, he walked out, closing the door. The three men waiting in the room stared at their visitors in silence. The windows – again barred – over-looked the front street where the jeep was parked, Partridge noted as Humble made introductions.

'Better sit down, I suppose,' the half-colonel behind a desk suggested. 'Although we can't give you long. We have things to do.'

'So have we, sir,' growled Humble. 'Like investigating a grim murder . . .'

Partridge, seated next to his chief, assessed the three men with interest. Lieutenant-Colonel Barrymore had spoken in a languid voice, was dark-haired with a trim moustache, thin-faced with an aquiline nose. Effortlessly, he carried an aura of authority and command.

The records showed he was only twenty-one years old but from his air of sophistication Partridge would have guessed he was in his thirties. He sat back in a swivel chair,

19

turning a short swagger cane between strong fingers. He pointed with the cane to the two men seated in hard-back chairs on either side of the desk.

'Captain Robson. Company Sergeant Major Kearns. Members of my unit.'

'Which unit is that, Colonel?'

'Classified.' He used the tip of the cane to push a typed sheet of paper across the desk. 'That explains.'

Partridge studied the other two men while Humble scanned the letter. Robson was twenty-two, more heavily built than the lieutenant-colonel. Brown-haired, he also sported a moustache, straggly, and his whole manner was more relaxed. He sat with an arm stretched across the back of his chair and his expression was amiable. He reminded Partridge of a country doctor. Again, he looked older than his years.

Kearns was tall, thin, clean-shaven and hadn't moved a muscle since they entered the room. His brown eyes reminded Partridge of glass marbles. He sat very erect and his expression was bleak, his jaw clenched. All three men had skin tanned the colour of mahogany.

'I can still ask you some questions. I'm going to do just that. It's my job,' snapped Humble, pushing the letter back over the desk-top, the letter from GHQ signed by a general.

'Let's hurry it up, shall we?' Barrymore suggested in his silken tone. 'I'm beginning to get irked.'

'Unfortunately Ionides can no longer be irked. You have met him, of course? All of you? Seeing as you have your unit stationed in the same building?'

Humble's gaze swept over the three men. Nothing changed in Kearns' expression. Barrymore tapped his small white teeth with the tip of his cane. It was Captain Robson who replied.

'Personally speaking, no. I gather he was stuck away up on the next floor. As far as I know I've never set eyes on the chap. Horrible business. Any clues – as to who did it?'

'The investigation is continuing.' Humble turned to Kearns who was studying Partridge like a hangman measuring him for the drop. Only twenty years old. Must be the youngest CSM in the British Army.

'What about you?'

'The same as Captain Robson.' There was a snap in his voice. He'd be a bastard on the parade ground, Humble thought. It was the sheer immobility of Kearns which fascinated Humble. He looked at Barrymore.

'What about you, sir? I've heard there are special units which slip into Greece to help the Resistance there. And Ionides was Greek.'

'Rather an obvious observation. That last remark.' Barrymore made no attempt to conceal the sarcasm. 'No is the answer. And now, I think we've told you all we can. I'd prefer this interview to draw to a close. You've read that letter . . .'

'Which authorizes you not to answer any question affecting military security. No, I haven't quite finished, Colonel Barrymore. I understand the three of you returned to Cairo forty-eight hours ago. That means you were all in the city last night. Where were you between the hours of nine and eleven? Last night. And *that* has nothing to do with military security.'

'If you must know . . .' Barrymore sounded as though he were having trouble stifling a yawn. 'All three of us were getting some well-earned kip aboard a houseboat on the Nile. The location is top secret.'

'Any witnesses to confirm your story?'

Despite his tan, the hint of a flush of blood appeared on Barrymore's face. He stood up and Humble saw for the first time his khaki drill trousers were thrust into the tops of gleaming leather cavalry boots. Walking to the door, he opened it.

'I am not accustomed to being insulted in front of subordinates. May I suggest the interview is concluded? That you both leave now. If you please.'

Humble stood up, nodded to Partridge, and strode out of the room. The door closed behind them as they headed for the lift.

'Botched that one, didn't I?' observed Humble. 'Sprawled right into it. Gave him just the excuse he was looking for to chuck us out. What did you think of them?'

'Funny trio. I couldn't get it out of my mind there was a lot of tension under the surface.'

'Which there would be if they've just returned from some mission to the Greek islands. They're Special Operations Executive – and commandos to boot.'

'SOE? Then that explains . . .'

'It explains a lot,' Humble interjected as they ignored the lift and walked down the staircase. 'It explains why some flaming desk wallah of a general at Grey Pillars provides Barrymore with a letter giving total immunity from questioning. It explains why he could throw me out on my ear. And we can't check their alibi. That houseboat is where the SOE plan operations. It's called *Tara*. Don't know why – but it's off limits even to us.'

Partridge waited until they were settled inside the jeep before he asked his question. First he paid off the chief urchin of the gang guarding the vehicle. 'Not enough!' the urchin screeched. '*Imshi! Yallah!*' Partridge bawled. They ran off, shouting obscenities.

'Did you notice Captain Robson qualified his statement that he'd never met Ionides? *As far as I know I've never set eyes on the chap.*'

'You spotted that, too? You're learning. Gives him an out if we came up with a witness who saw them talking together. Any idea how the murder was done?' he asked as he started the vehicle moving.

'From our visit in the night it seems impossible. The only

22

way out is the front entrance – guarded by the Sudanese receptionist. Our people searched the place from top to bottom. No one there. All windows are barred. You *can* get out on to balconies from certain rooms on the upper floors. But you're thirty feet from the ground. Yet the killer had to be behind that locked door Higgins tried before he went into the next room.'

'And we found traces of blood in the bathroom. My bet is Higgins sat on that lavatory seat quite a long time. I can't say I blame him – but that was when the murderer was cleaning himself up before performing his vanishing trick.'

'Unless the Sudanese receptionist was bribed?'

'I talked with Selim. I've carried out enough interrogations in my time to know he wasn't lying. You know something, Partridge? I've a hunch we're not going to solve this one.'

'This is a bloody waste of time. You do know that?' Humble rapped out as he pulled the jeep into the kerb in front of the Antikhana Building. It was dark, the street was deserted.

Partridge checked his watch. 'Ten o'clock. The exact time Higgins arrived back on the night of the murder. I want to walk right round the outside first. Then go inside – just like Higgins did.'

'You're on your own, laddie. I'll wait here. And watch it at the back. The native quarter . . .'

Partridge jumped down on to the pavement and began walking slowly away from the entrance steps. Although it was dark there was plenty of light from the street lamps. He looked up as he walked, stared at the projecting balconies with their iron grilles.

It was very quiet. The only sound the smack of his shoes on stone. No one about. Probably it had been like this on the night of the murder. He turned the first corner of the building and the side street was a canyon of gloom. He unbuttoned his holster flap, felt the butt of his Service revolver. Butterflies in the stomach. The silence became oppressive, sinister.

He turned the next corner, walking more slowly, trying to make no sound. Across the narrow street to his right loomed the ramshackle tenements of the native quarter. Black as pitch now. He looked up again. The roof of the building was a blurred silhouette against a distant background of star-studded sky. He heard a scuffling sound and his hands were moist. A half-starved cat scuttled across the street.

Completing the circuit, he saw Humble leaning over the wheel, the red glow of a cigarette near his mouth. He mounted the steps, pressed the bell. An SIB sentry opened the right-hand door, Partridge showed his pass, went inside, nodded to the Sudanese behind the desk.

'No one in the building?' he asked the sentry.

'Yes, there is, sir. Colonel Barrymore is still in his office. Professor Guy Seton-Charles is also working late. And Sergeant Higgins is sitting on the staircase.'

'Why?'

'Better, maybe, sir, you ask him that yourself.'

The heavily built ex-tank commander was seated out of sight on the sixth step. Hunched forward, hands tightly clasped, he looked embarrassed and stood up as Partridge appeared.

'Sorry, sir. It's just that I can't go up there alone. I'm waiting for Clanger Wilson, my room-mate.'

'Let's go up together. I'm on the way to the roof myself.' Partridge hastened to put the burly sergeant at his ease. 'Why Clanger?'

'It's his nickname. Nothing malicious. He's always knocking things over. Bit like a bull in a china shop. Everyone likes him. Just a bit of fun. Calling him Clanger.'

24

'I think you're sensible to wait for company,' Partridge assured him as they climbed the staircase together. 'Think I'd have done the same thing myself in your place. After all, we still have to catch the blighter. Does Colonel Barrymore work this late often?'

'He's still here?' Higgins sounded surprised. 'Never known that to happen before. Not that any of us have a clue what that lot do. We call them the Hush-Hush Boys.'

'Let's look in on him before we go on the roof.'

Partridge opened the door to the office where a light shone from beneath it without knocking. Barrymore was bending over a file behind his desk. He looked up, closed the file quickly and laid a hand flat on it.

'I saw the light,' Partridge explained quickly.

'What the devil do you mean invading my quarters without so much as a warning knock?'

'I've just explained that. I saw the light and thought maybe someone had forgotten to turn it off. And I smell smoke. Is that mineral water, sir?'

A metal wastepaper basket stood by the side of the desk with smoke drifting up from inside. Partridge had pointed to a large glass jug on the desk next to a tumbler. 'Yes. Your powers of detection are extraordinary.' Barrymore noticed Higgins standing in the corridor. He jumped up, strode towards him. 'What are you doing? Snooping around at this hour?'

Barrymore's back was turned when Partridge picked up the jug, doused the papers burning inside the basket. Stooping, he retrieved an intact remnant with a few visible words. *Report on Siros raid*. He turned to face the door. 'Higgins is with me. We were just making our way to the roof.'

'Then kindly make your way.'

As Partridge, cap under his arm, walked back into the corridor Barrymore slammed the door behind him. Going

25

back to the file, he emptied more sheets into the basket and set light to them.

Partridge was walking alongside Higgins towards the corner of the building when a door opened. A man of slim build wearing a pale civilian suit emerged from an office and locked the door. 'Who is this?' Partridge whispered.

'Professor Guy Seton-Charles. Boffin type.'

Twenty-three years old, Partridge recalled from his study of records at GHQ. Rejected for military service on grounds of poor eyesight. The thin-faced man walked towards them hugging a green file under his arm. Everything was thin. Hands, his long studious face. He wore rimless glasses.

'A word with you, sir.' Partridge produced his identity card. 'SIB. We haven't got around to interviewing you yet. What is your precise job here?'

'Difficult to be precise about anything. All problems have shades of meaning. I am concerned with propaganda to the mainland.'

'Mainland?'

'Greece. The authorities are getting it all wrong, of course. The left-wing ELAS *andartes* are the real guerrillas fighting the Germans. The Republican EDES lot are hopeless. But can I convince people here? Even if ELAS are Communist?'

He spoke in a pedantic petulant tone and was obviously launched into a lecture. Partridge stopped him.

'Propaganda? Greece? Then you must have worked with Ionides.'

'Never, my dear chap. No idea why those two – Gavalas and Ionides – were here. Making jobs for themselves, I suspect . . .'

'We must go,' Partridge interjected. 'We'll talk later.' He headed for the end of the corridor. 'Funny type.'

'We've given him a nickname. Cuckoo.' Higgins chuckled.

'I'll lead the way,' Partridge suggested tactfully and began to climb the stone spiral staircase. It was very narrow, curving sharply, and there was no lighting. He felt his way up the wall with one hand, emerging suddenly on to the rooftop.

It was flat, enclosed by a waist-high wall with an iron rail on top. Higgins led the way, heading for one of a row of cabin-like structures erected on the rooftop. Taking out a key, he opened the door, switched on the light and showed Partridge his sleeping quarters. Alongside either wall leading from the door to a window at the far end was a camp bed neatly made up with Army blankets. Higgins indicated the one to his right.

'That's where Clanger sleeps. Luckily we arrived at the unit early enough to grab a cabin. Better than being billeted in Kasr-el-Nil Barracks across the road. No privacy in that madhouse. I'll show you round. Not a great deal to see. Except the Pyramids.'

Partridge made for the side of the roof at the back. Behind him he heard Higgins relocking the cabin door. His macabre experience had shaken the ex-tank commander to the core. Partridge placed a hand on the iron rail perched half a foot above the wall-top, gripped it, tested its strength and peered over. The dark canyon facing the squalid tenements of the native quarter was like an abyss. It was very quiet as Higgins joined him and made his remark.

'I heard you hadn't been out here long, sir. Going into the native quarter is forbidden. For a very good reason. Lord knows how many squaddies have staggered in there dead drunk. They never come out. The body is found days later by Military Police patrols. Throat slit. Wallet gone.'

'So it would take a brave man to go in even stone cold sober?'

'Sober – and armed – he'd probably be all right. Let's look at something more savoury.'

They walked across to the wall overlooking the front

27

entrance. Below, Humble was smoking behind the wheel of his jeep. Higgins pointed south. 'There they are.'

In the far distance, by the light of a waxing moon, Partridge saw the dark silhouettes of the Pyramids of Giza. He pulled at his shirt. He was sweating but the temperature seemed to have dropped suddenly.

'My Gawd! Look at that. Here she comes,' Higgins commented.

What seemed like a black cloud was blotting out the moon, the Pyramids below. Partridge had the impression smoke from a huge forest fire was sweeping into the city. It was a sight which stayed with him for the rest of his life.

'*Khamsin*. Sandstorm. Ever seen one?' asked Higgins. 'You've a treat in store. Inside ten minutes that cloud will blot out Cairo like a London pea-souper. Better get back to your jeep – you'll be lucky to make it back to GHQ . . .'

Humble had the engine running when Partridge ran down the steps of the building. He glared and moved the gears as Partridge jumped aboard.

'I was about to leave without you. *Khamsin* coming.'

'How did you know?' Partridge asked as the jeep rocketed down the deserted streets, exceeding the speed limit.

'That breeze that's flapping your shirt, you stupid bugger. What kept you?'

'I think I know now how the murderer escaped without being seen.'

'Great! And you know who the murderer is?'

'No. No idea . . .'

'Great again! I think my hunch was right. We'll not be solving this one.'

And Humble was right. Up to a point. The case might never have been solved but for a man who hadn't even been born as they raced through the streets. A man called Tweed. Over forty years later.

PART ONE

The Moor of Death

1

May 1987. It was another rainy day in London. Tweed stood by his first-floor office window gazing across Park Crescent to Regent's Park. Seated behind her desk, his assistant and confidante, Monica, watched the Deputy Director of the Secret Intelligence Service.

'A penny for your thoughts,' she said. 'You're not here – you have that faraway look.'

'Harry Masterson,' he replied. 'Why has he chosen Greece for his holiday? Dammit, he's Sector Chief for South-East Europe. You'd think he'd want to get as far from that part of the world as possible.'

'He does speak fluent Greek – among his other languages.'

'And you saw him in Bond Street the day before he was due to start his leave. With an attractive girl you think was Greek.'

'So, it's simple. Harry is divorced, has lots of girlfriends. This time it's a Greek. Maybe she wanted to go there, felt homesick.'

'I'm not convinced.' Tweed, a compact, clean-shaven man in his forties who wore glasses, sat behind his desk, began cleaning the glasses with a handkerchief. Monica frowned. He often performed that action when he was disturbed. 'Harry can't take a proper holiday,' Tweed continued. 'He once told me he's bored in three days without a problem to get his teeth into. He's been out there for three weeks.'

'And not a word from him, you mean?'

'But there has been a word – if you can call this a word. I got in early this morning. This came in the post.'

Unlocking a drawer, he took out a package shaped like a cigar box. The wrappings were still intact although the package had been opened. Monica stood up, came round and stood by the side of her chief. The address was written in Masterson's clear bold hand. Marked 'Personal'. The stamps were Greek. Tweed lifted off the top packing where he had carefully slit along the edges. Inside was a cigar box.

'From Harry Masterson. I don't like it,' Tweed said grimly. 'It looks like pieces of evidence he's collected about an investigation he's working on. And sent to me in case something happens to him.'

'Aren't you over-reacting? What's inside the box?'

'See for yourself.' Tweed flipped back the lid. 'That girl you saw him with in Bond Street before he left for Athens. Is this her?'

He rummaged among a collection of papers, photographs and a small notebook. Selecting one of the photographs, he placed it on the desk.

'Yes, that's her,' Monica said, studying the picture. 'I'm sure of it. She looks slimmer in a white dress. Good figure. She was wearing a coat when I saw her. I wonder where it was taken? Looks like somewhere in Greece.'

'Look on the back. Zea. Wherever that might be. Notice anything odd about the picture?'

'There are a lot of expensive-looking pleasure craft moored behind her. And beyond, the buildings are stepped up a hill. What's odd?'

'I'm damned sure the girl didn't know her picture was being taken by Harry. She's looking at some book. I think he took it surreptitiously. That's suggestive in itself. I don't think he trusted her . . .'

'Don't use the past tense . . .'

'Come in,' Tweed called out as someone rapped on the

door. A slim, fair-haired man in his early thirties with an air of self-assurance entered. 'Marler, your timing is perfect as always,' Tweed commented. 'You know Greece fairly well.' He handed him the photo. 'Harry Masterson took this picture somewhere in Greece. Any idea of the location?'

Marler examined the print, turned it over, smiled drily. 'It all links up if it's Harry, doesn't it? An attractive female, a small port, very exclusive, millionaires' yachts. Nothing but the best for our high-life Harry. This is the port of Zea. It's along the coast road from the main Piraeus harbour.'

'Why so exclusive?' Tweed asked. 'Apart from the floating palaces? Drug traffickers can afford those boats these days – if they're at the top.'

'Because just behind Zea is the Royal Yacht Club. Nowadays it is officially the Yacht Club since Greece became a republic.' He picked up a magnifying glass from Monica's desk. 'Bet you a fiver some of these still have the initials RYC on their sterns. Are you on?'

'No. I'm fed up with losing money to you.'

'And you would have lost.' Marler was peering through the magnifier. 'Two of the yachts berthed do have those initials. A bit of rather nice snobbery,' he commented in his upper-crust voice. He laid down the glass. 'What's this all in aid of, if I may be so bold?'

'I'm worried stiff about Harry.'

'For what good reasons?'

Marler, dressed in an immaculate pale linen suit, blue-striped shirt, matching blue tie and handmade shoes skilfully weighted in the toecaps – 'useful for kicking your opponent in the balls' – sat down in Tweed's armchair. He lit one of his rare king-size cigarettes. Crossing his legs, the epitome of relaxation, he fixed his blue, ice-cold eyes on Tweed.

'Reason One, why choose part of his working sector for his holiday? Oh yes, I know he likes the sun, but the

33

Caribbean would have served. Reason Two, he always sends a rude postcard. No card. Reason Three, instead he sends this cigar box with stuff which looks to me like clues about an investigation he's conducting. Reason Four, Harry gets bored easily – so if someone has approached him with a problem which intrigues him he'd jump at the chance of occupying himself with it.'

'That the cigar box? May I see?'

'Over to you. See what you make of the contents. I've only had time to skip through them. I find the sending of that sinister.'

'Any note, letter, with it?'

'No. Monica saw him in Bond Street with that girl whose photo you're looking at.'

'When was that?' Marler asked.

'Three weeks ago. The day before he flew to Athens, I assume.'

'You *assume*?' Marler raised an eyebrow. 'These photos are a mix. Some obviously in Greece, some in this country. Don't know where.'

'I do,' said Tweed. 'That one of the outside of The Royal Oak Inn. I recognize it. Winsford. A village on Exmoor. So why do we have Somerset and Greece? Doesn't make sense.'

'Unless he hasn't spent his whole three weeks in Greece. The day he was seen by Monica he could have taken off for Exmoor. Gone on to Greece later. Suggests something the Greek filly told him led him to Somerset. Something he found there led him to Greece. A regular bloodhound, our Harry. Picks up a scent and won't let go.'

'The timing,' Monica agreed, 'suggests it could have been something the Greek girl told him sent him haring off to Somerset.'

'I wonder what,' muttered Tweed, sifting through the non-Greek pictures. 'This looks like Watchet, a tiny port on the Bristol Channel. One of the front, another of the

34

harbour. I remember that line of lampposts along the front with the small hill at the eastern edge of the harbour. Dunster High Street, not a doubt. The front entrance to the Luttrell Arms, leading hotel in Dunster. Another of a Tudor-style mansion behind a stone wall. Familiar. Near the Doone Valley if I remember right.'

Marler had emptied the cigar box and was fiddling with the base of its interior. He raised a thin sheet of wood pressed down on the base, extracted a folded sheet of paper.

'Seen this?' he enquired. 'The scene widens. Take a shufti.'

Tweed studied the opened sheet. Harry's distinctive writing. *MOD. Brigadier Willie Davies*. Ministry of Defence. Harry had visited the place, presumably before he flew to Greece, maybe even before he'd driven down to Somerset. There were two more words written on the sheet of paper. *Somerset Levels*.

Tweed felt a prickling of the hairs at the back of his neck, an unreasoned sense of foreboding. He became aware that Marler and Monica were watching him.

'Something's wrong,' said Monica.

'I hope not.' He passed the sheet to her. 'I don't think we've told you yet, Marler, that Brigadier Davies is our most friendly contact at the Ministry of Defence. He's also a member of the same club as Harry. They were close.'

'Chums, you mean?' Marler enquired. 'As well as a professional relationship? This business is getting a bit weird. So many strands. And what the deuce is – are – the Somerset Levels?'

'One of the most benighted and lonely spots in England. The area between Taunton and Glastonbury where they dig peat. In the time of Charles the First the sea used to flood in. Now they have constructed waterways – they look like canals. It is like a bleak marshland. I don't understand any of this – too many strands, as you said.'

35

He stood up and walked over to the window. It had stopped raining. Now they had May sunshine. The pavements were drying out, leaving damp patches. He stood with his hands clasped behind his back. He was, Monica knew, on the verge of taking a decision.

'I want Harry recalled from Greece immediately. Isn't his deputy for Greece, Patterson, at the British Embassy?'

'Yes,' said Monica promptly. 'Harry appointed him a couple of months ago. Patterson speaks Greek and has travelled widely in the archipelago. You're assuming Harry contacted him after he reached Athens.'

'Which he probably didn't,' Marler commented. 'Running his own investigation unofficially, he'd play it close to the chest. Why the MOD? Or again was it something the Greek girl told him? Incidentally, Monica, what made you so sure she *was* Greek?'

'When he stopped me he said something in a foreign language. She looked annoyed. Then Harry said, "The Greeks always have a word for it." Looking back, I almost think he was sending me a signal.'

'Fair do's,' Marler agreed. 'She is Greek.'

'And now,' Tweed said impatiently as he returned to his swivel chair, 'I want that call made to Athens recalling Harry. A direct order. He's to return instantly, the moment they locate him.'

Monica was reaching for her phone when it began to ring as a raven-haired girl with good bone structure came into the office. Marler jumped up, grinned, offered Paula Grey, Tweed's assistant, his chair. He spread his hands, adopted a theatrical pose.

'Lothario offers you his comfortable seat. How is it you look more ravishing every time I see you?'

'Flannel,' rapped back Paula. 'You think I haven't heard all about your women?'

She was crossing her legs when she stiffened. She was looking at Monica who had been talking on the phone. In a broken voice Monica nodded to Tweed to lift his receiver.

'Athens on the line . . . Larry Patterson for you.'

Tweed grabbed up his receiver. It became very silent and still in the office. They watched Tweed whose expression had become poker-faced. In a quiet controlled voice he asked several terse questions, said, 'Yes, of course,' five times, thanked Patterson for calling and replaced the receiver. Leaning across his desk, he clasped his hands, gazed at them and spoke in a monotone.

'There is no easy way to break this type of news. Harry Masterson is dead. He was found today at the base of some cliff called Cape Sounion. I gather it is some distance southeast of Athens. The cliff is very sheer and is three hundred feet high. They will be flying the body home.'

'Oh dear God, no! Not Harry . . .'

It was Monica who burst out like a stricken animal. Her eyes filled with tears. Paula jumped up, put an arm round her and helped her to her feet and out of the room. The silence was oppressive after the click of the closing door.

'Apparently, according to Patterson, he must have slithered over the edge early in the morning,' Tweed continued. 'About nine o'clock a coastguard launch patrolling the area on the lookout for drug smugglers spotted the body on some rocks at the edge of the sea.'

'Balls!' said Marler, his tone harsh. 'Which is what Harry would have said if they'd found me there. I know the area.'

'I'm listening,' said Tweed in the same monotone, twiddling a pencil between his fingers.

'Cape Sounion is about a two-hour drive along the coast road from Athens. It's the southernmost tip of Greece at that point. Perched on the summit of the Cape is the Temple of Poseidon. It's a lonely spot when the tourists aren't there. Beyond the temple the ground is covered with stubby grass which slopes gently towards the brink. You can easily see when you're coming to the end of everything.'

'So?' pressed Tweed.

37

'Harry had all his marbles – more than most of us. The idea that he slipped over the edge is fatuous.'

'So?' Tweed repeated.

'Harry was murdered. Absolutely no doubt about it. And I would like to know what the hell we are going to do about it.'

2

Action this day. A favourite maxim of Tweed's, borrowed from Winston Churchill.

Tweed had called for the afternoon what he termed a 'war conference'. Inside what Howard, Tweed's chief, insisted on calling the 'boardroom', six people were gathered round a large oblong table.

Like antagonists, Howard was seated at one end of the table, facing Tweed, who occupied the other end. Also present were Paula Grey, sitting on Tweed's right, notebook at the ready. Marler sat next to Bob Newman, foreign correspondent and close confidant of Tweed. Pete Nield, experienced agent, sat opposite Marler and Newman. Already the atmosphere reeked with tension and disagreement.

'Aren't we jumping to a lot of conclusions rather early in the game regarding this dreadful tragedy?' suggested Howard in his slow pontificating voice.

'It's not a game,' Tweed snapped. 'And Masterson's death does not sound like an accident.'

'Hold hard a jiffy . . .' Howard, six feet tall, plump-faced and perfectly tailored in a Chester Barrie navy blue suit, shot his cuffs to expose the gold links.

Oh God, thought Tweed, why did he have to turn up unexpectedly and attend this meeting? He stared hard at Howard as he spoke.

'Well, let's get on with it.'

'I was going to make the point that Patterson is already in place in Athens. He could take a look-see, send us a report. Oh, nothing personal, of course, but why is Mr Newman honouring us with his presence?'

'Because I asked him to. Because he knows Greece. Because he speaks Greek fluently and is flying out there with Marler.'

'Not necessary,' Marler interjected in his clipped tone. 'You know I work on my own . . .'

There was a heavy silence. Tweed kept the silence going while he deliberately arranged the pile of photos in front of him. Newman, in his early forties, well-built, clean-shaven, with thick sandy hair and a strong face, sat watching Tweed with a droll expression.

'I have to say,' Howard continued eventually, 'that I really don't see how Newman, able though he might be, fits in with such an assignment.'

Tweed launched his attack. 'He's fully vetted, as you well know. Patterson has only been in Athens for a short time. Let's get a few opinions.' He addressed Newman. 'Bob, you knew Harry Masterson. Can you see him stumbling off the edge of a cliff?'

'He was sharp as a fox. But I would like to collect a few more facts in Greece. Facts are what I go by.'

'Marler?' Tweed asked.

'So unlikely the idea is ridiculous.'

'Paula?'

'I heard he once left a party half-smashed and walked down the middle of Walton Street balancing a bottle of champagne on his head. The bottle stayed there. Sure-footed as the proverbial goat. Not a chance.'

'Pete?'

'Never in a million years.'

'Are you convinced?' Tweed asked Howard. 'If it was murder and we don't act fast the Prime Minister will call us to account.'

'I don't like blackmail,' Howard replied stiffly.

'Who does? You haven't answered the question.'

'Well,' Howard began, his manner breezy, 'first he's a fox, then he's a goat . . .'

'I don't find that the least bit amusing,' Tweed snapped.

'In that case, what do you propose?' Howard's well-fed face was flushed with annoyance. 'And I still maintain Marler could go on his own. Newman is surplus to requirements – I do realize he's rendered valuable service in the past . . .'

'Very generous of you,' Tweed interjected. The trouble was Howard realized Newman was wealthier than he would ever be. The foreign correspondent had made a fortune from his best-selling book, *Kruger: The Computer That Failed*. Tweed spoke decisively.

'Marler and Newman will travel to Greece together Masterson went alone – and see what happened to him.' He glanced at Paula but she was already recording his instructions.

'Marler's deputy, Harris, can take over the German sector in his absence. Agreed, Marler?' He went on as Marler nodded. 'The investigation covers two very different areas. Greece. Dealt with. Newman reports back to me over Patterson's scrambler phone at the Athens Embassy.'

'Why not Marler?' Howard bleated.

Tweed, in full cry, ignored the interruption. 'I shall drive with Paula to Exmoor and check that area. Pete Nield will come with us in a separate car. He will appear not to know us. He will come armed.'

'Why?' demanded Howard.

'Because I don't know what we're walking into. One man has already been murdered.'

40

'That has yet to be proved,' Howard objected.

'Everyone I asked believes that. I have an open mind but I'm taking no chances. We start tomorrow – before the scent goes cold. The contents of this cigar box Harry posted me will be checked by our experts in the Engine Room in the basement. I want someone to visit Harry's country cottage in Sussex. What was it called?'

'Clematis Cottage, near Apfield,' said Paula, continuing her writing.

'I will contact Jim Corcoran of Airport Security at Heathrow. He'll check the passenger manifests of all flights to Greece over the past three weeks.' Tweed looked briefly at Howard who had lapsed into silence. 'If we can find which flight Masterson used we may find the name of that Greek girl Monica saw him with in Bond Street.' He turned to Paula. 'How is Monica?'

'Harry Butler took her home. He'll pull her round. Should he go down to check Clematis Cottage?'

'Good idea. And tell him to look at a power cruiser moored at a landing stage a few hundred yards south of the cottage. He turns off to the right along the first track.'

'Is that the lot?' Howard enquired with a hint of sarcasm.

'No. We need photos of Harry Masterson run off by the Engine Room urgently this evening. Newman and Marler will need them when they're tracking his movements in Greece. And I want careful blow-ups of the photo of the Greek girl at Zea. Some for Newman and Marler, some for me to take to Somerset.'

'I think I'm going.' Howard stood up. 'I do have other work calling for my attention. I can't rubber-stamp all this in a memo . . .'

'So you'll have a little extra time for that other work calling for your attention.' Tweed smiled. 'Thank you for your cooperation and attendance.'

Howard withdrew, closing the door behind him as

41

though it were made of glass. Round the table there was a sense of relief.

'I have held back two intriguing points,' Tweed told them. 'Harry made a reference to a friend at court at the Ministry of Defence. I hope to visit him before you leave tonight. I can't imagine why Harry went there.'

'And the other point?' asked Marler.

'Endstation.' Tweed looked round the table. 'Like a clue to a crossword puzzle. Mean anything? Suggest anything? The word is written – in Harry's writing – on the back of a British postcard. Just that one word. *Endstation*.'

'Sounds like Cockfosters, the last station on the Piccadilly Underground,' Paula suggested.

'Which doesn't link up with Exmoor – or Greece.'

'The fact that he wrote it on a *British* postcard points to a connection with Somerset,' Newman remarked. 'Harry liked little tricks like that. And he may well have had in mind that cigar box could have been intercepted.'

'So?' enquired Nield.

'He'd write any clue in code. Some puzzle he'd hope Tweed could unravel.'

'Puzzle is the word for what he sent me,' Tweed commented. 'Paula, book tickets for Marler and Newman to fly to Athens tomorrow . . .'

'I've already made a note to do just that . . .'

'But no one moves anywhere, leaves London, until I've seen Brigadier Willie Davies. We need to know why Harry went to the Ministry of Defence.'

Escorted by a male receptionist, Tweed walked down the endless corridor past doors carrying the names of military officers. He clutched in his hand the pass he would have to surrender before being let out of the MOD.

Brigadier Davies, a tall red-faced man with lapel tabs of the same colour, rose from behind his desk as Tweed entered and the door closed behind him. They shook hands.

'Long time no see,' Davies remarked in his crisp staccato voice. 'Take a pew. Long time,' he repeated, sitting down again, 'then we have a queue from your outfit.'

'Harry Masterson, you mean?'

'The great man himself.' Davies tugged at his ginger moustache, ran a hand over thinning hair of the same colour. 'But since you authorized the interview you'll know all about it. Always good for a laugh, Harry. Say anything outrageous.'

'You said I authorized the interview?'

'Course you did.' Davies pushed a sheet of paper with typing across the desk. Tweed glanced at it. A printed heading. General and Cumbria Assurance Company – the cover name for the SIS at Park Crescent. The letter was brief.

Dear Willie – If you could give Harry your cooperation re this one I'd be greatly indebted. At the bottom was Tweed's signature. Forged. Typical of Harry, Tweed thought nostalgically. Break every rule in the book to get what he was after.

'A lot's been happening. My memory must be going.' He phrased the next words carefully. 'The trouble is he took off on a plane without leaving me a report. Just caught his flight after leaving you, I gather. Could you bring me up to date? What he asked, what you told him?'

'Weird case. Going back over forty years.' Davies stood up, extracted a bunch of keys from his pocket and unlocked a green steel cabinet. 'Took me a while to locate the file for Harry.' He grinned as he pulled out a blue file with a red tab attached and handed it to Tweed. 'Still classified.'

Tweed left the file unopened on the desk. The typed inscription on the front in faded letters carried a brief message. *Commando raid on Siros Island, Greece, February, 1944.*

43

'If you'd bear with me, Willie, I went off abroad as soon as I'd provided the authorization,' he lied glibly. 'It would help if you could tell me what Harry asked you. I'm not sure exactly how much he knew about this business.'

'Oh, he had his facts all lined up.' Davies clasped his hands behind his long neck. 'I'd offer you coffee but why poison a friend? Harry said he first needed details of that four-man commando raid on Siros in February 1944. I expect you know Siros is a large island in the Cyclades, a strategic stepping-stone to Piraeus, the port of Athens. Couriers passed through Siros from Cairo on their way to the mainland to contact the Greek Resistance. Actually, the Resistance was active on the island. German-occupied, of course. And the HQ of the German commander of the Cyclades group. A General Hugo Geiger. All this came from Harry before he looked at that file. And a bit more. I wondered how he'd come about the information.'

'Tell me about the bit more.'

'A four-man commando team made the raid. From Special Operations Executive. Commanded by a Lieutenant-Colonel Barrymore. Had with him a Captain Robson, a CSM called Kearns, and the Greek.'

'The Greek?'

'You didn't know about him? Chap called Andreas Gavalas. He had got out in a motorized caïque, reached Cairo months before. The idea was he knew Siros well. The Resistance lot, by the way, were the Republican crowd EDES. As opposed to ELAS, the Commie faction. Barrymore was taking a fortune in diamonds to hand over to a courier from Athens. Last time Cairo financed them. Turned their cooperation completely to ELAS shortly afterwards. Word was ELAS were doing the real fighting out there against Jerry, even though they were Communists.'

'And that was the extent of Harry's knowledge?'

'No. Weird business. He knew about the tragedy. After

they landed on Siros successfully the diamonds were handed to Gavalas to pass on to his Greek contact. The commando team was returning to the beach down a gully and found Gavalas lying dead with a knife stuck in his back.' Davies' expression became grim. 'It was a commando knife.'

'You can't mean that one of . . .'

'The three commandos? No. Barrymore immediately gathered his team together and asked to see their weapons. All of them, including himself, had their knives.'

'Weird, as you say. Why didn't the killer remove the knife?'

'Well, that's something I can understand. Apparently it had been driven into Gavalas with great force. Ever tried to pull out a knife from a dead body? It can take some doing – if it's rammed in deep. Barrymore tried to pull it out and couldn't manage it. So they scarpered pretty damn quick.'

'And Harry explained all this before seeing the file?'

'I think he wanted me to realize he wasn't on a fishing expedition, that he knew a great deal about the murder on Siros.'

'And was it eventually brought home to the killer?'

'Not as far as I know.' Davies made a sweeping gesture with his hand. 'Look at the range of suspects. The EDES section which knew Gavalas was coming. The Germans occupying the island. They patrolled constantly, I gather.'

'And the diamonds had been handed over before the Barrymore team left Gavalas the first time – alive?'

'No, they hadn't.' Davies pursed his lips.

'So the first thing Barrymore would do when he realized Gavalas was dead would be to check for the diamonds.'

'Which he did. They'd vanished.'

'What was a fortune in diamonds worth then? Any data?'

'One hundred thousand pounds. God knows what they'd be worth now. That covers what Harry told me before I searched for the file and he sat in that same chair reading it. His next request was what startled me. Tell you about it when you've scanned the file.' Davies smiled cynically. 'You can't, of course, borrow that file, photograph it, or make a single note. It's the regulations.'

'I know.' Tweed glanced up and caught the cynical smile. He understood. Davies knew Tweed's reputation for a photographic memory. He only had to read a long document once and he had total recall. Every word would be imprinted on his brain.

Five minutes later Tweed pushed the file back across the desk. He sat with hands clasped as he asked the question.

'And what was the request Harry made that startled you?'

'He asked me if I could give him the present whereabouts of Barrymore, Robson and Kearns – if they'd survived. I don't think I can take this any further, Tweed. It involves another department. Better ask Harry when you see him again.'

'Not possible, Willie.' Tweed paused. 'Harry is dead.'

Davies stiffened, his face froze. He opened a drawer, took out an ash tray, a pack of cigarettes and lit one. He dropped the pack back inside the drawer.

'Rarely smoke these days. You tricked me, Tweed. Not like you . . .'

'I thought you might close down on me. It's just possible he was murdered. I've thrown away the rule book. I'm going to find out how he died come hell or high water. You'd do the same thing if our roles were reversed.'

'You're right there,' Davies admitted. 'May I ask where and how?'

'In Greece. He's supposed to have stumbled off a three-hundred-feet cliff a good way south-east of Athens . . .'

'Bloody rubbish. Never!' Davies stubbed out the cigarette, drummed his thick fingers on the desk-top. 'Not

46

Harry. And you won't stop until you've found out what happened.'

'No, I won't.'

Davies stood up, went back to the cabinet, unlocked it, took out a thin blue file and laid it before Tweed. He sat down, lips tightly compressed before he spoke.

'You can look at that appendix to the other file. Same regulations apply . . . Hell, I don't have to tell you. When Harry asked for that information I didn't think I could oblige. I checked with this other department which keeps certain records. You see, Barrymore and Kearns stayed in the Army for a few years after the war. The girl who checks records like that is a tigress. Never gives up. I gave her all three names – Robson and Kearns as well as Barrymore. She located Barrymore easily. Then she obtained a copy of the phone directory of the same area. Came up with all three addresses. Better look in that file.'

A single sheet of paper. Tweed stared, unable to believe it. All the addresses were in Somerset. 'The last two are from the directory,' Davies explained.

'After all these years, they all live in the Exmoor area.'

'Odd, isn't it? Odd, too, that Harry died in Greece – not a hundred miles from the island of Siros from what you've told me.'

Tweed closed the second file, stood up slowly, his mind whirling. He thanked Willie, said they must have a drink soon. At the door he turned before he opened it.

'When I came in you said something about a queue from my outfit.'

Davies was standing close to him, hands thrust in his trouser pockets. He stood thinking for a moment.

'I wasn't too accurate there. You used to be with Scotland Yard. I made a subconscious connection.'

'What are you talking about?'

'A few days after Harry visited me someone else arrived – an ex-Chief Inspector from the Yard called Partridge.'

47

'Sam Partridge of Homicide? Now retired. I know him.'

'Might as well tell you the lot. Partridge carries no status here, of course. But he's a persuasive sort of chap. And coming so soon after Harry. Well . . . Long and short of it is he also wanted the present whereabouts of Barrymore, Robson and Kearns. I ended up giving him the addresses.'

'May I ask what was his interest?'

'He's still investigating a murder which took place over forty years ago. Never solved. Can't sit at home and cultivate a vegetable patch now he's retired. Very vigorous type.'

'The murder of Gavalas on Siros?'

'No. This is going to shake you. It did me. After Harry. Which is why I coughed up those addresses, I suppose. I'm sure there can't be a connection.'

'A connection between who?'

'The killing of Gavalas on Siros and the murder of some other Greek at the HQ of certain secret units in Cairo. Ionides I think he called him.'

3

'Jim Corcoran came through from Heathrow Airport Security,' Paula reported as Tweed walked into his office. 'We've got the data you need. Corcoran checked the computers. Harry flew out to Athens via Zurich on Swissair Flight 805. Ten days ago.'

'Which gave him about another ten days to poke about on Exmoor before he left. And I know now why he went there.'

'The news is even better. Harry booked two seats aboard the flight in advance. Guess the name of the passenger who sat in the seat next to him.'

'Not in the mood for guessing games. And I've got a mass of my own data to dictate to you . . .'

'A Christina Gavalas sat next to him.'

'My God, it's beginning to link up.'

'How?'

'Exactly how I've no idea. Ready for dictation? File One.'

Tweed stood quite still, eyes half-closed, while he recalled the contents of the Siros file. Paula took it down in her shorthand book, scrawled a fresh heading for File Two, recorded the three addresses Tweed reeled off.

'Two copies only,' he warned. 'One for Newman and Marler. The other for us.'

'Consider it done. Newman and Marler can collect the tickets from Heathrow if they're leaving tomorrow.'

'They are doing just that. I had a word with them on my way in. Let them have the first copy of the Siros file earliest.'

He was sitting behind his desk when the door opened and Monica walked in. She waved reassuring hands as Paula jumped up. 'I'm all right. Better back in the front line than moping at home.' She went to her desk. 'Can I help?'

'Yes,' said Tweed. 'Call the Yard. Superintendent Jack Richardson. Give him my best wishes. I need the home address of Chief Inspector Sam Partridge of Homicide, now retired.'

'Before you phone,' he said as Monica sat behind her desk, 'I want you to react quickly to this question. One possibly important clue from Harry's cigar box. One single word. Ready? *Endstation*.'

'The name of some operation. Codename.'

'Doesn't add up,' Paula intervened. 'It could have been

49

the codename for the raid on Siros. But there's no reference to any codename in the file. Also, Harry wrote it on a *British* postcard. That points to Somerset.'

She turned to Monica. 'Isn't all this pretty painful for you? You knew Harry well. Is it a good idea to come back yet?'

'Anything I can do to track down the swine who killed him. I want to be a part of this. I'll call the Yard.' She reached for the phone.

Tweed was heading for the door. 'Something else to pass on to Newman and Marler. Someone else is taking an interest in the Siros file. Partridge. What's the betting he's in Greece at this moment?'

'Do you think it's a good idea Newman going to Athens with Marler?' Paula asked after Tweed had left the room. 'They seem to fight like cat and dog. Square up to each other on every issue. Bob is early forties, Marler barely thirty.'

'And there, my dear, you have put your finger on it,' Monica assured her. 'They do scrap, I agree. But whereas Marler is quick off the mark, independent-minded – just the way Bob used to be until recently – Bob has become harder, tougher, wary. They could make an ideal combination once they're out there on their own. I think Tweed is banking on that.'

'What changed Bob? Made him a hard man? After all he was an international foreign correspondent. Still is, if a story interests him.'

'Ah, that was his experience behind the lines in East Germany when he went underground with a resistance group. A bitter, grim time, but he came through. Now, I'd better get on . . .'

When Tweed walked briskly back into the room Monica was putting down the phone. She waited until he had sat behind his desk, scribbled a note on his tasks pad.

'Did you know when you were at Scotland Yard they

had a nickname for you? Quicksilver Tweed, they called you, according to Superintendent Richardson . . .'

'A long time ago.' Tweed made a dismissive gesture. 'What about Partridge?'

'I have his phone number at Cheam. Thought I'd call him when you got back.'

'Yes, I'd like to talk to him personally.'

Monica dialled a number. She had a brief conversation with someone, then put her hand over the mouthpiece.

'Partridge isn't there. It's Mrs Partridge . . .'

'I don't know whether you'll remember me,' Tweed began, using his own phone, 'my name is Tweed . . .'

'I know you, it must be years . . .' She had a cultured voice. 'Sam worked with you at the Yard. We met once at a party. I recognize your voice . . .'

'Sorry to bother you, but I need to speak with Sam urgently.'

'He's not here, Mr Tweed. And I've no idea where he is . . .'

Tweed frowned, detected a note of anxiety in her voice now.

'Something wrong, Mrs Partridge? Why don't you know where he is?'

'You know how Sam is. He can't retire gracefully. Too active, restless. He's investigating some old murder case. I am worried. Before he left he said something he's never said to me before.'

'What was that?'

'He warned me never to open the door to strangers. Especially if they looked to be foreigners. He even had a spyglass fitted in the front door before he dashed off.'

'Dashed off where, if I may ask?'

'I've no idea as I said earlier. He packed his own bag. He's taken enough clothes to last him several weeks.'

'What sort of clothes?'

'Some of his old Army khaki drill suits. Plus a lot of

normal clothes – the kind of things he wears in this country.'

Tweed paused, wondering how to word it. 'Mrs Partridge, don't be alarmed by my call. It's something I'm working on connected with my insurance job as claims investigator. Wives are pretty clever where their husbands are concerned. They often spot a clue as to what they're up to. Have you any suspicions as to where he might have gone?'

'You're not thinking of another woman?'

Oh Christ, Tweed thought, are all marriages like this? Always the wives not a hundred per cent certain about their menfolk? Mrs Partridge went on talking.

'Sam's not like that. I'd know if it was anything untoward.'

'I phrased that badly. As you say, Sam is like the Rock of Gibraltar. It's his *destination* I'm interested in. I do need to contact him urgently.'

'Oh, I see what you mean. Sorry, Mr Tweed, I simply haven't a clue as to where he might be.'

'Here or abroad?' Tweed persisted, hating himself.

'I just don't know. He took off two weeks ago and I haven't had a word from him since. Mind you, he warned me that might happen. I just wish I could help . . .'

'That's quite all right. I'm sure you'll hear from Sam soon. By the way, I'd follow his advice. No opening the door to strangers, especially foreigners. I've no idea why he said that – but Sam usually knows what he's talking about. He'll explain it all when he gets back. Take care.'

He put down the phone and stared into the distance. Paula was typing the Siros file out, slim fingers skimming the keys.

'What was all that about?' asked Monica. 'And who is this Partridge character? Where does he fit in?'

'He called on Brigadier Davies after Harry had been there. Wanted the addresses of the three commandos who made up the team which raided Siros. You'll understand that bit when Paula gives you the file for a quick look before it goes to Newman and Marler. Where does Partridge fit in? I wish I knew. It's a peculiar business. Partridge told Davies he was investigating the murder of a Greek called Ionides over forty years ago in Cairo.'

'My God!' Paula paused briefly. 'That makes two murders. And both of them Greeks.'

'And Partridge warned his wife against opening the door to any foreigners. Greeks? Partridge has disappeared off the face of the earth, went off on some trip a fortnight ago. Destination unknown. I've got an awful feeling of presentiment. Harry walked into something too big even for him to handle.'

'But you'll find out what it is,' Monica told him.

'We'll try. Paula and I drive to Somerset tomorrow. You hold the fort. I'll keep in touch – for any messages from Newman.' He clenched his fist on the desk. 'One of us has to come up with something.'

4

'Ten minutes before we land,' said Newman and peered down out of the window of the Swissair DC9 as the plane banked and swung eastwards.

'And we've got damn all to go on,' Marler observed.

From thirty thousand feet Newman stared down as they left the sapphire blue of the Adriatic Sea behind and flew over a landscape of bleak mountains studded with *maquis* – scrub. Savage gulches cleft the terrain between the mountain ridges. A wilderness of rock. They were over Greece.

The air was incredibly clear, the sun shining brilliantly.

He felt he could reach down and touch the summits of the highest peaks. He looked at Marler sitting next to him, arms crossed, his face expressionless.

'If I were flying in to follow up a story I'd feel I had more than I normally had. We have to locate Christina Gavalas – the girl Harry flew to Athens with. We have copies of his photo to show round the hotels to find where he stayed. We've got Andreas Gavalas who went with the commando group forty odd years ago to check. We have the island of Siros to visit. We have Nick the Greek . . .'

'Who?'

'A driver who makes his living taking tourists from the Hotel Grande Bretagne on trips in his Mercedes. Nick is an old friend of mine. Very reliable, tough. He knows a lot about what goes on in this country.'

'You make it sound like a piece of cake. Anything else?'

'We have Cape Sounion to visit. I want to look at that cliff where Harry supposedly stumbled over the edge. And we have Chief Inspector Peter Sarris of Homicide in Athens. I once did him a favour – so he owes me one.'

'You know something, Newman?'

'You're going to tell me anyway.'

'I think we've got bugger all. And we should have brought someone to do the legwork.'

'If necessary, I'll do that while you prop up the bar at the Grande Bretagne,' Newman said quietly.

'I think Tweed is rushing it. I like a good basis of solid research.'

'He's moving fast before Howard writes Harry's death off as an accident.'

'I suppose it could have been just that.'

'You're forgetting the cigar box he sent. He knew he was walking a tightrope,' Newman said tersely. 'That he might not be coming back.'

'Trouble is I hardly knew Harry,' Marler reflected, still

54

keeping his voice low. The seats in front of them were unoccupied.

'But I did. And we're starting to descend. End of conversation.'

'Endstation,' Marler responded sardonically.

The big heat hit them like a heavy door as they descended the mobile staircase. Newman looked quickly round. Those bare hills loomed in close to the airport. The light was a glare. Mid-afternoon. Marler made a gesture as they walked towards the airport bus with the other passengers.

'Hardly Heathrow.'

'That has its advantages.'

But Marler had a point, he thought, as they boarded the waiting bus which would take them to the arrivals building which was smaller than any garage at London Airport. They passed the entry checks without any fuss and within minutes climbed inside a yellow taxi.

'Hotel Grande Bretagne,' Newman told the driver in English, 'and we're in a hurry.'

Marler glanced at Newman as they moved off. The driver had not understood the second instruction. That much was clear from his throwaway gesture. Marler marked up a notch in his companion's favour. Newman was concealing the fact that he spoke Greek fluently.

The Grande Bretagne is a solid-looking edifice standing on a corner of Constitution Square – Syntagma as the Greeks call it. The hotel looks as though it has stood there for generations, which it has. Inside they crossed the marble floor to reception.

'We have reservations,' Newman began. 'But first I would like a word with the chief receptionist.'

'You are talking to him, sir,' the man behind the counter informed him in perfect English.

Newman took an envelope from his breast pocket,

55

extracted a photo of Harry Masterson, laid it on the counter.

'I'm trying to find my stepbrother, Harry Masterson. I understood he stayed here. He may have left by now.'

The receptionist stared at the photo with a blank expression. Then he seemed to seek the right words.

'This, I regret to say, looks very like a man who fell off Cape Sounion to his death recently. There were pictures in the papers. I could be wrong, but they did give the name you mentioned.'

'Can't be the same man,' Newman protested. 'He did stay here?'

'Oh, no sir. I would have remembered. In view of . . .'

'Partridge,' said Marler. 'Does that name ring a bell?'

'Yes, it does, sir.' The receptionist transferred his attention to Marler. 'When I was serving my apprenticeship I went to Britain to learn the language. I was at the Gleneagles Hotel in Scotland. Plenty of partridge shooting up there. Which is probably why I noted this guest's name.'

'May I ask when he was here? Old chum,' Marler said smoothly.

'Let me check.' They waited. A small man wearing the dark suit of a hotel employee was lingering close to the counter – his eyes on the photo of Masterson. Newman stared at him and he wandered away. The receptionist came back.

'I was right. Mr Samuel Partridge?'

'That's him,' said Marler. 'Nice man. Told me he'd probably stay here. Best hotel in Athens.'

'Thank you, sir. Mr Partridge stayed one week. He arrived two weeks ago and then left. For the airport, I seem to remember.' He looked back at Newman. 'But Mr Masterson, no. He did not stay with us. If you would like to register?'

'Certainly.' Newman spoke as he began filling in the form. 'That small man who was standing near the counter. Who is he?'

56

'Oh, one of our temporary employees.' The receptionist made a resigned gesture. 'During the summer season we have to take on temporary staff. Unfortunate, between the two of us. They do not always understand the standards we set here.' He smiled with a certain satisfaction. 'Giorgos will not be with us after September . . .'

After opening his case in his own room, Marler walked along the corridor to Newman's. The foreign correspondent was standing with his hands on his hips, staring out of the window at the view of the distant Parthenon perched on the Acropolis.

'One up to me, I think,' Marler said pointedly as he sat in an armchair. 'Finding that Chief Inspector Partridge has trotted out here to have a look-see.'

'I'll give you that one.' Newman sounded absorbed. 'And Nick the Greek will be here shortly. I got lucky. I had his card in my wallet, the one with his home number he gave me when I was last out here.'

'What's the betting Partridge is now strolling round the island of Siros? You seem somewhat preoccupied.'

'Didn't you spot it?' Newman asked.

'Spot what?'

'One up to me. The receptionist recognized the picture I showed him of Harry because he said he'd seen it in the papers. What I want to know is how did they get that picture? He only became newsworthy when he was a smashed-up corpse at the foot of Cape Sounion.'

Giorgos slipped out of the side entrance of the Grande Bretagne, walking through the restaurant. There was no doorman on duty at this exit.

He hurried round to the far side of Syntagma Square where a row of phone boxes stood. Going inside a booth, he dialled a number and waited, tapping thin fingers on the coin box. If he was away too long that sod of a chief receptionist was going to notice his absence from duty. He spoke in Greek when a deep-throated voice answered.

'Giorgos here. I thought you should know two Englishmen have just arrived at the hotel. They are asking questions about Masterson. They have a photograph of him.'

'Another Englishman was there snooping around only two weeks ago. That man Partridge. This is getting dangerous. You have the names of these two new men?'

'No. But I can get them from the records. But only after the chief receptionist has gone off duty.'

'Get them,' the voice rasped.

'It may be late afternoon . . .'

'Get them,' the voice repeated in Greek. 'Call me the moment you have the information. And anything else about these two you can find out. We may have to take drastic action.'

Giorgos was sweating as he hurried towards the restaurant entrance door. And not only with the heat – it was in the high eighties. He was worried the chief receptionist might have sent someone looking for him to carry out some task.

He slowed down as he walked across the entrance and through the doorway leading into the main hall. A tall heavily built man in his forties, clad in a clean white short-sleeved shirt and spotless denims, was approaching the counter from the main entrance. He heard quite clearly what the new arrival said in Greek.

'A Mr Newman is expecting me. He arrived during the past hour or so. Could you tell him I am here?'

'Will do, Nick. It's getting hot early this year. He's in Room . . .'

Giorgos missed hearing the room number but made a mental note of two facts. If this was one of the men he'd phoned about then he already had a name. Newman. He fiddled with a plant in a large holder, moving it a few

58

inches. The receptionist put down the phone, said something impossible to hear, and Nick headed for the staircase.

Strolling after him, Giorgos mounted the luxuriously carpeted steps. He had earlier followed the two men after noting the floor they were making for over the lift bank, running up the staircase. He had been just in time to see Newman being shown into his room. Too far along the corridor to be sure which room. And he hadn't dared to follow Marler.

The Greek called Nick turned along a corridor, stopped at a door and knocked. The door opened and Giorgos clearly heard the voice of the man who had shown the photograph to reception welcoming him in English. He retreated back down the staircase, working out an excuse to ask the question.

'I think I know that man who just arrived, a friend of one of my cousins.' The chief receptionist stared at him. 'He did my cousin a good turn, if it's the same man.'

'What would the likes of you have to do with Nick? He drives a Mercedes. Rather out of your class. Don't waste my time. See that pile of luggage over there? Be ready to carry it to the cab when it arrives to take our guests to the airport . . .'

Marler stared straight into Nick's dark eyes as they shook hands. Firm grip. Hair, streaked with grey, cut short and trim. A strong face. A firm jaw. A hint of humour at the corners of the mouth. Marler was good at weighing up a man quickly. Formidable was the word which came to mind.

'Bob will do the talking,' he said and sat down.

'Take a seat,' suggested Newman. 'We're here about Harry Masterson who was killed down at Cape Sounion.'

'So, you think he was killed?' Nick sat down, crossed his powerful legs. 'The papers said it was an accident.'

'One thing while I remember, Nick. Officially I don't

59

speak or understand any Greek on this trip. You think it was an accident?'

'I said the papers did. They think he was drunk. I saw him drunk myself.' Nick smiled drily. 'I drove a friend to the Hilton one evening, carried her bag in for her. Beyond the entrance hall is a large seating area at several levels. A crowd was gathered, watching something. Masterson had perched himself on a rail no wider than my hand, was walking along it like a tightrope walker, a champagne bottle clutched in each hand. A fifteen-feet drop below him. He walked the full length of the rail, then jumped back on to the floor next to the rail on his left. Enough people saw his performance to recall it when the news came through from Cape Sounion a few days later.'

'And he was drunk?' Newman pressed, hardly able to believe it.

'No.' Nick smiled drily again.

'But you said he was.'

'I know enough about drink – and drunks – to recognize the real thing, and when someone is acting being drunk. Masterson was acting. Don't ask me why.'

'He was staying at the Hilton?'

'No idea.'

'And you think his death was an accident?'

'No. I watched his act at the Hilton closely. He was nimble as a goat. A big man but quick on his feet, reflexes as fast as mine. That type doesn't go stumbling over a cliff.'

Newman opened a briefcase, took out a cardboard-backed envelope, extracted three photos of Masterson. He held them while he asked the question.

'I need to know where he stayed. Do you know two men you can trust – really trust?'

'To do what, Mr Newman?'

'Take these photos round hotels in Athens and find out where he stayed. He might have used another name.'

'Yes. They use his name? No? Of course some will

60

recognize him from the pictures in the papers.' Nick was looking at a print Newman had handed him. 'I could do some of the checking myself – divide up the search. It would be quicker.'

'One thing puzzles me.' Newman handed three prints to Nick. 'I really need to find out how his picture got into the press. Doesn't make sense. No one was interested until he became very dead.'

'Yes they were.' Nick clapped his hands together. 'I've just remembered. It happened when Masterson performed his crazy walk with the champagne bottles at the Hilton.'

'What did?'

'They have a creep of a photographer who works the hotel restaurant at night. He was hanging around in the lobby while Masterson did his walk. And he had his camera equipment with him.'

'So what happened?'

'It could have caused a disaster, but Masterson had strong nerves. This stupid photographer took a picture of him with a flashbulb. Masterson wobbled, then recovered his balance and went on. There was a gasp from the people watching.'

'Stupid, as you say.'

'But that is probably where the newspapers got the picture from,' Nick continued. 'All these photographers are after extra income. He took the picture when Masterson was grinning at the crowd – and the picture in the papers was like that. Mind you,' he added grimly, 'that was the only picture he was allowed to take.'

'Somebody stopped him?'

'Yes. Several people protested. The receptionist rushed over and gave the photographer hell. Anything else I can do to help?'

'Drive us to the port of Zea, then on to Cape Sounion.'

'You have the time?' Nick asked. 'Two hours there and back. And it would be best to wait a couple of hours. The traffic.'

'A couple of hours from now then. You still have the Merc?'

'A new one. Parked outside. I'd better go check the meter.'

'Two more things, Nick. Does the name Ionides mean anything?'

'Hardly. It's a common name. I know two. Both shop-keepers. And the other thing?'

'Christina Gavalas,' Marler interjected. 'Does that name mean anything to you?'

'You are joking?' Nick was amused. Marler's expression remained blank. 'You both know Greece. Surely you have heard of Petros Gavalas?'

'You mean the legendary Resistance leader during World War Two?' Newman asked. 'I didn't make the connection.'

'Christina is his granddaughter. She hates him. The Gavalas family is a strange story. Maybe I wait until we drive to Zea and tell you then. If she is concerned in any of this you have big trouble on your hands, my friends.'

5

Leaving the room, closing the door, Nick glanced along the corridor to his right, away from the exit. A small man wearing the black clothes of one of the hotel staff stood making a fuss about closing a window.

Nick looked away quickly, made his way downstairs and out of the hotel to where his Mercedes was parked in the blazing sun. He used a finger to loosen his collar. The heat seemed even worse. Dry and like a burning glass as the sun shone out of a sky as blue as the Mediterranean.

He was polishing the bodywork, which already gleamed like glass, when the small man in black jacket and trousers strolled out of the restaurant exit and round the corner. He was smoking a cigarette as he stood admiring the Mercedes.

'That is a real car. You are taking one of the customers for a drive?'

'Who knows when business will turn up?' Nick stopped polishing and stood facing the little man, the same man who had sneaked up behind him when he first arrived and asked reception to inform Newman he had arrived. Dark eyes too close together between a thin ferret of a nose. A smear of a black moustache above full lecherous lips.

'What is your name – and why aren't you on duty inside the hotel?' Nick demanded.

'I am Giorgos. I am entitled to an afternoon break. You think it is a pleasure working in this heat?'

'Get yourself another job if you are not happy. They pay you, don't they? Now, move away from my car. I am busy even if you can fritter away the day.'

Nick turned his back on the little man, polishing the car as he watched Giorgos walking back up the hill towards the restaurant entrance. In the wing mirror he saw Giorgos pause at the corner, take out a notebook from his pocket and scribble in it before he disappeared. He had recorded the registration number of the Mercedes.

To conceal his action half an hour later, Giorgos waited behind a corner before joining a crowd of pedestrians walking over a street crossing. Nick was still working on his car.

Giorgos made his way along the top side of the square facing the pink-washed building which had once been the

63

Royal Palace. Now it was the Parliament since Greece had become a republic.

In the centre of Constitution Square is a park filled with a variety of trees and shrubs. Tall railings fence off the park from the pavement beyond. Walking rapidly in the opposite direction from the one he had previously taken, Giorgos slipped inside a phone booth. Again he dialled the same number. Again he had to wait for it to be answered.

He glanced at his watch. His off-duty period was almost over. At least the chief receptionist had gone home, the bullying bastard. The same heavy-timbred voice came on the line.

'Giorgos here. More news. I discovered the names of those two men. Newman and Marler . . .' He spelt them out. 'I think they will be going somewhere in a Mercedes with a Greek driver. The registration number of the car is . . .'

'Any sign of them leaving immediately?' the voice enquired.

'No. The driver is still cleaning the Mercedes. But they may leave at any time. A silver-coloured Mercedes.'

'I can have a car following them in ten minutes.'

'Let us hope they are in time. Oh, there is one more thing.'

'Yes?'

'This is hard work for me. Maybe a little dangerous. More money would be welcome.' Giorgos swallowed, then stiffened. 'Another twenty thousand drachmae would be welcome – if I am to continue this work.'

'Be at your place in the Plaka at nine this evening.' The connection was cut before Giorgos could say 'thank you'.

He was surprised at how easy it had been.

88°F. 31°C. They were driving down Syngrou Avenue, sitting in the back of Nick's silver Mercedes. It was early evening and the scalding sun shone out of the azure sky as clear as a sea without ships. Nick used a handkerchief to wipe sweat off the back of his hand, his forehead.

'Syngrou is the longest avenue in Athens,' he remarked. 'As you can see, it's mainly car showrooms. BMW, the lot.'

Newman glanced back again through the rear window. Marler, wearing the lightweight linen suit he'd changed into, was careful not to look back.

'Some problem?'

'I think we may be followed,' Nick replied.

'The black Mercedes with amber-tinted windows?' Newman suggested.

'That's the joker. We'll know more when we fork for Piraeus. Someone may have been on the lookout for you coming into the city.'

Ruler-straight, Syngrou Avenue, lined with dusty poplar trees, stretched away forever into the distance. Nick maintained the same speed, kept glancing briefly in his rearview mirror.

'What facts have you to back up that statement?' Marler demanded.

'The fact that one of the temporary staff at Grande Bretagne took an interest in your arrival. Followed us up the stairs when we used the elevator. He was peering round the corner when Mr Newman was shown into his room. The fact that later when I left the room he was hanging around in the corridor, pretending to fool with a window. The fact that he came and tried to get information out of me when I was cleaning the car ready for this trip. The fact that he made a note of my car's registration number. Which may explain that big black Mercedes keeping the same speed and distance behind us now.'

'Any idea who this character might be?' asked Newman.

'Name is Giorgos. Don't know his second name. He's a small creep with a small dark moustache.' Nick made a quick stroke above his upper lip. 'Dark hair. Now, let us see what that black Mercedes does. Here we take the right fork to Piraeus. Left for Cape Sounion.'

He swung the wheel and grinned. 'Still with us. If he stays with us to Zea we shall know.'

'How far from Syntagma to Piraeus?' asked Marler.

'Ten, twelve kilometres. We are entering Piraeus now . . .'

The buildings lining the street were lower than in Athens. Nick pointed out derelict sites between them, the legacy of the wartime bombing of Piraeus. They crossed the main city square with the imposing town hall on their right built like an ancient Greek temple. Then they were swinging round the curve of the waterfront of the main harbour.

They passed large car ferries with their doors open, exposing yawning caverns. Nick slowed down. He gestured towards the vessels.

'The big ferries. They go to Crete and Corfu and Rhodes. The small one is soon sailing for Siros.'

Newman jerked his head. The name of the vessel was clearly marked on its compact stern. *Ulysses*. The last cars and trucks were edging their way up the ramp, forming three rows.

'How long to Siros?' he asked.

'Two hours.'

Marler was staring at the wall of buildings to the left facing the waterfront. Four-storey blocks, they carried names of various shipping lines, most of which he recognized. Watching him in his rear-view mirror, Nick grinned again and gesticulated.

'The headquarters of so many shipping empires. Others have registered in Panama. Some of those big men have yachts which come in to Zea. Petros Gavalas has a small yacht there – what these people would call a rowboat. And still our friends are with us.'

'That black Mercedes?' Newman enquired, careful not to look back.

'Yes. And we have made too many turns for it to be a coincidence. Let us see what he does when we turn down to Zea.'

They had left behind the big shipping company buildings. Now they were driving along a narrow street which twisted and turned, following the indentations of the coastline. On the landward side were small old apartment blocks. Freshly painted, they had pots and tubs holding decorative shrubs standing on their balconies.

'It would cost you a fortune to live at Zea,' Nick said. 'Only the very rich have an apartment here . . .'

Staring ahead beyond the windscreen Newman saw a signpost to the right as Nick slowed to a crawl. *Zeas Port.* He turned down a sloping track leading to the sea and along a platform below a high stone wall. The small harbour was crammed with ships moored hull to hull – and each worth hundreds of millions of drachmae. The million-dollar class.

Nick drove along the jetty which curved round the exclusive harbour, protecting it from the sea. Executing a three-point turn, he pointed the car the way they had come. He was parked by the stern of a small yacht, *Venus III.* Jumping out, he opened the rear door.

'This is Gavalas' yacht,' he remarked. 'A very small fish.'

'How could he afford even this?' Newman asked.

'He buys cheap. During the oil crisis he buys it for one tenth of its value from a man who needs cash. Petros is cunning.'

'What happened to the black Mercedes?' Marler enquired, standing by Newman on the jetty.

'It stopped by one of the apartments on the hill, one man got out, carrying a violin case. Then it drove off.'

'Odd that,' Marler observed and lit a cigarette.

'Please?' Nick was puzzled. 'I do not understand.'

'The car follows us from Syntagma. He has no way of

knowing where we are going. We arrive here and they drop off one man at an apartment. Some coincidence.'

Newman was running up a flight of steps to a narrow ledge beneath the wall which was now waist-high. The view out over the harbour hit him. The emerald sea, very calm, sparkled with dazzling reflections from the sun. On the far side and further out a fleet of freighters waited, stationary, bows pointed towards the harbour, smoke drifting lazily from their stacks.

'For Christ's sake come down,' Marler called out.

Newman turned, leant his arms on the wall. It was so hot he could barely stand the heat. He stood looking down at the assembled craft. From one of the photographs taken by Masterson this was where he had stood when he took them. On the jetty just about the point where Marler waited.

He recognized the huddle of old apartment blocks, the hills rising behind, bare, mushroom-coloured, flecked with scrub. There had to be something here which would give a clue as to why Masterson had come to Zea. He walked down the steps and spoke to Nick, who was polishing the bonnet of the car.

'There's a whole queue of big ships, mostly freighters, waiting to come in.'

'The cargo docks on the other side,' Nick explained. 'They will be waiting for the signal from Marine Control to berth.'

Newman frowned as he saw Marler staring up at the bridge of the *Venus III*. He followed his gaze and sucked in his breath. Standing by the side of the bridge was a girl with a mane of black glossy hair, centre-parted. She had good bone structure and wore a polka-dot white dress with a thin belt hugging her slim waist. She held her right hand over her thick eyebrows, shielding herself against the sun. It was the girl in the photo Masterson had taken unawares.

Marler stared back with a dry smile. Then he raised his own hand and gave her a mocking little wave. Her mouth twitched. She waved back, then vanished. Nick also stood staring at where she had appeared, the cloth poised above the bonnet.

'Christina Gavalas,' he said in a low voice. 'That is very strange.'

'I want to have a word with her,' Newman said grimly.

A gangplank linked the vessel's stern with the jetty. Newman approached it, followed by Marler at a more leisurely pace. His movements were always slow and deliberate. Except in an emergency.

Newman reached the gangplank when three seamen came round the corner of the deck. They wore white sleeveless sweat shirts, blue pants. In their late twenties they were heavily built and two carried marlinspikes. One of them shouted at Newman in Greek, brandishing his marlinspike.

'What did he say?' Newman asked Nick, although he'd understood every word.

Nick laid a warning hand on Newman's arm. 'He says you are not allowed aboard. This is private property.'

'Tell him to get stuffed. I only wanted to invite the girl to join me for a drink.'

'I think we had better leave,' Nick warned again. He called out in Greek. 'We are just leaving. My passengers were admiring your beautiful boat.'

The Greek waved his marlinspike and the three crewmen walked out of sight. Marler was staring beyond the boats up at the apartment buildings above the small harbour. He saw the sun reflect off something, like one flash of a semaphore.

'Get into the car quick!' he ordered Newman. 'No bloody argument.' He pulled open the rear door and dived inside as Newman joined him. 'Nick,' Marler continued, 'move us out of here fast.'

Nick reacted instantly. For a large man he moved with surprising agility. He was behind the wheel when the shriek of several ships' sirens blasted over the wall. As the noise continued Nick started the engine. There was a heavy *thud*. At the same moment they heard a crackle of glass splintering behind them. The bullet passed between the heads of Marler and Newman, passed on through the open window of the front passenger seat beside Nick.

6

Nick accelerated along the narrow platform, braked, turned up the track leading to the main road. He glanced in the rear-view mirror. Newman and Marler both had their heads turned. The rear window had crazed, had a small hole in it.

'He fired from the top of one of those apartment buildings,' Marler remarked.

'We go up there, yes?' Nick enquired. 'We find the bastard before he can get away?'

'No!' replied Newman. 'Turn left. Head back for the town hall square. Find us somewhere we can talk. And somewhere you can hide the car.'

'I know a bar. Close to it is a bombed site. They will not find the car if I park there.'

'Do it,' said Newman. He turned to Marler. 'Is that why you tried to get me down off the wall?'

'Of course, my dear chap.' Marler was as calm as though he'd experienced an everyday happening. He adjusted the display handkerchief in his breast pocket. 'You normally catch on quicker. You had an absorbed look when you ran up those steps. Stood on that ledge like a target in a shooting gallery. Is it the heat, by any chance?'

His tone was mocking. He reached into his pocket and perched a pair of horn-rimmed glasses on his nose. 'They have seen me once. I don't think they'll recognize me so easily next time.'

'Those glasses make you look exactly like Michael Caine.'

'Flattery will get you nowhere. The lenses are plain glass.'

'You were expecting that shot?'

'Something like it. The black Mercedes follows us. Nick reports they drop one man carrying a violin case, then drive off. A violin case! Not much imagination there. Did they strike you as musical characters? A violin case,' he repeated. 'Just the thing for carrying a dismantled Armalite rifle. You are only alive because he had to assemble his weapon before he used it. I saw the sun flashing off his telescopic sight – which is when I told you to dive into the car. He was a better shot than I'd hoped. Very smart, too.'

'Why do you say that?' Nick asked.

'He had a bit of luck and used it. Those ships' sirens starting up muffled the sound of the shot.'

'They made one huge mistake though,' Newman said.

'Which was?' Marler enquired.

'Firing that shot, of course. Now we *know* someone murdered Harry Masterson.'

The bar was small, located up a side street, was furnished with plastic-topped tables, a plastic-topped counter. Only the floor had a hint of luxury. It was laid from wall to wall with solid marble. Nick had ordered *ouzo* for everyone. Newman asked for a large bottle of mineral water.

'We can't afford to risk dehydration,' he remarked, wiping the back of his neck with a silk handkerchief. 'First things first. That bullet-hole in the rear window of your car could be embarrassing for all of us. Can anything be done about it?'

'You don't want to report the attack to the police?' Nick asked, his broad tanned arms resting on the table-top.

'They could complicate life at this stage. Unless you insist?'

'I have many friends.' Nick drank half his glass of *ouzo*. 'I know a garage mechanic who will fix that overnight. A new window. No questions asked. OK?'

'OK,' agreed Newman. 'I pay the bill, of course. Next – when Christina Gavalas appeared on the deck of *Venus III* you said, "That is very strange." Why?'

Nick paused, refilled their glasses from the jug of *ouzo*. 'It is a bit . . . complex. Is that the word?'

'Tell me, then I'll know.'

'Petros is eighty years old, a ferocious tyrant. Pray you do not meet him. Born in 1907, he married when he was seventeen. His first wife produced two sons – Andreas and Stephen. Twins, but not identical. Andreas and Stephen also married when very young – only eighteen. It was the war in their cases, I suppose. That was in 1943 or 1944. After Andreas was killed on Siros his wife gave birth to Christina – Petros' granddaughter. Do you understand so far?'

'Perfectly,' said Newman. 'Go on.'

'At that time Petros fought with the Communists – the ELAS party. Andreas hated them. He escaped to Cairo, joined the anti-Communist party, EDES. Petros was furious. Called him a traitor. But blood is thicker than water. Petros had a grudging admiration for Andreas. When Andreas was killed in the Siros raid he swore to hunt down his killer. Then came the second tragedy.'

'Which was?'

'The other twin, Stephen, also hated his father and fled to Cairo to join the EDES forces. Then he, too, was murdered. Later *his* wife gave birth also to twins, Dimitrios and Constantine. Again, non-identical. But the strain had run out. They are peasants working on Petros' farm in Devil's Valley.'

'A whole lot of hatred,' Marler observed.

'It gets worse. After the end of the Civil War in Greece between EDES and ELAS – which nearly wrecked my country – in 1950 Petros married again when his first wife died. His second wife produced a son, Anton. Maybe because Petros was then forty-two and his new wife was twenty-eight Anton turned out to be very clever. You see the scope for bitterness in that family?'

'How did Christina react?' Marler asked.

'A magnificent woman now, she is torn between two moods. Greek loyalty to the family – and her detesting Petros who treated her badly. As I told you, it is complex. But that is why I thought it strange to see her on *Venus III*. Petros only keeps the boat so he can watch those millionaires – wait for another to become in desperate need of money. Then maybe he picks up yet another bargain. He owns farms. One near Cape Sounion.'

'So he is rich?' Newman pressed. 'What kind of farms?'

'The one in Devil's Valley is in a remote part of the interior of the peninsula between Athens and Sounion. A dangerous area to explore. He grows figs and olives. His headquarters is an old farmhouse in wild country – reached by a track off the main highway to Sounion. There are even rumours he has a working silver mine. That I don't know about – whether it is working.'

'Let me get this clear,' intervened Marler. 'Petros was a one-time Communist. His son, Andreas, was killed on Siros. OK so far?'

'OK,' Nick agreed.

'And,' Newman suggested, 'this fierce old Petros is a Communist although he's rich?'

'Not any more from what I hear. Petros was sickened of

politics by the Civil War. It lasted from 1946 to 1949. A lot of blood was spilt. At the end of it Petros said all politicians could burn in hell. He devoted himself to farming, making money, but he has never forgotten the murder of his sons.'

'How and where was Stephen killed?' Newman asked.

'The rumour is it happened in a street brawl in a native quarter in Alexandria. There are other versions.'

'And Christina wavers between supporting Petros and hating him?'

'So it is told in Athens.'

Marler grunted. 'The only fact that comes out of all this is that Petros – and Christina – could still feel bitter about Andreas' death on Siros. After all, Andreas was her father.'

'That is what I have heard,' Nick agreed. 'And now maybe we should drive back to Athens so I can have the window repaired.' He finished off his *ouzo*, glanced at Newman. 'We forget about Cape Sounion – after what happened at Zea? For today?'

'Back to Athens. Another day we could visit this Petros? I'd like to ask him some questions.'

Nick grinned. 'You have brought some good weapons with you?'

'No. Nothing.'

'You go in Devil's Valley, you go armed. All Petros' men have guns. I said it before. A very dangerous place. You want to come out alive. Back to Athens . . .'

Newman saw the diesel train perched up on an embankment as it headed into Piraeus. He caught glimpses of it between buildings as they left the harbour behind.

'That's the Metro line, is it, Nick?'

'Yes. It starts at the other side of the city. The last stop this way is Piraeus.'

Newman looked at Marler. 'Endstation?'

'Who knows?' Marler adjusted his horn-rimmed glasses, perched his head back and closed his eyes.

Newman stared out of the window as a motorcyclist drew level. The rider, wearing a crash helmet and tinted goggles, turned and stared straight into the car for a few seconds. Then the machine was gone, zooming ahead of them, weaving in and out along the traffic.

'If you don't mind,' Nick suggested as they turned on to Syngrou Avenue, 'I will drop you close to Syntagma Square. That window is conspicuous. I want to get the car inside the garage before a policeman sees it. Then I have another job. I wish to have a word with Giorgos. He will tell me who it is he is working for – who followed us in that black Mercedes.'

'He may not feel like telling you,' Marler suggested.

'I have my own methods of persuasion. I will get his home address from reception. Oh, while I was waiting to take you to Piraeus I contacted my two helpers. Each has a photograph of Masterson. They must have checked with twenty hotels by now. Soon we will know where Mr Masterson stayed. May I drop you here? Only a five-minute walk to Grande Bretagne.'

'That's fine.' Newman had taken out his wallet. 'Time I paid you – for the trip, the repair to the window, and fees for your helpers.'

'Later.' Nick jumped out of the car, opened the rear door. 'You are well organized. Changing your traveller's cheques so quickly.'

He was referring to the regulations which only allow any tourist to bring in three thousand drachmae. Newman had changed cheques for a large sum at the hotel. As they stood on the pavement, the heat still hammering them, he laid a hand on Nick's arm.

'We would like to be there when you question this Giorgos. I have a few questions to put to him myself.'

'Late in the evening would be best. He will be relaxed and not expecting a hard time. I call for you at ten o'clock? If I find the time is wrong, I call your room?'

'Ten o'clock. See you then.'

They strolled along the street as Nick drove away. A park stretched away beyond iron railings to their right. Kiosks selling newspapers stood by the railings. People were queuing to buy plastic bottles of mineral water.

A motorcyclist cruised past. Newman frowned, watched the rider sliding in between the slow-moving traffic. The machine disappeared, heading for Syntagma Square.

Arriving at the main entrance to the Grande Bretagne, Newman handed Marler his room key. 'Wait upstairs in my room. I'll be right with you . . .'

Newman followed Marler inside, paused, waited for a brief time, then pushed open the door and peered out into the square. Full of traffic. He scanned the area rapidly. He found what he was looking for further down the hill.

The motorcyclist had parked the machine by a meter, still sat astride it. The same motorcyclist with the orange-coloured crash helmet and tinted glasses who had passed them in Piraeus. Who had later skilfully guided the machine between cars when they were walking.

The rider removed the crash helmet, perched it between the handlebars. She reached up with both hands and draped her waterfall of black glossy hair over her shoulders. Christina Gavalas had arrived. Things were warming up, and not only the temperature. Newman closed the door, went up to his room.

Ten o'clock. On the dot. Nick led the way to his parked car. It had a new rear window. Newman and Marler had dined in the oak-panelled restaurant. It was still daylight as they sat in the back and the Mercedes took off down the hill which was almost traffic-free.

'He lives in the Plaka, this Giorgos,' Nick informed them. 'That is the old quarter of Athens. It spreads out at the foot of the Acropolis, climbs part of the way up the hill.'

'I know,' said Newman. 'Any news about where Masterson stayed?'

'No. It is strange. My helpers have checked all the main hotels. No luck. He must have stayed somewhere. Would he choose some cheap place?'

'Not our Harry,' Newman said positively. 'He liked a bit of luxury. Live high was his motto. Maybe the hotels don't like giving out information about their guests?'

'My helpers are clever. They take round an expensive wristwatch. Say they found it with a credit card in his name. They want to give it back. And they don't read the papers, so they don't know he's dead. They get a reply. No, he didn't stay with us.'

Dusk was falling. The sun had slid down behind the Acropolis. Nick had entered a maze of narrow, twisting streets. There was little space to spare if he met a vehicle coming the other way. Through the open window Newman heard the mournful strains of the *bouzouki* from the open doors of small restaurants and cafés. Sometimes it was Western pop music. Every second door seemed to lead to an eating place. The pavements were crowded with sightseers and customers.

Nick drove into a small square with a muddle of buildings on three sides. The fourth side was open to a large level area littered with stones. The Parthenon Temple, perched on the Acropolis, was an ancient silhouette against the darkening sky.

'Monastiraki Square,' Nick announced. 'We park here and walk back to Giorgos' place. That way we surprise him. And parking is difficult.'

'Damn near impossible,' commented Marler.

Nick led them a short distance along a narrow street,

77

then he turned up a wide paved alley sloping like a ramp, lined with more eating places, more *bouzouki*. Newman and Marler strolled behind him and suddenly he stopped, held up a hand.

'Something is going on. Look at the crowd. We must be careful.'

'Where does he live?' Newman asked.

'Down that alley to the right. You see that car?'

The police vehicle was empty, parked half on the worn stone pavement. The crowd filled the street, was stationary, was staring down the alley Nick had indicated. They joined the crowd. Newman drew back, mounted the two steps at the entrance to a restaurant to see over the heads. He sucked in his breath.

A macabre sight. Beneath an old metal wall lantern attached to the side of the alley stood a large wine barrel. From the top projected two legs, bent at the knees. The legs were clad in black trousers, which had concertinaed, exposing tanned skin.

'What is it?' Marler asked, perching beside Newman.

'Look for yourself . . .'

Uniformed police swirled in the narrow confines of the alley. Several formed a cordon, holding back the crowd. Two stood on either side of the barrel. As Newman and Marler watched they took hold of the legs, slowly hauled up the rest of the body. Black hair dangled from the upended head.

Nick came close to Newman, whispered, 'I'll get in there. I know a couple of those police. Back in a minute . . .'

As he shouldered his way through the crowd the two policemen laid the body on the stone cobbles carefully, face up. Nick spoke to one of the police in the cordon, was let through, walked up the alley, which was a flight of steps, stopping beside the barrel.

'Looked a trifle queasy,' Marler remarked, and lit a cigarette. 'Did you notice?'

'The body's hair? Lank and dripping. Some liquid dripped off the shoulders when they hauled it out.'

'And since it is a wine barrel one might assume that's what it contains. Wine.'

After a few minutes Nick shook hands with both policemen and pushed his way back through the crowd. He used a handkerchief to wipe sweat off his head as he stood close to them.

'It's Giorgos. He didn't die too easily. They reckon he was grabbed, upended and lowered into that barrel. It is more than half full of wine. They drowned him in it. Held him with his legs kicking, I suppose. Held him upside down until he stopped struggling. Drowned. Then left him like that – legs crooked over the barrel's rim. Someone decided to make an example of him. To keep your mouth shut.'

'They certainly made their point,' Marler observed coolly.

'Let's get out of here,' said Newman.

He felt sick as they made their way back to the car. The shops were still open, shops selling a load of junk as far as Newman could see. Wicker baskets, leather bags, sponges. The shops were crammed between the tavernas. The *bouzouki* music had become louder, reminded Newman of a funeral march. The crowds were denser. Suddenly the Plaka had become a nightmare.

'Back to the hotel, Nick,' he said as they sank into the car. 'Back to civilization and peace.'

Peace was the last thing they found when they returned to the Grande Bretagne.

7

Marler and Nick stood in the corridor while Newman unlocked his door and walked into the room. They followed and Newman stood stock still, his expression grim.

Two men in civilian clothes were searching the room, checking inside drawers, examining the wardrobe. A third man, also in civilian clothes, sat smoking a cigarette. Hawk-nosed, in his thirties, dark-haired, thin and long-legged, his old friend, Chief Inspector Peter Sarris of Homicide, regarded him with no particular expression. He made no attempt to get up, to shake hands. Bad sign.

'May I ask what the hell is going on?' Newman demanded.

'You will all sit down in separate chairs. Not on the couch. No one will speak unless I ask him a question. This is a murder investigation. What is going on?' he continued in the same level tone. 'Surely it is obvious, Bob? We are searching your room. Before you ask, I have a warrant.'

'Best do as His Lordship says,' Newman told his companions.

'No need for sarcasm,' Sarris continued in perfect English.

'I'd have thought there was every need. You expect me to like this? And tell those goons of yours I expect them to replace everything exactly as they find it.'

'Be careful to leave everything neat – the way you find it,' Sarris said in Greek to the two searchers, then switched back to English.

'Only you are permitted to speak, Bob. Where have you just returned from?'

'You know the answer to that question. The Plaka.'

'And how would I know that?' enquired Sarris.

'Because the Volvo police car parked near the alley where Giorgos' body was found had a radio. One of the policemen was staring at me. I'm sure he recognized me. My picture has been in enough newspapers in the past. And my guess is Giorgos had something on him which showed he worked for the Grande Bretagne. One of the uniformed police radioed in to headquarters, reported to you . . .'

'That's enough,' Sarris said quickly. 'I know you are a top foreign correspondent, but you'd have made a good detective.'

'. . . and this is Marler, my assistant, learning his trade . . .' Newman was talking rapidly before he could be stopped. 'My driver Nick I have used on previous visits . . .'

'I said shut up . . .'

'. . . and this afternoon we used him to take us on a peaceful tour round Piraeus and the port of Zea . . .'

'*I said shut up!*' Sarris, livid, was on his feet. He gave the instructions rapidly in Greek to the searchers. 'One of you take the Englishman there to his room. This Greek, Nick, is to be taken immediately to a police car and held at headquarters.' As his men moved, he stood over Newman. 'I have one more word out of you and you will find yourself inside a police cell.'

'On what charge?' Newman enquired amiably.

'Suspicion of accessory to a murder . . .'

'Which one? Harry Masterson's?'

Newman shot out the words as Marler and Nick were bundled out of the room. In time for both to hear what he said. Sarris waited until the door closed and then offered Newman a cigarette, took one himself and sagged back into the same chair.

'Did you have to do that?'

'Do what? I thought you wanted information.'

'You're a bastard.' Sarris spoke in a resigned tone. 'But a clever bastard. When you've finished your cigarette you will have to come to police headquarters.'

'Why waste time? Let's get on with it . . .'

Outside the hotel Sarris was in time to stop Nick being taken away in a police car. 'Where is your own vehicle?' he asked.

'Parked down the hill. The silver Mercedes . . .'

'You will drive it to police headquarters. One of my men will accompany you.'

Sarris drove Newman by himself in an unmarked police car. He began chatting amiably as soon as they drew away from the kerb.

'I have to do this, I'm afraid, Bob. How long is it since you were last here?'

'Two, three years. I'm not sure,' Newman replied vaguely.

'I can see you are going to be difficult to interrogate. Maybe one of your companions will be more forthcoming. You will all be interrogated separately . . .'

'Bully for you . . .'

'A little cooperation would help all round.'

'Not after you searched my room without waiting for me.'

'We have a new police headquarters. Very modern. All the latest equipment.'

'Bully for you . . .'

'It's on Alexandras Avenue. Built about a year ago.'

'You make it sound like the bloody Hilton.'

'There are some similarities. Although not with the Athens Hilton. One of the places your hired snoopers visited when asking where Harry Masterson stayed.'

'Keep talking . . .'

Sarris gave up. Skilfully he drove through the night. Headlights appeared, flashed past them. They were on Alexandras now. Close to the football stadium on the opposite side a small colossus of a building faced with white marble loomed. A very modern rectangular block twelve storeys high it soared up towards the night sky above a vast entrance hall. No premium on space for government buildings in Athens, Newman thought as he followed Sarris inside.

To the left was a reception counter. A uniformed policeman hastily donned his peaked cap. Sarris led Newman to an inner lobby with a bank of four lifts on the right-hand side. His office on the eighth floor overlooked Alexandras. Sarris used an intercom to order coffee.

'Now,' he said, facing the seated Newman across his desk, 'may we start at the beginning?'

'We arrived in Athens . . .'

4 a.m. Sarris in his crumpled shirt-sleeves was showing signs of strain. The ash tray was crammed with his cigarette stubs. Only one of them belonged to Newman.

'So,' Sarris summed up, 'it comes to this. You came here to investigate the accidental death of Harry Masterson, sensing a story. Marler came to learn the ropes, despite his being described on his passport as an insurance executive?'

'I told you. He's fed up with that job. He wants a more adventurous life.'

'The murdered man, Giorgos, took an interest as soon as you arrived at the Grande Bretagne. He saw the photograph you showed the receptionist. Later, he tried to get information from your driver, Nick. You thought he could be a lead. So Nick found out where he lived from reception. You went there with your two companions to question him. You were too late?'

83

'End of story.'

'Bob, you really should have been a barrister. You so neatly make all the facts fit what I know . . .'

'Presumably because they do fit.' Newman drank more coffee. His fifth cup. 'Haven't we just about covered everything – except for what happened to Harry Masterson? An accident, you said.'

'I gave you the official explanation at the moment. He was murdered.'

Newman, cup raised, stared at the Greek. For the first time since the interrogation had begun he was taken aback.

'You change your mind quickly, Peter.'

Sarris stood up, wearily stretched himself, then leaned over the desk, spread both hands flat and stared straight back. His tone changed, became grim, almost spitting out the words.

'You think I have lost my touch? Homicide is my profession, my business. I'm supposed to be able to recognize murder when I see it. You think I park my backside here all day? Let me tell you something. I've visited Cape Sounion. No one with the savvy Masterson had staggers round above that cliff and walks over it. And I met Masterson by chance.'

'When? Where?'

'That night at the Hilton when he pretended to be high as a kite, did his death-defying walk along the rail beyond the entrance hall. I was attending a party. When I walked into the Hilton Masterson was just beginning that charade. I watched him. I tackled him afterwards, asked him what the hell he thought he was doing. Drunk? He was more sober than I am now after all that coffee. I talked with him for maybe ten minutes. He was able, tough, alert and street-wise. And he had the women in the palm of his hand.'

'Women? Any particular woman that night?'

'Christina Gavalas couldn't get enough of him. More coffee? You look shaken . . .'

A few minutes later. Sarris stood by the window, had opened the blinds. The first light, the false dawn, was casting a glow over the dead city. The peak of Mount Lycabettus was a massive silhouette in the distance.

'Why?' Newman asked. 'Why the official line that it was an accident?'

'The tourist industry is sacred to Greece, the billions of foreign currency it brings in, a commodity we're a little short of . . .'

'Oh Christ! Not the *Jaws* syndrome again?'

'*Jaws*?'

'The film about a shark off a resort island in America. The mayor didn't want to know about any sharks. Again, it might have frightened the tourists away.'

'Ah, yes, I remember. I see what you mean. Yes, there is a similarity. Murder – especially of an Englishman – would be bad publicity. The British come here like lemmings.'

'So you buried the case?' Newman said bitterly.

'You will apologize for that insult.' Sarris left the window, stormed back to his desk and sat upright in his chair. 'The case is not closed for me. No mealy-mouthed politician gives orders here . . .'

'You have your apology. Unreservedly.'

'It is early in the morning.' Sarris made a resigned gesture. 'We are both fully stretched. But maybe now you understand why I hauled you in? Informers – more than one – had told me men were going round the hotels showing Masterson's photo, asking where he had stayed. I had one in that chair, accused him of being an accessory to murder. He told me Nick was his employer. I phone the Grande Bretagne. They tell me you are the one who hired Nick.

85

Then I get another call from my men in the Plaka, investigating a particularly brutal murder – and he tells me he has recognized you. Now, do you think I do my job?'

'OK, Peter. You move fast. I'll give you that. Ever heard of Petros Gavalas?'

'Why?'

'I did my homework back in London before I came out. You're not the only one who does his job properly.'

'And you found the wolf has his lair north of Cape Sounion – where Masterson was killed?' Sarris had walked over to a filing cabinet. Unlocking it, he sifted through several files, extracted a glossy print from one, laid it on the desk before Newman. 'Petros.'

Newman stared at the print. He had rarely seen a picture which made such impact. A head-and-shoulders photo, the subject gazing away from the camera. An aged, ageless man. Like a prophet from the Old Testament. A great crooked beak of a nose, the eyes large and glowing under thick eyebrows, the face long, terminating in a heavy jaw. A bushy moustache above a thin wide mouth, the lips clamped tight.

'He didn't know his picture was being taken?'

'No,' Sarris admitted. 'We used a telephoto lens from inside an unmarked police van.'

'So he has a track record?'

'No, he hasn't.' Sarris pulled his shirt away from under his left armpit. Despite the open windows beyond the blinds, and a fan whirling overhead, the room was like an oven. The big heat was building up.

'Then why do you have his picture?'

'We think he could be trouble. One day. He has many hectares on his big farm in the wilderness. He rules it like a private kingdom – fief? Is that the word? I thought so. Armed men on horses patrol this kingdom to keep out intruders. They say they carry guns for shooting vermin – birds which feed on the figs. He hates what he calls the

English. Holds them responsible for the death of his son, Andreas, on Siros. An explosive situation.'

'And his granddaughter, Christina, was with Masterson?'

'That night at the Hilton? Yes. I don't know why. Maybe she just fancied him. She is a very beautiful woman. And now, perhaps you should go home with the others.'

Sarris took the photo, put it back in its file, relocked the cabinet. He poured more coffee from a fresh pot brought in by a girl.

'If you believe Masterson was murdered isn't there something you can do about it?'

'What?' Sarris spread his hands. 'I have no evidence. No one saw him at Sounion. The pathologist isn't much help.'

'But what did he say?'

'What I said. He has no evidence. When the coastguard cutter took his body off the rocks at the base of the Cape it was a wreck of smashed bone – smashed almost to a pulp the pathologist told me – showed me. Not a pretty sight. He only had one conclusion. The way the body hit the rocks the stomach was intact – plus its contents. No trace of alcohol. Only mineral water.'

'Time for me to push off.' Newman stood up. 'The others are coming with me?'

'Yes.' Sarris smiled drily. 'Their stories fit what you've told me. You can all go home. Maybe you and Marler should really go home – back to London?'

'You're deporting us?' enquired Newman as he opened the door.

'Wish I could.' Sarris grinned, slapped Newman on the shoulder. 'Take care of yourself. Greece could be bad for your health . . .'

Nick drove his Mercedes along Alexandras as streaks of the real dawn painted the sky with vivid slashes of red and gold. Above a band of black receding night was a curve of pure cerulean, intense as a blue flame, warning that another scorching day was coming.

'Take us somewhere very quiet and lonely, Nick,' said Newman. 'Somewhere we can talk without interruption.'

'Lycabettus,' Nick responded. 'Very high, very lonely – at this hour . . .'

He swung off Alexandras. Soon they were climbing steeply up a road spiralling round the lower slopes of Mount Lycabettus. They drove higher and higher. And as they climbed, below them Athens receded, the view expanded. Newman gazed out of the window. Already the panorama was awe-inspiring. They went on climbing, Nick turning the wheel all the time, negotiating the large car round diabolical hairpin bends, blowing his horn in case a vehicle was coming down. They met no one by the time he stopped at the edge of a precipitous curve.

'End of the road,' Nick said, alighting quickly to open the door, but Newman beat him to it, stepping out and taking a deep breath of fresh clear air. Marler stood on one side, Nick on the other.

'How did you get on, Nick – with their questions?' Newman asked.

'I told the truth.' Nick grinned. 'Some of it. I told them you hired me when you were last here. That explained how you knew me. I told them I drove you to Piraeus to show you the sea, that we looked at the boats at Zea and then drove back. Thank God I had the rear window repaired. It would have been difficult to explain the bullet-hole.'

'I thought of that. Go on.'

'I told them you gave me pictures of Masterson to find out where he'd stayed. That reference you made to him just before we left your room tipped me off I could talk about that. I told them Giorgos was taking too close an interest in our activities, that you wanted to ask him why. So I obtained his address in the Plaka from one of the assistant receptionists – by saying I owed him some money. When we got there we found he was dead. I kept it simple.'

'Which linked up beautifully with what I told Sarris. How did you cope, Marler?'

'I coped. Much the same story Nick told. Kept it simple. I only answered what I was asked. No elaborations. I must say I didn't care too much for your description of me as your assistant.'

'You'll get used to it.' He stared down. 'God, what a view.'

The huge eye of the sun was already glaring down on Athens. A city of white buildings crammed cheek by jowl, spreading out towards the horizon, merging with Piraeus, once a separate port. From that height the immensity of the capital showed dramatically.

In the far distance Newman could pick out a shoehorn-shaped bowl which was the new stadium they had passed on their way into Piraeus. Beyond, the Mediterranean was already a shimmer of hazy blue. It was the sheer *density* of the city of three million inhabitants which astounded Newman.

'Where the devil is the Acropolis?' Marler asked.

'I show you . . .'

Nick ran back to the car, returned with binoculars, focused them. He pointed below into the middle of the endless congestion. 'There. Perched up with the Parthenon on top.'

'Incredible.' Marler gazed at the ancient temple through the glasses as Nick went on talking.

'Most people who first come to Athens think the highest point is the Acropolis. But Mount Lycabettus towers like an old volcano far above anything else. And we are not at the top.'

Newman looked up to where Nick pointed. The mountain soared up further. Perched on its summit was a church with a brown-coloured dome.

'The Church of St George,' Nick explained. 'You can reach it by the funicular at the top of Kolonaki.'

'Kolonaki? I remember that from when I was here before. District for the people with big money?' Marler remarked, handing back the glasses.

'Christina Gavalas has an apartment in Kolonaki,' said Nick.

'The key is somewhere down there,' Newman reflected, gazing down at the vast sprawl. 'The key to who killed Masterson.'

Nick drove them back down another equally hair-raising spiral road into the city. The streets were still quiet. Outside a few shops women were spraying water on the pavements with hosepipes. As soon as their backs were turned the water shrank into damp patches, then evaporated.

'Another hot day coming up,' Nick commented. 'So we all sweat again. Grande Bretagne?'

'You can sweat,' Newman said. 'I'm going to sleep.'

They approached Syntagma Square along Sofias Avenue, a street which Newman remembered ran straight from the Hilton to the square. They would visit the Hilton later.

Nick was stopped by red lights at the entrance to Syntagma and Newman leaned forward, staring through the windscreen. Nick nodded.

'It is the same car . . .'

'With the same registration number . . .'

The black Mercedes with amber-tinted windows was parked across the street from the main entrance to the Grande Bretagne. Behind the tinted glass Newman could see two men sitting in front, two more in the rear seats. Nick parked at the foot of the steps leading up to the hotel. Newman got out slowly, stood upright, stared at the car.

One of the front windows lowered slowly, moved by

automatic control. A head leaned forward, looking direct across the street at Newman. He stood quite still, hands in his jacket pockets.

In real life he looked even more like an Old Testament prophet than in the photo Sarris had showed him. Aged and ageless. The curved beak of the cruel nose. The eyes intense beneath the bushy brows, the craggy forehead. Their eyes clashed over the width of the street. Newman sensed a look of pure hatred, venomous. The window closed slowly, shutting out the gaze of Petros Gavalas. The black Mercedes slid away from the kerb and was gone.

8

Petros Gavalas sat beside the driver, his grandson, in silence as the Mercedes headed down Syngrou Avenue. A very big man, he had pushed his seat back to its fullest extent to give comfortable leg room – so far back that the henchman sitting behind him had cramped knees. As they approached the point where the avenue forked, he spoke in his gravelly voice.

'Dimitrios, take the turn-off to Piraeus.'

'I thought we were returning to the farm . . .'

'Later. I have phone calls to make from the apartment at Zea. You are a fool,' he continued. 'I told you to shoot the driver of their car – to discourage Greeks from helping the English. You missed.'

'But we did not miss with Giorgos,' Dimitrios replied as he turned down the right fork. He chuckled unpleasantly. 'That one had his fill of wine forever.'

'People should not ask for more money than has been agreed. And he was a Greek. He should have known better. He knows now.'

'We are going to kill those two Englishmen?' Dimitrios asked.

'Not yet, cretin.' Petros shifted his bulk: the heat was making him irritable. 'I have already given orders. They will be followed night and day. Let us first see what they are up to. They had better not come near the farm. And they would be most unwise to start asking questions about Andreas. I trust for their sakes they do not go anywhere near Siros.'

'Does it matter? If they do go to Siros?'

It was the wrong thing to say. Petros hit Dimitrios on the arm. He almost swerved off the road. Petros swore at him, turned to glare at his grandson.

'Any English who goes near Siros could be involved in the great betrayal over forty years ago on Siros. Someone will pay for that. With his life . . .'

Marler ran a bath as soon as he entered his room. He stripped off, donned a robe, waited for the bath to fill. He ached in every limb. They'd sat him in a hard-backed chair for the interrogation. Standard procedure . . .

The gentle tapping on the outer locked door startled him. All his mental alarm bells began ringing. He picked up the ebony-backed hairbrush he always packed, held it in his right hand. He opened the door suddenly, leaning against the side wall.

A woman stood in the opening, a woman with a mane of dark glossy hair, a woman in her early forties, a woman clad in tight denims emphasizing her long slim legs and a white blouse unbuttoned at the neck, which exposed the upper half of her full firm breasts. Christina Gavalas.

'Aren't you going to invite me in, Mr Marler?' she

92

enquired with a slow smile. 'People may talk if they see us standing here together.'

'All right, come in. If you must.'

'Such a warm welcome,' she commented as he closed and locked the door. 'I thought it was time we talked.' She eyed the bed. 'I am a little tired. I don't mind where we talk.'

'That makes two of us.'

Marler stood with his hands on his hips, his mind racing as she unlooped her shoulder bag, dropped it on the dressing table. She reached for the hairbrush he was holding. 'May I? I look a mess.'

She stood in front of the mirror, brushing her hair vigorously, watching him in the mirror. Putting the brush down, she turned, put her arms round his shoulders, clasped her hands behind his neck and kissed him on the mouth, pressing her strong body into his.

'To what do I owe this honour?' Marler enquired as she pulled her head away from his, still grasping his neck. He watched her greenish eyes, his expression bleak and showing no excitement. She arched her thick eyebrows, half-closed her eyes, presenting to him her open front. Marler remained still, without reacting. Let her make the running. Her right hand slid inside his robe, felt his naked chest, moved down.

'I took a fancy to you when I saw you at Zea. I thought that you'd taken a fancy to me. You did wave.'

Her English was perfect. Her technique for rousing a man was good. The roving hand took its time. She gave him her slow smile again. Then she removed the hand, used it to take off her earrings, tossing them on to the dressing table.

'We won't be needing those, will we?'

'If you say so.'

'The cool calm Englishman. I love them . . .'

Standing away from him, still facing him, she undid her

blouse, threw it on the floor. She wore nothing underneath it. She watched for the effect she was creating as she undid her denims, slid them down her legs, threw them on top of the blouse. She kicked off her flat-heeled shoes, shoes fit for running in, for moving around with the least possible noise, Marler noted. He raised both hands, palms towards her, rested them on her bare shoulders and threw her back on the bed. Dropping his robe, he followed her, lying on top of her as she giggled and wriggled.

'My name is Christina,' she said ten minutes later as they lay side by side.

'Christina What?'

Marler lit a cigarette he didn't really want, stared at the ceiling as she pressed against him, the black mane spread over the pillow.

'Does it matter? Tell me something about the man I have just made love with.'

'I am training to be a newspaper reporter. I was in insurance before. Bored the hell out of me.'

'And what story are you working on at the moment?' She snuggled closer, her hand splayed on his flat hard stomach.

'This and that.' He leaned on his elbow, stared down at her and his expression was grim. 'I like to know who I've played with. Christina What?' he repeated.

'Does it matter?' She pouted.

He jumped off the bed, told her to stand up. Puzzled, she got to her feet. She faced him, then gave the same slow smile.

'What is your relationship with Petros?' he demanded. 'Did he send you?'

'Petros? If I am going to be cross-questioned I can get that at police headquarters like you . . .'

She stooped to reach for her clothes. Marler grasped her

94

by her strong pointed chin, stood her erect. 'I answered your question, now you answer mine.'

'I am going . . .'

Marler raised his right hand and hit her hard across the side of her face with the flat of his hand. She reeled under the blow, fell back on the bed. Her eyes blazed. He saw now they were black with greenish flecks. She leapt to her feet. Before she could speak he hit her again on the other side of her face, the blow harder. She now had two red weals. She leapt up again, came for him with clawed hands. She had become a raging wildcat. He grasped both wrists before the fingers tore his face, forced them downwards. She aimed a knee at his groin. He turned sideways, took the thrust on his thigh, dropped both hands suddenly, then hit her with real force. She sagged on to the bed, glaring up at him.

'What is your relationship with Petros Gavalas? You're going to answer before you leave. I didn't invite you here . . .'

'Why don't you go and . . . yourself?'

She no longer spoke her perfect English. She had lapsed into Greek and he realized she was watching him closely. One tough cookie, this girl. She had taken quite a beating but still she was probing.

'I beg your pardon?'

'Nothing,' she replied in English.

She started to get up and he used one hand to push her down on the bed again, digging his fingers into her shoulder. Both their bodies were gleaming with sweat from what they had done together, from the later struggle. The heat was building up in the room and Marler felt parched.

'Can I have a drink?' she asked.

'No. What is your relationship with Petros Gavalas?' he said again.

'I am his granddaughter . . .'

'I know that. It isn't what I meant. And you know that. Did he send you here to extract information from me – by using any method?'

'He wouldn't do that! No Greek would do that to his own kith and kin . . .'

'So you came yourself? Why? Because you love Englishmen? I recall you said that.'

'I hate Englishmen,' she hissed, pulling her hair back from her face. 'I want to get dressed . . .'

'You couldn't wait to get your clothes off when you arrived. If you hate Englishmen why did you take up with Harry Masterson when he arrived?'

'Who?' She drew back as Marler broke loose. Grabbing her by her long hair, he twisted it, pulling her down on the bed as he sat on her stomach, his mouth tight, pinning her down. He jerked her hair and she opened her mouth to scream. His hand clamped flat over her lips, exerting so much pressure she couldn't use her teeth to bite him. Her dark eyes were full of hate.

'Harry Masterson,' he repeated. 'Stop lying. You were seen with him at the Hilton. Other places, too. Now, I'm going to remove my hand. Yell – try to – and I'll knock you out.'

He jumped up suddenly, walked to his jacket, took a cigarette from his pack and lit it. The unexpected change of tactics threw her off balance. She stood up warily, slowly reached for her denims, slid inside them, wriggled herself into them, watching him. Straightening up, she adjusted the slacks, still naked above the waist. She spoke quietly as she made the threat.

'I'm going to accuse you of rape. The Greek police don't like foreign men who rape Greek girls.'

'There's the phone. Call Chief Inspector Sarris. I'm sure he'd enjoy a session with us. That he'll be interested to hear how you gave the signal for a marksman down at Zea to try and kill me. The bullet missed me by inches.'

'What are you talking about? There was no shot. I would have heard it . . .'

Marler was certain that for the first time she was telling the truth. He kept the surprise out of his expression. She reached for her blouse and held it dangling from one hand.

'You might just have managed it,' Marler speculated.

'Managed what?'

'Driven Harry Masterson so crazy over you that he fell for it. When you lured him down to Cape Sounion so he could be killed.'

'No! No! That was something I didn't do. What do you think I am?'

'That's easy to answer.' He pulled his wallet from his jacket. Taking out a sheaf of five-hundred-drachma notes, he looked at her. 'How much? What's your fee? For . . .' He gestured to the bed.

'*You swine! You lousy bastard!*'

'And I have diplomas to prove you're right,' Marler assured her.

She crammed her feet into her shoes, slipped on her blouse, hastily adjusted it. She glanced in the mirror. Her hair was a wild tangle. Marler handed her the brush he had picked up before opening the door earlier. As she used it, brushing her mane vigorously, she again stared at him in the mirror as he donned his bathrobe. This time she had a puzzled expression. His deliberate changes of mood were confusing her. He disappeared into the bathroom, returned holding a glass of water.

'You said you were thirsty. Next time I ask questions please give me answers, then we'll get on fine together.'

She drank the water in two long gulps, handed him the glass. 'I've never met a man like you before. Harry wasn't . . .' She stopped speaking.

'"Harry wasn't like you",' Marler completed for her. 'Tell me – before you go – why did you take up with him?'

97

'He was asking dangerous questions.'

'Such as?'

'About the Greek Key.'

'What's that?'

'Just pray to God you never find out. See you around, Marler.'

'It sounds as though you gave her a rough time. Just like you're giving me one,' Newman grumbled. 'I was fast asleep when you hammered on my door.'

'Thought you'd want to know the latest developments,' Marler replied, unrepentant. 'That you'd rely on your assistant to keep you informed.'

Heavy-eyed, his hair tousled, Newman tied the cord of his dressing gown more tightly, drank some of the coffee Marler had ordered from room service. He pursed his lips as he replayed in his mind Marler's account of his adventure with Christina.

'You have been enjoying yourself,' he said eventually.

'All in the line of duty . . .'

'Don't say that to Tweed. Significant that remark she let slip – "if I am going to be cross-questioned I can get that at police headquarters like you . . ." *Like you*. She knew we had been taken there by Sarris. No motorcyclist with an orange crash helmet followed us that I saw.'

'I thought I caught sight of that black Mercedes when I was taken in the police car,' Marler remarked.

'Did you now?' Newman drank more coffee. 'Then that would prove she *is* working under Petros' orders, that he told her about our visit. Which means she was lying – about acting under Petros' instructions.'

'Oh, she's a lovely little liar. Makes it a way of life.'

'Except on two points, you said. She didn't hear a rifle shot at Zea – which is possible with those ships' sirens blaring. And she wasn't the one who led Masterson down to Cape Sounion. This business is full of twists. And what the blazes is the Greek Key?'

'Maybe it turns the lock to the whole mystery.'

'If we could ever find that key. I'm going back to bed.'

'And our next move is?'

'Keep Nick and his helpers looking for where Masterson stayed. We might start making enquiries about the Greek Key. Someone must know what it is. In short, keep stirring the pot until something rises to the surface. And maybe take a look at Cape Sounion. While we're there we could try to locate old Petros' headquarters in the mountains.'

'Think I've already stirred one pot. It's called Christina Gavalas. I left her not liking us a lot. Which was the object of the exercise.'

'Exercise is the word for what you did.'

'Did you tell Newman everything about Giorgos, Chief?' asked his assistant, Kalos.

'What do you mean, everything?' Sarris demanded.

He stifled a yawn as he gazed down at the traffic jamming up Alexandras. Nine in the morning. It would get worse. He flexed aching hands. He wasn't up to these all-night sessions.

'The knife rammed into his back under the shoulder blade.'

'No, I didn't. We keep that quiet. I kept Newman away from the pathologist. That knife bothers me. Doesn't make sense.'

'The fact that he was drowned in the wine barrel first, then the knife was stuck in later? The lack of blood proves that.'

'Precisely. And it *is* an old British commando knife. The war museum has a specimen. I compared them. The knife in Giorgos is an exact replica. Macabre. Some kind of symbolic gesture?'

99

'Or something to put us off the real identity of the killer?'

'Could be. I just hope Newman doesn't go poking round in Devil's Valley. Petros Gavalas controls that area like some medieval baron.'

'And what about the number of accidents that have taken place in that area? Hikers and mountaineers who never come back?'

'I've never been able to pin anything on the old villain – but I'm certain his men tossed them over precipices. No one penetrates his territory and survives. He's the old school. Comes from Macedonia. They play rough up there. Yes, I do hope Newman gives that one a miss . . .'

2 p.m. 90°F. 32°C. Newman was freshly shaved, showered, his brain was alert, he had eaten a large lunch in the hotel dining room with Marler and they had returned to his room with Nick who had arrived promptly.

'We're going into action,' Newman rapped out. 'We'll stir the pot, as Marler put it earlier. Not to make it simmer – I want it boiling over.'

'The weather is boiling over already,' Nick remarked as he mopped his forehead.

'We'll drive down towards Cape Sounion,' Newman went on. 'My bet is we'll be followed. That will confirm we are getting somewhere. We'll enquire at the main hotels in the coastal resorts to see if we can find where Masterson holed up. We'll ask openly about the Greek Key . . .'

'What is that?' asked Nick. 'Sounds like a night club . . .'

'That is what we want to find out. And Christina will be in a rage after what happened. She may make a wrong move. Let's get to the car.' He picked up a large plastic bottle of mineral water and they left the room.

Nick ran ahead while Newman and Marler walked down the empty corridor. Newman never used elevators if they

100

could be avoided, if a staircase were available: elevators could become traps.

'You know, Marler, I think we're missing something. Maybe something under our noses.'

'Why the doubts?'

'This mystery is full of twists, unexplained contradictions. Why was Christina aboard that yacht, *Venus III*, *if* she is supposed to hate its owner, her grandfather, Petros? Who is paying for that expensive apartment she has in Kolonaki? We must visit her there.' He corrected himself. '*I* must visit her. She may tell me more than she told you.'

'I whetted your appetite,' Marler said cynically.

'What did Masterson find out that decided someone he had to be murdered? What was the link between him and Christina? Don't forget – they first met in London. Why did Masterson visit the Ministry of Defence to ask about that commando raid on Siros over forty years ago?'

'My head begins to spin . . .'

'I wish we had one man here who is a master when it comes to a manhunt, to untangling a complex web.'

'You mean . . .'

'Tweed. I miss Tweed . . .'

9

A sea of grey unbroken cloud pressed down like a smothering blanket: not a hint of blue anywhere. A fine drizzle like a sea mist covered the desolate landscape, settled on the windscreen of the Mercedes 280E Tweed had borrowed from Newman. He drove slowly along the narrow country road elevated above the grim marshland on either side. Not a soul in sight. At two in the afternoon they had the dreary world to themselves.

'Are we going the right way?' Paula asked as she studied the ordnance survey map. 'I'm lost.' She glanced out of the window, settled in the front passenger seat beside Tweed.

'We're right in the middle of the Somerset Levels, the area Masterson noted down on a scrap of paper in the cigar box he sent from Athens,' Tweed remarked. 'This is where the sea used to flood in centuries ago. Now they cut peat. I want to get the atmosphere of this place.'

He stopped the car, but kept the engine running as he stared around at the bleakness. Paula, dressed in a windcheater and a blouse and pleated skirt, shivered.

'I find this place creepy. Look, there's some kind of a building over there under those willows.'

'One of the farms – the peat-cutting farms.'

Below the road there stretched a ditch full of stagnant water. Paula lowered her window and wrinkled her nose as an odour of decay drifted inside the car. She opened the door, stepped out to take a closer look.

The ditch was coated with an acidic green slime across its surface. Patches of black water showed here and there. In the distance stood the ramshackle building Tweed had called a farm. Its roof slanted at a crooked angle. Smoke curled up from a squat chimney. Another smell assailed her nostrils and again she crinkled them in disgust.

'That's the smell of peat. You can see this side of that farm where they're cutting it. And someone is coming . . .'

Tweed's grip on the wheel tightened as he stopped speaking. Paula turned again to look towards the collection of hovels he had called a farm. Two men were advancing towards them, one walking behind the other along a grassy path leading to where she stood.

Both wore stained old pea-jackets, grubby caps and

muddy corduroy trousers stuffed into the tops of rubber boots. Each carried over his shoulder a long-handled implement. One was some kind of vicious-shaped hoe, the other a long spade more like an iron scoop. Both walked with steady intent, wide shoulders hunched, primitive faces staring at the intruders.

'Get in the car quick!' Tweed snapped.

He had the car moving as she slammed the heavy door and then increased speed. Paula let out her breath, a sigh of relief. Tweed started the windscreen wipers going.

'I didn't like the look of them at all,' Paula said.

'A couple of ugly customers,' Tweed agreed. 'The peat diggers are an enclosed community shut off from the outside world. I know this area well. Went to school at Blundell's near Tiverton. Hated every minute of it – like being in prison. During my spare time I used to cycle for miles – including round here. Pedalled like mad down this miserable road. Even then it frightened me.'

'Why cycle here then?'

'Kid stuff. Got a thrill out of scaring myself. You know something . . .' He glanced across the dank marshlands. 'This would be a good place to hide a body.'

'I'm glad you kept the engine running. There seem to be a lot of willows growing in this wilderness.'

'The other industry here. See those clumps growing by that ditch running away from the road? They're called withies. Shoots from pollarded willows. The osier-workers cut them and make wicker baskets to sell. Chairs, too. They can keep busy all the year round. When they've used up the withies and are waiting for next year's crop they dig up the peat. Goes way back over a couple of centuries. The Victorians were very keen on wickerwork.'

'And where are we?' She was studying the map again. 'I do hate to be lost.'

'Sign of a good navigator. Westonzoyland is probably

the nearest point of civilization. We left the A372 and drove north. We're heading for the A39. We turn left on to that, head for Bridgwater and then west to Dunster via Watchet.'

'Got it. What was in that large package which arrived from Harry this morning with the Athens postmark?'

'Look in the glove compartment. Another mess of clues. And after glancing at them I haven't one. A clue. See what you make of it.'

She sifted the contents of the reinforced envelope with the address again written in Harry Masterson's distinctive hand. Pulling out something as Tweed switched on the headlights to warn any oncoming vehicle, she examined it and then unfastened a clip, wrapped it round her wrist, closed the clip.

'It's a girl's bracelet. Why would he send that?' she wondered.

'No idea.'

'It's quite beautiful. You've seen the symbol the pendant has been designed as in imitation jewellery?'

'No. I told you I only had time to glance at the contents before we started out from Park Crescent.'

'It's the Greek key.'

Through a hole in the lowering clouds a shaft of sunlight like a searchlight moved across the great sweeping brown ridges in the distance. Tweed nodded towards them as they travelled along a hedge-lined road, approaching a small town.

'Up beyond there is Exmoor. A lonely place for the trio who long ago raided that island of Siros. And why should they all settle in the same area?'

'Let's ask them . . .'

'I intend to. We're close to Dunster now.'

They passed a signpost on their right pointing down a

narrow road. *Watchet*. Tweed grunted and Paula looked at him.

'You had a thought.'

'Watchet. I checked it in guide books before we left. My memory was right. It's the only port between here and Land's End. A real port, I mean. In a small way of business. It exports scrap metal and wastepaper to Scandinavia. And, guess where.'

'We turn left soon according to the map. Can't guess.'

'I know where we turn. I remember the road. From Watchet there is the occasional ship plying between the Bristol Channel and Portugal. Turn here . . .'

At The Luttrell Arms Tweed waited until they were settled in their separate rooms before strolling down the staircase to tackle the manager. Each room had its name on the door. Tweed had *Avill*, a large and comfortable room with a door leading to a garden at the back. The manager, a tall, pleasant man clad in black, looked up from behind the reception counter as Tweed placed a photograph on the woodwork.

'Can you do me a favour, please,' Tweed began. 'Has this man stayed here recently?'

The manager stared at the print of Harry Masterson without a change of expression. He looked up at Tweed.

'It is, I am sure you will understand, company policy not to give out information about other guests. If someone came and asked the same question about yourself . . .'

'Special Branch.'

Tweed laid the card forged in the Engine Room basement at Park Crescent alongside the photo. The manager stared at it with curiosity. He had a quiet deliberate voice, the kind of voice used to pacifying impossible guests.

'I have heard about your organization. This is the first time I have met one of you.'

'So I would appreciate it if you would answer my questions in confidence. A question of national security.'

'Oh dear.' The manager paused. Tweed replaced the card in his pocket in case anyone came past them. The place seemed deserted. 'I do recognize him,' the manager said eventually. 'He stayed here about three weeks ago . . .'

'For how long?'

Keep them talking – once you've opened their mouths.

'Five days, Mr Tweed.'

'In what name?'

'Harry Masterson. A jolly man. Well-dressed. A joker – made me laugh.'

'And this person?'

Tweed removed Masterson's photograph, replaced it with the blow-up of the picture of Christina Gavalas which had arrived in the cigar box. He watched the manager intently.

'No question of scandal involved, I hope?' ventured the manager.

'I did say in confidence.'

'Of course. Yes, she came with him. They had separate rooms,' he added quickly. 'As a matter of fact, Mr Masterson had the Garden Room, *Avill*, the one you have, the best in the house.'

'And the girl?'

'The same room as your Miss Grey. *Gallox*.'

'Registered in what name?'

'Christina Bland. She wore a wedding ring. You see why I was concerned about a little scandal. Foreign, I thought.'

'Don't be concerned. What did they do while they were here? I realize that's a difficult question – but everyone has to pass this reception area when they come downstairs. Did they spend a lot of time out?'

'A striking couple.' The manager eyed Tweed as though to confirm he was the genuine article. 'Yes, they did go

106

out most of the time. They would have breakfast – I help with that when staff is off duty – and ask for a packed lunch each day. Then we wouldn't see them until long after dinner. We close that front door at eleven and late-nighters have to ring the bell for admittance. Twice I let them in at midnight. I thought maybe they had friends round Exmoor they visited. That's a pure guess. You will keep this between us?'

'You have my word.' Tweed paused, smiled. 'You will keep entirely to yourself the nature of my job?'

'Good Lord, yes, Mr Tweed. The privacy of the guests must be sacred.' He looked embarrassed. 'Yours is, of course, a special case.'

Tweed picked up the second photograph. He put it inside his pocket, turned away, then turned back as though a thought had suddenly struck him.

'In connection with the same investigation, would you happen to know any of these three men? A Lieutenant-Colonel Barrymore, a Captain Robson, a man called Kearns? I do have their addresses. Barrymore, for one, lives at Quarme Manor, Oare.'

The manager took his time fastening up the middle button of his black jacket. Giving himself time to think, Tweed guessed. So I've given him something to think about.

'Again in complete confidence, I assure you.'

'This is a strange business you're investigating, if I may say so.'

'Very strange, very serious, very urgent.'

'Well . . . The three of them are friends. Every Saturday night they dine here. Always the same quiet table at the far end of the dining room. A kind of ritual, I gather.'

'They were here last Saturday? Two nights ago?' Tweed asked quickly.

'Well, no. The colonel is very formal. Always phones himself to book the table in advance. They've missed

107

for three weeks. Probably on holiday. Only my guess, I emphasize.'

'Thank you.' Tweed paused. He looked the manager straight in the eye. 'When you wake tomorrow morning you'll possibly worry about what you've told me. Don't. Worry, I mean. It is Monday. If I am still here next Saturday I shall make a point of dining elsewhere. Then if they come back you won't have me in the room. We do consider people's feelings.'

'So it seems. I thought, if you won't resent it, that your outfit were more aggressive.'

'On the contrary, we find we get the best results by being exceptionally discreet. And the local police shouldn't know I am here. Then we can't have any gossip about my being in the area.' Tweed leaned forward. 'We keep it just between the two of us. So, sleep well.'

'Thank you, sir. And if it's not out of place, I hope you enjoy your stay here. I'm not worrying.'

Tweed went back upstairs and knocked on the door of the room named *Gallox*. 'Who is it?' Paula called out.

'It's me,' said Tweed. She called out again for him to come in.

'Just look at this,' she began as he entered. 'Isn't it marvellous?'

She was sitting on the edge of a huge four-poster bed with a large canopy. It gave the large room a medieval atmosphere. Five feet six tall, the mattress was so high her feet dangled above the floor.

'You should have plenty of room in that,' Tweed observed and sat in an armchair. 'I have just talked with the manager. A tricky conversation. I had to show him my Special Branch card before he'd tell me a thing.'

'I like him. There's something Dickensian about his appearance.'

'And he's a man of great integrity . . .' Tweed told her about their conversation. She listened, watching him,

108

and he knew every word was being imprinted on her memory.

'That's queer,' she commented. 'We thought it peculiar that those three men should end up living in the same part of the country. After all these years they obviously keep in close touch. Why?'

'They could have stayed friends,' Tweed pointed out. 'They were together during the Second World War. Occasionally it does happen. But I think there's more than that to it – the trouble is I can't imagine what.'

'So where do we start?'

'We drive over by the coast road to Quarme Manor. I checked it on the map. Oare is down some side turning. That is after we've had a cream tea at the best place in this village.'

'Why? The manager said they were all away somewhere.'

'I want to see whether Barrymore – for starters – really is away. And if so, where he's gone – if possible . . .'

'This is one hell of a road,' Paula said with feeling.

'Porlock Hill. One of the most diabolical in Britain.'

Tweed was driving up a gradient like the side of a mountain. Added to the incredibly steep angle, the road twisted and turned round blind bends. Added to that, a grey mist was coming in off the moor, coils of sinister grey vapour creeping down the road.

Tweed drove with undipped headlights to warn any oncoming traffic, ready to dip them at the first sign of lights from the opposite direction. Like Tweed, Paula was tilted back in her seat as though inside an aircraft taking off. They passed a road turning off to their right and Tweed nodded towards it.

'That's the toll road, as they call it. That's fun too – it goes down like a water chute slide with a sheer drop on one side towards the sea.'

They had bypassed Minehead before they started the ascent and Paula patted her stomach. 'At least I'm full. That cream tea was fantastic. I'll get fat as a pig. And we're going to miss that turn-off to Oare,' she warned.

They had reached the top of the hill and drove along the level. No other traffic in either direction. The mist was thickening, making it as dark as night. The headlights picked up an inn sign. Culbone Inn.

'I'll check here for that turn-off,' said Tweed, swinging off the main road on to a wide drive.

He returned after a few minutes, climbed back behind the wheel. 'They say it's the next turn-off. A mile or so ahead. Easy to miss. And the road to Oare is very narrow.'

'Sounds great. Just what we need – for a car this size. How big is Oare?'

'Hardly a hamlet. Very spread out, as I remember. Two manor houses. Oare Manor and Quarme Manor, the stately home of Colonel Barrymore.'

'What exactly are we trying to do?' Paula was sat forward, braced against the seat belt, trying to spot the turn-off. At this height the mist was thinning. A chilly sea breeze blew in through her window. She pressed the button to close it.

'It's damn cold. Can I put on the heater?'

'As high as you like.'

Paula glanced at Tweed as she switched on the heater. He seemed impervious to extremes of both cold and heat. He wore a new hacking jacket, a pair of grey flannels, and a deerstalker hat which should have looked slightly ridiculous. But it suited him, gave him a commanding air. He read her thoughts.

'Dressed to merge into the landscape. Wear a London business suit out here and I'd stick out like a sore thumb . . .'

'Stop! You turn off here . . .'

He'd just checked the rear-view mirror, something he

110

did every ten seconds. He swung the wheel and they began to drop downhill. The country lane was so narrow the Mercedes just slid past the grass verges on either side. Beyond them a bank rose, topped with dense hedges. It didn't help visibility as the lane spiralled down steeply, a series of sharp bends. But the mist had evaporated and now they moved through a weird half-light as they dropped and dropped. At the bottom they drove across a gushing ford, reached an intersection. Paula desperately searched the map as Tweed swung right.

'Close to Oare,' he said. 'I remember that ford. From what the publican back at Culbone told me we should soon reach Quarme Manor. On the right somewhere.' The Mercedes was crawling as they navigated the winding lane. Above them in the distance Paula saw great sweeps of the moor, like tidal waves frozen in mid-flight.

'You asked me a few minutes ago what we are trying to do,' Tweed continued. 'We are trying to discover why Harry Masterson came here, what he discovered which led him to fly to Athens. In other words, what is the link between Exmoor and Greece? And who murdered Harry . . .'

He peered through the windscreen, still keeping the Mercedes at crawling pace. 'We have arrived. There is Quarme Manor.'

Paula was alone inside the car. Tweed had driven it into one of the lay-bys carved out of the side of the lane at intervals to allow one vehicle to pass another. He had instructed her to keep all the doors locked while he was away.

'Where are you going?' she had asked.

'To explore round Quarme Manor first, then call to see if anyone is at home . . .'

She sat with the heavy long torch in her lap he always

111

carried when driving. It was still daylight and she could see up on to the moor. She had turned off the heater, opened one window a few inches. Suddenly she stiffened, leaned forward.

She was looking at a ridge behind and overlooking Quarme Manor. It was uncannily silent. The wind had dropped. And despite the fact there was a dense copse of trees huddled round the manor house she hadn't heard the cheep of a single bird.

The horseman was perched on the ridge, silhouetted against the pale grey sky. Even motionless in the saddle, she saw he was a tall man. He held something with a long barrel in front of him, held it across the horse and parallel to the ground. A rifle.

Where the devil was Tweed? She watched the horseman, standing so still he might have been a bronze statue. Could it be Lieutenant-Colonel Barrymore waiting and watching over his property? Then the horseman moved, although his steed remained still.

He raised the rifle to his shoulder. He settled the stock in position and tilted the rifle angle downwards. He was aiming at something – someone – moving inside or just outside the grounds. Oh, my God . . .! Tweed was the target.

She raised the lever which unlocked the door, jumped out into the lane, still grasping the torch. Raising it with both hands like a revolver, she aimed the torch straight at the horseman, pressed on the light. The beam cut through the grey light. She knew it would never reach the horseman but she flashed it on and off time and again.

The horseman shifted in his saddle. The rifle swung in an arc, was now aimed at the car. She ducked down behind the Mercedes, waited for the crack of the shot. Nothing . . . She raised her head, ready to duck again quickly. There was nothing to see. The ridge outline was bare. The horseman had vanished. She had distracted him.

112

Shaking, she climbed back into the car behind the wheel, closed the door quietly, pressed down the lock.

Leaving the car, Tweed had walked quickly down the deserted lane. Coming closer, he saw Quarme Manor was a large Elizabethan pile built of grey stone with a wing extending forward from either end. The distinctive chimneys festooned the tiled roof. A high stone wall surrounding the place soon hid the house. He came to the entrance. Tall iron grille gates. A name plate. *Quarme Manor*.

No sign of lights. There should be lights if anyone was inside. The two-storeyed mansion was shrouded in gloom – made darker by the copse of trees sheering up inside the wall. Tweed peered through the closed grille gates up the curving drive beyond. A particularly fine example of the Elizabethan period, the mansion stood four square and seemed to grow out of the moor. All the mullion-paned windows with their pointed arches were in darkness.

He walked on along the curving lane, following the line of the wall. The silence was so intense he could almost *hear* it. His rubber-soled handmade shoes made no sound. He came to where the wall turned at a right angle away from the lane, climbing the steep slope towards a ridge behind the manor. A narrow footpath followed the line of the wall. He began climbing.

He had to keep his head down. The path was treacherous with slippery stones concealed beneath brown swathes of last year's dead bracken. He felt damp on his face, squelchy mush underfoot. He paused to stare at a second dense copse of trees – this one outside the wall and beyond the path. Out of the corner of his eye he caught movement. He looked up at the sabre-like cut of the ridge crest. Nothing. He could have sworn something moved.

Reaching the point where the wall turned again, running parallel to the front wall alongside the lane, he explored further until he found an opening. The gap was closed off with a single wide grille gate which was padlocked. He bent down.

By the gate the ground was cleared and in the moist earth were clear traces of hoof-marks. A back entrance to Quarme Manor which would take the owner straight on to the moor. And recently someone had ridden a horse here. He peered between the grille bars.

A gravel path led round a spacious lawn with ornamental shrubs arranged here and there. The lawn was cut, the topiary well-trimmed. Such attention cost money. He returned the way he had come.

The left-hand grille gate leading off from the lane opened at a push. His feet crunched as he walked up the drive. Inside the large porch he found an old-fashioned chain-pull bell. He tugged at it, heard it ring inside. A light was switched on, illuminating a diamond-shaped window behind an iron grille in the solid studded door. The lantern suspended over the porch came on. The small window opened. Tweed had a glimpse of a woman's bony face before the window slammed shut. The door was opened half a foot, a chain in place.

'What be it?' the old woman demanded.

'I wish to see Colonel Barrymore . . .'

'He b'aint be available.'

'You mean he is away somewhere?'

'He b'aint be available.'

She repeated the words as though she had been taught to say them by rote. She was tall, late sixties, her grey hair brushed close to the skull, her expression hostile. She was closing the door when Tweed spoke more firmly.

'The colonel will want to see me. When do you expect him to be back?'

'Name?'

'I shall have to tell him you were uncooperative. And he won't like that . . .'

'Phone for appointment . . .'

She was closing the door when they both heard the sound of a car approaching. It stopped outside. A shadowy figure opened both gates after jumping lightly out of the car. Before the headlights blinded him Tweed saw it was a crimson Daimler. Swinging round the short curve, it pulled up for a moment. A face behind the wheel stared out, then the car continued on round the side of the house. To the garage, he assumed.

'This is Colonel Barrymore?' Tweed asked the woman who still stood by the door.

'Better ask him, 'adn't you? Doesn't welcome strangers, you know.'

'It's becoming somewhat apparent,' Tweed remarked drily.

He turned as he heard the crunch of boots on gravel approaching from the side of the mansion. A tall, slim, elegant man in his mid-sixties appeared and stood, studying Tweed with an expression of disdain. Thick black hair was brushed over his high forehead and beneath his aquiline nose he sported a thin dark moustache.

He wore a sheepskin against the night chill and cavalry twill trousers shoved inside riding boots gleaming like glass. How the devil does he drive in those? Tweed wondered. The voice was crisp, offhand, as though addressing a junior subaltern.

'Who are you? If you are selling something you can take your immediate departure. And is that your Mercedes parked in the way down the lane?'

'Which question first?' Tweed asked mildly. 'And my car is in a lay-by. Plenty of room for you to get past even in your Daimler. That's what lay-bys are for . . .'

'I asked that stupid girl to move it and she refused . . .'

'She's not stupid and she's quite right to ignore

115

intimidation.' Tweed produced his card. 'Before you say another word you'd better know who I am. And while we're talking identification, who are you?'

'Colonel Barrymore.'

He moved under the lantern to examine the card, then looked up. 'It's all right, Mrs Atyeo, I'll sort this out myself.' He waited until she had disappeared, then stared at Tweed, handing back the card. 'Special Branch? A bit off the beaten track, aren't you?'

'So is Siros.'

Barrymore stiffened, stood even more erect. He jerked his head. 'Better come inside, I suppose. Just wait in my study until I'm ready to see you.'

By the light of the lantern Tweed saw Barrymore's skin was a tanned mahogany. He stood pulling slowly at one of the kid gloves he was wearing, taking hold of each finger and sliding it slowly half-way off. Even the slightest of the colonel's movements was slow and calculated.

'I'll go and fetch my assistant first,' Tweed said. 'She'll be taking notes . . .'

He was walking away before Barrymore could react. He felt he had left Paula alone in the car quite long enough. She greeted him with relief, told him quickly about the horseman on the ridge.

'That was very bright of you,' he said gratefully. 'To think of shining the torch. Oddly enough, Colonel Barrymore wears riding boots.'

'The man who stopped his Daimler alongside me and rudely told me to push off?'

'The very same gentleman. Surely there was plenty of room for him to pass?'

'Oodles. What do you think of His Lordship?'

'You said it. Let's get back to the manor. We have a right tartar to deal with. Something odd about him. Cold-blooded is the word, I suspect . . .'

10

'Go in there. No notes will be taken. I will join you when I can.'

Barrymore turned his back on them and disappeared through a doorway. They were standing in a stone-flagged hall. At the back a huge staircase mounted to the first floor, turning on a landing. Grim-faced, Mrs Atyeo stood holding open a heavy panelled door.

'In 'ere is where 'e wants you.'

'Always wears his riding boots, does he?' Tweed enquired as he walked towards the doorway.

'Part of 'is uniform, 'ain't it? 'E is The Colonel.'

'In capital letters, it appears.'

Tweed entered followed by Paula holding her notebook, the bracelet she had taken out of Masterson's last envelope still dangling from her wrist. Mrs Atyeo's expression changed, became ashen. She was staring at the bracelet and shrank back against the wall to let Paula pass, closing the door behind them.

'Tartar is the word,' Paula commented. 'And for some reason Mrs Atyeo nearly had a fit when she saw this bracelet.'

'I wonder why. Keep wearing it. Sit over there, notebook poised. It puts you offside from the chair behind that desk may put the colonel off balance.'

The study was also a library. Three of the walls were lined with books. The door into the room was cut out of a bookcase wall and lined with green baize on the inside. The fourth wall was occupied by tall mullion-paned windows which overlooked the garden and the distant moor.

'Not very comfortable,' Paula remarked, staring at the tall hard-backed chair behind the desk, the spartan wood-blocks forming the floor, the lack of any soft furnishings and the desk which was a large block of oak. She shifted in her chair, trying to find a less awkward position. Tweed was looking at the books.

'What a man reads can tell you a lot about him. Military history of the Second World War, the campaigns of Wellington, a lot of travel books. None on Greece . . .'

'Prying, are we?'

The soft voice came from the direction of the well-oiled door which had opened silently. Tweed turned slowly and faced the colonel. He wore a dark silk shirt, a regimental tie, his cavalry twill trousers and the riding boots.

Tweed sat down in front of the desk, made no reply as Barrymore crept round the far side and sat upright in his chair, crossing his legs. The man moved like a cat. That was it, Tweed decided: cat-like in his movements and gestures.

'Well?' He waited for Tweed to respond but his visitor sat studying him. He glanced round at Paula. 'I said no notes.'

'And I said Special Branch,' Tweed snapped. 'A statement has to be taken of this conversation. If you object, we can always drive straight to London and conduct the interrogation formally. You know our powers.'

'Get on with it then.'

Barrymore opened a drawer. Taking out a ruler he held it between both hands. As they talked he bent the ruler slowly, then let it revert to its original shape. Substitute for an officer's stick.

'You've got yourself a good suntan, Colonel,' Paula intervened before Tweed began.

'Just back from the Caribbean.' He swivelled his gaze,

118

looking at her shapely crossed legs, her well-formed breasts outlined by her N. Peal cashmere sweater. Her windcheater was draped over the back of her chair. He took his time studying her. 'There are some lovely islands out there,' he went on. 'Not the package-deal spots. Islands with hotels like select clubs. Emphasis on privacy. The last bastions of a civilized holiday. Native servants to attend to your every wish. All the guests vetted. Word of mouth the only *entrée*. None of your wog nonsense like Marbella. You'd like it. I didn't catch your name.'

'Paula Grey.' She clamped her mouth tightly.

'Siros,' Tweed said suddenly. 'During the war you led a raid on the island.'

'Did I?'

'The Ministry of Defence files say you did.'

'Oh, you've been permitted to poke round the MOD?'

'No doors are closed to us. Especially when the murder of a Government employee is involved . . .'

'Which murder?'

The ruler was bent like a bow, close to snapping point. The colonel released the tension, straightened it. His eyes were dark under hooded lids. No trace of expression crossed his tanned face as he watched Tweed.

'The murder of Harry Masterson. You've met him? He was in this area – with a Greek girl.'

'He called here.' Barrymore paused. 'He asked a lot of damn-fool questions. Who was this Greek girl?'

'We're straying. You led the raid on Siros. Tell me what happened – what went wrong? And who came with you?'

'Someone knew we were coming. Cairo was a hotbed of gossip. We were carrying a fortune in diamonds to hand over to the Greek Resistance. To help finance them. Two first-rate men came with me. Captain Oliver Robson and CSM Stuart Kearns. Plus one Greek who knew the island. Andreas Gavalas. His job to hand over the baubles. Someone grabbed them off him. Mission aborted.'

'Haven't you left something out?'

'Probably. Over forty years ago? Is there much more?' He glanced at his watch. 'I've had a long journey. A bath would be welcome.'

He stifled a yawn, hand over mouth. Long slender fingers, more like those of a beautiful woman. Paula was writing shorthand in her book, recording every word. She looked up. Tweed was again waiting. She glanced at a side table near her elbow. A copy of *The Times* lay on it, folded open at the personal advertisements section.

'Andreas Gavalas was murdered,' Tweed said eventually.

'Top secret. They couldn't have let you read that file?'

'That was the most significant incident of the raid. Tell me about it.'

'Unpleasant. One of my few flops. The four-man party got separated. There was an alarm. Someone – forget who – said a German patrol had been spotted. We dived for cover. False alarm. When we found Gavalas he had a knife in his back – the diamonds were gone. We beat a hasty retreat – back to the beach for rendezvous with the motor launch. Then back to Mersa Matruh by night. That's a wog port on the African coast – inside the Gyppo border.'

'I know where Mersa Matruh is. What kind of knife?'

Barrymore slammed down the ruler. 'If you read the file you know. This isn't quiz time. A commando knife – as well you are aware. Embarrassing. I checked both Robson's and Kearns' equipment. Both had their knives. Showed them my own. Any more? I hope not.'

'One final question. Could you please – in a few words – give me your estimate of the characters of Captain Robson and CSM Kearns?'

It was the last question Barrymore had expected. Paula saw the puzzlement in his saturnine face. The colonel steepled his hands, a concentrated look in his dark eyes. Like a man reliving some experience of long ago.

'Robson was seconded from the Medical Corps. Steady as a rock in a tight corner. Cautious. Always looked where he was placing the next footstep. Never panicked. Dour.'

'And Kearns?'

'Courage came to him second nature. Fast on his feet, in his thinking. Could be impulsive. Didn't matter. Had a sixth sense for danger. In an emergency very audacious. Time you went.'

Tweed stood up, showed no sign of resenting the abrupt dismissal. Like the ending of a military inspection. Paula slipped her notebook inside her shoulder bag, walked after Tweed to the door without a glance at Barrymore.

Opening the door, Tweed stood aside and let her walk into the bleak hall. He glanced back. Barrymore sat behind his desk like a statue, hands still steepled, a glazed expression on his long-jawed face. Suddenly he seemed aware they were leaving. He stood up, remained behind the desk, bowed formally, said not another word as Tweed closed the door.

'You'll be leavin' now.'

Mrs Atyeo was waiting in the hall. She unclasped the hands which had rested on her thin waist, went to the front door, drew back bolts, peered through the diamond-shaped window, unleashed the heavy chain, opened it and waited as they filed past her into the night.

They paused under the lantern on the porch as the door was shut behind them. They could hear the bolts sliding back into position, the chain being fixed, a lock turned. The lantern went out, plunging them into darkness. Night had fallen.

Tweed looped Paula's arm through his and they made their way slowly down the drive. He waited until they were inside the car before he sighed and asked the question.

'What was your impression of Barrymore?'

'Nasty piece of work. Like a satyr. Did you notice how he was looking at me? Undressing me with his lecherous

121

eyes. I felt I was naked. Thinks a lot of himself. I can imagine him riding a horse inspecting his troops, riding very slowly along the line with an expression of cynical contempt. And he moves oddly – like a cat. Took those gloves off with a feline grace . . .' She paused and shivered. 'I'm glad you're back with me in the car.'

'You didn't think I'd leave you on your own in a lonely place like this, did you?'

Tweed was watching his wing mirror. Paula froze suddenly and then jerked her head round. A slim hatless man was walking alongside the car from behind them. He leant on the window ledge. She let out her breath, lowered the window. Pete Nield grinned, pulled at his small dark moustache with his index finger.

'How goes the battle?' he enquired.

'Where on earth did you spring from?' she asked.

'Pete has followed us in my Cortina all the way from London. I told you he was coming. He's been parked a short distance behind you ever since I left you.'

'In this road?'

'No,' Nield told her. 'I parked the car beyond a gate leading to a field. Then I sat in a hedge close behind you. I was ready to intervene when that character in the Daimler pulled up by you if he'd tried anything on.'

'But what about in Dunster?'

'Parked the car at the other end of the village. I still have to register at The Luttrell Arms – but I warned them over the phone I'd be late. They won't realize we're together. At the hotel, I mean.'

'You haven't told me what you spotted about the colonel,' Tweed remarked. 'Only that you dislike him. Irrelevant. Pete, get in the back of the car and listen. Now I want both of you to grasp this. Ready, Pete?'

'Jolly comfortable back here. Nice to see how the other half lives.'

'Masterson came down to Exmoor with the Greek girl,

122

Christina. All three men involved in a raid over forty years ago on Siros, a German-occupied Greek island, are living on Exmoor. Harry Masterson, I'm sure, knew that. From Christina . . .'

'Assumption,' interjected Paula.

'Listen! Our main task is to interrogate all three men. And *every* word said by these men is important. One of them may let something slip. There was something very peculiar about that raid on Siros. Now, Paula, you were there when Barrymore gave his version.'

'Well, he was very suntanned,' she said slowly. 'So he could have just come back from Greece . . .'

'Now we're getting warmer. You see, Pete, this Colonel Barrymore has a terse way of speaking. Typical Army officer. But when Paula remarked on his suntan he became positively loquacious – explaining at some length how he'd been to the Caribbean. No specific mention of locales. It was the only time he really opened up.'

'You mean he was lying?' Pete asked.

'Paula, when we get back to London, will type out the transcript of each of the three men's statements – including their description of what happened on Siros. You can read them, decide for yourself.'

'You also asked his opinion of the other two men,' Paula recalled. 'I couldn't see the point.'

'In the end the whole thing may hang on the *psychology* of these three men. Would one of them be capable of murder? And did you notice,' he asked Paula, 'that when I mentioned a murder, Barrymore said, "Which murder?" It sounded to me as though he was thinking of more than *one* murder. Who else could he be thinking of besides Andreas Gavalas who accompanied them on the Siros raid?'

'Harry Masterson?' suggested Nield.

'Or possibly a third murder over forty years ago – mentioned briefly to me at the Ministry of Defence. Back to

123

your car, Pete. We must tackle our next member of the trio.'

'Who is that?' asked Paula as Pete left the Mercedes.

'Captain Oliver Robson. He lives the other side of Oare. I was given directions at that pub at Culbone. Robson calls there for a pint occasionally . . .'

11

After the gloomy Quarme Manor the modern L-shaped bungalow perched on the hillside in the dark looked to be out of another world. Which, Tweed reflected as he stopped the car, in fact it was. A wild leap from the fifteenth century into the twentieth.

The residence was a blaze of lights, standing at the top of a tarred drive above the lane. A wide stone-paved terrace ran the full width of the frontage. Ornamental lanterns were placed at intervals along a stone wall below the terrace, shedding light over the long slope of rough-cut grass to the hedge by the lane. The white-painted gate was open.

Tweed studied the large bungalow carefully. Curtains were drawn back but it was impossible to see inside the picture windows from below. Searchlight beams flooded the night from each corner, illuminating all approaches. He drove in through the entrance slowly, glancing to left and right.

'They'll know we're coming,' he commented.

'They'll hear the car, you mean?' Paula asked.

'No. In each of the gateposts there are photo-electric cells. As we drove through that invitingly open gateway we broke a beam. It will have set off an alarm inside the bungalow.'

'I suppose it's wise to take precautions – living in such an isolated position on the edge of the moor.'

'Including spy cameras projecting from under the eaves? Every possible kind of security measure has been installed. I begin to see something Colonel Barrymore and Captain Robson have in common. When I trudged round Quarme Manor before going up to the front entrance I noticed the high walls were topped with barbed wire. And a straight wire ran beneath it. Electrified, I'm sure. Remember all the security precautions on the front door? Both places are like fortresses.'

'That's what the owners have in common?'

'No. Both of them are scared stiff of dangerous intruders. To an almost pathological extent it appears . . .'

He stopped speaking. He had parked the car at the top of the drive. The front door opened. Framed in the dark opening – the lights inside had been switched off – stood the silhouette of a man. Holding a pump-action shotgun. Aimed at the Mercedes point blank.

'I'll sort him out,' said Tweed.

'God! What a welcome,' whispered Paula. 'Worse than Quarme Manor . . .'

'Good evening.' Tweed had lowered his window. 'We are looking for Captain Robson. It says Endpoint on the name plate.'

'Who are you? What do you want?'

A trace of Scots accent. The voice clear, level in tone, controlled.

'Special Branch. My name is Tweed. We have just called on Colonel Barrymore . . .'

Tweed made it sound as though Barrymore had led them to Endpoint. He waited for a reaction, said no more. Silence is a potent weapon.

'You'd better come in then.' The shotgun was lowered,

125

still held ready for action as they alighted from the car and walked across the terrace. 'You have some identification?'

'Just about to show you. I'm taking my card out of my pocket . . .'

'It is very lonely out here. There have been two attempts to break in to my home. I'm Robson.'

As he looked at the card, shotgun tucked under his arm, Tweed studied Robson. Medium height, heavily built, but all of it muscle and bone, he was about the same age as Barrymore. And like the colonel his skin was deeply suntanned. The top of his rounded head was covered with an untidy thatch of brown hair and he had a straggly moustache of the same colour. Clad in shirt-sleeves rolled up to the elbows, his shirt was open-necked, but his well-worn grey slacks had a razor-edged crease.

'Better come in, I suppose.' He handed back the card. 'Special Branch? Sure you've got the right man? Let's go and make ourselves comfortable in the sitting room.'

'Oh, this is my assistant, Paula Grey,' Tweed introduced. 'Welcome.'

Robson hardly gave her a glance as he closed the door and walked across a hall towards an open door. A brown-haired woman of about the same age appeared wearing an apron over her dress.

'Who is it, Oliver?'

Tweed detected a note of anxiety in her voice. White-faced, she had an air of bustle. Robson gestured towards her.

'My sister, May. Looks after me. Keeps the place going. Be lost without her. It's all right, May. Barrymore sent them along. We'll chat in the sitting room.'

The moment she entered the hall the warmth hit Paula. Two old-fashioned radiators stood against the painted walls. The sitting room was long and large with a Wilton carpet wall to wall. Cosy-looking armchairs and couches were spread about and a log fire crackled beneath a huge burnished copper hood.

'Do take a pew, anywhere you like. This is my work room, too.'

He sat in an old swivel chair behind a desk with a scruffed top. A tumbler of something which looked like whisky stood next to a pile of newspapers. Robson stood up as they sat down.

'I'm forgetting my manners. What would you like to drink? I can do Scotch, white wine if you prefer . . .'

Paula had sat down close to him near the end of the desk. He stared suddenly as she adjusted the bracelet round her wrist. His right hand jerked, knocking over the tumbler. Liquid ran over the edge of the desk.

'Sorry. Damn careless of me . . .' He opened a drawer, took out a cloth and began mopping up the mess. 'Just back off holiday. Half here, half somewhere else.'

'I guessed that from your suntan,' Tweed remarked. 'You'd hardly have acquired that in this country. Go far?'

'Sailing off Morocco. Agadir and Casablanca. By myself. May can't stand the sea. Stayed back to guard the fort. Drinks?'

Both Tweed and Paula, notebook perched on her lap, asked for wine. Robson poured two glasses of Montrachet. Returning behind his desk, he produced a tobacco pouch and a pipe.

'Fire away.'

'I'm checking details of a murder which took place over forty years ago,' Tweed began. 'During your stint of duty in the Middle East.'

'A long time ago, as you say – that grim business when we made that raid on Siros. Barrymore was in command, but you know that – just coming from his place. Why has it become important now?'

'Because someone else investigating it has just been murdered. Ever met Harry Masterson?'

127

Robson's thumb, tamping tobacco in the bowl, remained poised for a second or two. Paula saw the pause. *Cautious* was a word Barrymore had used, describing Robson.

'Yes, he visited me. Jolly sort of cove. Life and soul of the party type. Asked some rum questions. What on earth is going on? "Just been murdered," you said.'

'That is what I am trying to find out. Could you tell me in your own words what did happen on Siros?'

'Who else's words would I use?' Robson smiled drily.

'And if you don't mind, Miss Grey will record your statement – for the record.'

'Of course not. Certainly she may. Special Branch. You have a system, I suppose. One thing I am entitled to, I assume. A copy of the statement. Siros.' He settled himself at ease in his chair, lit his pipe, watching Tweed from beneath his upswept eyebrows, his light blue eyes thoughtful. What a contrast to Barrymore, Paula thought: he's the soul of relaxation. And his house reflects his informal personality.

'Siros,' Robson repeated, puffed at the pipe, 'the main island in the Cyclades group. Shaped like a boomerang, a huge one. Steep cliffs along the southern coast – rising up to Mount Ida. Same name as the tallest mountain on Crete. No idea why. Siros was the headquarters of General Hugo Geiger, who commanded the German troops occupying the Cyclades . . .'

'Is Geiger still alive?' Tweed interjected.

'No idea. Bit long in the tooth by now if he is. Like our little group. Now . . . The Greek Resistance had made its own HQ on Siros. They thought hiding under the Germans' noses was a smart tactic. We were carrying a fortune in diamonds to hand over to the Resistance . . .'

'Who is "we"?'

'The colonel, of course. Myself. You wouldn't think I was a commando in those days. I'm a doctor. The Resistance lot were short of medical help. Plus CSM

Kearns, stout fellow. Lastly, the Greek, Gavalas. He was to be the contact with his own people. He'd escaped to Cairo. He was the one who carried the diamonds. To cut a long story short, we landed from the motor launch at night on the southern shore, made our way up a difficult defile cut in the mountainside – where the Germans would least expect a landing. It was wild terrain. Someone – can't remember who – sounded the alarm. German patrol. Every man for himself in that situation. We scattered, later re-assembled at an agreed rendezvous – and Gavalas was missing.'

'He'd handed over those diamonds?'

'No one knew. Unlikely. That rendezvous was several miles away on the *northern* slopes of Mount Ida. We were still to the south. We started searching for Gavalas. It was pretty dramatic – horrific. Barrymore found him. Dead. A knife sticking out from under his left shoulder blade. And the diamonds had gone. We headed back for the rendezvous with the motor launch due to take us off. Nothing else to do.'

'And the knife?' Tweed prodded gently.

'That made it more horrific. A commando knife. The colonel checked us. We all still had our own knives – including the colonel. Later we wondered whether the knife had been taken off one of the two earlier teams which had perished while raiding Siros.'

'Who by?'

'Could have been one of the Greek Resistance. Even a German soldier. Someone must have had quite a collection. There were six commandos who died on Siros.'

'And the value of those diamonds?' Tweed asked.

'A hundred thousand pounds. Wartime value.' Robson tamped his pipe, glanced at Paula writing in shorthand.

'One more question before we go, if I may. Could you please give me your assessment of the characters and temperaments of Barrymore and Kearns?'

129

'We make a good team. Kearns has a place on the way to Simonsbath, a stone's throw from here. The colonel is decisive, ice-cold in an emergency. The most controlled man I've ever known. Remarkable. Always ready for any danger, however outlandish. Never lets up his guard.'

'And Kearns?'

'A natural CSM. Very young in those days. Weren't we all? Your legendary man of action. But an excellent planner as well. The two don't usually go together. Could always see three moves ahead in the game. Still can. I think that sums them up. More wine?'

'Thank you, but I think we've taken up enough of your time.' Tweed stood up. 'Could I possibly visit your loo?'

'Of course. Remiss of me not to show you when you arrived.'

When he strolled back into the room Paula had slid her notebook inside her shoulder bag and was standing close to the picture window. Pete Nield would be out there watching and she was trying to signal to him they were leaving. Robson padded across and joined her by the window.

'I'm a lifelong bachelor,' he remarked, fiddling with his dead pipe. 'Not from choice. Once I was madly in love with a débutante. Can you imagine that?'

'Yes, I can. What happened, if I may ask?'

'Why not? It was all a long time ago. I thought my feelings for her were reciprocated. She left me standing at the church. Sounds like an old joke, but it happened. A telegram arrived. *Sorry, Oliver. It won't work. Very sorry. Diana.* And Diana was a Greek goddess in mythology. Went off and married a baronet. Rather put me off women. Present company excluded.'

'It must have been an awful blow.'

'It was a bit. She was a *silly* girl.' He made the comment with such vehemence Paula glanced at him. The eyes were like stones, the mouth twisted in an expression of bitter

130

irony. 'Her baronet hadn't a penny. Had to take a job . . .'

'Thank you for being so helpful,' said Tweed as he returned and stood on the other side of Robson. He tapped the long thin picture window. 'Good view by day, I imagine.'

'Yes, it is. A lookout point over the moor. As to helping you, my pleasure. I'll show you out.'

'You keep your home beautifully warm,' said Paula. It was the first remark which came into her head and she sensed Robson was embarrassed by his display of emotion.

'It has to be oil-fired central heating out here. Tricky during the oil crisis. We practically lived in this room. The log fire . . .'

In the hall the pump-action shotgun was perched in an umbrella stand, the twin barrels pointing at the ceiling. Ready to hand for the next caller, Tweed noted.

The door closed behind them and they climbed into the car. Before starting the engine Tweed looked back at the bungalow, at the security cameras. The viewing screen must be in a room he hadn't seen. 'Something odd about this place,' he said as he reached to turn on the ignition and then leant back. 'Look at the roof, the far end of the long stem on the bungalow. We couldn't see it when we arrived because of the dark and the glare of those searchlights.'

Paula stared through the windscreen. Projecting above the roof of the bungalow rose a wide circular column which reminded her of a lighthouse. Even more so because at the top was a circular rail and behind it the column was made of glass. She expected at any moment to see a slowly revolving light.

'The moon came up while we were inside,' Tweed pointed out. 'Which is why we can see it clearly now. It's like a watch tower. Mind you, when I went to the loo his sister, May, took me the full length of the bungalow behind the sitting room to the main bathroom. On the walls are fishing nets with those glass balls suspended they use to keep nets afloat close to the surface. And fishing rods crossed like swords. Very much a man of the sea, Captain Robson.'

'There's someone inside the lighthouse. I can see his shadow against the moonlight.'

'Time to go.'

'Why did you liken it to a watch tower?' she asked while he drove down the drive and turned back the way they had come along the lane.

'I passed the base of the circular column on the way to the bathroom. It had a curved door, closed. Inside there must be a spiral staircase. Watch tower? Because I think Robson uses it to keep a close eye on the approaches to his home. The ridge along the moor continues from Quarme Manor, runs above Endpoint.'

'They both gave me the impression they're waiting for something dangerous to arrive – Barrymore with that wall and an electrified wire you saw. Now Robson – again with all that expensive security. The kind of thing you expect to see protecting a Beverly Hills mansion.'

'As though they were expecting Nemesis,' said Tweed.

12

Tweed, who had studied the map of Exmoor, drove back the way they had come and then turned on to a country lane leading away from Quarme Manor. Paula watched his expression as the headlight beams followed the twists of the hedge-lined road. The darkness seemed eerie, the moor closing in on all sides.

'Pete is still following us if that's what you're wondering,' she remarked. 'I saw his lights a moment ago behind us.'

'I was wondering about the name of Robson's bungalow. Endpoint.'

'Rather obvious. The lane comes to a full stop below where his bungalow is perched.'

'I noticed that. Something else came back to me. One of those notes Harry Masterson sent back from Athens – wrapped up as a clue only I would understand, he thought. *Endstation*. Close to Endpoint, wouldn't you say?'

'My God! It never occurred to me. Was Harry pointing a finger at Robson?'

'Who knows? It's early days yet.'

'It's getting late nights. Where are we off to now?'

'To pay a call on the third member of the party which raided Siros all those years ago. CSM Kearns. If we can ever find his place in the dark. I've marked where I think it is on that map. Navigate, girl.'

'Maybe he won't welcome a surprise visit at this hour . . .'

'So, maybe we catch him off guard. It's odd the way the three of them live so close together.'

'Perhaps they've remained close friends even after all these years.'

'And you don't sound any more convinced than I am . . .'

It was a difficult drive even when the moon rose, casting a weird light over the landscape. The light became weirder as a mist began creeping down from high up the moor. Behind the phosphorescent glow Paula could still see the ridge crests sweeping across Exmoor like giant waves.

They met no other traffic. They passed no villages. For miles on their way towards Simonsbath they saw not even one isolated dwelling. They were alone in the desolate wilderness as Tweed descended a long curving road, lights undimmed to warn any vehicle approaching from the opposite direction.

'What on earth is that?' Paula asked suddenly.

Lights suddenly appeared further down the slope, lights close together on their right-hand side. Tweed frowned, slowed to a crawl. They were still several miles from Simonsbath from his memory of the map. Woods now lined either side, and the lights gleamed between the tree trunks, flashing on and off as the trunks momentarily obscured them. He stopped the car and stared through the windscreen.

'It's a small estate of modern bungalows. They're crammed pretty close together. Must have been built during the past ten or fifteen years.'

'And I think we may have pulled up just outside CSM Kearns' house,' Paula commented.

To their left inside a gap in the trees stood an old stone two-storey house perched higher up the slope. Surrounded by a high stone wall, there were two six-feet-high solid wooden gates. Tweed reached for his flashlight in the glove compartment, asked Paula to lower her window, switched on the light. A large metal plate carried the name. *Woodside House*. 'This is his place,' he agreed.

He continued to move the light over the solid wooden gates. On the roadside was a grille covering each slab of wood. Reaching over to the rear seat, he grasped a heavy wooden walking stick he had purchased in Dunster. He was never sure afterwards what had made him do this.

'Let's investigate,' he said, switched off the engine and extracted the ignition key.

He locked the car before walking round it to join Paula who stood staring at the gates. Carrying the stick in his right hand, the light in his left, he swivelled the beam to the side of the right-hand gate and saw a bell-push. He pressed firmly with his thumb and they waited.

In the distance beyond the wall there was the sound of

a door being opened, a door which creaked loudly in the heavy silence of the mist-bound night. Footsteps approached with a brisk tread across what sounded like a cobbled yard. Suddenly a ferocious snarl murdered the night, followed by barking.

'My God, what's that?' Paula asked.

'Guard dog.'

'Sounds as though it's short of food – and thinks we'd make a good dinner.'

'Who is it?'

A cultured voice. Terse. Commanding. Talking at them through a small window flap opened in the right-hand gate.

'My name is Tweed. Are you Mr Kearns?'

'Yes. What do you want?'

'Special Branch. I want a talk with you. Now.'

'You have identification?'

'Of course. Wait a minute.' The unseen animal was growling, its claws pawing at the inside of the gate. It couldn't wait to get out. Paula shivered. Tweed produced his card, held it up to the spyhole, shone his torch on it.

'Stand quite still when I open the gate. Move and you'll be torn to pieces.'

'Charming,' Paula mumbled under her breath.

The flap slammed shut. A sound of bolts being withdrawn, the turn of a key and the right-hand gate swung inward. They were still faced with the heavy iron grille. Tactfully, Tweed switched off his light. Also, he wanted to regain his night vision. He felt Paula tense beside him.

The tall figure of a man stood inserting a key into the grille with his left hand. His right gripped a chain holding a huge dog. The creature became excited again, baying and snarling, lunging forward.

'Quiet, Wolf,' the crisp voice commanded. 'Come in. He's harmless . . .'

'You could have fooled me,' Tweed rapped back.

'And who is this girl? Not also Special Branch? She can wait in the car.'

'She can come in with me, for God's sake. She's not waiting by herself out here in the middle of nowhere. And she is Special Branch. My assistant, Paula Grey . . .'

As this exchange took place Kearns was closing the grille and the gate, relocking everything. Tweed wandered up the slope paved with stone flags towards the house. Over a hundred years old if it was a day. Paula kept pace, anxious to distance herself from Wolf, which she had now identified as an Alsatian.

'Wait here,' Tweed said as they reached the steps up to the front door. 'Back in a moment.'

He walked swiftly in his rubber-soled shoes round the left side of the stone hulk. At the entrance to a wide passage a horse had recently relieved itself on the stones. Rounding the corner, he was confronted with a stable door, the upper flap open. A horse's head regarded him, poked itself further over the flap and whinnied softly. Tweed held out a hand, stroked its neck. Its smooth hair was wet. It had been ridden hard. And not long ago.

'Leave him alone. What are you poking round here for?'

Kearns' voice was harsh, demanding. He moved as quietly as Tweed. Turning, Tweed smiled apologetically, made a dismissive gesture.

'I'm fond of horses,' he lied. 'That's a very fine animal . . .'

'Come back to the proper entrance.' The Alsatian, snarling like a mad dog, lunged for Tweed, who instinctively raised his walking stick. Held by an expanding lead, it almost reached Tweed and Kearns hauled him back. 'Prowl round here and Wolf will have your guts for garters.' Kearns made the statement in a calm tone.

Tweed followed Kearns at a distance. He switched on the flashlight as though picking his way. To the side of the paved area rough uncut grass and weeds cluttered the earth up to the base of the wall. His beam reflected off something metallic. Pausing, he prodded carefully with the stick. There was a grinding clash of metal. Two sabre-like blades, saw-toothed, sliced across the lower end of his stick. Kearns swung round.

'What the hell do you think you're playing at?'

'You tell me.'

'You just released a trap. We keep chickens and we're plagued with vermin – foxes and such like off the moor. That could have amputated your leg.'

'Let's go inside then. As you suggested . . .'

Inside, a bleak square hall was dimly lit with a forty-watt bulb. The woodblock floor was highly polished, doors led off the hall and a wide oak staircase climbed to a landing before turning to the next flight. From a door at the rear a blonde woman in her thirties appeared smoking a cigarette in an ivory holder.

She had a good figure, wore a powder-blue blouse with a high neck and a classic pleated cream skirt. She watched Tweed with a speculative eye, ignoring Paula. Kearns' mouth tightened.

'My wife, Jill. We have gatecrashers.'

'Would you like some refreshment?' she enquired, still eyeing Tweed. 'Coffee? Maybe something to drink . . .'

Her voice was soft, husky, but Kearns answered for her.

'Not necessary. They won't be staying long. Better come into the mess,' he told Tweed.

'He means the dining room,' Jill explained. She stroked her shoulder-length hair with one hand.

'In here,' Kearns went on. 'Sit down. Both of you.'

The rectangular-shaped dining room was oak-panelled, had an oak dining table and was illuminated by another forty-watt bulb inside an old-fashioned shade suspended high above the table. An atmosphere of spartan gloom pervaded the room. Tweed and Paula sat on chairs at the table while Kearns took up a standing position.

137

'First, I'd like to see your identification again,' he demanded.

Tweed handed him the card and studied their host while he examined the document. Kearns was over six feet tall, a lean and rangy man with a clean-shaven face and strong bone structure. He stood very erect in front of the fireplace which was laid with logs but unlit. Paula suppressed a shiver. It was chilly.

Kearns was in his sixties but he had worn well. His hair was still dark, his complexion was deeply tanned. He carried himself with an air of complete self-assurance and his eyes were like two brown marbles. Never off parade, Tweed thought drily.

He was clad in a pair of dark slacks, sharply creased, and a navy blue polo-necked cashmere sweater. There were traces of dried mud on his dark brown shoes, the only flaw in his otherwise impeccable appearance. He dropped the card on to the table so Tweed had to reach forward to retrieve it.

'Get to the point,' Kearns said.

'I'm investigating an unsolved murder which took place over forty years ago in the Middle East.'

'Oh, that macabre Ionides killing in Cairo. Can't help you. Why bring that up now?'

'Because it may be linked with the recent murder of one of our people. In Greece. At Cape Sounion. Know it?'

'No.'

Kearns stood with his feet slightly apart, hands clasped behind his erect back. He glanced at Paula who was taking notes in her book on the table. She had kept her expression blank during Kearns' reply. This was the first reference to Ionides.

'There are two of you,' Kearns decided. 'Bad tactics to be outnumbered. I also need a witness . . .' He walked quickly to the closed door, opened it, called out. 'Jill, come

138

and join us. Just sit and listen with that remarkable memory of yours. Sit there.' He made brief introductions.

As he returned to his position in front of the fireplace Jill Kearns, still smoking, carrying a porcelain ash tray, sat at the head of the table. She studied Paula, who stared straight back. Hackles rising, Tweed noted.

'Don't see how a recent murder could be linked with the Ionides business,' Kearns resumed.

'Tell me about Ionides. You used the word "macabre".'

'Not much to tell. We had just returned from a mission . . .'

'We?'

'Three-man commando raid on a Greek island. Anti-khana – name of the building in Cairo where Ionides was slaughtered one night – was our official HQ. No one in the place knew what we were really employed for. Propaganda was supposed to be our job. Not even the CO of the building – Colonel Grogan – had a clue about us.'

'Tell me more about Ionides.'

'Some Greek who *was* working on propaganda – printing leaflets to send to the Resistance crowd. Two nights after we got back Ionides was apparently working late, alone in the building – a habit of his. Late one evening someone cut him to pieces. Blood all over the walls. He must have fought for his life – the room was a wreck. Ionides was slashed everywhere. Head pretty near severed from the body. Some maniac must have got in – and out. The Special Investigation Branch – equivalent of your crowd in the Army – never did solve it.'

'Did you ever meet a Harry Masterson?'

'Bluffed his way in here. Bit of a buffoon. Sent him packing.'

'You look very suntanned,' Tweed remarked, switching the topic without warning.

'I should do. Just back from windsurfing in Spain.'

'Your wife kept out of the sun from her appearance . . .'

139

'Didn't come with me. She hates the heat, loves the cold. Is this part of the interrogation? I haven't all night.'

'I have. And we're talking about murder. Maybe three murders. Where had you come back from just before the Ionides killing?'

'I told you. A three-man raid on a Greek island. Siros . . .'

'And the names of the other two men?' Tweed interjected quickly.

'The CO, Colonel Barrymore. A Captain Robson, medical officer.'

'And after all these years the three of you all live in the same area. Exmoor. I find that very curious – even strange.'

'Nothing to it. Barrymore and I stayed on in the Army after the war. Same unit. Robson got his demob soon after hostilities ended. Set up in practice as a doctor here. We kept in touch. When Barrymore and I left the Army we weren't sure where to settle. Robson offered to find us property round here. He knew the ropes. Barrymore and I told him what we could afford. Is that all?'

'Not quite. A Greek came with you on the Siros raid.'

'Oh, Gavalas.' Kearns shifted his stance, showed signs of growing boredom, even impatience. 'He was supposed to put us in touch with the Resistance group we landed to meet. Knew them, so he said. I had my doubts. There was a moment when we thought Jerry was near us in force. We scattered. When we met up Gavalas was missing. We found him in a gulch. Obviously he'd hidden there. He was dead. Knifed in the back. Commando knife, too. The colonel sorted that out. Checked that Robson and I had our knives. Showed us his own. Stickler for detail, the colonel. Not that we thought any of us had touched the Greek. Why should we?'

'For a hundred thousand pounds of diamonds that went missing.'

140

'Obviously taken by the assassin. Siros was crawling with odd characters. Fortunes of war.'

'Misfortunes in this case,' Tweed pointed out. 'For Gavalas. You ride much, Mr Kearns?'

'All of us do. One reason for living on Exmoor. And now . . .'

'Who is "all"?' enquired Paula.

Kearns turned his head as though he'd forgotten her presence and wasn't too pleased about her intervention. He stared at her coldly.

'The colonel and Dr Robson. As I was about to say before you interrupted, is that all?' He stared now at Tweed, looked pointedly at his watch.

'One more question. What odd characters? You just said Siros was crawling with them.'

'Republican Greeks, left-wing Greeks, Royalist Greeks, monks from the monastery. And the German occupation troops. Now . . .' He marched round the table to the door, opened it and went into the hall.

Jill Kearns, who had lit a fresh cigarette, leant across the table to Tweed. 'Are you staying somewhere near?' she whispered.

'Luttrell Arms, Dunster. You can get me there if something's bothering you,' Tweed replied in a low tone. He raised his voice. 'I think we may soon outstay our welcome, Paula.'

In the hall Kearns stood by the open front door. Somewhere close at hand Paula heard Wolf snuffling, growling, scratching at a door. Kearns had handed the dog's chain to Jill when they entered the place.

'Goodbye,' said Kearns stiffly.

'Just before we go,' Tweed persisted amiably, 'please give me your impressions of Colonel Barrymore and Captain Robson.'

Kearns' thin mouth tightened. 'The colonel is a first-rate commander. Can smell trouble a mile off.' He gazed straight at Tweed for a moment. 'Knows at once how to deal with it. No hesitation. Captain Robson was not a regular. More inclined to circle round trouble. Very determined in an emergency.'

'And that estate of new houses just down the road. Seems out of place.'

'Why? Occupied by businessmen, I gather. Probably commute to Taunton or Bristol. Like the country life. How would I know? I'll let you out now . . .'

Tweed and Paula prepared to follow him down the slope. Just before he stepped out Tweed glanced back. Jill Kearns stood watching him, holding her cigarette holder. She nodded at him.

'Goodnight,' said Tweed. 'Sorry to disturb you at this hour.'

'Any disturbance is welcome out in this Godforsaken wilderness.'

Kearns had both the wooden gate and the grille open when they reached him. He stood aside, said not another word as they walked out. The grille slammed shut behind them, followed by the main gate. Standing on the grass verge Tweed heard brisk footsteps retreating back towards the house.

'Well!' Paula blew breath between her teeth. 'That was really something. Imagine living with him.'

They climbed back into the car which was chilly inside. Tweed switched on the heater and tapped his fingers on the wheel before starting the engine. He was gazing at the glow of the estate lights in the mist.

'What was your impression?' Tweed asked as he fired the engine.

'A born CSM. Should still be in the Army, bawling contemptuous commands to his troops. Very self-contained. Could settle anywhere. A bloody iceberg.'

'And his attractive wife, Jill?'

'A manhunter. After more trophies to add to her collection.'

142

'That's pretty catty. Not your usual style . . .'

'I saw the way she watched you while you grilled Kearns.'

'She's a good few years younger than him – and it must get very lonely in that hideous old pile.'

'She's getting to you already.' Paula glanced at Tweed as he let the car cruise downhill. 'You devil, you're teasing me. I agree it can't be much fun married to the perfect CSM.'

'I thought he did that rather well – put on a clever performance. Just stopped short of caricature.'

'Tweed, what are you driving at?'

'Mr Kearns is a great deal more devious than you give him credit for. He was presenting a mask to us.'

'Talking about masks, I wonder about that peculiar little colony of bungalows,' she observed. 'They don't look real. Let's take a closer look. You know, they all look simply too good to be true to me.'

He slowed down even more as they passed the entrance to the estate and Paula counted six bungalows, three on each side of the cul-de-sac. All the dwellings had curtains drawn, lights on behind them. All had the usual status symbols of the upwardly mobile young and ambitious executives. Coach lanterns flanking each porch; more lanterns at the entrance gates to the drives; urn-shaped pots with evergreen shrubs like small exclamation marks.

'Like something out of the Ideal Homes Exhibition they hold at the annual Olympia exhibition in London,' Paula remarked. 'As I said before, they don't look real.'

'And Kearns, who lives on their doorsteps, doesn't seem to know a thing about them. Hard to swallow.'

'Makes sense to me. You said it yourself. He's a self-contained type . . .'

'I also said he was a good actor. What's the matter?'

They had left the bungalow estate behind, the road was now level, winding across the moor, open to it on either side. No hedges. In the moonlight on both sides smooth

143

dark slopes swept up to high ridges silhouetted against the night sky. Paula had stiffened, was staring up to her left.

'There's that ghostly horseman again!'

'Where?' Tweed reduced speed to peer up the slope where transparent veils of pale mist rolled slowly over the moor, assuming strange shapes. Tweed was sceptical. One patch of mist looked like a centaur, then dissolved. 'I don't see any horseman . . .'

'Up there on that dip in the ridge, for God's sake. And he's got his rifle again. He's aiming it . . .'

Everything happened at once. A Cortina came up behind them and overtook, slowing as it pulled in ahead of the Mercedes. 'Pete is still with us,' Tweed remarked. 'I still can't see . . .'

He broke off in mid-sentence. Paula was not given to seeing phantoms as he'd imagined. Perched in a fold between two ridge crests a man on a horse stood still as a statue, rifle raised. Tweed rammed his foot down on the accelerator, turning out to pass the Cortina which had stopped. There was a sharp *crack!* At the same time the sound of splintering glass. Paula jerked her head round.

'Both rear side windows are crazed . . .'

'Bullet,' Tweed said tersely.

He pulled up at a point where two copses of trees shielded the road on either side, forming a shield. In the rear-view mirror he saw Pete Nield crouched behind the parked Cortina, both hands raised, aiming up the slope. The hard detonation of three shots fired in rapid succession echoed through the night. Nield stood up, climbed back behind the wheel, drove forward and stopped alongside the Mercedes. Tweed lowered his window full depth.

'He tried to kill you this time,' Nield remarked. 'How the hell did he make it all the way down here from the Doone Valley?'

144

'Did you get him?' Tweed asked calmly. Beside him Paula gripped both hands tightly to stop shuddering.

'No. The range of fire was too far for a handgun. Frightened him off before he could try again. Saw him vanish over a cleft in the hills. You didn't answer my question. How could he make it here from the Doone Valley?'

'He'd have to know the country well, have ridden over Exmoor a lot.' Tweed splayed his hands on the wheel. Paula was amazed by his reaction: he was cool as a cucumber. She was still shaking. 'Also there's a moon up,' Tweed went on. 'An experienced rider could have come across country direct while we drove in a half circle slowly.'

'So it could have been either Barrymore or Robson?' Paula suggested. 'Kearns told us they all rode . . .'

'Or even Kearns himself. Time to get back for a late dinner to Dunster.' He glanced at her as he released the hand-brake. 'Don't forget – Kearns is closest and the horse I saw in his table was still saddled up. But the attempt on my life proves that we came to the right place.'

13

The horseman appeared in the middle of the road as they came close to Dunster along a quiet hedge-lined country lane.

He sat motionless on his horse, one hand held up, the other holding the reins. Tweed saw him clearly in his headlights. He turned them from dipped to undipped and the twin glare showed up the waiting man starkly. He lowered his raised hand to shield his eyes.

Pete Nield's Cortina, close behind the Mercedes now,

overtook Tweed's car. Nield drove with one hand on the wheel, his other slipping the .38 Smith & Wesson from his hip holster. Stopping the Cortina, he jumped out of the seat, lifted both hands, gripping the gun, aiming point-blank.

'Don't shoot!'

Tweed had stopped his own vehicle, dived out and ran forward. He stood beside Nield, studying the horseman who remained as still as a bronze statue. Tweed blinked, wondering if his eyes were playing him tricks. Then he spoke briefly to Nield before walking forward.

'You won't need the gun. Incredible. I know who this is . . .'

Standing by the flank of the horse, he extended a hand upwards. The horseman reached down to shake the hand. Both men stared at each other. The horseman was stockily built, in his sixties, sported a brown moustache which matched his thick hair.

'Chief Inspector Sam Partridge,' Tweed said.

'Ex-Chief Inspector. Now retired. You gave me quite a chase over the moors. Where are you staying?'

'Luttrell Arms, Dunster . . .'

'Like me. It's the only decent hostelry for miles. I'll join you there for dinner, if I may. And they know me simply as Mr Partridge. It's only about a mile now. Why don't you drive on and I'll follow?'

'We'll wait for you in the bar,' replied Tweed and went back to his car, waving to Nield to take the wheel of his own vehicle.

'What was all that about?' Paula asked as the horseman turned and began trotting towards Dunster. 'And who is that man? He tried to kill you.'

'There was more than one horseman out on the moor today.' Tweed sat behind the wheel, watching Partridge's retreating figure.

'More than one?'

'The man who tried to kill me and that chap. Ex-Chief Inspector Sam Partridge of Homicide. I knew him at the Yard when I served my stint before joining the Service.'

'I don't understand this too well.'

'Neither do I. The long arm of coincidence is stretching itself to breaking point. There has to be some logic in this business somewhere. Partridge called at the Ministry of Defence after Harry Masterson – talked with Brigadier Willie Davies, the chap I went to see.'

'I still don't see . . .'

'When Partridge called at the MOD he told Davies he was still investigating a murder committed over forty years ago. In Cairo. A man called Ionides.'

'In Cairo? But Gavalas was murdered on the island of Siros.'

'Exactly. Odd, isn't it? Two different murders nearly half a century ago. I'm looking into one, Partridge is investigating another. He's staying at The Luttrell Arms.' He switched on the ignition. 'We're meeting Partridge when we get back to the hotel. Should be an interesting conversation, wouldn't you say?'

They sat at a quiet corner table at the far end of the dining room at The Luttrell Arms. Tweed had requested somewhere they could talk on their own. The manager in his dark jacket and trousers had escorted them and whispered to Tweed after pulling out Paula's chair.

'This is the table those three local gentlemen sit at when they meet here every Saturday night.'

'Which three gentlemen?' Paula asked when the manager had gone.

'Barrymore, Robson, Kearns . . .'

Tweed looked across the table at Partridge who sat opposite to him. Paula sat next to Tweed and faced Nield, sitting alongside Partridge. She studied the ex-Scotland

147

Yard man. Beneath his thatch of thick brown hair his face was weatherbeaten, had the ruddy glow of a man who spends a lot of time out of doors. His grey eyes had a steady gaze, his nose was short, almost pugnacious, but his manner and way of talking were gentle. The pursed lips and the strong jaw gave him an obstinate look. Not a man who gives up easily, she decided.

'The three men who are my suspects,' Partridge commented.

'Suspected of what?' Tweed enquired, glancing up from the menu. He noticed Partridge hesitate, glance at Paula and Nield. 'My companions are both fully trustworthy,' he assured him.

'Of the murder of a Greek called Ionides back in 1944 in Cairo.'

'That's a long time ago,' Paula remarked.

'I was hardly out of my teens in those days. For some reason I never understood they attached me to the SIB – Special Investigation Branch,' he explained to Paula. 'Military equivalent to Scotland Yard. I had a fool for a superior – a Captain Humble. Funny name for him – he was anything but humble. Knew it all, so he thought. Knew damn-all from what I could see. He'd been with the police in Manchester before joining the Army . . .'

He paused as the waitress came to take their orders. Paula was studying him again. He wore a hacking jacket, old grey slacks, and by his side on the banquette rested a much-worn check cap. A perfect outfit for merging into the Exmoor landscape. Tweed sipped water and then encouraged Partridge to continue before he could ask what Tweed was doing on Exmoor.

'Tell me a bit more about the murder of this Greek. Ionides, I think you called him.'

'Which wasn't his real name. I'll come to that later.' Partridge rested his elbows on the table and began to talk animatedly. Almost like a man possessed, Tweed noted.

'It was a horrific murder. Took place late one evening after dark in a weird building called the Antikhana. Near the Nile and backing on to a native quarter. Ionides had escaped from German-occupied Greece and was officially working on propaganda fed back into his country. A British sergeant who was billeted on the roof found the body. Blood all over the walls, the furniture, the floor. He had been cut to pieces with a knife. Head almost severed from the body.' Partridge looked at Paula. 'Sorry, don't want to spoil your meal.'

'I have a strong stomach. Do go on.'

'Humble was in charge of the case. Came up with nothing. No one in the building at the time of the murder, apparently. Only one entrance – and a Sudanese receptionist guarded that. Main entrance doors kept locked at night after six. Murder took place somewhere between eight and ten according to the pathologist. So theoretically the murder couldn't have been committed.'

'The windows?' Tweed suggested. 'The murderer could have got out by one of them?'

'Impossible. Bars on all the windows. Security was tight. The case has remained unsolved to this day.'

'So what are you doing prowling round Exmoor?'

Partridge waited while drinks and starters were served. He rapped on the table with his left-hand knuckles, a quiet tattoo. He ignored his soup, started talking again as soon as they were alone again.

'It's a bit complex. Three commandos were based officially inside that building. Two days before the second murder they'd returned from an abortive raid on an island called Siros.'

'Just a moment, Sam,' Tweed interjected, 'you're losing me. You said "the *second* murder" and "*abortive* raid . . ."' What was the first murder?'

'The two questions are linked. The raid was abortive because attached to the three-man commando unit was a

149

Greek called Gavalas carrying a fortune in diamonds to hand over to the Resistance on Siros. They were desperately short of funds. On Siros Gavalas was murdered – knifed in the back. The diamonds he was carrying had gone. So, the mission was abortive. Two days later the three commandos were back in Cairo – *before* the murder of Ionides. You see where I'm leading?'

'Never like to assume anything, Sam. You must remember that from our days at the Yard.'

'Humble made a routine investigation of the murder of Ionides and then dropped the case. Something else came up. I was fascinated by the whole thing. The sheer brutality of the killing at the Antikhana. I kept on digging in my spare time. Ever since I've been convinced one of the three commandos was the killer of both men. On Siros, Gavalas. In Cairo, Ionides. The three men were Barrymore, Robson and Kearns.'

Tweed drank the rest of his soup while he thought. Nield, who was keeping quiet, had devoured his shrimp cocktail. Partridge was sipping his soup. Paula watched him as she went on eating her pâté. There were only three other couples eating late dinner.

'Sam,' Tweed began, 'you've spent your life as a detective. So far I haven't heard you produce a shred of evidence to back up this bizarre theory.'

'I told you I went on digging. I bluffed my way into Grey Pillars – as they called GHQ. I checked certain confidential records through a contact there. I found that Stephen Ionides – remember I said earlier it wasn't his correct name – was, in fact, Stephen Gavalas. Brother of Andreas Gavalas.'

150

14

Three people sat in what was known as the Garden Room – Tweed's bedroom with the door at the far end leading into the hotel's garden. It was elevated one storey above street level and at ten in the evening the curtain was closed over the locked door.

Paula sat in an armchair, her legs crossed, balancing a cup of coffee on her knee. On a couch Nield relaxed, nursing a glass of cognac. Only Tweed sat upright in a hard-backed chair. It helped his concentration.

'I think I'll pop off to bed, get an early night after all that riding,' Partridge had said as they left the dining room.

'So apparently there were two horsemen riding the moor while we were driving round,' Nield observed. 'Partridge was one, and the other is Mr X.'

'I was pretty mad when Partridge said he was the horseman behind Quarme Manor,' Paula reflected. 'Pointing that rifle at you – even if it was unloaded.'

'He used the telescopic sight to find out who I was,' Tweed reminded her. 'Must have had the shock of his life when he saw it was me.'

'But the other horseman near Kearns' place tried to kill you,' Nield pointed out. 'It's Mr X we want to track down.'

'That story about the Gavalas family still carrying on a vendetta worries me,' Tweed said. 'And I don't like the sound of the grandfather, Petros, who – according to Partridge – rules the family with a rod of iron. Sounds like a real ruffian.'

'Would anyone still carry on a vendetta after all these years?' Paula objected.

'The Greeks have a strong family sense. And an equally strong sense of family honour,' Tweed told her. 'According to Partridge two sons of old Petros were murdered. He could still be looking for the killers – or killer. Newman and Marler, who know Greece well, could fill us in on that angle best. Maybe when they return they'll have news.'

'But there is still no news from Athens?' Paula enquired.

'Nothing. I called Monica at Park Crescent while you were tarting yourself up in your room.'

'Tarting?' Paula grinned mischievously. 'Well at least he does notice when I freshen myself up.' Her expression turned serious. 'None of what we've learned gives us any data on poor Harry Masterson . . .'

She broke off as someone knocked tentatively on the door. Nield was on his feet in seconds, gun in hand. 'I'll check that.'

Tweed was also on his feet. 'Crouch behind the bed,' he ordered Paula. Switching off the main light, leaving the room dimly illuminated by table lamps, he moved his chair against the wall and sat down again. Nield approached the door silent as a cat. He stood against the wall to one side, grasped the key in the lock, turned it with great care, took hold of the handle with his left hand, threw it open.

A startled Partridge, still dressed, stood in the doorway. He glanced to his left as Nield slid the gun out of sight. Tweed asked him to come in and Nield closed and relocked the door.

'Very wise,' Partridge commented. 'And sorry to bother you at this hour. But I found things whirling round in my mind, facts I hadn't told you. A man called Harry Masterson was murdered while I was paying a visit to Greece . . .'

'What about this Harry Masterson?' Tweed asked after room service had delivered coffee. It was going to be a long night.

'I couldn't find out anything about his background – but I did discover he was squiring Christina Gavalas – that is Petros' granddaughter. Apparently they flew to Athens together. So I began to poke around.'

'Why? If you didn't know this Masterson?'

'Because where he went over the cliff – at a place called Cape Sounion – is close to the entrance to what the locals call Devil's Valley. That's where Petros Gavalas has his farm and his headquarters. It's hidden away in the hills near an abandoned silver mine.'

'Rather a flimsy connection,' Tweed probed.

'You think so? Masterson was with Christina Gavalas – and Cape Sounion was the location of his murder.'

'How do you know Masterson was murdered? Evidence, Sam – have you evidence? Something about the state of the body?'

'No. Just found by a coastguard cutter on the lookout for drug traffickers as it rounded Cape Sounion. Masterson's body was lying on some rocks. He'd plunged down two or three hundred feet.'

'I'm still waiting to hear some evidence,' Tweed insisted.

'Some years ago at a crime seminar in Athens I met a Captain Sarris of Athens Homicide. I visited him on this latest trip. He told me in confidence they couldn't prove anything, but Sarris was convinced it was murder.'

'Why?'

'He'd observed Masterson somewhere. Said he simply wasn't the sort of man to stumble over the edge of a cliff. Do you mind if I light my pipe? After all, you'll be sleeping here . . .'

'Light up! You think better when you're smoking, Sam. I can open the door to the garden later. Anything else?'

'Yes. There's a Greek called Anton riding around on Exmoor – Anton Gavalas, son of Petros. By his second wife. There was a rumour he slipped ashore off a boat from Portugal at Watchet.'

Tweed leaned forward. 'How do you know about this Anton?'

'Sarris told me just before I left to fly home. They keep an eye on the Gavalas family. I visited the harbourmaster down at Watchet. He told me ships do arrive from Portugal delivering cork. They take back wastepaper for recycling – there's a paper mill at Watchet. Then I ran into a roadblock.'

'What kind of a roadblock?'

'The harbourmaster. Got pretty indignant when I suggested maybe someone had slipped ashore without his knowledge. Pointed out his office overlooks the harbour.'

'You still think he came ashore illegally?'

'I phoned Jim Corcoran, Security Chief at London Airport. He checked all the passenger manifests – I'd hinted it might have something to do with drugs. No Anton Gavalas showed up. Maybe he flew in via somewhere like Manchester. Doubtful.'

'How could you know it was Anton?' Tweed pressed.

'Sarris showed me several photos of him.' Partridge looked surprised. 'Thought you'd be ahead of me there.'

'You remember how I used to be.' Tweed waved a dismissive hand. 'A stickler for precise facts. You've seen Anton, then? Here?'

'Riding across Exmoor. Doone Valley area. Using a monocular glass to study Barrymore's place, Quarme Manor. Then on to Dr Robson's bungalow. Same routine there. Later across country to Kearns' place. He knows where those three live.'

'And you know where this Anton is based?'

'No, dammit. And not for want of trying.'

'I'd like his description – unless you have one of those photos.'

'Sarris wouldn't release any.' He closed his eyes, sucked at his pipe. 'Late thirties. Hair black as sin. Small moustache, same colour. Nose of a hawk – like Petros. About five feet six. Nasty piece of work would be my guess. First-rate horseman.'

'And how do you know that?' Tweed went on.

'Followed him. Saw him riding by chance when I was on the moor. Kept well out of sight but one day he caught me. A cunning type. I rode round a big crag and there he was – waiting for me. Asked in a sneering way why I was following him. He speaks perfect English. Sarris told me he'd spent time at a riding school while in Germany. Somewhere in Bavaria. Close to the main railway line between Munich and Lindau on Lake Konstanz – facing Switzerland.'

'What on earth would this Anton be doing prowling round Exmoor?'

'Obviously sent by Petros to locate the three men who took part in that commando raid on Siros. Petros is still seeking vengeance on the man who killed his sons, Stephen and Andreas, all those years ago.'

'And you're doing the same thing, in a way. Still trying to identify the murderer. It's folly, Sam . . .'

'It gives me an interest in my retirement.'

'But it must be costing you a fortune,' Tweed protested. 'Can you afford all this?'

Partridge grinned, sucked noisily at his pipe. 'If I just had my pension, no. That keeps myself and my wife comfortable. We're modest in our life style. You see, an uncle of mine left me a large legacy. Came out of the blue. That finances my hunt. I never could forget that unsolved murder at Antikhana. Haunted me, you might say . . .'

He stopped speaking. Paula had recrossed her legs. She reached down to stroke an itch above her ankle. The bracelet which had remained concealed under the cuff of her cream pleated blouse slid down her wrist. She glanced up. Partridge was gazing fixedly at her wrist, his expression frozen. He realized she was watching him and smiled, looked away.

'I'd forget the whole business, Sam,' Tweed advised.

'I really came to your room to give you this.' Partridge produced a sealed manila envelope from his breast pocket, handed it to Tweed. 'In case I don't wake up one morning that's for you. Inside is the address and key of a safety deposit box. Nearly opposite Harrods in London. Not to be opened while I'm still alive and kicking. Agreed?'

'If you insist . . .'

'I do.' He checked his pipe, which had gone out again, tucked it in a pocket and stood up. 'This time I really am off to bed. Sorry to intrude. But it's been good talking with you – like the old days at the Yard.'

'Just before you go, Sam.' Tweed held up the envelope. 'Give me some idea of what I'd find if I ever visited that safety deposit.' Partridge hesitated, Tweed pressed. 'We worked together once – with Homicide. I'm entitled to an answer.'

'I've been building up a dossier on those three men. All the details are in a notebook inside the safety deposit. I'd like to leave it there.'

'Fair enough . . .'

Pete Nield had been fingering his dark moustache, studying the ex-detective. Now he spoke, his index finger pointed to stress what he said.

'Mr Partridge. On the ridge behind Quarme Manor you said you had used the telescopic sight on your rifle to look at Tweed – which is how you identified him. You also said your rifle was unloaded. Then you told us about following this Anton Gavalas over the moor. Was the Greek armed?'

Partridge turned to face Nield and frowned. 'Yes. He carried a rifle in a scabbard. I saw it clearly through my telescopic sight . . .'

'And your rifle was loaded then – because you felt the Greek was dangerous?'

'As a matter of fact, yes . . .'

156

'Are you still telling me that the rifle you aimed at Tweed was unloaded – knowing you might bump into that Greek again riding the moor?'

'I had the safety catch on.' Partridge paused. 'But you are right. It was loaded. I just thought it embarrassing to let Tweed know . . .'

'It's all right, Sam,' Tweed intervened. 'It's been a long day for you. Better get off to bed now. See you in the morning.'

'Goodnight everyone.'

On this note Partridge left the room. Nield followed him and locked the door. Returning to his chair he sat down and poured fresh coffee which he handed round.

'He's a nice man,' Paula remarked. 'I think he's under great stress.'

'He's also a liar,' Nield told her quietly. 'He lied about his rifle being unloaded when he aimed it at Tweed. Who knows what might have happened if you hadn't flashed your torch, distracted him?'

'Surely you can't suspect Partridge?' Paula said with a note of disbelief.

Nield grinned at her. 'I suspect everyone. Guilty until proven innocent. That's why Tweed employs me. And don't forget by his own admission he was in Cairo when Ionides – Stephen Gavalas – was slashed to pieces.'

'If he was involved he'd never have admitted that,' she objected.

'He's clever enough to know Tweed would find out sooner or later. Maybe he's under stress because *we* have arrived on the scene.'

'I will say that was smart of you to dig out the fact his rifle was loaded.'

'Simple logic. He could have carried night glasses if he just wanted to see what was going on. But no, he has a rifle.'

Paula turned to look at Tweed who had listened to this exchange in silence. He sat with his head rested against the

157

wall, eyes half-closed, miles away. She leaned forward, patted his hand. His eyes snapped fully open.

'A penny for your thoughts. A pound if you push me. And you look worried.'

'I am. About Sam. He's a man with an obsession. The most dangerous state of mind for a detective – or a spy. Fogs the judgement. That's not all.'

'So, tell me . . .'

'All this business about a Greek vendetta. I don't like that one little bit. That old hawk, Petros – he could have brainwashed his whole family into thinking they have one mission in life. To locate and revenge themselves on the man who did kill Andreas and Stephen – *if* it was the same man. And if Sam is right, Petros has harnessed the second generation to his obsession. Hence the arrival of Anton on Exmoor. I sense the kind of man Petros is. He reeks of ferocity and blood.'

'You don't normally use such melodramatic language,' Paula remarked.

'This isn't a normal situation. Not by a long shot. Literally. Someone did take a pot shot at me in the Mercedes a few hours ago. If we're not careful there could be more killings . . .'

'Which reminds me,' Nield suggested. 'In the morning I'll take the Merc to a garage in Minehead, get those windows replaced. I'll tell the mechanic it must have been a wild shot by someone out for sport on the moor.'

'There's a couple of other things, Tweed,' Paula continued. 'I wonder if you noticed Partridge's expression when my bracelet slipped from under my cuff? He stared at the Greek key symbol like a man transfixed.'

'Probably looking at your legs,' Nield joked. 'Enough to transfix any full-blooded male . . .'

'Oh, shut up! The other thing was when we met those three men. Barrymore, Kearns and Robson – all with dark suntans.'

'I did notice,' Tweed agreed. 'And they went to some length to explain where they'd been. Even Barrymore, who wasn't exactly voluble. Interesting that all three said they'd been away to places difficult to check – Morocco and the Caribbean . . .'

'Which, as I said earlier, means one of them could have just returned from Greece where Harry Masterson died.'

'Exactly. And the timing of their absence coincides with when Masterson was killed. Pure speculation, of course.'

'But odd that they should all be away at the same time,' she persisted.

'Now you're reaching,' Nield intervened. 'The month of May – the time when people who are free to go on holiday do. They avoid the crowds.'

'And that's not all,' said Tweed.

'It's enough for me tonight.' Paula stifled a yawn. 'But do tell me what else there is.'

'When we can I want to check Sam's story about Anton Gavalas.'

'How on earth are we going to do that?' she asked, standing up and clearing the coffee cups, arranging them neatly on a tray.

'When we can we visit Watchet. *I* ask the harbourmaster. Was there a ship which berthed from Portugal? *I* carry more clout than Sam, who is now retired. Did he see a man answering the description of Anton coming ashore?'

'Sleep well.' Paula bent down, kissed him on the cheek. 'Forget everything.'

'I'll try.' Tweed smiled grimly. 'I'm expecting developments. Maybe rather unpleasant ones.'

15

The following morning Paula was walking down the old oak staircase when Nield caught up with her. Both had breakfasted with Tweed. Paula had gone to her room to fetch her outdoor clothes, leaving Tweed to linger over his coffee in the dining room.

'I'm off to Minehead to fix the Mercedes,' Nield told her. 'You look thoughtful.'

'It's Tweed. He's worried. He enquired for Partridge before we had breakfast. The manager told him Partridge had early breakfast and had gone off to the stables. He's going to ride over Exmoor again. Tweed wishes he'd leave it alone – or cooperate with us.'

'Independent chap, our Mr Partridge. And, like Tweed said, he's obsessed with a forty-year-old murder. You can't reason with an obsession.'

'I suppose you're right . . .'

She half-opened the door to the dining room, then stopped, paused, and closed it again quietly. Checking the belt of her raincoat, she glanced up at Nield from under her thick eyebrows.

'She doesn't waste much time. I thought she was a manhunter.'

'Who?'

'You'll never guess who's sitting at Tweed's table. Jill, Kearns' ravishing blonde wife. She asked Tweed where he was staying just before we left Woodside House.'

'Tweed will handle her, maybe extract some information.'

'You could be right.' She hesitated. 'Do you mind if I come with you to Minehead, Pete? I can leave a note for Tweed.'

'I'd welcome the company . . .'

Tweed had been sitting quietly, sipping his coffee, sorting out in his mind what he had learned, when Jill Kearns walked into the dining room. Slipping off her suede gloves and her camelhair coat, she'd perched in the chair opposite him.

'I hope I'm not too early for you. Stuart – my husband – went off riding on the moor so it seemed an ideal opportunity to pop over and see you.'

She wore a tight-fitting powder-blue sweater which showed off her well-rounded breasts and had a polo-necked collar. Using both elegant hands she threw her shoulder-length hair over her shoulders, inserted a cigarette in the ivory holder, pausing before she lit it.

'Do you mind? My smoking while you breakfast?'

'Not at all. I'm only drinking coffee.'

'And there's no one else about, so it's an ideal chance for us to get to know each other better.'

'As you say . . .'

Tweed smiled to encourage her. She had excellent bone structure, a well-shaped nose, a full-lipped mouth painted with bright red lipstick. Her eyes were a startling blue beneath blonde arched eyebrows. She radiated animation and he guessed her age at something over thirty. About half Kearns' age. And very sexy.

'Let me tell you something about myself,' she began in the soft, husky voice he remembered well from the previous evening. 'My father was a squadron leader with the RAF in the Mid-East during the war. Stayed on afterwards as an adviser to the Egyptian Government. I was actually born in Cairo.' She cocked her head on one side,

161

staring straight at him. 'Is this all a frightful bore? It must be . . .'

'On the contrary, I'm always interested in the background of a beautiful woman.' She inclined her head, smiled impishly as she acknowledged the compliment. 'Please go on.'

'My mother was Clementine Hamilton. Born in Dublin . . .'

'That name rings a bell.' He waited.

'My brother, David Hamilton, is a Member of Parliament. I was born late. My mother was forty.'

'Was? You mean . . .'

'Both my mother and father are dead. A car crash. They were in a pile-up on the M25 . . .' She hurried on as Tweed began to say something. 'It's all right. It was quite a few years ago. Then I married Stuart – or he married me might be more accurate. His first wife died in a swimming accident. You'll have noticed the difference in age between my husband and myself. I found the younger men callow, quite boring. I didn't know Stuart at all well. He's very handsome – but looks aren't everything.'

'I suppose not,' Tweed commented cautiously.

She reached across the table with her right hand and placed it over his. Her hand was warm, the fingers supple as they entwined Tweed's.

'I need an ally, a confidant, someone I can trust . . .'

'I'm afraid I might not fit the role,' he began.

'Someone right outside this tight social circle on Exmoor. Wait,' she urged as he opened his mouth. 'Please, let me finish. I am becoming frightened. Something is wrong. Help me. Please.'

She released his hand but her eyes held his. Blue? More like *lapis lazuli*. For a moment Tweed was aware of himself standing mentally away from the table, observing his own reactions. The woman was getting to him, exercising all her charm, exerting an almost hypnotic effect.

162

He drank more coffee, gazed at the base of the inside of the cup. His brain began to tick over again. He chose his words carefully.

'What are you frightened of?'

'The atmosphere. As though something awful is about to happen.' She stubbed her cigarette, fitted a fresh one into the holder, lit it with a gold Dunhill lighter. Tweed reached across to the next table, put a clean cup and saucer in front of her, poured coffee from the pot. She said, 'No, thank you,' when he offered cream and drank half the cup of steaming black coffee. 'Thank you, Tweed. I needed that.' He sensed they were already on intimate terms as he asked the question.

'I'm afraid I don't understand yet – what atmosphere?'

'The moor, for one thing. Being shut up in Woodside at night – cut off from the world by high walls. Like being in prison. My only companion, Wolf, my dog.'

'And for another thing, Mrs Kearns?'

'Jill. Please call me Jill. Then there are Stuart's strange friends. Dr Robson and that Colonel Barrymore. Do you know they were in the same Army unit all those years ago? Now they *still* seem to be in the unit. They meet twice every week. Once here for dinner. On Saturdays. Then for lunch at The Royal Oak in Winsford each Wednesday.'

'Today is Wednesday . . .'

'I know. Which is why Stuart won't be back until late this afternoon at the earliest. So I'm safe. Driving over here in the hope of seeing you. And, Tweed . . .' She leaned close to him and he caught the faintest whiff of perfume. Something expensive. His mind felt dazed. 'They'll all be at The Royal Oak,' she went on in her soft, soothing voice. 'And the weird thing is the colonel – Barrymore – still acts as though he's in command of them. He's creepy. The way he looks at my legs sometimes. I know what he's thinking.'

'Listen to me,' Tweed began briskly. 'Nothing you've

163

said so far explains why you think something awful – that was the word you used – is going to happen.'

'They've all become so guarded – they seem to have closed ranks against some terrible force they fear is coming. Stuart has those dangerous mantraps concealed all round the house . . .'

'Mantraps?'

'Oh, yes.' She held the holder by the tip and waved it with an elegant gesture. 'He says they're to keep out vermin. I don't believe a word of it. The high walls would do that. Those gates are always kept closed. Stuart stays up half the night, pacing in his study. I can hear him as I lie awake. Now, do you see why I need a friend, an ally?'

'Why choose me? You have your brother David . . .'

'We're not close. He's very busy. I once tried to talk with him and he said it was all imaginings – that I should have married a younger man. We had a bit of a row after that.'

'I still say why me?'

'You're Special Branch.' She paused, her lips parted in a warm smile. 'It's more than that. The moment I saw you I felt that I could trust you. Are you going to turn me down flat?'

'I didn't say that. Can't you get away from Exmoor for a while? Spend a little time with a friend. Say in London?'

'Stuart wouldn't stand for it. He *expects* me to stay at Woodside. I'm his wife . . .'

'So talk to him about it – as you have to me . . .'

She shook her head. Her mass of blonde hair swirled in waves. Tweed wondered what it would be like to run his hand through that jungle of blondeness . . . His mouth tightened. Madness. *I want you to remember one thing, Tweed. Never get mixed up with any woman connected with a case you're working on. That is the road to certain disaster.* His mentor when he'd first joined the Yard.

'I can't,' she said vehemently. 'He's closed up inside himself. He always was too self-contained. I realized that after we were married. Too late. Can I come to you if things get worse?'

'If I'm still in Somerset. Why are these three men living so close together? Your husband, Robson and Barrymore.'

'Robson is a doctor. He came out of the Army at the end of the war. They kept in touch. When Stuart and Barrymore retired from the Service Robson helped them find homes. I didn't know any of this until after I was married. I never did like such a peculiar set-up. I'd better go now.'

Tweed stood up promptly, checked his watch. 'Actually, I have an appointment. I can't promise you anything . . .'

She slipped on her coat, left it open, stretching her breasts as she threw back her golden hair over the collar. Walking quickly round the table, she hugged him with both arms, pressed her body close to his and kissed him.

'It's early days for you and me,' she said.

Then she was gone.

The phone was ringing when Tweed returned to his room. He ran, knowing the ringing would stop as he reached for the receiver. He lifted it, said 'Hello.' The manager answered, said there was a call for him.

'That you, Tweed?'

Partridge's voice. Sounded as though he'd been hurrying before he used the phone.

'Yes, Sam.' A click, which told him the manager had put down his instrument. 'I think it's all right to speak now. Where are you?'

'Winsford. You take the road out of Dunster where you met me on horseback. Continue on until you come to a signpost on the right. I'll meet you at The Royal Oak Inn for lunch. 12.30 suit you?'

165

'I'll be there. Stay off the moor, Sam. We'll cooperate. I can tell you something about Masterson . . .'

'Really?' Still sounded in a rush. 'One thing you should know. Antikhana. You know where that is? What happened there a long time ago?'

'I'm with you.' Partridge was exercising caution, not trusting the phone. 'Go on . . .'

'I didn't like the look of Selim, the Sudanese on duty the evening it happened. Humble had questioned him. Superficially. I put him through the wringer. He was hiding something. No doubt about it. Selim vanished shortly afterwards. I think someone used a carrot and stick. The carrot, money. The stick, fear. Never seen again. Rumoured he'd gone back to Khartoum. My bet is he ended up floating down the Nile. Must go now . . .'

'Stay off the moor,' Tweed repeated.

'See you for lunch . . .'

The connection was broken. Tweed replaced the receiver slowly. He felt very unhappy about the call. Hands clasped behind his back, he paced the large room. Later he went out into the garden for some fresh air. He stood on a neat lawn, looking at the old castle which perched above the small town at the other end of the High Street. Beyond the wall at the end of the garden green fields stretched away. An atmosphere of pure peace. And the last thing he was experiencing was peace of mind.

Tweed checked his watch again. Fifteen minutes to twelve. He had studied his map of Exmoor, obtained from a newsagent down the High Street. He calculated thirty minutes would be ample time to drive to Winsford. He would give Paula and Nield until noon to get back from Minehead; if they didn't arrive he would leave a note and drive there alone. Someone tapped softly on his door.

'We were quick,' Paula told him as she entered the room followed by Nield. 'Both windows have been replaced.'

'That *was* quick.'

'I found a Mercedes dealer,' Nield explained. 'With a garage next door. I tipped them well before they started. Four men worked on the job. We're off to Watchet now?'

'No. Something came up . . .'

'She certainly did,' Paula commented, teasing him. 'You've come into close combat with the enemy, I see.'

She reached for Tweed's right shoulder, took something between her fingers off his blue bird's-eye suit and held it up. A long blonde hair. 'Good job we didn't get back earlier.'

'Sit,' Tweed commanded. He was irked by his carelessness. He'd wiped his mouth clean of Jill Kearns' lipstick. He should have checked more thoroughly in the mirror. 'I have a lot to tell – and not much time to tell it. We have to be in Winsford to meet Partridge at 12.30 . . .'

He repeated a concise account of his encounter with Jill Kearns; he had total recall for conversations. Paula and Nield sat and listened while he then went on and told them about the telephone call from Partridge.

'And now you're up to date,' he concluded.

'She doesn't waste much time,' Paula remarked, then clapped her hand to her mouth. 'Sorry, that was pretty catty. She sounds like a very frightened woman. But frightened of what exactly?'

'Or a first-rate actress,' Tweed pointed out. 'Sent by Kearns to probe me, find out what I'm really up to.'

'My own thought,' Nield interjected. 'And why should we assume it was Kearns who sent her? If she's having an affair with one of the other two – Barrymore or Robson?'

'You are a couple of cynics,' Paula observed.

167

'Pete could be right,' Tweed said. 'Someone may have sent her on a fishing expedition.'

'But what was your real impression?' Paula demanded, leaning forward, staring hard at Tweed.

'Not enough data yet. I'm in a neutral zone. And it's time we set off for Winsford. Same procedure, Pete. Paula comes with me in the Merc. You follow in the Cortina. When we get to The Royal Oak, sit at a separate table. You're not with us. Let's move . . .'

'It's Wednesday,' Paula said suddenly. 'That's the day those three – Barrymore, etc., have lunch at The Royal Oak.'

'And that had occurred to me when Partridge suggested meeting me there. No coincidence I'm sure. Sam knows what he's doing. So, when we arrive we don't recognize him unless he comes up to us. It's his game. Let him play it his way.'

Tweed had taken the right-hand turn off the main road to Dulverton, following the signpost to Winsford. The day was overcast and chilly, the winding road ahead deserted. Paula sat beside Tweed, gazing at the huge brown sweeping ridges of Exmoor towering in the distance.

'Look,' she said, 'it's coming back.'

Tweed glanced to his right. Along the high edge of the ridges a wave curled like a surf-crested sea. The mist crept down, blotting out the upper slopes of the moor, advancing remorselessly. Paula shivered. There was something sinister the way the grey vapour swallowed up the moor.

'I hope to God Partridge has reached Winsford,' Tweed remarked. 'Imagine getting lost in that stuff.'

'You would get lost then?'

'Well, it depends. I guess by now he knows Exmoor pretty well. The amount of time he seems to have spent roaming over it. He probably knows which gulches lead down into Winsford. I just don't like the idea of him being up there at all. Let's hope we find him at The Royal Oak, sitting with a pint in front of him. Then I'll feel better.'

Astride his horse Partridge spotted the first wraiths of mist higher up, wraiths which merged into a solid wave of grey as it rolled towards him. Time to head down for Winsford. Turning his horse, he was about to ride down a gully which would take him on to the main road when he saw the second horse.

It stood riderless, reins draped, head down as it nuzzled tufts of grass. The rider lay sprawled on the ground, face down, his head resting on a boulder. His riding cap was askew, tilted no doubt when the animal had thrown him. Or had he been taken ill, fallen from the horse, his head striking the iron-hard boulder?

Partridge gave a quick glance at the mist which was close now. Dismounting, he strode towards the stricken man. It would be the devil of a job getting him down to Winsford. He'd have to try and fold the unconscious man over his own horse. If he was still alive . . .

The thought made him hurry. At the very least he could have cracked his skull – hitting that boulder. Granite. The hardest of rocks. The mist was floating over the sprawled figure when he reached it. The dampness felt cold on his face. He stood astride the figure, stooped to examine it further . . .

You bloody fool! Suddenly Partridge's instinct for danger flared. *Reins draped* . . . No one falling from a horse had time to do that. He was straightening up when the figure came to life. Mist swirled round Partridge's head as hands like a vice gripped his ankles, toppled him face down. He fell heavily, was winded. He ignored the shock. Started to lift himself on his elbows, to whip over and over. He was seconds too late. He felt a dull ache under his left shoulder

169

blade as the knife was driven home. Then he plunged into a bottomless pit of darkness.

'What a lovely-looking place,' said Paula.

They were approaching The Royal Oak after driving past several thatched cottages. The ancient inn had a steep brown thatched roof. The thatch curved round arched windows close to the inn's sign, a painting of an oak tree. Several cars were parked outside.

Winsford was a sprawling village located at a point where several roads met. It nestled snugly below hilly green fields and as they entered the place Paula saw stately evergreen trees shaped like pepperpots. An oasis of civilization amid the grim unseen moor which loomed behind the mist.

'We'll go inside, get a bite to eat,' Tweed said as he parked the car. In his wing mirror he saw Nield's Cortina arrive and stop on the other side of a small green.

Outside, The Royal Oak was freshly painted, its walls a beige colour. Must have stood there for hundreds of years, Tweed thought as he locked the car and walked with Paula. She pulled up her raincoat collar: there was a chill in the air.

Inside, the large, low-ceilinged room stretched away into separate sections with wide openings leading from one to another. The bar was crowded and behind it a giant of a man in an open-necked shirt served drinks and joked with his customers. Mostly locals, Tweed guessed. A log fire crackled and there was an air of animation.

'Where do they all come from?' Paula whispered.

'I expect they ride or drive in from miles around. You've seen some of the lonely places people live in this part of the world.'

'No sign of Partridge,' she whispered again.

'He'll be along. He's a punctual chap . . .'

She gripped his arm. 'Someone else has arrived.'

170

Kearns strode in as though on parade. Clad in riding gear – pale grey jodhpurs thrust into boots which gleamed, a drab windcheater – he waved his riding crop at the barman. 'What is it today?'

'Hello, sir. Good to see you again. How about a nice chicken and mushroom pie? And your usual double Scotch?'

'That'll do . . .'

'Here's your drink. I'll send over the food. We've kept your table.'

Paula gribbed Tweed's arm again. 'The clan is gathering.'

Oliver Robson, also dressed in riding gear, but scruffily dressed compared with the CSM, appeared, smiling, exchanging words with several people. The barman spotted him at once, called out again over the heads of the crowd.

'Good morning, Doctor. Don't think you got that tan on the moor. Not this year. Nice to see you back . . .'

He repeated the menu and Robson nodded amiably, said he'd have a glass of white wine. His manner was tentative, Paula was thinking. Like a man who was shy. He took the glass and sat down next to Kearns who sat upright, looking everywhere except in the direction of Tweed and Paula. The two men were sitting at a window table where a third chair remained empty.

'Grab that table,' Tweed advised. 'You're hungry?'

'The chicken and mushroom pie smells good,' she replied as a serving woman passed them with a tray. 'And a glass of the white wine. The third member of the club is joining them . . .'

She sat down at a small round table for two after draping her raincoat over the other chair. Barrymore, also wearing riding gear, had stalked in, his manner stiff. The barman greeted him as 'Colonel' and Barrymore nodded when offered food. He took the chair between Kearns and Robson without saying anything and stared around. Like the chairman of the bloody board, Paula thought.

Tweed eased his way to the bar, gave his orders, waited while the wine was poured. Something made him glance over his shoulder. Barrymore had moved quickly. He was standing over Paula, a hand on her shoulder as he spoke. Paula gazed up at him, her expression cold, distant.

Turning back to the bar, Tweed paid the bill. Picking up the two glasses he edged his way out of the crowd in time to see Barrymore sitting down again at his own table. Paula's flawless complexion was slightly flushed. He sensed annoyance.

'You have an admirer,' he teased as he seated himself.

'Saucy swine. He had the nerve to invite me over to Quarme Manor. For afternoon tea, and maybe a drink, he said.'

'I'm sure you coped . . .'

'I told him he could phone me at The Luttrell Arms sometime. They serve tea there.' She paused, drank some wine. 'If you think I might get something out of him I'm quite happy to play along.'

'No! On no account are you to be alone with that man. On the other hand, if he does call you at Dunster, take your own decision. But only meet him in a public place. He's still staring at you.'

'I know. Staring at my legs. I was right. He reminds me of a satyr. And Pete is doing his stuff.'

Nield had perched himself on a stool close to the table where the three men sat. He was drinking a half pint of beer, gazing across the room.

'He identified them quickly,' Paula remarked.

'I gave him a verbal description of them. He has sharp hearing. Even with all this babble going on he'll be able to tell us what they were talking about.' Tweed checked his watch. 'Partridge is late. Very out of character.'

'The mist may have delayed him . . .'

'Not like him, not like him at all.'

They had finished their chicken and mushroom pies,

172

eaten some of the inn's excellent French bread, when the commotion started outside. Voices raised, the sound of running feet. Someone shouting. Tweed stood up.

'Back in a minute. I'll just see what's going on . . .'

'You look grim.' She spoke softly. The babble inside the pub was suddenly hushed. People stared out of the windows. Tweed slipped into the street, throwing on his coat as he walked. He paused to get his bearings. Beyond the small green was parked a Land Rover. A police car, its blue light whirling, was close to it. Uniformed policemen were gently pushing back the gathering crowd. Tweed took his card from his pocket, walked across the green. The grass was soggy underfoot. A uniformed inspector held up his hand.

'Please keep back, sir.'

Tweed, his eyes on the long sheath of folded canvas in the back of the Land Rover, showed the card. The inspector, a short and burly man, took the card, stared at it, compared the photograph with its owner, handed it back.

'Special Branch? We don't see much of you in this part of the world. I'm Inspector Farthing.'

'I may be able to help. What is inside that canvas bundle?'

'Something rather shocking. Brought down from the moor by the chap over there with the corduroy cap. A local, Lock. Goes shooting rabbits on the moor. He found the body inside a rock cleft. Pure luck. Rabbit he'd just shot fell inside the cleft. Nothing in the way of identification. No wallet. No letters.'

'Can I have a look?'

'Of course. I hope you have a strong stomach, sir . . .'

Tweed was moving to the back of the Land Rover when Paula joined him. He warned her it might be unpleasant. She bridled.

'Goes with the territory. Don't treat me like a five-year-old.'

173

'It's all right,' Tweed assured Farthing who had laid a hand on Paula's arm. 'She's my assistant.'

He heard a retching sound. Lock, the driver, was stooped over a ditch. Nimbly, Tweed leapt up on to the rear of the vehicle open to the sky. Paula followed. Tweed bent down, folded back one end of the canvas. What remained of the face of Partridge stared up at him, eyes open, sightless. He had been savagely slashed many times with a knife. Folds and slivers of flesh hung in flaps. The nose and eyebrows had almost completely disappeared. The clothes as much as anything identified him for Tweed. Paula sucked in her breath. Plunging both hands inside her windcheater, she clenched them into fists.

'I know this man, can identify him,' Tweed said, folding the canvas gently over the brutally ravaged face. He kept his voice low. Farthing crouched to hear him. The crowd of sightseers was still pushing close to the Land Rover. 'Sam Partridge,' Tweed said. He paused. 'A retired Chief Inspector of Homicide at Scotland Yard.'

'Thank God you were here.' Farthing grunted. 'You don't want to see, but all his fingers are missing. Cut off at the base. I'd say they're at the bottom of some other crevice. And all makers' labels have been ripped off the clothes.'

'Someone took trouble in the hope he wouldn't be found quickly – and by the time he was identification wouldn't be easy.'

Farthing breathed heavily. 'Then this case is going to raise one hell of a stink.'

'I'm sure of it. Can I make a suggestion? People rushed out of The Royal Oak to gawk. But three men are still sitting inside at a window table. Colonel Barrymore, Dr Robson and Stuart Kearns. Send a man in to ask them to come out and look at the corpse . . .'

'Study the reactions of each man,' Tweed whispered to Paula when they had moved to the rear of the crowd.

Kearns came out first, strode briskly to the vehicle, climbed into it. Farthing pulled back the canvas, exposed the hideously mutilated face. Kearns stood erect as he gazed down. No trace of emotion showed as he shook his head. 'Never seen him before,' he informed Farthing, jumped down and walked back to the inn.

Robson arrived next and Farthing greeted him more effusively. 'I am glad you were here, Doctor. You're the first medical man to see the victim. He's dead, of course. Do you know him?'

'Let's check before we make assumptions,' Robson replied in a relaxed voice. Tweed could just catch what he said. Robson stooped over the body, felt the pulse at the side of the neck, then nodded. 'He's dead. No doubt about that.'

'An ambulance has been summoned,' Farthing explained. 'But you have given us valuable assistance before. Any idea of the timing of his demise?'

'I could only guess.' Robson frowned. 'Something odd – you see the small amount of blood? Yet the face has been savaged. He was dead before the murderer did that.' His tone was dry and professional as he pulled open the windcheater at the top. 'I suppose you realize the head has almost been severed from the body? Look at that.'

Bile rose in Farthing's mouth as he crouched on his haunches beside Robson. An enormous red gash ran just below the throat, continued out of sight. 'We ought to wait for the forensic team from Taunton before I explore further,' Robson reminded the inspector.

'On the other hand he'll have to be shifted into the ambulance when it arrives,' Farthing pointed out.

'Then we'll go a little further, see if I can find out how he died. Not from that vicious slash across the throat. Again – not enough blood. He was dead when that happened.'

Robson unfolded more canvas to the corpse's waist. Gently he turned the body on its side. The head lolled like

175

the broken neck of a doll. Robson pointed to the back of the windcheater, to a wide rip and crusted blood below the left shoulder blade.

'I would imagine that was the death thrust. He was attacked from behind. A knife was plunged deep upwards, penetrating the heart. That came first.'

He was replacing the body in its original position, folding the canvas back, when the distant sound of a siren came closer. The inspector glanced up. 'Ambulance almost here. Now, Doctor, how long ago?'

'As I said, I can only guess. The Taunton pathologist will be able to give a more accurate diagnosis. During the past two hours I would say. Now, I'd better leave this to you . . .'

He was walking back to The Royal Oak to wash his hands when Colonel Barrymore appeared, strolling towards the crowd, which parted to let him pass through. He levered himself aboard the Land Rover, thrust both hands in his pockets, stared down while Farthing again exposed the face. Ambulance men carrying a stretcher paused behind the vehicle. Tweed stared hard as Barrymore glanced at Partridge's face.

'Must be the work of a lunatic,' he commented sardonically. 'No, I've never seen him.'

Leaping down from the Land Rover, he strolled back to The Royal Oak, presumably to finish his lunch. 'Cold-blooded bastard,' Paula hissed.

'He will have seen a lot of war casualties,' Tweed reminded her.

As they loaded the pathetic canvas bundle aboard a stretcher and carried it to the ambulance Paula stared round. The crowd was dispersing; some heading for The Royal Oak before closing time, others trudging to their homes, while a few men and women stood, unsure what to do next now the show was over.

The quiet country village seemed to have taken on a

macabre atmosphere. She looked up towards the overcast sky, a threatening gloomy pall; towards the moor where the mist was slowly retreating, exposing the sweep of the grim brown ridges. Somewhere up there a frightful murder had taken place. She hated the moor now and turned to Tweed.

'What do we do next? Did you notice anything about the way those three men reacted to looking at poor Partridge?'

'I noticed the absence of something.'

'Don't start talking to me in riddles.' She played with the bracelet composed of Greek key symbols. 'The murder of Partridge is reminiscent of what we heard about that other horrific murder of the Greek in Cairo during the war.'

'Which reminds me of something I should tell Farthing . . .'

He caught up with the inspector who was just about to climb into his car. Farthing looked at him with an impatient expression.

'Bringing those three chaps out of The Royal Oak didn't get us far. What was all that about?'

'They're all locals. I thought they might have seen Partridge. But there's something else you ought to do. Have you a notebook? Good. Note this down.' He gave Partridge's description of Anton Gavalas, spelt his name. 'I should put out an all points for him. Partridge told me he saw him riding all over Exmoor. And there was one occasion when the Greek confronted him, accused Partridge of following him.'

'We'll check . . .' Farthing held a microphone from the radio car in his hand and studied the description he'd noted down.

'I'll be at The Luttrell Arms in Dunster if the CID man put in charge of the case from Taunton wants to talk with me.'

'Roger . . .'

Farthing was issuing an all points bulletin for Gavalas as Tweed and Paula walked back to the Mercedes. Nield strolled out of The Royal Oak towards the Cortina.

Tweed drove back at speed to Dunster, overtaking the ambulance, his expression grim. Paula glanced at him, laid a gentle hand on his arm. He showed no emotion but she sensed he was concealing a feeling of deep shock.

'You're upset, aren't you?'

'I worked with Sam at the Yard once. He was a good friend and my mentor. I learned a lot from him. Facts, he used to say, concentrate on *facts*. Then the solution will come sooner or later. He was generous with professional advice. Not always the case. Now I have to hunt down the man – or men – who killed Sam and Harry Masterson. Whatever it takes.'

She was disturbed. She had never heard him express himself with such vehemence; almost as though he were prepared to throw away the rule book. 'I have a feeling this is important.' She dangled her bracelet. 'Harry wouldn't have sent this Greek key bracelet unless it pointed to something. I wish we knew what it means.'

It began to rain. Tweed turned on the windscreen wipers. The moor was lost in a veil of fine drizzle, disappearing like a monster retreating to its lair, Paula thought. A beastly day – in every way. Wet, chilly, a nightmare day. Tweed made the remark as they reached Dunster.

He turned into the High Street, the cobbled areas like sweating stones. No one about; people were huddled indoors. He swung the Mercedes into one of the parking spaces opposite the hotel.

'You could be right,' he muttered. 'Maybe the answer lies not here but in Greece. Let's hope Newman and Marler get lucky.'

178

PART TWO

Devil's Valley

⌐⌐⌐

16

11 a.m. 104°F. 40°C. The heat scorched them like a burning glass. The cloudless sky above the ferry was a molten blue. Newman lifted his hand, wiped his forehead. He was dripping with sweat. His shirt was sodden. The car ferry bound for Siros edged away from its berth at Piraeus, turned slowly through ninety degrees, headed out into the gulf.

Newman stood at the bow of the vessel, elevated above the car deck and below the bridge. The ferry to Siros was small compared with the giant five-deckers which plied between Piraeus and Crete and Rhodes. Below the bridge and stretching to the stern, trucks and cars were parked three abreast, filling the ferry which was open to the sky.

Nick had had to back the Mercedes on to the ferry up the ramp so, like the other vehicles, he faced the ramp for ultimate disembarkation at Siros. Marler, wearing an open-necked shirt loose outside his khaki drill trousers, appeared alongside Newman and grinned.

'Enjoying the weather, old chap? A super day for the trip.'

'If you say so, and not so much of the old chap.'

'Just an expression, old boy. Don't mind me . . .'

'I won't.'

Marler, damn him, looked as cool as a cucumber. Resting his hands on the rail, Marler stared ahead at the millpond sea where the sun reflected like wavelets of mercury. Newman had earlier rested his own hands briefly on that rail. Very briefly. Like touching a red-hot iron.

181

'What's the object of our trip to Siros?' Marler enquired. 'That is, assuming I'm permitted to be put in the picture.'

'No need for sarcasm,' Newman growled.

'Irony, not sarcasm. Big difference. Why the change of plan at a moment's notice? Sort of thing Tweed would do. We were going to check out Cape Sounion where Harry Masterson took his dive.'

'You have such a subtle turn of phrase, Marler. The enemy – whoever they may be – would expect us to follow Masterson's trail. Instead we're going to Siros – where over forty years ago a man called Gavalas was murdered during a commando raid. I want to see the place where it happened.'

'You think there's a link with Masterson's death?'

'Tweed said it was a possibility. And that commando raid came up in conversation when Harry visited that chap at the MOD.'

'And how on earth are we going to find the spot where Gavalas was killed on Siros?'

'Nick. He knows the island well, has friends there. But we'll have to watch ourselves every step of the way . . .'

'Which is why, I suppose, you had Nick kit us up?'

'That's why,' Newman agreed. He tilted his wide-brimmed straw hat to shield his eyes. Marler, who seemed impervious to the torrid heat, was hatless, his fair hair gleaming in the sunlight. 'Watch it,' Newman warned, 'Nick's coming.'

'It's very hot,' Nick complained as he hauled himself up the companionway leading from the car deck and stood mopping his neck with a large handkerchief which was already limp with moisture. 'You can get a drink inside. The only way to avoid dehydration. I came up for a breath of air. There isn't any.'

'Join us,' Newman suggested.

'No.' Nick shook his head. 'I'll get a bottle of orange juice, take it back. I'd better stay with the Merc. You know why . . .'

Ten minutes later Newman stood alone on the bow deck, a fresh bottle of orange juice in his hand. Four more unopened bottles stood on a nearby seat. He'd have drunk gallons of the stuff by the time they reached Siros, two hours' sailing time away. *You know why . . .* He recalled Nick's words.

It was Newman's idea that they travel to Siros armed. He had not forgotten the bullet fired at them at the port of Zea. And Siros, he suspected, was a sensitive area for someone. He felt confident they had slipped the leash by boarding the ferry at the last moment, but he was not a man to take unnecessary chances.

Hence the guns and ammo Nick had obtained from God knew where. A sniperscope rifle for Marler, one of Europe's top marksmen; a Lee Enfield .303 rifle for himself; a Smith & Wesson .38 revolver for Nick. And all concealed, carefully taped to the underside of the chassis of the Mercedes. Which was why Nick was staying down on the car deck. To keep an eye on the car and its hidden cargo.

An hour later the ferry was moving at speed across the surface of the incredible sapphire blue of the Mediterranean. It almost hurt Newman's eyes to stare at it as he maintained his vigil, thinking, planning his moves when they landed. Over to the port side he made out the tip of Cape Sounion where Masterson had died. He raised the field glasses looped round his neck and focused them.

Perched at its summit the near-intact temple of Poseidon, guardian of the sea, came up in the lenses. A vision of perfection. Newman sighed, dropped the glasses, looked ahead. He'd liked Masterson.

Passing the Cape, the ferry headed south-east direct for the Cyclades group of islands. Siros was the closest of the group but was still out of sight. Peace, perfect peace, Newman thought as the ferry ploughed on through a shimmering heat haze. Probably their tour of Siros would also be peaceful, quite uneventful.

Deep in the heart of Devil's Valley, not twenty miles north of Cape Sounion, Petros Gavalas sat on the veranda of his headquarters farm. He had just put down the telephone. A summer hum of insects drifting above the grass was the only sound.

The farm was huddled under a looming limestone crag, almost hidden from the air, nestled in a wide defile between scrub-studded hills rising like cliffs. Shifting in his cane seat, Petros yelled his instruction hoarsely in Greek.

'Dimitrios! Christina! Get out here fast. And tell Constantine to be ready to take off in the helicopter. Come on! You should be here now, damn you!'

He waited until his two grandchildren stood before him. Christina, clad in tight-fitting denims and a flowered blouse, looked down at him, took a cigarette out of her mouth and ran a hand through her long dark hair.

'Was that Anton?' she enquired anxiously. 'He is on his way back from England?'

'No. And Anton can look after himself. He has a job to do. So have both of you.'

He studied the thin-faced Dimitrios, who often acted as his driver. Forty-four years old, he had Petros' dark eyes, his cruel mouth. With more training, another five years, Dimitrios might become as ruthless as Petros himself, although the old man doubted it. He twisted his hawk-nosed profile, stared hard at Christina.

'That Englishman, Marler, you got information from. Did you sleep with him, you whore?'

'Of course not,' she lied smoothly, refusing to lose her temper with the old bastard. God, she thought, he's still living in 1947. The world has changed since then. But he'll never know it. Petros leaned towards her, reached out a gnarled hand to grasp her arm, to twist it. She was too quick for him: she stepped out of his reach.

'I told you once. That's enough,' she snapped. 'What job? Who phoned you?'

'Pavlos – from Piraeus.' Petros slumped in his chair with disgust. 'He had trouble getting through on the phone. Nothing works in this country any more. Since the colonels went . . .'

'Don't start that again,' she rapped back. 'What has happened?'

'Oh, nothing much.' He made a sarcastic gesture with his hands. 'Just that the two English – Newman and your Marler – are at this moment aboard a ferry bound for Siros. The chopper will get you to Siros ahead of them. The ferry left Piraeus at eleven this morning and arrives soon after one o'clock. It is now noon – so move your leaden feet. Christina, you will stay out of sight. If Dimitrios decides, you can meet your Marler and lure him into a trap.'

'He is not my Marler. You have said that twice. Say it a third time and I will not go . . .'

'You try to disobey me?' Petros heaved himself out of the chair, clenched his fist and moved towards her. 'I will beat you until you cannot move . . .'

'No more!' she shouted back. From the sheath attached to her belt she whipped out a long-bladed knife and waved it in front of her. 'Come one step nearer and I'll cut you open . . .'

Petros stood stunned. He couldn't believe what was happening. A woman was threatening him. Aware that Dimitrios was watching him closely, that he must not lose face to a mere female, he changed tactics. Slapping his thigh, he raised his large head, roared with laughter, then gestured at Dimitrios.

'You see! She is a true Gavalas. A real spitfire, my little Christina.' He turned back to her. 'Use that knife to cut open this Marler and I will buy you a beautiful dress from Kolonaki. Now, off you go! You are armed, Dimitrios?'

'Constantine has loaded shotguns and rifles aboard the chopper. He guessed it was an emergency . . .'

'Then what are you waiting for? If those two English go near where my son, Andreas, was killed in the war – you kill them.'

He stopped speaking as the sound of a helicopter's rotors starting up drowned all further conversation. He sank back into his chair as Dimitrios and Christina ran off round the side of the house. *Stephen and Andreas, vengeance for your deaths will be mine*, he said to himself. He felt great satisfaction.

He had four descendants – Dimitrios, Constantine, Christina and Anton. He believed all shared his obsession that the killers must be dealt with. He had dinned the idea into them since childhood and worried only about Christina. Women should not think – only obey.

Petros looked around the front of the farm while he waited to see the machine take off for Siros. It was a large building. The veranda ran thirty feet along the front. The once-white walls were grey with dirt. In places they sagged, were held up by huge beams of wood which served as props. Many tiles on the roof were broken. Petros never spent money on repairs unless he simply had to.

This meanness had helped make him rich. Money in the bank. That was *power*. And he owned a second farm way up north in Macedonia. A farm which boasted many scores of head of cattle. They provided the milk the tourists loved. And for making the cheese the tourists staying at the great hotels also loved. Goat's milk, which Petros preferred, was not liked by the visitors bloated with money.

The Sikorsky was airborne, flew along the front of the farm as it gained height. The pilot, Constantine, waved. Petros waved back. They would do the job. And the sight of the Sikorsky made him feel good. War surplus bought by another farmer at a knock-down price.

Petros had coveted the Sikorsky. One night during a heatwave summer he had led his grandsons to the farmer's fields. They had used flaming torches to set fire to his crops. He had been ruined. Only then had Petros approached him with an offer for the Sikorsky – an offer which would not have bought a second-hand car. Desperate for money, the farmer had sold him the machine. I'm a good business-man, Petros told himself. Now I wait, see what happens on Siros.

Aboard the ferry Nick sat behind the wheel of the Mercedes and started up his engine. They were coming in to Siros, the ramp would soon be lowered. Newman stood on the bow deck as the ferry began turning slowly through a half-circle, ready to berth stern first. Alongside him stood Marler, lighting one of his king-size cigarettes.

'Pretty-looking place,' he drawled.

Newman was carefully scanning the waterfront with his glasses, searching for any sign of a reception committee. The island was mountainous, one limestone giant rearing in the distance. Mount Ida, he assumed. The lower slopes were arid, studded with more scrub.

He blinked. The small port of Siros was crammed with stark white-walled two-storey houses. Huddled together and piled up the hill, they glared beneath the burning sun. The shallow-sloped red-tiled rooftops were stepped up the incline. He followed the route of several narrow walled roads which appeared to zigzag upwards. A rabbit warren.

The harbour was sickle-shaped, enclosed by two curving jetties. Inside the entrance a small fleet of fishing vessels and motorized caïques were moored. Along one jetty wall the golden strands of scores of fishing nets hung drying. The tavernas and shops lining the waterfront had a sleepy look.

'It's a working port,' Newman remarked, lowering his glasses. 'Not many tourists find their way here would be my guess. And I still wonder about that chopper which flew over us earlier.'

'Could have landed anywhere,' Marler replied off-handedly. 'I think we'd better join Nick . . .'

There was a bump as the stern touched shore by a stone causeway. The ramp was lowered, vehicles began moving off as Newman ran down the companionway, then slowed his pace. It was like moving inside a red-hot oven.

'You take it easy in Greece, old boy,' Marler needled him, strolling down the steps.

'And you don't let on I speak Greek,' Newman warned. 'That way we may hear something interesting.'

'Sir!' As Newman looked over his shoulder Marler gave a mock salute.

Cocky bastard, Newman thought, then quenched his irritation. He had better watch himself in this inferno. Nick had driven the Mercedes off and was waiting on the waterfront. Small boys were dancing round the gleaming car, touching it and then jumping back as Nick shouted at them.

'Where to first?' Newman asked, climbing in beside Nick while Marler settled himself in a rear seat.

'To meet my friend, Spyros. I sent him a radio message from Athens. He lives high up here in Siros . . .'

The car was moving, turning away from the waterfront into one of the narrow side streets. Almost immediately the street was climbing, twisting round narrow corners over the paved surface. On both sides they were hemmed in by the clean whitewashed walls as they ascended the labyrinth. Sweat started pouring down Newman's back. The tunnel-like streets, the blinding glare off the white walls – everything intensified the hellish heat despite the fact that Nick had opened all the windows.

'Where is everyone?' Newman asked. 'We haven't seen a soul.'

'Indoors. Resting,' Nick replied. 'Even for Siros today is very hot. It helps. If we see someone out we must wonder why. Who they are. Did you see that old Sikorsky with the blurred markings which flew over the ferry?'

'What about it?' Newman asked, glancing at Marler, who looked damnably cool and relaxed as he lolled in his seat.

'A woman passenger wearing dark glasses and a scarf over her hair was checking the ferry through binoculars. I think she was trying to find someone. Maybe us?'

'Cross that bridge when we come to it,' Marler responded.

'This is a good place to stop,' Nick went on. 'Then I can get the guns from under the car . . .'

He had reached a tortuous turn and pulled up half-way round so they had a view both down and up the street which was still deserted. Sliding under the car, he was less than a minute before he handed Marler his sniperscope rifle, followed by Newman's weapon. Scrambling out from under the car, he glanced round as he dumped a hip holster with his revolver on the front passenger seat.

'It's all right,' Newman assured him, 'we watched both up and down the street while you were under the car.'

Nick strapped on the holster while Marler raised his rifle and peered through the sniperscope at a fisherman walking slowly along a jetty far below. Nick slipped on a lightweight linen jacket he kept slung from a hook behind the driving seat. He left it open and grinned at Newman.

'It will be hot wearing this – but it conceals what I carry. You hide your rifles under that travelling rug rolled up on the floor in the back.'

'And now?' Newman asked.

189

'We meet Spyros who is waiting at the top. He will take us to Mount Ida – to the place where the Greek was murdered during the war . . .'

'They have disappeared,' said Dimitrios. 'One moment the Mercedes is driving up towards us, then it vanishes. What kind of a trick is this?'

'They're probably parked at the corner of the road down there. Where it turns a sharp bend. That church dome hides it from us,' concluded Christina.

She sounded thoroughly rebellious. She shook her dark mane, exasperated with her cousins' slave-like obedience to Petros.

Constantine shrugged his shoulders, irked by her attitude. This was not women's work. Like Dimitrios he was thin and bony and he sported a moustache which curved round the ends of his slit of a mouth. He looked after his moustache proudly: it had made him a big hit with the girls, really rolled them over. On their backs.

They were perched on the roughcast terrace of a house overlooking the port of Siros. Through his binoculars Dimitrios had observed Newman, Marler and Nick coming ashore from the ferry. It was Christina who had earlier confirmed they were aboard when Constantine had overflown the ferry.

The house belonged to Petros and was empty. Today was Wednesday. On each Monday a local woman came to clean up the place. Parked in front of the house was a battered Cadillac, paint peeling from its bodywork. Petros had bought it for a song from a man in need of money. The weapons transported aboard the helicopter were stowed inside the Cadillac. Shrubs sprouting blood-red flowers decorated the terrace in large Ali Baba pots. Christina put on her dark glasses, lit a cigarette.

'You won't need to use the guns,' she told them.

'We use them if they go near Mount Ida,' Constantine snapped at her. 'You remember what Petros ordered?'

'Ordered! You are like a couple of puppets he dangles at the end of a string. Harm the Englishmen and everything goes wrong. The police will hunt you down. Sarris himself might come. He only waits for his chance to put you all inside for ever. Then what happens to me? If necessary I will handle Marler, lead him and the others away from where it happened . . .'

Constantine grinned unpleasantly, made an obscene gesture. 'Ah! You and Marler. Petros was right. You will do as we tell you to do . . .'

His left hand gripped her arm. He froze. Her free hand had whipped out the knife from the sheath attached to her belt. He felt its point tickle his throat. Her black eyes blazed with fury.

'Let me go or I'll rip your throat open. God knows how many women you have had, you fornicator . . .'

He released her, stepped back carefully. The fear was written large on his face as she followed him and his back pressed into the terrace wall. It was only as high as his hips and there was a long drop to the paved street below. She rested the point of the knife against his breast bone. He breathed heavily. She was strong; if she pushed the knife a couple of inches more . . .

'You will never use that filthy gesture in front of me again,' she told him. 'You will not use the guns. We will find some other way of diverting them. You understand?'

'Yes, Christina. For God's sake . . .'

She sheathed the knife suddenly, turned away. Her expression was contemptuous. As she had always suspected Constantine was a coward. Dimitrios, careful not to interfere – he had previous experience of Christina's temper – stood staring through his binoculars. He lowered them quickly.

'You were right,' he told her. 'They had hidden behind

191

that corner. Why? Could they have spotted us? Impossible.
They are driving this way. We must leave in the Cadillac
quickly before they arrive, drive up towards Ida and see
what they do next . . .'

Nick turned yet another sharp-angled bend in the zigzag
road which went up and up. Newman glanced out of the
window on his side. Nick was a superb driver: he had
missed scraping the wall of a house by inches. They were
very high up now and Newman caught glimpses of the sea
which was an incredible mixture of brilliant colours –
sapphire, turquoise, *lapis lazuli*. No picture postcard had
ever captured this. The car slowed and stopped.

'Spyros,' said Nick.

An old hunchback, clad in peasant clothes and with a
face like a wrinkled walnut under his wide-brimmed straw
hat, sat perched outside a house. He was whittling a piece
of wood with a knife. He stood up, adjusted the angle
of his hat, opened the rear door of the car and joined
Marler.

Nick drove on as he made introductions. 'Spyros. Sitting
next to you is Marler. My other friend is Bob Newman.'

'I am pleased to meet both of you,' Spyros replied in
English and with quaint old-world courtesy. 'You take the
next fork to the right when we leave Siros port and climb
the mountain.'

He opened the cloth he had used to wrap the piece of
wood and the knife and continued whittling, careful to
keep the pieces carved off on the cloth. Marler stared at
the wood. It was beginning to take the shape of a madonna.
Spyros kept glancing up as he worked, checking their
position.

They emerged from the labyrinth of the port of Siros
suddenly. Ahead the road was no longer paved. A track
of white dust, it snaked up the mountain which rose sheer

above them. Before long they were driving along a ledge just wide enough to take the Mercedes. On Nick's side rose a sheer wall of limestone. Newman peered out on his side and the mountain fell away into a deep precipice. Far below a grove of olive trees spread their stunted branches. Beyond the grove the sea spread into the distance, ink blue.

'You're sure the Merc can get all the way?' Newman enquired in what he hoped was a casual tone.

'Spyros would not have let us come if it was not possible.'

'Good for Spyros . . .'

Newman glanced down again and began to feel the symptoms of vertigo. He averted his gaze, forced himself to concentrate on the track ahead spiralling up and round the mountain. At several points there were tracks leading off through gulches in the mountain. Newman would have given anything to tell Nick to turn into one of the gulches – away from the hideous precipice which was growing deeper and deeper. Had the old Greek sensed his fear? Still whittling at the wood, he said suddenly, 'We are very close now. The country will open out. We shall leave the abyss.'

'And then?' Newman prodded.

'We shall be at the place where Andreas Gavalas died over forty years ago.'

The Cadillac, driven by Dimitrios, had taken the other route on the far side of the mountain. Hidden inside a copse of olive trees, they had seen Nick heading up the seaward road.

'They are going where they shouldn't,' Dimitrios said. 'So, we get there first and wait for them . . .'

He had driven like a madman up the curving road with Constantine beside him, a rifle and shotgun resting in his lap. In the back of the car Christina sat tense and silent.

To her left the ground sloped away steeply but not precipitously. In the distance she could see the white-walled houses of Siros port – looking like a child's model.

'We turn here,' Dimitrios said and swung off the road inside a deep-walled gulch which snaked between lofty heights of limestone. The wheels bumped over rocks, shaking the vehicle.

'Why?' demanded Christina.

'We are now ahead of them,' Dimitrios condescended to explain. 'We will check to see they are going all the way. Then, if they are, we turn round here and go on up the mountain. There is a place where we can look down on them, see what they do.'

He had stopped at a point where the track widened and turned the Cadillac so it faced the way they had come. He had concealed the car out of sight of the gap at the end of the gulch. Daylight showed and way beyond it the intense blue of the sea.

'A place where you can look down on them?' Christina queried. 'You are taking your guns with you? Why?' Her hand clawed at Dimitrios' shirt collar as he was alighting. 'What are you planning to do?'

'You heard what Petros ordered. To shoot them if necessary. Now let go, you treacherous cat. At the end is the other road. We shall see their car pass if they have come this far.'

As Spyros had predicted, they had left the abyss behind. Ahead, below the sheer wall of the mountain, an area of flat scrubland stretched before them. Nick stopped the car, Newman stepped out, stretched and took another swig from the plastic bottle of mineral water. They had six unopened bottles: dehydration, as Nick was never tired of warning, was the greatest danger. Newman grimaced after drinking, replaced the cap. The liquid was tepid, tasteless.

The plateau of arid scrubland projected out from the mountain wall, then sloped steeply downwards. A wide deep parched gully led its winding way towards the distant sea. Its surface was cluttered with limestone boulders and pebbles. In winter, Newman guessed, it would be a gushing torrent. Now it was bone dry.

'Where?' asked Marler in his direct way.

Spyros pointed to the gully with his knife. The rocky gulch lay about two hundred yards away. Shielding his eyes, Marler gazed up at the towering mountain above them.

'What in Hades is that?'

Newman stared up. At the summit of Mount Ida, clinging to the edge of the rock, was perched a huddle of ancient buildings. Built of solid stone, one shallow-roofed building was hanging above another, perched at different levels and all joined in one complex.

'The monastery of Mount Ida,' Spyros told them. 'From there you see all over the island. During the war the German general, Hugo Geiger, established a lookout unit. He respected the monks. He said someone should live in peace in this frightful war.'

'Where?' Marler repeated again. 'Where exactly did this Andreas Gavalas die?'

'Inside the gully.' Spyros pointed the knife. 'I will show you the place . . .'

'Not yet.' Marler placed a hand on the old man's shoulder as he began to walk out into the open. 'Everyone back inside the car,' Marler continued, reaching inside for his rifle. He pocketed the sniperscope sight, picked up several spare magazines. 'Go on, get in quick,' he ordered. 'The lot of you.'

'May I ask why?' Newman enquired.

'You may. A mile or so back coming up the mountain I glanced down one of those side tracks leading into a gulch. I saw movement, a man watching. He dodged back out of sight. Before you venture into the open I'm going up there.'

He looked up the mountain which was fractured with deep fissures, some wide enough to allow passage for one man. Newman sucked in his breath at the prospect, thinking of the vertigo.

'You stay in the back, Bob,' Marler instructed. 'On this side of the car. Keep an eye on me. When I wave my rifle you can go into the open. Only then.'

He looped the rifle over his shoulder, wriggled his feet in his rubber-soled calf-skinned shoes to test their ankle support. 'If I'd known I'd have brought climbing boots. Can't be helped. I'll cope.'

'Watch it – for God's sake,' Newman warned.

'And I never knew you cared . . .'

Typical of Marler to mock just before he was attempting a climb fraught with risk, Newman thought. They settled in the car and Newman peered up. Marler was already a good twenty feet up a narrow fissure, finding a foothold on one side, then on the other.

17

'We climb up here. It looks straight down on the place,' said Dimitrios as he switched off the engine.

He had turned off the mountain road, backing the Cadillac into a cul-de-sac. Christina peered through the rear window. At the end of the cul-de-sac a wide defile led upwards between rocky walls. A primitive staircase carved out of the rock led out of sight.

'What is this? Where does it lead to?' she demanded.

'The monks made it ages ago.' Dimitrios grinned as

he gripped his rifle, opened the door and slipped out. Constantine joined him with his shotgun. Dimitrios thrust his head in through the rear window. 'Christina, you wait here. We're going up to a high point which overlooks the place. You hear shots, we will be back soon after. Then we drive back.'

'I told you, Dimitrios . . .'

They were gone, climbing the rough-hewn steps rapidly, Dimitrios in the lead. They disappeared round a corner. She climbed out of the car, left the door open, ran back on to the mountain road. From the view ahead she knew roughly where she was. She began running, jogging at a steady trot up the road.

She wore a lightweight jump suit and trainer shoes. As she ran she hauled her dark glasses out of her pocket, perched them on her nose. The stupid cold-blooded bastards. They liked their work: Petros had trained them well. They were true grandsons of the sadistic old ruffian.

Ten minutes later she was still running uphill, pacing herself. She was close to where the mountain ended, where the ground became flat, spreading out towards the sea on the other side of Ida. Pray God she got there in time . . .

Dimitrios crouched down, settled himself in the nest between massive boulders. He perched his rifle in the cleft of a rock, looked along the sight. Three men were alighting from the Mercedes parked at the edge of the plateau. Beside him Constantine aimed his shotgun.

They were positioned seventy feet above the three men. Both of the Greeks were excellent shots. The place Dimitrios had chosen was a meditation point used by the monks. High above them reared the overhanging monastery. Dimitrios glanced up once, then down again. He was satisfied no one looking down from the summit of Mount Ida would ever see them. An overhang of rock almost

completely obscured the view from that height. The overhang was two hundred feet above where they waited.

'Let them get well out into the open,' Dimitrios warned
his brother. 'Then there is nowhere to hide. We can pick
them off one by one.'

'Which shall I aim for?' Constantine asked.

'You don't. Leave it to me. If one dashes back for the
car, he's your dead meat for today. Any minute now . . .'

'Andreas was found lying dead somewhere near the top of
that gully,' Spyros explained.

Newman led the way, avoiding the numerous sharp rocks
which littered the ground, often almost hidden by scrub
grass. The heat beat down on the back of his neck. He tied
a handkerchief round it as he walked. It was very still and
silent at this height. No screech of gulls. A stillness which
was uncanny – and unsettling. He was the first one to hear
the sound of running feet approaching.

Breathing heavily, Christina appeared round the side of
the mountain, saw them, increased her pace until she
reached them. Holding his rifle loosely in his right hand,
Newman stopped and waited, suspicious. What the hell
was such an attractive girl doing up here in the wilderness?
He didn't like questions to which he had no answer. Nick
stepped forward.

'This is Christina Gavalas,' he informed Newman.

'Introduce me. Who is he? Quickly!' Christina demanded.

She was panting from her exertions, her breasts heaving
under the jump suit. Newman was careful to keep his
eyes on hers. They glowed with life. And she was the
enemy.

'Robert Newman,' Nick replied. 'The foreign correspondent . . .'

'And where is Marler?' Christina asked anxiously.

'Oh, he's gone to deal with a call of nature,' Newman told her easily. 'What are you doing up . . .'

'You are in great danger. There are men up the mountain with guns . . .'

She broke off as a man appeared from the direction she had come. At least six feet tall, he was clothed in a black robe and wore a black cylindrical hat. A priest. Member of the Greek Orthodox Church, Newman realized. His face was lined with age but he was erect, his movements brisk. He spoke in English.

'Welcome to Mount Ida. You wish to see the monastery? I fear the lady cannot enter.'

Newman took a quick decision. The priest, he estimated, was in his late seventies. Had probably spent all his life in this part of the world. Including the period of German wartime occupation.

'We are looking for the place where – over forty years ago – a Greek citizen called Andreas Gavalas died.'

'Was murdered,' the priest corrected him gravely, stroking his black beard. 'I was here when it happened.'

'You mean you saw what actually took place?' Newman concealed his excitement. 'You know who killed Andreas?'

'Damn that priest. He will have to take his chance.' Dimitrios carefully aimed his rifle at Newman's chest. 'Bull's-eye,' he gloated.

Constantine knocked the rifle barrel upwards. By some miracle Dimitrios avoided pulling the trigger. He glared furiously at his brother. 'Cretin! Why did you do that? Do it again and I will break your arm . . .'

'There is a priest down there,' Constantine protested.

'So? Since when did you go religious? Petros is an atheist – he brought us up to regard the whole Church as a swindle on the people. What does one less priest matter?'

199

'And Christina is down there. Are you mad? If your aim is bad you could hit *her* . . .'

'Since when was my aim bad?' He glanced down. 'Now look what you've done. They have started walking towards the gully – the place Petros said they must not reach.'

'The problem is solved then. Forget it.'

'No, I will not forget it.' Dimitrios grinned evilly, hoisted his rifle and tapped Constantine's jaw gently with the heavy butt. 'Interfere again and you'll need a new jaw. You understand? No distractions this time. A moving target? Bull's-eye. Again . . .'

He repositioned the rifle, rested it firmly in a cleft in the rock, thrust the butt firmly against his shoulder, lined up the sight, took the first pressure. One final squeeze . . .

The bullet slammed into the rock less than an inch from the hand on the trigger. A rock splinter cut Dimitrios' cheekbone. His rifle jerked up. This time it fired. The shot winged into the sky. A second bullet slammed into the rock between the two brothers crouched less than half a foot from each other. The third bullet struck Constantine's shotgun. He let go, yelled. The weapon dropped out of sight over the brink. They were scrambling out of the nest when a fresh bullet nicked the heel of Dimitrios' shoe. He jumped with sheer fright.

A hundred feet above them, perched on a ledge protruding from the mountain wall, Marler reloaded. He aimed down in seconds, pulled the trigger. The fifth bullet ripped a shard of cloth from Dimitrios' right shoulder. Before he followed Constantine, who was scrambling back towards the staircase, he risked a glance upwards.

He saw Marler on the ledge and beneath the huge overhang of rock. Constantine looked back, saw the few seconds when his brother was glancing up.

'Come on!' he yelled. 'He missed five times. He'll kill you with his next shot . . .'

'Stupid cretin!' Dimitrios yelled back as he also began to run. 'He aimed to miss . . .' Dimitrios was enough of a marksman to recognize shooting superior to his own. Feeling safe as he ran out of sight of the ledge, he jumped with fright again as a fusillade of bullets peppered the rock walls on all sides, showering him with sharp splinters. How could this be?

'Shoot the bastards!' Christina urged Newman viciously.

Newman was standing, legs braced apart, rifle aimed up at the mountain as he continued shooting at the fleeing figures still in view from below. Christina, eyes blazing, stared up at Marler, now edging his way back along the ledge – at her hated cousins disappearing from sight down the staircase. Newman smiled, lowered his rifle, reloaded.

'You're one lousy shot,' she informed him, her hand pressed into her hip.

'You think so?' He smiled again. 'I aimed to miss – just as Marler did. There's been enough killing. And we don't want to start up a fresh vendetta with your lovely family.'

'Blessed be the merciful,' said the priest.

'I don't know about that, Father.' Newman grinned again. 'I might agree – so long as the merciful are alive. Which isn't often the case if you read history. Now, where was Andreas Gavalas murdered? And what did you see?'

The priest led them to the gully wending its way down to the sea. Near the top, where tufts of bleached grass stood at the edge of the dried-up watercourse, he pointed. A smooth-sided cleft large enough to hide a man. This had been Andreas' temporary grave. The priest, taking a 'walk of solitude', had discovered the body by accident.

The hilt of a knife had protruded from beneath the left

201

shoulder blade and the man was dead. Hurrying back towards the monastery for help, the priest had met several monks who had accompanied him back to the cleft. The body had vanished.

The priest had reported the incident to General Geiger, the German commander-in-chief. Geiger had checked with the only patrol in the vicinity. Later he had told the priest he was satisfied his men had no knowledge of what had happened.

'Then who took away the body?' Newman asked. 'And did you see the British raiding party approaching up the gully after landing from the sea?'

'Yes. I saw them from the monastery. Perhaps that is why my steps led me this way. Presumptuous curiosity. Not a virtue.'

'How many men in the raiding party?' Newman persisted.

'Four. I watched them through field glasses before starting on my walk down here.'

'Four Greeks, you mean?' Newman asked casually.

'No. Three British soldiers and one man dressed in peasant garb. I presume that was Andreas Gavalas who knew the island. I knew they were British because they wore green camouflage raincoats.'

'Surely they would have been seen by that German lookout unit I heard was established in the monastery?' Newman suggested. 'If you saw them coming, the Germans must have done?'

'The British were clever – and lucky. They landed when a thick winter sea mist was covering this area. When I saw them through my field glasses the mist had parted for a short time. At that moment the watchguard unit was being replaced by new men coming on duty.'

'And have you ever heard a whisper as to who might have removed Andreas' body?'

The priest pulled at his beard, his eyes avoided

202

Newman's. 'It is a mystery,' he eventually replied. 'And now I must return if you will excuse me.'

'The whole business is peculiar,' Newman responded.

He stared round the scrub-covered platform. Very little cover for a raiding party which must have relied on the mist to reach the shelter of the mountain. Doubtless Andreas had known ways of penetrating the fastness. Marler was walking towards them at a jaunty pace, rifle propped over his shoulder, as Newman stared once again upwards. What a life – confined most of your days inside that fortress-like complex perched half-way to the sky. A large bird, probably an eagle, drifted off a tongue of rock and circled them high up.

'Can you take me back to Athens in that car?' Christina asked Newman. 'My cousins drove me up here in an old Cadillac. I have been abandoned.'

'All the way to Athens?' Newman queried in surprise.

'I'm not going back to the Devil's Valley – to where Petros is waiting to beat hell out of me. I've finished with that life.' She moved closer to him, her eyes enormous. 'I will pay for my passage. The last ferry leaves in two hours. You will take me? Please.'

'And how will you pay me?' Newman enquired ironically, expecting a certain answer. She had lowered her voice so only he could hear her.

'With information. About Harry Masterson.'

'You just bought yourself a one-way ticket.'

Marler arrived, brushed dirt off his jacket, grinned at Christina. 'You get around, little lady.'

She walked slowly up to him, a half-smile on her face. 'We met earlier, you may recall . . .'

'How could I forget?' He smiled sardonically.

'I do not forget either. I have something for you, Marler. A keepsake. Is that not the right word?'

She was still smiling when her right hand whipped up, palm open, and hit him with all her considerable force

203

across the face. The blow jerked his head sideways. She smiled again, watching the red weal which had appeared across his cheek.

'Now we are quits. Is that not the right phrase?' She turned to Newman. 'Now, I am ready when you are.'

The priest had lingered with Spyros a few yards away, as though reluctant to leave. His expression was a study in indecision. He seemed to make up his mind suddenly and walked to within a few feet of Newman. He took a deep breath before he uttered the words and then walked rapidly away towards the mountain.

'The disappearance of that body. There was something else on the island when it vanished. I suggest you look in that direction. I refer to the Greek Key.'

18

Nick drove the Mercedes back along the far side of the mountain, much to Newman's relief when he saw the ground beyond the brink sloped away gradually. It had been his idea to use this route after talking with Christina.

'Those two hard cases, Dimitrios and Constantine,' he pointed out to Marler before they started back, 'will travel in their Cadillac to Siros port. Then they'll ditch the car and fly back in their chopper. They landed on open ground just outside Siros according to Christina. They came here in that machine which overflew our ferry.'

'What's the plan?' Marler demanded.

'If we can catch up with that Cadillac I'd like a few words with them – and I guess you would. This time with our fists. Petros has to be discouraged from sending his jackals after us. I don't want to spend the rest of our time in Greece looking over our shoulders. When we get back to Athens *I* want a quiet talk with Christina on her own. I'm sure she has more information.'

'Why not me? I've known the girl a bit longer . . .'

'Oh, yes!' Newman's tone was ironical. 'You got to know her so well she pasted you one.'

'It was the only way I could hope to get her to talk . . .'

'It was the only way *you* thought you could get her to talk – and she didn't.'

'It's just possible you could be right,' Marler admitted reluctantly. He felt his face. 'She's a beauty but she packs a rare punch . . .'

'Which you richly deserved. Let's get over to the car.'

'May I enquire what is the next object of the exercise with her?'

'Christina met Harry Masterson in London, probably pointed him to Exmoor and those three ex-commandos. Why? Only she can tell me. So, old boy,' Newman went on, mimicking Marler, 'I'd appreciate it if from now on you leave the beauty to me. And on the way back we'd better assume those two thugs may be waiting to ambush us.'

They arranged the seating to anticipate the worst. Marler, loaded rifle across his lap, sat in front next to Nick. In the rear they placed Newman, Christina – sitting in the middle – and Spyros occupied the other corner. The hunchback was apologetic as Nick drove away from the plateau, heading for the far side of the mountain.

'I was not a great help to you, Mr Newman. The priest told you everything.'

'Everything? Are you sure about that? Who took away Andreas' body? And what is the Greek Key?'

'Don't ask me that.' The hunchback shuddered, clasped his veined hands tightly. 'I know nothing about such things.'

205

'But I do.' Christina pressed her shoulder against Newman, turned and gazed at him. 'Maybe later, when we are alone, the two of us should talk.'

'I'd welcome that.' Newman stared back at her. 'You speak very good English.'

'That was my mother's doing. I was lucky enough to be well-educated. And sometimes I think that is why my cousins – and Petros – hate me. They are still men of the soil. They think like peasants, behave like them. My mother was left money by a distant relative. She banked it secretly. Petros was furious. One night she packed me off to Zurich. To a school. I found I was good at languages. As well as Greek I speak German and English. I took a law degree. Then I made a mistake.'

'Which was?'

'I came back for my mother's funeral. Petros insisted I must pay my respects by staying in Devil's Valley for a time. Like a fool I agreed. Time went by. They all made me think their way. Now I have had enough of them for two lifetimes. We will talk later.'

Spyros had produced something from under his floppy jacket. Newman heard a strange sound, glanced across Christina. Spyros was clicking a length of black worry beads. His expression was anxious. Newman looked out of the window. The view was spectacular: a vast panorama stretching all the way down across the island to the sickle-shaped harbour.

There was tension inside the car. As they approached each bend Marler leaned forward, gripping his rifle, alert for any sign of the Gavalas brothers. He had warned Nick to be ready for an emergency stop at any second. Nick kept wiping a hand dry, then grasping the wheel tightly, staring ahead while he crawled round the bends.

The worry beads stopped clicking. Newman remained quite still. Spyros leaned forward, staring in his direction. Newman went on gazing out of the window as the car continued its steep and tortuous descent. Now he could pick out individual boats berthed in Siros harbour.

'My cousin, Sarantis, is an archaeologist,' Spyros began. 'Is that the right word?'

'He goes on excavations – digging up ancient sites. A lot of them round the Plaka district in Athens,' Newman encouraged him.

'That is so. But Sarantis likes places where there are few of his kind. Like Cape Sounion. The Temple of Poseidon.'

'Sensible chap.' Newman forced himself to stay relaxed. 'So what about Sarantis?'

'He is very old. Like me. But he has a wonderful memory for faces. He was near Cape Sounion when the Englishman, Masterson, was thrown from the cliff not many weeks past.'

'He saw it happen?'

'No. But he did see the two men who went to the temple shortly before the killing.'

'*Two* men? You are sure? You did say he was very old,' Newman reminded him gently.

'Eighty years. He recognized Masterson from the pictures later in the papers – the man thrown from the cliff, he said.'

'And the second man,' Newman probed. 'He could describe him? How does he know Masterson was thrown off – if he didn't see it happen?'

'I think he did, but he felt it was dangerous to admit that. He has a good memory for faces,' Spyros repeated, in the manner of the old.

'He described this second man to you?' Newman enquired.

'No. But you could ask him. He would tell you. He likes the English. Treat him gently, please. He is frightened by what he saw at Cape Sounion.'

'You have his address in Athens?'

'Athens? He lives here on Siros. In a house near the top

207

of the port. We could see him before you take the ferry back to Athens.'

'Let's do that,' Newman agreed. 'Maybe we've stumbled on just what we've been seeking. By pure chance – coming to Siros. I have experienced that when I was a foreign correspondent,' he told Marler, who was watching him in the rear-view mirror. 'A stroke of luck when you least expect it. And it opens up a whole new picture – maybe leading all the way back to Exmoor.'

'Sounds just a shade too easy to me,' Marler commented, switching his gaze to the view beyond the windscreen.

Approaching the outskirts of the port, Nick spoke in Greek to Spyros who gabbled vehemently in reply. Newman was watching the view out of his window, apparently taking no interest in the conversation, his expression blank as he absorbed every word of what was being said. Spyros was having second thoughts about mentioning Sarantis; Nick was reassuring him.

Driving down a narrow paved street, closed in again by the glaring white walls of the stone houses, Nick swung off the street up a curving walled ramp. The house was isolated from the town, grey shutters masked the windows, the brilliant red front door was closed. Marler leapt out of the car, gripping his rifle, and poked his head in the rear window to speak to Spyros.

'Is there a rear way out of this place?' he asked urgently.

Newman noticed he had released the safety catch on his rifle. He was tense, quick-moving. Spyros looked up at him and gestured.

'Round the other side. There is a terrace leading to a door. A flight of steps runs down into the street.'

'What's the matter?' asked Newman as he also left the Mercedes holding his own rifle.

'Something not quite right here,' Marler said tersely.

'What makes you think that?'

'Sixth sense.' Marler spoke to Spyros again. 'This Sarantis. Does he live alone? Any wife, servants?'

'No. By himself. A woman comes in each day . . .'

'Will she be here now?'

Marler was firing the questions. Frequently he glanced at the closed shutters. He frowned as he glanced up at the flat roof. 'Any way to get up there?' he demanded before Spyros answered his first question. Nick, who had switched off the engine, had caught the atmosphere, stood near the front of the car, his right hand under his loose jacket, close to the revolver.

'The woman comes only in the mornings,' Spyros replied. 'And round that corner there is a flight of steps leading to the roof . . .'

'I'll take the roof,' Marler snapped. 'Bob, you take the rear door. Nick, wait by the front door here . . .'

'You wait in the car with Spyros,' Newman warned Christina and ran after Marler.

'The front door is ajar,' Newman warned Nick. 'Synchronize our watches. OK? Eighty seconds from now we both go in. Caution is the word . . .'

Newman ran round the side of the house. Marler was taking the steps to the roof two at a time. The terrace widened overlooking the deserted street. Siesta time. Probably all day. The heat burned his back. The grey shutters were closed over the windows at the back. Newman arrived at a door painted a bright blue.

This door was half-open. Somewhere out of sight further down the street a car started up, sped away. Could mean nothing. He checked his watch. Thirty seconds to go. He stood to one side of the doorway, listening. The sound of the car departing had vanished. A heavy heat-laden silence descended on the terrace. No sound of movement inside the single-storey house. He had the feeling the place was empty. So why were both doors open?

209

Ten seconds. He took a firm grasp on his rifle, held it at waist level. Raising his right foot he kicked the door wide open, darted inside, pressed his body against a wall.

A drop of at least twenty degrees. Positively cool compared with outside. He was inside a large L-shaped living room. A lot of soft furnishing: armchairs, couches. An arched fireplace took up most of the opposite wall. His eyes swivelled, getting accustomed to the dim light. A desk pushed up against the right-hand wall. Its surface littered with papers. He could hear Nick prowling round out of sight. His eyes were fixed on the desk area.

A chair was overturned. The body of an old man lay sprawled on the tiled floor. He lay very still on his back, his eyes staring at the roughcast ceiling. His right hand stretched out, clawed except for the index finger pointing towards Newman as though in a gesture of protest. Nick appeared, gun in hand, followed by Marler who moved with the silence of a cat.

'Anyone in the place?' Newman asked. Both shook their heads. 'Get Spyros. Warn him. I think we're too late . . .'

'Dead as a dodo,' Marler pronounced in a neutral tone.

He was crouched over the body, had checked the neck pulse. He remained crouched on his haunches, his forehead wrinkled as he looked round. Newman was standing gazing down at the old man. He pointed to a scrape mark on the tiles close to the desk.

'Difficult to say what happened,' he commented. 'That looks like the scrape of his shoe. He could have stood up, slipped, cracked the back of his skull. No, I don't think so. Look at his wrist. It's been broken . . .'

'Which could have happened when he slipped. This floor is very highly polished. Makes for accidents.'

'And he broke his arm as well?' queried Newman.

He could now see the arm was turned at an unnatural

210

angle – it was fractured close to the elbow. He looked up as Spyros entered, followed by Nick and Christina. Spyros walked slowly to the body and his voice quavered.

'Is he . . .'

'I'm afraid so,' Newman told him. 'He is dead. Who is it?'

'My old friend, Sarantis . . . my oldest friend . . .'

Tears ran down his weathered cheeks. Christina wrapped an arm round his shoulders, hugged him. Taking out a handkerchief she wiped his face, whispering to him in Greek. She led him to one of the couches where he sagged, then looked up at her.

'You are very kind – all of you,' he said in English. 'I will be all right now.'

'I'll take up guard on the roof,' Marler said crisply. 'Keep a lookout. I don't think we should linger here very long.'

Then he was gone. Christina disappeared briefly, returned with a glass of water. Spyros accepted it gratefully, gulped down the contents. Christina, her expression grim, walked over and stared at the body. Her voice was harsh.

'Another killing?' she demanded. 'They tried to make him talk?'

'Who?' Newman enquired, propping his rifle more securely inside an armchair.

'Dimitrios and Constantine, of course.'

'Why "of course"?'

'Because of this.' Stooping, she pulled out a handkerchief from under the body. It was brightly coloured with a diamond-shaped design. On a cream area it was discoloured with something dark reddish which looked like dried blood to Newman. 'Dimitrios has a handkerchief like this,' she said coldly. 'The rotten swine.'

'Is that the only handkerchief of that kind in Greece?' Newman asked.

'Well, no. You can buy them in the shops in Athens . . .'

211

'Then you can't be sure. Give it to me. Nothing must be disturbed.'

Newman tucked the handkerchief back under the body in the same position she had dragged it from. He checked his watch. Spyros sat very still, staring at Sarantis as though wishing to imprint on his mind this last memory of his friend. A great mistake, Newman thought: and made by so many people.

'They were here,' Christina insisted. 'How did he die?'

'Painfully,' Nick whispered so Spyros shouldn't hear. 'His wrist was broken, then his arm. The shock could have killed him . . .'

'You see!' Christina protested to Newman. 'Sarantis worked up on that platform where we were. They wanted to extract information from him, the brutes . . .'

'We don't know who "they" were,' Newman insisted. 'We don't even know there were two of them . . .'

'Yes we do,' she hissed. Nick nodded as she went on. 'Go in the kitchen. There are the remains of a quick meal – *two* plates on the table, two dirty knives, two pieces of half-eaten cheese and two hunks of bread. Two wine glasses . . .'

Marler appeared, rifle held in both hands. 'I really think we should get away from this place.'

'My own thought,' Newman agreed. He looked at Spyros. 'When I first arrived at the back door I heard a car disappearing towards the port. What time is the next ferry?'

Spyros checked his watch. 'An extra one left about one half hour ago. Today there are a lot of trucks bringing supplies to Siros. You can catch the last ferry for Athens if you leave now. About one half hour for you to drive to the ferry. Then about one quarter of an hour before it leaves.'

'Time for a quick snack at a taverna on the waterfront,' Marler said firmly. 'I'm famished.'

'We inform the police?' asked Christina.

'Not from Siros,' Newman replied. 'We get caught up in this and it could take days, even weeks. We might even be suspected. I don't want to move Sarantis – but we haven't seen the condition of the back of his skull. He could have been hit over the head.' He looked at Spyros. 'Do you think you could keep quiet until the police arrive on their own? Even then, you'd be better to stay out of the whole tragedy. For your own sake.'

'I prefer to mourn in silence . . .'

'Then we'll drop you off at your house. I don't think you'll be bothered. Only that priest knows we were on Siros. I doubt if the police will go all the way up to Mount Ida. Let's move . . .'

'And the police?' Christina persisted.

'I'll make an anonymous call to headquarters from Athens,' Newman replied vaguely. 'We have things to talk about – you and I – when we get back to the city.'

19

Room 318 at the Athens Hilton had a spectacular view from the balcony across the city. In the distance the Parthenon perched on the summit of the Acropolis was silhouetted against a clear evening sky. Her arms folded, Christina stood on the balcony alongside Newman.

'It is very beautiful,' she said, 'especially when you think of man's age-long struggle to become civilized. Two steps forward, one step backward. You know they're going to come looking for me,' she added quietly. 'My horrible family. Petros will see to that.'

'Which is why I brought you here instead of the Grande

Bretagne. And you registered under an assumed name.'

'They will still track me down. They will tour the hotels. A few drachmae will change hands. They have photos they can show a bellboy, a reception clerk.'

'When you arrived dressed so differently? Wearing those huge dark glasses and your hair concealed under a scarf.'

'Maybe you're right, Bob. I wish I could feel as carefree as those people by the pool.'

She looked down to where guests sprawled round the large swimming pool, the water a deep turquoise in the sunlight. Even with the air-conditioning going full blast the large double room behind them was heavy with heat. Newman watched her while she gazed at the pool.

On their return to Piraeus aboard the ferry, Nick had driven them to Kolonaki, the Mayfair and Park Avenue of Athens rolled into one. He had left Newman and Christina there while he took Marler back to the Grande Bretagne. Christina had bought herself several new outfits and nightwear because all her clothes were at Petros' farm. Newman had paid with traveller's cheques and she'd made him promise to accept payment from her.

'I can go to the bank in the morning,' she had insisted. 'My mother left me all the money left her by her relative. There was quite a large sum even after paying for my education . . .'

Newman had braced himself for an ordeal. A woman buying clothes would take forever. He found he was wrong. Christina was decisive, could look quickly at a dozen outfits in her size, pick out one immediately, try it on in minutes, then buy it. They came closer together during the shopping expedition. Newman was always consulted as to whether he liked what she'd chosen. Twice he shook his head and she looked for something else.

Now she was kitted out with one evening dress and an adequate wardrobe for daytime. When she changed out of her jump suit she gave it to him, he rolled it up, took it outside the hotel and rammed it inside a litter bin. They would be looking for her dressed in that.

'Are we having dinner together?' she asked as they stood on the balcony. 'Or is that too forward of me?'

'The nicest possible way to put it. I've been hoping you would join me. We'll try the Ta Nissia here.'

'Super!' Her eyes glowed. 'Now, you've appointed yourself my bodyguard. Can you read a magazine or something while I take a bath?'

'Take your time . . .'

He was sitting by the large picture window spanning the end of the room when someone tapped on the door. He walked rapidly and quietly to the door. Leaving it on the chain, he opened it and Marler waved a hand through the gap.

'Embarrassing moment?' he drawled. 'I can come back. Give you another hour with her?'

'Shut up and come in. She's taking a bath before we have dinner downstairs.'

'The balcony,' Marler said tersely.

He waited until they were outside, then slid the door closed and lit a cigarette. 'No sign of the enemy at the Grande Bretagne yet. And,' he forestalled Newman, 'I wasn't followed. Do you realize you may be walking into a lethal trap?'

'What the hell does that mean?'

'Strikes me you're getting pretty cosy with Christina. That's OK as far as I'm concerned . . .'

'Oh, how very kind,' Newman interrupted ironically. 'Nice to have the Marler *Good Housekeeping* seal of approval . . .'

'Let me finish. It could be a set-up – organized by Petros to lure you into a trap. All this stuff she's been handing out about hating them, that they'll come after her. Has she had a chance to use a phone since you left us?'

'As a matter of fact, no.' Newman held up a hand. 'And before you waste any more breath, did you really think the idea hadn't occurred to me? If it is a trap I'll be walking into it with my eyes wide open – to see where it leads. Tweed has used the tactic very successfully himself in the past.'

'Pardon me for being alive.' Marler gazed down at the illuminated swimming pool. 'Plenty of talent down there. Look at that brown beauty sprawled on the grass. And, while we're on the subject, I did as you suggested. Called in at the British Embassy and contacted Patterson. Bit of a drip, but after seeing my identification he let me call Tweed on scrambler. You have to call him back when you can. Sometime tonight. Remember we are two hours ahead of London.'

'That means my going to the Embassy . . .'

'It's on Sofias Avenue – a ten-minute walk along it from here.'

'I know that, too. The point is Christina must be guarded during my absence. You're elected.'

'We need to fix a time, then. There's a large hall outside this room with armchairs. I can sit there – but I need to know when to be here.'

'Be downstairs by the bank of lifts at ten forty-five. When you see me leave you come straight up . . .'

'Ten forty-five? My, we are looking forward to an athletic evening.'

Newman punched him hard on the arm. 'Just piss off, Marler – and before you go, you told Tweed about our trip to Siros?'

'Of course. He said it was as he'd thought before I called – that the solution to Masterson's death lies out here in Greece.' Marler held up a warning finger. 'Don't forget, the last Englishman who got pally with the glamorous Christina was Harry Masterson. And he ended up as a pancake at the foot of Cape Sounion.'

'Again, your subtle turn of phrase. I liked Harry. Now, Marler, just piss off . . .'

Petros sat in his cane chair on the veranda of the farmhouse in Devil's Valley. His shirt front was open, exposing the hair on his barrel-like chest. Across his lap rested a shotgun. The sun had sunk behind the cliff-like wall of the mountainside to the west. The valley was dark with shadows like blue smoke.

His son and two grandsons stood outside the veranda, keeping their distance, showing their respect. Anton was the most confident. Still wearing his dark blue English business suit, he had loosened his tie and unbuttoned the collar at the neck.

Compared with his two nephews, Dimitrios and Constantine, who were clad in shabby peasant garb, Anton was small and dapper. He smoked a cigarette while he waited for Petros to speak – something the other two would not have dared do. Petros leaned forward.

'Anton is smart,' he began, his voice grating. 'He has just returned from England and the English don't even know he was there.'

'But Passport Control . . .' Dimitrios began.

'Tell me, tell these simple-minded cretins how you did it,' Petros suggested.

'It was easy. Just like that.' Anton snapped his fingers. 'An English gesture,' he lectured his nephews with a superior smile which infuriated them. 'You are right, Dimitrios. I was able to enter England without any check by Passport Control.' He paused. It amused him that he had fooled Petros, an old brigand – an illiterate who couldn't speak a word of English. Well-educated – at Petros' expense – he secretly despised his father. 'I think it would be unwise to reveal my route – it could be given away by Dimitrios in one of his drunken stupors.'

'Now, listen to me, all of you,' Petros growled. 'I taught you, since you were mere children, family honour demands that we revenge ourselves on the killers who dishonoured our family name. Your father, Dimitrios and Constantine, was Stephen, my son who was murdered in Egypt during the war. Christina's father, Andreas, was murdered on Siros. Not that she cares . . .'

'We know this,' Dimitrios muttered in a feeble show of defiance, but Petros heard him.

'Silence! Both of you are in disgrace. You blundered badly on Siros today. More of that later.' He sank back and the chair creaked. Hooding his eyes like a hawk, he spoke again.

'Anton. Tell us what you found in England. Make it brief.'

'There is a lonely area called Exmoor. Also a place like here called the Doone Valley. The three men who went with Andreas on a commando raid to Siros – Barrymore, Kearns and Robson – live close together on that moor. Which is strange. They are not related . . .'

'Tell them about the places where they live,' Petros prodded.

'Each house is well-defended. Like small castles expecting an invasion. One has television cameras watching all approaches. Another is guarded by a fierce dog called Wolf. The third has tall walls topped with barbed wire and a single separate wire. I was suspicious. I scaled a wall carrying a cat. I dropped the cat on the single wire. There was a flash. It screamed, died. Electrified. They are afraid – after all this time . . .'

'How did you find these three men?' asked Dimitrios.

'Christina went to England and used a newspaper advertisement which attracted the attention of a Harry Masterson . . .'

'That's enough,' Petros interrupted, eyes wide open. 'No need to give details. But which of the three is guilty, has our blood on his hands? Or were all three involved in both murders?'

'I don't know.' Anton made a resigned gesture with his manicured hands – hands which contrasted with the roughness of his nephews' who, Petros reflected, were poles apart. 'I made discreet enquiries in the pubs on Exmoor,' Anton continued. 'The three men meet twice every week – for lunch in one place, for dinner in another.' His manner changed, became more nervous as he talked more quickly. 'Then there was the strange incident of the murder of the Englishman, Partridge, on the moor.'

'Partridge, did you say?' asked Dimitrios, quick to sense Anton's change of mood. 'We know an Englishman of that name was poking round Athens, asking questions. That he later visited Siros.'

Anton looked at Petros before replying. The old patriarch nodded agreement for him to continue. 'It was the same man. There was an old picture of him in a newspaper reporting the murder. It is worrying – the report said he was a detective for most of his life with Scotland Yard. The Homicide Branch.'

'There was a man of that name in Cairo when Stephen was killed,' Petros reminded him. 'We found out later. He was one of the military detectives who supposedly investigated Stephen's death. Very young, he was. Is Partridge a common English name?'

'Not as far as I know,' Anton replied. He hurried on. 'That is why I returned here quickly. They were hunting for the killer.'

'And why should they think it was you?' demanded Dimitrios.

Anton hesitated again, looking at Petros. The old man frowned. It was a good question. 'Answer Dimitrios,' he ordered.

'I happened to be riding on a different part of the moor when he was killed,' Anton replied. 'Watching the homes of the three men who were the commandos.'

'I see.' Petros frowned and Anton shuffled his feet.

The old man turned on the two brothers, determined to humiliate them, to exert his authority. 'Now, tell us what a mess you made of things on Siros today. Describe in detail. Anton should know what fools his nephews can be . . .'

Petros sat staring into the distance while Dimitrios recalled the day's events. It was when he came to describe their visit to the home of Sarantis, the archaeologist, that he transferred his gaze to Dimitrios who seemed uncomfortable.

'Constantine,' he broke in suddenly, 'do you agree with all that Dimitrios has said?'

'Yes.' The more passive brother paused. 'We tried to make him talk, to tell us what he knew about where Andreas died. We broke his wrist, then his arm. The old fool slipped on the polished floor, fell over backwards and cracked his skull on the tiles.'

'Go on.'

'We decided to leave quickly aboard the chopper. We knew you would not want us to be tangled up with a police investigation . . .'

'So, you leave in the kitchen the cutlery and things you used to eat a quick meal. With your fingerprints on them, of course.'

'No, Petros! We wiped everything clean. Knives, the glasses. We would have put them away but we were afraid someone would arrive.'

'You ate when you first questioned him, then took him into the living room to apply more pressure?'

'That is how it happened.'

'I wonder whether to believe you.' He was silent for a moment. 'And these two Englishmen Christina reported on – Newman and Marler. You fouled that up as well. No information from Sarantis.' He raised his voice to a shout. 'Do I have to be everywhere to make sure you do the right thing? All of you, get out of my sight. No, wait!

220

Christina has disappeared. Last seen with those English.' His tone was venomous. 'Tomorrow you go to Athens, find her. Do not let her see you. Follow her and tell me what she does, where she goes. Later I decide what to do about her. Now, go! Prepare the meal. If you can do that properly . . .'

Petros sat alone on the veranda, a grim smile of satisfaction on his lined face. Frequently it was necessary to crack the whip to remind his family who was the chief. He looked up as Anton appeared and spoke, his voice low.

'While I have been away, Papa, has anyone been seen near the silver mine?'

'No.' He smiled bleakly. 'You worry too much. Leave me alone. I have to think.'

Despite the mild rebuke, Petros approved: it showed Anton was using his brain. At least one of the litter had turned out well. Odd it should be his second wife's only son. The wife who had died from overwork like the first – driven on by Petros' insistence they run the farm. Early in Anton's childhood Petros had realized he was the bright one. How he had scrimped and saved to educate the boy.

While Dimitrios and Constantine had worked in the fields, Anton had been sent to a select school near Berne in Switzerland – away from the fleshpots of Athens. A school where discipline was strong, where he had learned to speak English and German.

But Petros had taken the precaution of bringing him home during the holidays for Petros' own kind of discipline. He had hammered into the boy's head that his half-brothers, Andreas and Stephen, had been murdered – that the family must take their revenge. A cloud of poisonous hatred hung over Devil's Valley.

It had been a long struggle. First the Civil War from

221

1946 to 1949 between the Communists and the anti-Communists. Breaking out soon after World War Two had ended, it had gone on until the Communist guerrillas were defeated. So many wasted years.

Only recently had Petros been able to devote all his efforts to his vendetta. He had reached the stage where he was quite unable to realize it had become an obsession, filling his every waking moment. A stray thought crossed his mind. The Communists.

Why – after all these years – had the Russian, Oleg Savinkov, reappeared in Athens? He was one of the old school, a Stalinist. And the new man, Gorbachev, was a very different leader, they said. Savinkov, once called The Executioner, did not fit the new pattern Petros heard about in the cafés of the village he visited. To play checkers, to listen to the gossip. Above all to get the first hint of a farmer in trouble. Someone whose land or stock he might buy for a pittance.

Why had Savinkov changed his name to Florakis? The Russian did speak Greek fluently. And he had bought a small farm adjacent to Petros on the coast. But why had he made a point of meeting him when Petros was sitting alone in a café? The Russian had handed him an envelope crammed with drachmae. A large sum – so large Petros, greedy for money, had not accepted at once.

'What do you expect me to do for this?' he had asked bluntly.

'Only one thing – which fits in with your own purposes. You make sure no Englishmen visit the island of Siros and poke around up near Mount Ida.'

'You expect me to kill them?' Petros had demanded.

'It is up to you.' Savinkov had shrugged. 'Maybe you rough them up a bit. You could sabotage their car – the mountain roads are dangerous.'

'And how do I get in touch with you?' Petros had asked, testing Savinkov. 'Walk across to your farm?'

'Never. And you know me only as Florakis. That is why I am paying you . . .'

Since then Petros had kept the money inside the same envelope in his Athens bank. For Petros this was an act of unprecedented willpower. But one day he might wish to sever all connection with the man who had appeared like a ghost. Then he would throw the money back at him.

But why, he asked himself for the twentieth time, should Savinkov take an interest in the murder of Andreas all those years ago?

20

Inside a first-floor room above a taverna in the Plaka, the sole occupant, Oleg Savinkov, was also reflecting on the past. A wiry thin-faced man in his sixties, with blank grey eyes, he sat at a table in his shirt-sleeves and mopped beads of perspiration from his forehead.

The evening heat confined by the rabbit warren of narrow twisting streets was ferocious. He drank more mineral water; years ago he had stopped drinking any kind of alcohol. Years ago . . . In 1946 he had been a young man of twenty, known and feared in Greece as The Russian – or The Executioner. Sent to Greece by Stalin personally because of his talent – his talent for assassination.

1946. Stalin had agreed at Yalta that Greece should come within the British sphere of influence. But when the Greek Communist ELAS movement rose up in revolt and looked like taking over the strategic country – with its potential great Russian naval base at Piraeus – Stalin quietly betrayed his promise.

Savinkov had been smuggled into Greece from Bulgaria. His mission had been brutally simple: to assassinate all the leaders of the Greek right-wing EDES movement fighting the Communists. He had succeeded – up to a point. Five top EDES leaders fell victims to his high-powered rifle. Hence his nicknames – The Russian and The Executioner.

But he had failed to take out the chief EDES leaders. Enough remained at the head of their troops to defeat the Communist uprising eventually. Savinkov had decided wisely not to return to Russia: Stalin demanded one hundred per cent success.

By this time Savinkov had learned Greek fluently and he merged with the landscape, working on a remote farm in Macedonia. The years passed and he seemed to have become the forgotten man. That was until he received discreet word from the Soviet Embassy that someone important wished to meet him.

The visit of General Lucharsky, a Deputy Chief of the Soviet General Staff, to Greece was never reported in the press. By 1986 Savinkov was settled in the Cape Sounion area, owning a small farm growing figs and olives. He had saved money, obtained from a small bank a mortgage to buy the property. He had applied for the loan in the name of Stavros Florakis. Over the years he had obtained sufficient forged papers to establish a new identity as a Greek citizen.

Here he had taken a risk. After some hesitation he had contacted one of the Communist ELAS leaders who had gone underground, the man with whose group he was working when the whole revolt fell apart. It was a greater risk than he realized since this benefactor kept a discreet and distant line of communication open with the Soviet Embassy in Athens. But this man had seen no reason to inform on Savinkov – his own relations with the Russians had been precarious. Until 1986 . . .

Florakis-Savinkov drank more mineral water. He wouldn't sleep, he knew. The oppressive heat would last all night long. Plus the babble of voices and *bouzouki* playing which drifted upwards through the dense humidity and through the open window.

1986. He had been visited at his farm late one evening by the ELAS leader who had provided him with the papers of a Greek citizen. The man's arrival had been a shock – it was Savinkov's first intimation that he had been watched, that they knew where he was.

He had been invited to meet an 'important visitor' to Athens. That was after he had been asked a number of questions about his reaction to the change of leadership in Russia. Savinkov had been frank – thinking that if he was candid the invitation which worried him might be withdrawn.

No, he did not approve of Gorbachev's *glasnost*. This was not the real Communism he had risked his life for during the Civil War. It was a dangerous departure from Lenin's creed, and so on. To his surprise an appointment had been made for that same evening. His visitor would drive him to Athens.

His destination turned out to be the Hilton Hotel. He was escorted to a room on the second floor where a man wearing a lightweight grey business suit had opened the door and ushered him inside. Tall and lean with the face of a fox, he wore a pair of dark glasses and offered Savinkov vodka. He refused, mentioned that he had not touched alcohol for forty years.

'I am Colonel Gerasimov of the GRU,' his host said as they sat facing each other across a small round table.

General Lucharsky was confident his deception would

225

never be penetrated. His photograph had never appeared in a newspaper and the general public abroad didn't know of his existence. He was weighing up his guest as he poured himself a glass of the vodka, a fact Savinkov was aware of. Mention of the GRU had reassured him – as intended – since it was a GRU colonel who had accompanied him to the Bulgarian border in 1946.

'We are very worried about General Secretary Gorbachev and his crazy *glasnost*,' Lucharsky commented.

He had no doubts about coming straight to the point: Doganis, who had brought Savinkov to him, would have checked his outlook. And for a man of sixty-one Savinkov looked very fit – more like forty. Already Lucharsky was fairly sure they had selected the right man.

'He is ruining Lenin's work,' Savinkov agreed, 'but why am I here?'

He spoke slowly. It was many years since he had conversed in his native language. But he had taken the precaution of reading novels in Russian and he found the language coming back fast.

'You were once trained as a radio operator,' Lucharsky said. 'Is that not so?'

'Yes. Before I came to Greece to do a job in 1946 . . .'

'To kill reactionary Greek leaders.' Lucharsky leaned forward. 'We need a liaison man who can communicate by radio in English. I understand you are fluent in that language?'

'I learned it in the days when I served as a waiter in hotels here to make money to buy my farm. I keep it up by talking with English people during the tourist season . . .'

'Good. You are just the man we need.' Lucharsky smiled. His wide mouth made him look even foxier. A conspirator type, Savinkov was thinking. 'You will have to operate the latest type of transceiver. Doganis will train you in the use of the instrument, will give you the codes, the wavebands, the times for transmission. England, you see, is two hours behind Greece.'

England? Savinkov was startled. In the old days he used to think very fast and he found his brain moving into high gear again. The man watching him from behind the tinted glasses would be in his forties. He would show him he was not dealing with some dumb peasant.

'There could be a technical problem. Transmitting over that distance.'

'Doganis tells me you have high mountains, very lonely, near your farm. You could use one of your donkeys to take the transceiver to a peak. From there transmission will be top-class.'

'Yes, it would.' They had thought this out very carefully. Which gave Savinkov confidence. But he needed to know exactly what he was doing – and why. He sat up straight, staring at the glasses.

'In the old days I never operated in the dark. I must know what this is all about, Colonel.'

'An independent type. Good,' Lucharsky repeated. 'Really I have already told you. Gorbachev must be re-moved before he can do any more damage. There is a group inside Russia – high up – which is determined to replace him by a correct type of leader. The trouble is we have to be very careful. He has ears everywhere – inside Russia. So we have reactivated an organization outside the motherland. Partly here in Greece, partly in England. You will be the link. Doganis will deliver the messages you must send. At other times our associate in England will send you signals at certain times arranged in advance. That's it. And Doganis is your sole contact. Never go near the Soviet Embassy here.'

'Who am I communicating with in England?'

'The codename is La Jolla – a small place in America.

227

Doganis will explain everything. Oh, by the way, when you leave here he will drive you to a room we have rented for you over a taverna in the Plaka. I think that is all.' Lucharsky glanced at his watch.

'I don't see how this is going to bring down Gorbachev. And I will be risking my freedom. Greek counter-intelligence could trap me and I would be a spy.'

'You are right.' Lucharsky pursed his thin lips. They had reported Savinkov was intelligent and self-reliant. A thought occurred to him. 'You are not married, we know. What do you do for a woman when you need one? Any permanent girlfriend?'

'None. I would have had to entrust her with my secret. If we had quarrelled one day she might have betrayed me. I have an old woman who comes daily to the farm to cook for me and two men who work on the land. When I need a woman I go into the city here and pick one up. Always a different one. That way, no complications.'

'You are very well organized. And now you will excuse me?'

'I still don't see how you are going to replace Gorbachev – even operating a group safely from outside.'

This was the crunch. By now Lucharsky had made up his mind – time had not eroded Savinkov's training, his reliability, his faith in the cause. Lucharsky waved a hand as though swatting a fly.

'If necessary we await our opportunity – preferably when he is abroad – and kill him. You object to that?'

'Why should I? In the past I have killed enemies of the cause.'

Doganis had been waiting for him outside the room and had led him to a Citroën parked in front of the taxi rank outside the hotel. It had been a baking evening as Savinkov stared at the car.

'What happened to the Peugeot you drove me to Athens in?'

'We change cars. Frequently. It is good security. Get in. Now we will go to the Plaka. Inside the locked boot there is an old suitcase. Inside that is the transceiver. You start training tonight . . .'

And, Savinkov thought as he poured yet more mineral water, it was inside this room a year ago that Doganis had produced from a worn, shabby suitcase a superb large transceiver. They had practised half the night, Savinkov tapping the key while the machine was switched off. He had been surprised how quickly he had mastered the machine – so different from the one he had used in 1946.

Later that week Doganis had again visited his farm and the training had continued until Savinkov could operate it blindfold. His greatest shock had come that first evening here in this room when he had tackled Doganis about the clandestine organization working outside Russia.

'Colonel Gerasimov told me they have reactivated an organization – an apparatus – outside the motherland. What does that mean? I do need to know what I am doing,' he concluded aggressively.

'You might as well know. We may have to send a stranger to you with a message. This will identify him. The apparatus which has come alive again is the Greek Key.'

21

Newman escorted Christina through the large bar at the Hilton and down the staircase leading to the Ta Nissia, the main restaurant. It was located at a lower level from the vast entrance hall paved with solid marble. Christina paused at the bottom step and grasped Newman's arm.

'Oh, look, that tempts my taste buds madly.'

Facing them was a vast open fireplace and over the fire spits revolved slowly, cooking the food. The lower spit supported a whole roasting pig. On the long spit above it chickens were turning slowly and an appetising aroma drifted towards them.

'No need to consult the menu,' Newman joked. 'I've reserved a corner table . . .' He gave his name to the maitre d' who escorted them past a huge cold buffet table into a spacious room shut off from the outside world.

They settled themselves at the table and Newman sat alongside Christina on a red velvet banquette, his back to the wall so he could watch the whole room. He glanced at her as she studied the menu. 'You're looking superb in that dress, what there is of it. It suits your figure.'

She glanced at him wickedly. 'Maybe a little too revealing.'

'I'm happy.'

It was the one item of clothing they had purchased in Kolonaki she had not allowed him to see. A strapless, low-cut dress of black velvet, it hugged her closely. 'You'll have to be careful not to drop anything down the front,' he remarked, with a quick look at the upper half of her well-formed breasts.

'You would think of that.' She giggled. 'I've decided. No starter. Spit-roast chicken for me. And it's nice to have a man who's so well-organized.' She nodded towards the ice bucket where a bottle of champagne rested half-concealed beneath a white napkin.

'Veuve Cliquot.' He looked at the waiter standing to take their orders. 'We'll start on the champagne right away – and we can order now . . .'

She waited until they were alone. 'Are these the opening moves in an attempted seduction?'

'You brought the subject up.' He lowered his glass. 'First I need to hear all about Harry Masterson.'

'I thought there'd be a catch.' She sighed. 'What do you want to know?'

'Everything. From the very beginning. How you met him would be a good opening.'

'I like this place. It's the first time I've been here. Silly, isn't it?' She gave him a bewitching smile. 'I suppose it is because I live here. A strange room, very cleverly designed.'

He looked round. The walls were constructed of very solid rough brown stone. Set back into the walls at intervals were alcoves containing Greek pottery – beautifully shaped vases and jugs. A soft glow illuminated the room and the windows were high up and recessed into the solid stone. At 8 p.m. there were only a few tables taken, but more guests were filtering in. Newman refilled their glasses.

'Now, about Harry Masterson,' he said firmly.

'What a persistent man you are. Well, it's a long story . . .'

'We have all evening.'

'Petros still had me under his thumb. He persuaded me it was my duty to help find who killed Andreas and Stephen. We Greeks call it *philotimo*, a matter of family honour.'

'Go on.'

'He went about it deviously – like he does everything. I had to fly to Zurich. There I stayed overnight and bought a return air ticket to London. I'd flown to Zurich by Swissair. I used British Airways to fly on to London. When I got there I stayed at the Strand Palace. I then inserted a personal advertisement in *The Times* newspaper.' She paused. 'Petros had written the words. The advertisement read, *Will anyone interested in the Greek Key and who knows about Antikhana please contact me. Irene.*'

Newman sipped champagne to conceal the shock he had

received. Harry Masterson had been Tweed's sector chief for the Balkans, and that zone included Greece. Newman was also recalling that among the items Masterson had posted back to Tweed was a bracelet – a bracelet from which was suspended a symbol. The Greek key.

'What happened next?' he enquired amiably.

'Petros thought I might be contacted by one of three men – the men who were part of the commando raid on Siros when Andreas was murdered. A Colonel Barrymore, Captain Robson and Kearns, a company sergeant major. Whoever answered the advertisement was likely to be the murderer. So Petros thought. He felt sure they would have to find out who was enquiring after all these years.'

'I don't understand the Greek key bit.'

'I'm not talking about that. Too dangerous. For you . . .'

'There's no limit on danger.'

'Don't you want to know who got in touch with the phone number I put in the advertisement?' she asked.

'Go on,' he repeated, confident he already knew the answer.

'Harry Masterson. I was very taken aback. Then I thought it could be one of the three men using a false name. Especially because of the precautions he told me to take when he arranged to meet me.'

'What precautions?'

'I had to meet him at a certain place in Lincoln's Inn – where all the British lawyers are. It frightened me when I arrived at eleven in the morning. No one about. All those ancient courtyards. I thought it was a trap. I'd armed myself with an aerosol. He was very clever. The appointment was for the same morning he phoned. I only had less than an hour to get there.'

Yes, very clever, Newman thought. So typical of Harry – to select a rendezvous where he could watch her approach,

232

make sure no one was following her. A thought occurred to him.

'How would he know it was you?'

'On the phone he asked me where I was and to give a description of myself, what I would be wearing. I waited for ten minutes and decided no one was coming. At that moment he came round a corner. Again he was clever. I realized he couldn't be one of the three men – he was too young. But I thought one of them might have sent him. He took me a short walk to a public place in Fleet Street, The Cheshire Cheese pub. Lots of people about. I felt safe then.'

She paused and drank half a glass of champagne. The restaurant was filling up. As he listened Newman kept a check on the new faces; for one especially. The face of Petros. He'd recognize him: from the picture Sarris, the police chief, had shown him; and even more from that moment he had spotted Petros inside the black Mercedes when they had returned early in the morning from police HQ.

'We're inside The Cheshire Cheese,' he reminded her after their meals of spit-roasted chicken had been served.

'Harry had a way with women. I felt he was OK but I still asked who he was, what he did. He said he was with Special Branch, the British secret police. I asked him to prove it and he showed me a card with his photograph. I found myself telling him about the murders of Andreas and Stephen, why I'd come to London, about Barrymore, Kearns and Robson. He said he had ways of tracing them. I couldn't believe my luck. I asked him what his interest was.'

'And he told you?' Newman was intrigued to learn what piece of fiction Harry had invented to cover that question.

'He said it might just link up with a case he had investigated and never solved. We arranged to meet the following day after he'd made certain enquiries. I've no idea where he went . . .'

I have, thought Newman. To pump Brigadier Willie Davies at the Ministry of Defence. He let her eat her meal while he traced in his mind what had happened. It was all becoming horribly clear now – the tragedy of Harry Masterson.

Harry had been given a month's leave. Unmarried, Harry detested holidays, got bored within twenty-four hours. He'd seen the advertisement Christina had placed in *The Times* and reacted to it for a lark – anything to occupy his time.

The moment he'd met Christina he'd been hooked – but cautious – by her story, by Christina herself. Harry liked the ladies. He had still kept up his guard by pretending to be a Special Branch officer. That had impressed Christina, had given her confidence he could help her. But at any time Harry could pull out, pleading call of duty with another case.

'What happened next?' he asked as she pushed her empty plate to one side. 'And we need more champagne . . .' He mimed the request to their waiter.

'When he arrived next morning at the Strand Palace he was carrying a small case. He told me to pack, that we were going on a journey, that he'd traced not only Barrymore, but Kearns and Robson, too. I was shaken to the core. He said we had to drive to the West Country, to a place called Exmoor . . .'

She went on to explain how they had put up at a hotel in Dunster near the coast. Harry had then driven off to visit the three men now he knew their addresses.

'He made appointments?' Newman asked.

'No, he was devious. He phoned each of the three men and said he was making an enquiry on behalf of the Ministry

234

of Defence, that he would be with them shortly. Then he put the phone down before they could ask any questions. That way he knew they'd be where they lived when he arrived.'

'You'd told him everything you knew about the two murders – one in Cairo, one on Siros? And about Petros' vendetta?'

'Yes.' She smiled ruefully. 'Harry could get any secret out of a woman. I told him more than I intended to.'

'So what happened after he'd seen the ex-commandos?'

'He was suspicious of one of them. He wouldn't tell me which one. He told each of them the identity of the murderer was now known, that he was on his way to Athens to check with the chief of police. He thought the guilty one would follow us.'

Oh God, Newman realized, and he succeeded. At the cost of his own life. No back-up. That had been Harry's fatal blunder. But he had always been a lone wolf, brimming with self-confidence. Had he left behind a clue?

'Did he say anything about how the three men received him?'

'He was very amusing about Colonel Barrymore who tried to treat him like a common soldier. They had a violent argument. Harry ended up by telling him that if they'd had many colonels like him they would have lost the war. Then we flew out here.'

'What came next?'

'I don't really know.' For the first time she sounded depressed. 'We booked in at the Astir Palace at Vouliagmeni. That's a sea resort on the way to Cape Sounion . . .' Which is why we weren't able to locate where he stayed, Newman thought grimly. She continued as he watched her closely. 'He said he was going to see Chief Inspector Sarris. I don't know whether he ever did. He changed his mind a lot.' She sipped more champagne and leaned against him. 'I'm getting a bit tiddly. Lovely.'

235

He changed his mind a lot. Newman knew why Harry had done that: to keep Christina off balance in case she was passing on information to someone. He had never completely let down his guard with her.

'Then what happened?' Newman prodded.

'He told me over early breakfast one morning he was visiting Devil's Valley. He wouldn't say why. I'd told him about the silver mine. I think he was going to try and find it. I feel awful about that. I may be responsible for what happened to him.'

'What silver mine?'

'It's near the top of a mountain in Devil's Valley. Nobody has worked it for years. It's abandoned – but Petros forbids anyone to go near it. I don't know why. He has even told his shepherds who work near it to shoot anyone they see prowling in that area.'

'Which is against the law,' Newman remarked.

'Petros makes his own law. Harry was intrigued by that silver mine – why it was forbidden territory. I've never been near the place.' She shuddered, drank more champagne.

'So, when Harry set out on his last journey that morning he was trying to locate this abandoned mine. Any idea what the place is like?'

'Dimitrios once told me something when he was drunk. The shaft is still open. It goes down a long way, a vertical drop with the old cage which took down miners still suspended at the top. It sounded horribly sinister to me. But at the last minute before he left Harry changed his mind again. He received a phone call when he was getting ready to leave his bedroom. He said he might go first to Cape Sounion to meet the Englishman.'

'What Englishman? What time in the morning was this?'

Newman was watching her closely. Was she spinning him an elaborate yarn? Setting the same trap for him she'd set for Harry? She was such a beauty with her mane of

236

black glossy hair; by the light of the single lighted candle on their table her bare shoulders gleamed. A girl to dazzle any man.

'We'd had breakfast at six,' she continued. 'Neither of us could sleep that night. The phone call must have come through before seven in the morning. Harry went up to his room to take it. He looked pleased when he came back, said his ruse had worked. I presume he meant telling those three ex-commandos he was flying to Greece while we were on Exmoor. The caller had disguised his voice but Harry was sure he knew who it was. He wouldn't give me even a hint. Said it was dangerous . . .'

And it had been dangerous, Newman reflected grimly. It had ended in Harry's death. But what she had told him was confusing. Had Harry tried to locate the silver mine first before going on to Cape Sounion?

'Christina, did Harry know the exact location of the worked-out silver mine?'

'Yes. He had a map of the area he bought in Athens. He asked me to mark its precise location on the map, which I did. Afterwards I wished I hadn't done that. Harry could be very persuasive.'

'So can I.' He produced a large-scale map he'd purchased of the huge peninsular area stretching between Athens and Cape Sounion. 'Mark the location for me.'

She pushed back her empty plate, clasped her hands in her lap, turned to face him. 'No. The last time I did that a man died. I'm growing fond of you, Bob . . .'

'Cut that out,' he said brutally. 'Mark the bloody map. Now!'

'It's your funeral.' Her eyes flashed. 'And don't ever use that tone to me again.' She spread out the map, took the pen he offered, studied the map, then drew a cross at the top of a mountain.

'Petros is crazy,' she warned. 'You'd be crazy too if you went anywhere near Devil's Valley.'

237

'When was the last time you saw Harry? Alive, I mean,' he persisted, his voice cold.

'You bastard . . .' Her voice trembled. She was on the verge of tears. 'When he left the breakfast room and went straight to his hired car . . .' She fiddled in her envelope-shaped handbag for a handkerchief.

He put an arm round her back, rested his hand on her shoulder. 'No need to get uptight, Christina. But I knew Harry well. I have to know everything he did – planned to do. What about a spot of dessert? The strawberry gâteau looks pretty good – forget about your figure for tonight, even if I can't . . .'

'Flattery could get you somewhere.' She recovered her poise as he squeezed her shoulder. 'And I'd love some gâteau. And more champagne.'

He waited until dessert was served, until she was tucking into the huge quantity with gusto. 'To sum up,' he began, 'you went to London at Petros' command, inserted the advertisement, made contact with Harry. OK so far?'

'On the nose,' she assured him and winked.

'He drove you to Exmoor, after tracing Barrymore, Robson and Kearns. He went to see each man, told them he was flying soon to Greece. You arrived with him. What was your mood about the mission Petros had sent you on when you got back here?'

'Bloody bolshie. I'd had Petros up to here. The trip to London – and spending time with Harry – had snapped any bonds with Petros. I didn't care any more who had killed Stephen, Andreas. I'd never even known them. I was worried about Harry. Now I'm worried about you. If it's not a secret, what are you going to do next? Please . . .'

She laid a hand on his arm. Then she waited until he turned towards her and kissed him full on the mouth. 'Please,' she repeated. 'I've been honest with you.'

'Fair enough. I'm going to phone a man in London I

238

know after I've packed you off to bed. And Marler will stand guard. Outside your room.'

'Who are you phoning?' she pressed.

'My editor,' he lied. 'I am a foreign correspondent. Remember?'

22

Newman arrived at the British Embassy at eleven, well after dark. The large villa on Sofias Avenue was surrounded by a stone wall, looming up behind a Turkish-style church. Patterson, his contact, was a pain in the neck.

Impatiently, Newman waited in the hall as the round-faced man in his forties carefully examined his press card and then his passport. A typical bureaucrat, Newman thought: inflated with a sense of his own importance. Smooth-faced, he turned the passport pages with irritating slowness.

'For God's sake,' Newman snapped. 'You knew I was coming. Tweed warned you.'

'It is my responsibility who uses the phone,' Patterson responded in his bland voice.

'It's just a phone . . .'

'It's the scrambler,' Patterson reminded him pompously. 'I have to log all calls, be very careful who uses it. You have no diplomatic status . . .'

'*You* won't have any if I report you're obstructing me. You're on probation, don't forget.'

The blow struck home. Patterson's well-padded face flushed, he ran a manicured hand over his slick black hair. 'No need to be rude,' he bleated.

'Just realistic. Let's get on with it. Now. Tweed is wait-ing. Or have you forgotten London is two hours behind us? He likes to get home early to work on files,' Newman lied.

The phone was in a small room in the basement. A table, chairs pushed under it, the phone with the red button the only object on the table top. Newman sat down, reached for the phone, then looked up at Patterson who still stood waiting.

'Piss off, there's a good chap. This is confidential. Leave the card and passport on the table. Shut the door on your way out.'

Pressing the red button, he dialled Park Crescent. Paula came on the line within seconds. She sounded relieved to hear his voice.

'We wondered what the devil was happening to you . . .'

'Nice to be loved. Tweed about? I'm on scrambler from the Embassy in Athens.'

'He's here. Take care . . .'

Tweed sounded as fresh as sea air at nine in the evening. Newman plunged straight into a terse report of what had taken place since his arrival. Tweed listened without inter-rupting. At the end of five minutes Newman concluded his story.

'That brings you up to date. Doesn't really take us any further as to who killed Harry.'

'It might have done. You have a pipeline into this weird Gavalas clan – Christina. Whether she can be trusted is for you to assess. What do you think?'

'I'm leaning to the idea she has broken with the whole crew. But only leaning – she's pretty street-wise and could be a first-rate actress. Pity Harry hadn't told her who the mysterious Englishman who phoned him was. Could it have been one of the commando trio?'

'Yes. All three I visited had just returned from separate holidays abroad. All had a deep suntan – which they could

240

have picked up in Greece. The timing is right, too. One of them could have been out there at exactly the time Masterson was killed. I have the feeling the solution lies in Greece. That raid on Siros all those years ago. What intrigues me is the missing body – who took the dead Andreas away from that gulch? And why? I may fly out to join you when the right moment comes. What's your next move?'

'To explore that old silver mine in Devil's Valley. Something very strange about that – the way Petros takes such precautions to keep strangers away from the place . . .'

'Don't!' Tweed's tone was sharp. 'I don't like the sound of Mr Petros one bit. We may do it together later. You need plenty of back-up to go into a place like that. Harry Butler and Pete Nield would be useful. Plus Marler. At the moment Butler and Nield are on Exmoor, nosing around and picking up gossip about Barrymore, Kearns and Robson. How are you finding Marler?' Tweed asked casually.

'A pain. But I can handle him. One thing I will give him – he's a good man to go into the jungle with. I'll keep you in touch . . .'

'Don't go.' A pause. 'At this stage it seems like a vendetta directed by Petros against whoever killed his two sons, Andreas and Stephen. His main suspects being on Exmoor. Is that how you see it?'

'With the little data we have to go on yet, yes. Especially now you've told me about this Anton character. Christina hasn't mentioned him, which I find odd. Butler and Nield are on the lookout for Anton, too, I assume?'

'Anton has disappeared. I suspect he's flown by some secret route back to Greece. He didn't pass through London Airport – I've had the security chief there check the passenger manifests.'

'But it backs up the vendetta theory.' Newman paused and Tweed said nothing. 'Or is there something more?'

'I think this business could be much bigger, far more

serious than we realize. I can't figure out the link between Exmoor and Greece.'

'There has to be one?'

'If there isn't, then we're wasting our time. But who pushed Masterson over a Greek cliff?' Tweed paused again. 'After he'd visited Exmoor. We're missing something . . .'

Florakis – Oleg Savinkov, The Executioner – crouched at the top of the mountain above his farm. It was 2 a.m. and earlier he had received a coded signal he suspected emanated from inside the Soviet Embassy in Athens.

His suspicions were correct. But he would have been surprised had he known the hand which tapped out the message was that of Colonel Rykovsky, military attaché. Rykovsky had waited until the Embassy staff had gone home: hence the arrangement made via Doganis for Savinkov to be ready to receive the signal at two in the morning.

Savinkov had placed the powerful transceiver given to him in a small depression at the mountain summit. The telescopic aerial was extended as he checked his watch by the light of a pencil torch. Time to retransmit the message to England. And for that elevation was needed to cover the long distance.

His bony face was tense with concentration as he sent out the call signal, received immediate acknowledgement. He began tapping out the coded message, keeping an eye on his watch as he operated. Three minutes was the maximum agreed time for any transmission.

It was unlikely Greek counter-espionage would have detector vans as far south as this remote wilderness, but Doganis had emphasized the importance of security.

'Take no chances. You are the linchpin of the whole operation.'

'What operation?' Savinkov had asked.

'I don't know, but it's big, very big. It could change the whole course of history. That's all I've been told.'

The words echoed in Savinkov's brain as he completed tapping out the signal. He felt excited as he depressed the aerial, lifted the heavy transceiver back inside the shabby suitcase. It was a long climb back down the mountain to the farm but he would be there long before daylight.

One thousand six hundred-odd miles to the north-west another hand on Exmoor was already beginning the task of decoding the signal which had just come in from Greece. The unbreakable one-time code had been used, the novel the series of numbers referred to was Sinclair Lewis' *Main Street*. Half an hour later the message was decoded, written on the pad which had a sheet of protective plastic beneath the sheet to avoid any risk of an impression of the wording reproducing itself on the sheet beneath the plastic.

All equipment and preparations should be made immediately. Possible that target will land in Britain on way to or when returning from Washington summit. Potential timing September or October this year. The Greek Key.

23

'Gorbachev must go, he is destroying the military supremacy we have taken so many years to build up. His crazy *glasnost* will be the ruin of the Soviet state,' General Lucharsky said vehemently.

By which he meant the power of the Red Army, his faithful aide, Colonel Volkov, thought as they strolled side by side in full uniform in the Moscow park. Children played ball games on the grass in the warmth of the sunlight round them as they followed one of the many twisting paths.

Lucharsky had chosen the park for this conversation because it was impossible for them to be overheard. He walked very erect, hands clasped behind him, head bowed in thought. Volkov asked the question tentatively. He was not sure Lucharsky wanted to reveal details of the plan but his curiosity drove him on.

'How can we ever hope to achieve his replacement? The Politburo is now packed with a majority in his favour . . .'

'Ligachev,' the General said tersely. 'He is Number Two. He does not agree with the new madness. Once Gorbachev has been removed he will take over and the yes-men in the Politburo will swing behind him.'

'But how can the present General Secretary be removed?'

'He can be killed.'

The cold-blooded audacity of the statement astounded Volkov and he was silent for a few minutes as they continued their stroll. Lucharsky took off his peaked cap and ran his hand through his blond hair, enjoying the feel of the sun on his forehead.

'But it must be done outside Russia,' Lucharsky continued, 'at a suitable moment. I set the wheels in motion when I made my unofficial visit to Greece. There are plenty of hard men in the Politburo who will welcome a return to the good old days. Fortunately, Comrade Gorbachev is playing into our hands. He agrees we must do everything possible to spread our influence in the Mediterranean. But by peaceful means. You, Comrade, have been chosen to follow up my visit to Athens. Like me, you will travel there in civilian clothes – on an unofficial visit. We are offering the Greek government special trade concessions. While you are there you will carry verbal orders from me to Colonel Rykovsky, the military attaché at the Athens

Embassy. I will give you those orders just before you fly to Athens via Zurich.'

'Why Greece? What is happening there?'

Lucharsky changed direction, headed for a path which twisted through a wooded area of birch trees. He had spotted two men in plain clothes who had KGB written all over them. One had a pair of field glasses slung round his neck. He might be a lip-reader. They entered the wood.

'Because,' Lucharsky explained, 'it is too dangerous to plan a coup inside the motherland. Gorbachev is no fool. He knows he faces opposition and has eyes and ears everywhere. We must not underestimate him. So, we have reactivated an organization outside Russia, one which has not operated for years. It is composed of men who worked for Stalin, who have been forgotten. Shadow men.'

'And Greece is this base?'

'One of them,' Lucharsky replied enigmatically. 'We are using the KGB cell system. Only what you need to know is told to you. There is great dissatisfaction inside the Red Army, as you know. When Gorbachev has gone the Army will again wield all the power it once did after Stalin died.'

'But you implied this organization outside the motherland is made up of Stalinists,' Volkov reminded him. He was bewildered.

'So it is. We use them, then discard them. They may well be the scapegoat for the assassination of Comrade Mikhail if that proves necessary.'

'You mean they do the job for us and then we accuse them of being responsible?'

'Possibly. It would be better if we could spread rumours once Gorbachev has gone that he was the victim of hard-liners inside the Pentagon. We will play our cards as the game progresses. We wait for our opportunity – which may come within a few months. Our only chance to liquidate the mad dog is while he is outside Russia. There our allies can operate more safely.'

245

'I am at your service, Comrade General,' Volkov, a round-faced ball of a man replied.

'Who knows?' Lucharsky commented, adjusting his cap to a more jaunty angle. 'It might end up in promotion for you.'

Always dangle the carrot in front of the donkey, he thought. No point in explaining that those who helped would also have to be eliminated when the coup succeeded.

Inside his office at Park Crescent Tweed sat behind his desk staring into the distance. The desk-top was covered with neat piles of documents which he had just examined for the third time. The items Masterson had posted him from Greece and the notebook of Partridge he had collected from the safety deposit in Knightsbridge.

Paula sat at her desk checking through a file. Every now and again she glanced up at her chief. In another corner Monica bent her head over a card index, her dark hair tied behind her neck in a bun.

'Are we getting anywhere?' Paula ventured. 'After that phone call from Bob last night?'

'Listen, both of you.' Tweed sat upright in his swivel chair, hands clasped in his lap, his eyes alert behind his glasses. 'Let's go over what we have briefly. Damn all, as far as I can see.'

'Maybe more than we know,' Paula suggested. 'Basically it all appears to have started with two murders a long way off and a long time ago. Andreas Gavalas on Siros Island, Stephen Ionides – now revealed as Stephen Gavalas. Someone is trying to bury both killings.' She caught Monica's expression. 'Sorry – that sounded a bit callous . . .'

'But it may be true,' Tweed agreed. 'Go on.'

He was, Monica realized, conducting in reverse an exercise he'd often carried out with her. At a certain point of an operation he would sum up the main points, using

Monica to bounce off his ideas, to test their relevance.

With Paula he was listening to how she saw the situation – seeking a key element they had overlooked. Something simple; maybe a factor which didn't fit what they knew. Paula went on.

'We have met Barrymore, Robson and Kearns – the three men who were with Andreas when he was killed. The same three men were back in Cairo when Stephen was brutally murdered at the Antikhana Building. Both victims were brothers. It really stretches the long arm of coincidence to breaking-point – that the commando trio were in the vicinity of two murders. OK so far?'

'Go on . . .' Tweed had relaxed, listening with his eyes closed as he visualized what she was saying.

'Now we have two odd complications – which don't link up with what I've said so far. The mysterious disappearance of Andreas' body from Siros the night he was killed. And the arrival of Anton Gavalas on Exmoor making enquiries about the ex-commandos.'

'Something else odd about Anton,' Tweed pointed out. 'The way he vanished without leaving a trace of the route he used. We checked with the harbourmaster at Watchet. No ship left for anywhere when Anton pulled off his vanishing act.'

'Anything in Partridge's notebook?' Paula asked.

'Yes. According to Partridge Anton is well-educated and speaks fluent English. Yet Newman told me his nephews – Dimitrios and Constantine – are peasant types. And what game is Anton playing? In his notebook Partridge records Anton is a lone wolf with plenty of money at his disposal. Newman also said Christina hadn't mentioned Anton. They seem to want him to be the invisible man.' He paused and Monica asked who 'they' were.

'That is what we need to find out. Anton could be acting independently of old Petros. This vendetta business is complex, reeks of a long and dangerous hatred. You know,

I'm getting the impression someone is using the vendetta as a smokescreen – to hide something far more deadly. And who killed Masterson?'

It was Saturday night at The Luttrell Arms in Dunster. They always dined together on Saturdays. At the corner table at the far end of the dining room Colonel Barrymore occupied a seat facing the room with his back to the wall. Dr Robson sat beside him while Kearns was seated opposite the two men. They were at the coffee stage.

'Another large Scotch,' Robson called out.

'Of course, sir. Coming right away,' the manager assured him as he passed their table.

'Pushing the boat out a bit, aren't we?' Barrymore commented in a supercilious tone, glancing at his companion.

Robson's complexion had lost most of its suntan and was now a ruddy colour like a setting sun. It was his fourth double plus several glasses of Beaujolais. He stroked his thatch of brown hair, pulled at his straggle of a moustache, grinned amiably. As usual he was in high good humour.

'Thought we were here to enjoy the evening. Ever known me to be half seas over?'

'There's always a first time,' Barrymore continued in a lofty tone. 'And we have serious business to discuss. See that chap with the dark moustache, black hair, a hearing aid? Caught him watching Quarme Manor this morning. I challenged him.'

'You did?' Robson sounded amused and Barrymore glared at him. 'Where was he?'

'Up on the ridge behind the manor. Riding a horse.'

'Free country – in case you've forgotten.' He chuckled. His blue eyes lit up as his drink arrived. 'Thank you.' Lifting the glass, he swallowed half the contents. 'That's better.' He turned to Barrymore. 'So what happened when you *challenged* the chappie? Sounds like the corporal of the guard.' He grinned at Kearns who stared back, blank-faced, ramrod-backed.

'Had the insolence to tell me he was bird-watching,' Barrymore continued. 'Hence the field glasses trained on Quarme Manor. Rode off pretty sharp, I can tell you.' His tone changed, became silky. 'Gentlemen, I smell trouble. There was the Greek you encountered, Kearns.'

'And how can you be sure he was Greek?' Robson chaffed the ex-CSM. 'Wearing his *Evzone* outfit, was he?'

'No laughing matter,' Barrymore snapped. 'Tell him,' he ordered Kearns.

'Well, sir,' Kearns began, gazing at the colonel, 'his appearance for one thing. Olive-skinned, the facial bone structure. I've seen enough of them to recognize the breed. When I spoke to him he replied in English but with a slight accent. Greek.'

'Not Bulgarian or Yugoslav?' Robson enquired. He grinned again, drank more whisky. 'Would you know the difference?'

'Yes, I think I would,' Kearns responded stiffly.

'And what was he doing? More bird-watching?'

'Said he was on holiday, that he liked wild places. Asked me the way to the nearest pub. Told him Simonsbath, miles away from where we met. To test him. Later I saw him riding down a gully towards Winsford. Which *was* the way to the nearest pub. See what I mean, sir?'

'He knew the moor, tried to pretend he didn't. That's what I want to talk about. The enemy could be closing in. Need to take more precautions.'

Barrymore sipped his cognac and Robson glanced at the balloon glass. 'Time I had one of those . . .'

Pete Nield, sitting with Harry Butler three tables away, adjusted his earpiece. A snappy dresser, he wore a navy blue business suit and a large jewelled tie-pin in his pale red tie. The tie-pin, shaped like a flower, was a directional microphone. The wire attached to it behind his striped

249

shirt led to the miniaturized tape recorder in his jacket pocket. He spooned more fruit salad into his mouth as he listened.

Harry Butler, heavily built and clean-shaven, was dressed informally in a tweed sports jacket with leather elbow patches and a pair of grey slacks. He leaned over to whisper in Nield's 'good' ear.

'Reception OK?'

'Picking up every word,' Nield replied in an undertone and fingered his neat moustache.

The Engine Room wizards at Park Crescent had excelled themselves. Despite the presence of people at four other tables the directional mike was recording every word of the conversation at Barrymore's table. It had been easy for Nield to 'point' the microphone in the correct direction. A man fiddling with his tie-pin attracted no attention . . .

'You're not going to have a cognac on top of all you've had?' Barrymore enquired sardonically. 'You do have to drive home.'

'I'll get there.' Robson grinned again. 'I always do.' He signalled to the manager, pointing to the colonel's glass and then himself. The manager smiled, acknowledging the request. 'The other chappie,' Robson continued, 'the bigger one with the thin one you *challenged* . . .' His tone was mocking. 'Was he on the moor as well?'

'Never seen him before. As I was saying . . .'

'Had the thin one that hearing aid when you met him?' Robson persisted with the geniality of a man who has imbibed well.

Barrymore frowned, trying to recall the scene. 'Don't think he had. But he wouldn't need it, would he? Not out on the moor. Now, for the third time, I think we should review our defences. Too many people poking around. There was that Tweed who barged in on us all.'

'Special Branch,' Kearns remarked. 'I thought that rather strange. Despite the yarn he spun. Seemed to me he had an ulterior motive for calling on me. That man worried me.'

'Oh, just one of the horde of bureaucrats justifying his fat salary at the expense of the taxpayer.' Barrymore waved a languid hand. 'Wish I'd had him in the battalion. He'd have had to jump to it.'

'I suspect, sir,' Kearns persisted quietly, 'Tweed has had a spell in the Army. Something about his manner. And he'd done his homework. Knew about the raid on Siros. And the murder of that Greek chap, Ionides, at the Antikhana . . .'

'Hardly relevant.' Barrymore made a dismissive gesture.

'Are you certain, sir? Did anything strike you as weird about that body they brought down off the moor at Winsford?'

'Should it have?' The colonel was clipping the tip from a cigar. He lit it with a bookmatch as Kearns continued.

'The savagery of the attack.' Kearns paused. 'He was slashed to pieces. Just like Ionides all those years ago.' He turned his attention to Robson. 'You examined the body inside the Land Rover. Surely I have a point?'

'Somebody had really done a job on the poor chap. A broad-bladed knife would be my guess. Mind you, it was a brief examination.' Robson's tone suddenly sounded sober, professional. 'Fail to see the connection with Ionides.' He drank more of his large cognac. 'Thought we were assembled here to enjoy ourselves.' He chuckled. 'But you Army types never slough off your skin.'

'The fact remains,' Barrymore intervened irritably, 'we now have possible enemies on two fronts. The Greeks and this Special Branch lot. I just hope to God it isn't the Greek Key.'

'After all these years?' Robson scoffed and grinned. 'Come off it. Not like you to suffer an attack of nerves, Barrymore.'

'I never suffer an attack of nerves, as you put it,' the

251

colonel replied coolly. 'I'm just saying we should look to our defences. Just in case.'

'Put up more barbed wire,' Robson joked. 'Lay a minefield round Quarme Manor.' He hiccuped. 'Call out the guard!'

'I'm serious,' Barrymore said coldly.

'I fear you are. As for me, business as usual. Carry on with my local practice. Did you know the local paper is doing an article on me? *The Only Doctor in the Country who Rides to See Patients* will be the headline. Rather good.'

'Jill has gone up to London,' Kearns said suddenly.

'Why?' Barrymore demanded.

'To pick up a few things from the shops she said.'

'You should have stopped her.' Barrymore sounded angry.

'Well, sir, that isn't the easiest thing in the world . . .'

'You made the mistake of marrying a younger woman,' the colonel told him brutally. 'Wives should be kept under heel. In the Army they knew their place . . .'

At his table Pete Nield finished his coffee, glanced round the dining room. A couple was just leaving. Which left only the trio at the end of the room and his table occupied. He leaned close to Butler.

'Time to go, wouldn't you say? We're going to look conspicuous.'

'Agreed. Let's move the feet now.'

Nield waited until they were in the deserted hall and suggested a breath of fresh air. They wandered out under the ancient portal into a deserted High Street. Opposite the entrance the old Yarn Market with its many-sided roof was shrouded in shadow. A moon cast a pale glow over the silence. Barrymore's Daimler was parked across the road.

'How's the recording?' Butler enquired, thrusting his hands into his trouser pockets.

'Let's check. Inside the Yarn Market would be a good place . . .'

Taking the recorder out of his pocket, Nield turned the volume to 'low' as they stood under the roof. He pressed the button which reversed the tape. Then he switched on the sound and together they listened.

Another large Scotch . . . Of course, sir. Coming right away . . . Pushing the boat out a bit, aren't we . . .

Nield switched off. He gazed through one of the arched openings to the far end of the town. The eerie silhouette of the brooding castle loomed above the buildings. The sudden silence of night was uncanny.

'Perfect,' Butler commented. 'The voice tone is good. You can tell who is talking.'

'I think I ought to drive up to London tonight,' Nield suggested. 'Then Tweed can hear the tape in the morning. I can drive back here tomorrow if that's OK.'

'Do it,' Butler agreed. 'While you're away I think I'll keep an eye on the colonel.'

'Why choose him?'

'Sixth sense. As Tweed would say . . .'

24

Three people were seated round Tweed's desk as he listened to the tape for the third time. Monica sat crouched forward, her head turned to one side, her forehead crinkled with concentration.

Paula sat upright, notebook in her lap as she made notes. On the third replay she ignored the notebook, staring out of the window as she visualized the faces of the three men whose conversation was reeling out as they had talked over dinner at The Luttrell Arms.

Tweed was the most relaxed. He sat back in the swivel chair, his hands resting on the desk-top, no particular expression on his face. He glanced at Pete Nield, seated behind Paula's desk, who was smoking a cigarette while he watched the others. The recording ended, Tweed switched off the machine.

'Very interesting, most revealing. What they said. And the relationship between those three men.'

'The reference to the Greek Key?' Paula suggested.

'That possibly, but something else. Pete, describe to me how they were seated. You came in with Harry to find them starting dinner?'

'No. We carefully did it the other way round – to avoid calling attention to ourselves. Harry asked one of the staff when they normally arrived for their weekly dinner. So we were at our table when they came in. Other tables were occupied with guests so we merged with the background.'

'And how were they seated in relationship to the two of you?' Tweed repeated.

Paula looked puzzled. She couldn't fathom the reason behind the question.

'They came into the dining room about ten minutes later,' explained Nield. 'They walked past us. We had our backs towards them as they entered. You know the corner table where they sit?' Tweed nodded and Nield went on. 'Barrymore and Robson faced us. Kearns had his back to us the whole time. Which is why his voice comes across quieter.'

'I thought it was like that. Something said in their conversation could be very significant. I may have the lead I've been waiting for.'

'And you wouldn't care to tell us what that is?' Paula enquired.

254

'Not for the moment. In case I'm wrong.' Tweed smiled. 'Listen to the tape on your own a few times. You might get it.'

Paula glanced down at her notes, then clenched her fists with a gesture of frustration. 'You'll drive me crazy with your hints one of these days.'

Monica nodded sympathetically. 'I know just what you mean. He's been doing it with me for years.'

'If you agree,' Nield said, 'I plan to drive straight back to join Butler again on Exmoor. Have there been any developments at this end?'

'Bob Newman called from Athens . . .' Tweed gave him a concise account of their conversation, picking out the main elements of the data Newman had passed on. 'Does anyone spot something odd about what he told me? Bearing in mind the clear description he gave of the topography of where Andreas Gavalas was killed?'

Three blank faces stared back at him. Paula pursed her full lips and sighed. 'Here we go again – more mysterious hints. I give up.'

'I have two questions I'd dearly love answers to,' Tweed told them as he perched his elbows on the desk. 'The raid on Siros. The three-man commando team – with Andreas – land on a hostile coast. They make their way up a twisting gulch. That gulch is overlooked by a monastery perched on Mount Ida like the nest of an eagle. The Germans have established a permanently manned lookout post on top of that monastery looking straight down the gulch. Why, then, in heaven's name, did the raiding party choose that point to climb up the island? There must have been scores of other places safer for them to choose.'

'Does sound very strange,' Paula agreed. 'Plus the fact that the body went missing.'

'My second question,' Tweed went on, 'is what happened to the cache of diamonds Andreas was carrying to hand over to Greek Resistance fighters on Siros? In those days they were worth about one hundred thousand pounds – so Brigadier Willie Davies at the MOD told me.'

'Stolen by the man who murdered Andreas,' Paula said promptly. 'Maybe we're dealing with a case of simple robbery.'

'I don't think so,' Tweed objected. 'And I've been to see a leading diamond merchant in Hatton Garden I know. I asked him what a parcel of diamonds worth a hundred thousand back in 1944 would be worth today. I got a shock.' He paused, looked round. 'Any estimates? No? My contact could only make a rough guess. Something in the region of one million pounds sterling.'

There was a stunned silence in his office. Nield screwed up his eyes, thinking hard. Paula crossed her legs, tapped her pen against her teeth, then reacted.

'So we may be looking for something – or someone – showing signs of great wealth? What about Barrymore and Quarme Manor?'

Tweed shook his head. 'He bought it years ago. Probably for a song.'

'He has a Daimler,' Paula persisted.

'An old job,' Nield interjected. 'Looks glitzy but wouldn't fetch all that much. A cool million? The only thing I've seen in the area is that modern little estate of de luxe bungalows near Kearns' place . . .'

'We're looking for something pointing to one of those three men we've listened to on the tape,' Paula objected.

Tweed was hardly listening. 'That business of where they landed on Siros. And the missing body. The priest told Newman they had asked the commander of the German occupation troops about Andreas. None of his patrols knew a thing. And Geiger was convinced they were telling the truth. So who else on the island could have spirited away the body? There's only one answer.'

'Which is?' Paula asked.

'It had to be some of the Greek Resistance people. But which lot? And why on earth would they do that? Now our next job is to pay a visit to Guy Seton-Charles. You come with me, Paula.'

'And who might he be?' she enquired.

'A name in Partridge's notebook. A professor of Greek Studies at Bristol University. The intriguing fact is he was based in the Antikhana Building at the time of Ionides' murder.'

'How could he help?' Paula persisted. 'After all this time?'

'That's what I want to find out.' Tweed swung in his chair to face Nield. 'You come with us to Bristol in a separate car – then later return to Exmoor to provide Butler with back-up. I want those three men to be aware of your presence. It will put pressure on them, may force one of them to make a wrong move.'

'You've used that tactic before,' Monica commented. 'And it worked. You're doing the same thing with this Seton-Charles, aren't you?'

'Partridge found out something,' Tweed remarked sombrely. 'I am certain he was murdered because he approached the wrong man. Which man?'

The timing was better than Tweed could have hoped for. He was approaching Professor Seton-Charles' room when the door opened and a brunette in her early twenties rushed out. She was in such a rush she almost collided with Paula who was walking alongside Tweed. The door automatically closed behind her on spring-loaded hinges. Very slim, her intelligent face flushed, she stopped abruptly, clutching a green folder.

'I'm dreadfully sorry. I could have knocked you down.'

'I'm pretty sturdy . . .' Paula began, and smiled.

257

'You look really upset,' Tweed said quickly. 'Professor in a bad mood?'

'The sarcastic bastard! I'm not attending any more classes he takes . . .' The girl flushed again. 'Oh, Lord, I'm sorry. Are you friends of his . . .'

'Hardly.' Tweed acted on instinct. 'We've come to investigate him. Special Branch. What's the matter with him?' he asked persuasively.

'Everything! He's a bloody Trotskyite. Tries to brainwash us . . .' She paused. 'God, I'm saying all the wrong things.'

'Don't worry, we won't quote you.' He squeezed her arm. 'Do me a favour. We were never here. Agreed?'

'My pleasure. I'd better push off now.' She turned back for a last word. 'And I can keep my mouth shut. Give him hell.'

Tweed waited until she had disappeared round a corner at the end of the corridor. Then he knocked on the door which carried a name in gilt lettering. *Prof. Guy Seton-Charles.* The door opened swiftly. A man started talking and then stopped when he saw them.

'That's my last word, Louise. You have an IQ of minus . . .'

'Special Branch.' Tweed showed his card. 'You're alone. Good. May we come in . . .' He was walking forward as he spoke while the man backed away and Paula followed, closing the door. 'You are Professor Seton-Charles? This is Miss Grey, my assistant, who will take notes during the interview.'

'Interview about what?'

'The unsolved murder of a Greek called Ionides in Cairo over forty years ago. We can sit round that table. If anyone arrives to interrupt the interview please tell them you're busy, get rid of them.'

Tweed was at his most officious. He fetched two fold-up chairs from several rows arranged beyond the table. The room was furnished starkly; walls bare, painted off-white; the table for the lecturer to sit behind and address his class; windows on the far wall which looked out on to a roughcast concrete wall.

Guy Seton-Charles was a slimly built man in his early sixties, Tweed estimated. His face was plump and pale, and perched on his Roman nose was a pair of rimless glasses. The eyes which stared at them were cold and bleak and wary. He had thinning brown hair, was clean-shaven, his mouth was pouched in a superior expression. Prototype of the self-conscious intellectual, Tweed decided.

He was dressed informally in a loose-fitting check sports jacket, a cream shirt, a blue woollen tie and baggy grey slacks. Not a man who gave much attention to his personal appearance.

'This is an unwarranted invasion of privacy,' Seton-Charles protested in a high-pitched voice.

'Oh, I can get a warrant,' Tweed assured him, 'but then we'd have to hold the interview in London at headquarters. Might not be possible to avoid a certain amount of publicity . . .'

'There's going to be publicity,' the Professor spluttered. 'I can promise you that . . .'

'About a murder investigation in which you might be involved? No skin off my nose.' Tweed was seated on one of the fold-up chairs. He pointed to the chair behind the desk. 'Unless you want to sit down and hear why we are here. Make up your mind.'

'Murder investigation? About Ionides? You're a bit late in the day, aren't you?'

His tone was truculent, sneering, but Tweed noted he had sat in his chair, a significant concession. He frowned as Paula sat in the other chair, produced her notebook, rested it on her lap and waited, pen poised.

'Is she going to record my answers? A bit bureaucratic and official.'

259

'Oh, it's official.' Tweed's expression was grim.

'All about a forty-year-old murder?'

'Which may be directly linked with two more very recent murders.'

Behind the rimless glasses Seton-Charles' greenish eyes flickered. Tweed had the impression he was thrown off balance. He recovered quickly.

'Which murders? If I am permitted to ask. It all sounds so melodramatic.' A tinge of sarcasm in his voice now.

'We may come to that later. Let's go back to Greece – and Cairo during the war. You had a job and an office inside the Antikhana as a young man. Why weren't you in the Forces?'

'Didn't pass the physical, if you must know. My eyesight.'

'What was your job? Start talking, Professor. I'm a very good listener. It's your job – talking.'

'Even as a young man I had an interest in Greece. It's my subject,' he added pedantically. 'They said I could do my bit for the war effort by going to the Mid-East. I was packed off aboard a troopship round the Cape and landed up in Cairo. My job was to create propaganda to encourage the Greek Resistance . . .'

'Which side?' Tweed snapped.

'Oh, you know about that battle in high places? The SOE lot – Special Operations Executive – in Cairo had a fetish for backing the right-wing crowd. Wanted to bring back the King after the Germans were defeated. Wrong side altogether. The EDES people. The London end were brighter – possibly as a result of reading my reports.' He preened himself with a knowing smile. 'It was the ELAS organization who were killing Germans by the score . . .'

'The Communists, you mean,' Tweed interjected. 'After Russia had been attacked by Hitler, of course.'

'No need to be snide . . .'

'Merely stating a fact. You supported the idea of switching the airdrop of arms to the Communists. That right?'

'Yes. As I told you, they were really fighting the enemy – and London agreed. Churchill himself took the decision, so I heard. Killing Germans was his main aim in life in those days . . .'

'And Ionides was the man you worked closely with,' Tweed guessed.

'I wrote the text for leaflets in English. Ionides translated them into perfect Greek. I wasn't up to that then. I didn't know him at all well. We worked through secretaries. Hardly ever spoke a word to him. Very close-mouthed, our Mr Ionides.'

'Who do you think killed him so savagely? And why?'

'No idea. My billet was an apartment in another part of Cairo. I wasn't there the night it happened.'

'Quite so.' Tweed gazed at the concrete wall beyond the window, switched the topic suddenly. 'Where do you live, Professor?'

'You do jump about . . .'

'Just answer the question, please.'

'I bought a bungalow on a new estate near Simonsbath on Exmoor. Rather exclusive . . .'

'You work here in Bristol, yet you live on Exmoor?' Tweed's tone expressed disbelief. 'Why?'

Seton-Charles sighed heavily as though his patience was wearing thin. He spoke as though explaining a simple point to a child. 'With the motorway a lot of people commute between a home on Exmoor and Bristol. Businessmen as well as university professors, amazing as it may seem. My hobby is walking. I like the open country, the moor. Would you like a list of some other people who live exactly as I do? Your assistant could take down names, help to fill out your report.'

'Might be helpful,' Tweed agreed equably. 'Plus the occupation or profession of everyone living on that bungalow estate.'

Seton-Charles' expression went blank. Something like venom flashed behind the glasses, then disappeared. Tweed was puzzled so he kept silent, forcing the other man to react.

'I don't know anyone on the estate,' the Professor snapped. 'I keep to myself. I take students' papers home to work on. Any free time I walk the moors, as I've already told you. I was referring to the *bourgeoisie* who live in luxury pads near Taunton.'

'That bungalow you live in must have cost a packet,' Tweed observed in the same level tone.

'I have a huge mortgage, if it's any concern of yours. The colonel was very helpful.'

'The colonel?'

Tweed was careful not to look at Paula. He sensed she had frozen, pen poised in mid-air. Only for seconds then she relaxed as Tweed waited again. Seton-Charles was answering more slowly.

'Colonel Winterton. He owned the land the estate was built on – had some old barns pulled down. That was why he was permitted to build. With a restriction the houses should be one storey high.'

'Where can I find this Winterton?'

'No idea. I never met him. I dealt with his staff at an office he had in Taunton. It was a package deal – he arranged the mortgages where required. He was fussy about who he sold the properties to. You had to qualify.'

'How?' Tweed pressed.

'I don't know about the others. When he heard I was a professor in Greek Studies he accepted me. I think the other residents are brokers, solicitors – boring things like that. They leave for work before me, I get back when they've got home. We don't mix.'

'So you could give me the address of Winterton's office based in Taunton? I'd like that.'

'You're welcome to it. Except it's no longer there.'

'What do you mean? Stop playing the half-smart intellectual with me.'

'You don't know everything . . .' Seton-Charles paused. Paula could have sworn he changed like a chameleon, then recovered, changed back again. Something about the cold glint in the eyes. 'Once he'd sold all the properties he closed down the office and the whole outfit vanished.'

'Vanished?' Tweed's tone was sharp. 'Explain that.'

'The staff weren't local. They disappeared. The rumour was that Winterton pocketed his profits and went to live abroad.'

'The whole outfit didn't vanish,' Tweed objected. 'Who do you pay your mortgage interest and repayments to?'

'Oh, we found out that was handled by the Pitlochry Insurance Company. Winterton had simply acted as middleman, taken his commission. That's it. End of the trail.'

Was there a smug note in Seton-Charles' voice? Paula couldn't be certain. He sat behind the table, smooth-skinned hands linked together. Like a man satisfied he had closed all the loopholes.

'You visit Greece frequently?' Tweed said suddenly.

'I go to Athens spasmodically.' He was frowning as though he hadn't expected this thrust. 'I have links with the university there. Take seminars . . .'

'Your last visit was when?'

'A few weeks ago. I thought we started out with the murder of Ionides over forty years ago.'

'We did.' Tweed stood up. 'Which makes a good point at which to end our first interview.'

'Our *first* interview?'

'That's what I said,' Tweed replied and walked out.

They waited in the Mercedes loaned by Newman, waited in the car park. Tweed sat behind the wheel, Paula stirred restlessly beside him. There was no one else about and they were hedged in by cars on either side.

'What do you think of him?' Paula asked. 'And why did you insult him with that half-smart intellectual crack? Not your normal style.'

'To rattle him. I think it worked. *You don't know everything.* He got that far and stopped what he had been going on to say. Something funny about that new estate of bungalows near where Kearns lives. And Pete Nield, who often hits the nail on the head, remarked that estate was the only thing he'd seen on Exmoor worth a cool million. Something like that.'

'Where is Pete? He followed us down here from Park Crescent as you suggested, then dropped out of sight.'

'He's parked in the Cortina up the road. Again as I suggested. I want to see if Seton-Charles takes the bait.'

'Don't understand.' She gave a rueful smile. 'Par for the course – working with you. I still don't see why there should be something funny about the bungalow estate.'

'There may not be – but Seton-Charles is an experienced lecturer, used to fielding the sort of questions I threw at him. He answered fairly tersely, then went out of his way to explain a lot about the estate. I don't think he liked my asking where he lived. Now, who have we here?'

'Professor Seton-Charles – and in one devil of a hurry.'

In the distance the Professor was wending his way among the army of parked vehicles. He carried a briefcase and his hair was flurried in a breeze. For a man in his sixties he moved with great agility.

'Maybe it has worked,' Tweed commented. 'Pressure. Everyone remembers the last thing you say. I mentioned this was the first interview, suggesting I'd be back. One odd thing about our conversation. He only made a brief comment on my reference to two more recent murders. The *absence* of something so often goes unnoticed.'

'Well I didn't notice it, but I was taking notes. Are you going all mysterious on me again?'

'The absence of any later comment by the Professor. You'd expect almost anyone to come back to that – to ask again what I'd been talking about. Whose murders? He didn't . . .'

'He's getting into a Volvo station wagon. Do we follow?'

'No, too obvious . . .'

'He's a professor. His mind will probably be miles away while he's driving.'

'Seton-Charles,' Tweed told her, 'has a mind like a steel trap. He may have nothing to do with what we're looking for, but he has to be checked out. And carefully . . .'

Tweed waited until the Volvo was moving towards the exit, then turned on his ignition. He drove out of the slot slowly, turned into the main aisle as Seton-Charles shot at speed for the exit. 'Speedy Gonzalez,' Paula commented. Tweed arrived at the exit seconds after the Volvo had swung left. Perching with the nose of the Mercedes at the exit, he flashed his lights. Seconds later Nield drove past the exit, following the Volvo in Tweed's Cortina.

'There, it worked,' Tweed said with some satisfaction.

'You arranged with Pete to park outside?'

'Yes. I foresaw I might get lucky, pressure Seton-Charles into leaving. Pete will see where he heads for, who he meets, and report back to me.' He checked his watch. 'Three o'clock – we can make Park Crescent by early evening. We'll be driving into London when the commuters are pouring out.'

'Pressure all round,' Paula remarked as they left the car park. 'Butler and Nield showing themselves to the ex-commando trio. After Nield has tracked Seton-Charles. You think we're getting somewhere?'

'Time will tell. I'm waiting for someone to crack. Here – or in Greece.'

Monica looked up as they entered Tweed's office. 'Nield called ten minutes ago . . .' The phone started ringing. 'Maybe that's him.' A brief exchange, she nodded towards Tweed's phone.

'Just got in, Pete,' Tweed said. 'Any news?'

'Subject drives straight back to Exmoor, makes a call from a public box near Simonsbath. Which is strange.'

'Why?'

'He has a phone in his bungalow. They have overhead wires out here. A three-minute call – and he checks his watch.'

'And then?'

'Drives back to the estate and into his garage. He has one of those electronic devices so you can open it from inside the car. Something else odd I noticed. Perched on the roof of his bungalow is one of the most complex aerial systems I've ever seen – plus a satellite dish. A whole mess of technical gear. Change of subject. Gossip in the pubs reports a dog ferreting on Exmoor came home with Partridge's wallet in its mouth. A hundred pounds, all in tenners, intact. Banknote numbers in sequence. That's it.'

'You've done well. Get back to Butler in Dunster. Start a campaign of harassing all three men. Put on the pressure – but from a distance. And watch your backs.'

'Will do. 'Bye, Chief.'

Tweed put down the receiver, jumped up from his desk and began pacing the office as he rubbed his hands with satisfaction.

'Things are moving. It worked, Paula. Seton-Charles called someone from a public booth. Reporting my interrogation of him, I'm sure. We're on the right track.'

'At last,' said Monica.

'And I want you to call Inspector Farthing of Dunster police,' he told her. 'Partridge's wallet has been found. I'd like a list of everything inside that wallet. Someone may just have made the fatal mistake I've been waiting for.'

At the summit of the mountain where he used his transceiver Florakis-Savinkov completed sending the latest coded message to England. The pace was hotting up. Earlier he had been instructed to receive the signals from Athens weekly. Now it was twice a week. The radio traffic was increasing.

He was about to sign off when he was amazed to receive an order given in clear English. He blinked as he recorded the message. *From now on call sign changed to Colonel Winter.*

25

Newman was in shirt-sleeves as he drove along the coast road which twisted and turned and was empty of other traffic. It was twilight time, the most torrid period of the day as the earth gave up its heat and the atmosphere was cloying and humid. Nick sat beside him with a worried frown; beyond him the Mediterranean was indigo, a smooth sheet of water stretching away towards the hulk of a huge rock rearing up out of the water.

In the distance a toy-like temple perched at the summit of a cliff was silhouetted against a purple sky: the pencil-thin columns of the Temple of Poseidon where Harry Masterson had died. In the rear of the car Christina pulled at the tops of her slacks thrust inside climbing boots. She was perspiring all over. It had been one hell of a hot day and her nerves were twanging at what they planned to do.

'Tell me when to stop,' Newman called over his shoulder. 'We must be near now.'

'Round the next two bends. That structure we're passing is on the land of a farmer called Florakis. He sold it to a developer.'

Newman glanced at the ruin-like structure on the landward side. In the half-light it looked like an abandoned building site, as though the developer had run out of money.

'What is that place?' he asked.

'The beginning of a new hotel complex,' Nick replied. 'They are spoiling the whole coast with new tourist developments.'

The structure had a weird skeletal look. Two storeys high, it consisted of a steel framework for several buildings and he could see right through it to the hillside beyond, like staring through the bones of a Martian-type skeleton eroded by time.

'I still don't like the idea of you going with Christina into Devil's Valley,' Nick said for the second time. 'Petros has armed shepherds patrolling the area night and day. They all carry rifles. Tourists, amateur mountaineers who have gone in there never came out. They had "accidents". They fell over precipices, God knows what. I must warn you . . .'

'Thanks, Nick. You have warned me. You've done all you can.'

'Then stay away from that old silver mine. Please.'

'Of course. The idea never entered my head.'

Christina bit her knuckles to stop herself protesting. Newman *was* going into Devil's Valley with the sole idea of locating the silver mine. He had concealed his plan from Marler as well as from Nick. At first she demurred at his suggestion to act as his guide into the Valley. But he had the map she had marked when they had dinner at the Hilton two weeks ago.

'Stop the car round the next bend,' she called out. 'You can park it well off the road on a flat area. It is part of Florakis' land but farmers go to bed early because they rise at dawn.'

Newman pulled in, turned the car in a wide half-circle so it faced the way they had come. He switched off the engine. A brooding silence fell over the mountains which rose close to the road. In the back Christina shivered at the lack of sound. A moon was rising, casting a pale illumination over the arid mountain slopes, the still, endless sea.

'Nick,' Newman told him, 'I think the car would be concealed much better if you drove it back to that building site.' He looked at Christina who had climbed out and was standing alongside him. 'We could find that on the way back easily with the moon up, I assume?'

'Yes. It would be a good landmark . . .'

'And exactly where do we go to find the entrance to Devil's Valley?'

'Straight up that gulch. It's on Florakis' land but only for a short distance. I can show you on the map.'

Newman slipped on his sports jacket, took a pencil torch attached to the breast pocket, shielded it with his hand and opened the map. Christina traced the route up the gulch, showed where it led to the entrance to Devil's Valley. Newman held his hand so Nick couldn't see the cross which marked the silver mine.

'We'd better get moving,' he said. He checked his watch. Well after ten o'clock. He opened the glove compartment, took out Nick's revolver, slid it inside his hip holster, pocketed spare ammo. 'You won't fall asleep?' he asked Nick. 'We'll be away for some time.'

'Not me. I can stay awake all night. And I'll drive back to the hotel development and wait for you there.'

'See you. The rifle is in the back – just in case.'

'It will be in my hands until you return,' Nick promised.

Parked in the shadows of the steel framework, Nick was careful. He smoked the cigarette inside his cupped hand. The headlights of the car approaching from the Athens direction appeared only five minutes after he had arrived. He stubbed out the cigarette. It was the first vehicle he had seen for over an hour.

The headlights swung over the building site as the car slowed. They swept over his Mercedes. He opened the door, took a firmer grip on the rifle, the muzzle aimed through the gap. The car was stopping.

It backed slowly, very slowly. For the second time the headlights played over the Mercedes, for a longer period. Nick sat very still, raised the muzzle slightly, slipped off the safety catch. The car had stopped now. The headlights stayed on, beamed at an angle beyond his own vehicle, glaring on the building site, which took on a surrealist quality in the dazzle.

Nick had acute hearing. He listened in the heavy silence – for the opening of a car door, the crunch of feet on the loose stones covering the ground. Nothing. The silence grew heavier. Sweat began trickling down his neck. He sat immobile as a Greek statue. Nothing. The driver couldn't be a ghost . . .

'Hello, Nick. I could have shot you rather dead.'

Marler's voice, speaking through the open passenger seat window. How the hell could a man move so silently?

'Come on, Nick, where have they gone? Newman and Christina? I followed you from Athens, so where are they? Exploring Devil's Valley?'

Nick reached for the bottle of mineral water, took a long swig. He was in a state of shock. And couldn't decide whether to tell Marler the truth. Marler seemed to read his mind as he leant an elbow on the open window.

'Loyalty is a virtue. Especially for a Greek. I know that. I also know you wouldn't want something to happen to Newman – something fatal. The last man who made friends with Christina ended up at the bottom of a cliff. She's all Gavalas. So, tell me – Newman needs back-up. Desperately. We're talking about Devil's Valley.'

'Christina is guiding him to the entrance to the Valley. He is going to find the old silver mine. I know it. He said he wasn't but I know he was. They went up a gulch two bends further down the road.'

'Show me. And mark the location of that silver mine.'

Marler dropped a large-scale map of the area into Nick's lap. 'I don't know the exact location of the mine . . .' Nick protested.

'Do the best you can. Hurry. I'm driving my car alongside yours. Back in a minute . . .'

He parked his vehicle a few feet away from Nick's, doused the lights and walked to the boot. He appeared at Nick's window and the Greek stared. Marler wore mountaineer boots, had a long loop of rope coiled over one shoulder, an Armalite rifle over the other.

'You came equipped?' Nick said.

'I saw Newman and Christina buying boots in a shop. I guessed the rest. I'm a good guesser. Marked the map yet?'

He studied the map Nick had marked by the overhead light. He nodded, took the map, refolded it, shoved it inside his pocket.

'I'm off on my travels now. See you.'

'It could be dangerous . . .'

'I agree. For anyone I meet up there.'

*   *   *

271

Newman led the way up the gulch with Christina close behind. The moonlight helped. He was careful where he placed his feet: the gulch was littered with loose rocks. Sound carried a long way at night. He was relieved to hear no sound from Christina as she plodded up behind him. Which is why he heard the faint tumble of stones slithering.

He stopped, turned, grasped Christina by the arm, raised one finger to his lips. Unlike some women she didn't ask questions: she simply raised one thick eyebrow. He crouched down behind a boulder, pressing her down, and her shoulder rested against his.

'Someone else on the mountain,' he whispered.

'I didn't hear anything – and I have good hearing . . .'

Another slither of stones. One came over the side of the gulch and touched Newman's right boot. Christina nodded. Newman had been right. Someone was approaching and very close.

They were crouched behind the large boulder at a point where the gulch began to turn sharply above them to the left. Whoever was on the prowl couldn't be descending the gulch, thank God, Newman thought. For the stone to have slithered from immediately above them the intruder had to be moving higher up the slope. Could he see down inside the gulch? Newman slipped the revolver out of the holster and Christina gripped his other arm. He looked up and froze. He hardly dared breathe. He held his body tense – for fear of dislodging even a pebble.

Along the crest of the ridge above, the silhouette of a man was moving. In the moonlight Newman could clearly see the bony profile, the prominent nose, the sunken cheeks beneath prominent cheekbones, the curve of the mouth. Over one shoulder was looped a rifle. He was carrying something in the other hand – something heavy. Newman frowned and then felt his right leg begin to cramp. He gritted his teeth.

Christina, hunched beside him, kept perfectly still.

272

Newman was staring at the heavy bag the man was carrying as he climbed the mountain – he knew it was heavy from the way the figure sagged to one side. But it wasn't a bag. It was rectangular-shaped, like a metal box. Newman was certain it was a high-powered transceiver – and that size meant it was capable of transmitting over long distance. The silhouette disappeared behind the ridge.

'That was Florakis,' Christina whispered. 'Someone pointed him out to me in the Plaka.'

'You're sure? In this light . . .'

'Positive. I could see his profile clearly. And he is walking on his own land. What on earth can he be doing at this time of night?'

'No idea,' Newman lied. 'Let's get moving. How much further to Devil's Valley?'

'We're nearly there. Another hundred feet up this gulch and we cross the pass. Then it's downhill . . .'

They climbed higher up the gulch inside its shadow, the ground levelled out and Christina pointed. Beyond, a track descended into an arid steep-sided valley, the slopes studded with scrub. The crest of the far side was lower and, following the line of her extended arm, Newman saw a weird structure perched on the crest. It looked like a large shack, but there were no walls. Between the supporting pillars at each corner there was open space and moonlit sky beyond the apertures.

'The old silver mine,' Christina said. 'A track from that huddle of boulders down there leads straight up to it. Mules used to bring the ore from the mine down that track years ago.'

'You know your way back?' Newman enquired casually.

'I know every inch of this country. As a child I used to roam all over it. I liked to go down that gulch so I could cross the highway and swim in the sea.'

'Sorry about this. It's for your own good . . .' Newman swung round and clipped her on the jaw. He caught her as

273

she sagged and laid her carefully on the ground, placing her head on a soft tuft of grass as a pillow. He checked her pulse, found it was regular. Taking out the note he had prepared earlier, he tucked it inside the top of her slacks. Then he hoisted the rifle on his shoulder and started the descent, heading for the silver mine.

'There is someone coming up the track,' said Dimitrios and he slipped the safety catch off his rifle.

'You are imagining it,' objected Constantine. 'You see ghosts everywhere. Because of what is in the mine . . .'

'Someone is climbing that track,' Dimitrios insisted. 'I tell you I saw something move.'

'Now he says he *saw* something,' Constantine scoffed. 'In the past tense. Sure, he saw something move – a goat, maybe?'

Petros had sent them out as he did regularly – as another form of discipline, of keeping them under his thick thumb. And forcing them to stay up all night in the open toughened them. Petros had a dozen reasons for exerting his authority.

'Tonight you will go up and guard the mine,' he had ordered. 'One day there will be an intruder. Too many have been poking their snouts into my valley. And all accursed English. First there was Partridge – and he gave you the slip. Then came Masterson. Now we have more. This Newman, this Marler. Why so many so suddenly? Am I the only one who can scent danger? You go tonight . . .'

So they had climbed to the summit of the ridge close to where the mine reared up like a hideous eyeless monument. Constantine peered over the edge to where he could see stretches of the track as it mounted up to a point a quarter of a mile from where they waited.

Parts of the track were clearly illuminated by the moon; other parts were obscured by overhangs of rock, by the blackest of shadows. He could see nothing. From his ragged jacket pocket he pulled the bottle of *ouzo*. He handed it towards Dimitrios as he sneered at his brother.

'Drink some. It will steady the nerves of an old woman . . .'

'You talk to me like that and I break your scrawny neck, wring it like a chicken's.'

But Dimitrios snatched the bottle, tore out the cork and upended it. The liquid gurgled down his throat. That was better. He recorked the bottle, looked at Constantine and stiffened.

'What is it, cretin?'

'There is someone down there now coming up the track – a man with a rifle. A well-built man used to rough country.'

'Where?'

Dimitrios peered over the edge, saw nothing – only the wending track which came and went. Into the moonlight. Back into the shadows. He leaned over further, his mouth a thin slit, shoved the bottle into his own jacket, rested both hands on the rock, still staring down.

'Now you see ghosts.' He glanced at his brother. 'What are you doing?'

Constantine, always the quieter, the calmer of the two brothers, was checking his shotgun. He nodded with satisfaction. Then looked at Dimitrios.

'Inside ten minutes he will appear at the top of the track. We move now to that point. That is where we prepare the ambush.'

'And we drop the body down the mine . . .'

Marler had taken a short cut from the hotel site where Nick was waiting with the parked cars. He had scaled the almost sheer face of the mountain, working his way up a chimney hollowed out of the limestone. The map had shown him he would reach the pass far more quickly

275

than by following the route Newman and Christina had taken.

Now he heaved himself over the top and the pass was thirty feet below. He descended rapidly, reached the entrance to the pass, stopped, head cocked to one side. The rope was again looped over one shoulder, the rifle over the other. Someone was coming. He heard the stealthy movement of feet padding among the bed of pebbles. A thick needle-shaped column of rock rose up near the track. He slipped behind it.

Christina was in a cold fury. Her jaw was sore, but that was nothing. When she regained consciousness she had found the note tucked inside the top of her slacks. Its message was clear – to the point. *Christina, this expedition is too dangerous for me to take you any further. Sorry for the tap on the chin. Go straight back to Nick. I'll join you there. Later. Bob.*

The stupid swine. She could have helped him find the mine, showed him where to veer off the track so he reached it more quickly. She *knew* the country. He didn't. And her sharp eyes could have spotted any shepherd guards lurking . . .

The arm came round the back of her neck, lifted her off her feet. She used her elbows to thud into the midriff of her attacker, her feet to kick back at his shins. She wriggled like a snake and the pressure on her throat increased. The voice whispered in her ear.

'Don't want to strangle you. Relax. Go limp. I'll let you go. Be quiet. There may be others about. Ready?'

Marler's voice. She stopped struggling. He released her. She turned round. His expression was bleak. She swung her right hand with the speed of a striking snake. The flat of her hand slapped hard into the side of his face. His head didn't move.

'Make you feel better? Jezebel . . .'

'Why call me that, you bastard?'

'Because you've just led Newman into another trap – the way you did with Masterson . . .'

'You bloody idiot!' She waved Newman's note at him. 'Better read that. He socked me one, left me behind because he was worried about me . . .'

'Worried you'd betray him . . .'

'Read the bloody note.'

He shrugged, took the note, read it, then looked at her. 'OK. Tell me where he's gone.'

'To the silver mine. The crazy idiot. He's a suicide case.'

'Hardly. At least I hope not. Care to tell me exactly where this mine is?'

'You can see it from the end of the pass. I'll show you . . .'

Her long legs covered the ground in minutes. Marler had collected the rifle and rope he had left behind the needle of rock and hurried to catch up with her. At the end of the pass again she pointed, indicating the position of the silver mine. Marler frowned, then turned to her. She waited, hands on her hips, her expression contemptuous, eyes flashing. He lifted a hand and his slim fingers closed round her chin. She gritted her teeth, determined not to wince. The gentle way he handled her was a surprise. He turned her chin to examine it by the light of the moon.

'Sorry. I was checking to see how hard he'd hit you. Scarcely a bruise. Just enough to put you out. How long ago do you think he left you?'

She looked at her watch. 'I checked it just before we got here. I must have been out cold ten minutes. No more than fifteen.'

'Then I have to hurry. Anything you can tell me to help?'

She repeated what she had told Newman. She pointed out where the track ran up to the mine. But this time she tried to show where Marler could veer off three-quarters of the way up, cutting across direct to a point just below the mine.

'Got it,' Marler said. 'Do me a favour. Go back to Nick. I think I can make it faster on my own. And I don't want to have to worry about you.'

'I'm popular with the men tonight, aren't I? Marler, why are you waiting? Get there fast . . .'

Newman had caught the faintest hint of movement high up and out of the corner of his eye. Imagination? He remembered the man he'd only known as Sarge. The time when he'd trained with the SAS – the Special Air Service – Britain's élite strike force, so he could write a series of articles on them. Sarge had put him through the full course. And he'd survived it. Just.

If you even suspect you've seen something, heard something, smelt something – *assume the worst*. You've been seen. Sarge, the toughest man Newman had ever known, the sergeant who'd put him through his paces, had said something else. Get inside the enemy's mind. Sit in *his* chair. What would you do *if you were him*? Out-think the bastard . . .

Newman moved into the shadows out of the moonlight. He paused, took out the compact pair of night glasses he'd bought in Athens. His mouth was parched with thirst, with fear. His boots, his clothes, were coated with limestone dust from his journey up the track. Slinging the glasses from his neck, he took the opportunity to relieve himself against a rock. Then he took a swig from the small bottle of mineral water in his pocket. Now . . .

He leant against the side of the rock and raised the glasses, aiming them where he thought he'd seen something move at the top of the ridge to the right of the track. He moved the glasses slowly, scanning the whole ridge. He stopped. Silhouetted against the night sky was the outline of a man, a man peering over a rock parapet. Got you. He held the glasses very still. No doubt about it. One of the shepherd guards. And he held the high ground. Time to rethink.

Assume the worst. He'd been spotted. Coming up the track. So what would the enemy do? Wait for him where the track emerged at the top. The solution? Get off the track. Move up to the left. However rough the going. Head diagonally straight for the mine. He put the glasses back into his pocket. Began climbing higher, so long as he kept in the shadow. He nearly missed the defile spiralling up to his left.

It looked pretty steep, but rock projections formed a kind of ladder. He entered the defile, felt safe from observation. It was exactly like climbing a ladder. He placed his boots on each projection, hauled himself higher and higher. He began to feel the strain on his calf muscles. He was sweating litres with the effort. Keep going. He must be close to the top.

His head and shoulders projected above the defile without warning. He remained perfectly still. Listening. Sniffing. For the smell of a mule. The shepherd might well be patrolling on an animal. He turned his head very slowly. He had emerged just below the crest of the ridge. Keep below it. That was the mistake the shepherd had made. He could see the spectral outline of the mine. No more than a hundred yards to his left.

No sign or sound of anyone else. He rubbed the calves of both legs. No time to get cramp. He hefted the Smith & Wesson out of the holster, moved towards the mine in a crouch, placing his feet carefully. The ground was powdered dust. Easy to slip on. The mine came closer.

'The bastard has tricked us.'

Dimitrios stood at the top of a huge crag which gave him a view of the whole length of the ridge. Below him

Constantine waited, gripping his shotgun. Dimitrios clambered down and joined his brother.

'What do you mean?' Constantine asked.

'I saw him moving. He's nearly reached the mine. We'll have to hurry. He left the track, came up a different way.'

'Then let's get moving. If we lose him Petros will go mad.'

'Petros is mad. Maybe we don't tell him what happened. That shaft goes down forever. Who is to know? So long as you keep your big mouth shut. I lead, you follow. We've got him cornered.'

Newman approached the weird structure cautiously. There could be another guard hidden and waiting. Resisting the temptation to peer inside the shaft, he crawled slowly round, pausing at each of the four corners. The structure reminded him of a ruined Greek temple constructed of rusting iron. He peered round the final corner. Nothing.

He had completed one circuit round the mine. He chose the side furthest away from the head of the track, from where he had seen the immobile silhouette on the ridge. Straightening up, he looked into the mine.

No cage. Christina had said there was a cage at the top. But she had never been up here. Someone must have told her about a cage, had lied. He was looking down into an immense bucket made of iron. It was suspended by a chain windlass coiled at the top. He switched on his pencil torch, his hand well below the surface of the mine. At its base he saw remnants of ore. He thought his light reflected off veins of silver, but it could have been his imagination.

Newman was baffled. Why should Petros make such a fuss about no one going near the mine? Between the huge bucket – large enough to hide a crouching man – and the side of the shaft was a wide gap. He shone the torch down the shaft. The light penetrated only a short distance into bottomless blackness. A musty aroma drifted up to his nostrils. He swivelled the light and saw a huge chain dangling beneath the bucket. And something else he couldn't identify . . .

He heard the shuffle of feet hurrying across rock-strewn ground. He peered through the aperture and saw two men coming, still several hundred yards away. From the direction of the track. They dropped out of view, presumably into a dip in the ground. But he had seen the long barrels perched over their shoulders. Men with rifles. He glanced round quickly.

No cover. Anywhere. The ridge behind him was open, as exposed as the slope which fell away from it. And they could out-range him with those rifles. A handgun was useless except for closer quarters. He went very cold, thinking. He leaned over into the mine, took hold of the rim of the bucket, tried to move it. The bucket was so heavy he couldn't shift it a centimetre. He flashed his light on to the windlass chain holding it. The links in the chain were enormous. He recalled it had been built to hold God knew what tonnage of ore.

He slipped on the pair of gloves he had used when scaling the defile. Without them his hands would have been bloodied raw – clutching at razor-edged rocks to heave himself upwards. He gave one more brief glance to where he'd seen the two men approaching. Any moment now and they would climb up out of the dip into view. He lowered himself into the shaft, hanging on to the rim of the bucket. It remained immovable as the Rock of Gibraltar. Now for the tricky part.

Engulfed in the darkness of the shaft, he held on to the rim with his left hand, felt down with his right for the dangling chain attached to the base of the bucket. He was just able to clutch it. Every muscle in his body strained as he jerked the chain with all his strength, testing it. It held. He took a deep breath, let go of the rim and fell. He whipped his right hand round the huge chain a second before the full weight of his body pulled at him. Now he had two hands gripping the length of chain which continued at least seven feet below him. He could tell that because he'd used both feet to get a hold on the chain lower down. His right foot rested on one of the enormous links. His left foot slipped, dangled in space. He forced it upwards, felt for a foothold, found it opposite the other foot and hung there suspended. The bucket had still not moved. But something light but unyielding had brushed his face. He couldn't identify it. He took another chance.

Holding on with his right hand, he felt for his pencil torch with his left. Sweating like a bull, he switched it on. He estimated the two men would not yet have arrived in the vicinity of the mine. What he saw by the light so frightened him he nearly lost his grip.

Suspended by a separate chain from beneath the bucket was a man-sized skeleton. The skull was inches from Newman's cheek. A gibbering skull with one eye intact.

Inside the gloves his hands were suddenly greasy with sweat. He gripped the chain more tightly, scared stiff his hands would slip out of them, plunging him down the shaft. The eye twitched and Newman nearly had a bowel movement. Then he saw it was an insect perched in the hollow eye socket, something like a praying mantis. The light had disturbed it. The insect twitched again, then flew upwards. Newman switched off the torch, rammed it in his pocket, gripped the chain with his free hand. Just in time. The strain on his right hand was becoming unendurable.

In the brief seconds while the light had been on he noticed the skeleton was wired together, which explained how it could hang there. Jesus! What a companion to hang suspended next to. Newman concentrated on securing his grip with his hands, his feet. Then he heard movement at the top of the mine.

Two voices. Talking excitedly. Leaning over to peer down into the shaft. Now they were moving round as though to get a better view. Still chattering.

Then the beam of a powerful flashlight shone down into the darkness. The light swung slowly, probing the shadows. The angle of the light changed, penetrated deeper. Newman looked down and cursed inwardly. The flashlight was shining on the lower part of his dangling legs, illuminating them from the knees downwards. More chatter. Then silence. Followed by a metallic click. Newman recognized the sound. The release of a safety catch. The flashlight beam remained very steady now, shining on his legs. He realized his teeth were clenched tightly. The bastards were going to shoot him in the legs. Not one damned thing he could do. Except wait for the impact, the slipping of his hands from the chain, the plunge down the shaft until his body smashed against the base, however far that might be . . .

Marler, smaller than either man, held the rifle at a horizontal angle, level with his nose. He swung the butt to his left. It smashed into the back of Dimitrios' skull. He was collapsing when Constantine began to turn round. Marler reversed the swing and the barrel thudded with all his strength against Constantine's forehead. The Greek sagged to the ground, dropping his shotgun. Dimitrios' flashlight had vanished down the mine.

Marler leaned over, switched on his own flashlight. He called down. 'Anyone at home?'

'Me, for God's sake. Hanging on to a chain under the bucket.'

'Hang about. I need a minute. You can last that out?'

'What the hell can you do?'

'Haul you up.' As he had started talking Marler had picked up the looped rope he had laid quietly on the ground before creeping up behind the two Greeks. He was creating a large loop with a slipknot. He tested the knot, then picked his flashlight off the parapet, shone it down.

'I'm lowering a rope with a big loop. Plus a slipknot. I can see your lower legs. Can you slide them inside the loop? I'll haul it up slowly. You have to get it round your chest, under your armpits. Think you can manage that simple exercise?'

'Give it a go. Soon as you're ready. I have company . . .'

Marler ignored the cryptic remark, held the torch in his right hand, lowered the loop with his left. When it was level with Newman's dangling feet he had to swing it away from the wall of the shaft. Newman saw what he was doing in the beam of the flashlight, waited for what he hoped was the right moment and swung his feet off the chain. Marler jerked the loop up and it ringed Newman's legs. He warned that the light would go out and took the rope in both hands. He hauled it up slowly and Newman called out that it was sliding up over his body.

'Tell me when it's under your arms, there's a good chap . . .'

'Now . . .'

'Tricky bit coming,' Marler called out. 'I need both hands to haul you up. When you let go you'll swing against the side of the shaft. Try and cushion yourself. Piece of cake. If you're lucky.'

'Thanks for the vote of confidence . . .'

Marler had his feet and knees braced against the side of the mine. He had knotted the rope in a few places to ward off as much rope burn on his hands as possible. And Newman weighed a few more pounds than he did. He called down that he was OK and waited for the considerable increase in weight. Newman called back that he was letting go.

The rope had slid up under his armpits, the loop had tightened. He let go of the chain and swung outwards, his right hand palm up. It slammed into the wall. His hand stung horribly from the impact. For a moment he hadn't the strength to call up.

'OK to haul you in? Tell me, for Pete's sake,' Marler rasped.

The weight was greater than he'd expected. His knees were pulverized with the pressure against the side of the mine. Newman said something he couldn't catch. Can't mess around any longer, Marler told himself and began to haul up the excruciating weight.

Newman came up facing the curve of the wall, hands pressed into it to steady his ascent. His head appeared over the top, Marler arched his body backwards, gave one last heave. Newman's hands scrabbled at the edge of the mine, then he came over the top like a cork out of á bottle and flopped on the ground beside the two unconscious Greeks.

'This one with the shotgun was going to pepper you,' Marler remarked as he stooped over the unconscious Greek. 'I heard the charming conversation when I came up behind them. Relieved to be back in the land of the living?'

'You could say that. Who are these two jokers?' Newman eased his back up, rested it against the side of the mine, took off his gloves and flexed his aching fingers. 'Did you do a real job on them – or will they come round? If so, maybe I'd better put a bullet in their skulls.'

'Tweed said you'd become a hard man after that trip behind the lines in East Germany.' As he spoke he was searching the Greeks. He pulled out a bottle, uncapped it, sniffed, used his handkerchief to wipe the top and handed it to Newman.

'You need a pick-me-up. Drink. *Ouzo*.'

'Thanks.' Newman upended the bottle, swallowed, choked a little. He took another swig when he'd recovered. His whole body was aching. Legs, arms, hands, shoulders. 'Who are the bastards?' he asked again.

Marler was scanning a photo he'd taken from a grubby envelope. 'This one, as I thought, is Dimitrios. Taken with a girlfriend. Rather crudely erotic. I was pretty sure I recognized him from our little escapade on Siros. The other is Constantine. Meet the Gavalas brothers.'

'Let's hope I don't – on the streets of Athens. For their sake.'

'Feeling better? You have a hike. Back down the track to where Nick is waiting with the cars.'

Newman forced himself to stand, supporting himself with a hand on the wall of the mine. He drank a little more *ouzo*. Marler took the bottle off him.

'That's enough. We don't want you drunk. I'll be ready to go in a minute.'

Marler was emptying the rifle. He threw the cartridges down the slope, then held the rifle poised over the well. 'Might interest you to listen to this . . .' He let go and the rifle plunged down past the bucket into the black hole. Newman waited and his hand tightened on the wall. Seconds passed before they both heard the faintest of thuds. Marler looked at him.

'You could have sprained an ankle if you'd gone down there.'

'Ended up as a jelly. Safe to leave these two thugs?'

Marler was stooping over the Greeks, lifting an eyelid of both men. He straightened up. 'Out for the count for a while yet. Maybe I split a skull.' He emptied the shotgun, sent it down after the rifle. Dimitrios was wearing a sheathed knife under his jacket. Marler was about to toss it into the well when Newman stopped him.

'Let me look at that.'

He held the knife up to the moonlight and his voice was

grim. 'This is a standard-issue commando knife. I'd like to know how he got hold of that.' He dropped it inside the well. 'While I remember, thanks for saving my life . . .'

'All part of the Austin Reed service. You're an idiot, you know that? Coming up here by yourself. I followed you from Athens. Had an idea what you were up to, you crazy loon.'

'You could be right. Let's make with the feet. But I discovered the secret of the mine.'

'That's what I like. A bit of melodrama. Back to the track . . .'

26

Florakis lowered the transceiver into the cavity, concealed it with a flat rock, picked up the shotgun he had left inside the cavity before climbing the mountain. The transceiver was heavy. Now to investigate the two cars parked on his land down by the hotel site . . .

Dawn was breaking over the Mediterranean shore, flooding the unruffled sea with a variety of fantastic colours. Behind the wheel of his Mercedes Nick sat smoking another cigarette. The ash tray was crammed with stubs. Disgusting. He hauled it out from under the spring clip, stepped out of the car, then reached back in for his rifle. You never knew.

Christina was curled up on the back seat like a cat, fast asleep. Nick walked quietly across to a pile of rocks, lifted a few and emptied the ash tray, then replaced the stones. Crouched over, he froze. Someone was approaching from behind the steel framework. He remained crouched, aimed the rifle.

Florakis came round the corner, shotgun held in both hands. He stopped abruptly when he saw Nick, who straightened up, rifle still pointed. 'Good morning to you,' Nick called out in Greek.

'What are you doing on my land?' snapped Florakis.

'Parking off the road. You see any damage we've done?'

'We?'

Christina had woken, had heard the exchange. Running her hands through her mane, she sat up and looked out of the open window. Florakis glanced in her direction, grinned lewdly and turned his attention back to Nick.

'I charge a fee for screwing on my land . . .'

'Watch your mouth,' Nick responded sharply. 'Who the hell are you?'

'Stavros Florakis. I own this land,' he repeated. 'I'm telling you to shove off now before I blow a hole in you . . .'

'Keep very still,' Nick warned. 'You forgot your back.'

Florakis stiffened as he felt the muzzle of Marler's rifle press into the nape of his neck. Marler nodded again at Nick, who understood. 'Place that shotgun carefully on the ground, step over it towards me. A dozen paces will do, then stop.'

Florakis bent forward, laid the weapon down, did as Nick had ordered. He stood in the open as Newman walked past him, keeping out of Nick's line of fire. He went towards the Mercedes and called out to Christina. 'Give me the mineral water. I'm parched.'

He drank from the bottle, turned round, leaned against the car. He smiled as Florakis stared back bleakly. Yes, Newman thought, this is the man we saw on our way up the gulch, the man carrying a heavy transceiver.

'What's his name?' he called out to Nick. 'I couldn't quite get it.'

'Stavros Florakis. He owns Greece,' Nick replied in English.

A tough, wiry individual, Newman was thinking. Self-contained. A typical Greek shepherd. Except that he carried a transceiver up the mountain. The lined face suggested he was in his sixties. Newman's mind wandered. In his sixties. Weren't they all – Barrymore, Kearns and Robson. And Tweed had rabbited on about the missing link with Greece – between Athens and Exmoor. So, during World War Two Florakis would have been about twenty. Old enough to be in the Resistance. Which one? The instinct which had made him one of the world's best foreign correspondents was working again.

He took out his handkerchief, wiped the mouth of the bottle, turned as though to say something to Christina, and wiped the rest of the bottle clean. He turned round and smiled.

'Nick, I think we ought to apologize for trespassing on Mr Florakis' land.' He began to walk towards the Greek, holding the bottle by the neck, still smiling. 'It's thirsty weather. As a token of our regret I'd like to offer him a drink. Translate for me.'

Nothing in Florakis' neutral expression showed he'd understood every word Newman had said. He listened patiently as Nick spoke in Greek. Florakis was nervous: all these people appearing, seeing him out and about at dawn. The last thing he wanted was any talk of his nocturnal activities to reach Athens.

Newman extended the bottle, holding it by the neck. Florakis was also bone dry: he had forgotten to bring his water bottle. He nodded his thanks, grasped the bottle, took a good long drink, handed it back to Newman, who again grasped it by the neck and wandered back to the car.

'Nick,' he called over his shoulder as he reached the car, 'let him know we're leaving now. That if we come this way again we'll park elsewhere.'

While Nick translated Newman leaned in the window. 'Christina,' he whispered, 'give me that paper bag the bottle came in.' He slid the bottle inside the bag, holding it by the neck, then he pressed the top of the paper bag inside the neck and capped it. He now had Florakis' fingerprints.

'What was all that business about the bottle?' asked Christina as Nick drove them at speed back along the coast road to Athens.

Newman sat beside her in the rear of the Mercedes while Marler followed close behind in his own car. Newman was staring out of the window as the sun came up from behind the mountains and bathed the Mediterranean in its fierce light. The sea was now a smooth sheet of pure mother-of-pearl. An amazing country.

'Just fooling around,' he replied.

'And how was the fooling around in Devil's Valley? Marler did find you. Did you find the mine? And thanks for the sock on the jaw. I love you too.'

'Quiz time,' Newman said jocularly. 'So many questions.' He looked at her chin. 'No sign of a bruise. Just a gentle tap. Marvellous, isn't it? You save a girl from what could be a death-trap and she hates your guts.'

She looped her arm inside his, nestled against him so he could feel the firmness of her breast pressing into his body. 'Don't remember saying anything about hating your guts. And you evaded answering my questions.'

'I do believe I did.'

He looked out of the window again. They were covering the distance to Athens, seventy kilometres from Cape Sounion, in record time. They passed a hotel at the edge of the shore and tourists were walking the beach, swimming in the placid water.

'They make use of every minute,' he called out to Nick.

290

'They know what they do,' he replied. 'Later in the morning no feet will be able to touch that beach. The sand will be so hot it will burn them like a red-hot stove. They'll retire to their rooms, lie on their beds and sweat it out with nothing on.'

'What a lovely idea,' Christina whispered. 'Maybe we could lie on my bed at the Hilton with nothing on, sweat it out?'

'I'm dumping you there,' Newman said abruptly. 'Nick, make for the Hilton. Then have breakfast with Christina. When she goes to her room would you please sit in the lobby outside to guard her till I get back? A large tip will be my thanks.'

'Forget the tip, I take care of her.'

'Thanks a lot,' Christina snapped, her eyes flashing. She pulled away from him and stared out of her window.

'I have business to attend to, an editor to keep quiet,' Newman told her. 'And you may be in even greater danger now after what has happened. And don't ask me what.'

'Did you tell Christina about the skeleton?' Marler asked as he drove away from the Hilton.

'Nary a word. Nor about the mine . . .'

'Which means you're getting smart. *You* don't trust her.'

'Can it, Marler. Information like that is dangerous. You do realize who that skeleton is?'

'I think so. You tell me.'

'The missing Andreas. My guess is Petros was on Siros when the commando raid took place. He took the body of his son. He's stark raving mad. He must have had it buried, then after the war the bones were removed to Devil's Valley. Wired together – hidden in the mine. You know Greece well. Tell me again about *philotimo*.'

'And you're sure this is a smart move – what we're doing

291

now? Driving to police headquarters to see Chief Inspector Sarris?'

'I want Florakis' fingerprints checked against their records. Look, a sixty-year-old Greek, tough as they come, lugs a transceiver up a mountain. He's gaining altitude. That suggests long-distance transmission. Who is he contacting? So secretly? I've had this lucky break before as a correspondent. You are working on one thing, you stumble across something much bigger. Yes, I think it's a smart move.'

Very little traffic at seven in the morning. They were coming close to Alexandras Avenue below the soaring peak of Mount Lycabettus. Close to the new police headquarters.

'*Philotimo*,' Marler began, 'is the Greek code of ethics which rules family life. No one must dishonour the family. If they do, the disgrace must be wiped out. In extreme cases by killing the culprit. Even if it is a member of that family. Only then can the family have peace of mind. Petros is just the type of man to be soaked in the creed – in the crudest and most old-fashioned way. Just the man to go to extreme lengths.'

'Just the man to go right over the edge,' Newman commented. 'I think Petros is taking the attitude Andreas cannot be finally buried until his murderer is identified and executed. Petros is crazy as a coot. Revenge is the most self-destructive force that can take hold of a man.'

'And this is the main reason we're going to see friend Sarris?'

'No. I want the fingerprints on this bottle checked. We may have stumbled into something even more diabolical than Petros' desire for revenge.'

The Thin Man. The hawk-nosed, dark-haired Sarris sat listening behind his desk. His eyes never left Newman's.

He smoked one cigarette after another. But he listened without interruption.

'That's it,' Newman ended, his voice hoarse from talking, from his ordeal at the mine. 'The skeleton at the mine, the bottle on your desk with Florakis' fingerprints. The transceiver I saw Florakis carrying up the mountain.'

'Petros has committed no crime,' Sarris responded, stubbing a cigarette. 'Yet. Funny you should come to me with this news of a possible transceiver . . .'

'Possible?'

'You have no proof that was the object Florakis carried. But, as I say, it is funny you come to me at this moment. Have you ever noticed weeks, months, can go by with no clues in a case? Then, bingo! Within hours the clues pour in.'

'What are you talking about? I'm damned tired.'

'Have more coffee.' Sarris poured as he went on. 'A friend of mine is what you call in England . . . a radio ham. Is that right?'

'Yes. An amateur radio operator. Sometimes they're helpful – pick up Mayday calls over long distances. That sort of thing.'

'My friend picked up something strange on the airwaves. Someone transmitting a series of numbers – sounds like a coded signal. At the end there are a few words in English – from the man receiving the coded signal.' Sarris leaned forward. 'So maybe the operator sending the coded signal was transmitting to England.'

'A big assumption,' Newman objected. 'English is a universal language these days . . .'

'Judge for yourself. My friend has a tape recorder. He recorded the entire signal. You might like to hear it . . .'

Sarris pressed a lever on his intercom, spoke rapidly in Greek, sat back, lit a fresh cigarette. 'The cassette will be here in a moment.'

He was wearing a pale linen suit and even at that early

hour he looked alert. He watched his two visitors until a uniformed policeman brought in a cassette. Sarris picked up the cassette, inserted it inside a machine on a side table. 'Listen,' he commanded.

The cassette reeled out a string of pure gibberish for Newman. He glanced at Marler who was staring out of the window, showing no apparent interest in the proceedings. Sarris was checking his watch. After two and a half minutes he raised a warning hand.

The gibberish stopped. There was a pause. Then it came through loud and clear. In English. *From now on call sign changed to Colonel Winter*. Staring at Newman, Sarris switched off the machine.

'You have heard of this Colonel Winter?'

'No. Doesn't mean a thing to me.'

'Pity. I am thinking of informing the Drug Squad. The traffickers are becoming very sophisticated. Using coded radio signals to warn of a shipment on its way. The Drug Squad has radio detector vans. Maybe they'll send a couple down to Cape Sounion, try to get a fix on this Florakis.'

'And the fingerprints on that bottle?'

'We'll check them through our records. That could take time.'

'You can isolate Florakis' prints? I gave you that postcard I showed Christina while we were driving back. You've taken my prints. The card gives you Christina's. Eliminate hers and mine and you're left with Florakis.'

'I had worked that out for myself.' Sarris rose from behind his desk. 'Thank you for the information. Now I expect you'll want to get back to the Grande Bretagne, have a shave, some breakfast, then maybe some sleep. You've been up all night.'

'I had hoped for more from you,' Newman said as he stood up.

'I gave you the radio signal – which may link up with Florakis.' He paused. 'I will give you something more. I said earlier all the clues seemed to pour in at once. Yesterday we had a woman here with a weird story. A Mrs Florakis. About sixty and recently she took a bus tour to Cape Sounion. A widow, by the way. Married very young.' He smiled thinly. 'I see I have your attention?'

'Go on.'

'Her husband, Stavros Florakis, was killed in 1947 during the Civil War. In a battle with the Communist ELAS forces. It so happened a woman friend saw him die near Salonika. This woman also saw the Communists search the body, take his papers, then they incinerated the corpse. Something Mrs Florakis never understood. Still intrigued?'

'Stop tantalizing. You sound like my editor.'

'As I said, Mrs Florakis takes this bus tour. The bus stops off the road close to a new hotel building site. To let them get a good view of Poseidon. A man appears with a shotgun. He threatens the driver, tells him to get off his land. The bus driver argues. Mrs Florakis then hears the man with the shotgun shout, "I am Stavros Florakis. I own this land and you are trespassing." She gets a good view of this man. She gets a shock. He is not a bit like her husband. Then she remembers what happened to him. All this flashes through her mind in a few seconds. Then the bus moves off. She tells her story to me very clearly, but I am not impressed. We get so many crazies wandering in here. For good public relations I let her make a formal statement, which we filed. Now you tell me something that makes me think maybe I was wrong.'

'Florakis is an impostor,' Newman observed. 'So who is he?'

'Maybe – just maybe – the fingerprints you cleverly obtained can unlock his true identity.' He shook hands with Newman and Marler. 'Let us keep in touch, gentlemen . . .'

*   *   *

'So that covers what Newman told me, Kalos,' Sarris concluded as he clasped his hands behind his neck and relaxed in his chair. 'What do you make of it all?'

Kalos, his trusted assistant, was very different physically from his chief. Small and stocky, with thick legs and arms, he had a long head and intelligent eyes. In his early forties, he had been passed over for promotion several times but bore no grudge. It was Sarris' private opinion that it was Kalos' lack of height which had held him back. Most unfair, and Sarris had done his best to help him up the ladder. But who said life was fair?

'We've had a lucky break again,' Kalos decided. 'We ignored the Florakis woman – but she may have fingered the key link in the organization the Drug Squad is trying to locate. With no success. Unless it's political,' he mused. 'Not drugs.'

Sarris sat up straight. 'What does that mean?'

'My mind roams.' Kalos smiled drily. 'As you know there are people higher up who don't approve of a man who lets his mind roam. Never get fixated on one theory. My inflexible maxim, and stuff them upstairs.'

'You said unless it's political. Please elaborate.'

'Last year,' Kalos began, fitting his bulk inside the arms of a chrome-plated chair, 'a so-called Colonel Gerasimov visited us from Moscow. We were asked to guard him like royalty – but discreetly with plain-clothes operatives. He spent very little of his visit at the Soviet Embassy, a lot of it at the Hilton. He had three rooms booked and switched from one to another. I got curious and had him secretly photographed . . .'

'Without my permission,' Sarris chided him.

'You know me. When I visited Belgrade unofficially about this drugs problem I showed that picture to a Yugoslav – a Croat called Pavelic in the security services. I got him drunk and showed him the picture. He laughed when I said it was a photo of Colonel Gerasimov of the

296

GRU. He told me it was General Lucharsky, a Deputy Chief of the Soviet General Staff.'

'I remember. Do continue,' Sarris urged him with a quizzical smile.

'Yugoslavia is sensitive to power movements inside the Kremlin. Gorbachev suits the Belgrade Government fine. Pavelic, though, is a hardliner. He told me Lucharsky was "one of ours".'

'You didn't tell me that bit,' Sarris snapped.

'Why raise hares? You were up to your eyes in work. While in Athens the man at the Soviet Embassy Lucharsky spent most time with was Colonel Rykovsky, the military attaché. And an expert in communications.'

'How do you know that?'

'The Greek cleaning woman they employ when their menial staff is on holiday happens to clean my apartment.'

'Purely by chance, of course?' Sarris was leaning forward now, taking in every word. 'You do realize you are far exceeding the scope of your duties, my friend?'

'I like to know what is really going on.' Kalos ran a stubby finger round his open-necked collar and smiled drily again. 'It is hardly likely to affect my promotion prospects. And now we hear a Colonel Volkov will soon visit us from Moscow. Odd.'

'Why?'

'Pavelic, the Croat, was *very* drunk when we talked alone. He said to me, "I would not be surprised if you receive another visitor in Athens one of these days. Lucharsky's aide and confidant. A Colonel Volkov. Another sound man." Translation – another hardliner. These are not pro-Gorbachev men. So why do they travel to Athens, I wonder?'

Sarris sat thinking. Yugoslavia was a 'federation' of six different nationalities. A racial mix, and not all of them loving each other. Croatia, the Yugoslav state in the north, was the most rebellious, the most pro-Russian, the one closest to the real hard men in the Kremlin. Gorbachev's opponents.

'This is all speculation,' he suggested, testing his assistant.

Kalos ran a hand over the thin brown stubble which covered the dome of his head. 'You are right. Up to now. There is one more thing. When off duty I often amuse myself by following the military attaché, Colonel Rykovsky. He likes wandering inside the Plaka. He thinks he has lost anyone who might just be tailing him. Then he meets and spends time with Doganis.'

'Doganis?'

'A leading member of the Greek Key.'

27

'Where to now?' Marler asked as they climbed into his car.

'British Embassy. I'll rout that fat slob, Patterson, out of bed if necessary.'

'Be it on your own head.' Marler nodded towards the clock on the dashboard. 'Eight in the morning here is six o'clock back in London. Who will be at Park Crescent apart from the guard?'

'Tweed would be my bet. I think he's reached the camp bed stage by now.'

They both knew what that meant. Tweed started investigating a fresh case slowly. Then the tempo built up. He unfolded the camp bed kept in his office and took up a permanent vigil at his desk, often working well into the night.

At the Embassy on Sofias Avenue Patterson greeted

them in his shirt-sleeves, unshaven, sullen. He let them inside the hall without a word. No one else was about as Newman rubbed both hands together vigorously.

'The scrambler phone. It's an emergency.'

'When isn't it? And you might have shaved before invading the precincts of Her Majesty's Embassy.'

Ye Gods! Newman thought. How bloody pompous can you get? He grinned at Patterson. 'You look pretty rough yourself. Late night on the town?'

'I don't indulge. Like some people. I'll unlock the door – you know the drill. He can't come with you.' He jerked his thumb at Marler.

Marler said nothing. He produced his Secret Service card, held it under Patterson's nose, withdrew it when Patterson reached for it. The official bit his lip, made no further comment, produced a bunch of keys and unlocked the door leading to the basement. Newman ran down the steps after switching on the light.

Marler pulled out a chair as Newman sat down and pulled the phone towards him. Upstairs Patterson slammed the door shut with great force. Newman pressed the red button, dialled the Park Crescent number.

'Who is calling?' Tweed's voice, very alert.

'Newman here. Sorry to call at this hour.'

'That's all right. Very glad to hear from you. I was worrying. I slept here, got up with the dawn. Paula's here – she couldn't sleep and has just arrived. In case you need data taking down. Now, I'm listening . . .'

He listened without saying a word for ten minutes as Newman reported everything that had happened since they last spoke – including the trip into Devil's Valley and how Marler had saved his life. Glancing across the table he saw Marler spread his hands in a *What the hell* gesture.

'You shouldn't have gone in alone,' Tweed told him.

'I know that now. OK, I'll behave in future. Nowhere tricky without my chaperon. Now you know the lot.'

'And maybe we've come a long way – with the information you've given me and what I've gleaned at this end. A lot more of the pieces in my hands. Now I have to try and fit them together. I'd better warn you, I'll be phoning Peter Sarris to try and stop him taking any action. Yet. I'll cover you. What's the next move you plan?'

'Grilling Christina again about her relationship and movements with Masterson. That's what I came out for – to find out what really happened to Masterson. It looks like the Greeks to me. Petros and his vendetta. He's mad as a hatter.'

'And dangerous. Tread carefully. He'll be turning Athens upside down to locate Christina. But don't be too sure you've got to the bottom of anything. Someone may be using Petros as a gigantic smokescreen – to divert our attention.'

'From what?' Newman asked.

'I don't know. Just a sixth sense. There are some pretty peculiar characters involved. Including a Professor Guy Seton-Charles. At the moment he's in the West Country, holds a position at Bristol University. But he takes seminars at the university in Athens. Greek Studies.'

'Description?'

'Early sixties, looks younger. Slim build. Clean-shaven, thinning brown hair, Roman nose. About five feet eight. Intellectual type. Conceited manner. Most distinctive feature the rimless glasses he wears. Informal dress.'

'I'll recognize him. Early sixties again. So many of them are. Barrymore, Robson, Kearns, Florakis . . .'

'Which could be significant. Takes them back to World War Two – where all this started, I suspect. Another point about this Seton-Charles. He was stationed in the Antikhana Building in Cairo at the time of the Ionides murder.'

'A pattern is beginning to form,' Newman suggested.

'Yes, but it's like a kaleidoscope. New events shake it

300

up, give a fresh picture. One more thing before I go. And warn Marler – he can be impulsive. Petros is a very dangerous man. That crazy business about the skeleton in the mine. I'm sure you're right. It is the remains of Andreas. Watch your step, both of you. And has something else struck you just before I go?'

'I expect not, since you phrase it like that.'

'From your description Florakis' land adjoins Petros' – that is a strange coincidence. Might be worth following up. But cautiously. Keep in touch . . .'

As Tweed put down the phone the door opened and Monica came in. She greeted Paula, took off her raincoat, said she would be making coffee for everyone. Tweed waited until she returned with the tray and asked for black coffee. He was still working on automatic pilot, struggling to throw off the remnants of sleep.

'I woke early,' Monica said as she filled their cups. 'It was all going round and round in my head.'

'I can give you more – enough to make your head spin. Newman just called . . .'

He gave them both a concise résumé of the data Newman had provided. The two women listened intently. Paula made a few notes in her book. Monica absorbed it in her encyclopaedic memory. Tweed leaned back in his chair as he concluded.

'So what do you make of all that?'

'Florakis seems to be the key,' Paula said promptly. 'You've been looking for a link between Greece and England. The fact that he appears to be sending coded signals to somewhere here may be the missing link. That reference to Colonel Winter intrigues me. Colonel Barrymore?'

'Not necessarily . . .'

'But the thing I got from that tape recording Pete made

of the conversation at The Luttrell Arms was Barrymore still treats his two companions as though he's in charge.'

'Colonel Winterton,' said Monica. 'The man Seton-Charles told you had handled the property transactions for that bungalow estate near Kearns' house. Colonel Winterton, who disappeared once all the properties were sold. The Invisible Man.'

'Have you contacted Pitlochry Insurance then?' Tweed enquired. 'They were the outfit which actually loaned the mortgages.'

'I managed to get through after you left yesterday afternoon. I had trouble getting the manager to part with the information. I used our General & Cumbria Insurance cover to get him to open up. Said we'd had an enquiry from a Colonel Winterton about a property deal, that he'd given Pitlochry as a reference and . . .' She began choking. 'Coffee . . . went down the wrong way.'

Paula jumped up, accompanied her to the ladies' room. Tweed sat thinking. The plate at the front entrance read General & Cumbria Insurance Co. The cover had worked well. They pretended to be a specialized company dealing with top security protection for private individuals of great wealth. Officially, they also dealt with kidnapping insurance, negotiating with the kidnappers if a client was snatched. This explained all the trips abroad made by Tweed and his sector chiefs. They were even a member of the insurance industry's association – to complete the cover. Monica came back with Paula, dabbing at her mouth with a handkerchief.

'I'm all right now,' she said, sitting down behind her desk. 'I was telling you about Pitlochry. The manager said they'd found Colonel Winterton sound and businesslike. He confirmed that Winterton had simply acted as a middleman between clients buying those bungalows and Pitlochry supplying the mortgages.'

'He met him?'

'No, that was the odd thing. Odd to me. All the trans-actions were carried out by correspondence from the Taunton office and Winterton on the phone.'

'Did you manage to get any idea how he sounded?'

'Yes, by cracking a joke. Winterton had a very upper crust way of talking. Very much the colonel addressing the battalion – the manager's phrase.'

'Any forwarding address?'

'None. No one at Pitlochry has any idea where he is nowadays.'

'The Invisible Man,' said Paula.

'Another cul-de-sac,' Tweed remarked. 'Which reminds me – we still have no idea what Masterson meant by his note referring to *Endstation*. I feel certain that's a major pointer – either here or in Greece. Masterson was the cleverest interrogator I ever met. He was trying to tell me something. But what?'

'Dead end for the moment,' Paula said briskly. 'But I've come up with something.' There was a note of triumph in her tone which made Tweed and Monica stare at her. 'I didn't tell you while we were there. I thought I'd follow something up for myself.'

'Which was?' asked Tweed.

'You remember the evening we visited Colonel Barry-more when you interviewed him? I was sitting to one side. He had his copy of *The Times* folded back to the personal advertisement section. I memorized the date. Yesterday I went off to Wapping, checked their files. What do you think I found?'

'She's playing you at your own game,' Monica said and chuckled. 'Teasing you.'

'So I'll play along. What did you find?'

'An advertisement placed at the time Christina Gavalas was in England, the time when Harry Masterson was going around with her over here. The advertisement was this.' She read from a small pocket diary. '*Will anyone interested in the Greek Key and knows about Antikhana please contact me. Irene.* It gives a phone number for contact. I phoned the number. Turned out to be the Strand Palace. I phoned the hotel, said I was the sister of Christina Gavalas. Had she stayed at the hotel? They wouldn't play. So I jumped in a taxi and went down to the Strand. I sexed up the reservations clerk – naughty of me, I think he thought he had a date. He looked up their records. Christina stayed there at the relevant time.'

'But Irene is the wrong name,' Monica observed.

'I think she did that to protect herself. Not knowing who would come looking for her.'

'I agree,' Tweed said. 'Type out that ad with the date and add it to the file. You did a good job. Actually,' he admitted, 'I knew about the advertisement. Newman told me over the phone that Christina had explained to him during dinner that was how she met Masterson. He saw the ad and contacted her.'

'Thanks a lot!' Paula threw down her pencil. 'So I wasted my time.'

'Hardly. I didn't spot that newspaper in Barrymore's study – which shows he was interested. And in the near future I think you and I should drive down again to Exmoor to see how Butler and Nield are getting on. We know more than we did last time.'

He stopped as the phone rang. Monica grabbed her receiver and spoke briefly. Putting her hand over the mouthpiece she looked at Tweed.

'Talk of the devil. Pete Nield on the phone for you.'

'Sorry to phone you so early. I called on the off chance,' Nield explained. 'I'm talking from a public box. We put the pressure on and guess what's happened. The hunters have become the hunted. Harry and I are being watched by Barrymore and Kearns.'

'What do you mean?' Tweed's tone was sharp, alarmed.

'We each took one of them in turn and let them spot us

– riding on the moor. Now when we get up there they appear out of nowhere and stalk us! It's uncanny . . .'

'They know the moor better than you'll ever do. What was their routine before they turned the tables on you?'

'Robson rode to see patients during the day. He can go for ages without food or drink. His patients are scattered over a large area. Evenings he has a meal, presumably prepared by his sister. Then he retires up to that conning tower place and reads. After dark he draws the curtains. Goes to bed late.'

'And Kearns?'

'He rides the moor a lot. His wife, Jill, never appears. She hasn't been seen by either of us. Maybe he locks her up. As for Kearns, he rides up to the summit of Dunkery Beacon. Stays up there at night. God knows what he's doing. Can't get close enough. Weird bloke. A solitary.'

'Dunkery Beacon? That's the highest point on Exmoor . . .'

'That's right. Like to know about Barrymore?'

'Of course.'

'He's about one hundred feet from where I'm talking. Inside a newspaper shop that opens early. He's standing by the window, half-pretending to read a paper. But he's watching me. He came into the village on a horse tethered further down the High Street. He's also got a rifle in a scabbard attached to the saddle.'

Tweed thought quickly. 'Now listen to me. Butler is inside The Luttrell Arms? Good. This is what you do. The unexpected. You vanish. Pay your bills. Then both of you drive to Taunton. The colonel can't follow you on a horse. Hire fresh cars in Taunton. Quite different models. Book into the main hotel in Taunton, using assumed names. Change your clothes – buy new ones which completely change your appearance. Then switch your attentions to Professor Guy Seton-Charles. Track him night and day. Don't let him know you're on his tail. You can pick him

305

up tomorrow morning at his bungalow on that estate. Understood?'

'Will do.'

'And let Monica know the name of your new hotel, how we can contact you. Now, move!'

Tweed slammed down the phone. He started cleaning his glasses on his handkerchief. Monica watched, winked at Paula. She recognized the signs.

'Something has happened?' she ventured.

'Yes. The pressure worked . . .' He told them what had happened. 'Maybe crisis time is approaching.'

'And the object of the new exercise is?' Paula asked.

'To throw Barrymore and Kearns off balance. One moment they're being tracked by Butler and Nield. Suddenly the trackers disappear. I'll bet for the next week Barrymore and Kearns scour the moors looking for them, wondering where the devil they've gone. Also I'm pulling Butler and Nield out of the firing line. Maybe literally.'

'Don't follow,' Paula said.

'I didn't like the sound of the rifle Barrymore is carrying. You get shooting accidents on moors. And no one can prove it wasn't just that. And it's psychological warfare.'

'Don't follow that,' Paula said.

'We'll leave Exmoor alone for a week. Just when the hunters think they've scared off the opposition you and I arrive – asking more questions.'

They had breakfast brought in by the day guard, George. Sandwiches and coffee which they consumed at their desks. It was ten o'clock when Tweed asked Monica to put in a call to Chief Inspector Sarris of Athens Homicide.

'I met him once at a security conference in Geneva. He's very bright, but I have to try and stop him doing something. The timing is wrong. If he's not there, ask for Kalos . . .' Tweed spelt it out for her. 'He is Sarris' clever assistant.

Has a mind like a computer – especially where Greek history is concerned.'

Tweed returned to studying the file headed *Ionides*. Monica reported all the lines to Greece were busy. 'Probably travel agents booking holidays. I'll keep trying.'

'Fair enough. Meantime, try Brown's Hotel again. In Dunster I made an arrangement with Jill Kearns that if she came up to London we'd meet. I said I'd keep in touch with the hotel so I'd know when she was here.'

'I'm calling daily. She wasn't there yesterday . . .'

'Nield told me she's disappeared from Exmoor, that they haven't seen her for some time. Try now . . .'

'She's on the line,' Monica told him a few minutes later.

'Tweed here. When did you arrive?'

'Darling, how absolutely marvellous to hear your voice. So reassuring. I'm on my own. God, am I glad to be back in civilization. I was going out of my mind on that dreadful moor.'

'Can we meet today?' Tweed asked, stemming the flood.

'You asked me when I arrived. Late yesterday. Just in time to have tea. It's out of this world, tea at Brown's. Why don't we do that?'

'Good idea. I could get there about three-thirty. Would that suit you?'

'Gorgeous. I'll count the minutes. Don't be late. They have the most scrumptious strawberry cake. But it goes quickly. Oh,' she added as an afterthought, 'I'll have something interesting to tell you. Not over the phone, darling.'

'Three-thirty then. Goodbye . . .'

Tweed put down the phone as though it were hot. He sighed, took out his handkerchief, mopped his forehead in mock horror. 'Good job you didn't take that conversation down.'

'She's very attractive,' Paula said in a thoughtful tone.

'Swarms all over you.' He looked at Monica. 'But you did tape-record the conversation I had with Nield?'

'Yes, I saw you nod twice. It's recorded for all time. Want to hear it played back?'

'Later. Something Nield said was significant and now it's gone. I was concentrating on getting them out of Dunster. Damned if I can remember what it was. You listen to it, Paula. See whether something strikes you. Monica, try Peter Sarris again.'

'Chief Inspector Sarris? London calling. Mr Tweed of Special Branch would like a word with you . . .'

Tweed spent little time over exchanging greetings. 'Robert Newman, the foreign correspondent, has told me of his conversation with you, Peter. He's fully vetted . . .'

'He works for you these days?' Sarris enquired.

'No, he doesn't. But when he's after a story and comes across something he feels affects national security he tells me.' That covered Newman. 'I have a big favour to ask you. Hold off any action on this character Stavros Florakis. Give him enough rope and he'll hang himself. I'm at the early stages of the investigation.'

'What investigation is that? If I may ask.'

'You may. I'm investigating the death of one of my top men – Harry Masterson. Can't tell you what it's about yet. Point is Florakis' farm is close to Cape Sounion where Masterson died in suspicious circumstances.'

'Official verdict is an accident.'

'And the unofficial? I'm on scrambler.'

'So am I,' Sarris assured him. 'We had it installed when drugs became a major problem. Unofficially? I'm only expressing my personal opinion. There are people higher up who wouldn't like this . . .'

'Don't worry. This chat is totally confidential.'

'Masterson was murdered. I went to the Cape myself,

308

looked over the ground. No sane man could have stumbled over the edge. And Masterson was very sane – I saw him once at the Hilton. So, you want me to hold off the cavalry?'

'Please. We're at an early stage, Peter. I'm not sure at which end the key lies yet – yours or mine. Talking about keys, have you ever heard of the Greek Key?'

Sarris hesitated. Only for a second or two, but Tweed caught it.

'Doesn't mean a thing to me. Will we be seeing you out here?' he continued.

'Hard to say just now. How is Kalos? I remember him well at that security conference in Geneva. You have a clever assistant there.'

'Ah, but you are shrewder than some people here on the higher floors.' Sarris hesitated, this time for longer. Tweed waited, sensing the Greek was making up his mind about something. 'It is interesting you mentioned Kalos. He has made an important discovery. As you may know, Newman obtained Florakis' fingerprints. We were putting them through the computer. Kalos – as always – went his own way. He checked back through a card index of old records going back to 1946.'

'Sounds like Kalos,' Tweed commented.

'He came up trumps. An hour ago we were comparing the fingerprints of Stavros Florakis with another set under the magnifier. They matched.'

'Who is he really?' Tweed kept the excitement out of his voice.

'A certain Oleg Savinkov. Sent in by Stalin to murder leaders of EDES, the right-wing group fighting the Communists during the Civil War. Are you with me?'

'I have read about it. Go on.'

'Savinkov was nicknamed The Executioner, sometimes The Russian. So what is he doing as an impostor back in Greece? Someone has reactivated him. Can't be

Gorbachev. He's in the détente business. You still want me to hold off the dogs?'

'More than ever. And I will definitely be flying to Greece as soon as I can . . .'

28

Newman knew there was something wrong the moment he stepped out of the elevator on Christina's floor. Nick was sitting in an armchair on guard. He was smoking a cigarette and the ash tray on the marble-topped table was filled with discarded butts.

But it was Nick's reaction as soon as the elevator doors opened which warned Newman. Nick stood up abruptly and his right hand slid inside his jacket towards the Smith & Wesson revolver Newman had returned to him. When he saw who it was Nick converted the movement into scratching his armpit.

'Is she safe?' Newman asked.

'OK. But we have a problem, a crisis. Anton, one of her relatives, has arrived. He came up to this floor, then wandered off down that corridor when he saw me. Later he came back and went down into the lobby again. Could still be there.'

'A good moment for me to have a little talk with Christina.'

'Maybe not. She's very touchy. Like a bomb that could blow up in your face. It's Anton that did it. I told her. Felt I had to . . .'

'You did right.'

Newman went to her door, rapped in the special way

they had agreed. She opened the door after removing the chain and Newman realized she was in a bad mood. Her eyes looked larger than ever, she didn't smile, she turned her back on him and walked towards the balcony, arms folded under her breasts.

'Anton is here. They've found me,' she snapped before he could say a word.

'You haven't told me about Anton. Talk. And keep away from the balcony. If he's by the pool he could see you.'

'What difference does it make? He knows I'm here.'

· 'We'll handle that.' He took hold of her by the shoulders and turned her round, sat her down on the edge of the bed. 'Stay put.' He lifted the half-empty glass on the table, sipped it. 'Champagne. Bit early in the day.'

'I needed something to settle my nerves. The bottle's in the fridge. Fill it up for me.'

'Anything the lady wants, the lady gets.'

'Anything?' she asked as he brought back the refilled glass, handed it to her. She was wearing a cream blouse with the top three buttons undone. She wore no bra.

'Not that now,' he said. 'I have questions to ask.'

'Your eyes said something different.'

He moved away to a chair. She also wore a short pleated cream skirt. Her legs were stunning. Get your mind on the business in hand, he told himself.

'Stop it,' he snapped. 'Tell me about Anton. The full *curriculum vitae*. That means his life from the day he was born.'

'I know. I'm not illiterate – like Dimitrios and Constantine.' She sipped her champagne. 'Nor is Anton. He is Petros' son by his second wife – who was worked to death like the first wife. That makes Anton, six years younger than me, my uncle, for God's sake. Petros spotted he was bright. He spent money on his education, every drachma that was available.'

'What kind of education?'

'A good school in Athens. Anton was always top of the class. So he went on to a school in Switzerland. As well as Greek, he can speak German and English fluently. He's a natural linguist. An expert horseman – he learned to ride in Germany, then went on to Vienna for dressage. Petros wanted a gentleman in the family, someone who could mix at all levels of society. He's also a crack shot with any kind of rifle or handgun.'

'Where did he learn that? In Devil's Valley?'

'You're joking. When he came back here Dimitrios and Constantine hated him. The one thing they could do to make him look useless was to shoot. Anton flew to England, joined a shooting club. When he came back he could make Dimitrios and Constantine look like children with guns.'

'Happy families. How old is he?'

'Thirty-eight. He looks ten years younger. He dresses smartly. Oh, I've left a bit out. When he came back from Geneva he had a spell at Athens University. He came under the influence of an English professor. He still attends his seminars when this professor comes here in summer.'

'You know the name of this professor?'

She screwed up her thick eyebrows. 'A double-barrelled name. I met him once. Didn't like him. He reeks with conceit and self-satisfaction. But he's clever.'

'Try and think of his name.'

'Got it. Guy Seton-Charles . . .'

Newman had a word with Nick, who went straight down to the lobby by elevator. Returning to the bedroom, he found Christina sitting in front of the dressing table, brushing her hair. A bottle of mineral water and a glass stood next to her cosmetics.

312

'I've sobered up,' she announced. 'I drank two glasses of water. Do you think this is a good idea – my going down to the lobby with you if Anton is still there?'

'Part of the plan. If he's hanging about I want him to see you. And I want to see him – so I'll know him in future.'

'He's the most dangerous of my relatives. Because I'm well-educated too he resents me. And he has pots of money of his own. Money is power he says.'

'Where does it come from?'

'He runs a chain of shops in Athens and Salonika. They sell expensive television, video and radio equipment. Imported, of course. We Greeks don't make anything – except silverware. Anton is clever technically, too. He can build the most complicated high-powered radio equipment.'

'That's interesting,' Newman commented to himself. He went to the door as he heard the agreed rapping signal. It was Nick.

'Anton is still here. He's strolling round the lobby below the elevators. With a bit of luck we could see him by looking down. Without him seeing us.'

'That's not the idea. Come with us. Ready, Christina?'

'If you insist.'

They crossed the first-floor lobby. Nick had pressed the button, the elevator doors opened and they stepped inside. Newman gave Christina's arm a squeeze as the elevator descended. She made a moue, stiffened herself, stood erect.

'To hell with Anton,' she said.

'That's my girl,' Newman responded.

They stepped out into the main entrance hall. Below them, beyond a waist-high wall, was a deep well, a large reception area approached by steps from the even vaster marble-floored hall leading to the street. 'Over to your left, behind the pillar,' Nick whispered.

Several couples occupied some of the spacious couches at the lower level. A small man stepped from behind a pillar, lifted a small object to his eyes, held it there, then replaced it in his pocket.

Marler sat in an armchair at the lower level. He had a newspaper in front of his face. He dropped the paper, stood up, wandered over to where Anton was lighting a cigarette. Marler brushed past him, looking the other way. 'Excuse me,' he said in English and walked on a few paces. He took the camera he'd filched from Anton's pocket, fiddled with it, snapped it closed again and tucked it down inside the side of his slacks.

Anton still stood by the pillar. A small compact man wearing an expensive lightweight blue suit which Marler suspected was made of silk. He had a blue-striped shirt and a pale blue tie. Very dressy, Mr Anton. His pale face was plump and his black hair was brushed back over his high forehead. No parting.

As Marler approached he was feeling in his jacket pocket. He looked up, put out a hand to detain Marler, who stepped behind the pillar. 'A word with you,' Anton said, following the Englishman. 'You've just stolen my camera.' His right hand gripped Marler's arm and there was strength in the hand.

Marler wrenched his arm loose, shook himself, his expression bleak. 'Don't do that again.' He glanced down on the floor, pointed. 'Your bloody camera is down there. You dropped it, you stupid little man.'

Anton stooped with agility, retrieved the camera. As he stood up Marler hit him hard on the jaw with his clenched fist. No one sitting in the reception area could see behind the pillar. Anton sagged, the back of his head caught the pillar, he lay on the ground.

Marler hurried to the steps, ran up to the higher level where Newman waited with Christina and Nick. 'He's out cold. Time to move her. I'll inform the reception desk . . .'

'Nick, go out to the car. Be ready to drive us to the Grande Bretagne . . .'

Newman grasped Christina by the arm, guided her into a waiting elevator, pressed the button. As it ascended he talked fast. 'You kept most of your case packed as I suggested?'

'Yes. I can dump my cosmetic stuff inside in its sachet and be ready in two minutes.'

'Make it one . . .'

In the main lobby Marler was talking to the chief receptionist. 'A chap has collapsed behind a pillar down there. Just keeled over. May have had a heart attack.' He waited until the receptionist phoned for a doctor and rushed off, then asked a girl for the bill for Christina's room.

'Everything's paid up,' he announced as Newman emerged from an elevator, carrying a bag with Christina by his side. Behind him he heard the same girl receptionist call out. 'Phone for you, Mr Newman . . .'

'Take Christina to the car,' Newman ordered Marler. 'I'll be with you in a minute. God knows who this could be.' The girl behind the counter handed him the phone.

'Tweed here, Bob. There's an emergency. Call me back safely within the hour. No later . . .'

'Thanks a bundle.' Newman lowered his voice. 'We have a crisis at this end. I'll call back.' He slammed down the phone.

Nick was waiting outside at the end of a queue of taxis. He opened the rear door of his Mercedes and Christina dived in, followed by Newman. As Nick dumped her bag inside the boot Marler appeared at the rear window. 'Follow us to the Grande Bretagne,' Newman told him. 'Reserve a room for Christina in the name of Mrs Charles. Take over. Nick will be taking me back to the Embassy.'

'Will do.'

Nick turned into the traffic. Christina was producing a large silk scarf from her handbag. She carefully wrapped

315

it round her hair so it was concealed. Next she donned a pair of dark wrap-round glasses, then looked at Newman.

'Do I pass inspection?'

'Unrecognizable.' Newman felt relieved. Everyone was getting into the swing of quick escapes. And Nick was driving a devious route to the Grande Bretagne. Christina looped her arm inside Newman's and snuggled up against him as he glanced through the rear window. Marler was close behind.

'How the devil did Anton find me?' Christina wondered.

'Probably by showing a photograph of you to a member of the staff short of folding money . . .'

'But I arrived at the Hilton disguised.'

'And then paraded yourself on the balcony. There were loads of staff serving drinks to the sun-worshippers round that pool. I should have thought of that. I should also have thought of telling you to wear your scarf and glasses when we had dinner at the Ta Nissia restaurant. We'll be more careful at the Grande Bretagne.'

'And maybe,' Nick called over his shoulder, 'I should park this car at the Astir Palace across the road from the Grande Bretagne. They'll have the registration number by now. It means booking a room . . .'

'Book one. In a different name. Buy a case and a few clothes, including one of those peaked caps the Germans like to wear. We want to sink out of sight – and that includes you. And sleep in the Astir Palace room, if that's OK. Then you're available on the dot when we need you. Unless your wife would object?'

'Glad to see the back of me.' Nick grinned. 'Sorry about the traffic snarl-up, but no one can follow us into this.'

They had arrived at Omonia Square, the Piccadilly Circus or Times Square of Athens. Everywhere intersecting roads converged, the traffic was solid. The square was surrounded with second-class hotels, department stores. Nick tapped his hand on the wheel as he waited.

'Refugees from abroad flock to this area. The police don't mind. They know where to look if they're after someone. Miracles will never cease. We're on the move again . . .'

On the veranda of his farm deep inside Devil's Valley Petros was lecturing his two grandsons viciously. He gestured with a heavy fly-swatter as they stood in front of him.

'You, Dimitrios, are telling me again that several men crept up behind you that night at the mine, then clubbed both of you. Is that still your story?'

'It is the way it happened . . .'

'Liar! Cheat!' Petros moved with savage speed. The end of the fly-swatter whacked Dimitrios across the back of his left hand. Reinforced with leather, the swatter brought up an ugly weal. And Petros was still sitting in his chair. 'You lie in your teeth,' he snarled.

'It was like that . . .' Constantine began, then stopped when Petros turned to him. He braced himself for the blow but Petros relaxed in his chair, studying the end of the fly-swatter as he talked in a calm tone.

'You were both staring down inside the mine. You saw the legs of a man protruding from under the bucket. Had you shot him without hesitation – as I would – you would have turned round and seen the single man coming up behind you, the man one of you probably glimpsed before he knocked you both out. Clumsy fools.'

'Why do you say that?' Dimitrios ventured. He sucked his injured hand.

'Because I know the mine, know that for hundreds of yards it is surrounded with loose rock chippings. One man trained in field warfare, one very clever man, might make his way silently across those rocks without making a sound. One man,' he repeated. 'I refuse to believe that several men managed it. You are covering up for your idiocy. It was a trap, you realize that?'

'A trap?' Constantine sounded genuinely puzzled.

'Of course. One man – the man inside the mine – lets you see him. He leads you to the mine. His companion then creeps up behind you both. Constantine, you said you saw a rifle barrel just before it struck you. He did it like this.' Holding the fly-swatter by the middle of the handle, Petros swung it first one way, then the other. 'Were they the English?' he growled. 'You saw one man coming up the track.'

'Too far away to see him at all clearly,' Dimitrios broke in before Constantine could reply. It was a relief to be able to tell the truth.

'And you did a lousy job of not finding Christina,' Petros sneered. He was enjoying himself, taking them down a peg, showing who was boss.

'We did our best,' Dimitrios protested. 'So many hotels . . .'

'Oho! Your best. Your worst, you mean. You walk into the Hilton and try to bribe the chief receptionist! He knows it is not worth risking his fat salary to give out information. I would have gone after the menials – people like yourselves. A chambermaid, a cleaner. Someone who needs the money, someone who goes into every bedroom. Well, at least Anton is now looking. He will find her.'

'We could go back, try again,' Constantine suggested eagerly.

'Now you grovel.' Petros spat beyond the veranda. They took all the insults he heaped on them, he was thinking. It was a tribute to the power of his personality. His huge body emanated physical magnetism. He waved towards the scrub-studded mountains.

'Get out there in the sun. Tend the sheep. Make sure the other shepherds are not sleeping behind rocks. If you catch one, kick hell out of him.' He paused. 'That was curious that you should see Florakis climbing a mountain

318

at that hour. Keep an eye on him, too. Report to me when you find out what he is up to.' Petros could not resist one last dig. 'And forget about Christina – let Anton find her. Anton has brains.'

When Dimitrios and Constantine had left the farm, climbing up the track even a goat might find trouble negotiating, kicking up limestone dust which filled their nostrils, sweating in the afternoon sun, Petros remained on the veranda. His leonine head sunk on his barrel-like chest, he remained awake, thinking.

Always the hated English. Newman and Marler – those were the two English Giorgos had reported as registering at the Grande Bretagne. Giorgos who had ended rammed inside a cask of wine upside down in the Plaka.

Without any formal education, Petros possessed a native cunning, the devious mind of a peasant which sometimes could out-think the well-educated. Newman and Marler who had seduced Christina into joining them. They had been sent by whichever of the three men had killed Andreas on Siros all those years ago.

Which one? Colonel Barrymore, Captain Robson or Company Sergeant Major Kearns? Could all three be involved in the bestial murders? Because later – when the war was over – Petros had visited Cairo to learn what he could of the murder of his other son, Stephen, masquerading as Ionides. An Egyptian who worked as a cleaner at the Antikhana Building had told him. The same three men had been based in the building. In some way one of them had penetrated Ionides' real identity, had discovered he was the brother of Andreas.

Which one? Petros asked himself the question he had pondered a thousand times. Now Anton – clever Anton – had located them at some place called Exmoor. Why were they all living so close together?

It didn't matter! Petros heaved himself out of the chair, went into the farmhouse, returned with the box he kept hidden. He opened it. Inside, wrapped in newspaper, was the commando knife, the knife he had used all his strength to heave out of Andreas' back. The knife he would one day use to kill the murderer of his two sons.

Dapper and assured, despite his experience, Anton thanked the chief receptionist and walked out of the Hilton. The doctor they had summoned had been a nuisance. Anton had assured him he'd fainted, caught his jaw against the side of the pillar. He had also handled the chief receptionist cleverly. Just before he left he made the remark casually.

'It was the heat. I must have fainted just before my friends left the hotel . . .' He described Christina, Newman and Marler. 'Did they say which hotel they were moving to? Maybe not – as they left in a rush.'

'No, they didn't. As you say, they were in a hurry,' the chief receptionist had replied.

Which confirmed Anton's suspicions. He shrugged as he walked into the blazing heat, hardly noticing the change in temperature. He had found her once, he would find her again. But first there was more urgent business to attend to. He checked his watch – he was late for his appointment.

Let the bastard wait. He would be so relieved when he saw Anton arrive. He ignored the taxis. Their drivers had good memories. He made his way over the complicated crossing and walked briskly down Avenue Sofias towards Syntagma Square where the Grande Bretagne was located.

Anton smiled to himself as he thought how livid Petros would be if he knew where he was going, who he was going to meet and why. The old ruffian was living in the past.

Had no idea of what was really going on in the world. Wouldn't he be surprised one day when he found Anton was a Cabinet Minister? The Ministry of the Interior for preference. There you had real power.

Half an hour later he was walking through the maze of alleys and streets which made up the honeycomb of the Plaka. Was the plan already beginning to work? Sooner or later the man he was going to see would have to tell him what was happening. The clod who was still important to Anton. For the present. The man called Doganis. The Athens chief of the Greek Key.

'You're late,' Doganis greeted him. 'Why?'

Anton sat in a rush-covered chair in the room above a taverna, took his time about lighting a cigarette. He disliked this hulking brute but was astute enough to conceal his distaste. Doganis, a man in his sixties, was heavily built with broad shoulders and a large head of greying hair. His hooded eyes regarded Anton with a cold expression.

Anton studied his chief, careful to betray nothing of the contempt he felt. The huge soft hands holding a circular ebony ruler, the sagging jowls, the barrel-like stomach. Out of condition, out of touch with the modern world. One of the Old Guard. A gross monument of the Civil War days.

Doganis was also studying the dapper Anton. Ambitious, ruthless. A young upstart who had to be kept in his place. Dressed like a gigolo. Doganis had been ordered to tell him the next move in the operation; personally he thought it premature.

'You are going back to England soon,' he informed him. 'You'll be taking letters to Captain Robson, Sergeant Major Kearns and Colonel Barrymore. Two of the letters will be meaningless. The third you will have the honour of delivering to Jupiter.'

'Jupiter? Who is that?'

'The man who is reactivating the organization. Do not ask who he is.'

'Jupiter is a Roman god, not a Greek,' Anton remarked, feeling his way.

'Which confuses the issue, protects his identity. You travel to England again in a few weeks' time – after we have received an important visitor from abroad.' Doganis paused. At least they hadn't told him to reveal yet to Anton that the visitor was Colonel Volkov, aide to General Lucharsky. 'You can travel there by the secret route again, I assume? Again there must be no record of your visit to England.'

'It worked before, it will work again,' Anton told him boldly. 'You do your job, I'll do mine . . .'

There was a sudden cracking sound. Anton stared. Doganis, who constantly held something in his restless hands, had split the ebony ruler in two in his fury.

Anton was astounded. The grotesque obese Doganis he had put down as effete had enormous strength in his apparently flabby hands. Strangler's hands. Doganis pointed the jagged end of one half of the ruler at him. His voice was more sinister for its soft tone.

'Listen to me, Gavalas. We have laid a tremendous responsibility on your immature shoulders. I have only to report you have lost my confidence and you are dead in twenty-four hours. You have displayed arrogance. I find that disturbing.'

Anton swallowed. The room was dimly illuminated by an oil lamp on a side table. Doganis' huge shadow suddenly seemed to fill the room. He forced himself to speak respectfully. 'I apologize, Comrade. I wished to assure you all will go well.'

'And remember this,' Doganis continued, ignoring the apology, 'I may introduce you to our visitor. He may wish to brief you himself. Treat him with reverence. Phone me daily from a public call box.' He changed the subject without warning, watching the other man closely. 'Is everything quiet down at Cape Sounion? No sign of anyone becoming curious about Florakis?'

'No sign at all,' Anton assured him.

'You replied too quickly. What about Petros?'

'He is still planning his mad revenge on the English murderers of his two sons. He thinks of nothing else.'

'Useful. He will divert the attention of those two Englishmen, Newman and Marler. Go now. Your future depends on obedience to the cause.'

Anton stood up quickly, glad to leave the presence of this man who now frightened him. He hurried down the narrow staircase leading direct to the street. He paused before he walked into the deserted street.

He did not see the small stocky man with a stubble of brown hair waiting in the shadow of a doorway across the street. For the simple reason that Kalos did not want to be seen. Kalos wore a stained old jacket and baggy trousers. He raised the camera with the infra-red lens and snapped off three shots. Anton turned left and walked rapidly away.

I'm lucky, thought Kalos. Whoever he is left the building when the tourists and the locals are eating and drinking inside the tavernas. He already had inside his camera two shots of Doganis. At least he had known this senior member of the Greek Key.

Kalos had waited over an hour outside the apartment Doganis rented in the Plaka, then had followed him to this new rendezvous above a taverna. Maybe Sarris would identify the younger man who had just left after spending half an hour with Doganis. The Greek Key was apparently recruiting younger members. A bad sign. And Kalos wondered who, where, and how they were finding fresh recruits.

323

29

'Bob, what crisis?' Tweed asked. 'Where are you talking from?'

'The Embassy. On scrambler phone. Now, you listen . . .' Newman explained tersely what had happened. He was alone in the basement room: Patterson had pushed off after unlocking the door.

'So your main task,' Tweed said, 'is to guard Christina, hide her away from Petros . . .'

'Our main objective is to find out who killed Masterson. And the last person we've found yet who saw him alive is Christina. It may be significant that Petros – through Anton – is doing his damnedest to track her down. What's your problem?'

'*Your* problem now,' Tweed told him. 'I had Butler and Nield on Exmoor, tailing Professor Guy Seton-Charles. An hour ago I had an emergency call from Butler. He was at London Airport. Seton-Charles suddenly took off. Left his bungalow with a case, drove a devious route to the airport . . .'

'Devious?'

'He took the main road to London, then cut off down a side turning. Nield followed him and Butler cruised on along the highway. Later Butler saw Seton-Charles come back down a slip road. From that point Butler and Nield leapfrogged so the target wouldn't spot them. At London Airport Nield stood behind Seton-Charles as he booked a first-class return to Athens. He's in mid-air now. British Airways flight 456, departed London 2.35 p.m., arrives at

Athens 8 p.m. Both local times. Can you get to the airport and track him? Remember his description?'

'Perfectly. And I've loads of time.'

'I need to know who he *contacts*. Something very funny about the professor.'

'Leave it to me . . .'

The BA flight from London touched down at Athens Airport at 8 p.m. Newman, lounging in a seat near the exit, spotted him at once – Seton-Charles wore a light-weight linen suit crumpled from sitting inside the aircraft. The professor climbed into a taxi. Newman got inside the next taxi.

'I'm a detective,' he told the driver. 'Don't lose that taxi – and here's a thousand drachmae as a tip.'

'What has he done?' asked the Greek.

'That's what I'm trying to find out . . .'

Settling back in his seat, Newman took off his jacket, mopped his forehead. The interior of the vehicle was like a sweat box. He recalled a headline blazoned on a newsstand. *Killer Heatwave Hits Greece*. And the character who wrote that one up wasn't joking, he thought.

Half an hour later, after passing between endless rows of white-walled two-storeyed houses backed by arid hillsides, they entered the city. Seton-Charles' taxi pulled up outside its destination. The occupant got out, paid off the driver and without a backward glance carried his bag inside the Hilton Hotel.

Tweed had phoned Jill Kearns at Brown's Hotel an hour before he was due to have tea with her. He had explained something urgent had come up, an emergency he had to cope with personally. Would she forgive him? Could they make a fresh date for tea in a couple of days' time?

325

Jill had shown no signs of resentment, said she certainly understood he had a difficult job. She would look forward even more to their being together now she would have to wait a little longer to see him. He put down the phone and looked at Monica.

'She's still keen to see me. Meantime we'll see where she goes, how she spends her time, who she meets. I fixed this up while you were out.'

'Fixed up what?'

'At this moment Paula is sitting in the lobby of Brown's. Jill can't get out of either the Albemarle Street or the Dover Street exit without Paula spotting her. When she leaves, Paula follows.'

'Paula will recognize her?'

'You've forgotten.' Tweed relaxed in his chair, pleased with the way things were developing. 'Paula,' he reminded her, 'was with me when I visited Kearns on Exmoor at his horrible old house near that bungalow estate where Seton-Charles lives. Jill sat in the room during my interview with Kearns – as did Paula. They sat within six feet of each other.'

'Is this Jill bright?'

'A very attractive blonde, in her thirties, and very bright.'

'Then she may well spot Paula following her,' Monica objected.

'You think so? Before Paula left here she altered her hair style. I loaned her a pair of glasses with blank lenses. It's amazing how a pair of glasses alters a person's appearance. On top of that she left early enough to call at Simpsons in Piccadilly – to do some shopping.'

'What shopping? You can be so exasperating. You're enjoying keeping me in suspense.'

'She went to buy a white raincoat, one with a large collar which buttons up to the neck. You may have observed it is drizzling on and off. In that outfit Jill will never recognize her.'

'And what's your motive in this devious – typically devious, if I may say . . .'

'You just did.' Tweed grinned.

'Devious ploy I was going to say if you'd let me finish just one sentence.'

'I'm suspicious of the glamorous Jill Kearns. She may be acting on her husband's instructions. I'm giving her enough rope – two days of it – to hang herself.'

'You don't trust anyone, do you?'

'Especially not attractive blondes who flatter me, try to make out they think I'm the cat's whiskers.'

'Maybe for her you are.' Monica doodled on her notepad. 'She may be just what you need . . .'

She stopped speaking, feeling she'd gone too far. Tweed's wife had left him several years ago, had walked out to take up living with a Greek shipping magnate. Last heard of in Rio. Tweed showed no sign of having heard her.

'Now we're on our own, let's check the facts we have so far, what we're doing. I'm a good listener as you know.'

He relaxed in his chair, hands clasped in his lap, eyes half-shut. Monica began her survey of recent events, reciting from memory.

'Object of the exercise – to track down the killer of Harry Masterson . . .'

'I'm going to get that bastard,' Tweed said half to himself.

Monica paused, surprised by the vehemence of his tone, then went on. 'Harry was going on holiday, bored stiff with the idea. He sees the ad Christina Gavalas placed in *The Times*, signing herself Irene. Intriguing reference to the Greek Key, which is a mystery to us still. Christina tells the story of the murder of Andreas and Stephen during the war. Harry gets interested, fools her into thinking he's a detective. Together they visit Exmoor. OK so far?'

'Go on.'

'Harry visits each of the three men, one of whom the Gavalas family is convinced is the murderer. Robson, Barrymore and Kearns. Harry is probably the shrewdest interrogator we've ever had – so maybe he spots the bad apple. He then, God save his soul, lays a trap. He tells each of the three he's flying to Greece. Which he then does with Christina. Harry is killed at Cape Sounion.'

'And,' Tweed added, 'by the time Paula and I do the same run Harry did – visit those three on Exmoor – they've all been on holiday and have suntans. Which means one of them could have been to Greece while Harry was there.'

'What I just can't see is who could have tricked Harry and pushed him over that three-hundred-feet cliff.' Monica shivered. 'The big question is who could have gained Harry's trust?'

'Christina is the obvious answer. The obvious is often correct.'

'There is an alternative,' Monica mused. 'Someone else Harry had no reason to fear but who got the better of him.'

Tweed opened his eyes. 'That's a new idea you have there. Someone he met in Greece?'

'Doesn't seem likely,' Monica disagreed. 'Next thing, Newman and Marler go out to Greece, make contact with Christina, who seems to have changed sides. But that could be another ploy, this time to trap Newman. That woman worries me. I sense she's clever.'

'Not clever enough to fool Newman,' Tweed assured her.

'She may have fooled Harry. I gather she's very attractive.'

'Harry,' Tweed recalled, 'was a great one for the girls. After his wife divorced him because he wasn't home every night, Harry made hay, was a devil with women.'

'Bob Newman is single again,' Monica reminded him.

'After that brutal murder of his French wife in the Baltic.'

'No woman ever fooled Bob,' Tweed insisted. 'He might *pretend* to go all starry-eyed over someone like Christina – but he'd be fooling her. Go on with your summary.'

'Newman and Marler contact Christina. They hear about this old villain, Petros – obsessed with tracking down his sons' killers over forty years afterwards. An impossible mission . . .'

'Theoretically,' Tweed interjected. 'But his son, Anton, does find his way to Exmoor – and locates all three ex-commandos. Petros must be a man with a deep peasant cunning. Obsessed, I agree. An impossible mission? Maybe not. And those three on Exmoor are scared of something. Look how Paula and I found all three were living inside fortresses. As I said to Paula, they're like men waiting for Nemesis.'

'Next development,' Monica continued, 'we get all this weird data from Newman. And weird it is – Andreas' skeleton hanging inside that old silver mine. Macabre. Petros is obsessed.'

'No proof it is Andreas. Probable, yes. Certain, no.'

'Plus the strange trip to the island of Siros. Dimitrios and Constantine – according to Christina – tried to shoot Newman. And,' she pressed on, 'this is the hairbrained place where the three commandos landed – with a German lookout point perched in that monastery above them. Back to the present day, we have the murder of Giorgos – who worked for the Grande Bretagne and spied on Newman and Marler. Also macabre – ending head down in a cask.'

'I think the solution lies in Greece.' Tweed, suddenly alert, walked over to the window and gazed towards the trees of distant Regent's Park.

'Looks like it,' Monica agreed. 'That's further reinforced by this peculiar Seton-Charles character hurtling off to Athens. That might mean nothing – except for the devious route he took to London Airport. Harry and Pete handled that cleverly. But what do they do now?'

'They're already doing it. While you were out when Butler called from London Airport I sent them both back to cover Exmoor. Robson, Barrymore and Kearns are still holed up there. Change of tactics again. Butler and Nield will have gone back to checking on that curious trio. Later, I'll fly out to Greece. I want to question Petros.'

'That could be dangerous. Newman nearly got killed venturing into Devil's Valley.'

'Sometimes you have to take chances.' He was pacing restlessly. 'Harry was murdered at Cape Sounion. That's close to this Devil's Valley. And some swine murdered Sam Partridge on Exmoor. That Greek, Anton, was floating about when it happened. Two scores I have to settle. Someone is going to pay the price.'

Monica again was disturbed by the ferocity of his language, his bitter tone. She spoke quietly.

'Be careful. Don't get obsessed – like old Petros. You're losing your normal sense of detachment. You always said that was the fatal mistake . . .'

'Stop nagging me, woman.' Tweed stared at her. 'I'll work it out in my own way without your advice . . .'

He stopped, appalled at Monica's expression. She looked like a woman who had been whipped across the face. In all their long relationship he had never spoken to her like that.

'I'm dreadfully sorry,' he apologized. 'I do rely on your judgement – maybe more than you've ever realized. I feel like a man walking in a fog, a tired man,' he admitted. He stuffed his briefcase with tape recordings and files. 'I think I'll spend a couple of days in my flat, sitting in an armchair, thinking. I need something to happen which points the way.'

'It always does.' Monica smiled. 'Now you're following your usual method. Don't worry. You're under pressure.

330

I'm amazed you haven't blown your top before. And there's a lot of personal feelings you've had to grapple with. Go home, get some rest – or would you like some coffee first?'

Tweed said thank you but he wanted to get straight off. He put on his shabby Burberry, squeezed her shoulder and walked out with his briefcase. Monica stood up, went to the window to watch him walk round Park Crescent through the net curtains. She was frightened. Tweed was acting like a man obsessed with his problems.

He left the building. He paused on the front steps to button up the raincoat, glancing all round the Crescent in case there were hostile watchers. Then he headed for the taxi rank.

On the way he passed a newspaper seller with a poster propped against the garden railings. Tweed didn't even notice it – he was thinking about Monica. It read, *Reagan–Gorbachev Summit in Washington?*

30

'I'm scared stiff. I need someone to confide in.' Jill Kearns laid a hand on Tweed's knee. It was two days later.

Tea at Brown's. Tweed looked round the room, admired the wooden wall panelling, the moulded ceiling. The atmosphere of the place created an air of intimacy. Especially when you were with a woman.

They sat at a table in an arched alcove at the end of the lounge. Behind them was a fireplace and they were isolated from the other guests taking tea. He twisted round in his deep armchair to look at Jill. She was worth the effort.

She had twirled her blonde hair into a single long plait looped over her shoulder. And she was dressed for London. A pair of tight-fitting leather trousers thrust into boots which displayed her well-shaped legs. She also wore a tunic of some black material splashed with vivid-coloured oriental flowers. Tweed drank some tea before replying.

'What exactly is worrying you?'

'Stuart, for one thing . . .'

'And for another?'

Tweed helped himself to a scrambled egg roll, bit off half of it. On the table in front of them stood a four-tier stand of some of the best food he'd ever enjoyed. The lowest tier had delicate little sandwiches with the crusts removed; on the second and third tiers were selections of bread and more sandwiches. Logically, the top tier held a variety of cakes, including some chocolate eclairs. You worked your way up.

'The company he keeps,' Jill replied, squeezing his leg. She used the other hand to eat and drink. The room was full of couples and quartets whose conversation muffled what Jill was saying. 'Those two men, Captain – Dr – Robson, and Colonel Barrymore. The colonel gives me the creeps.'

'Why?'

'He seems to mesmerize my husband and Robson. You'd think they were all still in the Army and Barrymore was their CO – the way he talks to them. Loathsome sarcastic bastard.'

'I take it you don't like him . . .'

'Don't make fun of me.' She looped her hand round his left hand he'd rested on the arm of the chair. 'You'll help me, won't you, Tweed? I wish I could get you on the telephone. Give me your number. It would be nice if we could have dinner. More cosy.'

All in a rush. She'll proposition me soon, Tweed thought. I wish to God I knew what she's really up to. He asked a question to throw her off balance.

'How do you know all this – how Barrymore talks to them? I thought they met by themselves for dinner once a week at The Luttrell Arms.'

'Sometimes they come over to our place and talk half the night in the study. I eavesdrop.'

'A bit naughty, that.' He smiled to take the sting out of the comment.

'You've got a lovely smile,' she said.

'You overheard something that frightened you,' he probed.

Outwardly impassive, Tweed wasn't feeling too comfortable. A woman had come in and sat down at a small table at the side of the room. She had folded her raincoat and parked it on the other chair. She was watching them briefly over the top of her glasses with a cynical expression. Paula. She hadn't, he knew, missed the fact that Jill was clasping his hand.

'Stuart is reinforcing the defences, as he put it. He's even laid some of those beastly steel-teethed traps outside the walls of our house. Barrymore advised that. They're all strengthening their security. Just as though they were expecting a raid.'

'Perhaps they are. By who?'

She hesitated, pushed two fingers under his shirt cuff. 'I've no idea. I feel like a prisoner.'

'You escaped for now. You're sitting here, in the middle of London. Not on Exmoor.' He poured more tea and she leaned over to hold the teapot lid in place, her breasts brushing his arm. 'You're confiding in me, as you put it, although I can't imagine why.'

She released her hand, flopped back in her armchair, her long leather-clad legs stretched out in front of her. Paula raised her glasses higher up the bridge of her nose, adjusted her beret and looked away. Tweed wished she'd stop sending signals.

'Because,' Jill said, 'you put the wind up all three when

you came to see them. I heard Stuart talking to Barrymore on the phone after you'd left. He was agitated. He started to say "This man Tweed is dangerous," then he slammed the door of his study and I couldn't catch any more. If you can put the wind up those three you're the man for me, my ally.'

She remained flopped in the chair but still looked elegant as she spoke in a coaxing tone.

'What about dinner here tonight? Say eight o'clock. And you haven't given me your phone number yet.'

'Can't do that – give you a number. Security. What I can do is to have you called daily in case you've got a message for me . . .'

'And dinner?'

'I expect to be working till midnight. Dinner will be sandwiches at my desk. Sorry.'

'If you agreed to dinner . . .' She crossed her legs and watched him through her lashes. 'I might have more news to pass on to you.'

'I can't promise to be an ally,' he warned. 'And if you've really more to tell me, do it now.' He decided an eclair was pushing it and took another scrambled egg roll.

She took a pack of cigarettes from her large handbag, extracted a king-size cigarette when he shook his head, and lit it with a gold-plated lighter. In the mellow light her beautiful bone structure stood out clearly. He was tempted to change his mind, to say he could make it for dinner. She's a devil, he was thinking. Blowing out a stream of smoke, she smiled.

'I can read your mind, Tweed. You're reconsidering your decision about dinner.'

There was an aura about her which drew him to her. In her thirties, he reflected. Not such a huge difference in their ages. He drank half a cup of strong tea to get a grip on himself.

'How long have you and Stuart been married?'

'Ten long years. Oh, it was fun to start with. He's a good-looking bastard. I met him soon after he'd left the Army – at a party in Taunton. He had a sense of humour in those days. Then he became cold – and spent more time with Barrymore and Robson. That's when he started turning the house into the Tower of London – like the others. I could leave him any day now for the right man.'

'That might be traumatic . . .'

'No more traumatic than the way we live now. At nights he spends half his time riding over the moor up to Dunkery Beacon. He's not back by midnight.' She looked at him with a certain expression. 'So I make a point of pretending to be fast asleep when my lord and master rolls in.'

'Dunkery Beacon? That's the highest point on Exmoor. And it's pretty rough country. How does he manage in the dark?'

'He doesn't.' She leaned forward to straighten his tie. 'He only goes up there half the month – not before there's a half moon waxing. I spend my evenings watching the television rubbish. I lead the most exciting life.'

'At least he seems generous,' Tweed remarked. 'Your clothes, that lighter . . .'

'Paid for out of a big legacy my favourite uncle left me.'

Tweed checked his watch. 'Sorry, but I have to go . . .'

She sat up straight and her face was close to his. 'All right, I'll tell you. One night when the three of them were talking they left the study door open a bit. A few nights ago. I crept down the stairs. Do you want to know what I heard?'

'Up to you.'

'My reward for telling is you have dinner with me soon. Promise?'

'I'll think about it.'

'The trouble was I only heard a bit. Then one of the

335

treads on the staircase creaked. Barrymore came to the door and slammed it shut. I froze, still as a mouse.'

'Did he see you?' Tweed kept the anxiety out of his voice.

'I'm not sure. Before that happened Robson said they'd better watch out. He sensed that the Greek Key might arrive soon on Exmoor, that he'd heard Petros – I think that was the name – was looking for them . . .'

Tweed was getting anxious: it was after 7 p.m. and there was still no sign of Paula. Monica, who worked all hours, saw him check his watch.

'She'll be all right. Paula can look after herself.'

The phone rang, she picked it up, spoke briefly. She nodded towards Tweed's phone.

'It's Harry Butler. Says it's an emergency. Not like him . . .'

Tweed lifted the receiver. 'Hello, Harry. Where are you calling from?'

'From a public phone box in Minehead on the coast. We're staying at a tiny place called Porlock Weir, also on the coast. End of the road. Literally. It stops there. I decided we needed a new base. Not Dunster, not Taunton. Porlock Weir is tucked away. Has a toy harbour for boats. The only way west is to walk along the rocky shore. I can hear the tide coming in at night. High tide around midnight. Got a pencil handy? Good. We're staying at The Anchor Hotel. I'm in Room Three, Pete has Room Two. Telephone number is 0643 862753. Got it?'

'Yes. Something's happened?'

'The ex-commando lot have disappeared. All three. Robson, Kearns and Barrymore. They've left Exmoor . . .'

'How do you know that?' Tweed felt a chill creeping up his spine.

'I took Barrymore and Robson's residences – because

336

they're close together. Pete watched Kearns. We kept in contact with our car radios. Careful what we said. Not a sign of them. I decided to use bull-at-gate method.'

'What did you do next?'

'Called at each address after buying new outfits. Country stuff. Pete shaved off his moustache – after a lot of pressure from me. I wore a polo-necked sweater and a pair of tinted glasses. Not foolproof, but if one of them opened the door we'd know at least they were there.'

'And the result?'

'At Quarme Manor that old bat of a housekeeper, Mrs Atyeo, tells me the Colonel is not at home. Can't say when he'll be back. I chatted her up, but let's skip that. So I drove on to Captain Robson at his posh bungalow. His sister – when I coax her – says her brother is away in London. Pete had a rougher time at CSM Kearns' place. No answer to the bell-push so he scrambles over the gate. The dog comes at him – ruddy Alsatian type. Pete coped, bashed the beast on the nose with the barrel of his gun. They don't like that – a hefty bonk on the nose. Pete prowled round the place. It was after dark. No lights. No one home. That's it. They've gone. To London maybe. Robson could have lied to his sister. We feel we should have seen one of them go.'

'Not necessarily. Harry, both of you stay on at The Anchor – and pick up any gossip on the three men. Call Monica if there's a fresh twist. In any case, call daily. Take care.'

Tweed sat staring into the distance after putting down the phone. Monica watched him as she removed the cassette which had recorded Butler's conversation.

'He said something which triggered off a memory,' Tweed told her after a few minutes. 'Can't put my finger on it. We'll play it back later, see if I can spot what it was.'

He walked over to the wall where three maps had been

attached – maps carrying flags with names. A map of Exmoor. A map of the Greek area stretching from Athens to Cape Sounion. And a map of Athens which Monica had obtained.

On the Exmoor map flags with names located the homes of Barrymore, Robson and Kearns, the bungalow estate, Professor Seton-Charles' residence, The Royal Oak at Winsford and The Luttrell Arms – the two places where the trio met weekly for lunch or dinner. One flag pressed in close to Winsford carried the name Sam Partridge. Tweed picked up two more from a tray on a table and wrote Butler and Nield on each. He pressed these in over Porlock Weir.

The map of Greece carried fewer flags. One for Petros in Devil's Valley, another close by for Florakis. A third, perched at the edge of Cape Sounion, carried what amounted to an obituary. Harry Masterson.

The street plan of Athens was becoming crowded. At the corner of Syntagma Square where the Grande Bretagne was situated, three more names: Christina Gavalas, Newman, Marler. At the other end of Avenue Sofias a flag for Professor Seton-Charles at the Hilton. And, finally, at the police headquarters building on Alexandras, Peter Sarris and Kalos.

'Who is Kalos?' Monica asked.

'The Dormouse.'

'Sorry? Did I hear you aright?'

'You did. I met Kalos, Sarris' loyal assistant, at the security conference in Geneva. A small, stocky chap with a stubble of light brown hair peppered over his head. I nicknamed him The Dormouse – because that's what he looks like. We got on well together. When I go to Athens he's the man I'm hoping will tell me anything they know. Sarris is more cautious. Another reason for my respecting The Dormouse is his uncanny ability to track a suspect while merging with his background. Sarris told me that.'

'Maybe you'd better fly to Greece soon,' Monica suggested.

'All in good time.' He looked at the wall maps again. 'At least we have our forces well distributed – Newman and Marler in Greece, Butler and Nield on Exmoor. There's a name missing.'

'Who's that?'

'Anton. Trouble is he's a will o' the wisp. First he was back in Greece, then he slips into this country by some unknown means before slipping out again. I'd like to know how he managed that.'

After parking his car at The Anchor Butler went for a walk westward along the coast. It was dark and he passed several isolated cottages with lights burning inside. To his right he could hear the slap of the incoming sea hitting the rocks. He turned round, went back to The Anchor and into the bar. Nield was chatting to the barman, a young chap who polished glasses as he talked.

'They have a ghost prowling the beaches at night,' Nield said to Harry, who ordered half a pint. 'Meet John, the barman. Local.'

'Not exactly a ghost,' John told Butler as he served him. 'A few weeks ago the old crone, Mrs Larcombe – lives in the end cottage – swears she saw flashing lights out at sea. Then another light flashing further west along the coast. Can't take her seriously.'

'Bats in the belfry?' suggested Butler, only half-listening.

'Hardly. Sharp as a tack. Local nosey parker. It was about the time that Portuguese ship, *Oporto*, was due to berth at Watchet.'

Butler frowned. 'Surely not at night – no ship could get inside Watchet except in broad daylight.'

'They said it missed the tide, had to heave to offshore all night.'

339

Butler nodded, said to Nield he was hungry. Time for dinner.

Paula arrived back at nine o'clock. She took off her raincoat, sagged into the secretarial chair behind her desk, kicked off her shoes. Monica said she was making coffee. Paula grinned. 'Bless you.' Tweed leaned back in his chair, studying her.

'You look all in – and you're still wearing those glasses.'

'So I am. I'd forgotten them. Thank the Lord I was wearing my flatties. That Jill Kearns has the stamina of a goat.' Waiting until Monica had left the room, she looked at Tweed quizzically. 'I'm sure you could have ended up in bed with her. She's ravishing. And she's after you. You do know that?'

'The thought crossed my mind. Don't push it. Give me a report. About her movements.'

'Window-shopping for three days. Didn't buy a thing. Went all over the West End . . .'

'She didn't spot you?'

'Of course not. I wore that beret I had on in Brown's, took it off from time to time. Switched round my reversible raincoat – every conceivable variation . . .'

'But did she at any time use a public call box?' Tweed asked.

'Definitely not. This evening she had early dinner – at Brown's. Then went up to her room. I thought it was time to return. To report to "Sir",' she added with mock solemnity.

'And that's it?' Tweed sounded disappointed.

'Except I found out she always stays at Brown's when she comes to town.'

'How did you discover that?'

'I chatted up the hall porter.' She looked at Monica who had come back with a tray. 'You're an angel.' She drank half her cup of black coffee, then gazed at Tweed. 'Now, what did you find – apart from the fact that Jill has wandering fingers?'

Tweed gave her a concise summary of his conversation with Jill. 'Well, did you notice anything interesting or significant she told me?'

'Robson's reference to the Greek Key,' Paula said promptly. 'I also spotted it's the first time we've heard any of the Exmoor trio mention Petros – linking him to the Greek Key. Surely that is significant?'

Tweed pursed his lips. 'Significant of what? But Robson seems to have changed his mind. On Nield's tape – recorded during their dinner talk that night at The Luttrell Arms – Robson scoffed at Barrymore's mention of the Greek Key.'

'And now he's linked Petros with it – whatever "it" may be.'

'So I simply must confront Petros – interrogate him – sooner or later.' He caught Monica's dubious glance and looked away. 'I have something else to do urgently. Monica, try and get Jill at Brown's for me. She could be in great danger.'

'Why?' asked Paula.

'She always stays at Brown's – you just told me. They'll know that on Exmoor and I've just heard all three ex-commandos have disappeared. That they may have come to London . . .'

He broke off as Monica signalled she had Jill on the line. He took a deep breath and began talking. She must pack at once, book a room at the Stafford Hotel in St James's Place, pay her bill and take a taxi there. Yes, tonight. At once. He put the phone down and sighed with relief.

'Thank God for a woman who does what you ask without questions.'

'Proves what I said earlier,' Paula remarked and winked at Tweed.

341

He turned to Monica. 'Could you play back that recorded talk I had on the phone from Minehead with Butler? Paula, listen carefully to what he says.'

Paula rested her elbow on her desk, cupped her chin in her hand, concentrated. Butler's cool voice came through loud and clear. As the tape ended Tweed asked his question. 'Anything strike you as interesting – bearing in mind that jumble of clues Masterson sent me in a cigar box from Athens?'

'Nothing. I must be thick. And I'm tired and hungry. So what did I miss?'

'Probably nothing, as you said. It was a wisp of an idea I had. I wanted to see if it hit you in the same way. And I'm taking you out to dinner. Monica has stuffed herself with sandwiches – fortunately.'

'Wild exaggeration,' Monica protested. 'But I have eaten. And why "fortunately"?'

'Because I want to locate Barrymore, Robson and Kearns. May, Robson's sister, let slip he'd gone to London. Start phoning hotels. Those three will be together.'

'What makes you so sure?' Paula asked. 'Before I pop along to the bathroom to fix my face. I feel a wreck.'

'Because those three have stuck together for years – trapped by the past and their fear it may come back. They're haunted men.'

'The two murders forty years ago? You think they were all involved?'

'I doubt that,' Tweed replied. 'Put yourself in their places. I suspect two out of three are wondering which of them committed the murders. I also suspect the guilty man is cleverly manipulating the other two. Listen again sometime to the tape recorded by Nield at The Luttrell Arms. Now, hurry up – I have a raging appetite too!'

He went on talking as he put on his Burberry after Paula had gone to the washroom.

342

'We'll wait a week or two longer before I fly to Greece – wait and see if anything breaks. Newman and Marler will be pretty active out there. Their rooting around may provoke someone to make a false move, to surface. There's something going on we've missed. I sense it.'

'Take-off time coming,' Monica observed. 'Your usual method. First gathering all the data – which can take ages. Suddenly it will be all action. I'm starting already. What kind of hotel might those ex-commandos be staying at?'

'Not Claridge's or The Ritz.' Tweed had his eyes half-closed as he thought. 'One of them stole the present-day equivalent of a million pounds in diamonds after killing Andreas. So he won't throw it around, show he's loaded. Try the hotels in the medium-priced range. Maybe somewhere in Kensington.'

'You don't ask much, do you?' She was reaching for the yellow pages when Paula reappeared. 'This job could take forever.'

'You may get lucky. We must try,' Tweed said as he opened the door for Paula. 'One more point. From now on we'll codename the murderer Winterton, the ghost who sold those bungalows on Exmoor.'

31

Moscow. General Lucharsky was walking in the park again with his aide, Colonel Volkov. Both men wore civilian clothes and Volkov had to quicken his pace to keep up with the long strides Lucharsky was taking. The sunlight cast thin shadows from the trunks of birch trees. Mothers pushed prams with babies along the lower path as

Lucharsky headed for a dense copse of trees, mounting a curving path.

'You leave for Athens tomorrow,' he reminded Volkov.

'I am fully prepared, Comrade General . . .'

'I should hope so,' Lucharsky snapped as they entered the copse. 'Everything depends on your passing on the verbal orders to Colonel Rykovsky, to Doganis and Anton, the Greeks. Events are moving quickly. I hear the Gorbachev–Reagan summit will take place in Washington. More important, the British Prime Minister has invited the General Secretary to land in England en route for America. A stroke of incredible luck.'

'What is the position now?' Volkov enquired.

'Gorbachev has gone too far. He is signing a treaty in Washington for the withdrawal of intermediate missiles from Europe. If we let him do that he will go on for more disarmament. The Red Army's power will fade instead of growing. And we have some powerful allies. Elements high up in the KGB are worried. They yearn for the return of the days of Brezhnev.'

'So it is something drastic?' Volkov suggested as he pushed aside foliage from his pasty plump face. The path they were following was getting overgrown, was rarely used.

'Gorbachev will be assassinated,' Lucharsky announced in his calm clipped voice. 'The Troika took the decision last night.'

'That will be difficult, and who will take over? What is this Troika?'

'A lot of questions, Comrade. First, you remember that document I handed you yesterday when I was wearing gloves? An incriminating document.'

'Yes.' Volkov felt a chill crawl up his spine despite the humid heat which enveloped Moscow that day.

'I put it in your safe after you had read it. I locked the safe and said I would keep the key. You do recall this?'

Lucharsky asked in a mocking tone which had reduced subordinates to jelly. 'I only check your memory because you had drunk a lot of vodka.'

'At your urging . . .'

'I am a good host, although I stick to mineral water since the new General Secretary's expression of dislike for hard drinking. That document – locked away in your own safe – carries only your fingerprints. You would be shot within a week if that document was placed before the Politburo.'

'Why do you threaten me, Comrade?'

'Just in case you thought you could obtain swift promotion by betraying the Troika which, officially, does not exist.' Lucharsky stopped, faced his companion, gave him a Siberian smile. 'Of course we know you would never dream of betraying us. Now, you asked certain questions. Who will take over from Gorbachev? Answer: Yigor Ligachev, his Number Two in the Politburo. He has openly disagreed with *perestroika* and *glasnost*. He does not know what we plan, but once the seat is vacant he will be compelled to become the new General Secretary.'

'And the Troika?'

'The three-man council of high-ranking Red Army officers who have decided Gorbachev must be removed. I am their liaison with the men in the field who will do the job.'

Which was a lie. No point in letting Volkov know that Lucharsky was the top man among the three generals who made up the Troika.

'But who will carry out the assassination?' pressed Volkov, anxious to know the plan would really work.

Lucharsky folded his arms, swung again on his heels, staring through the foliage which surrounded them. On no account must they be observed. And Volkov's anxieties were transparently clear to the General. He must reassure him for the moment.

'The assassination will apparently be carried out by two Arab fundamentalists. Those fanatics are capable of any

345

mad action. And relations between Moscow and Iran are deteriorating. That way we avoid any danger of a confrontation with the Americans – in case rumours spread it was the work of the CIA. We need the time to establish Ligachev in power, to turn back the clock to Lenin's age. To renew the great military build-up.'

'Arab fundamentalists? That is clever,' Volkov agreed.

'So tomorrow you travel with the instructions inside your head to Athens,' said Lucharsky, resuming his walk over the path encumbered with undergrowth. 'Doganis is controlling the operation – although he doesn't know what is really involved.'

'And what does he think he's getting out of all this?'

'A shrewd question, Comrade. We have hinted at support for a new Communist uprising in Greece. Doganis sees himself as a future Prime Minister. It won't happen that way, of course.'

'But, Comrade, I speak no Greek,' Volkov protested.

'Which is why you are chosen. While at the London Embassy you perfected your English. Doganis speaks the same language.'

'Everything has been thought of,' Volkov remarked, impressed by the efficiency of the planning. Then something struck him. 'I don't see how British security – which is good – will be penetrated? What weapons will be used?'

'No more questions.' Lucharsky increased his pace. 'But I can tell you the special weapons needed are at this moment on their way to their destination. Now I leave you, as last time. Go to your mistress's apartment. That gives you a reason for sneaking into Moscow if you are recognized. Give me five minutes to get back to my car.'

He turned round before leaving the copse, stood looking down at Volkov. 'And don't forget that document plastered with your fingerprints, locked away in your own safe. The KGB would not treat you with kid gloves – not after reading that document. *Bon voyage*, Comrade . . .'

Lucharsky emerged cautiously from the trees, standing to glance round like a man enjoying the warmth of the sunshine. Then he hurried back to his car parked in a deserted side street. It stood outside the block which contained the apartment of a well-known general he knew to be on holiday at a Black Sea resort. A further precaution – just in case a KGB patrol noted down the registration number.

Once inside the Chaika, Lucharsky took a pouch from his pocket, selected a specially designed tool. It took him only five minutes to turn back the odometer fifty kilometres. His chauffeur logged all journeys and recorded the precise distance. There was now no record he had ever made this trip from the barracks.

Everything has been thought of. Volkov didn't know the half of it. Lucharsky had earlier decided that after Gorbachev had been eliminated all his collaborating subordinates would go the same way. Rykovsky and Volkov would die in a helicopter crash over the Caspian Sea. Florakis would be ordered to take out Doganis and the other members of the Greek Key. Then Lucharsky would send someone from Moscow to liquidate Florakis.

Yes, everything had been thought of.

Kalos took the call at police headquarters the following day when Sarris was absent from his office. It came from the chief of security at Athens Airport.

'That you, Kalos? Stefanides here. Your target just arrived. Colonel Volkov. In person.'

'Hold him till I get there. Make out you've received threats against Russian personnel. That you're bringing in a bullet-proof limo from Athens. I'll fix that before I leave. Hold him.'

'Will do. See you . . .'

Kalos followed the limo, driving an unmarked police car

himself. It took forty minutes to reach the airport. Damned hot, Kalos thought as they arrived. Late afternoon. Like a furnace. He watched Stefanides escorting a stocky man clad in a pale grey lightweight suit to the limo. He had thick black hair, was clean-shaven, a pair of large rimless glasses very like those Gorbachev wore. In many ways he was like a pocket version of the General Secretary. And his face was pasty and plump – making him stand out as a new arrival. An easy man to follow.

Kalos watched a porter dump two suitcases in the boot, started his own engine as the boot was slammed shut. The limo glided away along the main road into Athens. Kalos followed.

Destination: the Soviet Embassy. As Kalos had expected. He parked the Saab behind another car, settled down to wait. Kalos was good at waiting. He watched Volkov disappear inside the building, followed by the chauffeur carrying the bags. Ages would now pass while Volkov conferred with Colonel Rykovsky.

Kalos radioed in to his assistant at police headquarters that he was on surveillance, that it might take all night. There was no request for information as to where he was. Surveillance meant secrecy. And he didn't want Sarris to know what he was up to. Yet.

Twenty minutes later Kalos had a surprise. Two men emerged and started walking down the street towards him on the far side. Volkov had changed into a linen suit, wore a straw hat. The glasses and the walk confirmed to Kalos it was Volkov. They were smarter than he'd anticipated. Never underestimate the enemy: Sarris' favourite maxim.

The second man, also short but slimmer, wore a similar linen suit and a peaked cap favoured by German students. A beak of a nose with a dark smear of a moustache, neatly

348

trimmed, a man who made quick gestures with his hands. Colonel Rykovsky.

They hailed a passing taxi, climbed inside. Kalos waited until he saw the taxi moving in his wing mirror, did an illegal U-turn, tracked the taxi. In Omonia Square they paid off the taxi, gazed into a department store's windows. Not normal behaviour. Kalos felt a glow of satisfaction as he pulled into a parking slot which a woman had just vacated.

The two Russians moved slowly along the pavement, stopping to stare inside another window. Rykovsky glanced over his shoulder, scanning the street. Kalos was slumped behind the wheel, eyes almost closed. A taxi stopped, dropped a fare and both Russians moved.

As Volkov climbed into the rear Rykovsky gave the driver his instructions and followed his companion. The taxi pulled out into a gap in the traffic. Kalos grinned to himself as he turned out, one vehicle behind the taxi. Who were they going to meet so secretly was the $60,000 question.

Inside ten minutes the taxi entered the Plaka, driving slowly, wending its way amid the labyrinth of twisting streets. The two Russians alighted outside a taverna. *Papadedes*. That made sense, Kalos thought, as he watched the couple disappear up a staircase alongside the taverna. Papa made a nice income on the side out of that first-floor room sealed off from the taverna.

He rented it out at exorbitant prices to Athenian businessmen who took their mistresses there. The room was nicely furnished, including one of those sofas you could convert into a bed. Papa also supplied his clients with drinks – at only four times the price charged in the taverna.

Kalos turned into a side street, parked his car on the one-man wide pavement and the cobbled street. He felt in his pocket. Yes, he had the compact Voigtlander camera

349

he always carried. He got out, took up a position in a doorway where he could see the staircase entrance.

Something serious was going on. Why couldn't they have had their meeting inside the Soviet Embassy? That puzzled Kalos. And he was damn sure Volkov had disguised himself. OK, it was pretty warm. And the Russian had just flown in from Moscow. But that straw hat had been well pulled down over his face – and they'd spent very little time outside.

He was about to light a cigarette when he stiffened, reached for his camera, the unlit cigarette clamped between his lips. A tall heavily built figure was strolling towards the taverna. The Fat Man. An open-necked shirt, clothes hanging loosely from his body. Doganis. Senior member of the committee that controlled the Greek Key.

Kalos raised his camera, cupped inside his hand, waited. Doganis stopped suddenly, turned on the pavement, a woman collided with his huge bulk. He ignored her as he glanced down the street the way he'd come. Then he plodded on in his large trainer shoes, paused again to look back in front of the staircase entrance as though not sure of his whereabouts. Kalos took three quick shots as the Greek swivelled his outsize head. Full-face, profile – and behind him the name over the taverna. Then Doganis vanished. He'd slipped up the staircase towards the room where the Russians had gone. For a large man he moved with great agility.

Kalos pocketed the camera and frowned. He was disturbed. This looked even more serious than he'd suspected.

Inside the expensively furnished room Doganis stood gazing at the two Russians who sat at a highly polished English antique round table. A tray – brought up by a waiter from the taverna before anyone had arrived – stood on the table.

350

Two bottles of vodka, three cut glasses. Both men had a glass in front of them.

Doganis nodded to himself. Free of the anti-alcohol restrictions imposed by Gorbachev, they were indulging themselves. The slim supercilious Colonel Rykovsky stood up to make introductions. Doganis shook hands with Volkov, squeezing his hand in a vice-like grip. The Russian had trouble avoiding grimacing at the pressure.

'Vodka?' Rykovsky offered.

Doganis shook his head, lowered his bulk into the third chair at the table. He wanted a clear head dealing with these goddamn Russians who had let down Greece in 1946 during the Civil War: they had not supplied the weapons needed. Later the US President, Truman, had sent a military mission, arms by the ton. That was what had defeated them. Rykovsky remained on his feet, downed the full glass of vodka, and explained.

'I am leaving you now with Colonel Volkov,' he continued, speaking in English. 'He has a long message to give you. It must be transmitted by Florakis to Jupiter tonight. The first part, that is. The signal is so long it has to be divided into three parts – sent on three successive nights. You have a good memory?'

'You know I have,' Doganis growled, his large paws clasped on the table-top. 'Get on with it.'

'Volkov will tell you where one section ends, the next begins. When he has passed on the complete message Volkov will leave. Give him five minutes. Then go yourself, drive at once down to Cape Sounion. Florakis will be expecting you. I have already phoned him. I am now returning to the Embassy to call him and confirm you are coming. He will wait for you at that site where they are constructing a new hotel complex. You know it?'

'I do.'

'They have stopped work on it for the moment. Something to do with waiting for fresh materials.' Rykovsky waved an elegant hand. 'The main point is the complex is deserted. When you get back to Athens, call me at the Embassy. Use your normal codename. Simply tell me you have found a further supply of mineral water – despite the shortage owing to this infernal heatwave. Remember, all calls are monitored, recorded . . .'

'I know that.'

'And get down to Cape Sounion as soon as you can. Florakis will need time to code the message. Understood?'

'Yes.'

Rykovsky told Volkov he would see him back at the Embassy later. He was leaving when he turned back.

'Doganis, you do have transport to drive to Sounion?'

'My car is parked a quarter of a mile away. I know what I am doing.'

Rykovsky nodded, bit his lip, decided to say no more. The Greeks were a touchy lot. He was glad to get out of the room. Doganis was glad to see him go. He turned to Volkov. 'I am listening.'

The stocky Volkov knocked back another glass of vodka, saw the Greek's expression and refrained from refilling his glass.

'This is the message. I will say it slowly. There is a lot to remember. The first part concerns furniture vans . . .'

Kalos took two photographs of Rykovsky as he hovered at the exit from the staircase, looking to left and right. The Russian then walked briskly away to the left. Doubtless searching for a taxi. In his notebook Kalos noted down the precise time, as he had done when Doganis had arrived.

He was growing more puzzled. That left the gross pig, Doganis, upstairs with the new arrival to Athens, Volkov. Most peculiar. It was half an hour later before a second figure appeared. Volkov. He walked straight into the street in the same direction, straw hat rammed down concealing the upper half of his face. He stopped suddenly, lifted the hat as he stared round. Kalos took two more shots, waited until Volkov had disappeared, noted down the time. He had been precisely thirty minutes alone with Doganis. Most mysterious.

Unless he had been passing detailed instructions to Doganis – but why had Rykovsky not remained present? My God, Kalos was thinking: maybe Moscow doesn't even trust Rykovsky to hear what Volkov was saying. The cell system – carried to these lengths! The instructions must be incredibly secret.

Five minutes later, exactly, Doganis stood at the exit, lounging against the side, lighting a cigarette, scanning the street. A real professional, the overweight slug. Kalos risked it, took another photograph. Without a glance in his direction, Doganis walked off.

Kalos memorized the time, ran to his car, backed it into the main street, crawled after Doganis. That had been a difficult decision Kalos had wrestled with. Who to follow? Since they had met so furtively, he'd decided the Russians would probably return to the Embassy. You're my meat, he thought as he trailed after Doganis.

Kalos found he could drop back well behind his target. Among the tourists and locals crowding the Plaka Doganis loomed up among the other heads like a bear lumbering forward. He had parked his battered old Renault on an open stretch of ground. Kalos waited until he had eased his bulk behind the wheel and started moving. Then he followed him.

'Repeat the whole message back to me. Indicate where one section stops, another begins,' said Doganis.

'Get stuffed. I've memorized it perfectly,' Florakis snapped.

'Prove it.'

353

'I said get stuffed . . .'

The two men sat in the front seats of Doganis' Renault parked in the shade thrown by the skeletal structure of the new hotel complex. Florakis, wearing his shepherd's garb, cast a sneering glance at the bloated jelly beside him, reached for the door handle.

'I said prove it,' Doganis said in a quiet voice. 'That comes from the top. I have to tell them you've really grasped the message.'

'Play with yourself, you overblown melon . . .'

Doganis grasped Florakis by his arm below the elbow. He squeezed as Florakis swore and struggled to get free. There was a brief tussle, then Florakis' face twisted in agony. He was staggered by the strength of that fat man who he'd imagined was soft as a jelly. Doganis, with no expression, began to bend the arm. Florakis stifled a scream of pain.

'Now, let's try again, shall we?' Doganis suggested, releasing his grip.

'You stupid bastard,' railed Florakis. 'There's no feeling in my arm. And I have to tap out your bloody signal . . .'

'You're right-handed,' Doganis said mildly, gazing out of the window where an opening in the building structure framed the sizzling blue of the sea. 'I remembered that when I twisted your left arm. In any case, you'll be OK by nightfall when you do the job. Going to repeat the message? Word by word?'

'Blast you! Yes . . .' Florakis took a hold of himself, let his rage evaporate, then began reciting carefully.

'That's pretty good,' Doganis said fifteen minutes later. 'One more thing before you ride your donkey back to that cesspit you call a farm.'

'What's that?' Florakis asked sullenly.

'In future don't ever again forget I'm the boss. Now push off. I'll give you ten minutes to get clear before I drive back to Athens . . .'

Behind a boulder a short distance up the arid hillside under the scorching sun Kalos was watching. He peered through the field glasses he'd taken from his glove compartment. He'd followed Doganis all the way from Athens, keeping well back when he realized his quarry was taking the coast road.

He'd crested a hill with a clear view of the Temple of Poseidon atop Cape Sounion when he saw the Renault swing off the road behind the building site. Immediately he'd turned off the main road himself, jouncing over the rough ground into one of the many gulches which ended near the coastal highway. Parking his car well inside the gulch, he had climbed high enough to stare down at the site.

His glasses had brought up clearly the two men seated inside the stationary car. Kalos had recognized Florakis and he recalled finding the fingerprints which exposed Florakis' real identity. Oleg Savinkov: The Russian, The Executioner of the Civil War.

He waited until Doganis had driven over the crest on his way back towards Athens, then drove after him. He didn't expect to discover any new twist but he followed Doganis all the way back to the city. His eyes narrowed as he grasped that Doganis was heading back into the Plaka. He was even more startled when Doganis parked his car on the same open space and got out, then checked his watch and waited, lighting a cheroot. Kalos parked illegally in a one-way street and waited.

Thirty minutes passed before Doganis made his way on foot to the same street where he had arrived earlier in the day. Kalos guessed his destination was the room over Papadedes taverna and watched him disappear inside the entrance to the staircase.

Kalos parked his own vehicle in the side street he had used before. Standing in the doorway, he saw Colonel Volkov arrive five minutes later. He noted down the time below his record of Doganis' entering the building.

Very curious. This meeting was taking place without the presence of Rykovsky. He blinked and only took his camera out in time when a third figure walked down the street, paused by the entrance, glanced confidently around and vanished inside.

He wrote down the arrival time of Anton Gavalas. What the hell was going on?

32

'This is political dynamite,' Sarris snapped, staring at his assistant. He waved the file containing Kalos' report. 'We have to bury it. You want us both to lose our jobs?'

Kalos ran a hand over his stubble of hair, unperturbed by his chief's outburst. He clasped his hands and spoke with great deliberation, gazing out of the window where night was falling over Mount Lycabettus.

'Point One. We know Doganis is the most powerful figure on the so-called committee running the Greek Key. An organization of fanatical Communists which has lain fallow for a long time. In that file there is photographic proof that Doganis met with Colonel Rykovsky and the new man from Moscow, Colonel Volkov . . .'

'That's what I'm talking about,' Sarris protested. 'Our government hopes for closer relations with Russia now Gorbachev has proclaimed his policy of *glasnost* . . .'

'These people are not *glasnost*,' Kalos interjected in the same calm tone. 'They are hardliners – anti-Gorbachev. That swine, Pavelic the Croat, said as much to me when I was in Belgrade. He also let drop the name General Luch-arsky – who visited us last year as Colonel Gerasimov of the GRU. I stole his photograph from Pavelic's file when he was dead drunk. I followed him to the Hilton Hotel where he interviewed Florakis.'

'And now you've put Lucharsky in your report! I hadn't finished when you interrupted me. I don't make our government's policy. I think they may be a bit over-hopeful . . .'

'To the point of idiocy,' Kalos commented.

'Keep quiet. Our government hopes for more trade with Moscow. Maybe even sophisticated military equipment to make our army stronger than the Turks . . .'

'It won't happen. Let me go on,' persisted Kalos. 'Point Two. Rykovsky leaves Doganis alone with Volkov – which suggests even he is not permitted to hear some highly secret message from Moscow – from Lucharsky, maybe. Point Three. After that meeting I follow Doganis. To where? Another subversive rendezvous – this time with Oleg Savinkov, alias Florakis. Peter, this is a conspiracy I have uncovered.'

'That's an assumption . . .'

'And there is more – also backed up with photographic evidence in that file. Doganis drives back to Athens, to the same rendezvous in the Plaka. What happens now? Colonel Volkov arrives on his own – again Rykovsky is not privy to this clandestine meeting. Who else arrives? Anton Gavalas. Where does he fit in? He's supposed to be helping his crazy father – to locate the man who committed two murders over forty years ago. I repeat, it is a deadly conspiracy.'

'And I repeat I cannot show this to the Minister. He will blow his top.' Sarris softened his tone. 'Kalos, you know I'm right. If I thought there was the slightest chance the Minister would let us follow this up I'd hand him the file.'

'You're the boss.'

Kalos sat, motionless, still gazing out of the window. He

knew Sarris had judged the situation correctly. He was frustrated beyond belief. Sarris rose from behind his desk, took the report out of the file, separated the photographs.

'Kalos, I'm sorry about this. It really is to protect you as well as me.'

He went over to the shredding machine. Kalos watched impassively as Sarris fed in the photographs, then the typed sheets Kalos had produced on his own typewriter. A mess of shredded fragments showered into the plastic bag. The job done, Sarris sat behind his desk.

'I had no choice. Forgive me.'

'You are ordering me to cease my investigations?'

Sarris chewed his lower lip. 'I don't recall saying that. And you have an excellent memory. Just be careful, for God's sake. For ours . . .'

Kalos nodded, left the room and went back to his own office. He locked the door, went to his desk, unlocked a lower drawer and took out the duplicate file of the report Sarris had destroyed. There were also copies of the photographs: Kalos had developed them himself in his own dark-room in his apartment on the edge of the Plaka.

With the file tucked under his arm, he crouched down and turned the numbered combination on the door of his safe. Opening it, he used a screwdriver to prise open the slim secret drawer at the bottom. Dropping the file inside, he closed the drawer, shut the safe, spun the combination lock.

As he straightened up he thought how curious it was that Sarris had not asked him for the negatives: Sarris, who never missed a trick.

After witnessing the meeting between Doganis and Anton Gavalas, Kalos had again been faced with a difficult decision. Which of the two men to follow? They had left the building separately: Doganis had emerged first. Kalos let him go.

Ten minutes later Anton had appeared. Kalos had followed him. He was surprised when his quarry took a taxi which dropped him outside the Astir Palace Hotel on Sofias Avenue, only a short distance from the Grande Bretagne.

There was nothing else he could do about that so he returned to present his report to Sarris.

Inside his room Anton sat on the bed and dialled the number of Petros' farm in Devil's Valley. He had to wait some time before they made the connection with that remote area.

'Anton here . . .'

'You have found Christina?' growled Petros.

'Found her and lost her . . .' Anton explained briefly his experience earlier that day at the Hilton. He expected Petros to explode. Instead the old man said he needed a minute to think. Anton jumped in quickly.

'Isn't it time I returned to England? We should know what the commando killers are doing on Exmoor. This time I may find out whether all three were guilty – or whether it was only one of them.' He went on talking quickly. 'I have ideas for harassing them. As I told you, they already live in terror. They've barricaded themselves in their homes like men scared witless.'

'But we must find Christina . . .'

'Let those lazy sons-of-bitches Dimitrios and Constantine come back to Athens. She's here somewhere. All the idiots have to do is to bribe cleaning women, show them her photograph. Not approach the chief receptionist like that cretin, Dimitrios, did. Which is more important?' he pressed on. 'Tracking down Christina or tracking down the killer of your sons? I could be in England in a few days. This time I will be more aggressive.'

The word 'aggressive' decided Petros. He liked the sound of that. It appealed to his temperament. It was how he went about problems.

359

'Very well,' he said. 'When will you leave? You have plenty of clothes?'

'Probably tomorrow. And I packed a case before I came to Athens. In any case, I have money. Keep Dimitrios and Constantine down there for two days, then kick their asses, send them, tell them they can't come back until they've found her.'

Splendid, Petros thought. Anton was becoming more like himself every day. Very aggressive.

'You can use the special route to England you mentioned?'

'Absolutely.' Anton was standing up now, his voice vibrant with confidence. 'Don't worry if I'm away for a while. This time the job must be done . . .'

Anton put down the phone, realized he was sweating profusely. It wasn't the heat – although the room felt like an oven. He had managed to persuade Petros, the old fool, to agree. Now he was ready to carry out the orders Volkov had passed to him.

Anton was pleased so much responsibility had been heaped on him. It augured well for the future. He saw a top Cabinet post in a Greek Communist government in his grasp. Who knew? Maybe one day he would be Prime Minister.

Extracting a Swissair timetable from his case, he sat down, checked flight times. Flight SR 303 left Athens at 5 p.m., arrived at Zurich 6.45 p.m., local time. He needed a late flight: there was some more work to do before he left Athens in the morning. He turned the pages.

From Zurich another non-stop flight, SR 690, departed Zurich at 12.10 p.m., reaching Lisbon in Portugal at 1.55 p.m. Again local times. That meant spending only one night in Zurich. He always stayed at top hotels: with luck he'd find some willing married woman on her own to spend the night with.

Anton was careful with women. The married ones, away

360

from their husbands and out for a fling, were safest. No comebacks. No risk of some annoying entanglement. He checked the dates in his diary. His memory had served him well.

The freighter, *Oporto*, was not due to sail for several days. Then it would leave Portugal with its holds full of cork, bound for the Somerset port of Watchet. Later it would return with a load of wastepaper.

Plenty of time to get in touch with the skipper, Gomez. To warn him this time there would be a special cargo as well as himself. And to call Jupiter at the agreed time to have someone ready for the rendezvous at sea. The phone number, he felt sure, was a public phone booth. Most important of all, time for him to contact the arms dealer in Lisbon, to collect from him the special weapons which would go aboard the *Oporto*.

Anton called room service. 'Send me up a double Scotch. No ice. No lemon. Plus a bottle of mineral water.'

He sat down, tired from the concentration. Now the only remaining task was to contact Professor Seton-Charles at his seminar at the Hilton in the morning. He'd go along as a student. Pass on the instruction Volkov had given him for the Professor.

33

Seton-Charles had held three seminars for Greek students over a period of two weeks. Newman and Marler had taken it in turns to monitor his movements. The seminars were held in a conference room inside the Hilton. They were advertised on a board in the vast lobby, giving the whole two-week programme. Subject: The Greek Civil War, 1946–1949.

The tension was rising between Newman and Marler. Security on Christina had been tightened up to the hilt: they had learned from their experience at the Hilton. Well-disguised, a scarf concealing her hair and wearing her outsize tinted glasses, she had registered as Mrs Irene Charles at the Grande Bretagne.

Booked into a suite, she stayed there. All meals were sent up by room service. Newman kept her supplied with books and magazines. 'This is marvellous, Bob,' she told him one day. 'The first real rest I've had in years – and I'm reading like mad . . .'

To keep up their watch on Seton-Charles, Newman and Marler had very little sleep. They exchanged surveillance duty at the Hilton; one staying with Christina, the other eating and keeping an eye open at the Hilton. Marler complained after a few days of this ritual.

'I feel locked in. I'd like to be outside, trying to find more data on what happened to Harry Masterson. Maybe take a trip to Cape Sounion, see what's going on down there.'

'Feeling the heat?' Newman grinned as he used a sodden handkerchief to mop his neck.

'No. You're the one who can't stand it. Doesn't affect me.'

'I can stand the waiting better than you can,' Newman told him. 'We're doing what Tweed asked. Checking on Seton-Charles and guarding Christina.'

'And as far as we can tell the Professor hasn't gone outside the Hilton. Which is pretty weird. Maybe he uses the phone in his room.'

'Not for any calls we'd want to know about. He'll know they'd go through the hotel switchboard.'

'So maybe he sneaks out in the middle of the night.'

'I have a feeling any message will be smuggled to him

362

by someone attending one of those seminars. Probably he doesn't like the heat. He looks the type. I saw him go outside once and he came straight in again, glad to return to the air-conditioning. Patience, Marler.'

'You know where you can stuff that. As for waiting, you spent your life waiting as a foreign correspondent. Mostly holding up bars, from what I've heard.'

'Which shows your ignorance,' Newman rapped back. 'I was moving about, searching for fresh contacts. Time you got back to the Hilton. Don't fall asleep . . .'

'Up yours, chum.'

They had been drinking mineral water at the Grande Bretagne bar. It was eleven at night: Newman had come back sometime after he'd seen Seton-Charles go up to bed. He mopped his sticky hands when Marler left. It was going to be another torrid night.

They had booked two rooms at the Hilton. Whoever was on duty stayed up until he was pretty sure Seton-Charles had retired for the night. He then waited another two hours, sitting in the lobby. Just on the off-chance S-C reappeared. Then he went to his room, set the alarm for five o'clock. After taking a shower, he put out his outfit to wear in the morning. Which meant the man on duty fell into bed at about 2 a.m. For three hours of sleep. No wonder the relationship – never good at the best of times – was growing strained.

It was Newman who spotted Anton Gavalas attending the final seminar eleven days later.

Christina had shown him a group photograph. Petros flanked by his family at the farm, occupying the central position, sitting on the veranda.

'Looking like God Almighty,' Christina had remarked venomously. 'Dimitrios and Constantine are there – on either side. As you see, I'm relegated to the outside – the proper position for a female. And that . . .' She had pointed to a slim man standing with his hand on Petros'

363

shoulder. '. . . is Anton. Petros' favourite, the smooth bastard.'

Newman borrowed the photograph. He showed it to Marler at the first opportunity, pointing out Anton.

'Cocky-looking sod,' was Marler's only comment.

Eleven days later Newman was 'on duty' at the Hilton. He had eaten breakfast in the ground-floor restaurant, sitting four tables away from Seton-Charles who was looking limp from the heatwave.

Now he sat in the lobby on a couch close to the entrance to the conference room where the third and final seminar was taking place in half an hour's time. Newman wore a short-sleeved shirt, open-necked, a pair of loud check slacks. He was smoking a cigar, reading the *New York Times*. He looked like one of the many American tourists staying at the hotel.

Students – men and girls – began arriving, standing round, chatting. Age range: sixteen to twenty-five, Newman estimated. Some carried briefcases, others clutched files. Newman stretched out his legs, crossed them at the ankles. He wore green socks decorated with white diamonds, a pair of loafers.

Seton-Charles arrived in his shirt-sleeves, a pair of creaseless powder-blue slacks. Newman puffed at his cigar, glanced up as he turned to a fresh page. For a moment he glanced at the Professor, who looked down at him. Behind the rimless glasses perched on his Roman nose eyes as hard as diamonds skimmed over the seated man. Newman had a shock.

This was the first time they had looked straight at each other. The first time Newman had noticed those eyes. You're a cold-blooded bastard, he thought.

Then Seton-Charles was leading the students inside the conference room. Like a shepherd leading lambs to the slaughter. Why had that thought entered Newman's mind? He settled down, then glanced up again as a latecomer arrived, hurrying inside the conference room. Newman froze inside as the slim, smartly dressed man passed him. Anton Gavalas . . .

He stood up and wandered to a seat on the far side of the lobby. Startled as he was by Anton's appearance, Newman still noticed what else was going on.

A moment after the Greek had disappeared he observed a man who had been lingering outside the entrance come into the hotel. A small stocky man who reminded him of a dormouse. The newcomer also took a seat against the wall, settled himself, crossed his fat legs and began reading a Greek newspaper.

Newman forgot about him as he sat down to wait. He'd have given a lot to be an invisible witness to what was happening inside the conference room.

When Anton walked into the seminar the students were sitting down in the rows of chairs facing the dais where the Professor stood behind a table, arranging papers in neat piles. He paused, Seton-Charles looked up, Anton walked across the room and mounted the dais.

'Good morning,' he whispered. 'Jupiter has sent me with information . . .'

He had been going to say 'instructions', but then he looked at the eyes behind the rimless glasses. No sign of recognition. Ice-cold, they seemed to assess him at a glance. Anton began to wonder how high up in the power structure this man might be.

'Take a seat in the back row. Record a few things in this notebook. Make sure you're still here when the last student has left.'

The back row was empty. Anton sat down, perched the notebook he had been given on his knee, took out his gold Parker pen and listened as Seton-Charles began to lecture.

Seton-Charles was a natural orator, reminding Anton of newsreels he'd seen of Hitler. He started slowly, then worked himself up to a pitch of fanaticism, waving his arms. When he stopped the students applauded vigorously, then filed out. Anton pretended to make more notes until they were alone.

He stood up, approached Seton-Charles, who was gathering up his papers and stuffing them into a file. Again Anton mounted the dais. The Professor's hair was dishevelled from his oration and he was sweating profusely from his efforts and the heat.

'Yes?' he said without looking up.

Anton felt it was important to address this man respectfully. 'You are requested to catch Swissair flight 303 today to fly to Zurich. It departs at 5 p.m. Then tomorrow you fly on to London and return to Exmoor. That is the message.'

'That means they have managed it,' Seton-Charles said, half to himself.

He looked up and stared at Anton as though photographing his appearance on his memory. Anton felt he dare not ask what they had managed, who they were.

'So you are not surprised, I shall be on the same flight,' he explained.

'I shan't even notice you. Hadn't you better go now? At once . . .'

Anton flushed at the tone of curt dismissal. Without another word he left the room. His feelings were a mixture of fury and fear.

In the lobby Newman watched Anton leave. He wished he could have followed him. But his task was to keep up the watch on Seton-Charles. Tweed had made that very clear.

Newman observed the quick short steps Anton took as he crossed the marble floor and left the hotel.

He lowered his eyes to his newspaper when out of the corner of his eye he saw movement. The dormouse-like man had folded his newspaper, shoved it inside his pocket and was also leaving. It looked very much as though he had Anton Gavalas under surveillance.

Outside the Hilton Anton climbed into a cab, slammed the door. Kalos ran to his Saab parked a few yards away and dived behind the wheel after unlocking the door with one deft movement.

He followed the taxi into the traffic, his bead-like little eyes gleaming with interest. The route was back along Sofias Avenue, past the British Embassy, and round Syntagma Square. The taxi returned to the opposite side of Sofias and Anton paid the driver, disappearing inside the Astir Palace Hotel. The same place where Kalos had followed Anton after his rendezvous at Papadedes.

Several days earlier Kalos had decided a piece was missing from his report. He had phoned the Astir Palace and obtained confirmation that Anton *was* registered at that hotel. He could hardly use a false name: he was too well known in Athens.

Since then Kalos had endured a long vigil patiently. Anton had stayed inside day and night – until this morning. Now a fresh link was established – of a sort. Anton had a connection with one of the students attending the seminars; maybe even with the crazy-looking Professor Seton-Charles. The latter seemed unlikely.

Parking his car, Kalos wandered into the vestibule of the modern-looking hotel, a black glass block which did not fit in with the more traditional surrounding architecture. He arrived in time to hear Anton giving the receptionist instructions in Greek.

'I shall want my bill ready immediately after lunch. Then

367

you must arrange a car to get me to the airport by 3.30 p.m. The car must not be late.'

'Of course not, Mr Gavalas,' the receptionist assured him. 'I will deal with everything myself . . .'

He tailed off. His guest had walked away, was heading for the elevators. Kalos pursed his lips, wondering where Anton was flying to. Well, he would be there in good time to find that out.

In his room Anton called room service, ordered a large Scotch. The plane was leaving at 5 p.m. but he had deliberately arranged to arrive at the airport very early. The last thing he wanted was to bump into Seton-Charles.

Anton, a ruthless, hard man, had met some tough characters during his wanderings as a youth. But there was something about the Professor which disturbed him. The man reminded him of a cobra.

In the late afternoon Newman was driving a hired car towards the airport. He had seen Seton-Charles collect a travel folder from the reception desk in mid-morning. The Professor had returned to his room, reappearing for lunch. When he stepped out of the elevator he was carrying a case which he deposited with reception.

Newman had phoned Marler, phrasing his message carefully over the hotel phone. 'I'm tied up. Urgent business suddenly cropped up. Be with you this evening. Can you hang on there?'

'My pleasure . . .'

Arriving at the airport, Newman parked two vehicles behind the taxi Seton-Charles was travelling in. He stood behind him in the queue for checking in, heard the Professor being booked aboard Swissair flight 303 to Zurich, left the queue. Tweed must be informed at once.

Leaning against a wall, Kalos watched, took a quick picture of Newman. Earlier he had done the same thing when Anton arrived. Anton was flying to Zurich. Why? He waited until the queue had evaporated, approached the check-in girl.

'That Englishman with the thinning brown hair, rimless glasses. Where is he flying to?'

'I'm afraid we can't give out information . . .'

Kalos placed his police identity card in front of her, waited.

'Oh, I suppose that's different.' She hesitated, Kalos waited.

'He's a Professor Seton-Charles,' she said. 'First-class seat on Swissair flight 303. Departs 5 p.m., arrives Zurich 6.45 p.m.'

'Thank you,' said Kalos.

He thought about what he had learned as he drove back to police headquarters. Anton had arrived three-quarters of an hour ahead of Seton-Charles. A trick. Kalos was certain the two men were collaborators: they had taken the precaution of not appearing to know each other. They'd sit in different sections of the plane to keep up the masquerade. But Anton had attended the Professor's seminar.

He tapped his fingers on the wheel as he waited at a red traffic light. What the hell could he do now to find out where they had gone? Then he had an idea. Switzerland . . .

Arriving in his office, Kalos locked the door before he made the call to Berne, capital of Switzerland – and headquarters of the Federal Police. He was lucky. Arthur Beck, chief of the organization, was in his office.

Kalos spoke tersely, explained what had happened, gave details of the flight. He described both Anton and Seton-Charles. Could Beck help?

'Something to do with drugs?' Beck enquired, still speaking in English.

'Could be,' Kalos replied non-committally.

'I'll go myself,' Beck decided. 'Anything to help Peter Sarris. I have time to get a chopper from the local airport, Belp, fly to Kloten Airport outside Zurich. I'll be there to watch the passengers disembarking. Which is most important?'

'Anton,' Kalos said after a moment's thought. 'Maybe you will call me back. Sarris is up to his ears.'

'Consider it done,' Beck replied and broke the connection.

Kalos put down the phone. Sarris had no idea what he'd started, and Kalos had no intention of letting him know. If it all blew up in his face, Sarris could disclaim all knowledge of what his assistant had been up to. As he began to record the latest details in his secret file Kalos was worried. Had he been right to give Beck priority in watching Anton?

34

'Newman here, speaking on the Embassy phone. Can you hear me?'

'Very clearly, Bob,' Tweed assured him. 'What's happened?'

'Seton-Charles is on his way back to England. At least, I assume he is . . .' He gave an account of his recent discoveries, including the appearance of Anton.

'You're probably right,' Tweed agreed. 'He's a devious so-and-so. Remember how he tried to make sure he wasn't followed to London Airport on his way out. My guess is he'll catch another flight back here tomorrow. At least that means you only have to guard Christina. One of you can start poking around again. How are you and Marler getting on?'

'Like two long-lost brothers.' He nearly added, 'who hate the sight of each other,' but kept his mouth shut. 'First I'm going to have another talk with Christina about Anton. Do you really need both of us to stay on in this inferno?'

'Yes. If you can stand the heat.' Tweed paused. 'You see, when the right moment arrives I'm flying out there. I may need back-up. I must grill that scoundrel, Petros.'

'Be it on your own head. He's got armed shepherds patrolling the whole area.'

'We'll cope. Keep in touch . . .'

Tweed sat back and looked at Monica and Paula. 'One bit of good news. Anton still seems to be floating round Athens. I didn't like the idea of that Greek on the prowl over here. And Seton-Charles is probably on his way back to Exmoor. I sense things are hotting up. Monica, warn Butler at Porlock Weir about the Professor possibly returning. Maybe at long last we're getting somewhere.'

The grim news reached them the following day.

In her room at the Stafford Hotel Jill Kearns checked herself in the mirror. Her bedside clock registered 6.25 a.m. She eyed herself critically, fiddled with her single golden plait. That would have to do. And how many people would be about at this hour? Not the point, she thought: never appear in public except at your best.

She was wearing a form-fitting pale green sweater, a white pleated skirt and flat-heeled shoes. Just the outfit for her early morning walk before breakfast.

A girl of firm routines, she always walked on the moor every morning before breakfast. Always left the house at precisely 6.30 a.m. Stuart, for some unknown reason, found her routine irritating. 'Should be in the bloody Army,' he'd told her. He never accompanied her; at least he hadn't for the last few years.

She said 'Good morning' to the hall porter and went out of the hotel, turning left into St James's Place. No one else about, thank God. It was a fresh morning, was going to be one of those rare fine days with the sun shining and the warmth on your face.

Reaching the end of the deserted street, she came out into St James's Street. Again no one in sight. Only a Jaguar parked by the kerb a score of yards further down the street, facing her way, the engine ticking over. She took a deep breath and made for the pedestrian crossing.

She was half-way across it when she heard the Jag coming. It had started moving the moment she stepped off the pavement. She glanced to her right, then froze in horror. The car was driving straight at her.

She began to run, taking a diagonal course to cross the whole street. Glancing again over her shoulder as she reached a point just midway across where a side street opposite entered from St James's Square, she had a glimpse of the driver behind the tinted glass.

He wore a chauffeur's cap pulled well down over his head and a pair of tinted goggles like motorbike riders affected. She ran faster, thanking her lucky stars she was wearing her flat-heeled shoes. The Jag was turning now, coming at tremendous speed.

The radiator slammed into her, lifted her whole body and threw it against the railings of a basement area on the far side of the street. She twisted under the immense impact. Then her lifeless body lay sagged against the railings. Blood from her smashed jaw flowed down over her green sweater, spreading like a lake.

The Jaguar picked up more speed, vanished in the distance as it turned into St James's Square. Suddenly it was very quiet.

35

'You're not going to like this.' Monica, who had rushed into Tweed's office, paused for breath. In her hands she clutched a copy of the *Evening Standard*.

'You're back early from lunch,' said Tweed as Paula jerked her head up from the file she was studying.

'It's awful,' Monica went on, sinking into her seat. 'I know how you liked her.'

'What is it?' Tweed asked, very alert.

'It's in the stop press. A Mrs Stuart Kearns, staying at the Stafford Hotel, was killed by a hit-and-run driver early this morning.'

'Show me.' Tweed's tone was bleak. He read the item, looked at Monica. 'Let's get this in the right sequence. Which hotel did you track those three down to? Something like a theatre.'

'Barrymore, Kearns and Robson are staying at the Lyceum Hotel. A modest place just off the Strand, close to Trafalgar Square.'

'And it says here the so-called accident occurred in St James's Street. Not very far from the Lyceum. Phone up the place. I want to know if they're still there.'

He stood up, shoved his hands inside his jacket pockets, began pacing up and down close to the window, his brow furrowed.

'They've checked out,' Monica told him as she put down the phone. 'All three left mid-morning. No forwarding address.'

373

'Get Chief Superintendent Walton of Special Branch. Urgently.'

'Why did you say "so-called accident"?' enquired Paula.

'Because I don't believe it. Jill Kearns had all her marbles. That newspaper item says it happened before seven in the morning. How much traffic is about at that hour?'

He broke off to take the call. 'That you, Bill? Tweed here.'

'You on scrambler? Good.' Walton's voice was its normal buoyant tone. 'Are you still forging my Special Branch identity cards in that Engine Room? I don't know why I let you get away with it.'

'You supplied the original model for copying,' Tweed reminded him. 'We agreed total secrecy could only be maintained if we did the job. And if anyone queries one they'll be put through to you.'

'Someone has queried one,' Walton warned him. 'Recently. A Colonel Barrymore. I told him you belonged to my department, that he'd better answer any questions you put to him. Very supercilious, he was. Plummy-voiced type. Now, what can I do for you?'

'Early this morning a Mrs Stuart Kearns, staying at the Stafford Hotel, was killed by an alleged hit-and-run driver. There's a stop press in the *Standard*. I think it was murder. I'm going to give you details of three possible suspects. They were staying last night at the Lyceum Hotel off the Strand. I'd like you to phone Chief Inspector Jarvis of Homicide at the Yard. Warn him, but don't mention me.'

'Why not?' Walton enquired. 'You and Bernard were pals during your old days at the Yard.'

'Because I need to maintain a low profile. Here are the details, including the addresses of the three men. Incidentally, they've left the Lyceum . . .'

He read out where Barrymore, Robson and Kearns lived on Exmoor. Walton said OK, he'd call the Yard. Say he'd had a tip from a very reliable source. And they must have lunch one day.

'What are you up to?' asked Paula when Tweed had finished the call.

'Pressure. I want maximum pressure put on those three. It's possible one – or all – of them will break. Though I doubt it.'

'You really think they ran down poor Jill?'

Tweed began cleaning his glasses with his handkerchief. 'It's a long coincidence. The morning Jill is killed the three of them are staying at a hotel about half a mile away.'

'But you moved her to the Stafford for safety – and they only knew she always stayed at Brown's. How could any of them have found her?'

'I'm afraid I blundered. I may even be responsible for her death. By mistake, anyway. I think she was being watched during that afternoon I went to Brown's for tea. Someone got frightened of what she might have told me. I suspect I was followed when I walked up Albemarle Street and didn't notice.'

'That's ridiculous,' burst out Monica. 'You always check . . .'

'On the other hand,' Paula said quietly, 'I was following her for three days. I could have been spotted. And I was with Tweed when he visited all three men on Exmoor.'

'Pure surmise.'

Tweed dismissed the idea with a wave of his hand. Secretly he was pretty sure she was right. But it was not something he wanted on Paula's conscience.

'Then,' Paula continued, 'they would have seen her change her hotel to the Stafford. And I bet that was a morning habit of hers on Exmoor. To stroll over the moor. Always at the same time.'

'Forget it!' Tweed snapped. 'We have to decide what to do next.'

'What do you suggest?' asked Monica.

She sensed an atmosphere of depression in the room. Worse, a mood of guilt that one – or both – of her colleagues had caused the killing of Jill Kearns. Paula had sunk into a brooding silence, so unlike her normal buoyancy. It was Tweed who changed the mood.

'We take action. Monica, call The Anchor at Porlock Weir. Tell Butler – or Nield – to call me back urgently. He'll know what that means – use a public phone box. I want to find out if Barrymore and Co. have returned to Exmoor. Then we'll move.'

'How?' asked Paula, lifting her head.

'You and I will drive down there at once. Partridge was murdered on Exmoor while those three were there. Jill was murdered in London – while they were here. I'm going to ask each of them a lot of tough questions.'

Monica was already dialling The Anchor. She spoke for a short time, then put down the phone. 'Both of them are out,' she told Tweed.

'Keep trying at intervals until you get one of them. I want to be at their throats before they've had time to settle in.'

Monica nodded. Again she didn't like the vehemence with which Tweed had spoken. If he'd still been a Chief Superintendent at Scotland Yard in Homicide, they'd have taken him off the case. Too much personal involvement.

Zurich. Arthur Beck could pass in the street for any profession. Except that of Chief of Federal Police. In his mid-forties, he wore a light blue business suit, a cream shirt, a blue tie which carried a kingfisher emblem woven into the fabric. Plump-faced, his most prominent feature was his alert grey eyes beneath thick dark brows the same colour as his hair.

He sat alone in an office at Zurich police headquarters with a window overlooking the River Limmat, the university perched on the hill rising steeply from the opposite shore. Lifting the phone, he dialled Kalos' number. The Greek answered quickly.

'Beck here. I have some data on your Anton Gavalas. Ready?'

'That was quick. It was only yesterday. Go ahead.'

'Anton disembarked from the Athens flight, caught a taxi to the Hotel Schweizerhof which faces the main station. He had early dinner, then wandered down the Bahnhofstrasse to the lake. He sat on a seat watching the boats come and go. No one approached him. He made no phone calls from the hotel – I found that out after he'd left.'

'Left for where?'

'Let me tell you in my own way,' the Swiss said precisely. 'I checked with the porter after he'd returned from his walk. He went straight to bed. This morning he has a leisurely breakfast. Again, no one approached him. Then he leaves by cab for Kloten Airport, where he arrived. A model citizen, Mr Anton Gavalas. Always well-dressed. Walking down the Bahnhofstrasse he could be mistaken for a Swiss – except for his dark suntan.'

'What happened next?' Kalos asked.

'He produces a first-class ticket, checks in his luggage for the SR 690 flight bound for Lisbon . . .'

'Lisbon?' Kalos sounded surprised.

'Lisbon in Portugal,' Beck continued genially. 'The 12.10 p.m. that reaches Lisbon at 1.55 p.m. That's Portuguese time. Which means you can alert someone in Lisbon to meet the flight if you wish. End of report.'

'I'm very grateful.' Kalos paused. 'It almost sounds as though you followed him everywhere yourself.'

'But I did. My dear Kalos, when you're trapped behind a desk in Berne most of the time, reading files, it does you good to get out on the streets again. Stops you getting rusty – your mind going to sleep.' He added the last bit in case Kalos' English was not up to the colloquialism.

'I really am grateful,' Kalos repeated. 'I owe you one.'

'Indeed you do. But that's for the future. Good hunting . . .'

In his Athens office Kalos put down the phone and mopped his forehead. The heatwave was getting worse. There was a real shortage of mineral water.

Lisbon? Kalos was baffled. He added the data to his secret file. What could the connection be? And he had no way of checking, no link with Portugal he could use without Sarris' cooperation.

36

Anton landed at Portela Airport, changed a sum of Swiss franc high-denomination banknotes into escudos, the local currency. He never used traveller's cheques while moving about secretly: they left a trail which could be followed. Inside the taxi he opened his case, used the raised lid to conceal what he was doing from the driver.

Inside the suitcase was an executive case crammed with Swiss banknotes. He had been handed this by a woman who visited his room at the Schweizerhof in Zurich. An incident Arthur Beck had no chance of observing; the woman had reserved her own room at the hotel for the night.

Anton collected the equivalent of £5,000 in escudos, tucked the bundle into an envelope. He then counted out the equivalent of £10,000 in Swiss banknotes, transferred them to a second envelope and put them in another pocket. When he closed the lid, the executive case contained £100,000 in Swiss notes. He looked out of the window.

Lisbon was a galaxy of colour-washed houses: pink, blue, green and all of them pastel shades. The side streets were narrow and twisting. He paid off the driver outside the Ritz Hotel.

Speaking perfect English, he registered under the name Hunter, using the forged passport Doganis had supplied for his previous trip. The Portuguese were strict about examining passports. Inside his room he checked the time and ordered mineral water from room service. He would need a clear head for coping with the arms dealer.

He ate a quick dinner in the restaurant, keeping an eye on the time. It was still light when he took a taxi to Cascais, a resort and fishing village on the coast. The air was sultry, but nothing compared with the burning heat of Greece. He paid off the taxi on the promenade, found a cheap clothing shop and bought a large fisherman's pullover, a pair of trousers. His feet were shod in trainer's shoes which fitted him comfortably. Footwear was important: you never knew when you would have to move fast.

Checking the time again, he walked along the front, the package of wrapped clothes under one arm, the other holding the executive case which was well-worn and had a grubby look. He found a *fado* café which was crowded, went inside, sat at a table and ordered a glass of wine which he paid for.

He drank half the glass, asked the waiter for the washroom, disappeared inside it. He locked the door of the cubicle, undid the parcel. Within a minute he had pulled the trousers up over his own pair and donned the turtle-necked pullover. Flushing the toilet, he stuffed the wrappings behind it and walked out carrying the case.

He made a point of finishing the glass of wine, standing at the table as people pushed past him. The place was a babble of voices with a background of mournful *fado* music.

Personally, Anton preferred the *bouzouki*. He checked the time once more.

He walked along the front and it was dark now. Lights sparkled in the clear air, the Atlantic rolled in, threw its gentle waves on the shore. Carlos, a gnarled wiry fisherman, was waiting with his boat moored, a lamp shining in the tiny wheelhouse.

'Mr Hunter,' he greeted, 'my wife had your phone message, passed it to me.' Clambering ashore, he pointed. 'Everything is with us when you need.'

He was pointing at a donkey cart half-filled with hay, a donkey between the shafts and fastened to them with traces. Anton frowned, put his free hand on the animal's shoulders. The head peered round.

'She has to carry a weight,' he commented. 'And also stay by herself for some time.'

'She is good. You take the cart. Look at wheels. She carries weight. When you come back I take you with cargo to *Oporto*.'

'The freighter is at the harbour now? Gomez is expecting me?'

'All is ready, Mr Hunter. We take cargo aboard in the night. The *Oporto* sails when the sun rises. One day from this day. Sails for England.'

'Here you are, Carlos. I'll be back later.' Anton handed him the envelope containing £5,000 in escudos. 'Don't open that envelope until you're inside the wheelhouse. And turn down the lamp.'

'I'll do that. All the time God gives us. I nearly do not know you in those clothes . . .'

Anton led the donkey cart along the front back the way he had come. He had no trouble controlling the animal. He'd had a lot of experience in handling the creatures on Petros' farm. The main thing was that it was docile.

From the cafés he was passing came more *fado* music, the voices of men and women who had consumed large

380

quantities of wine. It was not a night when anyone was interested in what was happening on the deserted front. Arriving at a narrow side street, he guided the donkey across the road, parked it outside a shop which sold swimwear and which was closed. Just beyond was the entrance to the dimly lit Rua Garrett. The address Volkov had given him.

He left the bright lights and plunged into Stygian darkness as he picked his way over the uneven cobbles of Rua Garrett. One place was still open, double doors thrown back. He strolled past it, glancing inside. A big place with a cracked concrete floor – a service garage on one side, a ship's chandler on the other.

His glance showed him a gloomy cavern lit by oil lamps. On the garage side a car was perched on an elevated platform about a foot above a service pit. He walked in when he was satisfied only one person was inside.

'Mr Gallagher?'

'That's me. What do you want?'

'I've come to collect the merchandise, the type with a sting in its tail.'

'So, you're the one? Brought the money?'

'Of course.'

Gallagher was six feet tall and broad-shouldered. He spoke with an American accent. In his late thirties, his manner was offhand and he moved silently. Like a big cat. Anton studied the insolent expression, the restless eyes. The arms dealer was not a man Anton liked the look of. Still, he had come prepared.

Gallagher held out a large hand. He made the universal gesture with thumb and forefinger.

'I'd like to see the colour of your money first.'

'That is reasonable.'

'Wait! We need a little privacy for our business transaction.'

He walked over to the wall, pressed a switch and the

double doors closed automatically. The place was not so down at heel as Anton had thought. Sealed inside the cavern, the stench of petrol and oil grew stronger. Anton laid his case on the table, unlocked it, raised the lid and stood back. While Gallagher walked back to the case and picked up bundles at random, riffling through the banknotes, Anton hoisted his pullover a little higher.

'Just how much is here?' Gallagher demanded.

He had the flattened nose of an ex-boxer, a mass of untidy hair the colour of ripened wheat, a hard jaw. His pale eyes watched Anton, waiting for an answer.

'One hundred thousand pounds in Swiss francs. The agreed price in the agreed currency. For three Stingers. Plus six missiles.'

'Price just went up,' Gallagher informed him. 'Law of supply and demand. Been a heavy call for Stingers. IRA, Angolan rebels, Iranian nutcases. People like that. £145,000 is the going rate. Take it or leave it.'

'But the price was agreed,' Anton protested coldly. Volkov had been very clear on that. 'Your reputation rests on keeping to a deal once concluded.'

'Grow up, buddy boy. I said the going rate is the price. You can't raise it? Get lost.'

'I didn't say I hadn't got that much,' Anton replied. 'Since you insist, I'll pay it. But first I want to see the weapons.'

'You need to go to the bank?' Gallagher pressed, arms folded. 'Or is it in there?' He nodded towards the case Anton had shut and relocked. 'You came ready for the bad news? *I heard it on the grapevine,*' he sang the old melody and then laughed.

'I hid more money in the Rua Garrett earlier,' Anton told him. 'You'll never find it – but it's within a hundred yards of where you're standing. Now, show me the weapons.'

'Good to do business with a gentleman.' Gallagher grinned and walked back to the bank of switches and buttons on the wall. He pressed one and the elevated platform supporting the car rose up four more feet. The arms dealer lowered himself into the pit, pressed a switch which illuminated the darkness. Against one wall was a large canvas bundle. He unstrapped it, rolled back the canvas with care, exposing three Stingers and six missiles. He looked up.

'Satisfied?'

'Bring one up, plus one missile. No – take the middle ones in each case.'

'Leery sort of bastard, aren't you?'

Gallagher placed a Stinger and a missile on the garage floor, hauled himself up. 'Show you how it works.' He grinned again. 'You get value for money here. It's shoulder-launched by one man. Weighs only thirty pounds. It has a hundred per cent hit rate – mainly due to its infra-red heat-seeking system, plus its amazingly accurate aiming system. You fire in the direction of the aircraft and leave it to do the rest – home in on the target. God knows how many Soviet fighters it's wiped out back in Afghanistan. Take hold of it.'

Anton balanced the weight in both hands, surprised at its lightness. It looked like a mobile telescope with a wide muzzle at the front tapering to a slimmer barrel resting on his shoulder. To his right as he held it was a large rectangular plate. He peered through the aiming system.

'This is how you load it,' Gallagher said, inserting a missile. 'Don't pull the trigger or we'll both end up as red goulash.'

'I want a demonstration,' Anton remarked as he handed back the weapon. 'Don't argue. For £145,000 I'm entitled to check the damned thing works . . .'

Gallagher had driven them in his Volvo station wagon into the hills. Leaving Rua Garrett, Anton had noted the donkey still stood patiently with the cart where he had parked it; it looked as though it would stay there all night.

Gallagher pulled up at a lonely spot overlooking the sea. Getting out, he grasped the Stinger and the single missile concealed under a travelling rug. They picked their way past a cactus grove and Gallagher halted at the top of a cliff. Out at sea a lone fishing vessel was returning to port, navigation lights twinkling. Gallagher handed weapon and missile to Anton.

'There's your target. There's always one comes crawling back late.'

'I don't understand.'

'That fishing vessel. Get on with it. It's about two miles away. How far will your target be in the air?'

'Less than two miles. I still don't understand . . .'

'Oh, for Christ's sake! The missile is heat-seeking. That boat has a boiler in the engine room. Aim straight for it.'

'Won't there be an enquiry?' Anton inserted the missile, raised the Stinger, cuddling it into his shoulder. 'The police might start searching – when they realize what did it.'

'Except they won't. A month ago a similar fishing vessel blew up – the boilers they use are ancient as these hills. It will be recorded as another case of inefficient maintenance. They don't bother that much round here.'

Anton aimed at a point well below the wheelhouse. He squeezed the trigger, the missile left the launcher, curved in a low arc above the Atlantic at such speed he didn't see its flight. A dull boom echoed in the humid night. The fishing vessel turned into a pillar of flame after a brief flash. The flame died fast.

Lowering the Stinger, Anton gazed at the smooth surface of the sea. The fishing vessel had vanished. He lifted the Stinger, peered through the aiming device. He could see no trace of any wreckage.

'Satisfied?' Gallagher demanded. 'If so, let's get back to the garage.'

'How many in the crew?'

'Roughly half a dozen. Plenty more where they came from . . .'

'Drop me at the entrance to the Rua Garrett,' Anton told the arms dealer as they drove along the front. 'I have to bring my transport.'

'That the transport?' Gallagher enquired as Anton, carrying his executive case, alighted by the donkey cart. 'You'll get a long way with that. And I bet I know where you hid the balance of the money. In that mess of a hillside at the end of the street.'

'And you could search for years and never find it. See you at the garage. Don't wrap the merchandise until I'm there.'

'Anything you say, buddy boy . . .'

I don't think he's American at all, Anton was thinking as he led the donkey cart into the side street, following the Volvo. Under the accent, the over-use of American slang, he had detected traces of some unidentifiable Mittel-European language.

He left the donkey cart outside the open garage doors. Inside Gallagher had lowered the elevated car back over the pit. A careful man, Mr Gallagher. Anton continued down the dark tunnel of the narrow street.

He'd noticed when he first arrived that at the end the street stopped where a steep hill rose, its slopes covered with undergrowth and trees. He found a narrow path twisting up and followed it a short distance. Crouching down, he unlocked the case, lifted the lid.

He took a number of bundles of banknotes and stuffed them inside his pockets until his pullover bulged in an ugly manner. This would appear to be the extra money. He locked the case, made his way back down the tortuous path, walked back to the garage.

'Looks like you're going to have a baby,' Gallagher commented.

He stood by the control panel, pressed one switch, watched the garage doors slowly close, pressed another and the platform elevated above the service pit. Anton put the case down on a table, hoisted his pullover a few inches as he asked the question casually.

'Supposing I want to come back and ask you a question tomorrow. About the operation of the Stingers. You'll be here?'

'No. Anything you want to ask, ask now.' He lowered himself into the pit. 'I'll be away for a week in another country. A fresh deal.'

'Your regular customers – for servicing cars – will be pleased.'

'They know me. The doors are closed, I'm not here. Give me a hand. Take these, put them on that big table, the one with the sheet of canvas.'

When the three launchers and five missiles were laid on the top of the table, Gallagher hauled himself out of the pit. He towered over Anton. He spent the next ten minutes working rapidly, wrapping each launcher and missile in polythene sheets; then he arranged them on the large canvas already spread out. Rolling up the canvas, he fetched some straps and began securing the bundle. 'You can start relieving yourself of that money,' he suggested.

Anton pulled out the bundles of banknotes, laid them in stacks on the table-top. Gallagher was fastening the last strap when the Greek stepped back to pick up the case he'd stowed under the table. Gallagher had his back to him, stooped over the canvas-wrapped weapons.

Anton took out a handkerchief, blew his nose, kept the handkerchief in his hand, grasped the handle of the commando knife inside its sheath fastened to the belt under his pullover. He drew it out, stepped forward and rammed it with all his strength into Gallagher just below the left shoulder blade. Gallagher gasped, made a muted gurgling sound and slumped forward across the table.

'You really should keep to an agreed price,' Anton said.

Anton used two of the straps as makeshift handles to carry the canvas bundle to the donkey cart. At that, he staggered under the weight which must have been between a hundred and fifty and two hundred pounds. And Anton kept himself fit.

He dropped it into the cart and moved the hay to conceal the weapons. He hauled large handfuls close to the bundle, which caused it to sink, then dumped the hay on top. It took him a good five minutes to complete the job. Returning to the garage, he repacked the stacks of banknotes in the case, locked it and buried it under the hay.

Half an hour later he was leading the donkey along the deserted front. The cafés and discotheques were going full blast. From open windows the sound of guitars being strummed, of girls singing *fado*, drifted. At least it guaranteed an empty waterfront.

He had acted quickly clearing up the garage behind closed doors. Gallagher's dead body had been heaved into the pit. Anton had found an oil-stained canvas sheet to cover the corpse. Then he had pressed the button and lowered the elevated platform. He had doused the three oil lamps. Fortunately the control panel was near the doors: he had pressed the switch and dived into the street before they closed.

Carlos leapt on to the jetty when he arrived. Between them they lowered the weapons into his fishing boat. The Portuguese hid them under a pile of fishing nets. He wiped his hands on his trousers and looked at Anton, who asked the question.

'What about the donkey and the cart?'

'Will wait until I return from the *Oporto*. Then I go home. I saw a fishing boat out there die.'

'Sorry?'

'It blew up. Boom! They do not take care with boilers. I am careful. It is my living . . .'

'Has the coastguard gone out?'

It was an important question. Anton was thinking police launches might be prowling around.

'No.' Carlos spread his hands. 'They will not make the hurry. Maybe when the sun rises. Are we good to leave for the *Oporto*?'

'As soon as you can get under way . . .'

Anton felt relieved as he saw the shoreline receding. It would be a week before anyone started worrying about Gallagher's closed garage. That had been a bit of luck. As the boat chugged steadily towards the main harbour Anton wiped his forehead. They were away.

Gomez, skipper of the freighter *Oporto*, was well-organized. A short fat jolly man, he helped to bring the canvas-wrapped cargo aboard up a gangway lowered on the far side from the jetty where his ship was moored. Anton waited until Carlos was guiding his fishing vessel back to Cascais, then handed Gomez the envelope containing £10,000 in Swiss banknotes.

'The same amount as before. Where is the crew?'

'Below decks. I invented work for them when I saw Carlos coming. What they don't see, they don't know. Better I hide this in a safe place?'

'Very safe.' He knew Gomez would assume he was smuggling drugs. 'When do you sail? I have to complete some business.'

'At dawn the day after tomorrow.' He checked his watch. 'It is eleven-thirty. Yes, not tomorrow, the day after. That is OK?'

'Perfectly.' Anton, holding his executive case, decided to take it with him. He had to return to The Ritz, act normally, sleep there, have breakfast, then pay his bill. 'I would prefer it if I could slip aboard tomorrow and stay under cover until you sail.'

'What time? Your cabin is ready now.'

'Probably about midday. You can time arrival at our destination as you did when you took me before? At eleven o'clock at night? Again someone will be waiting to take me ashore.'

'There is a problem.' Gomez, his weatherbeaten face making him look more like sixty than forty, scratched his head. 'Last time I told the harbourmaster at Watchet we had engine trouble. Ah! I have it. This time, after you leave us, we will steam back a way down the Bristol Channel, turn round, and berth during the morning.'

'I'm counting on you.'

'Of course. You will be put ashore at Porlock Weir just as you were before.'

37

'I've never seen anything like this place,' Tweed said as they walked out of The Anchor. He had Paula on one side, Butler on the other. 'It's fascinating. A tiny world on its own.'

Tweed had driven down with Paula to Porlock Weir after he had warned Butler they were coming. 'Book us two rooms at The Anchor,' he had told Butler. 'I want to avoid The Luttrell Arms in Dunster this time. The idea is to surprise Barrymore and Co. You said they've all returned to Exmoor?'

Butler had confirmed the three men had arrived back the previous day. As they left The Anchor after a satisfying lunch he explained.

'Nield and I each have our own hired cars. We spent our time touring the whole area, checking for any sign of life at their residences. We split up, went to pubs to catch any gossip. It's common knowledge the three men took a trip away from Exmoor. You can't go to the loo down here without everyone knowing. Nield is out having another look-see.'

They crossed a narrow wired-fenced footbridge over seventeen-feet lock gates. A notice warned, *Closed Spring Tide*. Tweed paused, gazing at the oyster-shaped harbour behind the gates. Low tide. The harbour was a basin of sodden mud. A trickle of water ran under the footbridge out of the basin. Expensive power cruisers, moored to buoys, heeled over at drunken angles.

No one else was about as they followed a footpath past a small row of three terraced houses; all of them old, one with a thatched roof. Beyond, a shoal of pebbles led steeply down to a calm grey sea. Tweed stopped, taking in the atmosphere.

He looked back at the gabled hotel which was combined with The Ship Inn. Gulls drifted in the overcast sky, crying mournfully. Behind the coast the hillside, covered with dense trees, climbed. To the west the rocky coast stretched away and everywhere was a feeling of desolation.

'A quiet hideaway,' Tweed commented. 'Like the end of the world.'

'That reminds me.' Paula sounded excited as she delved inside her handbag. 'I found this in a pocket in my suitcase when I was packing to come down here. A brochure I picked up at The Luttrell Arms.'

She handed him a coloured brochure headed *Take*

the West Somerset Railway to Minehead. Below was a picture of an old-fashioned steam train. He opened it up and looked at the map inside as Butler peered over his shoulder.

The steam train started at Minehead, ran along the coast through the port of Watchet and later turned inland over the Quantock Hills, ending at Taunton. It began running on 29 March and shut down for winter on 29 October.

'*Endstation*,' said Paula. 'That clue Masterson gave you inside the cigar box he posted from Athens. He was drawing your attention to that old privately run railway.'

'And which is *Endstation*?' Tweed asked. 'Minehead or Taunton?'

'No idea. Don't you think I'm right?'

'Maybe.' Tweed folded up the brochure, handed it back to her. 'Hang on to it. It goes through Watchet, I see. The port where Anton probably came ashore from that Portuguese freighter.'

'Except he didn't,' Butler said. 'I checked that out. A two-storey building looking straight down on the harbour there is Customs and the harbourmaster. I followed him into a pub and got chatting. Told him a cock-and-bull story about how a friend had boasted he'd come ashore from that freighter without being spotted. The harbourmaster said bullshit. They keep a sharp lookout for suspicious characters trying to sneak ashore. It's this drugs problem. He was a solid ex-seaman type. Said it was impossible. I believe him.'

'Another theory gone down the drain. Let's wander west along the coast a bit. Looks pretty lonely.'

Butler led the way back across the footbridge and they walked down a road a short distance. It stopped abruptly and they had to pick their way across a treacherous surface of pebbles and small rocks.

'It really is the end of the world out here,' Tweed remarked.

391

'Maybe that's what Masterson meant when he wrote *Endstation*,' Butler suggested. Wearing a thick woollen pullover as protection against the damp sea mist drifting in, he walked with his hands inside his trouser pockets. 'There's an old dear back in one of those cottages who says she's seen ghosts – and lights flashing late at night. The barman told me so I called on her. A Mrs Larcombe. In her late seventies, but sharp as a tack.'

'I don't think you're right,' Paula objected. '*Endstation* is one of those two terminal stations on that railway – Taunton or Minehead.'

'What's got into him?' Butler asked her.

Tweed was striding ahead, peering at the ground, his Burberry collar buttoned to the neck. He seemed totally absorbed in his thoughts.

Paula told Butler about the death of Jill Kearns. He listened as she explained Monica's anxiety about Tweed becoming obsessed. 'And now his mind is full of three deaths,' she went on. 'Masterson's, of course, and Sam Partridge and Jill.'

'Don't see how they link up. One in Greece, one on Exmoor, one in London.'

'That's what he's trying to do – link them all together. Drop the subject, he's coming back . . .'

'I found traces of a wheeled vehicle,' Tweed announced. 'In a patch where sand showed.'

'No vehicle would cross that terrain,' commented Butler.

'And on the way back, could we call on Mrs Larcombe if she's at home? I'd like a word with her . . .'

The cottage was built of stone, roofed with red tiles mellowed by the years. Swagged lace curtains draped the windows, the front garden was barely three feet wide but the lavender borders were trimmed and there was not a weed in sight.

Approaching the cottage, Tweed noted there was an end window facing west where he had walked. Butler raised the highly polished brass knocker shaped like a dolphin and rapped it twice. A nameboard on the picket gate carried the legend *Dolphin Cottage*.

A tall sharp-faced woman opened the door. Her nose was prominent, she was long-jawed, her eyes alert, her mass of hair grey neatly brushed. Butler spoke to her for a moment, then gestured for Tweed and Paula to enter. Mrs Larcombe led them into what she called 'the parlour', invited them to sit down and Butler made the introductions.

'What can I do for you, Mr Tweed?' she asked, seating herself in a chintz-covered armchair.

'I'm in insurance. No, I'm not trying to sell you any policy. I'm Chief Claims Investigator for my company. A holidaymaker called Burns disappeared here a few weeks ago. Last seen late at night walking that way.' He twisted in his chair, pointed west. 'We've had a claim on the basis presumed dead. Since no body has been found I'm puzzled.'

'Funny goings-on round here.' Her eyes glistened, bird-like. 'No one believes me. They think I'm seeing ghosts. I know what I saw and heard.' She sat more erect.

'Could you tell me a little more?' Tweed asked quietly.

'It would be a few weeks ago – about the time your Mr Burns disappeared. Can't fix it exactly. Yes, I can. About the time the Customs at Watchet practically took that Portuguese freighter apart. Didn't find anything except a lot of cork. The rumour was it was carrying drugs.'

'What did you see and hear?'

'Close to midnight it was. I don't sleep well. I was looking out of my bedroom window which faces the way you pointed. I saw a light flashing out at sea. Like someone signalling. Then another light flashing from the shore. There was a ship at sea, a fairish way out.'

'You had your bedroom light on?' Tweed enquired.

'No, I didn't. I'd got out of bed in the dark and put on my dressing gown. I know where all the furniture is. I had the window open. It was a sticky night.'

'This ship you saw – it had navigation lights? Which is how you came to see it?'

'No, it didn't. But my sight is very good. No glasses, as you see. I saw it as a vague silhouette. I thought that was funny. What you've just mentioned. No navigation lights.'

'And that was all?'

She stiffened. She wore an old-fashioned black dress with a lace collar pinned with a brooch. 'You don't believe me?'

'Yes, I do. Because your night vision would be good – since you hadn't put a light on. Was there something else?'

'I went back to bed, leaving the window open for some air. I fell asleep quickly. Then I was wakened by a noise. I felt fuddled but I got up again. It was the engine noise of some vehicle approaching – from the same direction. I thought that funny. No cars drive over those pebbles. By the time I got to the window it was passing my gate. No lights. I ran to the front window because the noise stopped. I was worried – it sounded to have stopped by my front gate. I made a racket opening the front window – the thing sticks. As I looked out the engine started and the vehicle disappeared towards Porlock.'

'Without lights?' Tweed asked gently.

'No. As it passed the harbour the lights came on. The red ones at the back and dimmed headlights in front. Then it was gone.' She leaned forward, her eyes shrewd. 'Could it have been your Mr Burns?'

'Possibly,' said Tweed. 'No way of telling for sure. Could you describe what sort of vehicle it was? Even in the dark?'

'An odd-looking beast.' She frowned with concentration. 'High up off the ground. Behind the cab it was squarish. At a guess, canvas-covered.'

'Colour?'

'Couldn't tell.'

'White or cream?' Tweed suggested.

'Definitely not. It would have shown up more. A darkish colour. No idea who was driving – I was looking down on it, you see.'

Tweed stood up, took his glasses case out of his pocket, fumbled, dropped it on the dark floral-patterned carpet. The room was dim. He put his hand behind him, stopped Paula searching for it. He almost knocked over a vase of dried flowers. Mrs Larcombe stepped forward, took hold of the case, handed it to him.

'You'll be lost without this.'

'Thank you. And thank you for giving us your time. Your help is greatly appreciated.'

'*You* do believe me then?' Mrs Larcombe asked as she stood up to see them out.

'Oh, yes, I believe you.'

'Well, I'm glad someone doesn't think I've lost my marbles . . .'

Paula waited until they were walking back to The Anchor before asking the question. 'What was that business about your glasses case? There was no need to take it out of your pocket.'

'A final test on her eyesight. My case is dark-coloured. Even I couldn't see where it had dropped – it merged with the carpet. Mrs Larcombe has exceptional eyesight.'

'What do you think she saw then?'

'Some kind of covered jeep or four-wheel-drive vehicle which could negotiate that pebble ground easily. Now I'm phoning Colonel Barrymore. He's first on the list for some hard interrogation. His reaction to my calling him will be interesting.'

Inside his room at The Anchor Paula looked out of the window while Tweed made his call. She had a view down over the road which ended a short distance to the west, and the harbour with the dried-up channel where the sea would come flooding in.

Tweed's conversation with Barrymore was brief. He spoke tersely and concluded by saying, 'Then I will call you back within the hour.'

'He says he has to try and cancel an appointment,' Tweed told her. 'I think he's up to something. Let's have some coffee sent up and review what we've discovered. Butler is taking a well-earned rest . . .'

He called back exactly one hour later. This time the conversation was longer. Tweed's manner was even more abrupt. He closed by saying, 'Very well, if you insist. It will save me time.'

He looked grim as he replaced the receiver. 'I was right – he was up to something. He's phoned Robson and Kearns and invited them to join him at Quarme Manor. We'll be confronted by the three of them.'

'Including Kearns? But surely he must be distraught so soon after the death of his wife?'

'We'll see, won't we?'

38

Colonel Barrymore did not bother to receive them. When they arrived at Quarme Manor the door was unchained and opened by Mrs Atyeo. She ushered them into the hall and then indicated the door to the study.

'They'se waitin' for you in there.'

'Thank you,' Tweed said pleasantly. Followed by Paula, he opened the door without knocking. They were seated round a large oak table in the bay window. Barrymore,

Kearns and Robson. The colonel had his back to the window with Robson at his left and Kearns on his right. Tweed instantly realized that the seating arrangement forced Paula and himself to face the light while the others had their back to it. An old tactic. Barrymore remained seated, launched his onslaught as soon as they were inside the room.

'I see you've brought that girl again. This time I won't have her taking notes. You sit there and there.'

'Paula Grey is my assistant,' Tweed rapped back. 'She will take notes of the entire interrogation.' He sat down and dropped his bomb. 'Now we are investigating four murders which may all have security implications.'

'Four? What on earth are you talking about?' Barrymore demanded in his most commanding voice.

'One, Ionides at the Antikhana during the war.' Tweed waited to see if anyone would correct him, say 'Gavalas'. Three blank faces stared back at him. 'Two, Andreas Gavalas on Siros when you made your commando raid. Three, ex-Chief Inspector Partridge here on Exmoor.' He paused.

Paula was watching Kearns. He sat very stiffly, motionless, and his face was drained of colour, chalk-white. Tweed turned to him.

'Four, your wife, Jill. My condolences.'

'She was knocked down by some hit-and-run bastard,' Barrymore protested. 'And that's pretty bad form to raise the subject – to call it murder is madness.'

'Then why is Scotland Yard investigating it as a case of murder?'

'How do you know that?' Barrymore snapped.

'I have contacts. I'm Special Branch. You know that. You checked up on the phone with my chief, Walton.'

Robson, wearing a loose-fitting brown shirt, a plain brown tie, the knot slack below his throat, and an old check sports jacket, stirred. He turned to face Barrymore.

'You didn't tell me that.'

'Must have slipped my mind,' the colonel replied curtly.

Robson tugged at his straggly moustache, turned back to face Tweed. His pale blue eyes studied him for a moment.

'What makes you think Jill was murdered?'

'A cleaning woman inside one of the St James's Street clubs saw a Jaguar waiting by the kerb with its engine running. The moment Jill started to cross the street the man behind the wheel headed straight for her. Cold-blooded murder.'

Tweed waited again. Before leaving London he had changed his mind, had phoned Chief Inspector Jarvis in charge of the case. No description of the driver worth a damn. The silence inside the room became oppressive.

Paula was studying Kearns. He sat like a statue. Not a blink of an eyelid at Tweed's statement. Years of iron self-discipline as a CSM, she thought. Never show your emotions however tough the situation. She felt Tweed was treating him inconsiderately.

'Why have you come to see us?' Robson asked, leaning forward, gazing at Tweed as though deciding on a diagnosis.

'Because you're all suspects, of course . . .'

'How dare you!' Barrymore burst out. 'Are you accusing us? And what evidence have you to base that slanderous statement on? I want an answer.'

'I'll give you one. You were all members of the commando raid on Siros. Andreas Gavalas was murdered. A fortune in diamonds he was carrying for the Greek Resistance was stolen. You were all based at the Antikhana Building in Cairo. You had returned from the raid. Ionides was murdered. You were all here on Exmoor a good few weeks ago. Partridge was murdered. You were all staying in London at the Lyceum Hotel – only a short distance from St James's Street. Jill Kearns was murdered. How much more coincidence do you think I can swallow?'

398

Robson laid a restraining hand on Barrymore's arm. He asked the question in the manner of a doctor enquiring about a patient's symptoms.

'Why do you think that Jill was murdered?'

'Because someone who knew she always stayed at Brown's saw me having tea with her. Whoever it was became worried she might tell me too much.'

'Stretching it a bit, aren't you?'

'Possibly. Until I link it up with the fact you must all have known she made a habit of staying at Brown's, that she made a habit of going out for a walk at that time every single day of her life. The killer followed her to the Stafford where I asked her to go, hoping to ensure her safety. Where were you all at 6.30 a.m. that fatal morning?'

Barrymore opened his mouth to protest. 'What damned impudence. I'll see you in hell before . . .'

'Best to reply,' Robson intervened. 'We all got up early – the habit of a lifetime. Goes back to Army days. By early I mean about 5.30 a.m. None of us have breakfast. There were tea-making facilities in the bedrooms. I spent my time packing, then studied some medical journals. No one to verify that.' His smile was wintry. 'Barrymore had gone for a walk – I know that because I went to his room and there was no reply. Kearns was also out walking. It was a fine day. Doesn't help a lot, does it?'

'Not a lot,' Tweed agreed. 'You were out for a walk, Barrymore?'

'You heard what Captain Robson said. I'm getting a trifle fed up with you . . .'

'And I'm fed up with the fact that my old friend, Sam Partridge, was foully murdered,' blazed Tweed. 'I'll move heaven and earth to find out who did that.'

Paula glanced at Tweed in surprise. She'd never known such an outburst during an interrogation. Then she saw the supercilious smile of satisfaction on Barrymore's face. He'd needled Tweed. She glanced back as Tweed began cleaning his glasses on his handkerchief and nearly sucked in her breath. Tweed had put on an act. She tensed: she was witnessing a duel between Tweed and the three men. Kearns spoke for the first time.

'That cleaning woman. Did she get a description of the driver? And what about tracing the owner of the Jaguar?'

'Stolen from outside a night club near the Lyceum Hotel where you stayed. Some fool of a yuppie got drunk, left the keys in the ignition, was persuaded to walk back to his flat in case he was stopped by the police.'

Tweed stood up and Paula closed her notebook, which carried a complete record of the conversation. Barrymore remained seated, his voice sardonic.

'You know your own way out. Mrs Atyeo will be waiting to lock up after you leave the premises. Don't come back.'

Tweed sat behind the wheel of the Mercedes where he had parked it in a lay-by twenty yards or so away before arriving at Quarme Manor. Butler, who had followed them from Porlock Weir, then waited, parked behind the Mercedes, appeared at Tweed's window.

'Next move?' he enquired.

'I want to ask Robson something on his own. His Saab is in the courtyard. Let's hope he comes out soon. You wait here. Then if Barrymore appears, follow him.'

'There's a better place for me to wait. I can back my car just a short distance and into a field. That way I won't be conspicuous if he comes this way.' Butler paused. 'Is it a good idea my leaving you? I'm the one with the gun.'

'It's broad daylight still. Not to worry. You back your car – and where is Nield?'

'No idea. We'll see him sometime at The Anchor when he's good and ready. Does Barrymore know where you're staying?'

'No. I said I'd phone him back when he wanted to call me.'

Paula stretched her arms to ease the tension out of herself as Butler left them. 'Did you get anything out of that interview? It was a bit fraught at times.'

'Two things you might have noticed. The absence of one of them asking a question. And someone else did say something.'

'And now you're going to leave me dangling. I'll ask you again. You think they're all in it together? Or just one of them?'

'Just one.'

'I'm too smart to ask which. Lord, it's getting darker.'

Earlier there had been hazy sunshine during their drive to the Manor. Now low heavy clouds were rolling in, obscuring the crests and higher slopes of the moor. It began to spot with rain on the windscreen. Then the Saab came out, turned in the other direction and drove off.

'We've got him,' said Tweed and followed as the Saab vanished round a bend. He drove slowly and when they reached Endpoint Robson had disappeared. The Saab was parked just below the terrace and Tweed gazed towards the Doone Valley. When he got out he stretched his legs, pacing up and down.

'Time to beard the lion in his den,' he remarked and they walked up the steep drive. It was very quiet, a silence Tweed felt pressing down on him. Then he stopped. The drive continued round the right-hand side of the bungalow. Parked next to the end of the building was a canvas-covered four-wheel-drive vehicle. Dark-coloured.

Robson's sister, May, opened the door, welcomed them inside and showed them into the sitting room. She asked them to sit down.

'Oliver is writing out his medical records in the conning tower. I'll just fetch him.'

'Conning tower?' Tweed asked.

'Well, I think it looks more like a lighthouse – the tower at the end. But Oliver calls it the conning tower. Back in just a minute.'

Her thick hair seemed even greyer in the daylight. She wore a flowered print dress over her ample form. On this second visit Tweed noticed she had the same pale blue eyes as her brother, eyes which had a remoteness about them.

Robson appeared quickly, gave his shy smile. He took out his pipe as he sat down and began to fill it with tobacco from an old leather pouch.

'Something else?' he enquired.

'Yes. Sorry to trouble you again – but it was Barrymore's idea I met all three of you at his place. Going back to that morning at the Lyceum Hotel, you said you went along to the colonel's room and he was out for a walk. How did you know he was out?'

'First there was a *Do Not Disturb* notice hanging from the handle of his door. He always does that when he goes out – very security conscious, our CO. That way any burglar will assume someone is sleeping inside. Don't bother myself.'

'You said "first". What else was there?' Tweed persisted.

'I wanted to ask him something. So I banged on his door to make sure. He's a light sleeper, like most Army types. He was definitely not there. You sound like a detective.' He smiled to take any sting out of his remark.

'I used to be one.' Tweed paused. 'With Homicide at the Yard.' Robson nodded and puffed at his pipe as Tweed continued. 'What did the three of you do the night before in the evening – after you'd arrived at the Lyceum?'

'Barrymore had some business to transact. Kearns and I went to Rules for dinner. The colonel joined us later.'

'And after your meal you did what?'

'Kearns and I went back to the hotel. Barrymore went for a walk. Said he felt like a breath of fresh air. He's a keep fit sort of chap.'

Tweed stood up. 'Well, thank you. Sorry to disturb your work.'

'That's all right. Do you mind if May shows you out? I've quite a workload to get through. There's a bug going round and I've been rushed off my feet. I make quick notes after seeing a patient. Then when I get the time I make a proper record. Ah, here is May.'

'I was going to ask if anyone would like coffee?' she said.

'They're just leaving. Perhaps you'd show them out . . .'

She accompanied them to the front door, Tweed said 'Goodbye,' and she closed the door.

Tweed walked down the steps off the terrace and strolled round to the end of the bungalow. Paula followed as he stood looking at the four-wheel-drive vehicle. Along the bodywork of the passenger seat side at the front was painted a word. *Renegade*.

'Can't be the same one,' Paula whispered. 'Mrs Larcombe would have noticed that word. It's in huge letters and painted white.'

'No, she wouldn't have done,' he observed, 'it's painted on the far side – the wrong side when she looked out of her window.'

'Can I help you?'

It was May who stood just behind them. Neither had heard her approach on the tarred drive. Tweed smiled and indicated the vehicle. 'We were just admiring it. In bad weather it must be a godsend.'

'Oh, that isn't Oliver's. He borrows it from Mr Kearns.'

39

Inside the isolated public call box near Simonsbath Seton-Charles pulled at his lips with his thumb and forefinger. He was waiting for the phone to ring, had been waiting a good ten minutes. Jupiter insisted he arrived in good time.

His car was parked off the road amid a clump of trees: an empty car left in the middle of nowhere in full view could attract attention. He looked round through the windows for the fifth time. The deserted road spiralled away up on to the moor. Mist curled down over the ridges. If the call didn't come soon it was going to be a difficult drive back to his bungalow.

He shivered. The chill seemed to penetrate the box. He felt the cold after his stay in Athens. He grabbed the phone when it began to ring.

'Clement here,' he said. 'Speaking from . . .' He gave the number of the call box, reversing the last two digits.

The voice began speaking immediately, the tone clipped, the accent upper-crust. No time wasted on greetings. Straight into the instructions.

'We need two furniture vans for the move. In Norwich there's a firm called Camelford Removals. Just gone bankrupt. Selling everything off. Purchase two vehicles, large ones. Pay in cash to save time. Store them in the barn at Cherry Farm in Hampshire. Make sure the doors are double padlocked. Two sets of keys. I want you to drive there tonight after dark. Put up at a hotel in Norwich.'

'I can't drive two vans back myself . . .'

'Think, man. Store one in a garage in the Norwich

area tomorrow. Drive the other to Cherry Farm. With a motorbike inside. Use the bike to get back to Norwich. Then drive the second van back to the farm. The bike is expendable. I want both vehicles at the farm two days from now. Camelford Removals' address is . . . Got it?'

'Yes,' said Seton-Charles. 'You're sure the vans will still be available? Not already sold?'

'My dear chap, the advertisement said they have six vans they want to shift. Bound to be at least two left, providing you're in Norwich first thing tomorrow. That's it . . .'

The connection was broken. Seton-Charles hurried back to his Volvo station wagon, backed it on to the road, started driving for his home on the bungalow estate.

He had no idea of the identity of the man who had called him. He thought the codename Jupiter rather pretentious, but driving along he realized Jupiter was a first-rate organizer. Now he'd drive to Norwich during the late evening, find a hotel. He'd have to park his Volvo in a lock-up, buy a second-hand motorcycle.

When he'd purchased the two furniture vans he'd park the motorbike inside one, then drive it to Cherry Farm, an uninhabited farmhouse he'd visited earlier. Next he'd ride the bike back to Norwich, collect the second van, drive it to the farm. Finally, he could use the bike to ride back again to Norwich to pick up his Volvo. The bike would be dumped in some convenient wood. Job done.

But what could Jupiter want with a couple of furniture vans? He couldn't even guess. But the operation – whatever it might be – was under way. And there had been a hint of urgency in the way he'd been given his instructions.

'Do go easy on Kearns,' Paula said as Tweed parked the Mercedes just short of Woodside House. 'Remember, his wife has just been killed.' She looked up. 'Good Lord, it's Pete.'

Nield leant on the edge of Tweed's window. He looked very tired. He winked at Paula and then spoke to Tweed.

'It's a small world, as they say. Seton-Charles has come back from Greece. I've been checking for days. He's just returned to that bungalow of his at the end of the cul-de-sac after making a covert phone call.'

'Covert?'

'I saw his Volvo parked outside his bungalow so I hung around. He has his own phone, as you know. So what does he do? Drives to a public call box near Simonsbath.'

'A long call?' Tweed asked.

'Let me tell it my way. I follow him. He hides his Volvo in some trees, walks into the box, then waits at least ten minutes.'

'That sounds like a professional. He has an arrangement to be at a certain call box at a specific time. Go on.'

'The phone rings. He snatches it. Conversation lasts precisely ninety seconds. Then he drives back here. His car is inside his garage. What do you think?'

'He bears watching.' Tweed looked closely at Nield. 'You've had a long day, I'd say.'

'Bit frayed. I could do with a sit-down and a half pint.'

'Then drive back to The Anchor now. If Seton-Charles put his car away it doesn't look as though he's going anywhere tonight. We'll see you for dinner. Go and relax.'

'Thanks. You're still prowling?'

'We're calling on friend Kearns. If he's home.'

'He is. I saw him ride in on his horse a while ago. I'll get moving . . .'

'Wait for that beastly dog to appear,' Paula said as Tweed pressed the bell-push beside the gates.

A light came on over the distant porch. Kearns came out slowly. He was carrying a heavy stick. He shone a

406

flashlight and the powerful beam reached the gate, blinding Paula. Tweed half-shut his eyes.

'No dog,' Paula whispered. 'Funny.'

'It's you,' Kearns greeted them. 'I suppose you'd better come in. I'd like it kept brief, whatever it is.'

'Of course,' replied Tweed.

They followed him carefully up the centre of the path, keeping clear of the rough grass and the mantraps it concealed. Kearns led them into the dimly lit hall. Outside it was twilight; dusk was gathering over the moors. Paula dropped her handbag, scrabbled on the floor and picked it up.

Tweed hardly noticed: he was thinking Kearns was getting careless about security. The inner heavy wooden slab doors had been open when they arrived; only the grille gates were closed. Where was the dog?

There was a sudden ferocious snarl from behind a closed door as Kearns passed it. A heavy thud, as though the Alsatian had hurled its bulk against the far side. Kearns hammered a clenched fist against the door.

'Shut it!' he growled.

The first sign of tension – of emotion – he had shown. He took them into the same dining room with the oak table and the panelled walls. Again the lighting was dim. White-faced, Kearns sat at the opposite side, gestured for them to join him on the far side.

'What is it now?' he demanded.

'I know this is a grim time for you,' Tweed began, 'but we need as much information as we can get about your wife's murder. And memory has a habit of fading fast . . .'

'You are convinced it was murder?' Kearns asked, his large hands clenched, the knuckles showing white. His brown marble-like eyes stared at Tweed.

'Yes, I think it was. It's not much consolation – but since the Yard is also convinced they'll do their best to hunt down the killer. An ordinary hit-and-run driver who's probably never caught can cause even more anguish.' He looked round the room. 'The place looks well looked after. Have you got someone in to help?'

'I've done it myself.' Kearns stiffened his back. 'I don't want any other woman inside the house now Jill's gone.'

'I understand. Incidentally, at Quarme Manor I gathered you went for an early morning walk the day you left the Lyceum Hotel. So did Barrymore – on his own. Did you by chance see him while you were out?'

'Strangely enough, no.'

'Why "strangely"?'

'Because,' Kearns explained, 'he always walks in St James's Park when we're in town. Which is where I went. No one else about at that hour. I didn't see any trace of him.'

'One more question, then we'll leave you in peace. I called in on Dr Robson while I was on my way here. He had a four-wheel-drive vehicle parked by the side of his bungalow. It's got the word *Renegade* painted on the side opposite to the driver's seat. Said he'd borrowed it from you.'

'That's right. But it isn't mine. I borrow it from a chap called Foster. Stockbroker type. Lives in the bungalow nearest the main road – on the left as you face the cul-de-sac. We do a lot of that on Exmoor – exchange things on loan. It saves money.'

'How old would this Foster be?' asked Tweed.

Kearns looked surprised at the question, but answered. 'I'd say about forty. Like most of them on that estate.'

'And when did they all move into those bungalows?'

'Fifteen years ago.'

Tweed stood up. 'Thank you for bearing with me. You have some friends you can talk to? I know myself what it's like – stuck on your own in a house when your wife is gone.'

Paula glanced quickly at him. She realized Tweed was

recalling the time when his own wife had left him for a Greek shipping magnate.

'Oh, yes. In Winsford,' Kearns replied. 'I'll survive. Let me show you out.'

As they crossed the hall they heard the Alsatian. Now it was moaning and whining behind the closed door. Tweed thought that it sounded as if it were mourning the death of its mistress.

It was dark as Kearns used his flashlight to guide them to the exit. He said 'Goodnight', locked the grille gates and walked slowly back to the house. Tweed and Paula returned to the car. He sank behind the wheel, took a packet out of the glove compartment and smoked one of his rare cigarettes. Paula kept silent for a few minutes before she spoke.

'You're ruminating.'

'A lot to think about. That four-wheel-drive vehicle, *Renegade*. First it seems to belong to Robson, then Kearns and now this man, Foster. The question is, who drove it along the coast near Porlock Weir about midnight? No way of telling.'

'So we can't pursue that line of enquiry – assuming that it's worth pursuing.'

'Then there's the weird psychological set-up between the three men – Robson, Barrymore and Kearns. That must be quite something.'

'I'm not following you.'

'Use your imagination. Three men take part in that commando raid on Siros all those years ago. Andreas Gavalas is murdered with a commando knife. One of them did it . . .'

'But Barrymore checked their weapons after they found the body.'

'So, the killer carried an extra knife, knowing what he was going to do in advance. A hundred thousand pounds' worth of diamonds – now worth a million – went missing.

409

When Barrymore and Kearns leave the Army they settle on Exmoor, close to Robson – who found accommodation for them. I don't think the three of them conspired to murder Andreas. Just one of them.'

'I'm being dim – what about the psychological set-up?'

'It's diabolical, like something out of a Tennessee Williams play. Nobody knows who did it. But two out of the three *know* they didn't. So two of them who are innocent must have wondered all these years which man was a murderer. That makes for almost unbearable tension.'

'So why stay together?'

'That's the truly diabolical part. There's another factor locking them together – fear of Petros and the Gavalas clan coming to Exmoor for revenge. They're trying to protect one another.'

'You're right,' Paula said slowly, 'it's a macabre relationship.'

'Let's get moving.' Tweed shook himself alert. 'I want to take a quick look at that bungalow estate down the road.'

He parked near the bottom of the hill with the engine still running. In the night they had a good view of the six bungalows with whitewashed walls, three on either side of the cul-de-sac. Curtains were closed. Behind them lights shone. The coach lamps in the porches were all lit. No sign of life.

Each dwelling had a low wall, also whitewashed, bordering a trim lawn inside. All the gardens had the grass cut. No cars were parked either in the road or on a drive. All neatly tucked away inside the garages attached to the bungalows. On the roofs of five of them were the same conventional television masts. Only Seton-Charles had the complex structure with a satellite dish.

'I tell you again,' Paula said, 'it doesn't look real. If robots walked out I'd hardly be surprised.'

'Best get back to The Anchor . . .'

He was releasing the brake after moving the gear into drive when she touched his arm. He put the brake back on and turned to her.

'What is it?'

'This.' She was holding a small white stick she'd taken out of her handbag. 'Remember when we arrived at Kearns' place – I pretended to be clumsy and dropped my handbag on the floor. I'd seen this on the woodblocks.'

'What is it?'

'I'm pretty sure it's French chalk. Let me test it.' She held the stick, rubbed it on the cuff of her cotton blouse. A white mark appeared. She brushed at it with her fingers and it vanished. Opening the glove flap, she balanced the makeshift shelf on her knee, rubbed the stick across it. The substance appeared as small grains of powder. She bent forward, sniffed at it. 'No smell.' Moistening her index finger, she dabbed it in the powder, tasted it. 'No taste. It is French chalk.'

'I fail to see the significance.'

'You know I make some of my dresses. I use it for marking. And there's another purpose it could be used for.'

'Now you're keeping me dangling.'

'Kearns' complexion – normally ruddy when the suntan has worn off – is white. We put it down to grief. I think he used this stick of French chalk to alter his complexion, to simulate grief. It must have dropped out of his pocket. I think he used it to touch up the effect just before he appeared at the door. There is a mirror in the hall. And I noticed traces of white powder on his jacket lapel.'

'My God!' said Tweed. 'And Howard still thinks I'm wrong to introduce women into the Service.'

40

They arrived back at The Anchor and found Butler and Nield having a drink in the bar. Nield sat at the corner table with his head leant against the wall, his eyes half-closed. It was early for business: they had the place to themselves.

'Don't get up,' Paula said as Nield stirred. 'You look all in.'

'Application to the job in hand.' Nield smiled. 'Your boss expects non-stop action,' he said as Tweed arrived with the drinks: mineral water for himself, a glass of white wine for Paula. 'I've been driving over those moors until they seem to start moving.'

'Application!' Butler snorted and drank from his half-pint glass. 'That's what we're here for.' He lowered his voice, speaking to Tweed, who sat next to him. 'Barrymore left Quarme Manor soon after you'd gone. Drove into Minehead. Made a call from a public box. Funny thing to do – he has his phone at home.'

'How long a call?'

'Between one and two minutes. I was going to time it but found my watch had stopped. Then he drives straight back to Quarme Manor.'

'Odd,' Tweed agreed. He looked round the table. 'Does anyone know whether Jill Kearns used to take that Alsatian when she went for her early morning walk on the moor?'

'I do,' Nield said. 'The answer is yes. Came out in a chat I had with the barman over there. She was well-known for those walks. Always started at 6.30 a.m. on the dot. The dog always went with her. For protection as much as company, I imagine. A lonely place, the moor.'

'That means the dog was pining for her,' Tweed remarked. 'And why am I worried about Mrs Larcombe down the road? Something she said. It will come back to me. What is it?'

Paula plucked at his sleeve. 'Look outside.' He twisted round, gazed out of the window. Two men and two girls clad in denims and windcheaters were getting out of a Land Rover covered with a canvas roof. They walked off towards the harbour. 'You see,' she said, 'another of those vehicles.'

Butler nodded. 'Four-wheel drives? They're pretty common – Pete and I have seen a number while we've driven around.'

'And there,' said Tweed, 'goes another theory I had. Every time I think I've got somewhere it turns into a dead end.'

'Like Porlock Weir,' Paula chimed in and sipped more wine.

'One thing I'd like you to do,' Tweed said to Nield, 'is check on the inhabitants of that bungalow estate near Kearns' place. Any titbit you can pick up.'

'First target the electoral register,' Nield replied. 'Then go on from there.'

'Why the interest?' Paula asked.

'Two remarks you made. That it didn't look real. And that you almost expected robots to emerge. Incidentally, the pathologist at Taunton told me Partridge was killed by someone who knew just where to insert the knife. Another thing, Pete,' he went on, 'I need to know whether Kearns still takes those night rides up to the summit of Dunkery Beacon . . .'

'Certainly not at the moment. Only when there's enough moonlight to see his way. Tricky riding those moors at

413

night even for a really experienced horseman.' He drank more beer. 'Well, that should keep my days filled.'

'There's more for you.' Tweed smiled at Nield's expression. 'You'll cope. I'd like you sometime – in daylight – to get up to the top of Dunkery Beacon and poke around up there. With Butler's help you'll manage. Plus, of course, keeping an eye on the other two. I wouldn't want you to have time on your hands, to get bored.' He finished his mineral water and stood up. 'I fancy a breath of fresh air. Want to come, Paula?'

'Lovely idea. Help to work up an appetite for dinner. That remark you made about the pathologist's comment again points the finger at the commandos.'

'Any news from Greece?' Tweed asked Butler as he donned his Burberry. 'You check regularly?'

'As you requested. Not a word. Monica didn't seem worried. She said Newman only calls when he has something solid. Same with Marler.'

'See you.' Tweed nodded to the barman, opened the door, paused. 'Pretty blustery out there.' He took his old waterproof hat off a peg and rammed it over his head. Paula wrapped a scarf round hers.

'Gale warnings round all coasts,' the barman called out.

'Which means a sleepless night,' Tweed remarked to Paula. 'Our bedroom windows both face the front.'

'Harry and Pete will be OK. Theirs face the back. I'm OK . . .'

The wind hit them as they plodded west along the road and then over the track which was still moist from the morning tide. To their right they could hear the crash of the sea against the rocky shoal. Spume, caught by the wind, blew off the wave crests and they felt it on their faces as they walked against the nor'wester.

'Are we staying here long?' Paula asked, her mouth close to his ear.

'I haven't decided. We may push off back to London

within a day or two. I've stirred up those three ex-commandos again. One of them may be nudged into making a wrong move. I'm stumped, Paula. And this doesn't seem the right place for any funny goings-on. That vehicle Mrs Larcombe saw would have to drive on through Porlock village even before it could turn up Porlock Hill. Too much risk of being seen.'

'That's not so. Harry told me about the toll road.'

'Told you what?'

'A very lonely road which turns up the hill just outside Porlock Weir. Apparently it turns up and joins the main road to Culbone. Sheer drop on one side. Harry's point was, that is the direct route to Quarme Manor and Endpoint – even on to our Mr Kearns' place. You take the first left off the main road like we did during our last visit. No one would see you driving that route late at night.'

'I've had enough of this,' said Tweed. 'We'll turn back.'

The wind was hammering them, making it difficult to walk over the sliding pebbles. They reached the track and were hurrying towards The Anchor when Tweed grabbed Paula's arm.

'Let me take a quick look at the harbourmaster's office. It has a notice behind the window.'

He took out a pencil torch, went close up to the deserted building. He shone the beam on the cardboard clock with adjustable hands. *High Tide 10.50 p.m.* The sea was already surging inside the channel which fed the harbour.

'I hope we decide to go back to London,' said Paula. 'If it's going on like this.'

Arriving back in the bar, they hung up their raincoats and got rid of their headgear. Butler and Nield sat at the same table. Tweed offered drinks.

'Not for me,' said Butler. 'I'll stick with this half pint – you may want to send me off somewhere.'

'I'll have a second,' Nield decided. 'I'm not going anywhere. Except to bed after a good dinner.'

'Harry,' Tweed said as he sat down, after calling out the order to the barman, 'have you shown Masterson's photograph to the barman here?'

'No. You told us to keep quiet about him – unless a lead turned up. It didn't.'

Tweed pulled an envelope from his breast pocket, extracted the matt print inside. When the barman arrived with Nield's drink he tapped the print.

'Recognize him? A friend of mine. Said he might stay here a few days. I owe him twenty pounds he lent me when I found I'd left my wallet behind. Can't trace him.'

The barman took hold of the print, studied it with half-closed eyes. He pursed his lips. 'You couldn't add a pair of tinted glasses? And a yachting cap – one of those peaked efforts with gold braid.'

Tweed took back the print, handed it to Paula. 'You're the artist.' She opened her handbag, delved inside, her hand came out holding a felt-tip pen. She frowned for a moment, then started working. She added tinted glasses and a yachting cap. Tweed was startled: it was just the type of gear Masterson would go for. He handed it again to the barman.

'Yes, that's him. Came in here half a dozen times. Thought I knew him when you showed me it first time. Now I'm sure. Had a whizz of a girl with him. Long dark hair and eyes a man could drown in. Spoke good English, but she looked foreign.'

'How long ago was this?' Tweed asked quietly.

'Seems like months ago. A lot of weeks anyway. It's coming back to me. Engaging sort of guy. I remember him asking about the colonel. Did he come in here? I said now and again. Mostly in the evenings.' He handed back the print.

'The colonel?' Tweed queried.

'Yes. Colonel Barrymore. Lives over at Quarme Manor near the Doone Valley. Gloomy old place.'

'Thank you,' said Tweed, and gave him a pound coin.

Paula crossed her legs. She swung one foot up and down. Studying the mud on her shoe, she asked the question.

'Does that mean we'll be staying?'

'I'll sleep on it.'

The *Oporto* mounted a huge wave, the deck tilting at a steep angle. Even in the dark Anton, clinging to the rail, could see its foaming crest. Knowing what was coming, he tightened his grip. The freighter hovered on the crest, then plunged downwards into the chasm. All around him Anton could see giant walls of water which seemed about to overwhelm the vessel. The plunge continued, as though it was heading for the bottom of the ocean. It was pitching and tossing at the same time.

The wind tore at his sodden windcheater, threatening to rip it off his body, howling in his ears. He had just returned from a perilous trip to the hold crammed with baled cork. Twice each day he checked the canvas-covered Stingers, tucked away by Gomez next to the bulkhead.

Anton had taken the precaution of tucking a thread of cotton pulled from a shirt under one of the straps. If anyone fooled around with his precious cargo he would know. The cotton thread was still in position when he made his recent check. As the *Oporto* regained its equilibrium in the trough, Anton ran up to the bridge before it started climbing another mountain.

He opened the door to the wheelhouse and the wind snatched it from his grasp. It took all his strength to pull the door shut. Behind his wheel, Gomez glanced round, his expression impassive as always despite the fury of the storm. Anton hung on to a side rail, ignoring the mate who understood no English.

'Where are we?' he asked.

'Just abreast of Ushant in France. To the east.' Gomez

made a quick gesture to his right, then grabbed at the wheel.

The freighter was heading downwards again, its bow flooded with teeming sea. Anton thanked God he was a good sailor. But the view from the bridge was terrifying. An army of tidal-size waves moved towards them from all directions.

'Are we keeping to schedule?' he asked anxiously. 'I mean with this storm.'

'We shall be heaving to off Porlock Weir two days from now. On schedule.' Gomez gave him an evil grin, showing the gold in his teeth. 'If we survive . . .'

Seton-Charles looked like anything but a professor in Greek Studies as he drove back to the Victorian bed-and-breakfast boarding house in Norwich close to midnight. He wore a boiler suit used for gardening. Before leaving his bungalow he had smeared the overalls with a mixture of oil and grease.

He had decided to leave for Norwich early and had driven off ten minutes after Tweed and Paula made their way back to Porlock Weir from Kearns' house. Now he would be in Norwich, ready to visit Camelford Removals, first thing the following day.

Well along the A303 he had seen a truck drivers' café and had pulled in alongside a giant twelve-wheeler. Inside the café he ordered a mug of steaming tea and sat down at a table close to the door. The place was full of drivers, some chatting, others slumped over their own mugs. A juke box playing pop records had added to the noise and the place was filled with blue smoke.

After drinking half the mug of tea, Seton-Charles had left. On his way out he paused to button up his suit at the neck. He eyed the row of caps hanging from wooden hooks. He took a cap with a plastic peak and walked out.

418

He didn't try it on until he reached a lay-by well clear of the café. It fitted well enough. And for the rimless glasses he normally wore he had substituted his spare pair of horn-rims.

After reserving a room for the night at the boarding house, he ordered a plate of fish and chips and another mug of tea at a cheap café. While he ate he studied the town map he had bought from a newsagent. He decided to take a look at Camelford Removals. He parked the Volvo round the corner from the warehouse, surprised to see lights inside. The figure of a man was silhouetted against a grimy window.

'I've come to take a look at a couple of furniture vans,' he informed a short middle-aged man who introduced himself as Mr Latimer, owner of the bankrupt business. 'They mayn't be what I'm after, but I come on spec . . .'

He slurred his vowels and spoke with a coarse accent. Latimer showed him the four vans still for sale. Seton-Charles chose the two largest, then began haggling over the price, which was expected. He bargained carefully: not offering too little but refusing to agree to Latimer's first price.

They compromised and Seton-Charles pulled a bundle of well-used fifty-pound notes from a pocket in his stained overalls. He paid the agreed deposit and Latimer held several of the notes up to the naked light bulb suspended over a roughened table.

'Done,' he had said. 'You'll collect soon? Pay the balance before you drive them away?'

'Only way to do business. Night . . .'

As he settled between grubby sheets that night Seton-Charles was satisfied. Within two days he'd have both vans hidden away in the barn at Cherry Farm. Although God knew what Jupiter wanted them for.

41

At the Grande Bretagne Newman had caught on to the game Christina was playing. She was holding back on supplying more information to keep him there as a protector against Petros and the Gavalas family. He was on the verge of threatening to leave – to force her hand – when something happened that decided him to be patient a little longer.

The killer heatwave had broken. It was a mere 80°F. September temperature. Marler arrived at 9 a.m. in Newman's room, sprawled on a sofa. He lit a cigarette.

'Well,' said Newman, 'get on with it. What's happened?'

'Patience, chum. You know I've been paying frequent visits to the Cape Sounion area. Object of the exercise to keep an eye on Florakis traipsing up the mountain at night with that transmitter.'

'You're sure it is a transmitter?'

'Absolutely. Took a pair of high-powered night glasses with me. Spent night after night watching him. It's stopped.'

'What has?'

'Do listen. Florakis has stopped making his excursions with the jolly old transmitter. I realized something last night – out of the blue, so to speak. It coincides with no moon.'

'You mean he only transmits when there's a moon? Doesn't make sense.'

'Transmits for about two weeks – when the moon's waxing and waning. Only possible explanation? It's important to the man he's transmitting to. Something else happened. Equally important. Tweed wants to interview friend Petros, I believe?'

'Yes he does. When he can get out here . . .'

'Better make it soon. That snide Dimitrios spotted me watching by the sea shore. Crept up on me. Thought I must be deaf and blind. Put down his rifle, came up behind me, grabbed hold of me. Thought he was going to throttle me, silly ass.'

'So why not tell me what happened next?' Newman asked in a resigned tone.

'Just going to. He ended up flat on the ground, arms pinned to his sides, my knee in his groin. He gave me a splendid opportunity to get him talking. He talked.'

'And how did you accomplish that feat?'

'As I said, we were by the edge. No one about. Still dark. I dragged him to the water's edge. Goes down deep there. Held his head under water three times. He thought I was going to drown him. Which I would have done if he hadn't opened his mouth.'

'Get on with it,' Newman snapped. 'What did you learn?'

'Within two weeks Petros is leaving Devil's Valley. He's owner of a cattle farm in the far north. Macedonia. Tweed would have trouble finding him there. Two weeks,' Marler repeated. 'Up to Tweed, wouldn't you say?'

'I'll call him from the Embassy. But first I'm going back for a word with Christina. You made Dimitrios talk. I'm going to do the same job on her about Anton.' A thought occurred to him as he grasped the door handle. 'Surely you've blown it. Dimitrios will go straight back to Petros and tell him what happened?'

'Doubt that. I warned him. If I heard he'd said anything the next time I saw him would be the last. For him. And he's going to keep quiet for another reason. If he told Petros he'd spilt the beans the old man would kill him.

421

You'll want me to guard Christina when you go to the Embassy, I take it?'

'I'll want you to do just that. Stay with her.'

'Hurry it up, then. I'm short of sleep.'

Christina had just finished drying her washed mane when Newman entered her room. She threw it back over her shoulders.

'How do I look?'

'Never mind that.' His voice was harsh. 'Marler and I will be leaving if you don't start telling me everything you know about Anton. You're on your own.'

'No!' She was appalled. 'Petros will find me. He'll kill me.'

'That's your problem. A family tiff . . .'

'Tiff! Don't you realize yet what he's like?'

'Start telling me then.' Newman perched on the edge of the bed. He folded his arms and stared out of the window, not looking at her as she slumped into a chair.

'I'm frightened. I've told you so much about them already. If Anton found out he'd be even worse than Petros. Anton is cruel.'

'I'm still waiting.' He looked at his wristwatch. 'But not for long.'

'You're a bastard . . .'

'I have diplomas to prove it. Stop stalling.'

She sat down in a large armchair, curled herself inside it like a cat, exposing her long legs. He made a point of not admiring them as she began.

'Anton is one of those people who can do anything. An expert at scuba-diving. Good with boats. Anything mechanical. He can design and build a word processor, a video recorder, a transceiver. And repair them if they break down. He's experienced with hydraulics. He got an estimate for a lift to be installed in his warehouse at Piraeus, thought it too much – so he built the damned thing himself. He's a good horse rider, but I told you that . . .' Once started, she didn't stop. 'He's an expert on handguns and rifles. A crack shot with both. Won some kind of trophy once at Bisley in England. For God's sake, isn't that enough? Oh, and he's a hell-raiser with the women. I think I told you that before.'

'A bit of an all-rounder,' Newman mused.

'He's also good at carpentry. Very good.'

'Carpentry?'

'Building anything out of wood. He made all the furniture for his room at the farm in Devil's Valley. That's the only decently furnished room. The rest is a slum.'

'Why didn't you tell me this before? People must know his many talents.'

'No, not many. He's very secretive. He likes his image of playboy. It amuses him to fool people. I loathe him – and I've never understood him. One more thing, he can fly any kind of light aircraft. Cessnas, Pipers, etc. He belonged to a flying club, then resigned once he'd mastered flying. Said he was bored with it. I think he craves excitement, new worlds to conquer. And he's very ambitious – to become one of the most important men in Greece. I really think I've given you the lot.' She watched him through her eyelashes. 'Do I still get protection?'

'You do. For as long as we can manage it. I have to go out for a short time. Marler will stay with you.'

'He'd better keep his distance,' she said viciously and picked up a hairbrush, 'or I'll crack his skull with this.'

'Argue it out with him while I'm gone.' Newman grinned. 'All I think he wants is kip – sleep. Alone . . .'

Tweed put down his office phone after asking Newman to call him daily. He sat for a few minutes, thinking. Paula and Monica were careful to keep quiet while they worked.

'Paula,' he announced, 'we have to fly to Greece – and soon. Inside the next couple of weeks. Monica, book a couple of first-class return tickets via Zurich. Open date. Bob has just told me Petros is leaving Devil's Valley for some other farm he has up in Macedonia. No one knows the territory up there. Marler and Newman do know Devil's Valley. I need to interrogate the old villain. He's crazed with a lust for vengeance. I want to find out whether he had Masterson killed.'

'How will you go about it?' Paula asked.

'I shall go into Devil's Valley with someone who speaks Greek as an interpreter. I'll grill him at his farm – the only way to get at him. He never comes to Athens – or rarely – so Newman said.'

'That could be dangerous,' Paula protested. 'He sounds mad as a hatter. And Newman told us earlier the area is crawling with armed shepherds.'

'We'll cross that bridge when we come to it.'

'I don't like it,' Paula insisted.

'No one asked you to.' He regretted the words as soon as he had spoken. 'I'm sorry, that was rude. I'm confused about this whole business. There seems no rhyme or reason to it. Unless the whole thing revolves round Petros.'

'You could ask Peter Sarris for help,' Paula suggested.

Tweed shook his head. 'No police until we know what we're getting into. We'll rely on our own resources.' He looked at Monica who had just made the phone call. 'All fixed up?'

'Two open date return tickets via Zurich booked.'

'Is this why we returned here so quickly from Porlock Weir?' enquired Paula.

'Yes. I felt I was getting out of touch with the position in Greece. Butler and Nield can keep a watch on any developments on Exmoor. You have your bag packed, Paula? Good. I may decide to leave suddenly for Athens.'

424

'Why go via Zurich?' Monica asked. 'Instead of flying direct?'

'I want to consult Arthur Beck. We'll call him before we leave. He often knows what's going on. And there are direct flights to Athens from Zurich.' He paused. 'So there are also flights direct from Athens to Zurich.'

'Oh Lord!' Monica groaned. 'He's being enigmatic again.'

Midnight. The storm had abated when the *Oporto* was rounding the tip of Cornwall. The sea now was just choppy as the vessel hove to west of Porlock Weir. On deck on the starboard side Anton held the flashlight and directed the coded signal towards the distant shore. Then he waited.

Gomez stood alongside him close to the gangway which had been lowered over the side. At the foot of the steps waves lapped over the metal platform. The canvas-wrapped Stingers, recovered from the hold, lay at Anton's feet. He wore a waterproof windcheater, thick seaman's trousers tucked inside rubber boots and over this gear a dark green oilskin. His suitcase was protected with another oilskin lashed round it with rope.

'You will need luck to make contact a second time,' Gomez commented.

'The crew are all below decks?' enquired Anton.

'As arranged – except for a lookout who can be trusted.' In the dark he smiled. 'He has been paid to be trusted . . . Look. Over there.'

Anton had already seen the light flashing its return signal from the shore. He checked the number of flashes, then sent a brief final signal, acknowledging, and rammed the flashlight inside a pocket of the oilskin.

'Now we have to wait. But not for long, I suspect . . .'

He was right. As the freighter rocked slowly under the

425

surge of the sea the sound of an engine approaching reached his acute hearing. The night was moonless but soon both could see the white wake of the small boat. Anton reached down and hauled up with both hands the heavy weight of the canvas bundle. Gomez picked up the suitcase with one hand; with the other he raised a pair of night glasses to his eyes, leaning against the rail as he scanned the shoreline. They were two miles out. To the east he picked out the lights of Porlock Weir. He lowered the glasses.

'Be very careful when you go down the gangway. The steps will be slippery. You are carrying a heavy weight.'

'I'll be all right. And when I've left you're turning round and sailing out to sea, ready to come back tomorrow?'

'Do not worry. No one will know we arrived off England earlier.'

The small grey-coloured motorboat, powered by an outboard at its stern, was close. Gomez could make out the figure of the solitary man aboard. As before, he wore a Balaclava helmet under a dark green oilskin. He cut the power, the boat glided forward, bumped against the platform. Balaclava hurled up a mooring rope. Gomez caught it with his free hand, the glasses looped round his neck, made the rope fast to the rail.

Anton stood on the top platform, slowly went down, step by step. He rested the bundle on the rails on either side, letting them take the weight, sliding it down. The moored boat ground up against the *Oporto*'s hull, made a grating sound. Anton was half-way down when the sea lifted the freighter, then dropped it. Anton lost his grip, the bundle tumbled down the remaining steps, landed on the lower platform. He swore in Greek, grabbing the rails to recover his balance.

Balaclava leant forward, took hold of the cargo, heaved it up and lowered it quickly inside the boat. Anton stepped off the platform and joined him. Gomez called down, dropped the mooring rope he had untied and Balaclava hauled it in, dripping, looped round the handle of Anton's suitcase.

Anton sat down as his companion started up the outboard, grabbed the tiller and guided the boat away from the *Oporto*. He was just in time. A large wave lifted the boat, would have hurled it against the freighter, but Balaclava had steered the boat round. He headed for the distant shore.

The motorboat was coming in close to the rock-strewn coast. Behind it cliffs loomed, hiding them from the mainland. Anton was careful not to stare at the eyes which looked out through the slit in the Balaclava helmet.

He had no idea of the identity of his companion. When he had landed on his previous trip to Exmoor the same man had met him, wearing the same gear. Because of the loose flapping oilskin he wore it was impossible for Anton to guess Balaclava's height, build or age. Only the voice was distinctive. Upper-crust, clipped. On the rare occasions when he spoke.

As they approached the shore, the boat pitching and tossing, the engine was cut out. Balaclava crouched over the tiller, peering ahead, steering the craft towards a slope. There was a grinding sound as the keel rode up over rocks and pebbles, stopped.

'Take the weapons, put them in the vehicle.'

Anton heaved up the bundle, stepped out of the boat and staggered to the canvas-covered four-wheel-drive vehicle parked close to the shoreline. He used his shoulder to ease up the flap at the rear, hoisted the bundle higher, lowered it inside on top of a pile of coiled ropes. The wind whipped at his oilskin, blew it round his legs as he let the flap drop and went back for his case.

Balaclava had taken an axe attached to the side and began hammering at the deck. The axe was heavy, its blade

427

honed like a razor. As he worked chips of wood flew up and he protected his eyes by holding one arm across them. He paused as Anton lifted out his case, turned to him.

'The sea goes down a hundred feet here. We have to lose this boat. Don't stand there watching me – keep an eye out along the shore.'

The axe began to sweep down again in thudding arcs. Inside a few minutes the boat was holed. Balaclava went on working, enlarging the gaping cavity. He was only satisfied when the hole was a foot wide, then he hurled the axe into the waves and returned to the vehicle. Climbing into the rear, he shifted the Stingers and covered them with the mass of rope. Jumping back on to the shore he gestured Anton to join him.

'We want to heave the boat over the edge. Give me a hand . . .'

They stood near the bow on either side and pushed with all their strength. The boat slid slowly backwards, the outboard poised over the edge. They straightened up, stretching their strained arms, took hold of the boat again. One more prolonged heave and the boat was floating. It filled rapidly with water, drifting just offshore. Then it went down stern first. The bow hovered above the surface, disappeared.

Balaclava strode towards the vehicle, climbed in behind the wheel and Anton sat beside him. They drove off without lights, heading away from the sea, bumping and jostling over the rough terrain.

The driver switched on his lights as they reached the track past the cottages. He never gave a glance at the darkened dwelling where Mrs Larcombe had talked with Tweed. He drove on along the road at higher speed, passing The Anchor Hotel, continuing towards Porlock.

Reaching the toll road, he swung the vehicle up the steep

curving slope. At the top he turned right again along the coast road. Beyond Culbone he turned left off the main road down on to the winding country lane which eventually led to the Doone Valley. For the first time he broke his long silence.

'Here is the key to the small house where you spend the night. It is unoccupied. And here is a pencil flashlight so you can find your way round it. The electricity is cut off. You will find canned meat, a tin opener, a loaf of bread, butter, knife, two bottles of mineral water inside a brown paper parcel in a downstairs room. Also a sleeping bag. The place is unfurnished. We'll park the vehicle in a garage alongside. But take the weapons into the house. Sleep with them by your side. And here is a sheathed knife for protection – to be used only in an emergency.'

Anton took the weapon. 'This is a commando knife,' he commented. 'I brought a couple with me . . .'

'Listen!' Balaclava was concentrating on negotiating the road which dropped as it twisted between high hedges. 'Keep that knife. Now, in the morning you take the weapons to Cherry Farm. You remember how to get there from the drive we took last time?'

'Yes. It's near Liphook in Hampshire.'

Balaclava stopped the vehicle at a bend where he could see in both directions, pulled an ordnance survey map from the door's pocket. 'Use the flashlight and show me the location of Cherry Farm. Your route is marked part of the way in pen – driving along side roads. That way you should avoid all police patrol cars.'

Anton unfolded the map, studied it with the aid of the light. He pointed to an area. 'The track to it turns off about here.'

'Good. Keep the map. Burn it when you get there. And you've plenty to keep you occupied when you do get there. You will find you have company. You give him the password – Sandpiper.'

'What does he say in return?' Anton asked.

'Nothing.' Balaclava chuckled, a hard cynical sound. 'You'll recognize him. Tomorrow morning you drive this contraption to Taunton.' He hauled a slim folder from the same pocket. 'I've marked on this with a light pencil cross the car park where you leave this vehicle about ten in the morning. You park at the very back where there's a thick hedge. Hide the cargo under that hedge while you're away hiring a car from Barton's – they are marked with a pencilled circle. And here is a driving licence in the name of Partridge for hiring the car. Drive it to the car park. Collect the cargo. Then head for Cherry Farm. You leave this vehicle in the car park and you must be on your way by eleven o'clock. I will have the vehicle collected. Understood.'

'Let me check this.' Anton was studying the street plan of Taunton with the aid of the flashlight. He found the cross and the circle. 'All clear. But why can't I drive straight on to Cherry Farm now? Or am I dropping you somewhere?'

'Of course not. I have transport waiting not far from the house where you spend the night. And travelling at night is dangerous. You could be stopped and checked by a patrol car. You should have thought of that yourself.'

'You are right,' Anton agreed quickly. There was something in Balaclava's manner, in his contemptuous tone, which frightened him.

'Needless to say, you burn the Taunton map soon after you have left Taunton behind. Now listen carefully. I said earlier you will have plenty to occupy you at Cherry Farm. Something that will test your skills as a carpenter and hydraulics expert. So *listen*. There are two furniture vans at the farm. This is what you have to do . . .'

By early afternoon the following day Anton was driving his hired Austin Metro close to Liphook in Hampshire.

The Stingers and missiles were in the boot, concealed under a load of groceries he had bought in Glastonbury.

On both sides of the country road the flat fields stretched away beyond low hedges. The sun was shining and he hadn't passed another vehicle for several miles. He drove round a bend and slowed his speed, recognizing he was very close. Anton had the most retentive memory for routes and geography. Across the road were freshly fallen leaves. Autumn was coming. Soon September would become October.

He stopped the car alongside a closed gate with a gravel track beyond. He sat listening for several minutes, listening for the sound of the distant approach of any more traffic. Nothing. He got out, opened the gate which carried the legend *Cherry Farm* in white paint. Driving up the track a few yards, he stopped the car again, got out and went back to close the gate. Attention to detail.

The field alongside the track was spongy grass. As he drove further he passed large lakes, the product of rain which had fallen three days earlier. Poor agricultural land. He followed the curve of the track and Cherry Farm came into view.

A long low two-storey building made of brick with a tiled roof, it had two squat chimney stacks and a large barn to the right of the farmhouse. The place had a deserted look and he drove slowly, his eyes scanning the whole area in search of a sign of life.

Beyond the large barn stood two long sheds with corrugated iron roofs. The doors to both were closed. As he drove closer he saw the farm had an abandoned look. Undergrowth was smothering the tiny garden in front. Ivy creeper sprawled up the brickwork like a giant spider, its tentacles crawling over the closed shutters.

Had something gone wrong? Where was the man he was supposed to meet? He drove on round the back of the farmhouse, parked the car in a muddy yard, switched off the engine and listened again. There is no silence more eerie than that of a deserted countryside.

Anton remained behind the wheel, checked the knife in the sheath attached to his belt. No cattle, no sheep. No animals of any kind. More lakes standing in the soggy field behind the farm. No birds chattered or wheeled in the clear blue sky. Then the back door opened. Seton-Charles came out to meet him. Anton hid his astonishment.

'Sandpiper,' he said.

'You have the weapons? Good. We'll get them to their hiding-place inside the house. Then drive your car and park it inside the first shed beyond the barn. There are doors at this end . . '

Seton-Charles stood in the kitchen, watching Anton through his rimless glasses as the Greek ate ham sandwiches, drank mineral water. Seated at the table, Anton ignored the Professor. There was a distinct sense of unease between the two men. It had been different in Athens when Seton-Charles had lectured him at the university. Anton finished his meal, decided to establish his authority from the beginning.

'I'm in charge here. You know that?'

'So I was informed.' Seton-Charles' tone expressed no enthusiasm for the arrangement. He leaned against the dresser, folded his arms. 'What role are you playing here?'

'You leave this farm from time to time?' Anton asked cautiously.

'Not without your permission. I prepare the meals from now on. I give you any help you may need with your work. What work?'

'Communications,' Anton persisted. 'How do we keep in touch with Jupiter?'

'We don't. There is a phone in the hall. He calls us. We

make no calls, have no contact with the outside world. You buy fresh food supplies in Liphook when we need them.'

'And might anyone come poking around here?'

'No. Haven't you seen the state of the farm? The land is useless, waterlogged half the time. The next farm is miles away. Now, if you don't mind, I'd like some idea on what I'm supposed to help you with. The two furniture vans are hidden inside the huge barn, one behind the other.'

Satisfied with the security, Anton dabbed at his mouth with a silk handkerchief. He twisted round in his chair to stare hard at the Professor.

'You saw the short planks of wood still in the boot? I bought them at a timberyard on the way. You've seen the two boxes on the floor here?'

'Yes.' Seton-Charles stared down at the containers, made of heavy wood and like tool boxes. The lids were open. Inside one was a collection of wires, steel slides and other electrical-type equipment. The second box looked like a carpenter's and was crammed with planes, saws, screwdrivers and other tools. 'What are you up to?' he asked.

'A complex operation. Each of those furniture vans has to be fitted with a large sliding panel in the roof – electrically operated. The hydraulics will be difficult. And inside each van I'll be building a platform with steps – the platform top to be about three feet below the roof, fitted with a chair I'll clamp to the platform.' Anton grinned. 'Guess what all that is for?'

'I'm not in the guessing game,' Seton-Charles said coldly.

'We're in the business of building two mobile rocket launchers.'

433

make no calls, have no contact with the outside world. You
buy fresh food maybe in Uptown, when we need them."

"And what anyway, come poking around here?"

"No, Hawai'i. Look past the state of the [illegible]. The land
is nothing, waters [illegible] [illegible] [illegible] [illegible] [illegible] farm is miles
away. Now if you don't mind, I'd like some such on shat.
I'm supposed to help good with the two lifetime who are
hidden inside the jar," Jane said, "of the others."

"Satisfied with the answer," Ajlon nodded at the mouth
with a stiff handkerchief. He twisted round of his time to
entertained at the Fyr[illegible].

"You are the [illegible] [illegible] that [illegible] still in the door," I
brought them at a inconvenient the way. You're with the
two books on the floor there?"

"Yes," Snowe-Davey, stood down, at the entrance
made of heavy wood and dry spot boxes. The door was
open. Inside one was a cardboard drawers, steel sheet and
other electronic equipment. The second box bought
like a cupboard and was stuffed with wires, tapes, wires,
screwdrivers and other tools. A bolt was put at at a
table.

"A camera operating flash of those features was too
to be lined with a large plastic panel in the roof. Cautiously
he said, "Technicalities will be actively. And inside box
too. I'll be building a platform with steps — they'll then
step to the main direction below the roof, fitted upward
that. I'll climb to the platform beneath ground." Guess
what all that is for?"

"I'll run to the grinding part," Ashton Charles said coldly.

"We're on the business of hidden investment rocket
frontier,"

PART THREE

The Greek Key

42

'We're coming in to land,' said Paula and gripped Tweed's arm. 'This is the bit I never like.'

'Look at the view over there out of the starboard windows,' he suggested and squeezed her hand.

They were aboard Swissair flight 801, approaching Zurich's airport, Kloten. The machine was banking and Paula saw framed in a window the magnificent sweep of the Bernese Oberland range, its peaks snow-capped. She sucked in her breath as she watched the mountain summits silhouetted against a backdrop of cloudless azure sky.

Tweed had taken one of his snap decisions. They had left London Airport at 9.30 a.m. and were due to arrive at 12.05 p.m. Before leaving Tweed had phoned Federal police chief Arthur Beck, an old friend. Beck was meeting them at Kloten. What worried Tweed was the closeness of their connection with the Swissair flight taking them on to Athens.

Flight 302, bound for Athens, departed from Kloten at 12.30 p.m. It gave them no time at all to check in on the fresh flight and Tweed needed time to consult with Beck. As the plane descended he laid his hand over Paula's and she turned and smiled.

'I'm OK now. Just a brief fit of nerves. Do you think Monica has got through to Newman, warning him we're coming?'

'It all depends on how early Newman makes *his* daily call to her. At least we know where to find him. The Grande Bretagne . . .'

Paula hardly realized the plane had landed as it skimmed along the runway. Beck was waiting for them at Passport Control. He wore civilian clothes and a Tyrolean hat with a little feather in the hat band, dressed like a man on holiday. The grey eyes under the thick brows gleamed as he spotted Paula. He took her arm.

'Welcome to Zurich, Paula.' He kissed her on the cheek. 'We bypass all the checks.' He looked over his shoulder as he led her to a side door which a guard unlocked. 'You'd better come too, Tweed. We have time to talk.'

Tweed smiled to himself. Beck had developed a soft spot for Paula when they'd met previously in Geneva. And he had organized their arrival so no one would notice them. He followed Paula along a corridor and into a starkly furnished room with maps on the walls.

'Thank you,' said Paula as Beck pulled out a chair for her from under a table. 'But what about our cases? Shouldn't I go to the carousel?'

'All taken care of, my dear. I phoned Jim Corcoran, security boss at London Airport. When you checked in a special small red label was attached to your luggage and Tweed's. Two of my men are at the carousel now, collecting your things.'

'Am I permitted to join you?' Tweed enquired mischievously.

'As a special favour, my friend. This is Kloten security chief's office I have borrowed. As you see, there is coffee and sandwiches. You would like some, Paula? Good.'

On the table was an electric warmer with a transparent flask of coffee perched on it. Sandwiches wrapped in cling-film. A telephone with a red button. Tweed sat down and stared at the instrument as Beck spoke while he poured coffee.

'Monica called you from London, spoke to the security chief and left a message. Can you call her urgently?'

Tweed looked at a clock attached to the wall with a red

second hand sweeping the dial. 'We're going to miss our flight we're booked on for Athens. It leaves at 12.30 as I told you.'

'So . . .' Beck waved a hand. 'It has been delayed. A bomb hoax. All passengers have to identify their luggage laid out on the tarmac before they board. That takes time.' He smiled. 'One of the advantages of being Chief of Police.' He sat next to Paula as he addressed Tweed. 'So, make your call, then we can talk.'

I should have guessed he'd tie it all up for us, Tweed thought. He reached for the phone, pressed the scrambler button, dialled Park Crescent. Beck and Paula talked in whispers while Tweed was calling London. She liked the Swiss: he had a wicked sense of humour. She put her hand over her mouth to suppress laughter and then noticed Tweed's expression as he replaced the receiver.

'Is something wrong?'

'Later,' he replied and looked at Beck. 'Greece. Have you heard anything unusual on the grapevine?'

'No. Unless this comes under the heading of un-usual . . .' For five minutes he recounted his two conversations with Kalos. He recalled how he had followed his quarry, kept an eye on him while he had spent a night at the Schweizerhof and then boarded a plane for Lisbon the following day.

'Lisbon?' Tweed's expression was grim. 'Are you sure, Arthur?'

'Of course I'm sure. I followed him myself to the airport. Later I checked with the pilot that he was on board. He was.'

'Sorry. That was a silly question. How long ago?'

'Ten days from today.'

'Hell's teeth.' Tweed stood up, began pacing the room. 'And I was congratulating myself that he was safely back in Athens. I'm getting this all wrong.' He looked at Paula. 'I said the solution lay in Greece, not Exmoor. Maybe it's the other way round.'

439

'Do we go on?' Paula asked.

'Yes. And we'd better hurry.'

'Might be as well,' Beck agreed. 'The baggage check should just about be over. You'll have to identify your own stuff. It will be all that's left on the tarmac . . .'

He hugged Paula, shook hands with Tweed. 'Anything more I can do to help – you give me a call.'

'You've helped a lot already,' Tweed assured him and they followed the Swiss to the aircraft.

They had eaten lunch. The plane was thirty thousand feet up and well south over the Adriatic Sea before Paula asked the question.

'You had bad news when you talked with Monica?'

'It's getting worse. Like the Klein problem we faced last year, the body count is rising. Butler called Monica. You remember that nice sharp old lady, Mrs Larcombe, we called on at Porlock Weir? This morning a neighbour noticed she hadn't taken her milk in. She started worrying, called the police. They found the front door unlocked and Mrs Larcombe battered to death.'

'Oh, that's awful. She was so bright for her age. Bright for any age. What do they think happened?'

'The *police* think some drunken youths called, pushed open the door when she reacted to the ringing of the bell, attacked her and walked off with fifty pounds she always kept in ready cash under her mattress. They found two empty beer cans in the front garden. No fingerprints.'

'I did catch your emphasis on "police". What do you think?'

'I'm convinced it was staged. Drunken youths don't remember to wipe beer cans clean of fingerprints. Something bothered me about what she said to us and I couldn't recall it afterwards. Now I can.'

'What was it?'

'When that four-wheel-drive vehicle stopped outside her house at midnight she opened the front window. She said that window *creaked*. My guess is the driver heard that creak. And no one believed her when she said she saw flashing lights out at sea and up the coast. She saw them all right.'

'I still don't follow,' Paula commented.

'That was the first run – bringing something, or someone – landed on the coast. There must have been a second run last night, an important one. They couldn't risk her seeing them – so they called on her, she opened the door, and that was it. The fact that she opened the door is significant.'

'Someone she knew?'

'I think so. She was a shrewd careful woman. And I noticed she had one of those spyglass things in her front door. She could see who was there before she opened it. Yes, someone she knew – or knew of. A respected citizen.'

'What a brutal thing to do.' Paula shivered. 'To kill an old lady like that just on the off-chance she looked out of her window at the wrong moment.'

'But we are dealing with a ruthless killer. Look at the score – Sam Partridge, Jill Kearns and now Mrs Larcombe. The stakes must be very high.'

He peered out of the window. The air was crystal clear, without a cloud. He looked down on the intense blue of the Adriatic. A tiny blur of white on the blue located the wake of a ship moving south: the ship was invisible.

'When we get to Athens,' he went on, 'someone must go to the Embassy to call Monica. I want her to contact Roberts of Lloyd's of London, get him to check the shipping register.'

'Why?'

'Remember what Beck told us about Anton. He took a flight from Zurich to Lisbon. Roberts can check the

441

movements of any vessel sailing from Lisbon about ten days ago – a vessel bound for Watchet on the Somerset coast. The killing of Mrs Larcombe backs up a vague theory I'd developed – that the way Anton slipped in without any record was that he came ashore from some vessel during the night. Hence those flashing lights Mrs Larcombe really did see.' He grunted. 'And now he may be back on Exmoor again. I don't like that at all. Monica must warn Butler.'

'And you think Jill was killed because she knew too much?'

'I have another idea about that. She may have been run down simply to divert our attention away from Exmoor to London.'

'That would be too horrible,' Paula protested.

'I said we're up against a ruthless killer.' He looked round the interior of the aircraft. They were travelling first-class and the section was three-quarters empty, which enabled them to talk freely. He peered out of the window again, checked his watch, settled himself back in his seat. 'Less than one hour to Athens. I have the feeling we're going to stir up a hornet's nest.'

The heat hit Tweed like a hammer as he emerged from the aircraft on to the mobile staircase. He walked down the steps and, with Paula by his side, made for the main building.

'God!' said Paula. 'It's baking and you don't like the heat.'

'So it's a good job you reminded me to wear my safari jacket and tropical drill trousers. Now, let's get the show on the road . . .'

Newman was waiting for them in the reception hall. He grinned as he came forward, shook hands with Tweed, hugged Paula, took her case.

'I phoned Monica early and she told me your flight details. I have a car outside. Straight to the Grande Bretagne? Marler is there, looking after Christina.'

'Straight to the Grande Bretagne,' Tweed replied. 'Sarris must not know I'm in town. We have to organize an expedition into Devil's Valley. I must see Petros, cross-examine him.'

'That will have to be planned carefully,' Newman remarked as he sat behind the wheel and drove off after storing their cases in the boot. He sensed tension in Tweed, that he was in one hell of a hurry.

Forty minutes later they were sitting in the room Newman had booked for Tweed. Newman relayed to him all the details about Anton he'd extracted from Christina. As he listened, sipping mineral water in his shirt-sleeves, Tweed's expression became grimmer.

'A man of many talents,' he commented as Newman concluded his report. 'And now I'm sure he's returned to England.' He told Newman the news Beck and Monica had given him in Zurich. 'I don't like the sound of any of this. But when can we get down to Devil's Valley? Tomorrow?'

'That's pushing it. You'll need protection – and an interpreter. Petros doesn't speak English, you don't speak Greek. I think we have just the man. Nick the Greek, our driver. I've kept him on ice. He's holed up at the Astir Palace just across the square. He's even protested about the extra fee I pay him, saying he's doing nothing for it. Do you want to talk with Christina?'

'Yes.' He looked at Paula.

She shook her head, smiled impishly. 'Better you see her on your own. I'll cramp your style. I bet you have her eating out of your hand.'

'I doubt that.' Tweed finished off his second glass of mineral water. 'But one-to-one conversations normally get off the ground better.'

443

'Especially when you're with an attractive girl,' Paula went on.

'Oh, do shut up.' Tweed put on his jacket. 'Just going to the bathroom. Back in a minute . . .'

Paula waited until he reached the door, then called out. 'Don't forget to comb your hair!' Tweed gave her a glare and vanished.

'You do twist his tail,' Newman commented.

She became serious. 'I'm trying to relax him. I'm really worried about him. He's got the bit between his teeth over this business. He's become obsessed.'

'Can you explain that quickly? I'll be taking him along soon to Christina.'

'It started with Masterson's death. You can't kill one of Tweed's sector chiefs and expect him to shrug it off like Howard might. Then Jill Kearns – and he took a fancy to her – was murdered in London. Before that his old friend Sam Partridge was killed on Exmoor. And now an old lady in her seventies, a Mrs Larcombe, he interviewed has been battered to death at Porlock Weir. That was the last straw, I suspect. All the killings could be linked. If he decides Petros is in some way responsible I don't know what he'll do. Which is why I'm petrified about this Devil's Valley visit. Tweed has lost his sense of detachment.'

'Thanks for telling me. I'll bear it in mind. Now I must call someone.'

Newman went to the phone, dialled a number, perched on the edge of the bed. 'That you, Nick? Can you get over here for a talk? In about five minutes? Good. My room. See you . . .'

Tweed came out of the bathroom as he put down the phone. 'We'll be having a conference about the trip to Devil's Valley while you talk with Christina,' he told Tweed. 'Nick, Marler and myself.'

'The sooner the better. I'm ready for Christina. What about you, Paula? Going to peek at the shops?'

444

'She'll be joining us,' Newman said firmly. He seemed to have taken command of the situation, noted Paula. Noted it with relief.

Newman escorted Tweed to another room on the same floor. When he rapped on the door in a certain sequence it was opened by Marler. He gazed at Tweed, then at Newman.

'You might have told me he was coming. About time,' he continued, looking at Tweed. 'Glad to have you on board. We need to take some action.'

'You'll get all you can handle soon,' Newman promised him. 'Be a good chap, push off to my room. Here's the key. Tweed wants to talk with Christina.'

As Marler left he walked into the room, followed by Tweed, and introduced him to Christina. 'My Editor-in-Chief . . .'

Christina was sitting on a sofa, her back propped against one end, her long legs stretched out. She wore a low-cut emerald green dress, strapless, and backless to the lower part of her spine. She put down the book she was reading and stared at Tweed with her large eyes as Newman left the room, assessing him. Then she swung her legs off the sofa and sat with them crossed, one bare arm rested along the top of the sofa.

'Do sit down. Pull up a chair close to me. You look like a man who can take care of himself.'

'I've survived so far.' Tweed moved a chair, sat down so their knees were almost touching. She was a woman who liked close combat, who liked to touch a man if he passed inspection. Tweed had a feeling he'd done just that. And he wanted her to talk. She asked him if he'd like a drink. He said mineral water would be fine. She reached out to a table standing at the end of the sofa, poured him a glass from a collection of bottles, then she helped herself to a glass of white wine. She raised her glass.

'Here's to us.'

'To us . . .'

'And you're not an editor.' She peered at him over the rim and sipped some wine. 'You have the eyes of a policeman. They're nice eyes.'

'I was once a policeman.' He had decided frankness – up to a point – was his best tactic with this shrewd and glamorous creature. 'What can you tell me about the Greek Key? I need your help. Very badly. A lot of people have already died here and in England. I suspect more may die unless I find out what is going on.' He took off his glasses, laid them on the table. 'I need all the help I can get.'

'Will Newman or Marler be coming back?' She watched him through half-closed eyes.

'Not unless I summon them. I wasn't thinking of doing so.'

He had trouble keeping his eyes off her beautifully moulded shoulders. The dress fitted her snugly; her well-rounded breasts projected against the cloth. She leaned forward and kissed him full on the mouth.

'That was for starters, Tweed.'

'The Greek Key?'

'A group of the most dangerous men in Greece. Shadow men who operate in the dark. The police can't find them. They live secret lives. Does that sound melodramatic?'

'Yes. But it sounds just what I'm looking for. Tell me more.'

'So you don't really need your glasses to see?'

'Only long distance. When I'm driving. Times like that. Then I forget I'm wearing them. Tell me more,' he repeated.

'I've told you too much already. You want to get me killed?'

'No. I'd go a long way to prevent that. Is Anton a member?'

She blinked, lowered her eyes. He could have sworn the suggestion came to her as a great shock. That she was

446

thinking back over incidents she had observed – trying to link them up with his question.

'I never thought of that.' She opened her full red lips and ran the tip of her tongue along her lower lip. 'I can trust you?'

'You must decide that for yourself.'

'When my mother sent me to the university – she's dead, Petros killed her with overwork on the farm – there was an English professor, Guy Seton-Charles.'

'What about him?' Tweed asked in the same quiet tone.

'There were rumours. He came to lecture from England each year. Behind his back they called him The Recruiter.'

'Who were "they"?' His voice was very soft now, careful not to disturb her mood.

'You will protect me?' She leaned close again and her eyes were enormous. She slowly removed her earclips, placed them on the table.

'Yes,' he said. 'Providing you do exactly what I tell you when the time comes.'

'You're a nice man. Some of the students who attended the Seton-Charles lectures stopped going to them.'

'Who was he recruiting for?'

'The Greek Key.' Her smooth-skinned face was almost touching his and he caught a waft of perfume. He told himself to move back but he was frightened of breaking the spell. 'I asked what it was and they wouldn't tell me. You asked me if Anton was a member. He attended the lectures and finished the course. After that he was a changed man.'

'Changed in what way?'

'He used to lay women like rows of beans. He still kept his playboy image outwardly – but he seemed to have become colder, more purposeful – dedicated. That's it. *Dedicated*.'

'Dedicated to what?'

447

'I don't know. Really, I don't, Tweed. As though he'd found some mission in life. Almost like a religious conversion. But he's an agnostic. That's all I can say.'

Tweed eased his chair away. He stood up. Christina also stood up and walked towards him. He had a curious gleam in his eyes. He saw his glasses still on the table, picked them up. Before he could put them on she grasped him.

'Let's do it. Now.'

He sighed, shook his head. 'Christina, I said I would protect you. I will. But I can't if we get involved with each other. I must go. Pack your things ready for a quick departure. All except your night things.'

'I have to say thank you.'

She pressed herself against him, kissed him again.

'You'll be leaving tomorrow,' he told her.

'Unless Dimitrios or Constantine or Anton reach me tonight.'

'Which do you fear most?'

'Anton. Of course . . .'

'He is no longer in Greece. And you will continue to be with someone until you leave. It may be a woman.'

'What use will she be? In an emergency?'

'More deadly than a man. I must go. Lock the door and only open it for the special knock. You do have confidence in me?'

'Completely.' She ran her hands through her hair. 'We will meet again?'

'If possible. It depends on how things develop . . .'

He waited outside the closed door until he heard her lock it. His hands were wet with perspiration. And not from the heat.

Four people sat round a table in Newman's room. Newman himself, Nick the Greek, Paula and Marler. Two litre bottles of mineral water stood on the table with four glasses. The bottles were almost empty. Tweed was introduced to Nick who clasped his hand in a firm grip and gazed straight at him. Tweed liked what he saw.

'Bob,' he said, 'take Paula along to Christina and introduce her. I want you to stay with her, Paula. Only open the door to the special knock Bob will demonstrate.'

Paula looked amused as she stood up and smoothed down her skirt. She stood close and whispered. 'Better go into the bathroom and comb your hair again. Clean up your mouth at the same time.'

Newman had reached the door with Paula when Tweed stopped them. 'Wait a moment.' He looked at Nick. 'I understand you can find weapons. We'll all be away when we go to Devil's Valley. Paula should have some protection. A small handgun. Can you obtain one for her?'

Nick, still seated, rolled up his left trouser leg and revealed the holster strapped to it. He pulled out a small gun, a .32 Browning automatic. He showed it to Paula.

'Do you know this gun?'

'Yes. It's a Browning. I've practised with it. That would do nicely.'

'And spare mags.' Nick handed her the gun and hauled the mags out of his pocket.

Paula dropped the mags into her handbag. She examined the Browning, released the magazine from the butt, made sure there was no bullet up the spout, all the time holding the weapon pointed at the wall. Nick watched with approval as she rammed the mag home again, dropped the weapon inside her handbag.

'You know the gun,' he said.

Tweed laid a hand on her shoulder. 'Only to be used in extreme emergency – if Christina's or your own life is in danger. You have no permit to use that in Greece. But if push comes to shove I'll square it with Peter Sarris. Take care.'

'And *you* take care,' she said vehemently. 'This whole secret expedition to Devil's Valley is madness . . .'

'Now go along with Bob and make friends with Christina.'

When they had gone he excused himself. Inside the bathroom he checked his appearance in the mirror. He should have done that before he'd left Christina. His hair was mussed up; traces of lipstick showed on his mouth. Christina had deliberately let him go like that – knowing there was another woman with him. Just to show Paula. Women! Thank God he'd kept control of himself.

He had a wash, used a tissue to clean off the lipstick. When he had combed his hair he went back into the bedroom.

'What's the plan?' he asked, sitting down at the table.

'She's quite a girl, Christina,' Marler remarked cynically.

'Don't you start.' Tweed jabbed his index finger at Marler. 'I said what's the plan?'

'Crack of dawn tomorrow we start out,' Marler began in a languid tone. 'We drive to the entrance near Cape Sounion. You go in on foot with Nick. He speaks Greek, he's the interpreter, and he knows the way. And we've devised back-up . . .'

Marler explained the details and Tweed listened in silence. He nodded when Marler had finished. 'You've been out here a while. You know what you're doing. At least, I hope so. I approve the plan.'

'It will be tricky – the timing,' Nick interjected. 'Dangerous, too.' He was looking at Tweed. 'What type of gun would you like? I can get most . . .'

'I never carry a gun.'

Tweed stood up. 'I have to attend to something now.' Newman came back into the room, using his key to unlock the door. 'I'm off to the Embassy,' Tweed told him. 'I have to talk to Monica, get her to contact Roberts at

450

Lloyd's. And warn Butler Anton is probably back on his patch.'

'I'll come with you,' said Nick. 'We pass the Astir Palace on the way to the Embassy. I can pick up another Browning from under my car in the garage.'

'I can go alone. I know the way. I studied a street plan of Athens before I left London. No one will recognize me.'

'I'm coming with you,' Nick persisted. 'Petros could have men watching this hotel. They would see you arrive with Newman and make the connection.'

'You're right. Thank you.'

Tweed cursed himself inwardly for not thinking of that. Maybe the heat was getting to him. They were crossing the road to the Astir Palace when Nick made the remark.

'It will be touch and go whether we survive in Devil's Valley.'

43

Dawn was breaking over the Temple of Poseidon when the two cars pulled off the coast road close to the skeletal hotel building site. Nick drove the Mercedes with Tweed beside him. Behind them Newman drove a hired Peugeot with Marler as his passenger.

'I'll drive,' he'd told Marler when they started from Athens in the dark. 'We want to get there in one piece.'

'I was a racing driver once,' Marler informed him.

'I know. You must have been a menace to the other contestants. I don't want to end up in the sea . . .'

Tweed stepped out of the Mercedes and stretched. He was wearing a pair of mountaineer boots purchased in

Kolonaki. He'd worn them for the rest of the previous day to break them in.

Nick lifted up the travelling rug on the rear seat, took hold of the twin-barrelled shotgun. He had a fresh Browning strapped to his leg, a .38 Smith & Wesson in a hip holster under his loose jacket.

'A walking armoury,' Tweed had joked.

'We'll need it,' Nick had replied without a smile.

While Nick was collecting the weapon, locking the car, Tweed gazed at the fantastic colours of sky and sea. A spectrum of rose pink, cobalt and sapphire sea. An incredible sight you wouldn't find anywhere else in the world.

'Ready?' asked Nick.

'On a job like this the thing is get moving. No palaver.'

Nick led the way behind the complex and they plunged into the wilderness of limestone bluffs looming above donkey trails which twisted and climbed. There was no sound once they'd left behind the screech of the gulls over the sea which soon vanished from view. Nick placed his feet carefully, treading wherever possible on tufts of grass to deaden the sound of his footfalls. Behind him Tweed followed suit, watching for any sign of human life.

He wore a wide-brimmed straw hat, his safari jacket, tropical drill trousers tucked into the tops of his boots. Despite Nick's long sloping strides, Tweed had no trouble keeping up with him. In London he'd taken to rising very early, walking two miles round the deserted streets every day. At the weekends he drove down to Surrey, parked his Cortina and climbed the North Downs. He was in better shape than for years.

They crossed the pass and began to descend into Devil's Valley. The tortuous path twisted as it dropped rapidly round boulders of limestone. Both Nick and Tweed carried water bottles slung over their shoulders. Nick carried the shotgun in his left hand and paused as he came to each man-high boulder. He peered round it cautiously, waved to Tweed to proceed, and walked on.

The sun was climbing in a clear turquoise sky. Already it was becoming very hot: the heat from the previous day had never dissipated during the night. As they progressed deep inside the valley Tweed cast frequent glances up at the ridges enclosing them to east and west. No sign of movement. Only the occasional sheep came into view, head down as it searched for nourishment among the scrub grass.

Tweed saw a weird squat structure perched on the ridge against the eastern skyline. He guessed it was the abandoned silver mine where Newman had had his nightmare experience. They arrived at the base of the valley and the path ran to left and to right. Nick paused, drank from his water bottle, wiped sweat off his forehead. Tweed wrapped a large silk handkerchief round his own neck to mop up the sweat.

'What's that thing?' Tweed asked, pointing to a crumbling high building. A series of chutes ran at angles and all the metal was rusty. The derelict structure stood at the foot of a path climbing up the eastern slope.

'The old ore-crushing plant where they extracted the silver,' Nick explained. 'Hasn't been used for years. Donkey trains brought down the ore. Have you noticed how quiet it is? And no sign of anyone.'

It was the first conversation they had had since they started out. They had agreed in the car they wouldn't speak during the descent into the valley. Nick had explained that voices carried a long distance.

'Well, isn't that our good luck?' Tweed commented and drank from his own water bottle.

'It's too quiet. And I have not seen one single shepherd. That I do not like.'

'Why not?'

'It is almost as though they know we are coming. Fifteen more minutes' walk along this path to the left and we see Petros' farmhouse . . .'

It was creepy. Despite the glare of the sun burning down Tweed found the silence unnerving. Now they had to pick their way among a bed of stones and rocks and he realized they were walking along the path of a stream. In winter it would be a gushing flood.

Tweed paused to glance round. Dante's Inferno. That was what it reminded him of. The deep valley, the mountains closing in, the heat trapped in the wide gulch they were moving through. It was the sheer aridity of the slopes which appalled him. Scrub, nothing but scrub.

By now his boots and clothes were coated with fine limestone dust. It clung to his wet face. Nick turned and walked back to him. He scanned the slopes and shook his head.

'Maybe we should go back,' he suggested.

'Why?' asked Tweed.

'Look at that flock of sheep grazing high up on the mountain. No shepherd. There should be a shepherd. Something's wrong.'

'How many shepherds has Petros?'

'Between twelve and fifteen. It is a big farm. And all those men are armed.'

'I'm not turning back now. I have to see Petros. Let's keep moving.'

Nick shrugged. 'OK. Petros' farm is round the next bend. We approach very cautiously . . .'

The long tumbledown building with a veranda stretching its full frontage came into view. Nick stopped abruptly. The desert-like atmosphere was transformed. Tweed gazed at the olive groves climbing up behind the farmhouse, small stunted trees with tortured twisted trunks. On the empty

454

veranda stood a large wickerwork chair. Tweed noticed the cushions were depressed – as though someone had sat there recently. The silence was even more oppressive.

'I am responsible for your safety,' said Nick. 'I think that we should turn back at once. We are walking into a trap.'

When Newman had introduced Paula to Christina the previous day and left them alone the atmosphere had been frigid. Christina eyed Paula up and down, lit a cigarette and then asked her casually, 'You're Tweed's woman?'

Paula tensed, then relaxed. 'Not in the sense you mean.' She decided she'd start as she meant to go on. 'Let's get one thing straight between us. I'm here to protect you. Just like Newman and Marler were. We're going to be penned up inside this room. Even at night because I'll be sleeping in the other bed. We'll use room service for all meals, including breakfast. Two women cramped together like that is a recipe for an explosion. There won't be one. Now, shall we start all over again?'

By the following morning they were chatting like old friends. It was Christina who brought up the subject when the waiter had taken their breakfast things away.

'Have they gone into Devil's Valley?'

'I think they're somewhere in Athens. On some checking job.'

Christina sat close to Paula, laid a hand on her arm. 'I can tell you are fond of Tweed. I like him myself. If he's gone into Devil's Valley he'll be killed. Petros hates what he calls English. He thinks an Englishman killed both his sons during the war.'

'Tweed can look after himself . . .'

'Then that *is* where he has gone?'

Paula bit her lip. She'd been indiscreet: Christina was quick. And very worried. Which increased the anxiety

Paula was feeling. Christina gripped Paula more firmly, her tone emphatic.

'I know the area. Petros and his men know every inch of that Godforsaken wilderness. Even if they've all gone – Tweed, Newman and Marler – they won't survive. Your friends are committing suicide. Their bodies will never be found. They'll be dropped down the old silver mine shaft . . .'

'Don't.' Paula began to feel sick. Christina had conjured up such a vivid picture. 'I didn't say that's where they were going.'

'But it is, isn't it? You said Tweed can look after himself. Petros is crazy. He has no mercy, no feelings. He lives only for revenge. Don't you understand? He's obsessed.'

Obsessed. Paula was shaken. Tweed, also, she felt was obsessed. What would happen when the two men confronted each other? She got up out of her chair, began to pace round the room. I'm doing what Tweed does, she suddenly thought.

'You have to do something,' Christina insisted. 'Now.'

Paula stopped by the telephone and smiled. 'I think I'm going to do something which will lose me my job.'

'Do you mind? If it saves Tweed – and the others?'

Paula checked the phone book, picked up the receiver, dialled police headquarters, asked for Captain Peter Sarris.

Keeping well away from the farmhouse which was overshadowed by a limestone crag, Tweed walked slowly forward over the dusty ground. Nick walked alongside, gripping his shotgun in both hands, the muzzle parallel with the earth.

'You interpret for me,' Tweed said. 'I'll try to make it a quickfire conversation.'

'With who?'

'I sense there are people here – all around us . . .'

He stopped speaking as a large tall man emerged from

456

the farmhouse. He had a hooked nose and thick eyebrows, a lined face. For a man of eighty his movements were vigorous. He carried a double-barrelled shotgun similar to Nick's and was followed by two much younger men. From Newman's description they were Dimitrios and Constantine. Both carried rifles.

'I am Petros,' the old man announced as he descended the steps. 'Bring me a chair, Dimitrios,' he ordered.

Nick translated as Dimitrios carried the wicker chair into the sun. Petros sat in the chair, crossed his legs, laid the gun over his lap, the barrel aimed at Tweed's stomach. The safety catch was on. Seated in the open, Petros reminded Tweed of an Old Testament patriarch. His presence radiated authority and domination.

Dimitrios padded well to the right while Constantine also came into the open, taking up a position on the left – making it impossible for Nick to cover both men. He aimed his gun direct at the old man's chest.

'You were expected,' Petros said, and grinned.

'My name is Tweed. I hold a senior position in the British Special Branch. That is our version of a secret police force. I am investigating the deaths of Andreas and Stephen Gavalas, among others.'

'Listen to him!' Petros threw back his great head and roared with laughter. 'He expects me to believe his lies.' His manner changed, became menacing. 'The main thing is you are English. I hate all English. You made a big mistake coming here, a fatal mistake.'

'You are blind, old man? You can't see my friend has a gun aimed at you point-blank?'

'At the first sign of movement you are both dead. *You* must be blind. Have you overlooked Dimitrios and Constantine?'

Tweed had not overlooked them. They stood, feet slightly apart. Dimitrios had his rifle aimed at Tweed, Constantine aimed his weapon at Nick. Sweat was running down Tweed's neck into the already sodden handkerchief. More sweat trickled from his armpits. But inside he was as cold as ice as he held the old man's eyes.

'There have been more murders. One of my men, Harry Masterson, came here. He ended up at the foot of Cape Sounion. Don't say you've never heard of him. It was in the papers. You were responsible for his murder?'

Petros' eyes gleamed, locked on Tweed's. He patted his shotgun, as though to check it was there. There was pure hatred in the dark eyes.

'No,' he said eventually, 'I know nothing about that. He must have been the man who came into Devil's Valley by night weeks ago. We couldn't find him. You should have asked Florakis.' He waved his left hand towards the western ridge. 'He owns a scrap of land over there, two hundred hectares or so.'

'You call that a scrap of land?' Keep him talking, Tweed was thinking.

'I own two thousand hectares here.' Petros made a grand gesture. 'Another thousand in Macedonia. If I had killed your man I would tell you. Why not? You will not leave here alive . . .'

'You are a member of the Greek Key?'

Petros scowled, screwed up his thick eyebrows. 'You know too much, Mr Tweed. Yes, during the Civil War I was a member. But when I found they were controlled by Moscow I left them. You think I want some commissar telling me what to do?'

'So you won't like the idea that Anton is a member?'

'You lie!' Petros' face was distorted with fury. He uncrossed his legs and his shotgun barrel shifted, pointing into space. 'You dare to say that to me, English? Your time has come. I will listen to no more of your filthy accusations. You are at the end of your life . . .'

*　　*　　*

458

Tweed said the first thing that came into his head, something which would distract the old ruffian. 'You know about those diamonds which were taken from Andreas' dead body on Siros? A fortune.'

He reached up, removed his hat, scratched at his head, smoothed down his hair. 'Order your grandsons to freeze.' Nick translated rapidly.

The first shot hit the ground between Petros' splayed feet, kicked up a puff of dust. The second bullet struck within inches of Dimitros. The third a foot behind Constantine. Petros' gnarled hands gripped the sides of his chair. He sat motionless.

On the top of the eastern ridge Marler squinted through his telescopic sight, the crosshairs centred on Dimitrios' chest. At the summit of the western ridge Newman held his own rifle, aimed at Constantine. The telescopic sight brought up the Greek so close he felt he could reach out and touch him.

Tweed put his hat back on his head. There was a dry smile on his face. 'You really think I'd wander into this place without protection? My men are marksmen, as you may have realized. They could have killed both Dimitrios and Constantine – their bodies would be lying in the dust. Had you moved, Nick would have shot you dead. Who would have carried out your mission of vengeance? If anyone attempts to move they will be shot. Now, can we continue?'

'You are a brave man.' Petros spoke slowly, glancing up at the ridge crests. 'You are also a clever man. OK. Talk.'

'Let's talk about Anton. He went to England many weeks ago by a secret route. You sent him, I suspect. His mission? To locate three men. Colonel Barrymore, Captain Robson and CSM Kearns, the same three men who accompanied Andreas on the fatal raid on Siros. Am I right?'

Petros drew a hand across the grey stubble of his unshaven face and stared at Tweed. It was a long minute before he replied. Tweed could feel the furnace-like heat radiating up from the ground.

'You are right,' Petros told him. 'That was the first stage in my plan to kill the man responsible.'

'You know which one did it? Anton found these men?'

'We don't know which one. Yes, he found them. All living so close together. I thought that strange.'

'Then Anton returned, told you what he had discovered. But it took you only part of the way. Because you still didn't know who murdered Andreas on Siros, stole the diamonds, then returned to Cairo and killed Stephen, masquerading as Ionides? The killer must somehow have found out his real identity. That worried him sufficiently for him to decide Stephen also must die. Why was Stephen living in Cairo under an assumed name?'

Tweed waited while Nick translated. He was trying to keep his questions short, to encourage Petros to continue the conversation, but he had to extract the whole story.

'You are right,' Petros said again. 'About Anton's first trip to England. And the rest. The EDES mob sent Stephen to Cairo as a spy. They gave him false papers under the name Ionides.'

'Maybe it was the right-wing EDES which killed Andreas?' Tweed pressed on.

'No. They had their headquarters on Siros, under the nose of the German commanding general, Geiger. They wanted the diamonds. They would never have killed one of their own.'

'What about the Germans? Maybe one of them did the job, found the diamonds, took them?'

'I thought of that.' Petros paused. 'This will sound peculiar. I arranged a truce with General Geiger. He agreed. He did not want a bloodbath. A Greek killed in battle is one thing. But killed by a German soldier who steals from him, that is another. We met under a flag of

460

truce. He was a reasonable man. He said he knew which patrols were near the area that night. He would question them himself. I knew I could trust him. Later he sent me a message. Only one patrol was near the place where we found Andreas. None of them had even discovered the body.'

'So that leaves the three commandos?'

'Yes. Now, I think we end this . . .'

'Wait! Anton is now in England again. Did you send him – or was it his idea? Did he persuade you it would be a good idea?'

For the first time Tweed saw doubt in Petros' expression. The old man stirred uncomfortably, looked away from Tweed towards the farmhouse and beyond.

'It was his idea,' he said slowly. 'He pressed hard for me to agree. Mr Tweed, do not remove your hat again. Do not make the signal a second time. Look behind the farmhouse . . .'

Tweed turned his head. Then he knew the reason for the absence of shepherds when they had made their tortuous way into Devil's Valley. A group of about a dozen men in shepherd's clothes stood scattered above the farmhouse, concealed beneath the overhang of the crag where neither Marler nor Newman could possibly see them. He had been out-manoeuvred.

'I have only told you all this because I knew you would never leave this place alive,' Petros told him. 'You see they are all armed.' He stabbed a finger at Nick. 'Now you are marked for the first shots. As you drop I shall move very quickly – which I can – inside the house. Away from your marksmen who will not react until you make the signal. Then it will be too late. So, Mr Tweed, you should never have come here . . .'

'Keep him talking for just a minute,' Nick whispered in English.

Tweed did not ask why. 'You haven't asked about

461

Christina. I know where she is. She is under my care. And not in Greece.'

The fury returned. The hands clutched at the chair. 'You hold her as a hostage? I do not believe it. I would do that, but you are not such a man . . .'

'A different subject,' said Tweed, seeking the maximum distraction, 'Why did you wait for so many years before trying to locate the three commandos? It doesn't make sense.'

Petros' eyes seemed to start out of his head. His right hand clenched the chair as he spat out the words. A streak of near-madness glittered in his expression. Obsessed, Tweed thought – I'm facing a man obsessed . . .

'First there was the Civil War . . . then the years of work to make money, to build up the farm . . . you need money to conduct a manhunt. I had my family to bring up. The years passed quickly, too quickly. And all that time the thought never left my head. I must track down the killer of my sons. I live with that each day. That is what keeps me going. *Revenge*. And now your time is up . . .'

Marler was a long way below the eastern crest where he had shot from. He knew he was taking a desperate gamble – that he was leaving one flank unguarded. But he had heard the tumble of rocks sliding, which meant someone was moving beneath the overhanging crag protecting the farm.

He knew he had assessed the geography correctly: Newman, perched high on the western ridge, couldn't possibly see beneath the great crag. As he made his rapid descent, his rifle looped across his back, he was helped by his small stature, by his slim build, by the fact that he was moving down the sandy bed of a dried-up stream – which enabled him to move silently.

He avoided shifting even the smallest pebble which might

give away his presence. His small feet skipped down the twisting bed. Then he slowed down, peered round the precipitous wall of the crag. The roof of the farm lay below. Under the shelter of the crag stood a group of shepherds, well spaced out, each holding a rifle or shotgun to his shoulder. Marler unlooped his own weapon.

Tweed could now hear the sounds which Nick's acute ears had picked up. The putt-putt beat of helicopter motors approaching fast. The machines appeared suddenly and at the same moment. One Alouette came over the western ridge, the second appeared over the eastern crest. Police choppers.

Petros stared upwards, exposing his thick neck. The chopper which flew in from the west was already dropping. Sarris was behind the swivel-mounted machine-gun, the glasses he had used looped round his neck. The window was open. A policeman beside him used an amplified loudhailer to shout the message in Greek.

'Drop your weapons or we open fire . . .'

A shepherd concealed behind a large boulder raised his rifle. He aimed for the pilot's cabin. There was a single report. The shepherd crumpled, shot in the back. Marler switched to another target. The shepherds panicked, hoisted their rifles to shoot at the chopper. Sarris' machine-gun began its deadly chatter, sweeping across those at the highest level. Shepherds threw up their hands, sagged to the ground.

'Run, Tweed . . .'

Nick darted forward, rammed the muzzle of his shotgun under Petros' jaw, shouted at him to get inside the house. The old man jumped out of his chair, fled for the veranda. Tweed was already running towards the house. On the western crest Newman saw one shepherd aiming his rifle over the rooftop at the running figure. He squeezed the

463

trigger. The shepherd dropped his weapon, took two paces forward, fell flat on his face.

Both Alouettes had landed. Uniformed police holding guns dropped to the ground, ducked under the whirling rotors, spread out, surrounded the farm. Sarris strode up the steps and into the farmhouse. Tweed held an axe he had snatched from the kitchen wall.

'Better late than never,' said Sarris.

44

They drove along Alexandras Avenue and pulled up outside police headquarters. Sarris had driven Tweed back from the helipad where the chopper landed after flying them from Devil's Valley. In the rear seats were Newman and Marler. Nick was driving his Mercedes back on his own; a uniformed policeman was bringing back Marler's hired Peugeot. Sarris switched off the engine, lit a cigarette.

'What was that business about the missing commando daggers at Petros' farmhouse?' Tweed asked.

'Six of them,' said Sarris, 'all collected from British commandos the Germans captured raiding the Cyclades islands. General Geiger apparently kept them as trophies. One night Petros and some *andartes* broke into his villa, walked off with them. Petros has kept them in a glass case at the farm.'

'I heard your conversation with him in Greek,' Newman commented. 'The old maniac used to gaze at them every evening before he went to bed – to remind himself of his mission of vengeance. I'd say there were five, not six, in Geiger's villa. The sixth could have been the knife which killed Andreas. It was Petros' lot who found the body and removed it – and remember the knife was still sticking in Andreas' back.'

'But how did you know Petros had this macabre collection?' Tweed asked.

'I had one of his shepherds in my pay. He's the man who dropped flat and survived when I opened fire. I had to twist Petros' arm to find out what happened when I noticed the case was empty.'

'And what did happen?' Tweed pressed. 'I have a reason for asking.'

'Petros eventually admitted they disappeared many weeks ago – about the time Anton left for his first trip to England.'

'Which *may* explain who killed Sam Partridge,' Tweed remarked.

'Why the doubt?' asked Marler.

'Because the three men on Exmoor would also have access to the weapon – when they were in the Army. We still don't know who the killer is. What will happen to Petros?' he asked Sarris.

'He'll end up behind bars. Maybe in a padded cell. Now, was your crazy expedition worthwhile?'

'Yes. I'm convinced Petros had nothing to do with the killing of Masterson. Which is why I came here. I also believe Petros was kept alive by his dream of vengeance, that he might never have taken any real action. The dream would have gone.'

Sarris opened the door. 'Let's go to my office, get a drink. I'm parched.' He looked at Tweed as he climbed out of the car. 'There's someone waiting to see you. And you'd better say thanks to her very nicely.'

Tweed asked the question suddenly, hoping to catch Sarris off balance. 'What precisely is the Greek Key?'

'It's an ancient symbol. You must know it. You see it used on embroideries, it appears in the friezes of temples.'

'Freeze is the word – what you all do when the phrase is mentioned.'

Tweed followed Sarris inside the building while Newman and Marler brought up the rear. They waited and then stepped inside an elevator. When they walked into the office Paula, who had been reading a magazine, dropped it and rushed to Tweed, hugging him.

'God! You're crazy,' she exploded. 'I warned you. Sarris sent a radio report from the chopper. You walked into an ambush.' She released him, stood back, spoke in a solemn voice. 'And I know I disobeyed your instructions. So I expect to be sacked.'

'Stuff and nonsense. I owe you my life.' Tweed sank into a chair while Sarris ordered coffee and mineral water over his intercom. 'But where is Christina? Is she on her own?'

'Of course not!' Sarris snapped. 'Paula phoned me. Before I drove to the helipad I left orders for a plain-clothes man to go to the Grande Bretagne to guard Christina – so Paula could come here.' He looked at Newman and Marler who had also sat down. 'Officially you were not involved. Which is why I've confiscated your rifles. They'll get lost. I won't ask how you obtained them.'

'That's big of you,' said Newman. 'Considering Marler shot down a shepherd who was aiming his rifle at the cabin of that chopper you were flying in. You could be cold meat on a slab now.'

Sarris grinned, looked at Tweed. 'Is he always so independent and aggressive?'

'Yes,' Marler interjected. 'A pain in the arse. But we did hold the situation until you arrived.'

'I think you all went mad,' Paula said and sipped at the cup of coffee served by a uniformed policeman. She was watching Tweed: there had been a major change in his mood and manner. The vehemence and tension seemed to have drained out of him.

A man came in and Tweed looked up. The Dormouse.

He stood up, smiled and shook hands. 'Good to see you again.'

'I would suggest,' Sarris began, 'that Kalos takes you for a ride away from here. That you ask him the question you put to me downstairs. I'd like the rest of you to stay while we cook up an official report, something that will make my superiors happy. The truth – but maybe not the whole truth . . .'

The Dormouse drove Tweed to the Plaka. He apologized for the transport, his battered old Saab. 'No one notices it,' he explained, 'which is why I favour it. Now the question.'

'What is the Greek Key?'

'I'll tell you when we reach my flat – that and a lot more. It's politically sensitive, which is why Sarris suggested we get out of police headquarters.' He manoeuvred the vehicle carefully inside the labyrinth, stopped outside a taverna, his engine still running. 'See that – Papadedes. Note the entrance to the staircase alongside – Papadedes hires out the room upstairs to men taking a woman up there. But other people have used that room. I will tell you in my flat.'

He parked the car inside a narrow alley climbing steeply up towards a hilltop. His flat was above a shop selling baskets and leather handbags to tourists. Tweed settled himself in an armchair after a good wash in a tiny bathroom. He felt more civilized after getting rid of the mixture of dried sweat and dust.

Kalos fussed about, making coffee. He placed the cup on a small round table next to the chair, produced a tin jug and two glasses. '*Retsina*,' he explained. 'If you do not like it leave it. And here is mineral water. Some bread with a little cheese – made from cow's milk. I do not think goat's milk cheese would appeal.'

'Very good of you, Kalos.' Tweed sipped at the

467

retsina. It tasted resinous. 'I like it. Now, can we talk?'

'The Greek Key,' Kalos began, settling himself in another armchair, 'is a highly secret underground organization of hardline Communists. It is run by a committee but the man who counts is Doganis, in his sixties . . .'

'Ah,' said Tweed, 'another man in his sixties. So he goes back also to the Second World War.'

'That is true.' Kalos leaned forward, tapped Tweed on the knee. 'And these are very hard men indeed. They are bitter because they just failed to take over Greece during the Civil War. We were saved by the American President, Truman. He sent a military mission, tons of arms. Now they have surfaced again. They are anti-Gorbachev.'

Tweed stiffened, put down his glass. 'Their activities are confined to Greece?'

'I don't think so. From the records, during the Second World War there were strong rumours the real controller of the Greek Key was an Englishman based in Cairo. Let me tell you what I have discovered.' He took a file from his briefcase. 'This is my secret report. You can read it later. Now, we start with the clandestine visit of General Lucharsky to Athens . . .'

Tweed ate the bread and cheese, listened grimly as The Dormouse described what he had found out. Lucharsky . . . Colonel Rykovsky. The arrival later of Lucharsky's aide, Colonel Volkov . . . the link with Doganis . . . Florakis, alias Oleg Savinkov, The Executioner . . . Pavelic, the Croat hardliner who had provided Kalos with secret information while drunk . . .

'This Pavelic,' Tweed said eventually, 'he is in touch with Moscow?'

'He boasted he had underground links with the hardliners inside Russia who hate and fear Gorbachev's reforms – that Gorbachev would not last much longer.'

Tweed recalled that Marler had seen Florakis carrying

a modern transceiver up a mountain on his land. The Dormouse listened with a gleam in his beady eyes.

'Who is he transmitting to?'

Tweed opened up, telling him about the three ex-commandos living on Exmoor; the long-ago murders in Cairo, on Siros; about the killing of Sam Partridge – who had been in Cairo as a very young man; the killing of Jill Kearns and Mrs Larcombe and the story the old lady had told Tweed.

Kalos nodded. 'We have uncovered a major conspiracy controlled by the hardline anti-Gorbachev faction in Moscow. I just cannot see where it leads.' He handed his file to Tweed. 'I would like you to read that – it includes times and photographs of the conspirators . . .'

Tweed read the file, automatically memorizing every detail. He studied the photos. Kalos sat with his hands clasped in his ample lap, waited patiently. When Tweed had finished he handed back the file.

'My God, it looks far worse than I ever dreamed. Could you get me copies of those prints?'

Kalos delved into his file, produced a large envelope which he passed to Tweed. 'I anticipated your request. I made copies myself in my own darkroom. All the dates are written on the back. I have signed my name and used a police headquarters rubber stamp. Sarris knows nothing of this. He destroyed the original file in my presence.'

'Sarris is involved?' Tweed asked.

A shake of the stubble-covered head. 'I'm sure he guessed I had already prepared a duplicate file. It was significant he did not ask for the negatives of those prints. Sarris would never forget a point like that. Except deliberately. We understand one another. Why do you think he suggested I took you away from HQ for a talk?'

'Of course.' Tweed smiled. 'It is just that I have a habit of trusting no one.'

'A very good habit. What are you going to do now? You

believe one of those three ex-commandos is the real head of the Greek Key?'

'I do now.'

'But which one? You have interviewed them all twice. Surely one of them let something slip? You are known for your flair for interrogation.'

'I think I know who it is.' Tweed paused. 'The devil of it is I have no proof.'

'And this Professor Seton-Charles you mentioned. The Recruiter, as Christina called him when talking with Newman. He too is involved?'

'Up to his ruddy neck would be my guess. Again, no proof. You asked me what I'm going to do. I'm very grateful to you, Kalos, for your cooperation. What you've dug up all on your own has filled in a lot of gaps. I am returning to England as rapidly as possible. The solution lies there.'

'Let me phone Sarris, see where they all are.' Kalos picked up the phone, dialled, spoke in Greek, waited, then spoke again at greater length. He put down the phone. 'Sarris tells me they are all at the Grande Bretagne, waiting for you. I hinted you may be leaving. He thinks that a good idea – after your experience in Devil's Valley. He looks forward to seeing you again.'

Tweed stood up. 'Thank you once more for everything. I am sure we will meet again.'

'There is always a next time in our work. I will drive you to the hotel.' The Dormouse smiled shyly. 'It has been a great pleasure to deal with you. I suppose you realize you may not have much time left to stop whatever is planned? They have been working on it for over a year.'

'That's what worries me. *I* don't think we have much time left. One more thing, could you leave Florakis alone? He sounds like the communications link. I don't want that disturbed.'

'I can persuade Sarris to agree to that. Now, as you say, you are short of time . . .'

They were all waiting for him in Newman's room: Newman himself, Marler and Nick. Newman told him Paula was still guarding Christina in her room.

'You see,' Nick intervened, 'I noticed at the farm that Dimitrios and Constantine were missing. I checked the bodies myself. I think they are in Athens, searching for Christina. It may be days before they hear Petros has been arrested. Sarris said he was keeping it out of the papers.'

'We are all leaving by a Swissair flight tomorrow,' Tweed told them. 'It leaves at 5 p.m., arrives at Zurich at 6.45 p.m. We stopped in the square on the way back and I bought tickets for everyone.' He dropped a folder on the table. 'Better collect your tickets now.'

'Why Zurich?' Newman asked. 'Why not a direct flight home?'

'Because we are taking Christina with us. I promised her protection. She will stay with our friend in Switzerland until this is all over.'

'May I make a suggestion?' said Nick.

'Go ahead.'

'You may well need strong protection until you have safely left Greece. If you take a taxi with Christina and Paula to the airport, Newman and Marler could follow close behind in the hired Peugeot the police returned.'

'That's good thinking,' agreed Tweed.

'But in case of emergency none of you is armed. Sarris took your rifles, as he took my shotgun. But I was not searched – I think that was deliberate.' He opened his jacket, took it off, exposing the hip holster carrying his .38 Smith & Wesson. Unfastening the holster, he laid it on the table. Pulling up his trouser leg, he unstrapped the holster containing a small Browning automatic, laid that on the

471

table. Then he emptied his jacket pockets of spare magazines and looked at Marler and Newman.

'Take your choice.'

'But we'll never get through airport security,' Newman pointed out.

'Yes you will. Because I will drive ahead to the airport to make sure it is safe. If I am standing leaning against my car when Tweed's taxi arrives, all is well. I then go to the men's room, followed by Newman and Marler. They hand the guns back to me.'

'Very bright,' Tweed agreed again.

Marler grabbed the Browning before Newman could object, saying he was smaller and wasn't going to lug the heavier Smith & Wesson about. Newman grimaced.

'Trust him to find the easy way.' He looked at Nick. 'You said you were running low on petrol.'

Nick jumped up. 'So I go and fill her up now. Do it at once is my maxim. I will be back later.'

Newman waited until they were alone. 'Tweed, shouldn't someone go to the Embassy, call Beck, warn him we're coming?'

'I was about to do that myself . . .'

'I feel like a walk. Give me his Berne number and I'll make the call.'

Tweed took out the pad he always carried with a sheet of plastic to stop the imprint of what he wrote being reproduced on the sheet underneath. He wrote down Beck's number from memory, gave it to Newman. After studying it for a few moments, Newman held the sheet over an ash tray, set light to it.

'I'm on my way . . .'

Tweed was left alone with Marler, who ran his hand through his fair hair before asking his question.

'What about Andreas' skeleton hanging inside that silver mine?'

'It *was* Andreas. Sarris told me he had questioned Petros

472

after I told him about its existence before we left the farm. Petros admitted he had kept the skeleton until he had administered justice – his phrase – to the murderer of his sons. Sarris sent a couple of men up to find the skeleton. I suppose it will be buried in due course. The whole episode shows Petros was crazy with his obsession.'

'And you're no further for'ard with who killed Masterson?'

'Yes, I am. After cross-examining Petros before the choppers arrived I'm convinced he told the truth. He had nothing to do with Masterson's death. So we're looking for someone else – which is what I came here to find out.'

'Any ideas?'

Despite their ordeal in Devil's Valley Marler looked fresh and ready for anything. He had cleaned himself up in the bathroom and emerged a new man.

'A lot,' said Tweed. 'I've been fed a whole load of new information. The trouble will be checking it out – and I'm not sure how much time we've got. You'll all be chasing your tails when we get back home. But Zurich comes first. Not that I expect it will be anything but a stopover . . .'

Beck met them at Zurich the following evening and they travelled from Kloten Airport to the Hotel Schweizerhof in two unmarked limousines. Inside the second car Christina was escorted by a plain-clothes policeman.

'She will be taken into the mountains,' Beck explained when they assembled in Tweed's corner room overlooking the Bahnhofstrasse and the main station. 'In a house near Santis,' he went on. 'Is there someone who needs smoke in their eyes? I didn't see anyone following us from the airport.'

'No. Just keep her out of harm's way,' Tweed replied. 'I'll give you a call when I'm sure the coast is clear. And we'll pay the expenses.'

'Oh, there will be a bill.' Beck smiled and sat down as Tweed gestured towards a chair. 'I have news. Is it for your ears only?'

'Everyone here knows what's going on.'

Tweed waved a hand, embracing Newman, Paula and Marler. When they arrived Christina had said she'd be taking a bath. She had been quite happy that Gustav, her guard, should stay in her room and drink coffee.

'I realized Anton Gavalas was important to you,' Beck began. He had chosen a chair next to Paula. 'I checked with Interpol in Paris, asked them whether anything unusual had happened in Lisbon. It has.' His voice became grave. 'And about just the time Anton was in the Portuguese capital. A murder.'

'God! Who was it this time?' Tweed asked.

'An unsavoury international arms dealer who went by the name of Gallagher. He ran a garage, apparently – as a cover for his real activities. He had been watched as he travelled all over Europe. No evidence. He was found stabbed in a service pit in his garage. Could there be a link with Anton?'

'Any idea what kind of knife was used?'

'Yes. It was left in the body. People don't realize it can be very difficult to withdraw the weapon if it is driven in deep. This one was. A British commando-type knife.'

'That sounds like Anton.'

'There is more. Some guesswork . . .' Beck waved a dismissive hand. 'But the dates are right. Anton stayed one night at The Ritz. The following day a Portuguese freighter carrying a consignment of cork for England sailed. The *Oporto*. After a few days it arrives at some port called Watchet in Somerset, unloads the cork, takes on board a cargo of wastepaper. Is this relevant?'

'More so than you might ever dream,' Tweed urged him on grimly.

'The *Oporto* had been shadowed by French aircraft.

474

French Intelligence, the *Direction de la Surveillance du Territoire*, had discovered the *Oporto* had visited Tripoli in Libya before arriving in Lisbon. Their aircraft lost it because of a storm and only picked it up again after it had left Britain and was sailing apparently back to Lisbon. Another storm drove it close to Brest. They sent out cutters and boarded it in French territorial waters. Anyone losing interest?'

'I'm fascinated,' said Paula. 'You're leading up to something.'

'I enjoy a little drama – as Tweed here sometimes does. They found in the hold an armoury of Sam missile launchers, missiles, hundreds of rifles and forty thousand rounds of ammunition. At the time there was an Irish fishing boat near Brest. Fodder for the IRA. Paris is certain of it.'

'I don't like the sound of this,' Tweed commented.

'Then you won't like the rest much. The DST interrogated Gomez, the *Oporto*'s captain. He wouldn't give any information. But a member of the crew he had rebuked did talk. He said before the ship reached Watchet it heaved to and someone carrying a large bundle was off-loaded into a waiting motorboat. The craft then headed for the British shore.'

'Did he recognize – I mean, see – anyone in the motorboat he could describe?'

'No. He was concealed behind the bridge and frightened of being found. End of story.'

'Or the beginning,' said Tweed. 'Sam missile launchers. That frightens me. What *was* landed on that remote stretch of Somerset coastline? And why? For what purpose? Those are the questions we must find answers to. And the solution lies back home in England.'

45

London. As soon as Tweed arrived back at Park Crescent he worried away like a beaver at the problem. He assembled all his helpers in his room, issued a whole series of instructions.

Newman, Marler, Paula and Monica were there. Everyone had to know what the others were doing. The Director, Howard, back from a long holiday, lounged in a chair, listening. He made a typical comment as he brushed imaginary specks of dust off his immaculate navy blue suit.

'This is costing us a fortune. Your trip to Athens alone . . .'

'Are you saying we are wasting our time?' Tweed enquired.

Paula sat behind her desk watching Tweed. He had lost his earlier manner of a man obsessed: seeing Petros had cured him of that. It was now the normal Tweed: calm, dogged, speaking in a controlled tone. Paula felt enormously relieved.

'No,' Howard replied. 'Not after hearing all the details. I don't like that business Kalos told you about General Lucharsky, Colonels Rykovsky and Volkov – above all the connection with Doganis. It does sound as though the hardline faction inside Russia – the anti-Gorbachev lot – has succeeded in establishing a power base outside Russia.'

'And that base is over here. All we have to do is to find it.'

'You make it sound so easy,' Howard observed.

'What gets me,' Paula persisted, 'is how they were able

to do that under our noses.' She frowned. 'Unless it was set up a long time ago and has recently been activated.'

'Monica,' said Tweed, 'double-check with Roberts, our man at Lloyd's. I want all details of the movements of that Portuguese vessel, the *Oporto*. Paula, drive down to Exmoor with Newman. Find out on the spot whether Butler and Nield have discovered anything more about movements in that area. Especially about Anton – and Seton-Charles, who seems to have vanished off the face of the earth. Marler, Interpol have persuaded Lisbon to send me that knife used to kill Gallagher. It's arriving at London Airport aboard this flight.' He gave him a sheet of paper. 'In the custody of the pilot of the plane. Bring it back here. I want to check if it really is a commando-type weapon.'

'We stay at The Anchor at Porlock Weir?' Paula suggested as she took from a cupboard the small case she kept packed for emergency trips.

'It's out of the way, a good place to stay under cover. And you can check on Mrs Larcombe's murder. Bob, you get out of the car short of the hotel, register as though you don't know Paula. It can come in useful to have a secret reserve.'

'And I'll have my Mercedes back, thank you very much.'

'Goody,' said Paula. 'I'll get to drive it. At ninety down the motorway,' she joked.

Tweed gave her a look as she left with Newman. Marler raised himself slowly from his chair. 'I'd better push off to the airport before you think of something else . . .'

'Just like old times,' Monica said when Marler had gone. 'It's all go – the way I like it.' She reached for the phone to call Lloyd's. 'Do you really think Anton is back in this country?'

'He's somewhere over here. What I'd like to know is what he's doing,' Tweed answered sombrely.

* * *

It was raining heavily at Cherry Farm in Hampshire. Anton could hear it beating down on the roof of the huge barn where he was working. Perfect weather: it kept potential snoopers indoors. Inside the second furniture van, parked behind the other vehicle, he turned round as Seton-Charles appeared and climbed up the lowered tailboard.

'How are you progressing?' the Professor asked.

'I will show you. We are far advanced.'

Anton moved a tool box on the floor among the straw, used his screwdriver to lever up the hinged floorboards. Beneath was the secret compartment he had constructed to store the Stinger launchers and the missiles.

Seton-Charles gazed round the interior of the huge vehicle. At the front, behind the driver's cab – shut off from the interior – Anton had erected a wooden platform, railed, and with steps leading up to it. A special wooden chair he had designed with an adjustable back was clamped to the platform floor.

Anton inserted a missile into the launcher, carried the weapon up to the platform, and sat in the chair. Reaching down, he depressed a switch. There was the faint sound of electrical machinery on the move. A large panel in the van's roof slid open, exposing the roof of the barn six feet above the top of the van.

He settled himself into the chair, raised the launcher, the stock pressed firmly into his shoulder. The Greek swivelled the weapon through an arc.

'Imagine open sky, a plane approaching three thousand feet up. I press the trigger, the heat-seaking device homes on the target. *Boom!* No plane. Satisfied?'

He didn't give a damn whether his companion was satisfied or not. The main thing was *he* knew it would work. He climbed back down the steps, detached the missile, wrapped it separately in a polythene sheet, did the same thing with the launcher, made sure they were safely tucked away and closed the floorboards. Then he rubbed dirt over the joins, moved straw over the compartment.

'Now I have to do the same job with the other van. It all takes time.'

'Maybe I could help by going in to Liphook and fetching the new food supplies?' Seton-Charles suggested.

He was getting housebound. Anton had not allowed him to leave the farm since he had arrived. The Greek shook his head. He had grown a thick moustache; he wore a greasy boiler suit and wore the type of cap affected by the average farm worker. His British boots were smeared with caked mud.

'I get the food,' Anton told him. 'You said Liphook. Do you not realize I buy each time from a different town? Where is your sense of security?'

'I am sorry. That was a foolish mistake . . .'

'Which could have been fatal. Let us go into the farmhouse – I want to check the two rooms we have prepared for the prisoners. They will be brought here within the next few weeks . . .'

They entered the farm by the back door: Anton insisted that they never used the front entrance which was kept permanently locked. He led the way up the old staircase and along the corridor to the two rooms facing the back. They were separated by the bathroom.

Each door had two locks and a bolt Anton had fixed. In each door was a spyhole with a cap which closed down over it on the outside. They could look in but an occupant could not see out. He opened the first door, walked inside. The room was starkly furnished.

An iron bedstead screwed to the floor over which was spread a straw-filled palliasse and two blankets. An Elsan bucket in the corner for the performance of natural functions. Anton told Seton-Charles to operate the light switch which he had installed in the corridor. He walked over to the windows he had double glazed. No way of breaking out there – especially as the shutters were closed and padlocked on the outside.

'Who are these prisoners?' Seton-Charles asked.

'Just two men.' Anton continued as though talking to himself. 'I must remember no pork. Lamb and chicken is their diet – and somewhere I will find Turkish coffee. In a supermarket in Winchester, probably.' He looked round. 'Yes, all is ready for our visitors.'

'I would like to know what is going on,' Seton-Charles protested.

'Patience. In the meantime, when you are not helping me as labourer you can study your Greek books. Jupiter stressed in his last call you must remain here.' Anton grinned unpleasantly. 'And do you think you would sleep well at night if you upset Jupiter?'

Paula and Newman stayed for several weeks at The Anchor. When Newman phoned Tweed from a public call box one evening Tweed said he wanted them both to remain there until recalled. They were to explore the whole area, to listen to gossip in pubs, to try and find the route Anton used to *leave* the country.

'I don't think he boarded a ship the way he probably came in,' Tweed said. 'We've been very busy here, contacting every airport in the country. No passenger manifest shows that he left by a scheduled flight. And remember, Christina told you he was a pilot, experienced with flying light aircraft . . .'

When he put down the phone Monica queried his decision.

'You have a lot of people in one area. Paula, Newman, Butler and Nield. Isn't that overkill?'

'I'm deliberately saturating that district. I feel it in my bones the solution lies on Exmoor.'

'Anything interesting from Bob? I know it's on the tape I can listen to, but I find your comments more informative.'

'Everything seems normal. Dr Robson visits his patients

480

– riding his horse. He works long hours. Barrymore makes infrequent phone calls from the phone box in Minehead.'

'Isn't that peculiar? Surely you said he has a phone of his own at Quarme Manor?'

'Apparently it often goes on the blink, as Newman expressed it. Something to do with the overhead wires getting blown down. It's the stormy season down there. Gale Force Ten and heavy seas.'

'What about Kearns?'

'He leads a strange life. When there's a moon he rides up to Dunkery Beacon, stays there a while. Butler has watched him through night glasses. He sits on his horse, still as a statue. Then he disappears for a while before riding back to his house.'

'Makes sense to me,' said Monica. 'The poor man has lost his wife. He just wants to be on his own. And he's trying to keep his sanity by maintaining old habits.'

'Another funny development – Paula found this out from lunching in pubs on Exmoor. Kearns doesn't meet his chums Barrymore and Robson any more. No Saturday night dinners at The Luttrell Arms, no Wednesday lunches at The Royal Oak, Winsford. He has cut himself off from them completely.'

'You can't tell how grief will affect people.'

'It's a very major change in relationships,' Tweed pointed out. 'For years those three acted as though they were still members of an Army unit. Kearns walking away is bound to affect the other two, Barrymore and Robson. Psychologically, I mean. We are still seeing the thing develop.'

'You'll get there in the end,' Monica encouraged him.

Tweed took from a drawer the commando knife which had killed Gallagher in Lisbon. That had been a frustrating exercise. At the last moment the Portuguese police chief had refused to send the weapon direct to London: Marler had arrived at London Airport several weeks before, only to find the pilot had nothing for him.

The knife had been ultimately despatched to Interpol in Paris. Which was the correct procedure. Tweed's friend, Pierre Loriot, had immediately flown it to London, but it had all taken precious time. Then there was the report from Lloyd's of London on the *Oporto*.

The typed document had confirmed all Tweed had been previously told. The vessel's clandestine call at Tripoli in Libya. Its voyage from Tripoli back to Lisbon – the arrival at that port coinciding with Anton flying from Zurich to the Portuguese capital. The shadowing of the vessel by French aircraft, culminating in its seizure after leaving Somerset off the port of Brest. The discovery of the large armoury of weapons which, Paris was certain, was destined for the IRA. Another dead end, as Tweed termed it, leading them nowhere further.

It was now November. Rain fell in a slanting downpour outside as Tweed put the weapon back in the drawer.

'I'm missing something,' he said. 'I feel it is under my nose and I can't see it. Get out all those tapes of phone conversations. I want to listen to them again. With a fresh ear.'

The dacha was located in the hills north-east of Moscow. There was a colony of them nearby where the bigwigs relaxed in summer, but this one was isolated. It was used for high-security military conferences in the hot season.

General Lucharsky stopped the Chaika a few hundred yards away from the shuttered building, switched off the engine, walked the rest of the way. His gleaming fur-lined boots crunched in the crisp hard snow; there had been a light fall the previous night. The temperature was eight degrees below freezing and he pulled up his military great-coat collar, revelling in the invigorating air.

The building was made of timber. Steps led up to the veranda overhung by the projecting roof. The place was surrounded with birch woods flaked with white. Sunlight reflected off the snow crystals. Lucharsky climbed the steps, stood by the front door and looked around. He listened carefully and heard nothing in the heavy silence. He had not been followed. He rapped on the heavy door four times slowly.

When the door opened two men, also wearing the uniforms of generals, appeared. Lucharsky put a finger to his lips. With a swift gesture he indicated that they should follow him. He led the way back down the steps and into the woods. His arm brushed a branch and crusted snow fell on it.

'Why could we not stay in the dacha?' asked a short stocky general with stubby legs and thick eyebrows under his peaked cap. General Budienny.

'Because it may be wired for sound,' Lucharsky told him contemptuously. He towered over both his companions. 'Out here no one can hear us.'

He stopped inside a hollow encircled with trees. The Troika was assembled. Lucharsky kicked snow off his boots before continuing. The third man, an expert on armoured divisions, listened.

'The plan is proceeding,' Lucharsky informed them. 'I have now heard Gorbachev will land in Britain at the invitation of British Prime Minister Thatcher. We have him.'

'On the way to or back from the Washington summit?' asked Budienny.

'En route to Washington. Except his plane will never land. In one piece, that is. The missiles are in place.'

'How do you know where he will land? London Airport?' persisted Budienny.

'We don't know yet.' Lucharsky waved a gloved hand. 'It makes no difference. The missiles are located in a central

483

position close to many airfields – including RAF military bases. They are mobile. Can be moved to the correct area as soon as we get the precise data.'

'How do you know all this?'

Lucharsky sighed. 'We have direct communication with the man who will control the operation. By radio. A complex route. But coded signals are received by one of our men at the Black Sea naval base of Novorossiisk. He is an excellent radio operator and brings me the signals regularly to Moscow.'

'Routine is dangerous,' Budienny objected. 'And our necks are on the block.'

Lucharsky sighed again, his expression saturnine. 'Since that naval base is so important a courier flies frequently to Moscow to report on progress about enlarging it. Our man is that courier. And before you suggest he could be searched he carries the messages verbally in his head, then tells me.' His tone became mocking. 'If your fears are now allayed perhaps I can proceed? The plan has taken on new dimensions.'

'What are those?'

'As Number Two in the Politburo, Ligachev – who has openly disagreed with Gorbachev's so-called reforms – will automatically become General Secretary. He knows nothing, of course, of what we plan.'

'But what are these new dimensions?' Budienny repeated.

'Once Ligachev is in power the real hardline element inside the Politburo will take over. Those men Gorbachev has not yet got rid of. Then next year, in 1988, we launch the limited attack.'

'Attack?' Budienny's eyes gleamed.

'We manufacture a border incident – as Hitler did against Poland in 1939. Our armies, brought close to the western frontier at night when the American satellites are blind, invade West Germany. We outnumber NATO enormously

484

with our tanks. With our artillery and our air force. We shall reach the Rhine in three days.'

'That means World War Three,' Budienny objected.

'No. We stop at the Rhine. We announce we are going no further. The Americans will be in the middle of their presidential election. Everything will be in confusion in Washington. You think they will want a conventional *limited* war – a three-day coup – to turn nuclear? To risk New York, Chicago and Los Angeles become incinerated ash-heaps? Then we have in our hands the Ruhr, the great German powerhouse of armament production. We become the greatest power on earth.'

'And who will bring down Gorbachev's plane over Britain?'

'I told you before.' Lucharsky clapped his gloves together without making a sound. 'Shi-ite Muslims. They will end Gorbachev's regime of anti-Leninist idiocy . . .'

46

At Cherry Farm Anton stood inside the second furniture van and surveyed his workmanship. He wore his boiler suit and his cap: he had developed the habit of wearing it all the time except when he went to bed. In the little spare time left over he had visited pubs some distance away, drinking beer while he listened to the locals' chatter. Anton could now talk with the accent of a working man. Holding a power tool in his right hand he turned to Seton-Charles.

'Well, you have seen the second demonstration. The sliding panel works, as it does in the other van.'

The two men stood close together; space was cramped.

Near the driver's cab Anton had erected another platform with steps leading up to it; a chair with an adjustable back was clamped to the floor below the sliding panel.

But the rear part of the van was crammed almost roof-high with old furniture – as was the van behind them. To leave the van they had to squeeze past the projecting legs of tables and a large wardrobe among other items. This was a precaution Jupiter had insisted on when he had given instructions to Anton after his landing on the coast.

'Then, if by chance you are stopped,' Balaclava had explained, 'the police will see a van stacked with furniture which will hide the launch platform . . .'

Before starting work on the rear van Anton had visited various furniture auctions, storing the junk he had purchased in the front van. Seton-Charles had studied the stack of local newspapers Anton had bought all over Hampshire, looking for furniture auctions. He had been surprised and pleased at how many there were.

'Let me see the panel open again,' Seton-Charles suggested. 'I want to be sure it works every time.'

Anton shook his head. 'The generator makes a noise. I tested it several times while you were inside the farm, keeping a lookout for snoopers. God, I've driven a long way, buying everything I needed from different shops. No one will have a clue about what we were constructing.'

'But why does each van need a small generator to operate the panel,' asked Seton-Charles, whose knowledge of mechanical problems was zero. 'Surely you could have used the power from the van's engine.'

'Which shows how much you know. For one thing the van will be stationary when we launch the missiles, the engine turned off. The driver will warn us over his walkie-talkie when the plane is in view. Only then do we open the panel.'

'It seems very well organized,' Seton-Charles agreed. 'That smell of fresh paint is turning my stomach. Was it really necessary to change the name on the outside?'

'Again, Jupiter's orders. We don't want any connection with Camelford Removals, the bankrupt outfit in Norwich you bought them from. Now we are Smith's Removals of Birmingham. There are two such firms in the city.'

Anton had spent hours with a paintbrush, first obliterating the old names, waiting for the paint to dry, then substituting the new names. But Seton-Charles had a point: the barn, with its doors closed at both ends, reeked of the stench.

'Tonight we'll open the rear doors of the barn after dark, let the smell out,' he decided. 'We'll take it in turns to stand guard while those doors are open. Later I'll rub dirt over the fresh paint . . .'

He stopped speaking as the phone extension he had rigged up from the farmhouse began ringing. He sent Seton-Charles back to the farmhouse, picked up the phone.

'Alfred Moss speaking.'

'Are both containers ready yet?'

The same supercilious, upper-crust voice Anton disliked. Like a commander giving orders to lowly subordinates. He took a deep breath.

'Yes. They are ready to move to the port.'

'Your two guests will be arriving today. Noon at the arranged meeting place. Foster and Saunders will be travelling with them. I must go. My garden is being ruined by magpies and goldcrests. I'd like to convert the place into a closed circuit. Don't be late . . .'

Anton put down the phone and swore in Greek. Arrogant bastard. But he was clever. In a few words – seemingly innocent if overheard – he'd conveyed a lot.

The two men who were bringing the prisoners to the lonely crossroads were called Foster and Saunders. They would give the password *magpies*. Anton would reply with *goldcrests*. He ran to the doors, opened one, closed it, snapped the padlock shut on the outside, ran into the farmhouse. Seton-Charles stood in the kitchen, waiting for the news.

'I have to leave at once. I'll come back with the prisoners. Be ready to open the shed doors . . .'

'Is it wise to keep on using the same Austin Metro you hired in Taunton? We've had it for weeks. And what about payment to Barton?'

'Jupiter arranges fresh payments in cash. It's risky changing cars, using that driving licence. I must be off . . .'

Driving at a modest pace along a winding country road, Anton reflected on the past. He kept a close eye on the dashboard clock, but he didn't want to arrive early. Hanging about – even in the middle of nowhere – was dangerous. A police patrol car might become interested.

He was thinking about Petros and his lust for revenge. Anton had never shared his father's one-track outlook on life. He had simply gone along with him for years; originally to make sure the money for his education was forthcoming. He had played up to the old man like mad. Later he had borrowed from him to help set up his chain of radio, television and video shops. Then he had met the man who had changed his life. Professor Guy Seton-Charles.

Anton had attended the first lecture at Athens University out of sheer curiosity. More intelligent – and cynical – than the other students, it had not taken him long to see through the professor. Under the guise of lecturing on Greek Studies, it had soon become apparent to Anton this was a course in political indoctrination. In the Communist creed.

In his turn, Seton-Charles had spotted Anton as the cleverest, most cold-blooded and ambitious of his students. Just the material he was looking for. They had formed an alliance rather than a friendship. Anton had decided the West was on its way out; the future belonged to Russia.

So convincingly did he appear to embrace Communism

he was in due course invited to join the Greek Key as a junior member. The fact that his father, Petros, had supported the Greek Key during the war helped. Anton simply saw it as the quickest route to power in Greece. That was until Gorbachev replaced Brezhnev. *Glasnost? Perestroika?* This was no route to a Communist takeover of Greece.

Recruited to the inner councils – after expressing his anti-Gorbachev sentiments – Anton had become a trusted member of the conspiracy. And then there was the detail of Petros' collection of British commando knives. It was Doganis who had suggested how these might come in useful when he learned of their existence.

'Steal them,' he advised Anton, before his first trip to England. 'You may have to kill someone. You could do that? Good. If it comes to that, use one of those daggers. It will confuse any investigation. The English are poking around still trying to find out who killed Andreas Gavalas. Use one of those daggers and they will go back over forty years, ignoring the present. An excellent smoke-screen . . .'

Anton glanced at the clock again, increased speed. When he arrived at the crossroads a Ford station wagon was pulled up inside the trees. A man dressed in a smart blue navy pinstripe suit appeared. He wore pigskin gloves. Anton noticed they were soiled, which did not go with the smartness of the rest of his appearance. He pulled up, switched off his engine, looked round and listened. The only sound was the crunch of the man's shoes on a gravel track where the Ford was standing.

'Excuse me,' the man said, standing by Anton's open window, 'I'm looking for the Magpie Inn.'

'I can tell you how to get to the Goldcrest Inn.'

'Thank God. Oh, my name's Foster. It's been a fraught business. We have them in the back of the station wagon. Hands bound behind their backs, ankles tied, their mouths taped, eyes blindfolded. Saunders is over there and will help. How are you going to move the merchandise?'

'Under the travelling rugs in the back of *my* car. One on top of the other . . .'

Seton-Charles ran out as Anton arrived back at Cherry Farm. The Greek lifted the corner of a rug and exposed the two captive Shi-ite Muslims dressed in prison garb. They untied the rope round the ankles of one man, manoeuvred him out of the car. When he tried to struggle they frogmarched him inside the farmhouse, up the stairs and into the prepared room.

'Dump him on the bed,' Anton ordered. 'He'll be safe while we get the other one inside . . .'

Five minutes later they had both men in their separate rooms. Anton held a Luger pistol while Seton-Charles tore off the tape and removed the blindfold. The Shi-ite blinked in the unaccustomed daylight and glared. Anton gestured towards the canvas sack he had dragged up the stairs. From its open end protruded the head of a slaughtered pig taken from the chest freezer in one of the sheds.

'Any trouble with you and I kill you, then you'll be buried in a grave with this pig.'

'No! No! No . . .!'

Anton watched the man's terrified expression. It had worked. The only form of intimidation which would quell a Shi-ite. The Muslim religion regarded the pig as the most unclean and horrific of animals. Anton waited behind the pig lying on the landing floor while Seton-Charles released the prisoner's hands. The Shi-ite rubbed his wrists to get the circulation going and all the time he stared at the pig's head as though hypnotized.

Anton waited until Seton-Charles had left the room, then threw inside a bundle of clothes: three suits in different sizes, underwear, shirts, socks and shoes.

490

'You get out of that prison garb, choose the clothes which fit you best, wrap the others in a bundle. We'll collect them when we feed you. Put your prison stuff with the bundle.' He aimed the Luger at the trembling Shi-ite's head. 'If you try to get away I will shoot you dead. Then you will share eternity with a pig.'

Seton-Charles closed, double-locked, bolted the door. 'Let's hope one of those suits fits him.'

'One will fit well enough. A man escaped from prison doesn't always have the right clothes to wear. Now haul the pig sack along to the other room and we'll repeat the process . . .'

He watched as Seton-Charles heaved the heavy sack along the corridor, his rimless glasses perched on his nose. Anton had been careful not to comment on the fact, but he had been surprised at how useful the professor had been. He was stronger physically than the Greek had realized. He had proved a useful workmate during the conversion of the vans, handing up tools to Anton on the platform, finding the right screws, and a psychological change had taken place in the relationship of the two men.

Seton-Charles now accepted Anton was boss and he prepared good meals for them. Something I might have foreseen, Anton thought: the professor was a bachelor who lived alone, looked after himself and was fastidious in his habits. They paused in front of the second reinforced door.

'That latest phone call I had from Jupiter,' Anton told him. 'We've reached the stage of closed circuit.'

'What's that?'

'We stay under very close cover. We don't leave the farm for anything unless it's essential.'

'Then the operation must be close?'

'Soon,' Anton assured him, 'it has to be soon.'

491

47

Tweed had 'broken silence'.

He had sent out a general alert all over Europe to counter-espionage chiefs, to his personal underground network of informants. The message was always the same.

Any data on past and present movements of Anton Gavalas, citizen of Greece. Suspected member of hardline Communist group the Greek Key. Also identical data on Professor Guy Seton-Charles, British citizen, Professor of Greek Studies at Bristol University, England, and Athens University, Greece. Data required extreme urgency. Tweed.

Copies of a photograph of Anton – made from the print inside the file Kalos had provided for Tweed – accompanied the request. But only a word description of Seton-Charles was sent. Tweed realized they had made a bad mistake in not photographing the professor.

Howard wandered into Tweed's office a week after the messages had been sent. It was his blue pinstripe suit day. He perched his buttocks on the edge of Tweed's desk, adjusted his tie, smiled at Monica who was stunned by such amiability.

'Any progress from the boys abroad?' he enquired.

Tweed winced inwardly at the phraseology. 'Nothing that gives us any kind of lead. Later this afternoon I have a meeting with the Prime Minister. I thought it was time she knew about this business.'

He waited for the explosion of outrage. It didn't come. Instead, Howard ran his fingers over his plump pink face and nodded approval. 'I was just coming in to suggest maybe we ought to let her know. Frankly, I'm surprised you didn't seek an earlier conference.'

'No hard facts to go on. Ever since Masterson was killed it's been like seeing shadowy figures in the mists of Exmoor. You aren't sure whether you actually saw anything or not. It may be a tricky interview. She *does* like facts. Oh, Paula is on her way here, driving up from Somerset. I just hope she gets here before I leave for Downing Street.'

'And why is the delightful Paula driving back to London? She could have reported over the phone from that public call box in Minehead.'

'She said she had information she'd sooner give me face to face.'

'Sounds intriguing. I suppose you couldn't record her report so I could play it back later?'

'I'll do that.'

Howard glanced at the machine on Tweed's desk, the neat piles of cassettes. 'You've been listening to those things yet again? The tapes of Butler's phoned reports and that clandestine job Nield did during dinner at The Luttrell Arms? You still think you've spotted which one of the three is the killer?'

'Yes.' Tweed stood up, began pacing slowly. 'But no proof. In case anything happens to me I typed out a secret report which is inside a sealed envelope in the safe.'

Howard stood up, pulled down his jacket at the back. 'Damned if I could point the finger at any of them. And God knows I've listened to them often enough. Why be so cryptic?'

'Because I could be wrong. The main thing at the moment is two people have gone missing. Anton Gavalas. I checked with Sarris and there's no sign he has returned to Greece. Then Guy Seton-Charles has vanished off the face of the earth. He'd accumúlated several months' leave, so Bristol University informed us. He said he was going abroad. No trace of him on any airline passenger manifest.

493

And he always flew everywhere – again according to Bristol.'

'So, we're up the proverbial gum tree. Good luck with the PM.'

On this encouraging note Howard left the office. Monica stopped studying her file. 'He's also worried. Like you are. And although I hate Howard's guts, his instinct is sometimes very sound. I wish you hadn't said that thing about in case anything happens to you. It's tempting fate.'

'Don't be so superstitious,' Tweed chided.

Monica slammed her pencil down on her desk. 'Have we got one damn thing to go on after all this effort?'

'Two things. When I was interviewing old Petros at his farm he mentioned there had been rumours during the Second World War that the Greek Key was controlled by an Englishman in Cairo.'

'Seton-Charles was in Cairo . . .'

'So were the three commandos. The second thing also came from Greece. Kalos told me a radio ham – a friend of Sarris' – had picked up a coded message. At the end there was an instruction in English. *From now on the call sign is changed to Colonel Winter*. History can be changed by such chance happenings.'

Paula arrived early when Tweed and Monica were standing by the window, drinking tea. She was behind the wheel of Newman's Mercedes. As she parked by the kerb further along the Crescent Tweed saw the automatic radio aerial retracting, sliding down inside the rear. He frowned, held his cup in mid-air.

'What is it?' asked Monica.

'Nothing. Just an idea.'

'She's made very good time. And she seems to be in a rush – she's almost running. And her clothes!'

494

Paula was wearing a pair of tight blue denims and a windcheater. An outfit neither of them had ever seen her adopt before. Paula was classic pleated skirts and blouse with a well-fitting jacket. She disappeared inside the entrance below them.

'I'll make her coffee,' Monica decided. 'She's had quite a long drive. Back in a minute. And I think something's wrong.'

Tweed had his back to the window when there was a knock on his door, he called, 'Come in,' and Paula appeared, carrying in one hand her briefcase, in the other her small travelling case.

'What's the matter?' he asked, coming forward.

'Does there have to be something?' she asked, went to her desk and dumped two cases. Her voice was cool, too cool. She turned, leaning against the desk, and smiled wanly as he gave her a hug, kissed her on the cheek. She was a shade too controlled.

She took off her gloves slowly, placed one neatly on top of the other. Then she folded her arms, tilted her chin in the defiant look he knew so well. She was white-faced and there were dark circles under her eyes.

'I drove like a bat out of hell to get here.' She smiled again at his expression. 'But within the speed limit all the way.'

'What's the matter?' he repeated.

'You really are the most perceptive man.' She paused. 'It's good to be back.' Another pause. 'I've just shot two men.'

Tweed concealed the jolt he'd felt. 'Why not sit down and tell me about it? Monica is coming with coffee. The Browning automatic I sent down by courier was for you then? Not for Newman or Marler, as I thought?'

'They've given me hell, those two.' She sat down, crossed

495

her legs. 'I gave them hell back. Am I – or am I not – a fully-fledged member of this outfit?'

'Very fledged.' He smiled and drew a chair close to her. 'I have always shown you that's the way I feel, surely?'

'Yes. *You* have. Want to hear about my target-shooting – with live targets?'

Her voice was steady but Tweed sensed tension under the surface. He fetched a bottle of cognac and a glass from a cupboard, poured a hefty snifter. 'Get that down inside yourself.'

'Thanks.' She held the balloon glass in both hands to drink – to stop the glass shaking, Tweed suspected. 'My, that's made a difference.' She relaxed against the chair-back, her normal colour started to return. 'I hardly know where to start. I suppose it was Marler who saved my life. He arrived soon after I did.'

'Because I decided we needed every possible person down there. Exmoor is a vast territory to cover. And why not start at the beginning? When you'd arrived with Newman at Porlock Weir . . .'

Monica had phoned ahead and there were two rooms reserved for them when Newman and Paula carried their cases into The Anchor. They reached Porlock Weir in the early evening – Newman had encountered heavy sea mist drifting across the road. The moor was blotted out.

They had a conference with Butler and Nield over dinner and divided up duties. Newman took charge, made the suggestion. The dining room was almost empty so they could talk easily.

'We have three people to watch – Robson, Barrymore and Kearns. Nield, you take Robson. I'll keep an eye on Barrymore. That leaves Butler for Kearns . . .'

'No go,' Butler informed him. 'Tweed has given me the

job of checking out the people who live on that bungalow estate near Kearns' place.'

'And I'd like to help Harry, if he doesn't mind,' Paula said. 'I was the one who thought there was something odd about the place.'

'Be my guest,' replied Butler with enthusiasm. 'I've been helping Nield watch the three commando types. The electoral register in Taunton is our first check,' he told Paula.

'Then I'll have to take on both Barrymore and Kearns,' Newman decided. He grinned at Paula. 'You're just about as bloody . . . independent as Marler.'

'You were going to say bloody-minded,' Paula told him. 'Maybe I am. Do I get the order of the boot?'

'I'll overlook it this time. Eat your dinner, it's getting cold . . .'

The problem solved itself the following day when Marler turned up at The Anchor, sent down by Tweed. Secretly Newman had been relieved the previous evening: Paula would have protection, working with Butler. He was careful not to point this out to Paula.

While Paula and Butler visited Taunton, Newman gave Marler the task of shadowing Kearns in his hired Peugeot. Apart from Newman, they all travelled in hired cars. It took a week for Butler and Paula to come up with a list of names of the owners of the bungalows on the estate. Once she had the names Paula took to visiting The Royal Oak at Winsford where she was soon firm friends with the heavily built barman. She always arrived before the crowd at lunchtime, always came alone.

Bit by bit she told Jack, the barman, about herself. 'I'm recovering from an illness – convalescent leave they call it, the insurance company I work for. And when I was a kid I used to come down to Taunton to visit relatives . . .'

Her psychology was shrewd: country folk liked to know who they were talking to. Gradually she extracted from

Jack information about the occupants of the bungalow estate. The one day she avoided was Wednesday: she had seen Barrymore and Robson lunching at their usual table. They were still keeping up the ritual meetings, but Kearns was not there with them. She checked his absence on two Wednesdays before avoiding that day.

'Thinkin' of buyin' one of those bungalows when it comes on the market?' Jack commented to her one day. 'You'll be lucky. A funny set-up that lot, you mark my words.'

'Funny in what way?' she asked.

'Ever 'eard of a bungalow estate put up fifteen years ago and not one of the original owners has moved? Six bungalows there are. Six men. You'd think at least one would have moved on. New job, somethin' like that. Not a bit of it. They're all still there. And keeps themselves to themselves.'

'You mean you've never met one of them?'

'Now I didn't say that, did I, miss? One of them came in here soon after they'd all moved in. Chap called Foster. Didn't take to 'im. Drank gin and tonics while he chatted. La-di-dah type.'

'What did he chat about? It sounds like a mystery. I love mysteries,' Paula glowed.

'Said he was an investment counsellor, whatever that might be. Works in Bristol. His wife has some big job overseas. Never seen 'er. Said his friend, Saunders, also had his wife abroad. Some job with the UN in New York. Funny sort of married life. Wouldn't suit me – visiting the missus once or twice a year.'

'You mean the wives never come here?'

'That's about the long and short of it. Then there's the crank. Professor Guy Seton-Charles. Bachelor. Something to do with Bristol University. In summer they mows their lawns at the weekends. That's about all you see of 'em. Stuffy lot, if you ask me.'

Paula swallowed a piece of her chicken and mushroom

pie, the day's speciality chalked up on a blackboard. She sipped at her glass of white wine. Jack was polishing yet another glass until it came up gleaming like silver crystal.

'I heard there was a Mr Simon Morle living in one of the bungalows,' she said casually.

'Maybe. I wouldn't know. They're there and yet they're not there.' People were beginning to fill up the tables. He turned to another customer. 'What can I get you, sir?'

That was the night they had the most almighty row back at The Anchor.

They were all assembled for dinner at their usual table. Paula sat between Newman and Marler. Butler and Nield faced them, and Nield, inadvertently, lit the fuse.

'Saw you today, Paula. I was tracking Robson when he tried to call on Kearns. Got no joy. I thought Kearns must be out. Robson pressed the gate bell several times, no one came out, so he pushed off. I had wondered whether Kearns was ill.'

'I think he is,' Paula replied. '*I* saw Robson call, then drive off. A few minutes later Dr Underwood – we met him in the bar if you remember – called. Kearns came out and let him in.'

'What did you mean, Pete?' Marler asked. 'You said you saw Paula. Driving along the road?'

'No. Parked in her hired Renault inside a gateway overlooking that bungalow colony – and Kearns' place.'

Marler turned to Paula. 'What the devil were you doing there?'

'Observing that bungalow estate. You can look down on it. It's odd – one woman seems to clean the lot. Furtively.'

'How do you mean?' Nield enquired.

'She always slips in by the back doors. She has a key to each of them. I've used night glasses to watch her after dark . . .'

'*After dark?*' Marler's tone expressed incredulity. 'How long have you been keeping up this vigil?'

'For about two weeks.'

'You do realize it's only a matter of time before you're spotted,' Marler persisted in a cold voice. 'It's madness.'

'I have already realized that.' She said the words deliberately, disliking his tone. 'I saw the solution today. There's a riding stable near Dunster which hires out horses. In future I'll ride – which means I can get on the moor, check the area from different angles.'

'You bloody well won't . . .'

'Partridge used a horse,' she snapped. 'For the same reason, I suspect. He could see more from a horse.'

'And look where it got him.' Marler leaned his long white face – his Grecian suntan had long since faded – close to hers. 'It got him a knife in the back. You should be armed. You shouldn't be doing it at all.'

'No one's going to stop me,' she said icily, staring hard at Marler. 'If you feel that way, get me a weapon . . .'

It was Newman who calmed the atmosphere. He knew Paula was seething at the unspoken suggestion that she couldn't take care of herself. He remembered times when Tweed had put her in the front line to toughen her up. Standing up, he said he was driving into Minehead to call Tweed, to ask him to send a Browning automatic with spare magazines by motorbike courier. While he was away the rest of the meal was eaten in silence.

The following morning after breakfast Newman tapped on Paula's door. Inside he handed her a Browning and spare mags.

'So, I've come of age,' she said and smiled drily.

'How are you going to carry it on a horse – so it's easy to get at in an emergency?'

She produced a makeshift but neat holster made of blue denim and took hold of the Browning where she had laid it on a table. Releasing the magazine inside the butt, she checked to make sure there wasn't a bullet up the spout, pushed the mag back inside the gun and slipped it inside the holster. Two straps of the same material were attached to it.

She was wearing tight denims thrust inside riding boots and a padded windcheater. All purchased the previous day. Then she strapped the holster to her right upper leg close to her crotch. Parading round the room, she made a gesture with her slim hand.

'I'm on a horse. You meet me. Would you notice it?'

'No. It blends in perfectly. How on earth did you make that holster?'

'By staying up half the night. I cut material from the bottom of my jeans – tucked inside my boots you can't see where I took it from. Then a lot of careful sewing.' She came close to him, kissed him on the cheek. 'I expected you to flare up like Marler last night. Thanks for your vote of confidence.'

Newman shrugged, grinned. 'You are one of the team. Marler's got a short fuse. What did that cleaning woman you saw down at the estate look like?'

'Middle-aged. Medium height. About a hundred and twenty pounds. Grey hair tied back in a bun. I've got several photographs of her. I was carrying my camera with the telephoto lens. Should we send the film to Tweed?'

'Let me have it. Maybe in a few days one of us will have to go up to London. You'd finished the film?'

She handed him the spool. 'Yes. And I've a fresh one in the camera. The one you're holding has pictures of all the men living there. Plus pictures of the bungalows. Including Seton-Charles' place with that weird complex of TV aerials attached to his chimney.'

She hid the Browning with its holster and the mags at the bottom of the wardrobe, then picked up neat rows of shoes and spread them over the gun. Straightening up, she looked at Newman.

'After that row at dinner last night I feel like a walk along the coast. I didn't get much sleep and I'm feeling restless.'

'Let's go . . .'

It was dark but the gale had slackened to a strong breeze as they strolled along the track westward. Paula glanced at the cottage where Mrs Larcombe had lived, then looked away. Newman was careful not to refer to it.

'What are the others doing?' she asked as they picked their way across the pebbles.

'We're keeping up the watch on the commandos. Kearns appears to have recovered, but he's limping a bit. Maybe he twisted his ankle. Butler followed one of the men who live in those bungalows to the Somerset and Cornwall Bank in Bristol. Watched him draw about a thousand pounds in fifties. He's reported it to Tweed who has now started a discreet check on where that money comes from.'

'Anything new on the commandos?'

'Not really, blast it. Robson still rides to see his patients at all hours. He has one old duck who delights in using her bedside phone and calling him out late at night. Lives in a creepy old mansion near Dulverton. Barrymore is still making calls from that public box in Minehead. Kearns has no help in his house -- looks after the place himself, does his own cooking. Army type, I suppose . . .'

He stopped speaking as Paula grasped his arm. They were some distance west of Porlock Weir, walking close to towering cliffs. 'I heard something funny, a sinister noise,' Paula whispered.

Then Newman heard it. A crumbling sound, the noise of grinding rocks. He looked above them, grabbed Paula's hand, shouted at her to run. They headed for the sea. Behind them the sound increased, grew to a rumbling roar. At the water's edge Newman turned and Paula swung round with him. She gazed, appalled.

By the light of the rising moon they saw a gigantic slab

of cliff sliding down from the summit, a slab which broke into smaller pieces as it rolled towards the beach. Enormous boulders bounded downwards towards where they stood, their backs to the sea. The boulders lost momentum, came to rest two dozen yards away. A sudden silence descended. Paula shivered, huddled closer to Newman.

'It's OK,' he said. 'That's it.'

'My God, if we hadn't run we'd have been under that.'

She pointed towards a dark mass of rocks piled up the height of a two-storey house. They were making their way back, keeping to the edge of the sea, when Paula pointed again.

'Who can that be?'

In the distance, close to the track, a man on horseback was riding away from them. Hunched forward, close to the horse's head, it was impossible to make out his shape, guess his height. He reached the track and the horse broke into a gallop. When they arrived back at The Anchor there was no sign of any horseman and they hurried inside to report the landslip.

The violent incident took place next day.

48

Grey mist was curling over the high crests as Paula rode her horse over the high ground behind the bungalow estate. It lay about two hundred yards below her and from this angle she was able to observe features she had not seen before.

Behind the end of the cul-de-sac a path led down into a dip invisible from the road. An old barn-like structure huddled in the dip, a building with half-doors. Both upper halves were open and two horses' heads peered out. This was her first realization that someone living on the estate rode the moors.

She saw movement, the opening of a back door in Seton-Charles' bungalow. Lifting her glasses looped round her neck, she focused. It was the grey-haired cleaning woman, carrying a mop and a plastic bucket. Paula remained perfectly still: people rarely looked *upwards*.

The woman opened a gate in the back garden fence, walked into the next garden. She put down mop and bucket, fiddled with a bunch of keys, inserted one in the rear door of the bungalow and disappeared inside with her cleaning equipment.

Paula dropped her glasses, rode on, slowly circling the estate. As usual, no sign of cars. They had probably all driven off to their jobs. The cars she had seen earlier, arriving back in the evenings, were Jags and Fords. No Mercedes or Rolls-Royces, but the cars they drove still cost money. There seemed to be no shortage of that commodity.

She had watched them at weekends cutting their lawns with power mowers, big machines which did the job quickly. It was late November and she gave a little shiver: the cold clamminess of the approaching mist rolling down the slopes was making itself felt.

She kept moving slowly, like a rider out for a gentle morning bit of exercise. For the moment she was sheltered from the estate by a gorse-covered ridge. She guided her mount up the side and perched on a small rocky hilltop which gave a bird's-eye view. The two horsemen seemed to appear out of nowhere.

One moment she was alone on the hilltop, the next moment they rode out from behind a concealed ridge and confronted her. They stopped about two dozen feet away, staring at her. She noticed several things as she casually dropped her right hand over the holster.

They were experienced riders: neither had his feet inside the stirrups. Probably because they had mounted their horses in a hurry. She recognized their mounts as the horses which had peered over the half-doors. One man was tall, lean-faced and with jet-black hair. His cheekbones were prominent, almost Slavic. The other was short and heavily-built with an ugly round face and a mean mouth.

Both were in their forties, she estimated. Both wore windcheaters and slacks thrust into riding boots. The Slavic-faced man raised a hand, unzipped the front of his windcheater, left it open. The ugly man began guiding his horse, took up a position on her right side. She responded by turning her own horse.

'I like to face strangers,' she informed them and smiled.

'Why are you spying on us?' Slav-Face demanded.

'It's normal to introduce yourself in this part of the world,' she replied. 'I'm Paula . . .'

'And I'm Norton. Now, I'll ask you again – why are you spying on us?'

His right hand slipped inside his windcheater, emerged holding a gun. A 9mm Walther automatic as far as Paula could tell. She froze. The weapon was aimed point-blank between her breasts. Paula glanced to her left. A ridge higher than the hilltop masked the road. No help from that direction – even if Nield came driving along.

'This is moorland open to the public,' she snapped. 'You think you own Exmoor?'

'Gutsy, eh?' Norton commented. 'Now answer the question.'

'I ride all over the place. I don't know what you're talking about. And it's illegal to threaten someone with a weapon in this country.'

'She says it's illegal, Morle,' Norton said to his companion, still staring at Paula. 'She says she doesn't know what I'm talking about.'

His voice was cultured; high falutin' some would have called it. Almost a caricature of Marler's drawling way of speaking, but with an underlying sneer. Norton and Morle. Paula recalled the names she'd recorded while Butler examined the electoral register. These were two of them: she had all five names in her head.

'So if she doesn't know what I'm talking about,' Norton continued, 'how come she's been sitting in a parked car up the road day after day, watching the bungalows through field glasses?' He still held the gun levelled at her. 'I think maybe we will continue this discussion inside my bungalow, have a real cosy chat.'

Paula had been frightened when the two men first appeared. Now she remembered Newman putting her through her paces at a quiet spot on the North Downs. And he'd gone through the Special Air Services course before writing an article on the SAS. *Faced with a gunman there's always something you can do – say – to distract him, if you're armed* . . . And now, unsure of survival, she had gone as cold as ice.

'So you've confused me with someone else,' she said. 'Parked in a car, my foot. A horse is my form of transport here. You can tell the difference between a horse and a car? This is not very encouraging – when Foster asked me if I could take on the job of helping clean the bungalows.'

'He did what?' Norton's forehead crinkled with puzzlement. He turned to Morle. 'Do you know anything about this? He must be clean out of his . . .'

As he spoke the gun sagged, the muzzle aimed at the ground. It took seconds for Paula to haul the Browning from the holster, to grasp the butt in both hands, to aim it. Norton saw movement out of the corner of his eye. He began to lift his own gun. Paula fired twice. Norton slumped, was falling from his horse, when Morle ripped down his zipper, shoved his hand inside, began to haul out a gun. Paula had swivelled the Browning, her knees clamped to her horse to hold it steady. Twice more she fired.

Morle grabbed at his saddle with one hand, slowly toppled. A loud explosion echoed. Paula thought she was hit. Then she saw Norton had pulled the trigger in a reflex action as he hit the ground. The bullet winged across the moor.

The men's two horses galloped off in panicky freedom. Paula's mount threatened to rise up on its hindlegs. She pressed a firm hand on its neck, made soothing noises, dismounted, trailed the reins and approached Norton, still gripping her Browning. He lay unconscious, his fingers had dropped the gun. She bent down, felt his neck pulse. It beat steadily. Blood oozed from his right shoulder.

Standing up, she ran across to examine Morle. He also was unconscious. A red stain spread across his slacks close to his left hip. Again she checked the pulse. Again she felt its regular beat. Thank God, she thought and stood up, deciding what to do.

Two minutes later she was riding fast along the track which led to Exford, a four-mile trek. She left the horse at the riding stables she had hired it from. Nothing more to pay. Walking along the road, she entered the field where she had parked her Renault, got behind the wheel.

She drove across country, turned on to the A396 and arrived via Minehead at Porlock Weir half an hour later. To her infinite relief Newman and Marler had just returned to The Anchor.

Tweed drank three cups of coffee while he listened to Paula's story in his Park Crescent office. She spoke tersely, with not a wasted word. On his desk lay the sheet of handwritten names she had given him – the occupants of the six bungalows. He already knew them from the earlier report Butler had given him on the phone. He squeezed her hand as she concluded her account, stood up and went back behind his desk.

'So Newman and Marler cleaned up the mess,' he said.

'They were marvellous. I wondered if they'd say I'd made a mistake stopping at the first public phone box on my way back to Porlock Weir. That was when I phoned the police, refused to give a name and told them there'd been a shooting incident near the bungalow estate close to Simonsbath. That they'd better send an ambulance. I felt I couldn't just leave them there. Marler said he'd have done just that . . .'

'Marler would,' Tweed commented drily.

'But Bob said I'd done the right thing. He took the Browning, spare mags and my makeshift holster. They were going to end up in the sea. Bob also said it was lucky Norton's gun went off by chance. That would confuse the police investigation.'

'Eat your ham sandwiches,' said Monica. 'You need something inside you.'

'Now you mention it, I'm famished.' She devoured one sandwich and Tweed waited, glancing at his watch. 'Am I holding you up?' she asked.

'No. Our tame accountant is due soon. Butler reported that he had followed Foster twice to the Somerset and Cornwall Bank in Bristol. He saw him draw about a thousand pounds in cash each time. He heard the teller address him as Mr Foster. Perry has the details and is in the Engine Room phoning God knows who to trace where that money came from. It's so often the money which helps us find out who people really are.'

'Well, there is something wrong about that bungalow estate. I said it was funny when we first saw it,' Paula said defiantly.

Tweed nodded. He understood her attitude. She was bound to suffer a reaction from the experience sooner or later. And the sooner the better.

'It's the first time I've shot anyone,' Paula went on and sank her teeth into a fresh sandwich.

'They're only injured,' Tweed assured her. 'Newman drove over to the estate after you'd left in the Mercedes. He arrived as they were carting those two thugs into an ambulance. He showed his old press card and they recognized the name. He called the hospital later.'

Tweed omitted to tell her Norton was in a coma, that Morle was still unconscious. Police were waiting by their bedsides ready to take statements.

'More alarming,' he went on, switching her mind to another topic, 'Marler arrived at the estate and flourished his fake Special Branch card, so the police let him in. The bungalows are all empty. The cars have gone. Most sinister of all, they can find not a single fingerprint. Everything has been wiped clean. You were so right about that estate.'

'What does that mean – no fingerprints?' Paula asked.

'I think you discovered the secret base of sleepers established fifteen years ago by the Englishman who controls the Greek Key. A base which was recently activated – and has now been evacuated – thanks to your encounter with Norton and Morle. We have now made copies in the Engine Room of those photos you took – and circulated them to every police force in the country. We also have their names.' He glanced down at the list on his desk.

Foster, Saunders, Norton, Morle, Sully.

'Anything else?'

'Yes. Before I sent out the European alert I circulated the registration number of Seton-Charles' Volvo station wagon over here. And Newman visited Bristol University with a police artist. They used several students to build an Identikit picture of the professor. Copies of that have gone out.'

'Will anyone take much notice?'

'I think so,' Tweed said grimly. 'I named him suspected terrorist planner. Highly dangerous.'

509

'Talking of terrorists,' Monica chimed in, 'there's an interesting story I cut from a recent copy of *The Times*. Two Shi-ite Muslim killers were air-lifted by a chopper from Gartree Prison exercise yard. Most audacious. They killed an Iraqi diplomat.'

Tweed wasn't listening. Paula had remembered a further incident.

'There was a big landslip when Bob and I were walking from The Anchor one night along the coast . . .' She described the experience. 'They've put up a big notice. *Warning. Keep clear. Danger of cliff falls.*'

The phone rang. Monica answered, looked up at Tweed. 'Perry is ready to emerge from the basement with his report on the Foster bank account.'

'Tell him to come up.'

Perry was a small, precise, neatly dressed man who wore pince-nez. Monica thought he was a giggle but he had a shrewd financial brain. Clutching a blue file, he sat on the edge of a chair facing Tweed. He glanced at Monica and Paula.

'This is highly confidential.'

Tweed compressed his lips. 'You should realize by now Paula and Monica know more about what's going on than you ever will.'

'Then I will commence.'

He opened his fat file but Tweed glanced at his watch. He had to leave soon for his appointment with the PM. And now Paula had brought information – facts – which made his interview well worthwhile.

'Just tell me in a few words what you've found out.'

'Very well, but I think you should read the file later. The enquiry took longer than I expected. It is a devious trail – and I had to get Walton, head of Special Branch, to vouch for me before the bank manager in Bristol would talk. Then I had to use your name for Europe . . .'

'I know. Chief Inspector Kuhlmann of Wiesbaden in

510

Germany called me. So did Beck in Zurich. Do get on with it.'

'Foster originally had twenty thousand pounds in his Bristol account. He's closed it now. The money was telexed from the Deutsche Bank in Frankfurt. They received it from the Zürcher Kredit Bank in Zurich. That's the end of the road.'

'What does that mean?'

'Zürcher Kredit received the funds from Liechtenstein. That's an iron door no one can open. Not much help, is it?'

'On the contrary, it fits into the pattern which is appearing so rapidly at last. Thank you, Perry. Yes, I suppose you'd better leave the file.'

He waited until they were alone. 'A secret Soviet base is set up fifteen years ago – in hardline Brezhnev's time – at that bungalow estate. It's screaming at us now. Those five men in their early forties would be in their mid-twenties when they slipped into this country. They'd have identities cooked up at Moscow Centre's Documents Section. A Colonel Winterton – whom no one ever met – bought a piece of land with an old house on it. Marler found that out from pub gossip. He had the house knocked down, the six bungalows built in its place. All ready for the *Spetsnaz* unit to move in . . .'

'*Spetsnaz?*' Monica queried.

'You know – élite Soviet troops equivalent to our SAS. Trained to merge into the landscape of a foreign country. They were probably originally intended to assassinate specific key figures in the defence of this country. The leader of the Greek Key, an Englishman living on Exmoor, was their commander.'

'I know what they are,' Monica protested, 'but surely you're reaching, as the Americans would say. Guessing . . .'

'I'd sooner say I'm deducing the solution from clues now in our hands. They always kept to themselves. Foster

511

visited The Royal Oak and chatted to the barman. Luckily barmen have good memories. Foster makes a point of telling him two wives have jobs abroad – which makes the place sound more natural, as opposed to six bachelors, including Seton-Charles. Having fed the barman that much – knowing it would be spread round the district – Foster never goes back there again. Paula finds one woman is cleaning all six bungalows . . .'

'In her forties, too, I'd say,' Paula interjected.

'That's very peculiar,' Tweed continued. 'Six men, all strangers apparently when they buy their bungalows, use the same woman. In England? Not likely. Now Perry tells us Foster draws large sums from a fund which originated in Liechtenstein. So we can't trace where the money came from. Now we hear they've all disappeared, leaving not one fingerprint behind. Everything those men did is shrouded in secrecy. Except the two in hospital. It stinks of *Spetsnaz*.'

'And it wasn't due to the shooting incident Paula was involved in,' Monica stated. 'How do I know that? Because I know how long it takes to clean my flat. To erase all fingerprints from six bungalows must have taken days of meticulous work by that woman. They were leaving anyway. Doesn't that mean an operation is imminent?'

'It means we have very little time left to trace them,' Tweed said grimly. 'And I have very little time to keep my appointment with the PM.'

'Anything more we can do?' asked Monica as he put on his Burberry. It was typical November weather outside, a heavy drizzle.

'Only wait. And hope. We've thrown out across the country all the information we hold. I'm off.'

'One other thing while I remember,' Paula said. 'Nield heard this in a pub. Kearns' dog kept on moping and whining for Jill. He shot it recently and buried it in the garden at the back of his house. Put up a wooden cross inscribed, *In loving memory of Jill*.'

'Damn!' Tweed hardly heard her as the phone began ringing and Monica picked it up. 'I can't talk to anyone . . .'

'It's Marler. Says it's very urgent.'

'Make it quick,' Tweed said after grabbing the receiver.

'Newman visited the hospital after hearing Morle was talking. Arrived, found Morle had a serious case of fever, high temperature. The policeman told Bob what Morle had mumbled. One word over and over. Then Newman heard it. Stinger. The police chap thought he was talking about the drink. *Stinger*. Do you get it?'

'Yes.' Tweed found he was gripping the receiver tightly. He said thank you and put down the phone.

'Bad news?' Paula asked.

'The worst. Now we know what Anton brought ashore. Stinger rocket launchers and missiles. God help us.'

He ran down the steps to the ground floor, forced himself to pause at the exit, glance round. Across the road stood the usual news seller. He stopped briefly to buy an *Evening Standard*. And this time he stared at the poster summarizing the main news.

Gorbachev To Meet Thatcher At Brize Norton En Route Washington.

49

Jupiter lay very still in bed inside his house on Exmoor. In the dark he ticked off in his mind the list of tasks dealt with. Everyone was now in place. It was 30 November: Gorbachev would land at Brize Norton on Monday 7 December.

Land? He would be blown to pieces in mid-air. The meeting with the British Prime Minister would never take place. Within days, Yigor Ligachev, Number Two in the Politburo, would take over as the new General Secretary. Ligachev had no time or sympathy with *glasnost*, with *perestroika*, and all the other nonsense. He had openly said so.

Jupiter had been trained as a youth in the hardline school. The world must be made safe for Lenin's Marxist principles. Only the Red Army could achieve the final victory. And I, he thought, will have contributed an essential role to that eventual victory I won't live to see. The Red Flag flying over Buckingham Palace, the White House in Washington. No, that would take more years than I have.

He smiled as he thought of the final signal he had transmitted to Greece. He had changed the scenario. The weak link was Florakis. It was ironic – that Florakis would pass on to Doganis the signal tomorrow, signing his own death warrant. *Closed circuit.*

Driving along the coast road to Cape Sounion just before dawn, Doganis hunched his huge, seemingly flabby bulk over the wheel. It suited him to be up early: he no longer slept well and woke with his brain churning with excitement. Everything had gone so well. Using Petros' insane lust for revenge as a smokescreen had completely foiled the opposition. He pulled up close to the hotel site, leaving his engine running.

'I have a fresh signal,' the lean-faced Florakis said as he got into the passenger seat. 'But why do I need the transceiver?'

'Put it in the boot,' Doganis ordered.

He waited until they were driving along the winding highway before he answered. Florakis glanced at Doganis who stared straight ahead: he disliked him intensely, this mountain of flesh, gone to seed. He should keep fit, an activity Florakis prided himself on.

'We are moving the location where you transmit from,' Doganis informed him. 'It is dangerous to transmit from the same area too frequently. You said it was a short message. Two words. What are they?'

'Closed circuit. That was all. Then he signed off.'

I guessed right, Doganis thought. And the timing is correct. Soon the operation will be accomplished. Unlike Florakis, he knew this would be the last signal. He went on talking as he drove closer and closer to Cape Sounion. And his own timing was correct – it was still half an hour before dawn.

'In future you will transmit from the summit of Cape Sounion. There is no one about at 2 a.m. I will show you the ideal place I have found – a dip in the ground beyond the temple.'

He stopped the car at the entrance to the track leading up from the highway. He told Florakis to fetch the transceiver. Inwardly Florakis sneered at this; the flabby bastard hadn't even the strength to lug the transceiver uphill.

They walked in silence past the restaurant and hotel which showed no lights. Then they climbed the twisting rocky path to the summit. Doganis wheezed, apparently with the effort. They reached the elegant Temple of Poseidon, its columns silhouetted in the dark.

Doganis led the way past it and down the slope towards the cliff edge. The ground was covered with scrubby grass and Doganis stopped at the edge of a bowl. He pointed one thick finger.

'That is the place. You make all future transmissions from here . . .'

'I see. But why bring the transceiver? I am not going to use it now.'

'Because you will not need it any more.'

515

Doganis raised his huge hands, clamped them round the throat of Florakis. The Greek was taken by surprise, but not frightened. Doganis had gone mad – even to imagine he could cope with a man of Florakis' strength. He tried to knee Doganis in the groin, but the attacker had turned sideways and the blow struck his thigh. Florakis felt a flash of fear. It had been like hitting the leg of an elephant. The pressure on his windpipe increased. Lights appeared before his eyes. Doganis' face seemed enormous as he began to bend Florakis whose back arched in a bow. If the process continued his back would be broken. Panic took hold. He kicked futilely with his right foot at Doganis' leg. It felt like striking ebony. Then he sagged, lost consciousness as Doganis went on strangling him.

Satisfied that he had done the job, Doganis let him slump to the ground. They were perched on top of the slope. Doganis used one foot to lever the prostrate corpse. It began to roll. The momentum increased. Like a broken rag doll Florakis vanished over the edge of the cliff. Doganis grunted with satisfaction, flexed his hands.

'I am arresting you for cold-blooded murder,' a quiet voice said behind him.

The Dormouse stood about two dozen feet away, further along the top of the ridge where it curved inland. He stood, a tiny figure, with his hands clasped behind his back, staring at Doganis, at the sea behind him which stretched away like a sheet of black steel. Stood as though about to make a speech.

'You came alone?'

Doganis could hardly believe it, looked round for re-inforcements.

The plump tiny figure looked so absurd. There was no sign of anyone else.

'Yes,' said Kalos. 'I have been watching your apartment

in the Plaka for days – and nights. I followed you in my Saab without lights. You were so intent on your murderous plan you never dreamed you might be followed.'

'And you think *you* are going to arrest *me*?'

Doganis began to move slowly towards Kalos who remained quite still. Hands still clasped behind his back as Doganis crept along the ridge, padding silently.

'Is this the way you killed the Englishman, Harry Masterson?' he asked.

'Yes. You might as well know it since you will end as food for the fishes. Masterson was also deceived like Florakis – by thinking I was a fat weak slob. I told him I could show him where the leader of the Greek Key lived. He was making too many enquiries about us. He was confident he could handle me. And he was stronger than Florakis.'

'Stay where you are,' Kalos ordered. 'Do not take one more step towards me. I have handcuffs behind my back. I am taking you in.'

Doganis continued his ape-like progress. A sound came from inside him, a rumbling noise which was his version of a chuckle. He raised both hands, ready to grasp this doll round the throat. He would be able to lift him off his feet, throw him over . . .

Kalos brought both hands from behind his back. They held the 9mm Walther automatic he had extracted from the holster strapped to the middle of his back. He fired once, aiming to disable. The bullet struck Doganis in the left shoulder. He stopped. Then he came on again. Kalos fired again. At the thigh. Still Doganis moved forward like an enraged bull elephant. Kalos shifted his aim, shot him through the heart.

Doganis slumped slowly to the ground on the seaward side of the ridge, on to the slope. Like Florakis, his huge bulk began to roll. He caught a medium-sized boulder a glancing blow and the loosened boulder also started to roll. Kalos stood watching as Doganis' body reached a steeper section of slope, picking up speed. The gross corpse shot over the brink, dropped out of sight to fall three hundred feet, followed by the boulder.

He walked over to the transceiver Doganis had intended hurling off the cliff. He embraced its sides with both hands, his gun slid back inside his holster, and staggered back to his Saab, preserving Florakis' fingerprints on the handle.

50

Three men paced the snow-bound barracks square south-west of Moscow. In the centre of the group strode General Lucharsky, flanked by the other two members of the Troika. Their boots crunched the hard snow and they had the square to themselves: all officers and men were moving out aboard military transport for the annual manoeuvres in the Ukraine which would be watched by Lucharsky.

The timing suited Lucharsky admirably. He would be out of the way when the imminent crisis broke. His companions waited for him to speak. He kept them waiting. An assertion of his authority. A bitter wind whipped at his white bony face.

'Everything is prepared,' he said eventually. 'We are so far advanced radio communications are being cut. The weak links in the Greek Key are being eliminated. It all depends now on Jupiter in England.'

'Gorbachev has played into our hands,' commented General Budienny. 'Thank God he is landing in England. But British security is very good. Is Jupiter better?'

'The commander of the *Spetsnaz* unit which has been

activated is an ex-soldier in the British Army. A formidable man. He will find a way. Meantime, General Budienny, your armoured division will remain here ready to seal off Moscow should a crisis arise.' He stopped and stared hard at the stocky, wide-shouldered general. 'But on no account must you move unless you receive a direct order from Yigor Ligachev to preserve stability.'

'Of course not, Comrade General. My division has always had to stand by for that role – even under Brezhnev.'

Lucharsky resumed his walk in the square where they could not possibly be overheard. 'And the one general who might rebel because he is a *glasnost* enthusiast will be taking part in the Ukraine manoeuvres. At the slightest sign of resistance on his part I will have him arrested. So what can possibly go wrong?'

'You were worried at one time when your KGB associate warned you the British agent, Tweed, was in Greece.'

'Until I heard he was concentrating on that crazy old idiot, Petros. Then I knew he had taken the bait – incensed by the killing of his sector chief, Masterson, which is why I ordered Masterson's liquidation. You can forget Tweed. He is confused, like a ship without a rudder, sailing round in circles.'

Snow had begun to fall again, heavy flakes which drifted down out of the pewter sky. Lucharsky paused, bent down, scooped up some in his gloved hand and rubbed it on his face.

'That helps the brain to become alert, Comrades. The first snow of winter – the winter which will descend on *glasnost* and freeze it to death.'

1 December. Tweed had not returned to his office the previous day. He had to wait at Downing Street to see the PM. And when he did meet her the meeting had lasted far longer than he had anticipated.

Now he was walking in Regent's Park with Paula. The

wind was biting and he wore his British warm topcoat. Paula clutched her own coat collar at the neck as they made their way across the deserted open spaces.

'Let us go back to the beginning,' Tweed said. 'I still have the worrying feeling I have missed something.'

'You've done everything you can,' she assured him. 'It is a matter of waiting for a break.'

'But we have so little time left. Gorbachev lands at Brize Norton on Monday 7 December. That leaves only six days. So, recall how it all started for me.'

She summarized the early events and Tweed listened in silence. 'Then,' she went on, 'there was the murder of Sam Partridge on Exmoor. You had to identify him for that local policeman . . .'

She broke off as he stopped, gripped her arm. 'That's it. Why did I have to identify him?'

'Because his wallet was missing. And later discovered with plenty of money inside it – by a dog ferreting in the Doone Valley.'

'So robbery was certainly not involved.'

'They were new notes. The numbers ran in sequence,' Paula reminded him. 'No thief with half a brain would risk spending them.'

'Back to the office.' Tweed's tone was firm. 'I want to see the list Marler sent us of what was in that wallet. *Something* was missing.'

'Sam's driving licence.' Tweed's voice held a note of triumph as he sat behind his desk and studied the list. 'It wasn't in his wallet. That's what is missing. And he drove down to Somerset. He told me he parked his car in the street at Dunster.'

'Then why hasn't someone reported its presence – parked there all this time?' Monica objected.

'Because someone – maybe Winterton himself – drove

it away and parked it in some hidden place on Exmoor. Maybe an abandoned building. They didn't want the car – they're using the licence. Which means they probably hired a car on the strength of Partridge's driving licence.' He scribbled on his desk pad, tore off the sheet. 'Paula, here's his address. Call the Vehicle Registration people in Swansea immediately. Find out the licence number.'

'Which could take God knows how long. They don't move fast,' Paula warned.

'Tell them you're Special Branch.' He produced his card. 'And tell them I need a reply within one hour. That we are searching for an escaped terrorist. Dammit, they're using computers. Within one hour . . .'

It was one hour and ten minutes later when Vehicle Registration phoned back with the number. Tweed called the Commissioner of Police, identified himself, gave him the number. He had hardly put down the phone when it rang again. Newman reporting from Exmoor. No change in the situation.

Tweed explained what he wanted, gave him the licence number and urgent instructions. 'I want all four of you on this. Divide up the area into sectors. Then drive round to every place where you can hire a car. Show them the number. If someone used the licence to hire a car their records will show it. I need any information you can get within twenty-four hours.'

'We have as long as that?' Newman asked cynically.

'Quicker if you can.'

At Cherry Farm the balance of power had changed, much to Anton's chagrin. It had started with a phone call from Jupiter. He told Anton in his cryptic way that three more guests would be arriving. Foster, Saunders and Sully.

At the appointed time Anton drove the grey Austin Metro Seton-Charles had hired in Taunton weeks before

521

to the crossroads where he had taken delivery of the Shi-ite prisoners. A Ford station wagon and a Vauxhall Cavalier stood parked alongside each other on the verge. The lean-faced smartly dressed Foster he had met before came towards him.

'Tawny Owl,' Foster greeted him.

'Night Heron,' Anton replied, wondering why Jupiter had thought it necessary for them to exchange agreed codewords when he knew Foster. There were two men in the Vauxhall who waited inside until Anton led the way, driving at the head of the convoy back to Cherry Farm. He didn't like the look of any of them. They had the smell of hardbitten professionals, almost as though they had undergone military training.

Foster introduced his companions after his two cars were hidden in the second shed. In the large kitchen at the back Seton-Charles examined the new arrivals through his rimless glasses. He also did not like what he saw. Foster, quick-moving and quick-talking, wasted no time.

'This is Saunders, my second-in-command. If I'm absent you take orders from him. This is Sully. We've brought our own food supplies. Sully will cook for the three of us . . .'

'Seton-Charles has been doing the cooking,' Anton interrupted. 'He can do the meals for all of us.'

'I said Sully will cook for us. You two look after yourselves. Now, where are the Stingers, the mobile launching platforms?'

Anton took them upstairs into the bedroom he occupied, opened a cupboard. Over his left arm was looped the handle of a walking stick with a hardened tip. He used both hands to push his clothes, suspended from a rod, to each side. Foster grunted.

'We'll need a better place than this in case a patrol car comes poking around.'

'Will we?' Anton snapped. 'Then find them yourself.'

Foster dropped to his knees, crawled inside, felt around the wooden planked floor. Anton looked at Seton-Charles, raised his eyebrows. *Bighead* his gesture conveyed. Sully, smaller, slimly built and also very fit-looking like the others, caught the expression.

'We can do without the sarcasm,' he growled.

Foster hammered hard at the back of the cupboard with his knuckles, expecting a hollow sound. He gritted his teeth – he had almost broken his knuckles on solid wood. He crawled out of the cupboard, stood up.

'All right, I can't find them,' he said and his tone was more polite.

Anton stepped inside, pressed hard with the tip of the stick on a knot of wood in a corner. There was a loud *click*. The rear panel opened inwards a few inches and Anton pushed it wide open, held it, revealing the compartment beyond with a long canvas bundle on the floor.

'You hold the panel open,' he warned. 'There is a spring-loaded hinge which closes it automatically. You haul that out . . .'

They stood inside the front furniture van after squeezing past the auction junk Anton had purchased. Seton-Charles had been told to stay in the farmhouse to keep watch. Holding a launcher with a missile inserted under one arm, Anton mounted the steps to the platform, followed by Foster and his two companions.

Anton settled himself in the chair, pressed the switch and the panel in the roof slid back. Foster stared, glanced at Sully and Saunders who also gazed up. 'Who created all this?' asked Foster.

'I did,' said Anton.

'Jesus, I'm impressed. The other van the same?'

'A replica of this one . . .'

There was an argument about who would drive each

523

van, who would use the launchers. Anton refused to give way. 'I've been trained in the weapon's use by the arms dealer. I'm firing one of the launchers. Who the hell drives is your problem.'

Foster compromised. He and Anton would fire the launchers; the vans would be driven by Saunders and Sully. He asked about communication and Anton produced a walkie-talkie from a leather sheath attached to the platform. 'The driver has his own, tells the launcher when the target is in sight. Anything else?'

Foster asked about the Shi-ite prisoners who would be left dead inside the vans, their hands pressed on the launchers to leave fingerprints. Anton told him about the dead pig he was using to keep them passive. Foster nodded. 'Except when it is on view,' Anton continued, 'I keep it in the chest freezer in the shed. I rigged up a generator to power the freezer.' Foster nodded again, then raised the delicate topic.

'You heard from Jupiter that before we leave nothing must be left to show we were here?'

'Yes. When the call was finished I asked Seton-Charles to dig a grave in the field at the back for the pig.'

'You know what will occupy this grave?' Foster asked quietly.

'Look, I've just told you.' Anton stared at Foster, who stared back with a poker-faced expression. Was he grasping what he'd been told, the Greek began to wonder. Maybe this cold-faced man wasn't too bright? 'It will be occupied by the pig,' Anton repeated.

'Together with Seton-Charles. He's expendable.'

2 December. An atmosphere of tension was building up inside Tweed's office at Park Crescent. There had been no further reaction to the long list of enquiries they had sent out. No one had called about Anton's photo or the

Identikit picture of Seton-Charles which had been widely circulated.

None of the four men scouring Exmoor had reported back on the phone. Tweed, Monica and Paula spent their time listening once more to the tapes of the conversations recorded. They reread the files, including the report Newman had dictated about their visit to Greece. They searched desperately for something they had overlooked. Late in the evening Monica brought more coffee and asked her question again.

'Can't you tell us anything about your interview with the PM?'

'At a certain stage – closer to 7 December when Gorbachev will land at Brize Norton – I shall recall Newman, Marler, Butler and Nield from Exmoor. They must stay there a day or so yet in the hope they find two things – if Sam Partridge's driving licence was used to hire a car in the area, and the route used by Anton to leave the country secretly. When they arrive back we hold a meeting. Then you will hear what has been decided.' He paused. 'I can tell you the PM was convinced I am right, that we have her full support to indent for any weapons we may need. And that two Westland helicopters have been put at our disposal. At my suggestion they are being equipped with swivel-mounted machine-guns and the words "Traffic Control" are being painted on the fuselages. They are at a private airfield called Fairoaks near Woking in Surrey.'

'What's the idea?' Paula asked.

'I should give the credit to Newman. He phoned me in the middle of the night and I outlined the situation. He knows what's coming. So does Marler. Newman made those suggestions.'

Paula glanced at the camp bed made up in the corner. 'So you didn't get an undisturbed night's rest.'

'I don't expect any of us will during the next five days . . .'

He stopped speaking as Howard strolled into the room and sat down in the armchair. He carried a sheaf of photo-prints.

'No developments yet, I assume? It's a tense time.'

'Nothing,' Tweed replied. 'And there's always tension at this stage.'

'As you know,' Howard remarked, 'I'm a bit of a car buff. It struck me that that *Spetsnaz* unit Paula uncovered must have moved to a new base prepared in advance.'

'I agree.' Tweed wondered what he was getting at.

'We know Foster has a Ford station wagon, Saunders a Vauxhall Cavalier, Seton-Charles a Volvo station wagon – from the information supplied by Vehicle Registration at Swansea. Sully left his Jag behind in the bungalow garage, so we can forget that. It occurred to me they won't dare hire fresh cars – they'd have to show their driving licences. With me so far?'

'So far, yes.'

'That means they'll have to use the same transport to move about. But they may respray their vehicles to disguise them.'

'Highly possible,' Tweed agreed.

'So I have used photographs of those three cars and traced them on a sheet of paper. But I filled the colours in with a solid black. Then I had these photocopies made. If we're looking for those cars from a chopper and use these photocopies we won't be fooled by any change of colour. They're all fairly common makes of car. We'll spot them by their shapes.'

He reached forward, dumped the photocopies on Tweed's desk and sat back again. Tweed studied the copies.

'I think this is a clever idea,' he decided. 'Everyone involved in the search will have a copy.'

'Then I need one,' said Howard and took back a copy.

'What for?' asked Tweed.

526

'Because I'll be in one of those choppers. You can ride in the other machine.' He raised a hand as Tweed started to protest. 'Don't argue. I'm good at spotting cars. And if you tell the PM I'll never speak to you again.' He stood up. 'So that's settled. I'm fed up with fighting the war from behind my desk with paper darts.' He glanced at Monica's stupefied expression as he left. 'And better give Monica a brandy. Looks like she needs it.'

'My God!' Monica burst out when Howard had gone. 'I'd never have believed it.'

'You always did underestimate Howard,' Tweed told her, and then the phone began ringing.

There was dead silence as Monica grabbed the receiver. She listened, looked at Tweed. 'It's for you. Peter Sarris. Athens.'

Tweed greeted the Greek police chief, then kept silent for five minutes. Gradually he hunched closer to the phone. When he put it down he stared bleakly into the distance for a long minute before speaking.

'It's very close,' he said gravely. 'Doganis strangled Florakis on Cape Sounion, sent his body over the cliff. He didn't know Kalos was following him. Doganis admitted he'd killed Harry Masterson. Apparently he's as strong as an ox. Kalos had to shoot him.'

'What does it mean?' Paula asked.

'It means the Soviet hardliners back in Russia – probably led by General Lucharsky – are wiping their tracks clean. Killing off anyone who could betray them. 7 December is definitely zero hour. Pray for a break soon.'

51

Friday, 4 December. At Cherry Farm the atmosphere was strained and becoming worse. Five men were living in close proximity inside the farmhouse. Anton had agreed with Foster's decision that no one must appear outside. The temperature was low and a biting wind swept across the waterlogged fields and rattled the closed shutters.

The Shi-ite Muslims, shivering with cold, had complained they were freezing. They were given extra underclothes and left to cope. Conditions were little better for their five captors. There was a tantalising pile of logs on one side of the large fireplace in the living room. No fire could be lit: smoke from the chimney would show a passer-by the place was inhabited.

There was no electricity, no gas, no water. All services had been cut off from the supposedly abandoned farm. Seton-Charles cooked a meal for himself at midday using Calor gas for the stove – an item he had bought on his way back from Norwich. He had very little left.

In the living room Anton and Foster pored over two ordnance survey maps, planning out the route to the general area of Brize Norton. Saunders and Sully stood behind them as they crouched over the table. They all wore extra clothes brought with them: woollen pullovers and two pairs of socks.

'Transport,' Anton said suddenly. 'We've talked about it but taken no decision. I'll drive the Austin Metro and park it so we can get away afterwards, then get inside the furniture van.'

'It's a risk, I agree,' said Foster. 'And I'll take the Ford station wagon – again a risk. But not so risky as trying to hire different vehicles. We'd have to show our driving licences. The Vauxhall can stay here.'

'What is the escape route?' Anton demanded. He stood with his arms folded. 'You fobbed me off before but I want to know now before we talk any more about routes.'

Foster compressed his thin lips. 'Very well. We're close to doing the job. Afterwards we abandon the vans, then drive back to Exmoor. We leave the way you came in – by motorboat from the beach at Porlock Weir. A ship will be waiting for us outside the three-mile limit. An East German freighter. The East Germans are not nearly so keen on *glasnost* as Gorbachev.'

'Another point – I'd like to discuss it with you alone.'

'Really?' Foster's cold grey eyes narrowed. 'Let's go take a breath of fresh air.'

The air outside the back of the farmhouse was more than fresh: it was bitter. Foster thrust his hands inside his jacket pockets. Until he was twenty-five years old he had been used to the razor-edged wind sweeping across the Russian Steppes. Fifteen years in England had made him more susceptible to the cold.

'What is it?' he demanded.

'I have decided I can't shoot Seton-Charles. Killing that arms dealer in Lisbon was child's play. He was a stranger. Seton-Charles introduced new opportunities into my life. I don't like him – but he's become a part of my life.'

Foster stood more erect, held himself stiffly as he stared hard at Anton, reassessing him. Anton forced himself to gaze back but inwardly he felt nervous. Suddenly he felt the force of the *Spetsnaz* leader's personality.

'That calls for a change of plan,' Foster informed him, his tone grating. 'I have been watching Seton-Charles. I thought he was no more than a theorist. He is dedicated – more dedicated than you will ever be. He will drive one of the furniture vans, Sully the other. That leaves Saunders and myself to operate the launchers.'

'But I can do that,' Anton protested. 'What would I do?'

'You drive the escape vehicle. When we met the second time at the crossroads and drove back here a Post Office van overtook us. He passes along the road at the end of the track every day, Sully tells me. First time early in the morning.'

'That's right. Seton-Charles told me. What's the idea?'

'On the morning of Monday 7 December, we stop the driver, seize his vehicle. No one notices a Royal Mail van.'

'What do we do with the driver?' Anton asked.

'Kill him, dump the body in that grave Seton-Charles dug. I'll do the job.' Foster's lip curled. 'I don't think you're up to it.'

'But I can fire one of the launchers . . .'

'But you won't. You've trained us. The Stinger is a weapon it is easy to use. Now, you can stay out here while your balls freeze – assuming you have any. I'm going inside to look at those maps again. Saunders and I are going to reconnoitre the route to Brize Norton.'

He walked inside the farmhouse, closing the door quietly. Anton shivered in the wind. The look in Foster's eyes, his manner, had frightened him. But he had to admit Foster was well-organized: they had brought with them three pairs of the type of overalls worn by furniture removal men. They had spent time rubbing dirt into them, crumpling them to take away the appearance of new garments.

Anton went back inside to find Foster and Saunders bent over the maps. Foster was tracing a route with a pencil, careful not to touch the maps. He looked up as Anton returned.

'And we'll be taking your Austin Metro for the reconnaissance – no one will know about that vehicle.'

*   *   *

530

Friday, 4 December. It was late afternoon when the call came through to Park Crescent from Newman. Monica told Tweed he was on the line and pressed the recording button.

'I've found out Sam Partridge's driving licence was used to hire a car. Weeks ago – and the car is still on hire. Someone with an upper-crust voice phones Barton's – the car hire outfit – and an envelope of money to extend the hire is pushed in the letter box at night. Barton's is in Taunton. The car is a blue Austin Metro, registration number . . . God, I called at enough places before I found the right one.'

'Good work, Bob. We'll circulate that car's details immediately. Now, can you contact the others within the hour? I want everyone back here tonight. It's an emergency.'

'I'm calling from the Minehead phone box. Couldn't find an empty one in Taunton – so I drove back here like a bat. Butler and Nield happen to be at The Anchor now. We'll be on our way within half an hour. Don't go, Marler has news for you. Here he is . . .'

'I know how Anton slipped out of the country,' Marler drawled. 'Got back here to find Newman monopolizing this box. Anton is an expert pilot of small aircraft. Remember – Christina told Newman. Dunkeswell Airport, a small private airfield south-east of Tiverton. He flew out in a Cessna.'

'You're sure? There's a manifest to prove it?'

'Like hell there is. I identified myself to a pilot, showed him Anton's photo, told him he was a leading terrorist. He went as white as a sheet. I had to exert a little pressure – you don't want to hear about that. Briefly, Anton paid this pilot a large sum in cash . . .'

'To fly him back to Lisbon?'

'Not quite. Anton insisted on flying the Cessna himself. Took the pilot along as passenger. The pilot flew the

531

machine back to Dunkeswell. The controller of the airfield was away, doesn't know what happened.'

'Another question answered. You're coming back to London. A disaster is imminent.'

'If weapons are in order,' Marler responded, 'I'd like a rifle with a telescopic sight. See you . . .'

On her other phone Monica was finishing giving details of the Austin Metro to the Commissioner of Police. She put down the phone, her eyes gleaming with excitement.

'It's all happening at once. Like it so often does.'

'And these things come in threes,' said Paula.

The call from Norwich came at 7 p.m.

Waiting for Newman and his three companions to arrive, Tweed had a meal of ham sandwiches, followed by fruit, with Paula and Monica. Extra camp beds had been erected in the office next door where the two women slept overnight. They were all beginning to feel housebound when the phone rang.

Monica frowned as she answered the call, listened, asked several questions, then put her hand over the mouthpiece.

'It's Norwich police headquarters. A Constable Fox. Calling in reply to our circulating Seton-Charles' Volvo description and registration number. Sounds tentative. He's called the General & Cumbria Assurance cover number we used.'

Tweed picked up his phone, asked how he could help.

'Constable Fox speaking, sir. In response to your enquiry re the Volvo station wagon.' The youthful voice hesitated. 'My inspector wasn't sure I should call. I keep a careful record in my notebook of even trivial incidents. You never can tell when the information may be needed.'

'Very sensible,' Tweed encouraged him. 'Do go on.'

'Back in October late one night. I can give you the date

in a minute. Left my notebook in my tunic pocket. As I was saying, I was on duty and I saw this Volvo park near a corner. A man got out and walked round to a furniture removal firm selling off bankrupt stock. It was eleven at night so I was curious. Especially as he could have parked in front of the warehouse. Am I wasting your time, sir?'

'Please go on.'

'There were lights in the warehouse so I thought I'd better check. This chap goes inside after Latimer answers the door.'

'Latimer?'

'The proprietor of the firm selling off the vans, Camelford Removals. When I saw it was Latimer I thought it must be OK, so I pushed off. Then the next morning I was walking near the same area when I saw the Volvo driver pass me behind the wheel of one of the furniture vans. Trouble is his description does not tally with your Identikit. He wore horn-rims and an old cap.'

'But the registration of the Volvo is the same as the one we sent out?'

'Quite definitely. I checked that in my notebook.'

'Could you contact this Latimer, persuade him to wait until I arrive? He'll be paid for his trouble. And can you wait for me at the station until I arrive? It will be after ten.'

'I'm on night duty again. And behind enquiries counter tonight. Latimer practically lives at the warehouse. I can phone him.'

'My name is Tweed. I'm coming. Your recording of trivial events could end up in promotion. I'm leaving London now . . .'

As Tweed had guessed, Constable Fox was in his early twenties. A thin, pale-faced man, he had an earnest manner and blushed when he was introduced to Paula. Tweed was careful to show him his Special Branch card. Fox took the card, studied the photograph inside the plastic guard, stared carefully at Tweed and handed it back. He was carrying the Identikit picture of Seton-Charles in an envelope.

Outside police headquarters he opened the rear door of the Cortina for Paula, closed it, then joined Tweed in the front.

'Latimer is waiting for us, sir. I didn't give him any idea who was coming.'

'Very sensible,' said Tweed again, then concentrated on Fox's directions. They reached the furniture warehouse in a few minutes and a short middle-aged man opened the door as they pulled up. 'That's Latimer,' Fox whispered.

Tweed introduced himself and Paula, showed his card, and with only a cursory glance Latimer invited them inside. They sat round a rough-surfaced wooden table and Latimer drank tea from a tin mug. Tweed took the envelope from Fox, extracted the Identikit picture and pushed it in front of him. 'Is that the man who bought a furniture van from you?'

'Two vans. No, it doesn't look like him. He wore horn-rimmed glasses, not rimless, and a driver's cap.'

Tweed looked at Paula, pushed the Identikit towards her. 'You are the artist. Mr Latimer, please describe as best you can the type of glasses, the kind of cap. Miss Grey will convert the picture under your guidance . . .'

He changed places so Paula sat next to Latimer. She produced a small clipboard and a felt-tip pen from her capacious shoulder bag and worked on the picture, altering it from Latimer's instructions. Then she pushed the picture in front of him.

'That's the chap. Magic it is, the way you did that. I've a good memory for faces. No doubt about it.'

'You said he bought two vans. He had someone with him?' Tweed enquired.

'No. Collected them both himself, one by one. Both the same day. Was gone about eight hours before he came back for the second job. Twin vans, they was. Only one left now.'

'He spoke with an educated accent?' Paula enquired.

'No. Workingman's lingo.' Latimer scratched his head. 'Mind you, it didn't sound it came natural to him.'

'He paid by cheque?' Tweed probed.

'No. Cash. Fifties. I held them up to check them. You can't be too careful these days. Funny sort of bloke. And that cap didn't fit him too well.'

'You said you had only one van left,' Tweed reminded him. 'Is that the same as the two you sold to this man?'

'Came from exactly the same stable. Want to see it?'

'Yes, please.' Tweed looked at Paula. 'Did you bring your camera?'

'Always carry it. Plus flashbulbs . . .'

They were there another half hour. Paula took pictures of the van from different angles. Tweed then persuaded Latimer to drive the furniture van into the street, deserted at that hour. Paula peered out from a top-floor window in the warehouse, looking down on the van with her camera. In the street below Tweed saw three flashbulbs go off. Then Paula waved her hand.

Latimer backed the van further away, stopped it at the entrance to another street, presenting her with a sideways angle. Three more flashbulbs went off. Tweed told Latimer he could drive the vehicle back into the warehouse.

'What's this all about?' he asked as he climbed down from the cab.

'A gang of very dangerous terrorists. Now, I want to pay you for your time.'

'On the house, Guv. If it's bleedin' terrorists I'm 'appy

to oblige. Shoot the bastards when you catch up with 'em.'

'Thank you for your cooperation. I'll bear your advice in mind. Now,' he said to Paula who had reappeared with Fox, 'we have to get moving. And Constable Fox, I'll be recommending your work to your inspector when this is all over . . .'

It was 2 a.m. when Tweed and Paula arrived back at Park Crescent. All the lights were on in the building behind closed blinds. They went straight down into the Engine Room in the basement where the staff were waiting. Paula handed one of the technicians her film, Tweed told him to develop and print immediately, then to produce two dozen copies.

His office was full of people when he opened the door. A large table had been moved in and round it sat Howard, Newman, Marler, Butler and Nield. The remnants of a meal were on the table and Monica was pouring more coffee. Marler sat smoking one of his king-size cigarettes.

'Any joy?' he enquired.

Tweed explained what they had learned as Paula took a spare seat at the table. Most of his listeners looked weary except for Howard and Marler who appeared fresh and alert. Howard raised the query.

'What on earth would they need two furniture vans for?'

'Remember the Stingers,' Marler told him. 'That reference to them we got from Morle rambling in high fever. Those vans are mobile rocket launcher platforms. Who notices a furniture van? It stops, they drop the tailboard and fire the missiles from the rear opening.'

'Oh my God!' Howard was appalled. 'Hadn't we better contact the PM?'

'And alert the SAS?' Newman suggested.

'We're on our own,' Tweed said quietly. 'SAS teams are guarding the Brize Norton perimeter. The PM calls us her private insurance policy. And while I remember, each one of you must carry one of these cards. Force Z is what she's termed us – Z for zero hour.' He dropped a pile of fresh identity cards he'd collected from the Engine Room on the table. 'Sort them out. Each carries an individual photograph. Including one for you, Howard – if you still insist on coming.'

'I do.'

'All security personnel at Brize Norton have been informed about Force Z. If you run into one of them you'd better speak quickly, then show the card.'

'How the hell do we go about this?' Howard demanded.

In reply, Tweed walked across to a wall map he had pinned up. It covered Oxfordshire, Wiltshire, Berkshire, Hampshire and London Airport. A tiny village called Liphook came just within the large circle he drew with a felt-tip pen.

'We have to think ourselves into the mind of Winterton.' He glanced at Howard. 'That is the codeword for the Englishman directing this operation.'

'Who is Robson, Barrymore or Kearns, you still think?' Paula asked.

'Yes. Based on the fact that Petros heard during World War Two that the Greek Key was controlled by an Englishman located in Cairo. The fact that the *Oporto* seaman who talked saw Anton being taken ashore near Porlock Weir by a man disguised with a Balaclava. The facts which came out of the tape recording Nield made of their conversation at The Luttrell Arms. The fact that the secret *Spetsnaz* base was situated on Exmoor. The fact that the murders of Andreas and Stephen Gavalas took place when those three men were nearby. The fact that Partridge and Mrs Larcombe were murdered on Exmoor. The fact that when Jill Kearns was run down in London those

537

three men were staying at a hotel not a quarter of a mile away.'

'I get the point,' Paula agreed. 'But now you've withdrawn everyone from Exmoor. Shouldn't someone be keeping an eye on those men now we're so close to the climax?'

'Yes. And you're elected.'

There were protests at the idea. From Howard. From Paula. 'I want to be in at the finish,' she objected. 'I believe I have contributed to the investigation . . .'

'Agreed,' said Tweed. 'You were the first one who spotted – and persisted – something was wrong with that bungalow estate. To mention only one thing. But from what Newman told me on the phone all three men are still on Exmoor . . .'

'It's too dangerous,' Newman snapped. 'She's already had her taste of gunpowder confronting Norton and Morle. And Winterton may have left the area by now.'

'He hasn't.' Tweed was emphatic. 'I haven't had time to tell you – but the Chief Inspector at Taunton has set up roadblocks on every route east out of the area. Barrymore, Robson and our friend, Kearns, are well-known. If one of them – Winterton – tries to leave Exmoor I'll know within minutes.'

'So that explains why we were stopped by the police near to Glastonbury,' Newman commented.

'And Paula will again be armed.' Tweed took a Browning automatic and spare mags from a desk drawer, placed them in front of her. 'Now, are you happier?' he asked her. 'Your job is to see which of the three makes a move.'

'I'll settle for that.'

'Good. Now maybe we can get on. I've tried to think myself inside Winterton's mind. He would know in advance there was a good chance Gorbachev would land in Britain to meet the PM – he would have found that out from Moscow, I'm sure. The hardline faction is there. He knows Gorbachev is coming, but where will he land? London Airport? Possible, but unlikely. Lyneham Air Force Base in Wiltshire? A good bet. Brize Norton in Oxfordshire? Another good bet – because security would be easier to set up rather than at London Airport. Makes sense?'

'Yes,' said Marler. 'How does he go on from there?'

'He sets up an advance base . . .' Tweed went to the wall map and waved his hand round the circle he had drawn. '. . . somewhere inside this area. This gives swift access to whichever landing point is chosen. The furniture vans will be hidden there. But I don't think we'll see them from the air until Gorbachev's aircraft is approaching Brize Norton on this coming Monday. Today is already early Saturday . . .'

'Surely as soon as daylight comes,' Howard intervened, 'we can fly over the area in the choppers. We might just see something.'

'No go,' Monica informed him. 'I called Fairoaks Airfield where the machines are being equipped and repainted. They said Sunday morning was the earliest they could be serviceable.'

'So we wait until Sunday,' Tweed announced. 'In any case, most of you look as though you could do with a good rest. I want you on top form when we fly in those choppers. Anything else?'

'Bob,' Paula suggested, 'could I use your Mercedes? I'll drive down there as soon as this meeting breaks up. Then I can grab a few hours' sleep at The Luttrell Arms and start searching. God knows, I'm familiar with Exmoor by now.'

'As a very special favour.' Newman stifled a yawn. 'Yes.'

'I don't think we should all be airborne.' Butler spoke for the first time. 'Nield and I were talking about that – after Monica explained what she knew of your plan. We'd both like motorcycles, equipped with radio so we can contact you in the chopper.'

'I'll think about that.' Tweed checked his watch. 'Now, if there's nothing else . . .'

'Weapons,' said Marler. 'What's available? We'll need a variety as I see it.'

'Everything you want. The PM gave me *carte blanche*. An armoured car is delivering an arsenal and standing by at Fairoaks. You'll get your rifle with telescopic sights. Handguns. Grenades. Take your pick when the time comes.'

'One final point,' said Paula. 'You still think you know the identity of Winterton?'

'Yes. But no evidence. And I expect him to stay in the background during the operation. On Exmoor. Maybe you'll spot who he is.'

Paula said nothing. She opened her hand and a stick of French chalk rolled on the table.

52

Saturday, 5 December. It was after midnight when Foster took Anton into his bedroom at Cherry Farm, closed the door. Fatigue was registered on the faces of both men and tempers were getting short.

'Those Shi-ite prisoners are getting restless,' Foster opened with. 'What did you tell them they were here for?'

'That they were hostages for an exchange of two men kidnapped in Beirut. That negotiations were proceeding but they took time. They think we're British Government agents. You'd best leave them to me.'

'With pleasure. I have enough on my hands. Practising

weapon drill for one thing. It's Saturday and everyone is feeling the strain. Today we keep under cover. Get some rest. We have to be on top form tomorrow and Monday.'

'Tomorrow is Sunday. What happens then?'

'We do a trial run. Saunders and I found two perfect places to hide the furniture vans as close to Brize Norton as we need to be. Your turn to empty the Elsan buckets. Do it before you go to bed . . .'

He stopped as he heard the phone ring downstairs. Automatically Anton turned towards the door. Foster pushed him out of the way. 'I'm taking all calls now.'

He hurried down the creaking wooden staircase into the hall where the phone was perched on a table. He lifted the receiver and gave the agreed false number. The familiar cold distant voice spoke.

'Is everything ready for the Monday conference? All delegates fully briefed?'

'Yes. We've checked the conference site. I'm double-checking it tomorrow, Sunday, to make sure nothing has been overlooked.'

'I should hope not at this stage. You'll give me a report when we meet? That's all.'

Foster put down the phone, knowing that would be the last call he would receive from Jupiter. The reference to 'when we meet' was a hint they would meet aboard the East German freighter, *Stralsund*, which would be waiting for them at the mouth of the Bristol Channel. Only then, after all these years, Foster thought, will I know who has been controlling us on Exmoor.

'Any crisis?' asked Anton, who stood at the foot of the stairs.

The question confirmed to Foster he had been right to stop Anton operating one of the two precious launchers. He was growing more nervous by the hour. Foster glanced at the phone.

'How is the bill for the calls made on this phone paid

541

for? You said earlier you had a phone booth you called at certain times.'

'All taken care of by Jupiter. A local solicitor in Taunton receives the bills, pays for them from a large sum Jupiter sent him in cash after instructing him over the phone.'

Foster was satisfied: it was tiny details like this which could upset all their plans. Jupiter never seemed to miss a trick. Anton was still standing by the staircase.

'What is it?' Foster snapped. 'Time we all got some sleep.'

'That Post Office van . . .'

'Don't shit yourself. I'll kill the driver. You can just bury him. And dump the Elsan closets we've been using for lavatories on top of the body. We leave this place neat and tidy. Don't forget to keep your gloves on – no fingerprints.'

'The Post Office van,' Anton began again. 'If you'd listened I was going to say it's a long drive to Porlock Weir. We'll need to top up the tank with petrol . . .'

'And we still have plenty of the stuff left in spare cans in the boots of the two cars we came here in. And also dump all our sleeping bags in that grave. Now, push off . . .'

He called after Anton as he was mounting the stairs. 'How much mineral water left?'

'A dozen litre bottles. I have kept a watch on supplies,' Anton rapped back.

'Good for you.' Foster's mind was checking other details. They would take the oil stoves and lamps which had provided heat and illumination with them. They could be thrown into ditches one by one on their way to Brize Norton. He went upstairs, nodded to Saunders who sat in a wicker armchair in the corridor where the Shi-ites were imprisoned. Saunders had a Luger lying in his lap. Any trouble in that direction and he'd crack their skulls with the Luger barrel, which was their ultimate fate anyway.

It was Foster's turn on the duty detail to watch the approach to the farm from the front window. Later in the night Seton-Charles and Sully would take over. Rest for everyone. Sunday would be a busy day – making the trial run to Brize Norton.

In Tweed's office at 3 a.m. everyone had left to get sleep except for Monica, Tweed and Butler. Newman had remarked that Butler had had more sleep than any of them, so he could make the report on Exmoor. With a cup of black coffee in front of him, Butler spoke tersely.

'You'd almost think they were setting out to look normal. Dr Robson still rides the moor at all hours to see patients. One old semi-invalid lady at Dulverton is always calling him in the middle of the night to her decrepit mansion. He goes . . .'

'How does she call him? Do you know?'

'By phone. She has an extension by her bedside upstairs. Barrymore drives into Minehead after dark to call someone from that public box we use. Pub gossip has it his housekeeper, Mrs Atyeo, is threatening to walk out on him. No one knows why – she's been there for years. Kearns still goes riding during the night. Nield was driving along that lane which leads to the Doone Valley after dark. He noticed Kearns' horse tethered beneath some trees at a lonely spot midway between Quarme Manor and Endpoint.'

'So Kearns could have been calling on Robson or Barrymore?'

'That's what Pete said. He didn't hang around – he'd have been seen. Barrymore and Robson still have lunch together at The Royal Oak each Wednesday. Dinner together every Saturday at The Luttrell Arms. Oh, and one night Marler was trying to follow Kearns on his horse riding up to Dunkery Beacon. Near the summit Marler heard a single loud explosion – a cracking sound like a grenade detonating. He couldn't find out what had been going on.'

'Unless Kearns was destroying something,' Tweed

543

suggested. 'I think you'd better get some shut-eye, Harry. There's a camp bed for you. Second door on the right when you leave here . . .'

For the next half hour Tweed was on the phone. He called Frankfurt, where Marler's deputy was standing in while his sector chief was away. He called Vienna and spoke with Masterson's deputy to check the Balkan sector. He called Berne and spoke with Guy Dalby about the situation in the Mediterranean. Finally, he called Erich Lindemann in Copenhagen, the sector chief for Scandinavia.

'All quiet,' he commented as he put down the phone. 'Except in Vienna where they report extensive military manoeuvres in the Ukraine. Under the command of General Lucharsky. Which they always carry out at this time of the year.'

He stretched his arms, got up and walked round to ease the stiffness out of his limbs. Monica marvelled at his stamina, his encyclopaedic memory which forgot nothing.

The staff running the European sectors were based in a building further along the Crescent – together with the complex technical communications, including satellite reception from the weird seeing eyes orbiting in space. Tweed suddenly returned to his swivel chair.

'I've overlooked something vital. Imagine the position of that *Spetsnaz* group. They've lost their Exmoor base, they're blown. After they accomplish their mission – as they hope – they need an *escape route*. Contact Roberts at Lloyd's. Ask about any Iron Curtain vessel sailing off our shores.'

'Sorry. Roberts is taking a weekend holiday. Don't know where. I could try to ask someone else . . .'

'Don't. Roberts knows the need for secrecy. Monday will have to do.' He took off his tie, loosened his collar. 'I'm going to get some sleep.'

Monica was already folding back the blankets from the

camp bed in the corner for him. She plumped up the pillow. He was taking off his shoes when he stopped.

'I wonder what happened to that cleaning woman Paula saw at the bungalow estate . . .'

'Bed,' said Monica firmly. Then she swore. The phone was ringing. She listened for a moment, then looked at Tweed. 'It's Paula. Calling from Somerset. I can tell her you're asleep . . .'

'I'll take it.' Tweed grasped the receiver, standing in his socks. 'Something wrong? You should be in bed.'

'So should you, but I took a chance. I'm talking from the public box in Minehead. I got lost in the dark. Don't worry – I called The Anchor and the night porter will let me in. Lucky I've stayed there before. The main thing is I wasn't stopped by any police checkpoint. That worried me.'

'That was because you were *entering* Somerset. The checkpoints are concealed. They're checking everyone *leaving*. I'm glad you called. In the morning contact Inspector Farthing in Minehead. He's reliable – the chap who turned up when Partridge's body was brought down from Exmoor into Winsford. Tell him frankly about the three men you're watching. You'll need help.'

'OK. Will do. Now, get some rest . . .'

'Bed,' Monica repeated. 'Stop thinking. Sunday is going to be hell.'

He put his head on the pillow, his mind churning. Then he fell fast asleep.

Sunday, 6 December. Foster was up early at Cherry Farm despite his night duty. They ate a hurried breakfast while he outlined the plan. 'I will be going over the route with Seton-Charles and Saunders. We'll use Anton's Austin Metro. That's the safest vehicle. I want several places where the furniture vans can be hidden *east* of Brize Norton

545

– the direction Gorbachev will be flying in from. The hiding-places have to be well away from the airfield perimeter. Security there is already ferocious.'

'What will I do?' Anton asked truculently.

'You will help Sully clean up this place. Ready for instant departure tomorrow. As soon as we've grabbed that Post Office van and dealt with the driver. Stack all the Elsan closets except one by the back door. What's that?'

He stood up, ran to the back of the house. Round the table they could now all hear what Foster's acute ears had caught. A steady chug-chug of a helicopter's motor. They froze as Foster peered out of the back door he had opened a few inches.

'Only a Traffic Control chopper,' he said when he returned. 'We get moving in the Metro now.'

Inside the Wessex helicopter – roomy enough to take ten men – Tweed peered out of the window from his seat. Newman sat in front of him by the door where the swivel-mounted machine-gun was positioned. A member of an airborne division sat beside him, his beret slanted at a slight angle. He was satisfied Newman could handle the weapon. They'd had a practice shoot while the machine hovered above Fairoaks Airport. The target, a pile of wooden crates, had been shattered by Newman's first burst. The airfield had a notice at the entrance. *Closed for Repairs.*

Marler was travelling with Nield in the second machine which was not visible. The radio op was keeping in close touch with its twin helicopter. Tweed was impressed with the swift conversion job. Both machines carried the legend *Traffic Control* in large letters. Only Butler was somewhere on the ground, riding one of the two waiting BMW motor-cycles. Nield had said, 'Thanks, but no thanks. I'm not riding one of those death-traps.' Butler had made a rude reply and wheeled his bike aboard the other Wessex.

The second machine had landed on a deserted main road, waited briefly while Butler disembarked with his BMW near Brize Norton, and had immediately taken off.

Tweed stared down at Cherry Farm from two hundred feet. Raising the glasses looped round his neck, he scanned the buildings carefully. No sign of life. He dropped the glasses and spoke into the microphone, part of the headset he had attached to himself.

'Nothing down there, Bob. That place has been derelict for a decade at least.'

They flew on as the airborne soldier, Harper, shifted to the seat on the starboard side and raised his own glasses. Very little traffic on the roads at this hour. The wind was strong and Tweed was thankful he'd had the foresight to take Dramamine as the chopper rocked like a boat in a storm.

At the last minute Howard had been forbidden to join them, much to his chagrin. The PM had phoned. 'Someone must be there to mind the shop . . .'

But every member of the search party had copies of the car outlines Howard had produced – together with Paula's photographs of the furniture van seen from different angles. Everyone – including Butler riding his motorcycle round the country lanes – was concentrating on detecting a furniture van. Except Tweed who kept studying the car silhouettes, with an Austin Metro added.

They had been cruising round the edge of the forbidden flying zone over Brize Norton for an hour without seeing anything. Marler came on the radio from his machine at regular intervals. 'Nothing to report.'

Then Tweed saw the Austin Metro.

Behind the wheel of the Metro Foster was driving along a winding country lane east of Brize Norton, close to the village of Ducklington. He saw the chopper appear over a ridge straight ahead about half a mile away. Beside him Saunders leaned forward. In the rear seat Seton-Charles peered out of the window.

'Yes, it's that bloody Traffic Control machine,' Foster snapped. 'Something funny about it – there's no traffic round here.'

He slowed down as a large copse of trees masked them from the helicopter. The copse was beyond a bend in the road. Glancing to his left, Foster saw a crumbling barn, the roof still intact, open at both ends. He looked in his wing mirror. Road deserted, behind as well as ahead. He jammed on the brakes in an emergency stop. Saunders was thrown forward; only his safety belt saved him diving through the windscreen.

'What the hell,' he rasped.

Foster made no reply. He swung the Metro through ninety degrees, drove off the road straight at the ancient farm gate. As the car hit it the gate fainted, collapsed inwards. Foster drove over it and continued across the field, pulling up inside the barn.

'Let the bloody thing find us in here.' He switched off the engine. 'At least we've found four possible places to site the vans tomorrow.'

'The chopper's coming,' warned Seton-Charles.

'You must have imagined it,' Newman commented. 'I didn't see a car.'

'Please keep flying along the country road below us,' Tweed instructed the pilot. He raised his glasses again as he replied to Newman. 'I tell you, I saw an Austin Metro. It matched the outline. And it was darkish – could have been blue.'

'We'll find it . . .'

'Which is exactly what we're trying to do.'

548

They were flying at eight hundred feet – the minimum altitude permitted because they were close to the forbidden flying zone round Brize Norton. The pilot followed the winding course of the empty road below. Tweed had the glasses screwed tightly against his eyes. He scanned every likely hiding-place.

A dense copse of evergreens came up in his lenses, a copse which straddled the road where it turned a bend. He ordered the pilot to circle it so he could study it from every angle. Where the devil had the Metro gone to? The pilot completed one circuit, commenced another.

Tweed saw an isolated barn standing in the fields a short distance from the road. From that height he looked down on the sagging roof. Nothing. Anywhere.

'Fly a mile or two, behind that ridge we came over. Then turn and come back,' he ordered.

Inside the Metro the chopper sounded like a giant bee circling. Saunders was sweating. He mopped his forehead. Foster sat patiently, gloved hand tapping the wheel. Saunders stiffened, lowered his window. A blast of icy air came inside.

'We might as well keep warm,' Foster told him.

'That chopper's going away. I can hear the engine sound receding. We've done the job. We might as well get back.'

'Not yet. It could be a trick. Go away and then come back – find us in the open.'

'You're assuming it's looking for us.'

'I always assume the worst. We wait . . .'

Five minutes later they heard the helicopter returning. Foster stared ahead in silence. It wasn't his way to say, 'I told you.' He waited half an hour until the machine had flown off a second time, then started the motor, backed on to the road, drove back the way they had come.

The Wessex cruised round the approaches to the

perimeter of Brize Norton air base for another three hours. They frequently crossed the Vale of White Horse, maintaining the permitted altitude of eight hundred feet. Tweed's eyes were aching from staring through his field glasses. As they returned to Fairoaks, coming in to land, Newman made his comment.

'Well, you were wrong about the Metro. And we've found damn-all. Marler reports the same result from his machine.'

Tweed had a map of the Brize Norton area spread out on his lap. He had marked with a cross the place where he was sure he had spotted the Metro. Using a ruler, he measured three miles in each direction from the cross, then drew a circle with a diameter of six miles. He handed the map over the seat to Newman.

'That's the area we concentrate on tomorrow.'

'Why? We never found your Metro.'

'For that very reason. I could have been wrong – the car could have belonged to anyone. But it did a vanishing trick. And we scoured the ground without finding it. I think it went into hiding. That's highly suspicious. I scanned every road after it disappeared. No sign of it.'

'If you say so.'

'And,' Tweed added as they were landing, 'I'm changing the dispositions of Force Z tomorrow. We need more men on the ground.'

They drove back to London to spend the night at Park Crescent, to see if any further information had come through. Butler left his motorcycle at Fairoaks. 'Didn't see a thing,' he reported as they drove back. 'But I have a few more roads to check – to the east of the air base.'

'Which I'd guess is where Winterton's men would place their missile launchers,' Tweed remarked. '*East*. Because that's the direction Gorbachev's plane will fly in from. And

I have to call the PM when I get back. She was insistent on that for some reason I can't fathom . . .'

They had just arrived back at Park Crescent when Paula called from Somerset. 'I'm speaking from Minehead again,' she opened. 'I've had quite a day. The police brought back a woman's body found in the Somerset Levels – that sinister area we crossed on our first trip here.'

'I remember. Sounds a bit grisly.'

'A peat digger found a hand sticking out of the place where he was digging. When Inspector Farthing told me I had an idea. I asked to visit the mortuary. It was the cleaning woman from the bungalow estate. I showed Farthing the photo I'd taken. She'd been shot once in the back of the neck.'

'They were cleaning up before they left. No macabre pun intended.'

'And Farthing has been very helpful. He's put two men in plain clothes to help me watch the commando trio. They're all still here. That's it.'

'Take care. I have an important call to make.'

The four men sitting in his office and Monica watched him as he called the PM on scrambler. He listened, said he understood and put down the phone. He looked around at Newman, Marler, Butler and Nield.

'She's just heard from Moscow Gorbachev will be flying here in *four* Ilyushin 62s.'

'Four?' Newman enquired. 'I know he's unusual but how can he do that?'

'It's a clever Soviet precaution – security. No one will know which of the four machines Gorbachev and his wife will be aboard. Maybe the PM gave him a hint of possible trouble. I don't know. Now, we've eaten, so everyone get some sleep. Tomorrow is the day.'

Monday, 7 December. 7 a.m. Sully lay in the road covered
with blood near the entrance to Cherry Farm. It was real
blood: Foster, against Anton's protests, had used a knife
to cut his forearm lightly. He had then smeared blood all
over Sully's face and neck. Inside the farmhouse Seton-
Charles was using sticking plaster to cover the flesh wound.

Nearby Sully the Austin Metro had its bonnet pushed
against a tree trunk, positioned at an angle across the road.
The driver's door was wide open. George Hobart, driving
his Post Office van, slowed, then stopped as he saw the
body sprawled in the road. He jumped out. Only twenty-
two years old, he wore his Post Office cap, unlike the more
veteran postmen who went bareheaded.

'Nasty accident,' said Foster, appearing from behind a
tree. 'It just happened. Could you take him to hospital?
We've no transport.'

'Of course I'll help.' Hobart approached the 'body' and
swallowed. 'He looks in a bad way.'

'Something for your help . . .'

Foster reached into his breast pocket, hauled out his
wallet, dropped it on the road at Hobart's feet. He was
slow retrieving it and Hobart bent forward to pick up the
wallet. Foster pressed the muzzle of his Luger against the
back of Hobart's neck, pulled the trigger. The old method
of execution used in the motherland when he'd been young.
Hobart slumped to the ground.

Saunders appeared with a large wheelbarrow. Foster
picked up the dead youngster and his cap, askew, dropped
off. When he'd dumped the body inside the wheelbarrow

and Saunders was taking it towards the farmhouse Foster picked up the cap. Climbing into the cab of the large van, he drove it off the road along a track into the woods opposite the farm entrance.

Then he checked his watch. They'd all better give Anton a hand to fill in the grave. He got behind the wheel of the Metro, closed the door, backed it on to the road and drove it back to the shed. They'd be on their way in fifteen minutes.

Tweed wore a thick woollen pullover, a heavy sports jacket, a woollen scarf round his neck, and corduroy trousers tucked inside knee-length boots with rubber-grip soles.

The Wessex chopper was again flying at eight hundred feet and Tweed sat in the same seat, map in his lap, binoculars looped round his neck. In front of him Newman sat holding the handle of the swivel-mounted machine-gun by the closed door. On the starboard side the airborne soldier, beret slanted at exactly the same angle, sat peering out of the window through his field glasses.

There had been very little conversation since the machine took off from Fairoaks. There was an atmosphere of rising tension inside the helicopter. Then the pilot passed on the message to Tweed through his earphones.

'Marler and Butler have landed. They are on the ground.'

'Thank you,' said Tweed.

Marler would now be driving the Land Rover waiting for him at the appointed rendezvous, a crossroads in the middle of nowhere near Ducklington village. Butler would be riding the BMW motorcycle which had been transported to the crossroads by truck during the night. All arranged by Tweed over the phone in the early hours. Nield was at Fairoaks, running the radio control room set up inside an administrative office.

Tweed studied the area he had circled on the map the

previous day. He was gambling everything that the attack would be launched from somewhere in that area. It was logical. And Winterton had shown himself to be logical in everything he organized.

The second chopper would return to Fairoaks. At the last moment Security Control at Brize Norton had sanctioned one machine, not two. Tweed gathered they did not take Force Z too seriously. He raised his glasses as they crossed the Vale of White Horse. They were moving into the danger zone.

The furniture van driven by Foster, with Saunders alongside him, turned off the road into the worked-out chalk quarry. It had been carved out in a semi-circle. A chalk cliff enclosed it on the west, south and north sides. To the east it looked out across open country and the sky. Foster backed the vehicle until it was facing due east with the rear of the van a few feet away from the cliff. Then he stopped the engine.

They jumped out, went to the back, lowered the tailboard and went inside. Foster led the way, squeezing past the piles of old furniture. He climbed the steps to the platform, sat in the chair and pressed the switch. The panel in the roof slid back. He settled himself in the chair, picked up the Stinger launcher, inserted a missile.

He picked up the walkie-talkie Anton had specially amplified to increase its range. Holding it close to his mouth with his left hand, he spoke.

'Coastguard Number One in position.'

There was a crackle. Then he clearly heard Sully's voice.

'Coastguard Number Two in position . . .'

Marler drove the Land Rover along the narrow country lane at speed. He was moving through open country so he couldn't miss anything. He was following routes which

Butler had not covered the previous day but which were inside Tweed's circle. Half a mile behind him Butler followed on his motorcycle.

He reached a crossroads and drove straight on. Round a bend he was confronted with a tarring machine taking up the whole road. A workman came up to him.

'Didn't you see the bloody diversion sign, mate?'

'No, because there wasn't one.'

'Must be blind as a bat. You can't pass.'

Marler swore, turned the Land Rover and went back to the crossroads. He turned right just as Butler appeared over a rise. He drove on, more slowly: there were clumps of trees on either side, clumps which became woodland. He turned a corner and saw a sign in the distance. *Diversion*. The sign pointed right at a point where the road forked. Marler frowned, then drove his vehicle straight at the sign, sending it into the ditch as he took the left fork.

On the floor lay his rifle, telescopic sight attached. They had installed a small transceiver, complete with microphone. He had tested it earlier and it was tuned to the waveband Nield was operating on at Fairoaks. He turned the wheel as the winding road curved round another bend. Then he slowed to a stop.

At the base of the chalk cliff Foster saw four Ilyushin 62s flying one behind another coming in from the east. He grabbed the microphone. 'Coastguard One reporting. Four blackbirds in view. Repeat, *four* blackbirds. I'll arrest three and four. You take one and two. Over.'

'Four blackbirds sighted,' Sully confirmed. 'Will take one and two. Over and out . . .'

Marler had stopped where the rear of a large furniture van was parked half inside a wood. Beyond, the trees had been felled by storms, leaving the sky open. On the tailboard sat Seton-Charles, eating a sandwich. A rug covered his lap. He threw back the rug and pointed an Uzi machine-pistol point blank at Marler. Somewhere beyond the pile of furniture Marler detected signs of further movement. Behind him he heard the sound of an approaching motorcycle.

'Stay very still. Hands in sight,' rasped Seton-Charles, dressed in overalls. 'Wait like that till the biker has gone.'

Marler raised both hands in the air. 'Drop them!' screamed the professor. 'In your lap.' Marler let his hands drop. The BMW was very close. He hoped Butler had seen his gesture. The BMW slowed down, turned out to pass Marler's stationary Land Rover.

As he cruised slowly past Butler tossed the grenade he'd extracted from his saddlebag into Seton-Charles' lap. Marler ducked, fell crouched on the floor. There was an ear-splitting *crack!* Marler's windscreen shattered.

He looked up, grabbing his rifle. Seton-Charles was plastered all over the furniture. Blood and flesh strips everywhere. Marler saw movement high up at the front of the van. The mass of ancient furniture had saved Sully. His head peered over the top. Marler shot him through the forehead.

He leapt out and ran to the right side as Butler ran to the left. They met on opposite sides of the cab. Empty. Somewhere beyond the trees a vehicle's engine started up, moved off. Marler ran to the rear, pushed his way inside, leapt up the steps. Sully, flopped over the back of the chair, was dying but not dead. He looked into Marler's eyes as the Englishman bent over him. His eyes were glazed. The bullet had missed the brain and his expression showed a glimmer of hatred.

'Anton,' he whispered. 'Bastard ran for it. In Post Office van. Ex . . .' Then he died.

*   *   *

556

Foster aimed his launcher to take out Ilyushin Number Three, the plane carrying Gorbachev. He waited for the first two machines to disintegrate. Then decided he could wait no longer. In his concentration he failed to hear the sound of the chopper.

Aboard the Wessex Tweed was scanning the countryside below. He swept over a chalk quarry, then swung his glasses back again. The van came up clearly in his high-powered glasses. So clearly he could see the open panel in the roof, the man seated inside holding something rammed into his shoulder.

'The chalk quarry!' he shouted into his mike. 'It's there . . .'

The airborne soldier swung open his door. Icy air blasted into the chopper. Newman aimed his gunsight, pressed the trigger, swept the opening in the roof with bullets. Inside Foster was training the Stinger's sophisticated gunsight on the third Ilyushin. The chopper pilot – at Tweed's urgent request – had earlier ignored regulations, descending to one hundred feet, and now he hovered. In response to Newman's shouted request. He held the trigger back in the firing position. A stream of bullets laced Foster's back and chest. Blood splotches burst out of his overalls. He sagged in the chair. His last reflex action was to fire the launcher's missile.

But as he'd slumped the barrel had dropped, was now aimed inside the vehicle. The heat-seeking missile *whooshed* from the launcher, sped the few feet towards the vehicle's engine, which was still warm.

'Climb!' Newman shouted.

The pilot reacted instantly, began to ascend vertically. Tweed was staring at the quarry. As the missile detonated there was a blinding flash, a low rumble like thunder. The climbing chopper rocked from side to side as the blast hit it, then steadied. Tweed and Newman gazed down.

The furniture van had disappeared, blown into a million fragments. A cloud of white chalk dust rose from the quarry. Tweed searched in vain for any debris which might be a relic of the van. His hands were sweating and he wiped them on his handkerchief as the airborne soldier hauled the door shut. The interior of the machine was like an ice box from the raw wind which had penetrated inside.

'Fairoaks reporting,' the pilot said, his tone calm. 'Marler has intercepted Vehicle One.'

'Thank God! Tell Fairoaks Vehicle Two also intercepted. Pass the message to Marler,' Tweed told him.

Overhead the four Ilyushin 62s were continuing their descent to Brize Norton. Tweed finished wiping his hands, put on a pair of gloves. He spoke again to the pilot.

'Please return to Fairoaks. We have unfinished business to attend to.'

54

Monday, 7 December. 'I will be driving down to interrogate Colonel Winterton,' Tweed told Monica, Newman, Butler and Nield in his Park Crescent office. 'Before he leaves the country.'

'On Exmoor?' Butler queried. 'You know who he is?'

'Yes. Monica has heard from Roberts at Lloyd's. The Shipping Index shows the only Iron Curtain vessel off our shores is an East German freighter, the *Stralsund*. At this moment it is unloading timber at Swansea. It sails for Rostock in the Baltic before the end of the day. That means it could heave to after dark at the mouth of the Bristol Channel. Ready to take aboard Winterton.'

'You really know who he is?' Monica asked. 'And he is one of the three ex-commandos?'

'Yes to both questions.' He turned to Butler. 'We left Fairoaks in a hurry. You talked with Marler. Why did he wait instead of coming with us?'

'Apparently just before Sully died he told Marler Anton had fled in a Post Office van. Heard the grenade I threw, then the shot Marler fired, I suppose. Ran for it. Headed for Exmoor, according to Marler. He's going after him. Trouble was the chopper we didn't use had a mechanical defect. And the pilot of our machine insisted on a thorough check-up before he'd fly Marler anywhere. That blast from the quarry really hit us.'

'Up to Marler, then. You heard me call Paula. She'll wait to meet us in the Mercedes by the call box in Minehead. Newman, you can come with me. Butler and Nield, you stay here. We're desperately understaffed if something else breaks.'

The phone rang. Monica said it was the call Tweed had booked to Arthur Beck at Federal Police headquarters in Berne. Tweed took the phone.

'Arthur. Check with Sarris, I suggest. But I think it's safe to send Christina back to Athens. Send me the bill.'

'No bill.' Beck chuckled. 'But now you owe me one. And don't think I won't call in the debt when it suits me. 'Bye.'

Newman stood up. 'I'm ready to leave when you are. As it is, we won't reach Exmoor before dark. Winterton could be aboard the *Stralsund* if we don't move. I'll drive the Cortina.'

'We need to be armed.' Tweed opened a drawer, took out from it a Smith & Wesson short-barrelled .38. Plus a shoulder holster. 'The armourer recommended this for me. You agree?'

559

'You never normally carry a gun. I'll give you some practice at a quiet spot on the way. Yes, that's OK. A hip holster would have been better. But it's short-barrelled, shouldn't snag if you have to snatch it out. I'm keeping the Magnum .45.'

'That blows a hole as big as a cave through your target.'

'Which means it does the job.'

Newman had become harder since he first knew him, Tweed reflected. His experience behind the lines in East Germany. Newman seemed to read his mind.

'Why is Winterton boarding an East German vessel?'

'Because the East Germans are not sympathetic to *glasnost*. And I doubt he'll report precisely what he was involved in. We'd better go.'

'Do give us a clue,' Monica begged. 'About the identity of this Winterton.'

'He must have needed to keep contact with the *Spetsnaz* group when it moved to a new base close to Brize Norton, wherever that was. So, he needed a phone he could use which wasn't his own – in case we'd put a phone tap on it. Which I wouldn't risk. A phone, Monica . . .'

It was early evening, just before dark, when the Wessex carrying Marler approached Dunkeswell Airfield south of Exmoor. On his lap Marler nursed his rifle with the telescopic sight as he peered out of the window. 'Can you land somewhere close to Dunkeswell, but not on the airfield?' he asked the pilot.

'Might manage it. You spoke in time. Not yet dark. How long a walk do you fancy?'

'No more than five minutes. It's an emergency.'

'When isn't it? There's Dunkeswell.'

Marler looked out of the window, frowned. Two main runways crossed each other almost at right angles. One had lights on at either side. Ready for a plane to take off?

The chopper was descending towards a deserted country road. Marler grabbed his rifle, headed for the door after one last word.

'Land me on that road. Then you'd better take off, head back for Fairoaks . . .'

He tore off his headset, splaying his feet as he made for the door. The machine was rocking gently. He felt it touch down, opened the door, dropped to the ground. Ducking to keep clear of the rotors, he ran towards the main airport building. He reached the open gate at the main entrance as an old Rover driven by a middle-aged man appeared from the opposite direction. The car stopped, half-turned to drive through the entrance. The driver lowered his window, leaned out.

'Who are you?' he enquired, staring at the rifle Marler held in his right hand.

'Don't go in there,' Marler warned. He used his left hand to extract his Special Branch card, shoved it in the driver's face. 'And who are you?'

'I'm the controller of this airfield. Those damned gates should be kept closed. I've told Abbott before . . .'

'Who is Abbott? Quick. There's probably an armed terrorist inside.'

'Maintenance mechanic. Odd-job man. Really runs the place . . .'

'Where do I find this Abbott?'

'Should be inside that office with the lights on . . .'

'Drive off. Up the road. Unless you want to risk getting shot.'

Marler darted inside the entrance, crouched low as he ran, rifle gripped in both hands. He avoided the office door, which was closed. Very carefully he raised his head, peered in through the window. Then he ran back to the door, turned the handle, threw it open. He had found Abbott.

The mechanic was sprawled forward over a desk. Blood

was congealing from a hole in the side of his skull. Marler felt the neck pulse. Nothing. In the distance he heard the sound of a light aircraft starting up. He ran outside, keeping close to the side of the building, peered round the corner.

A Cessna was taxiing slowly along a runway. As he watched, it turned. The engine revolutions increased in speed. He raised his rifle, peered through the sight. Inside the cockpit a face wearing a pilot's helmet jumped at him. Anton Gavalas. The machine began to move forward along a course parallel to the building. Moving target. Marler held the crosshairs fixed on the Greek's head. He took the first pressure on the trigger, waited until the small plane was opposite him, pulled the trigger rapidly three times.

He saw the perspex craze. The aircraft proceeded on down the runway. Marler thought he'd missed. The machine began leaving the ground. It was gaining height when the nose dipped and plunged swiftly down on to the runway. The tail was poised in mid-air. Then the fuel tanks exploded. Fire enveloped the Cessna, a fierce blaze which was smothered with a cloud of the blackest smoke. Silence suddenly descended on Dunkeswell.

'Lord, I'm glad to see you.'

Paula jumped out of the Mercedes parked by the call box in Minehead as the Cortina driven by Newman pulled up. It was dark as Tweed stepped out and she hugged him. 'They go to bed early here,' Tweed commented, glancing along the deserted street. He squeezed her, let her go as Newman approached.

'Look what Inspector Farthing gave me.' She took them both by the arm, guided them to the Mercedes and pointed at the dashboard. A mobile phone unit had been attached. Tweed got in behind the wheel, pressed the switch which operated the aerial and watched it slide down out of sight in the wing mirror.

562

'No, elevate that,' Paula protested as she got in beside him and dropped her shoulder bag in her lap. 'It helps contact. Farthing has a policeman with a walkie-talkie watching each of the houses. Barrymore, Robson and Kearns. They report back to a radio car and I hear their observations over that phone. In a kind of code I can understand. They're all at home. Farthing has been marvellous.'

'I have to get moving,' Tweed said as he elevated the aerial. 'Bob, take Paula with you. Drive to The Anchor and keep your eyes open.'

'For what?' Newman asked.

'In case he gets away from me. I'd say a four-wheel drive – heading past The Anchor and west over that pebble beach. And cover him with that Magnum. He's lethal. Out you get, Paula.'

'I'm coming with you.' She spoke calmly and produced from her bag the Browning. 'I can protect myself. I did with Norton and Morle.'

It was the controlled way she spoke which stopped Tweed arguing. He shrugged, glanced at the call box. 'Has Barrymore used that this evening?'

'Not so far.'

'Then we'd better move off.' He waved to Newman, drove through Minehead and climbed Porlock Hill. The Mercedes purred up the steep ascent. At the top he passed Culbone Inn, continued along the coast road, took the first turning to the left.

'It's the Doone Valley,' Paula said quietly as they descended the steep winding lane, crossed the ford at the bottom, turned right. Towards the Doone Valley.

'We located the two furniture vans they were using as mobile missile launcher platforms,' Tweed remarked. 'Just in time. One was blown to bits. Marler found a dead Middle Easterner in his. Maybe a Shi-ite. They were going to be left behind as the scapegoats. Monica read out a news story about two Arabs being airlifted from Gartree Prison. Shi-ites.' He stopped and backed the car through a gap in the hedge into a field, switched off the lights. 'No one will see you here. Keep the Browning in your lap until I get back.'

'You've stopped midway between Quarme Manor and Endpoint.'

'Lock all the doors,' Tweed said, then he was gone.

He pressed the bell. The man who opened the door was dressed in a leather windcheater unzipped down the front, cavalry twill trousers tucked into riding boots, a woollen scarf round his neck. The hall beyond was as cold as the biting wind moaning across the moor.

'May I have a word with you, Dr Robson?' Tweed asked.

'Come in, my dear fellow. Can't give you long. I'm expecting a call from a patient. They phone me at all hours. Goes with the territory as the Americans say.'

All this as Robson closed the door, led the way into the sitting room. The curtains were almost drawn with a gap where they should have met. Tweed sat down at a polished wooden table as Robson gestured and then sat opposite him. His host moved an old-fashioned doctor's bag on to the floor by his side without bothering to close it.

'I've come to arrest you for murder,' Tweed said. 'Quite a few murders. You've probably heard on the news your plan failed. Gorbachev is now in Washington.'

Robson's face crinkled into a smile. His pale blue eyes watched Tweed as he pulled at his straggly moustache.

'I don't follow any of this. You look sane enough.'

'One thing which pinpointed you was your conversation at The Luttrell Arms over dinner. Barrymore referred to the Greek Key. You pooh-poohed the idea. Out of character. When you all had houses like fortresses. Especially this place. I asked my man Nield, who was recording secretly, who was *facing* him. Barrymore was. So were you. The tape sounded like someone had spotted the tie pin microphone Nield kept fiddling with to get the right angle. And you made the mistake of asking Barrymore if Nield was wearing an earpiece when he met him on the moor. Only a professional would spot that. You spotted it. Hence your strange remark – considering you were all supposed to be scared stiff someone was coming from Greece to avenge the murder of Ionides . . .'

'Gavalas . . .' Robson stopped. His expression changed. The eyes were blank and cold.

'I never told you Ionides was a Gavalas,' Tweed remarked.

Robson sat very still. The only illumination was a plastic-shaded bulb which hung low above the table. Robson reached down into his bag. He pointed the Luger as Tweed reached inside his jacket.

'Don't bring your hand out with anything in it but your fingers. I still find your reasoning feeble.'

'Winterton – as we codenamed the killer – needed access to a safe phone. You wouldn't like using the one here. Your sister, May, could have overheard you. Where is she?'

'I sent her off for a holiday to my brother's place in Norfolk . . .'

'You needed access to a safe phone,' Tweed continued, 'to keep in touch with the *Spetsnaz* group you'd set up on that bungalow estate, to give orders when they'd moved to their new base. You kept visiting the bedridden old lady down in Dulverton at night. She has an extension upstairs by her bedside. That means the main phone is downstairs – the one you used.'

'Pure guesswork. You're crazy . . .'

'The first thing which drew my attention to *you* was when I heard you'd found homes for Barrymore and Kearns on Exmoor. Two reasons would be my guess, as you call it. Camouflage, in case suspicion centred on this area. Three suspects – and you made Barrymore look the most suspicious. I heard in Greece the voice changing the call sign in English over Florakis' transceiver. Very upper-crust. Very Barrymore. You mimicked him. The second reason for bringing your two commando friends here was a genuine fear of the vindictive Petros.'

'Why should I fear him?' Robson moved his left hand and then held it still: he had felt the need of his pipe, his prop.

'Because you murdered Andreas Gavalas on Siros. Another guess. You took a spare knife on the raid to do the job.'

'You'll be accusing me of stealing the diamonds next.'

'Of course you did. Which is why Andreas was killed. He was going to hand them to the right-wing EDES people. Probably you were told by your controller in Cairo to keep the diamonds for future use . . .'

'And I live in such luxury,' Robson sneered.

'Not for you. But it must have cost Colonel Winterton – again a pointer towards Barrymore – a packet to build that bungalow estate ready for the *Spetsnaz* group you'd been told to establish. Plus financing them in little businesses to give authentic backgrounds for them when they arrived from Russia. Plus buying the Stinger launchers and missiles from Gallagher, the Lisbon arms dealer. By then those diamonds were worth far more than the original hundred thousand pounds.'

'And what other murders am I supposed to have committed?' Robson enquired sarcastically.

'Stephen Ionides in the Antikhana Building for one. There was a lot of blood. My guess – again – is you wore an Army waterproof buttoned to the neck to save your uniform.'

'Oh, really? Entering the realms of fantasy now, are we? I suppose you worked out how I escaped when there wasn't even a convenient fire escape?'

'Poor Sam Partridge worked that out. There was a strong iron rail elevated above the wall on the roof. You took inside a briefcase – or something – a length of knotted rope. When you had cleaned up the blood from your hands in the bathroom you went back on the roof. You dropped the rope over the rail on the native quarter side – an equal length on either side. You shinned down the wall, holding both pieces of rope with the knots. Reaching the empty street, you simply hauled one length of rope down and coiled the lot in a loop. Very easy to lose that inside the available native quarter.'

'Any reason for all these acrobatics? And my killing Ionides?'

'Commandos *are* acrobatic. And Ionides – who was really Stephen Gavalas – had become suspicious of the killing of his brother, Andreas. You tied up a loose end.'

'Two murders so far. Any more?'

'It's not amusing. Mrs Larcombe's death was a fresh pointer – clue, if you like. She was a careful woman. Who would she let in to her house at night without fear? The local doctor. You said you needed to use her phone for an emergency?'

Robson ran his tongue briefly over his lips. In the dim light there was moisture on his brow, but the muzzle of the Luger aimed at Tweed's chest was steady.

'One thing which put me off the track,' Tweed went on. He had to keep Robson talking. 'Barrymore kept making clandestine phone calls from a public box in Minehead. What was wrong with using the phone at Quarme Manor?'

An unpleasant smile. 'A touch of romance, Tweed. Barrymore has fallen in love with a woman in London, hopes she will agree to marry him. But not sure of his chances. If it doesn't come off he'll still need Mrs Atyeo to run Quarme Manor. So he goes to extreme lengths to make sure she doesn't know anything. She might up and leave.'

'Extraordinary.' Tweed was momentarily non-plussed. 'A small domestic detail I never dreamed of.'

'Like your theories. All bits and pieces . . .'

'Which complete the jigsaw. And expose the face of Dr Robson. The killing of Sam Partridge on Exmoor was another pointer. The knife was driven in at exactly the right angle, the pathologist told me. A doctor would know how to do that. Much better than ex-commandos who had grown rusty with the passage of time. And Harry Masterson, who visited you, sent me a clue. *Endstation*. A clever clue. Pointing in two directions – here to your bungalow, Endpoint, and describing the atmosphere down at Porlock Weir, the end of the world. Harry was clever – I think he guessed it was you. He hoped to get confirmation by telling all three of you he was flying to Greece – to see which one of you turned up when he arrived.'

'I didn't.' Robson gripped the trigger of the Luger more firmly under the lampshade. 'I'm holding this gun on you because I appear to face a lunatic with a gun under his own arm.' He glanced at his watch.

'No. You sent a message to Doganis to do the job for you.' Tweed noted the glance at the time – which must be running out. But like a real professional, Robson was curious as to how he had tripped up. 'And,' Tweed went on, 'you fired at my Mercedes, aiming to miss – you couldn't afford the furore which would follow my murder at that stage. But you aimed – literally – to throw suspicion on Kearns. I'd just left his house.'

'You simply have no proof of these mad assertions.'

'Then take me up into the conning tower where you spend so much time at night. That curious structure which is supposed to be a watch-tower. Then I can satisfy myself there is no transceiver up there. Plus an aerial which automatically elevated while you were transmitting to Florakis in Greece, receiving messages from him. The retracting aerial on a Mercedes gave me that idea.'

The Luger wavered, then steadied. Robson's eyes became colder still. No smile. The bedside manner had vanished. His face became a frozen image, reminded Tweed of pictures of the statues on Easter Island.

'You're clever, I'll grant you that. But it was all in a great cause. Lenin's cause which I embraced when I was a young man. The cause Gorbachev is trying to pervert with his mad *glasnost*.'

'You killed Partridge because he was getting too close to the truth,' Tweed went on. 'You killed Mrs Larcombe because her window creaked and you heard it that first night you collected Anton Gavalas off the *Oporto*. You couldn't afford to risk her seeing you the second time when you brought the Stinger launchers ashore.'

'Dear me.' Robson's lips curled cruelly. 'You have worked it all out.'

'And you killed Jill Kearns in London. Why?'

'Simply to divert attention to London from Exmoor. She was a foolish sort of woman . . .'

Tweed saw movement by the gap in the curtains out of the corner of his eye. There was a tremendous smashing sound, glass breaking under a hammerblow. He thought he saw a rifle butt. Robson glanced at the window, swung the Luger round. Tweed reached up, grasped the plastic shade, pulled it down over the bulb. There was a brief flash, the room was plunged into darkness. Tweed threw himself sideways on to the floor as the Luger roared. Confusion. Bodies moving, feet running. A door shut. A vehicle's engine started up, moving at speed down the slope, skidded as though turning along the lane.

Tweed felt his way into the hall, along the wall, opened the front door. The sound of a second vehicle starting up, driving along the lane towards Quarme Manor. He ran down the slope, ran all the way back to where the Mercedes

569

was parked, jumped in behind the wheel. Paula had released the locks as she saw him coming.

'Two vehicles driving at speed along the lane,' she said tersely. 'First a four-wheel-drive job, like we saw parked by the side of Robson's house. Then a car. Couldn't see the make.'

'We must hurry.' Tweed was driving through the gateway, turning along the lane, lights full on, driving away from the Doone Valley. In his wing mirror he saw a police patrol car coming up behind him. He passed Quarme Manor, reached the ford gushing with deep water, drove through it. Behind him the patrol car stopped half-way through the ford. He drove up the hill, kept going when he turned right on the coast road, heading back towards Minehead.

'The Toll Road!' Paula shouted.

He was almost past it, swung the wheel, began the descent and slowed as he nearly took them over the brink. They arrived in front of The Anchor and Newman was just climbing into the Cortina. He left it as Tweed approached, dived into the back.

'Two vehicles heading for the pebble beach,' he reported.

'I know. It was Robson . . .'

'Robson?' Paula gasped. 'I thought it was Kearns.'

They had driven along the track, began bouncing across the pebble-strewn beach. Something jumped up under the Mercedes, there was a loud clang. The car stopped. Tweed jumped out, began running over the pebbles, careful not to lose his footing. In the distance both vehicles had also been stopped by the terrain. He glimpsed two running figures, a hundred yards between them. Behind him Newman ran with Paula, ready to catch her arm if she slipped. Then the searchlight beam came on, aimed at the foot of the looming cliffs. The light shone from the edge of the sea.

570

It took Newman a moment to grasp the searchlight was mounted at the bow of a motorboat which had been driven up on to the edge of the beach. Tweed ran on past the sign reading, *Warning. Keep clear. Danger of cliff falls.* He passed an empty Renault, then the four-wheel drive vehicle.

Robson was caught in the searchlight beam as he kept to the lee of the cliffs. A shot rang out. The bullet sang past Newman's head. Paula was fumbling for her Browning when Newman saw inside the beached boat a bulky figure, clad like a seaman, aiming a gun. He swung up the Magnum, gripped in both hands, fired two shots. The seaman was hurled back, tried to recover his balance, toppled, fell over the stern of the boat. His body drifted with the outgoing tide.

Robson, hair awry, flung up a hand to shield his eyes against the glare of the light supposed to lead him to the boat. Tweed saw the tall figure a hundred yards from Robson reach inside a satchel slung from his shoulder. He hoisted his right arm like a cricket bowler, threw an object high up the cliff.

His hand delved again inside the satchel, came out and his arm hoisted a second time. There was a deafening crack on the cliff top above Robson. Tweed stopped, grabbed Paula by the forearm to halt her. She was gasping for breath as the second grenade detonated.

From high up on the cliff they heard a muttering rumble, prelude to a cataclysm. A vast slab of cliff broke free, slowly slid downwards, then faster. Robson looked up, opened his mouth. A cascade of rocks roared towards him. He turned to flee. The cascade engulfed him, like a rising tide, swallowing him up to the waist. In the searchlight beam he was a man half buried alive. He opened his mouth again and screamed and screamed, waving his arms. Then a Niagara of boulders stormed down, bounding against each other. One struck his head and seemed to telescope it deep into his body. Paula gulped.

A fresh fall of massive rocks poured down, tumbling over each other like some mad race. The head vanished. The boulders piled over the invisible corpse, building a grisly funeral pyre. Slowly the noise receded, the cliff settled, returned to stability as a great cloud of dust, a dense fog, spread over the whole ghastly scene.

Kearns, still carrying the satchel, walked back to Tweed, his wrists held out, as though waiting for handcuffs.

'He killed Jill,' he said in a choked voice. 'It had to be one of them. I've lived with the conviction Robson or Barrymore killed those Greeks during the war. But we were afraid of Petros, so we stuck together. I followed you the previous walk you took along here, saw the landslip. I kept several Mills hand grenades when I left the Army. I tested one up at Dunkery Beacon the other night – to make sure they were still working. I'm ready to go.'

'Two questions,' Tweed replied. He opened his hand, exposing the stick of French chalk he'd taken from his pocket. 'Paula picked that up in your house – you used it to simulate grief, to chalk your face. Why?'

Kearns walked a few slow paces until they were on their own. 'When Barrymore phoned, asked me to come and meet you at his house, I'd been sobbing like a child – because of Jill. So I had to clean up my face somehow. I used that stick of French chalk – the one Jill used when she occasionally did a bit of dressmaking.'

'I see.' Tweed changed the subject. 'During the raid on Siros, why land below a German lookout post?'

'Bravado. Barrymore's. And because of the lookout there were few German patrols at that point. Made tactical sense – we relied on a sea mist to cover us, which it did most of the way. Now, I'm ready to go.'

'Then go,' said Tweed. 'I don't recall ever seeing you here. Leave Exmoor. Petros is in prison. Go,' he repeated, 'build yourself a new life.'

'Thank you . . .'

572

'I said go!'

As Kearns walked slowly away Tweed stared towards Porlock Weir. No sign of activity: they were too far west for the thunder of the falling cliff to have been heard. 'Poor devil,' he commented. He glanced at the pile of rocks where the dust was settling. 'It will be months before they find out what is under that lot, if ever. Now, let's get rid of that boat.'

Standing on either side of the motorboat, Tweed and Newman exerted all their strength. They heaved it upside down, pushed it over the pebbles, which made a grinding noise. The craft slid over the edge, floated for some distance half-submerged, drifted out to sea.

Kearns had managed to start up his Renault while they were occupied and it disappeared into the distance. Between them they tackled the Land Rover which still had the key in the ignition. Within ten minutes Newman had driven it to the water's brink. One final shove propelled it off the pebbles and it sank from view.

'Back to The Anchor,' Tweed ordered. He put an arm round Paula who was shivering with reaction. 'You need a good stiff drink. It's all over. Détente is intact – for better or worse. And I'll report to the PM on the quiet about Lucharsky and his allies. It's up to her what she does after that.'

Epilogue

*It is reported that Deputy Chief of General Staff, Andrei
Lucharsky, General Budienny, and a third unnamed
general, together with their aides, Colonels Rykovsky and
Volkov, perished while flying in a helicopter over the
Caspian Sea. The pilot saved himself by parachuting from
the machine. No further details are available of this tragic
accident.*

Extract from December issue of PRAVDA.

'Odd that so much top brass should be committed to one
chopper,' Tweed commented after reading the report. He
handed it back to Monica. 'File it.'

The Power

FOR JANE

CONTENTS

CONTENTS

CONTENTS

Prologue

Carmel, California, February. The man, windbreaker open at the top, exposing his thick neck, forced the screaming girl inside the one-storey log cabin. One large hand gripped her long blonde hair, the other shoved at the small of her back.

Joel Dyson, one-time society journalist, now a successful member of the notorious international paparazzi, crouched in the undergrowth at the edge of the clearing in the wood. His film camera was aimed at the struggling man and woman as they disappeared through the open door. He had their faces perfectly recorded on film.

The cabin door slammed shut from the inside. The crude edifice was perched in the centre of the clearing, shut off from the outside world by the dense screen of encircling trees. The shutters were closed across the windows but Dyson could still hear the girl's screams of terror.

He glanced down at the ground where his tape recorder was in motion, the revolving tape registering the horrific screaming which suddenly stopped. Had the man struck her in the face to shut her up? There was a loaded pause which Dyson found more disturbing than what he had seen and heard earlier. The stillness of the wintry forest had a menacing atmosphere. Something warned Dyson the silence was ominous.

He had his film camera ready for another close-up when the cabin door opened. He expected two people to emerge, but only the man appeared. He came out, closed the door, rammed a key into the lock, turned it, tossed the key on to the roof. Why had he done that?

The answer surfaced a moment later as smoke drifted out from behind one of the shutters, then the window burst into flames. God! He was leaving her there to burn to ashes. Dyson caught the expression on the man's face, a look of vicious satisfaction, his skin streaming with sweat despite the cold of the early morning. Instinct made Dyson switch off the recorder, haul the tape free, ram it into the pocket of his duffle coat. The man was staring towards Dyson's hiding place. Grabbing a gun from inside his belt, he walked slowly towards where Dyson was crouching.

Had he detected some movement? Dyson had the man's face in his film lens again and the expression was grim, determined. A full-length shot now, showing the gun. Dyson saw the cabin suddenly flare into a raging inferno. Roof ablaze, about to collapse on the girl inside who must be unconscious, maybe dead? The quiet crackle of the flames erupted into a roar.

The man paused, glanced back. Dyson's camera had recorded his initial advance, the pause, the cabin flaring into a funeral pyre. The man turned towards the undergrowth, began that familiar slow deliberate tread. Time to get the hell out of it. Alive if possible. Dyson was thoroughly scared.

Still crouching, he backed away from the undergrowth screen. Camera looped over his shoulder, the tape nestling safely in his pocket. He reached a copse of trees, stood up, resisted the temptation to run. The ground was littered with dry leaves. For the moment his flight was covered by the powerful roar of the dying cabin. He had to get as far away as possible before his flight made too much noise. It was a long way to his Chevy parked inside the woods out of sight of the nearby road.

He paused, heard the deliberate tramp of heavy feet on the leaves behind him coming closer. And there would be others the man could call on – if he dared risk that. On the

2

edge of panic Dyson reached the foot of a tall pine tree. *No one ever thinks of looking up*.

'It's my last chance to survive . . .'

Dyson said the words to himself as he shinned agilely from branch to branch. Higher and higher. He had to reach the cover of the foliage. Clawing at branches he heaved himself inside the prickly cover, straddled a stout branch with both legs, waited, terrified.

Through a small hole in the dense screen he could see down to the base of the giant pine. The man appeared, wiped sweat off his left hand on his denims, his right hand gripping the .38 Police Special. Dyson froze when the man paused at the base of the pine, head cocked to one side, listening. In the next minute Joel Dyson knew he could be dead, his body toppling down through the network of branches until it landed at the killer's feet. With the film camera looped over his arm, the tape in his pocket. It would be all over.

The cold was penetrating Dyson's duffle coat, his hands were frozen. The man below seemed impervious to the temperature made worse by trails of a mist off the Pacific Ocean which were now drifting amid the trees. Dyson forced himself to remain motionless. He'd begun to wonder whether his actions had been worth it – even for so great a potential prize, a vast fortune.

For a few seconds his thoughts filled his mind paralysed with fear. He looked down, blinked. The man had gone. He heard the heavy footsteps withdrawing, crunching dried leaves, retreating towards the cabin which must now be a pile of smoking embers.

Dyson checked his watch. 8 a.m. He compelled himself to stay motionless in his hiding place for half an hour. The man could have set a trap, moving away a short distance and then waiting. But in the deathly silence of the mist-bound forest Dyson had heard the sinister footsteps fading away and no sound of anyone returning

'Move now,' he told himself, 'before he seals off the whole area . . .'

Despite the veils of grey mist Dyson had no trouble making his way back to the parked Chevy. He walked rapidly, treading on soft moss wherever he could. At intervals he paused, listening for any signs of pursuit. Nothing. He hurried towards the parked car.

As he threaded his way between the tree-trunks Dyson came alive again, thinking furiously. The nearest airport was San Francisco International. But they'd be watching and waiting there, he felt sure. Far safer to drive the much longer route south through California to Los Angeles Airport. The all-powerful forces the man controlled wouldn't expect him to take that route.

From LA he could catch a flight to London. There he could transfer to another flight direct to Zurich in Switzerland. Julius Amberg, president of the Zurcher Kredit Bank, owed him. Dyson's mind went back several years.

Bob Newman, the famous international foreign correspondent, had done him a bigger favour than he'd realized at the time. Dyson had taken some embarrassing photos of Amberg with his mistress in Geneva. He'd been going to sell them to *Der Spiegel*. Amberg was hitting the headlines at that time, acting as go-between in a big financial take-over.

'Give those pics to Amberg,' Newman had urged. 'He is a powerful man and you might need his help one day. Forget the money just for once, Joel – important allies are worth their weight in gold . . .'

Reluctantly, Dyson had agreed. Now Amberg could repay the 'debt' by holding the film and the tape in his vault. What safer place in the world to hide a fortune?

As he came closer to his Chevy Dyson checked in his mind any loopholes in his plan. He voiced his thoughts aloud in a bare whisper.

'The Chevy was hired in Salinas. They'll take time

tracing the car, the description and registration number. I'll dump it in LA. By the time they track it I'll be long gone . . .'

He approached the concealed vehicle cautiously. *They* might just have found it. God knew there were enough of them – and professionals to their fingertips . . .

An hour later he was driving south along the coastal highway, crossing the bridge at Big Sur. Hardly any traffic. To his right the wind off the ocean blew against the side of the car. Huge waves created a curtain of white surf rising thirty feet high. Dyson had reached Santa Barbara when the shock hit him.

The tape recorder! In his haste to escape the man he had left the machine on the ground. It wouldn't take *them* long to visit his insurance company – to check the serial number of the machine with his insurance policy. Jesus! They'd then have a positive identification of who had crouched in the undergrowth near the cabin. Up to that moment Dyson had half-cherished the illusion it would take them time to finger him.

It was a very worried Joel Dyson who reached Los Angeles, crawled with the traffic, handed in his Chevy and took a cab to the airport. Here he walked into another piece of bad luck.

He entered the vast concourse, carrying the bag containing a set of clothes he'd been careful to purchase at several shops after handing back the Chevy. He bought a United Airlines return ticket to London -- the return was to throw off his track anyone who traced the reservation.

The flight left in three-quarters of an hour. Dyson was congratulating himself on his speedy departure as he checked in his bag. That was when he heard the crafty voice as he left the counter.

'Found a chick in London who's dropping her panties for the wrong man?'

'What?'

Dyson swung round and stared at a small man with a face closely resembling a monkey's. Which was why he was known as the Monkey. Nick Rossi was a small-time operator who watched the airports in the hope of picking up useful information he could peddle to the press for a small sum.

'I'm taking a well-earned holiday,' he snapped. 'And if I'm lucky I'll find an available chick. Sorry, Nick, no sale.'

'Which is why you're taking your camera with you?'

The Monkey grinned knowingly. A dead half-smoked cigarette was glued to the right-hand corner of his thin lips.

'You should know opportunities hit you in the kisser when you least expect it. Keep out of the rain . . .'

Dyson hurried away, swearing foully under his breath. He had thought of offering the Monkey a fistful of bills to keep him quiet – but that would have whetted his greedy appetite. Dyson only relaxed when the jumbo jet had taken off, swung out over Catalina Island and the Pacific Ocean, then turned east back over the mainland on its non-stop eleven-hour polar route flight to London. A double whiskey provided by the stewardess also helped.

His mood of relaxation didn't last long. As the machine flew on through the night, still climbing, he furtively glanced round, checking the other passengers. His chance encounter with Nick Rossi could prove fatal. Had *they* had time to rush a man aboard at the last moment? He doubted it. A second glass of whiskey relaxed him again.

Dyson dared not go to sleep even though most of the passengers of the half-filled jumbo were now comatose. The film camera nestled on his lap, concealed under a newspaper. Frequently he put his hand inside the pocket of his coat folded on the empty seat beside him. He felt relieved when he found the tape was still there . . .

Bob Newman. The name kept repeating itself in Dyson's mind as he disembarked at Heathrow. He changed his plan of action on impulse. Instead of immediately buying a

6

Swissair ticket to Zurich he hurried outside the concourse, climbed into a taxi and gave the driver the address of Newman's flat in Beresforde Road, South Kensington. In his haste, he failed to notice the small stocky man in a dark belted raincoat who watched him, followed him, signalled with his hand, stroking the left side of his face as a grey Volvo appeared. Then the man ran to a phone box.

'Ed, here. London Airport. The subject came in off the LA flight, walked out, took a taxi somewhere.'

'Did he now?' The gravelly voice of Norton was abrasive. 'With a tail, I trust?'

'The grey Volvo was passing. We had three cars cruising round . . .'

'I know that. Nick Rossi came across good. Wait there. Don't go to sleep. The subject may come back. Report to me any developments.'

'I'll stay tuned . . .'

The stocky man realized the phone had cut out, the connection broken. Typical. He had never seen Norton, had only heard his gravelly American voice on phones. He had commented on this to another member of the unit.

'That's your good luck,' his colleague had warned. 'No one knows what he looks like. You ever meet Norton, know who he is, you're dead . . .'

Arriving at Newman's flat, which faced the church of St Mark's, Dyson told the cab driver to wait. An elegant slim blonde girl answered the door, but made no attempt to invite him inside. Dyson produced an old press card carrying his photo.

'Sorry to disturb you. I'm Joel Dyson, an old friend of Bob Newman's, I need to see him urgently. He's expecting me,' he lied.

7

'He didn't say anything . . .'

'He wouldn't. Our business is confidential. And urgent,' he repeated. 'Matter of life and death.'

My death, he thought. The blonde examined the press card, looked at him, seemed uncertain how to respond as she handed back the card. Dyson forced himself to smile, to relax. She didn't smile back at him, but nodded.

'Have you something to write down an address? He's with the General & Cumbria Assurance Company in Park Crescent. Twenty minutes from here by cab . . .'

Thanking her after he'd scribbled in his notebook, Dyson, camera looped over his shoulder, hurried back to the cab, gave the driver an address in Soho. Earlier, on his way from the airport, he had glanced back a couple of times through the rear window. He didn't notice the grey Volvo driving one vehicle behind the cab. He really had little anxiety that he could have been followed.

Joel Dyson had badly underestimated the energy and power of the force reaching out towards him. During the eleven-hour flight from LA his San Francisco apartment had been turned over, examined for clues under a microscope. All main Californian airports had been checked – hence the swift contact with Nick Rossi. Wires had hummed between the States and Europe. Arrangements for the target's 'reception' had been made. Identity had been established by the tape recorder.

En route to the Soho address, Dyson was contemplating the value of the film and the tape. *Five million dollars?* No. *Ten million dollars* at least. The man would find ways of raising the money when faced with total destruction. Joel was on a big high when he left the cab in a street in Soho. He never even noticed the grey Volvo which slowed, then parked.

*   *   *

8

'Need to use your copying room for a film and a tape, Sammy. And I'm in a pissing great hurry,' Dyson told the cockney owner of the shop.

Outside it appeared to be an outlet for soft-porn films. But Dyson knew London well and had used the cockney's facilities in the past.

'Cost you, mate,' Sammy told him quickly. 'I don't let just anyone muck about with my equipment. Extra charge in case it's illegal, which it probably is.'

'Just watch the door. I don't want interruptions,' Dyson snapped. 'And here's your outrageous fee.'

Before disappearing into the back room he dropped two one-hundred dollar bills on the counter. Sammy, a ginger-haired hunchback, suppressed a whistle of surprise. He held the bills up to the light. They looked OK.

When Dyson came out of the room he had four canisters inside his bag. Two originals – film and tape – and one copy of each. Nodding to Sammy, he walked into the street, hailed a passing cab, told the driver to take him to Park Crescent.

Dyson had taken another impulsive decision the moment the cab had moved off from Beresforde Road – changing his next destination to Sammy's in Soho. Much safer to have twin sets of the film and the tape – one hidden in London, the other in Zurich. He prayed Newman would be at Park Crescent.

Inside a first-floor office at the Park Crescent HQ of the SIS, Bob Newman sat drinking coffee with Monica, Deputy Director Tweed's faithful and long-time assistant. Of uncertain age, Monica wore her grey hair tied back in a bun. Seated behind her desk, she was enjoying a chat with the foreign correspondent. In his early forties, of medium build, and clean-shaven, his hair brown, with a capable manner, Newman had been fully vetted and had often worked with her chief.

'I said Tweed was away,' she remarked. 'Actually he's in Paris. Expected back any time now.'

'He's like a dragonfly,' Newman commented. 'Zig-zagging all over the place. I think he likes travel.'

'You're one to talk,' she chaffed him. 'As a foreign correspondent you've been everywhere—'

She broke off as the phone rang. It was George, the ex-Army man who acted as door-keeper and guard down-stairs. Monica frowned, looked at Newman, said 'Who?' for the second time. 'Tell him to wait – and keep a close eye on him.'

'Someone for you,' she said as she put down the phone. 'A man called Joel Dyson. Says it's desperately urgent he sees you at once.'

'Joel Dyson? How the devil did he know I was here? He used to be one of my journalist informants. Nowadays he has sunk to the level of one of the paparazzi. Takes pics of so-called celebrities – married – enjoying a tumble with the wrong woman. Sells them to the press for huge sums. I suppose I'd better see him, but not up here.'

'The waiting-room,' Monica decided. She phoned George to give him instructions. Newman said he'd like her to come with him as a witness. 'I'll bring my notebook, then,' she replied.

Facing George's desk, the waiting-room was a bleak bare room with scrubbed floorboards, a wooden table and several hard-backed chairs. It was not designed to encourage visitors to linger.

Monica was surprised at how smartly Joel Dyson was dressed. While driving down through California he had stopped at a motel, hired a room, stripped off his duffle coat, denims and open-necked shirt. Substituting from his bag an American business suit, a Brooks Brothers shirt and tie, a vicuña coat, he had then slipped away from the motel unseen by the proprietor, his room already paid for the night.

A small slim man, in his thirties, he had a plump face with pouched lips, a receding chin and an ingratiating smile. Monica instantly mistrusted him. Her second surprise was his voice. He spoke with an upper-crust English accent. Joel could switch from convincing American to equally acceptable English with ease. He had, in fact, British nationality.

'How the devil did you find me here?' Newman demanded.

'No need to get stroppy. Called at your apartment. You do have a nice taste in blonde companions. She said you'd be here.'

Molly! Newman groaned inwardly. He was on the verge of gently ending the friendship – she was quickly showing signs that she expected him to take her seriously. Now he'd have to speed up the process of disengagement.

'Didn't know you were mixed up with insurance,' Joel went on cheerfully. 'Come to think of it, what an ideal set-up to learn people's dark secrets.'

He had been fooled by the brass plate outside which was engraved with *General & Cumbria Assurance* – the cover name for the SIS. Not asked to sit down, he was still standing.

'What is it you want?' Newman snapped. 'I happen to be very busy.'

'Insurance companies have top-security safes.' Dyson smirked at Monica who had sat down at the table and was making notes. She stared at him blankly, then dropped her eyes to the notebook. Which fazed Dyson not at all.

'I have a tape and a film,' he went on, addressing Newman, 'and they're a bombshell. I'll keep the originals and you store the copies. In case anything happens to me.'

'And what might happen to you?'

Dyson waited until he'd slapped his case on the table, unlocked it, produced two canisters, which he slid across to Monica.

11

'I may end up dead,' he said quietly.

The seriousness of his tone, the abrupt change from his previous breezy manner intrigued Newman. He was half-inclined to believe Dyson, but still not fully convinced.

'And who would want to kill the world's most popular paparazzo?' he enquired ironically.

'Don't like that word. I'm a highly professional photographer, one of the best – if not *the* best. And I can't answer your question.'

'Can't – or won't?' Newman snapped again.

'Pass.'

'Then get to hell out of here and take your junk with you.'

'The contents of those two canisters could shake the world, shatter Europe to its foundations, destroy any influence Britain has internationally. I'm running scared, Bob – scared as a rabbit with the ferrets inches from its tail.'

Dyson took a cigarette from a gold case and Newman tried an experiment: he used his own lighter to ignite the cigarette. Dyson couldn't hold the tip still, his hand trembling like a leaf in the wind. Reluctantly, Newman decided he was not putting on another of his chameleon-like acts.

'If we agree to keep this stuff we have to know where to get in touch with you,' he said. 'Otherwise, forget it.'

Newman had noticed something when Dyson had extracted the two canisters inside his case. Rammed in on top of some clothes which looked new – and American in style – was a film camera with a coiled hanging strap.

'I've got to rush now,' Dyson protested, lifting his case off the table.

'I said, how do we get in touch with you? Where will you be staying?'

'Contact that Swiss banker you introduced me to. Julius Amberg in Zurich. Look, I'm going to miss my plane . . .'

12

'Then shove off.'

Monica escorted him to the door, nodded to George to unlock the front door. Dyson disappeared like the wind.

'I'm taking these canisters straight down to the explosives boffins in the Engine Room for testing,' Monica said the moment she came back.

'Wise precaution,' Newman agreed. 'Then what?'

'Put them in Tweed's safe until he gets back . . .'

The driver behind the wheel of the grey Volvo, still parked within sight of the building where Dyson emerged, signalled to the driver of another car, a silver Renault, parked behind him, by stroking a hand over his head. 'Volvo' picked up his mobile phone as Dyson stepped inside a taxi he'd hailed, dialled.

'Jerry here again.'

'Developments?' Norton's gravelly voice demanded.

'Subject called at a soft-porn shop in Soho. Came out, took another taxi to a Park Crescent building. Went . . .'

'Park Crescent? God Almighty, not there! Number of the building?'

'General & Cumbria Assurance.' The driver gave him the number. He had strolled round the crescent and back to his car while Dyson was inside. 'When Dyson left the Renault took over—'

'General & Cumbria.' Norton had interrupted him, sounded to be thinking aloud. 'I know what that place is. What was Dyson carrying – when he left?'

'Just his bag . . .'

'He must have left them there for safe keeping.' The voice became even grimmer. 'We'll have to take out the whole building. You'll be needed to prepare the vehicle – and the explosives. The job must be done in the next forty-eight hours. Get back to headquarters . . .'

PART ONE

The Massacre

1

Two days later Paula Grey was following the other guests into the large dining-room of Tresillian Manor for lunch. The Elizabethan gem was located on an isolated stretch of Bodmin Moor in Cornwall. She had been staying with friends in Sherborne when the call from Tweed came through early in the morning.

'Paula, a strange emergency has arisen. I'm just back from Paris and I had a call from Julius Amberg, the Swiss banker. He sounded frightened. He's flown over here from Zurich to a friend's house on Bodmin Moor . . .'

He had given her careful directions where to turn off the A30, which spanned the moor. She had said she would drive there at once.

'I'll be there in time for lunch,' Tweed had continued. 'I am bringing a heavy bodyguard – Butler, Nield and Cardon. Armed. Which is what Amberg begged me to do.'

'What on earth for?' she had asked.

'He wouldn't say on the phone. He was calling from Tresillian Manor. Apparently he flew from Zurich to London Airport this morning, called me here at Park Crescent before I'd arrived. He then caught a Brymon Airways flight to Newquay Airport and called me again from Bodmin Moor. He has his own team of guards with him but doesn't have that much confidence in them. He spoke as though in fear of his life. That isn't like Amberg. We'll all meet up at the manor . . .'

It had been a pleasant drive from Sherborne for Paula – a cold February morning with the sun shining brilliantly out

17

of a duck-egg blue sky. Pleasant until she had turned down the side road across Bodmin Moor. The sense of isolation had descended on her immediately, the bleak deserted moor closing in on her.

She had stopped the car, switched off the engine for a moment, listened. Not a sign of human life anywhere among the barren reaches of gorse-covered heathland. In the distance she saw a dominant cone-like hill rising up – Brown Willy. It was the silence which seemed menacing.

Despite the sunlight, a sense of doom gripped her. Of impending tragedy. She shook off the dark mood as she started up the car and drove on.

'You're just being silly,' she told herself.

Tresillian Manor was hidden from the outside world because it was located in a bowl. Wrought-iron gates were wide open with a curving drive beyond.

Lousy security, Paula thought as she drove in past the stone pillar carrying the name of the house on a brass plate. Tall firs surrounded the estate, isolating it further from the outside world. Paula gasped as she turned a corner, slowed on the tarred drive.

Built of grey stone, it was a smaller manor than she had expected but a beauty. Stately gables reared up at either end. A massive stone porch guarded the entrance. Six cars, including a Rolls, were parked below the terrace which ran the full width of the house. Mullion windows completed the architectural masterpiece.

'Welcome to Tresillian Manor,' a small portly man greeted her. 'I am Julius Amberg. We met briefly in Zurich.' He peered over her shoulder. 'Where is Tweed?'

'He's coming down with his people from London. I'm sure he'll be here shortly.'

Behind Amberg stood a blank-faced heavily built man. Paula was shown a cupboard where she divested herself of her trench-coat. She kept her shoulder-bag, inside which nestled her Browning .32 automatic.

18

Drinks were served in a room Amberg called the Great Hall. Spacious, lofty, with a sculpted plasterwork ceiling, it seemed as old as time. A few minutes later Paula followed the other guests across the large entrance hall into a long narrow dining-room. The table was laid for lunch. Paula counted twelve places. Plenty of room for Tweed and his contingent.

She glanced at her watch. Unusual for him to be late. Her stomach felt queasy again: she must have eaten something the previous evening which had disagreed with her. She'd be relieved when Tweed *did* arrive. The sensation of imminent catastrophe had returned. She studied Amberg, who sat at the head of the table.

The Swiss banker, in his fifties, wore his black hair without a parting, slicked back from his high forehead. Under thick brows his blue eyes were shrewd, his face clean-shaven and plump. He smiled at Paula, who sat on his left.

'Tweed is usually so prompt.'

'He'll be here any minute,' she assured him.

She looked down the table at the other six men, none of whom had spoken a word. All were in their thirties and wearing black suits. She suspected they were hired from a private security firm in Switzerland. They didn't inspire her with confidence – there had been no one at the entrance gate, and Amberg had opened the door himself with only one guard behind him.

'It's very good of Squire Gaunt to rent the manor to me at such short notice,' Amberg continued. 'Even though I have spent longer periods here before. And the butler and kitchen staff.'

'Squire Gaunt?'

'He owns the manor. The locals call him Squire. He finds it rather amusing in this day and age.'

'Where is he?'

'Oh, probably riding across the moor. While I'm here

19

he stays in a cottage he owns at Five Lanes.'

He looked up as someone knocked on the door. The butler who had served the drinks earlier appeared, his manner apologetic.

'Excuse me, sir, Cook says she is ready with the luncheon whenever it suits you.'

Mounce, a Cornishman, wore a black jacket, grey-striped trousers, a white shirt and black tie. A tall, heavily built man, he had the perfect manners for a butler, Paula thought.

'I'll let you know in a minute, Mounce,' Amberg replied.

'Very good, sir.'

'Gaunt has an excellent cook,' Amberg chattered on as Mounce closed the door. 'I hope you will like the lunch. Asparagus mousse for a starter, followed by venison with wine. She is so good I'd like to steal her off him.'

'Sounds wonderful,' Paula said automatically.

The mention of food had brought back the queasiness. She was about to speak when Amberg checked his watch.

'Perhaps we ought to start. I'm sure Tweed will understand. In any case, that will probably bring him post-haste!'

'Mr Amberg . . .' Paula lowered her voice. 'Will you please excuse me for a moment? You showed me where the toilet is. Do start the meal – I'll only be a moment.'

'Of course . . .'

As she stood up she looked out of the windows overlooking the curving drive. A postman had appeared, riding slowly on a cycle. She recognized who was arriving from the blue uniform, the peaked cap pulled well down over the forehead, and for a second sunlight flashed off the red and gold badge. Perched on the front carrier was a large canvas bag.

'The postman's on his way here,' she said to Amberg.

'Mounce will attend to him.'

Amberg was slowly drumming his clenched knuckles on the table. Intuitively she guessed it was not with impatience but with nervousness at the non-arrival of Tweed and his men.

As she left the dining-room and crossed the wood-block floor the front doorbell rang. Mounce appeared, used both hands to pull down the edges of his jacket, walked erectly to the door. Paula, carrying her shoulder bag, entered the toilet, walked down two stone steps, closed and locked the door. It was heavy wood, insulating all sound from the rest of the manor.

Mounce opened the door and stared at the postman. Wrong time of the day. Also it was not the usual postman who stood with a heavy bag looped over the left shoulder. The postman held a parcel in the right hand which was extended to the butler.

As Mounce glanced down, noticed it was addressed to Julius Amberg, the postman's right hand slid swiftly inside the uniform jacket, emerged holding a long stiletto knife. It was rammed upwards into Mounce's body, carefully aimed to penetrate with great force between two ribs. Mounce grunted, an expression of amazement creased his face, then he slumped to the floor, still clutching the parcel.

The killer stepped inside, hauled the body clear of the threshold, quietly closed the front door. Stooping, the figure checked the neck pulse. Nothing. Straightening up, it whipped off the cap, shoved it into the bag, grabbed a Balaclava helmet from inside, pulled it over its head, adjusted the eye slits.

It next extracted a pistol with a wide short barrel from the bag, walked over to the closed kitchen door, opened it wide. The 'postman' was inside, door closed again, before the four occupants – Cook and three local girl helpers – had time to react. Grasping its nose with its left hand, the intruder fired the pistol, the tear-gas shell aimed at the flagstone floor. The gas filled the sealed room – all the windows were closed against the cold.

The four women were choking and reeling as Balaclava produced a leather sap like a small truncheon. Methodically Balaclava ran round the kitchen, coshing each one on the head. Up to this moment the 'postman' had worn leather gloves. For the next weapon sensitive finger control would be needed. Stripping off the leather gloves carefully, hands encased in surgical gloves were exposed.

The 'postman' checked the time. Two minutes since the butler had been dealt with. On the central table lay a silver tray with mousse in individual glass bowls. Venison and other items were cooking in a modern oven against a wall. A hand switched off the cooker – no point in risking a fire. Glancing round at the unconscious forms slumped on the floor, Balaclava extracted an Uzi machine-pistol from his bag. A firing rate of six hundred rounds a minute. Balaclava left the kitchen, closed the door.

Able to hold a breath for a minute, the 'postman' sucked in air. Rubber-soled shoes made no sound as Balaclava approached the dining-room door. A hand hovered, grasped the handle, threw the door open.

Seven men stared at the Balaclava-clad figure holding the Uzi. For a brief second in time they froze. They had been expecting the butler whom Amberg had summoned by pressing a wall bell. That brief second was fatal. Balaclava pressed the trigger, aiming first at the guards, spraying them as Amberg jumped to his feet. The last six bullets stitched a neat row of red buttons down his shirt front, buttons which rapidly enlarged. The banker fell backwards, sagged into the seat, hit the rear of the chair with such force the top half broke. He was grotesquely sprawled at a reclining angle, supported by the intact lower half. His face stared sightlessly at the ceiling.

The assassin extracted the empty magazine, which had

held forty rounds, and shoved it in a pocket, then inserted a fresh mag. Walking round the table, he emptied it into already inert corpses. Best to be sure.

Cradling the Uzi, Balaclava brought out a glass spray bottle two-thirds full of sulphuric acid. The spray was aimed at Amberg's face, the plunger pressed. A jet of acid enveloped the face from the bridge of the banker's nose to the chin. Replacing the cap, the assassin thrust it into a pocket, shoved Uzi and empty mag into the bag still looped from the shoulder. After leaving the dining-room, the door was closed.

In the hall the Balaclava helmet was removed, dropped inside the bag, replaced by the 'postman's' official cap. The front door was opened with gloved hands, closed from the outside, the bag was placed on the front rack of the cycle propped against the wall. The 'postman' rode off down the drive.

'Well, I delivered the parcel,' the assassin commented aloud with cold-blooded indifference.

2

Paula checked her appearance in the toilet mirror. She was feeling better, stomach settled, but rather weak. 'Not bad,' she said to her reflection. 'A bit white round the gills.'

Her image stared back. An attractive girl in her early thirties, long raven-black hair, good bone structure, calm eyes which missed nothing, a firm shapely chin. She wore a cream blouse with a mandarin collar, a navy blue suit, pleated skirt, flesh-coloured tights and soft-soled loafers.

Paula had been sick. Which left her with a washed-out

feeling. She had cleaned up the basin. She suddenly felt empty, hungry.

'Maybe I could tackle a little venison,' she said to herself as she mounted the steps, unlocked the door.

She took two paces into the hall, stopped. Mounce lay flat on his back near the closed front door, the handle of a knife protruding from his midriff. A red stain discoloured his white shirt. The Browning .32 automatic was already in Paula's right hand. She edged against the wall, listened, looked.

All doors closed, including the dining-room and the kitchen. She forgot her weakness, glanced up the staircase. Was the killer still in the house? Her loafers made no sound as she crossed the floor, bent over the butler, whose hand was still clutching the package. The 'postman'...

Her mind was racing as she quickly checked his carotid pulse. Dead. What the hell was going on? She straightened up, approached the dining-room door. She listened before her left hand reached out for the handle. Another solid door which shut out all sound. She revolved the handle slowly, using her handkerchief to avoid leaving finger-prints, opened the door suddenly, stepped one pace inside, her gun ready to swivel on any target.

'Oh, my God!'

She had the presence of mind to whisper the words. Her mind struggled to take in the macabre horror. It was a massacre. Two guards were still seated, sprawled across the table in lakes of dark red blood. Some security, she thought bitterly. Four other guards had toppled out of their chairs, lay on the floor in pools of blood. She closed the door quietly, still wary that the killer might be inside the manor. Facing the door, she bent down again and checked the pulses of the two men on her side of the table. Nothing. Corpses ready for the morgue.

Sucking in her breath, she moved to the top of the table where Amberg's body was bent over the broken-backed chair. Paula was about to check his neck pulse when she suddenly saw his head. She gasped, trembled with shock. Julius Amberg was faceless. Large parts of the flesh had been eaten away. Even as she watched, the original face was rapidly being converted into a skull.

Forcing herself to stoop closer, her acute sense of smell caught a sharp whiff. Some kind of acid? Why? Why this extra barbarity? She stood up, looked round the walls of the panelled dining-room – panelled from floor to ceiling. A beautiful room – which seemed to emphasize the horror of what she was witnessing.

Her eyes whipped up to the ceiling, then gazed at it. Like the Great Hall, where they'd had drinks, the plasterwork was sculpted in an artistic design of scrolls and ripples. But what caught her attention was a disfigurement. A vivid splash of blood spread immediately above the banker. One of the bullets must have hit an artery, sending up a spurt of blood. As she watched, a drop fell, landed on the relics of Amberg's skull-like head.

She looked at the table. In front of where she had been seated she had thrown her napkin over her place setting – which was probably why the killer hadn't noticed the absence of a guest. In any case it was clear he had moved with great speed to complete his devilish work.

'Get a grip on yourself,' she said under her breath.

She felt terribly alone but she went back into the hall. *The staff!* Inside the kitchen. She paused before opening the door, fearful of what she would find.

'Not them, too,' she prayed.

Another faint whiff met her sensitive nostrils when she eased the door open. Tear-gas. Four bodies sprawled on the stone-flagged floor. Swiftly she checked their pulses. She was startled to find they were all alive. Unconscious, but *alive*. She assumed the plump older woman, clad in white overalls and a white cap slumped near the venison, was Cook. Paula took a cushion off a chair, eased it gently

25

under her head. The younger girls, also clad in white overalls, were less likely to have suffered serious damage.

It was then she noticed the cooker had been switched off, which puzzled her. She was careful not to touch the dials. Fingerprints. She opened a window to let in fresh air to clear the remnants of tear-gas and, warily, explored the rest of the ground floor.

One door led to a study furnished with expensive antiques. Another opened on to a large living-room with french windows at the back facing a gap in the firs framing a view of the bleak moor beyond. The sight emphasized her solitariness. Paula ploughed on, entering the Great Hall. Empty, like the other rooms. The long stretch of windows looked out on to the drive. Two cars were approaching.

Tweed climbed out from behind the wheel of the Ford Escort followed by the sturdy Harry Butler dressed in a windcheater and corduroy trousers. Behind them Pete Nield and Philip Cardon left the Sierra.

'Sorry we're so late,' Tweed began and smiled. 'We were held up by running into a convoy of those travellers – gypsies, whatever. I hope Julius will excuse . . .'

He had spoken rapidly and stopped as he saw Paula's expression, the gun she was still holding in her right hand. His manner changed instantly.

'What's wrong, Paula? Trouble? What kind?'

'The worst kind. And I'd expected Bob Newman to come.'

It was the type of pointless remark made by someone suffering from delayed shock – by someone who had held herself together by sheer will-power and character. No longer alone, she was giving way. She made a great effort: they had to be told.

'Newman had gone off somewhere,' Tweed replied. 'Monica left a message on his answerphone to come and see her. She'll tell him where we've gone.'

Tweed had deliberately answered her question to introduce a whiff of normality back into her life. Middle-aged, of medium height and build, he wore horn-rimmed glasses. He was outwardly the man you pass in the street and never notice – a characteristic which had served him well as Deputy Director of the SIS. He walked quickly up the steps, put his arm round Paula, squeezed her.

'What's happened here?'

'It's ghastly. No, that isn't data, which is what you always want.' She took a deep breath. 'They're all dead.'

'Who exactly?' Tweed asked calmly.

'Julius Amberg, his guards and the butler, Mounce. Eight corpses waiting for you inside that lovely house. The postman did it . . .'

'Tell me more later. I'd better go and see for myself. This postman you mentioned has gone?'

'I haven't had time to search the upper floor. Downstairs is clear.'

'Harry,' Tweed said, taking command immediately, 'go upstairs and search for a killer, who will be armed. Take Philip Cardon with you.'

'On my way . . .'

Butler, a 7.65-mm Walther automatic in his hand, entered the manor followed by Cardon also gripping a Walther. As Paula and Tweed followed them they saw Butler, holding the gun in both hands, creeping up the wide staircase. Cardon was a few paces behind, sliding up close to the wall, starting at the upper landing.

'They're in here,' Paula said. 'Prepare yourself for something pretty awful. Especially Amberg's face.'

Tweed, wearing a trench coat over his navy blue business suit, paused. Hands deep inside his trench coat pockets, a stance he used to adopt when interrogating suspects in the old days when he had been the youngest

27

Scotland Yard superintendent in the Murder Squad, he stared at the dead body of Mounce.

'I'd like to know what is inside that package the postman delivered. But we mustn't disturb anything until the police get here. We'll call them in a minute,' he said, glancing at the phone on a table against the hall wall. He listened as Paula thought of something else.

'The kitchen staff behind that door were attacked with tear-gas, then I think the killer knocked them unconscious with something. One of the three girls has an ugly bruise on her head. They're all alive, thank heavens.'

'Pete.' Tweed addressed Butler's partner, a very different character. Slim, dressed in a smart blue suit under his open raincoat, he had neat dark hair and a small moustache. 'The staff are unconscious in the kitchen . . .'

'I heard what Paula said, Chief.'

'Go and see what you can do for them. Get a statement if any of them recover and are up to it.'

'I'll get it all down on my pocket tape recorder,' Nield assured him.

He produced the miniaturized recorder the boffins in the basement of Park Crescent had designed. Giving Paula a smile and a little salute, he headed for the kitchen.

'Now for it,' Paula warned.

She opened the door to the dining-room. Tweed walked in ahead of her, stood still after taking two paces. His eyes scanned the carnage, stared briefly at the red lake on the ceiling, walked slowly past each body until he arrived at the head of the table.

'It's a blood bath,' Paula commented. 'You won't like Julius Amberg's face. It's been sprayed with acid.'

'Ruthless,' Tweed said, looking down at his old friend. 'Also intriguing. Julius has – had – an identical twin brother. Julius was Chief Executive of the Zurcher Kredit Bank in Zurich, the driving force. Walter, the brother, is Chairman, does very little except draw a fat salary.'

He looked up as Butler appeared at the door, the Walther still in his hand. He nodded to Tweed.

'All clear upstairs. No one else is here.' His gaze swept round the room. 'Bloody hell.'

'A perfect description,' Tweed responded. 'Lucky we were late. Paula, how did you avoid this massacre . . .?'

His expression changed. His hands jumped out of his pockets and he was alert as a prowling tiger.

'My God!'

'What is it?' Paula asked.

Tweed had grasped something everyone else had overlooked. His own remark about being lucky to be late triggered off the alarm bells inside his head.

'*We* were supposed to be the targets. I must phone Park Crescent instantly. This is a major emergency.'

'I'll call them immediately,' Butler said, ran into the hall and picked up the phone. He was dialling as Tweed hurried into the hall. 'Shouldn't be long now . . .'

'Hurry!' Tweed urged him. 'Park Crescent could be in terrible danger . . .'

It took Butler several minutes – he had to dial again and Tweed stood close to him. Butler listened, nodded and handed the phone over.

'Pray God I'm in time,' Tweed said as he took the instrument.

3

'Tweed and the others have driven down to a Tresillian Manor on Bodmin Moor,' Monica told Newman as she closed a file on her desk at Park Crescent.

Newman had just arrived in response to the urgent call from Monica waiting for him on his answerphone at his flat. He took off his favourite Gannex raincoat, hung it on the stand, settled in a chair facing her desk.

'Bodmin Moor? That's Cornwall. Who are the others and why has he gone down to that remote spot?'

'He took Butler, Nield and Cardon with him as guards . . .'

'A heavy delegation. As guards? That's unlike Tweed. Were they armed? What's going on?'

'Yes, they were armed.' Monica sounded disturbed. 'He was going to meet a Swiss banker, Julius Amberg, who flew in from Zurich.'

'Amberg. That nasty little berk, Joel Dyson, knows Amberg. A very odd coincidence. Has Tweed seen that film or listened to the tape?'

'No, they're still in the safe. He hadn't time. It was action stations from the moment he arrived and took the call from Amberg – begging him to hurry to Cornwall.'

'More and more mysterious. And why did you call me?'

'Tweed wanted you to drive down there if you contacted me in time. I think it would be pointless your going now. The meeting at the manor was for lunch. It will all be over—'

She broke off as the phone began ringing. Picking up the receiver she started to announce 'General & Cumbria Assur—'

'Monica, this is Tweed. You recognize my voice? Quick.'

'Yes, is something . . .'

'Exit One! Exit One! *Exit One!* For Christ's sake . . .'

'Understood.'

Monica rammed down the receiver, took a key from a drawer, knocked over her chair in her haste. Inserting the key in a metal box attached to the wall, she pulled down a red lever, slammed the door shut. The moment the lever

30

was operated screaming alarm bells alerted every office in the building – including Tweed's.

'Emergency evacuation!' Newman shouted to make himself heard as he jumped up, grabbed his Gannex. Monica stuffed her Filofax in her handbag and Newman held the door open. Men and women were already moving down the staircase. There had been rehearsals: no one panicked. They kept moving.

In the entrance hall George, the guard, was slamming down a phone. He had a clipboard in front of him and ticked off people as they filed out through the front door. The bell in the hall was more subdued.

As Newman reached the entrance hall with Monica he glanced at Lisa, the fair-haired girl who operated the switchboard. He saw row upon row of red lights. Every phone was – had been – in use. Lisa snatched up her coat and handbag, as Newman asked the question.

'So many calls all at once?'

'Switchboard jammed,' Lisa replied quickly. 'Except for Tweed's line, which is separate.'

'I had a crazy call,' George commented, ticking off more names. 'Some nutcase said he was phoning from Berlin, had an urgent message. Been jabbering away for five minutes . . .'

Howard, the Director, appeared at the foot of the stairs. Immaculately dressed in a Chester Barrie business suit from Harrods, tall, plump-faced, he had thrown off his usual lordly manner. He stood by the desk next to George.

'Better leave,' said Newman as Monica vanished through the open doorway. 'It was Tweed himself who sounded the alarm from long distance.'

'I'm staying here until the last man and woman has left the building,' Howard said quietly.

Newman was surprised and his previous opinion of Howard as a pompous woodentop changed. He nodded, slipped outside ahead of a fresh file of staff coming down

31

the staircase. On the doorstep, standing to one side, he froze.

A maroon-coloured Espace station wagon was parked alongside the building. Newman went down the steps, stood close and ran back inside the hall as the fresh batch of people walked rapidly off round the Crescent. They were assembling out of sight round the corner in Marylebone Road as planned.

'George,' Newman said as the guard showed the list to Howard. 'There's one of those large Espaces parked just outside.'

'Ruddy 'ell,' George blazed, 'I'd have seen the blighter if I hadn't had that loony from Berlin on the blower.'

'Which is precisely why he was on the phone.'

'Time to leave,' Howard announced, gesturing towards the list. 'All present and correct. Present out of danger, that is. Fancy a quick stroll, Bob?'

'That will do me . . .'

They followed George out of the building, down the steps, turning left along the curve. All three men gave the Espace a quick glance then strode briskly towards where the staff were waiting. It was very quiet in the Crescent and no one else was about. Thank God, Newman thought.

'There was no one inside that vehicle,' he informed Howard.

'Let's hope we don't make fools of ourselves.'

'You've overlooked one point,' Newman commented. 'All the lines were jammed up with calls – phoney calls is my guess. If this is what I think it is we're up against a genius of a planner.'

'I'll call the Bomb Squad from one of the offices along Marylebone Road,' Howard decided. 'It's probably all a false alarm.'

'That doesn't link up with the avalanche of calls – including the crazy one to George,' Newman reminded him. 'I'll stay here.'

32

They had rounded the corner and Newman stayed behind a wall in a position where he could watch the building. He saw a silver Renault parked just beyond the far side of the Crescent. That was the moment when the world blew up.

Newman had put on sun-glasses he used for driving when the sun was low in the sky. There was a blinding flash. An ear-splitting roar. A cloud of dust dense as a fog. A brief nerve-wracking silence, succeeded by a sound like a major avalanche crashing down a mountain. No shock wave, which puzzled Newman.

The dust cloud thinned. He stared, hypnotized. The Espace had vanished. The section of Park Crescent which had been SIS headquarters was a black hole. Masonry rumbled as it slid down on to the pavement, out across the street. What staggered Newman was the clean-cut destruction of the target. On either side of where the building had stood as a section of the Crescent the walls stood scarred but erect. It was as though a vertical rectangular wedge of a giant cake had been sliced away. The sinister rumble of more debris slithering down over rubble continued, grew quieter, ceased. RIP, SIS headquarters.

Newman glanced across the Crescent. The silver Renault had disappeared. Howard came running up to him.

'What the hell was that? I called the Bomb Squad . . .'

'Hope they brought their sandwiches. No work left for them.'

'Oh, dear God!'

Howard stood like a man transfixed as he gazed at the ruin.

Automatically, he used both hands to adjust the knot of his tie, a mannerism Newman had noticed before when Howard was under pressure. With an effort he pulled

33

himself together, looked back at the small groups of people standing on the pavement.

'It's cold,' Newman said. 'Some of them are shivering. Send them home. Tell them to stay there pending fresh orders.'

'Best thing to do.'

Like a zombie Howard walked back slowly and began talking to his staff. Newman stood very still, thinking about the silver Renault. Odd – the way it had been parked at that observation point and had then disappeared. By his side Monica was recovering from her shocked state.

'Tweed should know about this urgently.'

'How can I reach him?'

'I have the phone number of Tresillian Manor. He might still be there.' She extracted her Filofax and a notebook. On a sheet of paper she wrote a number, handed it to Newman. 'Tresillian Manor.'

'Howard will be back in a minute. He may want a word with Tweed. More likely the other way round . . .'

The driver of the silver Renault was stopped temporarily in a traffic jam in the Euston Road. He picked up his mobile phone, dialled a number.

'Ed here. The property has been liquidated. The contract closed . . .'

'What about dispossessed occupants?'

Norton meant dispossession of their lives.

'A general evacuation took place a few minutes before we closed the contract.'

'It did?' Norton's American twang was a rasp. 'Could anyone have carried out the film and the tape?'

'I'm sure they didn't. No one carried anything which might have contained the canisters.'

'Any sign of Tweed? You have his description. No?

34

That I don't like. We'll have to trace him. He's due for a long holiday, a permanent one . . .'

'I'll report back in.'

Ed was talking into air. Norton had slammed down the phone.

'The Bomb Squad sent the top brass,' Howard observed while they stood in Marylebone Road near the corner of Park Crescent.

'Is it any wonder?' Newman remarked.

The door of a cream Rover opened and Commander Crombie, chief of the Anti-Terrorist Branch, stepped out. Several trucks had arrived, Bomb Squad operatives in protective gear were cordoning off the crescent, evacuating buildings. Other men stood in front of the pile of rubble.

'You're not here for a story, Newman, I trust?' were Crombie's opening words.

A powerfully built man with broad shoulders, in his forties, clean-shaven with a large head, he wore an over-coat with the collar turned up. As he spoke his eyes scanned the area of devastation.

'No, of course not,' Newman snapped.

'Just checking. You saw this thing happen? Any casualties?'

'None,' Howard assured him. 'We evacuated the building in the nick of time. I'll explain why later. The IRA?'

'I don't think so,' said Newman.

'How would you know?' Crombie demanded aggressively.

'No shock wave. Look, I'll show you where I was standing when the Espace blew itself to pieces . . .' He was walking fast and Crombie, a fit man, was hurrying to keep up. 'It was a maroon-coloured Renault Espace parked outside,' Newman continued tersely. 'Don't ask me for the registration number – I didn't get it – we were intent on saving our lives. Here is where I stood.'

'And no shock wave, you said?'

'Exactly. Look at the garden railings opposite. Not a scratch on them. *All* the blast went *one* way – into the building. From what I've seen of photos of IRA bomb damage the blast flies in all directions.'

'That is true. Excuse me. I'll want to see you later.'

'When you're ready . . .'

Newman walked rapidly back to where Howard was escorting the last three staff members into a taxi. Monica was still standing on the pavement.

'I'm going to call Tweed from a phone box in Baker Street Station,' Newman said, hardly pausing.

'I'll come with you,' Howard decided.

'Me too,' Monica said. 'There's something Tweed should know. We might just have a link.'

'Tweed here, Bob,' the familiar voice responded when Newman had dialled Tresillian Manor.

Tweed listened in silence as Newman reported concisely the events leading up to the catastrophe. Monica was squeezed into the box with him. Howard stood outside, erect, hands clasped behind his back, looking none too pleased at being excluded.

'Any casualties?' Tweed asked at one stage, expressed relief at the news. He listened as Newman told him about the visit of Joel Dyson two days earlier. Newman then handed the phone to Monica who explained that no one had seen the film or listened to the tape and that both had been still in the safe when the building was wrecked. Tweed asked to speak to Newman again.

'Bob, I'm speaking from Cornwall, as you know, so I'm phrasing this carefully. The phone doesn't appear to be bugged, but still. Now! Do you remember – no names – a

36

place down here we once stayed at overnight?'

'Yes.'

'Drive down to the same place as soon as you can. Make sure you're not followed.'

'For Pete's sake, I'd know . . .'

'*Make sure!* Now put Howard on the line. Tell him I am short of time.'

'Wherever you are I want you back in London quickly . . .' Howard began.

'No! Now listen to me and don't argue. You'll need a fresh base . . .'

'There's that concrete horror down at Waterloo . . .'

Howard was referring to what the public thought was the new HQ of the SIS. Pictures had appeared of it in the press but it was purely for low-level admin.

'I said listen to me!' Tweed snapped. 'I suspect we're up against the most powerful network in the world – and don't ask me to identify them yet. That network is out to exterminate all of us. I'm not sure why yet. You've got to go underground. Move the whole of our staff – and yourself – to the training mansion at Send in Surrey. It's surrounded with large grounds and is well guarded. That is if you value your life. And I'll only phone you at Send.'

'I don't like running . . .'

'We're all running from now on, Howard. Running to survive. Think of the lives of your staff.'

'All right. Send it is. A bit of peace and quiet might be quite a change. What are you going to do?'

'Go underground.'

4

'Lord, it's marvellous to be outside in this fresh air,' Paula said as she walked with Tweed, climbing up the moor.

Below them Tresillian Manor was a miniature house huddled in its bowl. Butler walked a few paces behind. He had insisted on accompanying them for their protection.

Tweed had earlier phoned the police after talking to Cook, who had recovered quickly. She had not been optimistic about an early arrival.

'No good phoning Padstow. The police station's just a cabin and most of the time no one is there. In the phone book they advise phoning Launceston but I think your best bet is Exeter. That's a real headquarters.'

Tweed had phoned Exeter. He had sensed the inspector's shock at the other end when he'd given details of the massacre waiting for him.

'Never 'ad anything like that. Might be best if I called Lunnon.'

'Just so long as someone gets here fast,' Tweed had snapped and put down the phone.

The ground was hard, ribbed with rocks, covered here and there with gorse. As they climbed higher Paula pointed to a rocky eminence rearing up in the distance from the shallow bleak moor surrounding its base.

'That's High Tor. I once climbed—' She broke off. 'I wonder who that is? There's a man on a horse at the summit of the tor.'

Tweed looked up. Too far away even to guess at what he

looked like, the horseman remained stationary for a brief interval and Tweed had the impression he was studying them through field-glasses. Then he was gone.

'Saw you, mate,' Butler said with unconcealed satisfaction.

Tweed and Paula swung round. Butler was holding a small slim monocular glass, another sophisticated device created in the basement at Park Crescent. It operated like a high-powered telescope.

'A big chap,' Butler continued. 'Wearing a deerstalker hat. That's all I observed before he vanished.'

'You really are a wizard,' Paula commented. 'The equipment concealed among your clothes.'

She turned round, started walking, stopped and grabbed Tweed by the arm.

'Up there, midway down High Tor. I saw the sunlight flash off something. More binoculars.'

'That horseman again,' Tweed suggested.

'No, it's someone else. Look at the bottom of the tor.'

On the level, a long way below the summit, a horseman was riding off at a furious gallop. Tweed frowned as Butler came alongside them, Walther in his right hand.

'This is sinister,' Tweed said. 'We have the massacre at the manor, which I'm convinced was supposed to include us. The killer was probably instructed to wipe out the whole lunch party without knowing his targets – with the exception of Julius Amberg. And now we are under surveillance. Then there was the Park Crescent bomb.'

'I can't see any one outfit – however large and well organized – synchronizing both atrocities so close together. Not one in London and the other in Cornwall. Amberg only phoned you this morning,' Paula reminded him.

'Except that is what appears to have happened,' Tweed rejoined.

39

'A motorcade is approaching the manor,' Butler warned.

They all turned round and looked down on the distant road snaking over the moor towards the entrance. Three police cars and one private car leading the procession.

'Better get back,' Tweed said. He looked at Paula. 'How are you feeling now?'

'Tons better.' She patted her stomach. 'All's well. That dried toast Cook made me was just what I needed.

'That's a terrible thing which happened at Park Crescent,' she went on as they hurried back down the sandy track. 'At least no one was injured or killed. I don't understand what's going on.'

'A wholesale and frighteningly professional attempt to wipe us all out. And I have only two clues as to who is behind this extermination campaign.'

'Which are?' Paula asked, not expecting Tweed to tell her.

'The fact that so few people know the location of our HQ, that so few knew we were due to arrive at Tresillian Manor. Those go together. The other clue is Joel Dyson . . .'

He stopped speaking as they neared the entrance and out of the front of the private car, a Volvo station wagon, a tall, lean and lanky figure stepped. The last man on earth Tweed wanted to meet at this juncture.

'No one mentions the Park Crescent outrage,' he warned. 'Not unless someone else mentions it first. We don't know about it.'

'What's the matter?' Paula enquired.

'Don't you recognize him? That's our old friend and my sparring partner, Chief Inspector Roy Buchanan of the Yard.'

*   *   *

'Tweed. Miss Grey.' Buchanan was formal in his greeting. As though we were mere acquaintances, Paula thought. 'And who, may I ask, is this?' Buchanan demanded.

'You just did,' Tweed told him in a neutral tone. 'Harry Butler, one of my staff. There are two more inside. Pete Nield and Philip Cardon – guarding the place and looking after the staff of four, who are in a state of shock. It's a blood bath,' he warned.

'Which is why I flew down here in a helicopter. At the request of the Commissioner.'

What's going on? Tweed wondered. The Commissioner of Police. As high up as you could go. Why? Buchanan was a calm and highly efficient detective. Detached in manner, his thick brown hair was neatly trimmed, as was his moustache. His grey eyes were alert and shrewd. He took charge immediately.

'Let's walk up the drive, give me a chance to get an idea of the surroundings. What were you doing out on the moor?' He asked suddenly as they neared the manor, followed by the cars. A typical thrusting question aimed at catching off guard Buchanan's target.

'We went for a walk to get the atmosphere of what's inside there out of our minds,' Paula replied.

'I was addressing Tweed.'

'Same answer,' Tweed said.

'I gather from what you told Exeter,' Buchanan continued, 'this Swiss banker, Julius Amberg, invited you down to lunch and you arrived late. I spoke to Exeter myself before boarding the helicopter at Battersea.'

'You gathered correctly,' Tweed replied.

'Look, Tweed, I understand there are eight bodies inside the mansion, shot to death . . .'

'Seven. The butler was stabbed.'

'A detail. You're answering questions like a suspect . . .'

'A detail!' Paula burst out. 'It wasn't a detail to Mounce the butler. It was his life. In his forties, I'd guess.'

41

Tweed smiled to himself. Paula had vented her indignation to give him time to cope with Buchanan.

'Possibly not the best way of phrasing it,' Buchanan agreed. 'But this is a murder investigation.'

'Why has the Commissioner intervened?' Tweed snapped, using Buchanan's surprise question tactic against him.

'Well . . .' Buchanan was thrown off balance. 'First there is the scale of the crime. Then an important foreigner is involved. Amberg was a member of the BIS which meets in Basle. The Bank for International Settlements.'

'We *are* aware of what the initials stand for,' Paula told him drily.

'Is that your only explanation for this unprecedented intervention of the Commissioner?' Tweed pressed.

'It's the only one you're going to get,' Buchanan snapped.

He paused. Paula guessed he was annoyed at losing his cool. He stood staring at the manor, with its curved Dutch-style gables surmounting the towers at either end. He studied the large window behind which was located the Great Hall. The grey, mellow stone and the mullion windows showed up at their best in the sunlight.

'It's beautiful,' Buchanan remarked and Tweed recalled that one of his interests was architecture. 'To think such a tragedy should take place in such an ideal setting. Who owns it?' he asked suddenly. 'Amberg?'

'No. A man called Gaunt. The locals call him Squire Gaunt. He's rented it to Amberg before,' Paula replied.

'How do you know that?' Buchanan demanded.

They were walking again. As they approached the mansion Philip Cardon came out of the front door, waited for them on the terrace.

A small well-built man of thirty, Cardon was the most recent recruit to join the SIS. Clean-shaven, he had an amiable expression. An expert linguist, he had penetrated

42

the inner fastnesses of China, speaking Cantonese and passing for a native.

'That's Philip Cardon,' Tweed remarked.

'I asked you how you knew this Squire Gaunt owns this little jewel,' Buchanan persisted.

'Because Julius Amberg told me,' Paula replied. 'That was just before lunch was served, the lunch the poor devils never got a chance to sample.'

'Wait a minute.' Buchanan paused at the foot of the steps leading up to the terrace. '*You* were here before this massacre took place? I understood you all turned up later.'

'You understood wrong,' she rapped back. 'And can we go inside before I explain? It's cold out here.'

'Yes. And you've got a lot of explaining to do,' Buchanan informed her grimly.

An hour later Buchanan had taken separate statements from Paula and then Tweed. Scene of the Crime teams were still swarming over the manor, mainly in the dining-room. A doctor who had arrived with them had officially pronounced that all eight corpses *were* corpses. Photographers and fingerprint men were still busy with their different tasks.

Cook had supplied umpteen cups of tea, secretly grumbling to Tweed at the amount of sugar they put in a cup.

'It's bad for them. Don't they know anything?'

'Only their own jobs,' Tweed had replied wearily.

Buchanan's interrogations had been intensive. At the end he felt sure Tweed and Paula were concealing information but he realized he'd never break them. On each he sprang his bad news near the end of the interrogation.

'Miss Grey, something strange is going on.'

'It most certainly is.'

'I have grim tidings from London. Your headquarters at

Park Crescent has been totally destroyed by the most massive bomb. Not a stone left standing.'

He waited. She saw the trap and nodded her head. Crossing her shapely legs she responded.

'Isn't it dreadful?'

'I'd have expected you to ask whether there were serious casualties.'

'Oh, we know all about it – and no one was even injured, thank heavens. Bob Newman happened to be talking to Monica in Tweed's office. They noticed the Espace parked outside and evacuated the building just in time.'

'And how do you come to know that?' Buchanan asked in his most persuasive tone.

'Because Bob – Newman – phoned the news to us.'

'He knew you were down here, then?'

'Only because Monica told him. She had the phone number of Tresillian Manor and Bob phoned in the hope we were still here.'

'You do realize,' Buchanan said, bearing down on her, 'that the only explanation of the two outrages – the massacre here which might have included you as victims and the bomb outrage at Park Crescent – suggests someone is trying to exterminate the SIS? Now who would want to do that?'

'I wish to God we knew,' she said fervently. 'No idea.'

'I see.' He sounded as though he didn't believe her. 'And you were the only one who saw the mass murderer. The fake postman. If only you'd seen his face.'

'He was too far away. I knew – I thought – it was a postman because of his blue uniform ribbed with red. And the sun flashed off his badge, as I told you. Plus the satchel perched on his front carrier.'

'Which undoubtedly hid the machine-pistol he used. I find it difficult to believe that when you were inside the toilet you didn't hear the shots.'

44

'It's a heavy door. The door into the dining-room is also heavy, assuming he closed it.'

'Can we try an experiment . . .?'

Buchanan escorted her out of the study, gave instructions to one of his detectives armed with an automatic, warned everyone what was going to happen. He then accompanied Paula to the large toilet and closed the door. Mischievously, Paula sat on the closed oak lid of the toilet.

'Let's do it properly.'

She had omitted to tell him she had been sick and had the satisfaction of seeing Buchanan look embarrassed for the first time. They waited. After a short interval someone tapped on the outside of the door which Buchanan opened.

'What is it, Selsdon?'

'I've just done it, sir. Fired six shots out of the dining-room window – with the door into the hall open.'

'Thank you. Go and do something useful.'

'I never heard a thing,' Paula said as they re-entered the hall.

'I must admit neither did I . . .'

Buchanan's interview – even longer – with Tweed produced no fresh information, which Buchanan found frustrating. He said as much to Tweed.

'I find this unconvincing and unsatisfactory.'

'The first is your suspicious mind, the second I agree with completely. I've answered all your questions.'

Which was true. But Tweed had omitted certain data.

No reference to Joel Dyson's visit to Park Crescent.

No reference to a film.

No reference to a tape, stored in the safe with the film, a safe now buried under tons of rubble. In the study, alone with Tweed, Buchanan stood leaning against a table, jangling loose change in his trouser pocket.

'I may want to talk to you again.' His manner was casual

45

and Tweed, knowing Buchanan's ploy of throwing a witness off balance at the end of an interview, braced himself for the unexpected. 'Incidentally,' Buchanan continued, 'the whole country knows you're down here.'

'How could they possibly know that?' Tweed asked quietly.

'Your presence here has been linked with the massacre. In a stop-press item in a London evening paper. Reported also on the radio and in a TV newsflash. You were named – Deputy Director Tweed of the SIS, et cetera.'

'I still don't understand,' Tweed persisted.

'Neither did I, so just before flying down here I phoned the paper, the BBC and ITV news editors. They all told me the same thing. An anonymous caller contacted all three, told them to check with the Exeter police. Reporting the massacre all the media were careful to use the phrase "it is strongly rumoured that eight people have been shot to death at Tresillian Manor", et cetera. Then your rumoured presence was reported.'

'I find this extremely sinister. Only the killer could have had that information. But why broadcast the crime?'

'You tell me,' Buchanan said, again sounding frustrated. 'You're going back to London?' he went on. 'Where will you operate from now?'

'You can try my flat in Walpole Street. It's up to Howard to answer the second question.'

'That's it, then. A fleet of ambulances has arrived to take away the bodies. The dead guests' cars have been driven away for examination. Any idea where I can contact this chap Gaunt?'

'None at all,' Tweed replied as they went into the hall.

Two white-coated men were carrying out a covered body on a stretcher towards the front door. The man at the rear called out over his shoulder.

'This is the last one from the abattoir back there.'

'The forensic team seems to have finished the job,'

Buchanan remarked. 'I understand they've gone, so I think I'll be gone too. I'll be up half the night when I get back. What about you?'

'We'll try and persuade that nice cook to make us some tea. Sustenance to fuel us for our trip away from here.'

'As you wish.'

Paula came out of the Great Hall at that moment. Buchanan looked at both of them, didn't make any effort to shake hands and walked out.

'I don't think he likes us much,' Paula observed.

They went to the door and watched Buchanan driving off followed by the last patrol car. Tweed put an arm round her shoulders and briefly told her what Buchanan had just told him. Paula was stunned.

'On the radio, TV and in the paper! I feel frightened. Is this place a death-trap?'

'We'll be out of here soon.'

They had wandered out on to the terrace and as the cars' engines faded the silence of the moor descended on them. It was late afternoon and would be dark within the hour. Paula was taking in deep breaths of fresh air to cope with what Tweed had told her. After a few minutes they were going inside when she grasped Tweed's arm.

'Listen . . . Horses' hooves.'

They waited as the clip-clop came closer. Two riders appeared, approaching the manor along the drive – a man and a woman. Tweed went back out on to the terrace as the newcomers halted at the foot of the steps. The man, large and with a hawklike face beneath a deerstalker, barked out his question.

'Who the blazes are you?'

'I might ask you the same question,' Tweed snapped back.

'I'm Gregory Gaunt. And I just happen to own this damned place.'

47

5

'Welcome to Tresillian Manor,' Gaunt said breezily. He had accompanied the girl to leave the horses in a stable on the left side of the house. 'I thought Amberg and all his guests would have pushed off by now. It was a flying visit from Zurich.'

'Stop here a moment, please,' Tweed said as they reached the terrace. 'There's something you should know before you go inside. You're in for a ghastly shock.'

'Shock? What kind of shock?' boomed Gaunt. 'A burglary? Is that it? Spit it out, man.'

Gaunt was six feet tall, heavily built, muscular and about forty, Tweed estimated. His complexion was weather-beaten under thick sandy hair and he seemed to be a man of the great outdoors. Under prominent brows his eyes were swift-moving and intelligent. His manner was dominant without being domineering. Tweed sensed he was in the presence of a strong personality and he could see why the locals called him 'Squire'.

'I'm forgetting someone,' Gaunt went on. 'This is my girl friend, Jennie Blade. Say hello, Jennie.'

'Greg, I don't need a prompter,' Jennie drawled. 'Hello, everyone. Who is that peach of a man who just came out?'

It was Philip Cardon, joining Butler and Nield, who had heard voices. Cardon smiled at her as Tweed made introductions. Paula and Jennie eyed each other up and down like two cats warily summing up the opposition. Jennie switched her gaze back to Cardon.

'Life is looking up, Greg – becoming interesting again.'

In her late twenties, Jennie was attractive. Five feet six tall, her riding outfit emphasized her superb figure. Her slim legs were encased in jodhpurs. Golden hair fell in smooth locks to her shoulders. Her face was triangular – a wide forehead, thick gold brows and a good bone structure tapering to a pointed chin below full red lips. Strong competition, Paula admitted to herself.

Bearing in mind the girl's presence, Tweed gave a terse account of the tragedy. He explained that Amberg had invited them down to lunch because he had been a friend of Tweed's. He omitted mentioning that Paula had witnessed the aftermath.

'I don't believe this,' Gaunt rumbled. 'Police trampling all over my property. And why should anyone want to harm Julius, a Swiss banker? I'm going to see for myself.'

'I'll come with you,' said Jennie.

Cardon stopped her. He took her arm as Gaunt marched inside. She looked at him through half-closed eyes.

'Better not,' Cardon advised her.

'I'll be all right if you'll come with me,' she replied, openly flirting with him.

'Glad to be of service,' Cardon agreed, who seemed not averse to accompanying her anywhere.

Tweed slipped in ahead of them. He found Gaunt standing very erect and still in the dining-room. The tablecloth, stained with pools of blood, was still there, to say nothing of the dark brown lakes on the ceiling and carpet.

'My God! Looks as though you were right.'

'I'd hardly make it up,' Tweed responded. 'And Amberg's face had been splashed with acid after being shot dead. He looked like a skull.'

He watched Gaunt's reaction but no emotion showed on the Squire's face. He walked slowly to the head of the table and stood looking down where Amberg had lain over the broken chair.

'Cost me a bloody fortune to clean up this place,' Gaunt rasped. 'And there are holes in the panelling. That will have to be attended to. Damned expensive.'

'Greg is money-conscious,' Jennie said as though she felt it diplomatic to explain Gaunt's apparent mercenary attitude. 'It's understandable. Keeping up a place like this these days is a drain on his purse.'

'Do you mind not discussing my personal affairs with a stranger,' Gaunt rapped at her. He looked at Tweed. 'I return from a day away which I enjoyed and find this. I still can't take it in.'

'How did you spend the day?' Tweed enquired.

'None of your business. You sound like a policeman.'

'*Greg!*' Jennie spoke sharply. 'It was a polite question.' She turned to Tweed. 'He has a small cottage at Five Lanes on the edge of the moor. The arrangement was we'd stay away from here from eight in the morning until now. Amberg holds – held – business meetings here.'

'Do belt up, Jennie,' Gaunt said with less force. 'You know something, Tweed? I don't feel like staying in here. Let's repair to the living-room. Thank God the staff survived. It's hell getting fresh servants.'

'He won't admit it,' Jennie whispered to Tweed as Gaunt marched out, 'but he's in a state of shock. Would you please join us for some tea? If Cook is up to it. I'll go and have a word, maybe give her a hand.'

'I'll come too,' Paula said.

She glanced at Tweed who was gazing out of the window into the distance. The light was fading and night fell over the drive like a menacing shadow. Knowing they were hemmed in by the desolate moor, Paula shivered.

'Where are you people off to when you leave?' enquired Gaunt.

They had just devoured a huge tea of sandwiches and

home-made fruit cake. They sat in the living-room on couches and armchairs. Gaunt faced Tweed and Paula while Cardon sat on a couch next to Jennie. Butler and Nield had chosen chairs facing the windows which they watched constantly – no one had closed the curtains.

'London,' Tweed lied smoothly. 'There shouldn't be a lot of traffic on the roads at this hour.'

'I'd have expected you to stay somewhere down here until the morning,' Gaunt persisted.

No one had mentioned the bomb outrage at Park Crescent to their host. He reached for a box of cigars and, when everyone refused, lit one for himself. It was quite a ritual: trimming the tip off, after rolling it close to his ear, then using a match to ignite it. He took a deep puff and sighed with enjoyment.

'That's better. After today. Tweed, I have been wondering what happened to all the cars Amberg and his guests must have arrived in. Amberg always had a Roller.'

'The police drove them away for further examination.'

'Fat lot of use that will do them.'

'It's surprising what forensic specialists can detect.'

'You really do sound like a policeman.' Gaunt's eyes gleamed as though scoring a bull. 'What do you do for a living?'

'I'm an insurance negotiator.'

'Insurance!' Gaunt jumped up. 'Oh my God! I'll bet my insurance doesn't cover damage caused by mass murder.'

'Depends on how the policy is worded,' Tweed said in a soothing tone.

'Blast it, Greg!' Jennie raged. 'Stop being so obsessed with money. You should be worried about how this terrible experience has affected the staff.'

'It hasn't,' Tweed assured her. 'The police brought a doctor with their team. He examined your staff, said all they'd suffer from were temporary headaches. Celia, the new girl, was tapped only lightly on the head.' He saw

51

Paula watching him, startled by his recent slip of the tongue. He covered it, looking at Gaunt. 'The reason I know about the forensic business is the chief inspector – a man called Buchanan – explained to me why they needed the cars. Incidentally, he said he would need to talk to you.'

'He won't be welcome, I can tell you that.'

'You said,' Jennie began, to ease the tension, addressing Tweed, 'that this fake postman delivered a parcel which poor Mounce was still clutching when the police examined him. I wonder what it contained?'

'A technician opened the package outside in the garden,' Tweed told her. 'You'll never guess what it contained. A box of Sprüngli truffle chocolates.'

'I find that rather beastly,' Jennie commented.

'Sprüngli?' repeated Gaunt, who had sat down again. 'A firm in Zurich – where Amberg came from.'

'I don't think Buchanan overlooked that,' Tweed remarked drily. Checking his watch, he stood up. 'I think we really ought to be going. Thank you for your hospitality.'

'It was nothing,' Gaunt said gruffly.

Jennie looked at Cardon. 'I live in Padstow in a rented flat. Here is a card with my phone number. It's a strange port – located on the estuary of the River Camel. Greg and I go there quite often. At this time of the year it's so gloriously quiet and hidden away. If you're down that way do come and see me, won't you?'

Tweed kept a blank expression. Padstow was their real destination.

The door to the hall had been left ajar as though Gaunt was expecting a phone call. The bell began ringing at that moment. Gaunt walked briskly out of the room. He was back again, almost at once, looking rather annoyed.

'It's someone for you, Tweed. Wouldn't give a name. People are so rude these days. No manners at all . . .'

Tweed closed the door behind him, crossed the hall, picked up the phone. All the staff had gone home – Jennie had explained they arrived early in the morning and cycled home again in the evening.

'Tweed here.'

'Hoped I might catch you,' the familiar voice said, deadpan. 'I'm back at the Yard – flew to London from St Mawgan Airport. Exeter has been on the line. I wondered how someone got hold of a postman's outfit. Now we know.' Buchanan paused, waited.

'All right, you want me to ask how. So – how?'

'They stole the uniform of the genuine postman from his cottage at Five Lanes.' He paused. 'They've just found his body, throat slashed open from ear to ear.'

6

Tweed drove the Ford Escort with headlights undipped as he followed the lonely road in pitch darkness across the moor, heading back to the A30. Paula, acting as navigator, sat beside him while Cardon was alone in the back. Behind them Nield, driving the Sierra, had Butler sitting alongside him. He used the red lights of the Escort to warn him of oncoming bends. His own headlights were dipped to avoid a blinding glare in Tweed's rear-view mirror.

'Why are we going to Padstow?' Paula asked.

'To go underground until I've identified the enemy.'

'Not like you to run,' she probed.

'A tactical retreat. We may be up against the most

53

powerful and dangerous enemy we've ever confronted.'

'What makes you think that?'

'First, Amberg begs me to join him at Tresillian Manor. With a lot of protection. Maybe we were the targets for the killer as much as he was.'

'And second?'

'Within a short time of the massacre a massive bomb destroys Park Crescent. Diabolical synchronization?'

'Not plausible,' she argued. 'I still maintain that no one could have timed the two events so close together.'

'I suspect the whole plot was triggered off by the arrival of Joel Dyson two days ago from the States. That conjures up a very powerful network with a long reach. Also, how many people knew the location of SIS HQ? The top-flight security services in Europe – and America.'

'You make it frightening,' Paula commented.

'You should be frightened. It must take a vast network to organize all that. Which is why we're spending a day or two in Padstow. Right off the beaten track.'

'So it could be unfortunate,' Cardon suggested, 'that by chance Jennie Blade lives in Padstow.'

'It doesn't help,' Tweed agreed, 'but I've booked rooms at the Metropole – which is in a strategic location. I stopped there overnight with Newman a few years ago.'

'And Philip,' Paula teased Cardon, 'you seem to have fallen for the golden lovely.'

'Fooled you, didn't I?' Cardon chuckled. 'She was pretending to take a fancy to me, that she thinks I'm the best thing since sliced bread. I wondered immediately: "What's this girl really after?"'

'Didn't know you were a cynic about women.'

'Not a cynic,' Cardon told her cheerfully. 'Just a realist. Are you offended?'

'Not in the least. Now I think you've got your feet on the ground. And what on earth is this ahead of us?'

Tweed had slowed. In his headlights red and white cones

barred the way with a large notice. It carried the word DIVERSION and an arrow pointing to the right up a narrow lane. It was raining now and between the wipers he had set in motion Tweed saw men in yellow oilskins and peaked caps. A burly individual waved a red lamp and walked towards the driver's side of the car as Tweed stopped, keeping the engine running. In the back Cardon had his Walther in his right hand, inside his windcheater.

'Sorry, buddy,' the burly man with the lamp shouted as he came closer. 'There's been a multiple pile-up on the A30. Go this route and you're back on the highway a short way to the west . . .'

Accent and language were muffled American, Tweed noted.

'Tweed,' Paula whispered, 'I've checked the map and the only turn-off to the right is a dead end. That is, before we reach the A30. The lane he's diverting us to leads close to another tor with a stone quarry close by.'

'Could I see some identification?' Tweed asked through his open window.

'What the bloody hell for?' The man's face turned ugly. He was reaching inside his slicker as he went on. 'You can't get through . . .'

'Don't do it!' Paula warned.

Her Browning automatic was pointed past Tweed at the man outside. He withdrew his hand as though he'd burnt it. He was looking uncertain and then turned to signal to the other men when Tweed reacted.

Ramming his foot down, he shot forward, scattering cones like ninepins. Men jumped out of the way and a missile of some sort landed on the bonnet, burst, spread a light grey-coloured vapour.

'Tear-gas!' Tweed snapped.

He closed his window, driving with one hand, maintaining his speed. A glance in his rear-view mirror showed him the Sierra roaring after him. He heard two reports.

55

Shots had been fired. Nothing hit his vehicle. A quick second glance in the mirror showed him the Sierra rocketing up behind him: no apparent damage.

'Thank you, Paula,' Tweed said. 'I was suspicious but you confirmed it. A multiple pile-up? On the A30 in February and at this time of night? And a road crew with an American foreman? The whole set-up was phoney, stank to high heaven.'

'So what had they waiting for us up at that dead end?' Paula mused.

'A *dead* end – for all of us,' Cardon suggested.

'You have a macabre sense of humour. It doesn't bear contemplating – out in the middle of that moor . . .'

She started checking her map again. Tweed was driving at speed, lights undipped, swerving round corners. He was anxious to reach the main road.

'What worries me,' he said, 'is how did that gang of thugs know we would be travelling along that road at this hour? Again it suggests a powerful, well-organized network. I get the feeling our every move is being monitored.'

'We're close to the A30,' Paula warned. 'As to how they could know where we were – Buchanan told us your presence down here was reported by all the media. They could have flown down from London to St Mawgan Airport – arranging in advance for hire cars to be waiting. And this is where they stole the equipment from . . .'

Tweed had slowed down, paused at the T-junction on to the A30 to look both ways. Yards to the left, road repair equipment was stacked on a verge, flashing lights illuminating cones and other material. Tweed drove out, turned right to the west, his headlights showing a great belt of the road descending a long hill. No other traffic in sight. The rain had stopped but the road surface gleamed in the moonlight.

'You could be right, Paula,' he remarked. 'There would be time for the opposition to fly down from London. But these are people who can move like lightning. I still find it puzzling why the anonymous call was made to the media. I'm going to pull in here, have a word with Pete Nield, make sure they're both all right.'

Paula saw a lay-by was coming up. Tweed signalled, pulled off the main road into it. He stopped, still keeping his engine running as the Sierra drew in behind him. It was Butler who got out of the car, used a torch to check the side of his vehicle, then walked up to Tweed who had lowered his window.

'You handled that well, Chief,' he commented. 'Nothing like a reception committee to welcome us to Cornwall.'

'I heard shots,' Tweed replied.

'You did. One bullet went wide. The other ricocheted off the side of the Sierra. I just found the point where it dented the metal. Maybe time we moved on . . .'

They were driving again through the night along the deserted A30 when Paula made her suggestion.

'There are only three people who could have co-operated with the killer who committed the massacre,' she said.

'Gaunt or Jennie Blade,' Tweed anticipated her. 'And we saw two people on High Tor. But who is the third?'

'Celia Yeo, the young red-headed girl who was helping in the kitchen.'

'Why pick on her?'

'Because I ask questions. After the police doctor had examined the staff he remarked that the one who had got off lightest from being coshed was Celia. Said he was surprised she had become unconscious – so slight was the bruise on her head.'

'Not very conclusive,' Tweed objected.

'There's more. I talked to Cook when Celia was outside in the scullery. Apparently the girl she recently replaced was knocked down by a hit-and-run driver, had both legs broken. Celia turned up at the manor offering her services

57

the following day, which Cook thought was rather odd.'

'Still not sufficient to convince our jovial Chief Inspector, Roy Buchanan,' Tweed persisted.

'There's more still. I had a little chat with Celia on the quiet. She's a mulish type, hard as nails, and has avaricious eyes. That girl would do almost anything for money. And she lives in Five Lanes – where the real postman came from. I think I'll drive over there and talk to her again. Her day off is tomorrow. And I saw her sneak back across the grounds with a scarlet tea towel in her hands. She said she'd hung it out to dry – it was still dripping water. She could have hung it from the branch of a tree at the edge of the estate to signal to the killer – signal to him that Amberg had arrived. I don't think she'd known what was going to happen.'

'Bit of a far-fetched theory,' Tweed commented.

'Hold on, Chief,' Cardon called out. 'Paula has made a pretty solid case for your so-called far-fetched theory.'

'If you say so,' Tweed responded impatiently, concentrating on his driving. 'One thing I insist on, Paula. You're not going back to Bodmin Moor on your own.'

'Maybe Bob Newman will come with me – if he's reached Padstow . . .'

Paula saw why Tweed had referred to the Hotel Metropole's strategic position as soon as they arrived. Perched high up, it looked down on and across the estuary of the River Camel. Gleaming like a sheet of quicksilver by the light of the moon, it appeared to be about a quarter of a mile wide from Padstow to the opposite shore.

Parked outside, in the forecourt in front of the large Victorian building, was Newman's Mercedes 280E. Its owner appeared from inside as Tweed was registering for his party. Newman frowned at Paula, slipped her a sheet of folded paper as he passed her, which she palmed. He walked outside as though he'd never seen them before in his life.

She showed Tweed the note as they travelled up in the lift to their rooms. Tweed had a suite, No. 11, on the first floor, while Paula's double room was on the second.

'Come down and see me within five minutes,' Tweed told Paula after he'd read the note.

Butler and Nield, acting as guards, had rooms close to Paula's. Tweed had requested this at the desk.

'Miss Grey is recovering from a serious illness,' he had informed the receptionist. 'Pneumonia. She might need assistance walking when she leaves her room . . .'

Paula closed her room door. The lights were on, the curtains drawn. She moved swiftly, sensing the urgency in Tweed's order. Opening her case, she threw the lid back, lifted out her favourite navy blue suit, hung it in the wardrobe, hurried back to the lift.

Tweed had a much larger room with a sitting area. He stood in the middle, still wearing his trench coat in spite of the heated atmosphere. Handing her the note, he began pacing like a caged tiger. The note was terse.

Meet me in my car – parked halfway up Station Road. Have phoned H. Very big trouble. H. wants you to call him. Have found safe phone. Bob.

'You said you were ravenous just before we reached here,' Paula reminded him.

'Food will have to wait. I phoned the dining-room. They will serve us later.' His brusque tone softened. 'But you can go straight down to dinner – you've had a pretty rough day.'

'Nothing doing. I'm coming with you.'

'So is Butler . . .'

Outside the hotel an icy breeze blew from the north. As they climbed the hill Paula asked her question.

'Why do they call this Station Road?'

59

'Because at the bottom of the hill behind us is a building which is the old station. Now it's Customs & Excise. The trains don't run here any more. Haven't for years. The line was eliminated long ago. Here we are. You sit next to Bob. Maybe he'll be better company than I am tonight. While I remember, Bob, I'd like to borrow your field glasses.'

Newman drove to the top of the road, turned right down New Street. Lined with two-storey grey stone terrace houses, it made Paula feel they had arrived in old Cornwall. Newman paused, pointed to a wooden cabin set back from the road. No light in the windows.

'Believe it or not, that's the police station. Unmanned. So, if we hit trouble, don't expect any help from the police.'

'Comforting,' Paula commented.

Newman swung right again down St Edmund's Lane, an even narrower and bleaker street at night. It descended steeply and it too was hemmed in on either side with old grey stone terrace houses. No one about, not a soul, and the lighting was dim. Newman paused for a moment, pointed to a gap in the wall to their right with a shadowed pathway leading uphill.

'That's a short cut on foot back to the Metropole.'

'I wouldn't advise going up there after dark,' said Butler, seated next to Tweed.

It was the first thing he'd said since they had entered the car. Paula, feeling edgy, took the remark personally.

'I suppose that was for my benefit. Harry, I'll have you know I *can* take care of myself.'

'I wouldn't go that way at night myself,' Butler told her equably.

Newman drove to the bottom of the lane and Paula leaned forward, anxious to get some idea of Padstow's layout. Turning to the left along a level road, Newman gestured to his right.

'That's a dock beyond the car park with the estuary on

the far side. I'm now driving along a one-way street. If I'd turned right at the bottom of St Edmund's Lane it's two-way traffic. Ahead is the harbour, a complex system. I can show you better in the morning. Tweed, I decided it might be better if I stayed elsewhere as an unknown reserve. I have a room overlooking the harbour in the Old Custom House, the building on your left. It's a very good hotel. And there is your phone box. I have to park a bit further on. See you in the morning?'

'Yes. We'll be walking past your hotel at ten o'clock on the dot. Good night. Take care . . .'

Newman had paused, while Tweed and Paula got out of the car. Butler followed them, crossed to the carpark where he had a clear view of the old-fashioned red phone box. The raw wind hit them as Tweed struggled to haul the door open and Paula dived inside with him. It was with some trepidation that Tweed dialled Howard's number at the Surrey mansion.

'Who is this?' Howard's voice enquired after Tweed had been passed through an operator.

'Tweed. I gather you wanted to talk to—'

'Is that a safe phone?' Howard interrupted, his voice tense.

'It should be. It's a public call box. If you don't mind I won't say where I'm speaking from.'

'Oh, damn that, I don't care. As long as you're well away from London . . .'

'I am . . .'

'Tweed, the situation is desperate, unprecedented. You'll hardly believe what's happening.'

'Try me,' Tweed suggested quietly.

'As you know, our HQ has been totally destroyed by the bomb. But I can't get through to the PM. He seems to have cut himself off from me. Every time I try to reach him some fool of a private secretary feeds me a load of codswallop as to why I can't contact him. But I know the PM is in

Downing Street. The secretary let that slip.'

'I see. Any theory as to why this is happening?'

'Well, the PM is having trouble with Washington. He needs America's support, as you know, over Europe and the Middle East. Washington is being very distant with London.'

'Precisely who in Washington?' Tweed enquired.

'I gather it's the Oval Office. President March himself.'

'Rather a rough diamond, I've heard.'

'Should never have been elected,' Howard stormed. 'Just because he's a powerful orator, talks the language of the people.' He sighed with disgust. 'The people – and some of them he mixes with are hardly out of the top drawer.'

'What you're saying is we've lost the PM's support? Even with this bomb outrage?'

'It would seem so. I can't believe it.' Howard sounded to be in despair. 'I really can't believe it,' he repeated, 'but it's happening.'

'I want you to call Commander Crombie . . .'

'I spoke to him a few minutes ago. At least *he* is talking to me. He said it was too early to be positive, but his experts have found relics of the device which detonated the bomb. It's definitely not IRA, Crombie says. A very sophisticated and advanced mechanism was used – something they've never encountered before. The press will continue to say it was the IRA, and Crombie won't contradict them.'

'He sounds to be moving fast.'

'Something else difficult to believe. Crombie has teams working round the clock on clearing the debris – three shifts every twenty-four hours. I think it's discovery of this new device which has electrified him.'

'Howard, phone Crombie on my behalf. Tell him it is very important to find amid that mountain of rubble my office safe. It contains a film and a tape recording. They

62

could be the key to all that's happening. I'm guessing.'

'You usually guess correctly,' Howard admitted. 'I will make that call to Crombie – mentioning you. What do the film and the tape contain?'

'If I knew that I might know who is masterminding these attacks on us.'

'Could take weeks to find,' Howard warned. 'And then it may be crushed to nothing – or its contents will be.'

'That's what I like about you, Howard – your eternal optimism. Just call Crombie.'

'I've said I will. Have *you* any solid ideas?' Howard pleaded.

'One or two. Give me a little time . . .'

Tweed's expression was grave as he left the box with Paula. Butler strolled across the road to meet them. The alert bodyguard was smiling.

'Cheer up! We'll break this thing sooner or later. Oh, while you were on the phone Newman came back for a moment on foot. Full of apologies. He forgot to mention that Monica took a call from Cord Dillon earlier in the afternoon before the fireworks display. Dillon is somewhere in London.'

Tweed stared. Cord Dillon was Deputy Director of the CIA. A very tough, able man – what was he doing in London at a time like this?

'Dillon wants to talk to you urgently.' He handed Tweed a folded piece of paper. 'Newman gave me that to hand on to you. The number of some London phone box. You can reach Dillon between 9.30 a.m. and 10 a.m. at that number tomorrow morning. Monica said it sounded as though he was keeping under cover. Wouldn't say where he was staying.'

'Let's get back to the Metropole . . .'

Tweed walked beside Paula, told her the gist of his talk with Howard. They turned up St Edmund's Lane. Butler was following several paces behind them, reeling as though

63

he was drunk. His right hand gripped the Walther inside his windcheater as they plodded uphill and took the long way back, ignoring the short cut to the hotel. Paula was relieved: the path which turned off the lane was a tunnel of eerie darkness.

'What on earth is going on?' she asked. 'That business about not being able to reach the PM. I'm scared.'

'With good reason. Interesting that Washington business – and now Dillon turns up out of the blue. My thoughts are turning towards America.'

'Why America? Because of Dillon's arrival?'

'Not entirely. Something rather more sinister.'

'Sorry. Perhaps I'm being rather thick. Probably fatigue. And I do want to drive with Bob Newman back to Bodmin Moor tomorrow to talk again to Celia Yeo. What is it about the States which has suddenly grabbed your attention?'

'America,' Tweed repeated, half to himself, 'where there is so much money and *power*.'

'Power?' Paula queried.

'Work it out for yourself.'

7

Feeling dopey when she woke the following morning in her double bedroom, Paula bathed, dressed for the moor, fixed her face in two minutes and only then pulled back the curtains. She stared at the view in disbelief. Something very weird had happened overnight. The River Camel had disappeared!

She stared at the vast bed of sand, rippled in places, stretching from shore to shore. When she phoned Tweed he said he was just ready for breakfast, so why didn't she come down to the suite?

She was closing her door when another door opened and Pete Nield appeared. He fingered his moustache and grinned.

'Good morning. Just checking to make sure you're not wandering off on your own.'

'Makes me feel like a ruddy prisoner,' she mocked him. She liked Pete. 'I'm on my way to Tweed's suite. Come and join us.'

'What on earth has happened?' she asked as Tweed unlocked his door and ushered her inside. She went over to his extensive bay window which gave a better view. 'The river has vanished.'

'Leaving behind a vast sandbank,' he explained as he joined her. 'There's a very high tidal rise and fall here. The tide is out now.' He pointed to his left through a side window. 'That rocky cliff protruding at the edge of the town blots out a view of the open sea. Straight across from us is Porthilly Cove. No water there at all at the moment. There is a narrow channel which remains along the shore of that weird village over there.'

'Where is that?'

'Place called Rock. A small ferry shuttles back and forth between Padstow and Rock. At low tide – now – the ferry departs from a small cove at the base of the rocky cliff. When the tide rises it departs from the harbour.'

'What a strange place. This is my idea of Cornwall.'

She gazed to her left, beyond Rock towards the invisible Atlantic. The far shore was forbidding. Climbing up steeply was a wilderness of boulders, scrub and heathland. A sterile, inhospitable area. Yet further in past Rock there were green hill slopes undulating against the horizon as the sun shone out of a clear blue sky.

'You haven't heard that tape on the recorder I had hidden in my pocket when I talked to Cook,' Nield pointed out. 'It doesn't add much to what Buchanan later told us.'

'Let's hear it quickly, then get down to breakfast,' Tweed urged.

He stood with Paula staring out at the endless sandbank. Nield placed his small machine on a table, ran through the first part, then pressed the 'play' button.

'I spent time putting her at her ease,' Nield explained. 'Now, listen . . .'

'Cook, can you tell me what you saw when the kitchen door was opened and closed again?' Nield's voice.

'It was an 'orrible shock, I can tell you . . .' Cook's voice quavered, then became firm. 'He was standin' there with this awful gun. A short wide barrel – bit like a piece of drainpipe. He aimed at the floor, something shot out and the place was full of a greyish sort of vapour.'

'The tear-gas,' Nield's voice broke in gently. 'But you probably had a good look at him?'

'Like a nightmare. That woollen hood over 'is 'ead with slits for the eyes. He moved gracefully, like a ballet dancer. But those eyes – without feeling, without any soul. A chill ran down my spine. Those eyes were blank – like a ghoul's eyes.'

'What happened next?' Nield pressed, still gently.

'We're all choking. Tears running down our faces. Then this beast walks straight up to me and 'its me on the 'ead with something. I just dropped to the floor and didn't know what was 'appenin' till I came round . . .'

'That's the relevant part,' Nield said. He switched off the recorder. 'There's more but nothing informative.'

'Interesting that reference to moving with the grace of a ballet dancer,' said Tweed. 'Time for breakfast.' He picked up a copy of the *Daily Telegraph* which had been slipped under his door. 'The late edition. They must fly them down.' He showed them the headline.

66

HUGE IRA BOMB DESTROYS LONDON
BUILDING

'That's not the significant item. I'll show you in the dining-room.' Butler joined them outside and they took the lift to the ground floor. Tweed held on to Paula's arm, keeping up the fiction that she was an invalid.

In the dining-room Tweed sat with Paula at a table with a panoramic view of the harbour over the grey slate rooftops of the small port. After ordering a substantial breakfast of bacon and eggs he folded the paper, handed it to Paula.

'That's the intriguing bit,' he told her, keeping his voice down.

'GHOST' ROADBLOCKS IN WEST COUNTRY
LAST NIGHT

Paula read the text below the headline. The gist was that a series of roadblocks had been established on all the main routes out of Cornwall. Motorists had been stopped and told it was a census to check the amount of traffic passing through. The strange twist was that no police force or council office had any knowledge of them.

'What is this weird business?' she asked Tweed.

'Not reassuring,' Tweed replied quietly. 'They – whoever they are – were looking for *us*. Again it confirms my fear about the extent of the vast network we're up against. To be able to organize something like that so rapidly.' He smiled. 'Enough to put me off my breakfast – but it won't.'

'It's like a noose closing round us,' Paula commented.

'Oh, we'll find a way of eluding them.' Tweed checked his watch. 'I must be at that phone box to call Cord Dillon just after nine thirty.' He glanced across at a distant table where Butler sat with Nield. 'Luckily you'll have some reliable company while I'm away.'

'But I'm coming with you to the phone box,' she insisted.

'Certainly, Paula, I fancy a drive to Bodmin Moor myself,' Newman told her. 'I'd like to get the atmosphere of where this ghastly massacre took place. Odd there's nothing about it in the paper. Meat and drink for the tabloids.'

They were standing outside the phone box while Tweed held the door half open in case someone else tried to use it. Tweed swung round.

'That's something else I find sinister – the absence of any report about the massacre at Tresillian Manor. It looks as though someone has silenced Roy Buchanan – and he's a man not easily silenced.' He looked back the way they had come as Cardon loped towards them, smiling.

'Morning, everyone. What a beautiful day. Sorry to be late but I slept in. I usually do if nothing's happening.'

'Too much *is* happening,' Tweed snapped.

'Bob is taking me for a drive to Bodmin Moor,' Paula reminded Cardon.

'Can I come too?' Cardon asked. 'Butler and Nield are ample guard for Tweed.' He grinned at Newman. 'Carry your bag, sir?'

'As I told you, we're going to interview one of the servant girls who works at Tresillian Manor,' Paula said. 'I think she might not say a word if too many people arrived. But thank you, anyway, Philip.'

'I could stay with the car if you're keeping it out of sight,' Cardon persisted.

'We'll be doing just that,' Paula agreed.

'Take Philip with you,' Tweed ordered. 'I don't like this idea of yours, but as you're being obstinate I'll only let you go if you have two men with you. Now, I must make that phone call . . .'

*   *   *

At the London end the receiver was lifted swiftly when Tweed had dialled the number. He instantly recognized the distinctive American voice that answered.

'Who is this calling?' Dillon demanded.

'Tweed. Monica said you wanted to talk to me urgently.'

'Monica was dead right. Are you OK? I walked to Park Crescent . . . Say, where are you calling from?'

'Public phone box . . .'

'Like me. I said I walked to Park Crescent – saw your building. A hole in the wall. Are you sure you're OK?'

'I wasn't inside when it happened,' Tweed assured him. 'Neither was anyone else. They were warned in the nick of time. Why are you in London?'

'Tweed, I'm on the run. In Washington I'd have ended up on a slab. This is a tough one. Certain people – a small army of professionals – are out to liquidate all of us. They're controlled from the very top. We haven't a hope.'

'Cord, I need to know what it's all about. Up to now I'm in the dark. Shadow-boxing. Give me a lead, for God's sake. Where are you staying?'

'At a crummy little London hotel which I've just left. I can see the entrance from this box. Keep moving is the name of the game. Survival. I called to warn you to do just that – if you want to go on living.'

'Cord, I need data,' Tweed said grimly.

'It's about a guy called Joel Dyson – some film he took, a tape recording he made. That's all I can tell you till we meet some day. If we're both still standing up. Get out of the country, Tweed. One thing I'll give you – the only other American you can trust is a Barton Ives, Special Agent, FBI. He knows it all. I'm on my way. Jesus! I don't even know where I might be safe.'

'Cord.' Tweed spoke with great emphasis. 'Head for Switzerland. For Zurich. Stay at the Hotel Gotthard – same name as the pass south into Italy. It's a three-minute walk from the main railway station.'

'I'll think about it . . .'

'Don't. Just do it. I'll meet you there when I'm able to make the trip.'

'You could be right. Jesus!' Dillon repeated. 'They are arriving at my hotel. I've left my bag inside a locker at one of the main terminals. Got to go now.'

'Cord . . .'

'One more thing, Tweed, then I'm moving. You ever meet a man called Norton, shoot him before he kills you . . . *Norton*. Got it . . .?'

The connection was broken.

8

Ed, a small pock-marked American, dialled the new number for Norton as he stood inside a phone hood in Piccadilly Underground Station. Norton kept constantly on the move, never stayed at the same place for more than one night.

'Who is it?' Norton's abrasive voice demanded.

'It's Ed. I've been staring at wallpaper since we tracked Joel to London Airport.'

'*We?* Bill tracked him to the Swissair flight he boarded for Zurich . . .'

'Well, we're a team . . .'

'You're a schmuck who takes orders from me. And we have more schmucks in Zurich. Guess what happens.'

'No idea,' Ed replied cautiously.

'You always were short of ideas. The people waiting at Zurich Airport lost Joel. Can you believe it?'

'Yes, you just told me . . .'

'Don't get smart-ass with me. I had another team grouped by the entrance to Amberg's Zurcher Kredit Bank in Talstrasse. Guess again.'

'No . . . You really had Zurich sewn up.'

'Wrong again. I *thought* I had Zurich sewn up. So, Joel walks into the Zurcher. Never comes out again. The staff leave, the doors are locked. Still no Joel. You have one guess.'

'Beats me . . .'

'Seems most things do. Joel must have been let out the back entrance – which the schmucks who call themselves operatives didn't know about. You know Zurich. You know Joel. Get out there to Zurich pretty damned fast. Find him. Got it now?'

'Sure. And when I do find him?'

'Goddamnit!' There was a pause and Ed would not have been surprised to hear a snarl. 'I'll tell you what you do . . .' Norton's voice had gone deceptively soft. 'You break his fingers one by one. You break his arms, his legs, until he tells you where he's hidden what we must find fast. And then you snuff him out.'

'Got it . . .'

'I do hope so, Ed,' the soft voice went on. 'For your sake.'

'What about Tweed?' Ed ventured.

'He's still around. Not for long. He's a walking corpse. And when you get to London Airport don't forget to buy Swiss currency.'

'I had thought of that.'

'You amaze me . . .'

The phone went silent.

Tweed was stunned when he left the Padstow phone box and was joined by Butler. Nield waited on the far side of the road. Tweed had never known Dillon be frightened of anyone. So what group could have scared the tough American, made him start running?

'Where is Paula?' he asked.

'She went off with Newman and Cardon towards the harbour. They're collecting the car ready for their drive to Bodmin Moor.'

'I don't like it,' Tweed commented. 'Lord knows what they will run into on that blood-soaked moor . . .'

Newman had led Paula and Cardon to the harbour to show them the complex layout. Paula saw there was an inner harbour full of water, which puzzled her since the tide was out. She stopped to look at a large luxurious cabin cruiser with an array of radar equipment. *Mayflower III*.

'That's cost somebody a bomb,' she remarked.

A gnarled old fisherman sorting out his orange-coloured fishing net near by looked up. Paula smiled at him and he walked over to her.

'Admirin' the Squire's boat? It could sail to Europe in bad weather.'

'The Squire?' Paula queried.

'Yes. Squire Gaunt. Lives on the moor. Comes down 'ere quite often and takes her out for days.'

'To somewhere in Europe?' she asked casually.

'Ah! No one knows. Keeps a tight mouth on his doin's, does the Squire. You'll excuse me, lady. This won't earn a crust of bread. Enjoy yourselves.'

Newman led them back into the car park. He pointed to a single-storey building.

'Harbour Master's office. I enquired there about the tidal rise and fall. Seven point six metres, they told me.'

'That's fantastic.' She did a quick calculation. 'Over twenty feet.'

'I'd say you need to be skilled sailing round here,' Newman commented, leading them along a quay.

72

They reached a narrow footbridge linking one side of the harbour with the other. As they strolled over the white metal bridge Paula stopped, looked down. She realized they were walking over a large lock gate. To her left was the inner harbour full of water, to her right a drop like an abyss to a mudbank. Water trickled through the gate. Only then did she see an outer harbour, exposed to the sea.

It lay to her right and was a basin of mud. Small craft moored to the walls were canted over at a drunken angle. Beyond the closed lock gate on the seaward side a thin channel of water led out of sight towards the ocean. Newman pointed across to the outer jetty enclosing the waterless harbour.

'That's what they call the Pier. When the tide starts coming in you catch the ferry to Rock from some steps on the far side. Now you have to take that coastal path to the cove further out where there is still water.'

Paula saw a flight of steps leading up to a steep path which disappeared behind a new development of flats, directly overlooking the river.

'Wouldn't like to live there,' she remarked. 'No wonder they're all for sale. It must be as lonely as hell.'

'Padstow is pretty much hidden away,' Newman agreed. 'Which is why Tweed has chosen this place to give himself a little time to think. Turn round and you'll see the whole of the little town.'

Paula swung round. Beyond the harbour and the quays a densely packed series of old buildings was stepped up like a giant staircase. Newman checked his watch, looked at Cardon.

'Now I think it's time we headed for Bodmin Moor and bearded this Celia Yeo – if you can do that with a girl. Philip, you sit in the back and keep your eyes open . . .'

*   *   *

There was a little more traffic on the A30 as Newman swooped down a huge slope and then whipped up the other side. The sun shone down on the moor out of a clear blue sky but Paula found it no less hostile. A strong wind beat against the side of the Mercedes 280E as Newman made his suggestion. He perched dark glasses on the bridge of his strong nose, then rammed a black beret on his head.

'Paula, I think you ought to disguise yourself. We've no idea what may face us at Five Lanes. It's possible we won't want to be recognized.'

'A smart idea,' she agreed.

She took a pair of dark glasses from her shoulder-bag. After putting them on she took out a scarf, wrapped it over her raven-black hair and framed her face. Both actions completely altered her normal appearance. Newman grinned.

'You look like a madonna.'

'Just so long as I don't look like the contemporary Madonna. I suppose not – I'm wearing too many clothes.'

'While I'm waiting with the car,' Cardon called out, 'I'll sit hunched up like a midget.'

'You look like a midget normally,' Newman retorted, which was unfair. Cardon stood five feet ten tall and was very muscular.

Paula called out a warning to Newman. 'We're approaching the turn-off to Five Lanes. Celia lives in a cottage called Grey Tears on the outskirts.'

'Let's hope that peculiar name isn't prophetic,' Newman remarked.

Grey Tears was a small single-storey stone dwelling set in a hollow outside the village of Five Lanes. It was almost on the moor and Paul noticed that High Tor reared up as a clear-cut cone against the blue near by. Newman parked the car in another hollow off the road and followed Paula who was lifting a brightly polished knocker carved in the form of a sheep's head and hammering it down.

'That polishing job doesn't look like Celia to me,' she whispered.

The ancient wooden door swung inward to reveal a stooped crone wearing an overall over her flowered dress. Her lively eyes studied the new arrivals.

'We have come by arrangement to see Celia Yeo,' Paula began. 'She told me this was her day off from her job at Tresillian Manor.'

'Not one of we locals will ever work there again. Not after what 'appened yesterday. 'Orrible.' She clamped a worn hand to her lips, the hand of a worker. 'Dearie me, we're not supposed to talk about that to anyone.' She brightened up. 'Still, I 'aven't told you anything, come to think. Celia's gettin' ready to go out.'

'Well, perhaps you wouldn't mind telling her a lady has arrived who'd like a word with her.'

'See what she says . . .'

The door was closed slowly, not rudely, in their faces. Newman, keeping his voice down, stared at Paula.

'Why didn't you mention your name? Just your first name? There are other Paulas in the world, so it wouldn't have positively identified us.'

'Intuition. I have a feeling Celia may be reluctant to talk to me.'

They waited several minutes. Newman paced backward and forward and Paula bit her lip to stop telling him to for God's sake keep still. Then the door opened slowly again. Newman studied Celia. She had an odd-shaped head, almost misshapen. Not a lot of intelligence and her eyes reminded him of a cow's. Celia pulled the door to without closing it and stood outside with them.

'What was it you were wanting, miss?' Sullenly.

'We agreed to meet today, Celia. There are a few questions I'd like to ask you.'

75

The servant girl's eyes opened wider. She stared at Paula like a startled fawn.

'It's you, miss. I never recognize you till you spoke.'

Newman glanced at Paula. Wearing ski pants tucked inside the tops of leather boots and a windcheater, she looked very different from when she had arrived at the Metropole. Celia's eyes swivelled to Newman, gazed at the eyes she couldn't see behind the glasses.

'Who is he?'

'My brother,' Paula said quickly. 'Now, about yesterday. That tea towel – the bright red one I saw you bringing back from so-called drying. It was a signal, wasn't it?'

'Information costs money.' Her manner was suddenly truculent. 'I've no boy friends. No man ever looks twice at *me*. I have to get something out of life, don't I? Like money.'

Newman took out his wallet. He extracted a twenty-pound note, saw her expression, added another one to it. He held the banknotes folded between his fingers.

'First, answer my sister's question, please.'

'You guessed right,' Celia said after a brief hesitation. 'It were a signal. I was paid a hundred pounds just for doin' that after the guests arrived for lunch. Then another . . .'

She stopped in mid-sentence. Celia was dressed for going somewhere. Above her shabby raincoat she wore a bright yellow woollen scarf. Her frizzy hair did nothing to improve her appearance.

'Who paid you to do that?' Paula asked quietly.

'I 'ad nothing to do with those awful murders at the manor!' she burst out. 'So don't you go thinkin' I did.'

'I'm sure you didn't. Who paid you, Celia?' Paula asked again.

'A man . . .' She hesitated. 'Never seen 'im before,' she went on quickly. 'And I've left a pot on cooker for Mrs Pethick. Talkin' about payment, before I says any more I want me money.'

76

Newman handed over the forty pounds to her. She grasped the notes eagerly, shoved them deep into a pocket of her raincoat. Glancing back inside the house, she retreated, opening the heavy door wider.

'Before I tells you more I must attend to pot. It will boil over and then Mrs Pethick will throw me out. I need these lodgings . . .'

The door closed in their faces with a heavy thud. Paula looked at Newman.

'Tweed was right. The massacre was diabolically well organized. And I think she does know who paid her.'

'So do I . . .'

They waited. There were no sounds from inside the small primitive dwelling. Five minutes later – Newman had timed her disappearance by his watch – he voiced the same worry that had entered Paula's head.

'I think she's run off. There's probably a back way – let's check.'

At the rear of the cottage the 'garden' was a miserable vegetable patch. There was also a back door. Closed. Paula took off her glasses, looked towards High Tor, pointed.

'There she is. That flash of yellow. She's headed out across the moor.'

'And,' Newman replied grimly, 'she was on the verge of saying her paymaster was going to pay her another hundred pounds today. God knows what she's walking into. We have to catch her up. Before it's too late . . .'

Newman began running along a track which led towards the base of High Tor. He could still see the flash of yellow scarf in the sunlight. He was surprised at the speed Celia Yeo could keep up as she ran. Behind him Paula followed. When they were out of sight of the cottage Newman grabbed his .38 Smith & Wesson out of the hip holster.

Paula lost sight of Newman as he kept up a marathon pace, descended into a deep gulley. She came to a fork in the path. Which way? She chose the left-hand path, kept on running, her eyes watching the ground which was uneven, making it easy to stumble.

She was nearing High Tor when she realized she had chosen the wrong fork. Newman was racing up the east side of the tor. No sign of Celia. 'Might as well go on, see where this leads to,' she said to herself.

She paused for breath and the ominous silence of the moor descended. A silence she could *hear*. Not even a hint of birdsong. The undulating moor stretched away on all sides, in a series of gorse-covered hillocks, cutting her off from any distant view. Paula shivered and then looked up. The view upwards was even less reassuring.

She was close to the west side of High Tor. Unlike the shallow slopes she had associated with it, at this point from the peak it fell sheer into an abyss. At the base she saw a tumble of huge boulders. She was about to resume running when she caught sight of movement at the summit.

'Oh, God, no!'

She spoke the words aloud. Even at that height Celia was easily identified by the yellow of her scarf. She stood perched on the edge of the fearsome drop. Why? Seeing her – and what happened next – took a matter of seconds.

Celia seemed to push out her stomach and Paula realized there was someone – out of sight – immediately behind her. One moment she was poised there. The next moment she plunged into space, her body cartwheeling in mid-air as she fell and fell and fell. Her scream of terror echoed over the moor as Paula watched in horror. The scream was cut off suddenly. It might have been her imagination, but Paula thought she heard the dreadful thud as her body hit the boulders. The silence of the moor returned like a threat.

Paula ran like mad, heading for the point where Celia had landed. Once, she glanced up briefly, but saw no one.

Whoever had shoved Celia into eternity had kept well hidden. Paula slowed down as she saw what remained of the servant girl.

She was sprawled, face up, over a boulder of massive size. Paula shuddered as she thought of the impact. She kept running until she stood by the boulder. Celia's spine was arched over the rock, her neck twisted at an angle. Blood and brains which had oozed from her skull were already drying in the sun. Without hope, Paula bent down, checked the carotid artery. Nothing.

She was about to close the eyes, staring sightless up at the summit where Celia had started her death plunge, when Paula decided not to touch anything. She wasn't sure at that moment why she took this decision.

She was breathing heavily when she glanced up again at the summit. Newman stood on the edge, staring down. She beckoned to him. Cupping her hands round her mouth, she called up to him.

'Come down, Bob.'

Her words echoed round the moor, recalling that terrible scream.

Newman's legs had never stopped moving since he started to climb High Tor. Boulders and smaller rocks were scattered across the surface above him. He couldn't see the summit and he had long since lost sight of Celia as he followed the twisting path.

As so often happens with climbing heights, he reached the summit suddenly. Flat-topped, it had more rocks – some perilously close to the edge, he saw in time. With the gun still in his hand, he walked slowly to the brink, gazed down. He sucked in his breath at what lay below.

He could see the bright yellow scarf *now*. A small flash of colour on the tiny crumpled form lying across a huge boulder. He was startled to see Paula looking up, her right

79

hand raised as she beckoned, then cupped both hands against her mouth.

'Come down, Bob.'

Her cry was faint but he heard the words clearly. He waved to acknowledge he had heard her. Had Celia thrown herself over? Seemed most unlikely. Newman stood where he was for a moment, looked round. Just behind him was a patch of grey sand. Clearly imprinted in it was the outline of a large fresh footprint. Much larger than Celia's small feet. And, he recalled, she had worn flat-heeled walking shoes. The imprint showed small indentations inside the outline. Studded climbing boots. Celia had been brutally murdered – shoved over the precipice.

The view from the summit of High Tor was panoramic and he could see over the moor for miles in every direction. Newman took a small pair of field-glasses out of his coat pocket, removed his dark glasses, began to scan the moor. He must have missed the murderer by minutes.

Through the lenses he saw how rough the country below was. Deep gullies where a horseman could ride unseen. Stretches of dense gorse which could mask sunken paths. Avoiding the footprint, he walked to the four points of the compass to look down the slopes. No sign of anyone, but there were boulders the size of houses. He decided he must hurry back to join Paula.

9

'I really hated leaving her like that,' Paula said. 'And I wish I'd closed her eyes.'

'Don't worry about it,' Newman said. 'You did the right thing.'

They had hurried back to the car from High Tor and were now driving back towards Padstow along the A30. Cardon stirred in the back.

'I make the body count ten now,' he observed. 'Eight wiped out in the massacre at Tresillian Manor. The postman at Five Lanes. Now this Celia Yeo is number ten.'

'All right,' Paula said edgily. 'Now we know you can add up.' She returned to the previous subject, which was gnawing at her nerves. 'We can't just leave Celia lying out there. Supposing it rains tonight? I know that must sound silly . . .'

'Not at all.' For a moment Newman drove with one hand and put an arm round her, gave her an affectionate squeeze. 'I had two reasons for not touching her. They have an advanced fingerprint technique these days which can sometimes take a print off flesh. You'd have had to touch her eyes to close them. But my main reason is we should leave everything for the police without disturbing anything.'

'When they eventually find her,' she snapped.

'Oh, they're going to find her today. When we get back to Padstow my first job is to call Buchanan from that phone box outside the Old Custom House. I'll disguise my voice. That's another reason for handling it this way – if Buchanan knows we were there when it happened Lord knows how much more time would be wasted while he questions us. Maybe several days. And I suspect time is something Tweed is short of.'

'You've made me feel better,' she said. 'But why are we visiting Tresillian Manor?'

'Can't you guess? I think it might be significant to find out whether Gaunt and Jennie Blade are at the manor. Bearing in mind what happened at High Tor.'

* * *

Spiky hedges lined the section of the side road leading to the manor. At one point where the fake diversion had been set up Paula pointed to an open gate leading on to the moor.

'We told you last night about the ambush, Bob. I think they hid their vehicles inside that gateway.'

'Tweed took a chance crashing through,' Newman commented.

'What would you have done, then?' Paula challenged him.

'Exactly what Tweed did . . .'

No one was about as they entered the drive to the manor. As it came into view and they drove closer Paula noticed the curtains were closed over the dining-room windows. Again they left Cardon to mind the car while Newman and Paula climbed the steps to the terrace, walked into the large square porch. Paula pressed the bell and quickly the door was opened on a heavy chain. Cook peered out. Behind her loomed a shadowy figure.

'Well, what do you want?'

'It's me.' Paula swiftly took off her glasses, whipped off her scarf. 'We talked yesterday.'

'Lordy me, never recognized you.' She released the chain, opened the door wide. 'Cousin Jem is here with his shotgun. Come in and have a good strong cup of tea.'

'That's kind of you. This is my friend, Robert,' she introduced Newman. 'I was hoping Squire Gaunt was here.'

'Been gawn 'ours. Both of 'em. One took the Land-Rover, the other a horse. Not sure which took which. I was out back in kitchen. There's a proper upset 'ere. Two girls never came for work – don't expect as we'll ever see them again, considerin' what 'appened yesterday. I 'as to serve meals in the Great Hall for the master and Miss Blade. The police said they 'ad to seal the dinin' room . . .' It was all pouring out in a torrent as though Cook was glad to talk to

82

someone she could trust. 'But Wendy's turned up – worth the other two of 'em, she is. Police said they'd be comin' back later.'

'Thank you, Cook. I wonder if you'd mind not mentioning our visit? It's a surprise for the Squire. And I don't think we have time for that cup of tea, but thank you.'

'We've been told not to say a word to a soul. I hope Celia's keepin' her mouth shut. She'll be back tomorrow. Don't worry, dear. I won't say a word to anyone about your visit.' Her ruddy face creased into a grin. 'Me, I likes secrets . . .'

Newman said nothing until they were heading back along the drive. The reference to the police returning had alarmed him. He made his remark when they were driving back to the A30.

'That was interesting. Both Gaunt and his girl friend could have been on the moor near High Tor.'

'But not the one in the Land-Rover,' Paula pointed out. 'We'd have heard it. Pity we don't know which one was on horseback . . .'

Newman swung out on to the A30. He was just about to drop out of sight down a steep slope when he saw a car a long way off in his rear-view mirror. A patrol car turning off down the road to Tresillian Manor.

'That was a damn near run thing,' he commented, 'which Wellington remarked after Waterloo. Now, Padstow, here we come, so I can make my phone call to Buchanan. And Cook little knows that poor Celia is keeping her mouth shut,' he said grimly. 'For ever . . .'

Paula waited with Cardon in the Mercedes in the car park opposite the Old Custom House. It was the most impressive building in Padstow, a solid block of an edifice, three storeys high. From the roof projecting up was a large dormer with two closed wooden doors. Paula pointed to it.

'At one time, ages ago, they must have hauled cargo up there from the street.'

'It's ancient history,' Cardon agreed. 'I wonder how Bob is getting on . . .'

Inside the phone box Newman had dialled New Scotland Yard. When the operator answered he spoke quickly through a silk handkerchief stuffed into the mouthpiece.

'Get me Chief Inspector Buchanan and 'urry it up. I'm callin' about a new murder on Bodmin Moor. Don't interrupt me. Just get 'im. I'll call back in five minutes and expect to be put straight through or I'll ring off again.'

He replaced the receiver. It was the only way to ensure Buchanan had no time to do what Newman was certain he'd try to do – trace the call. He looked at his watch and dialled the number again in exactly five minutes.

'I called a few minutes back. Put me on to Buchanan. Now! Or forget it.'

'Chief Inspector Buchanan speaking,' the detached voice answered after a moment. 'Who is this?'

'No names, no sorrow. Just listen and take this down. There's a fresh corpse at the western base of 'Igh Tor outside Five Lanes. Servant girl who worked at the manor. Thrown down from the top. And you'll find a big footprint on summit. I s'pose you likes clues.'

'Thank you. Now if you'll just give me your name . . .'

'You're the detective . . .'

Newman put down the receiver. No time to trace that call – even with the sophisticated equipment they had now which could often pinpoint a location in three minutes. Stuffing the silk handkerchief into his pocket he stared across the car park at his Mercedes. Paula and Cardon had company. Drawn up alongside was a Land-Rover: the occupants Jennie Blade and Gaunt.

* * *

'A hearty welcome to Ye Olde Port of Padstow,' Gaunt had called out jovially as he stopped the vehicle.

'Hello again, Philip,' Jennie greeted Cardon with a fetching smile. 'We must have a drink together sometime. Oh, Paula, I'm ignoring you,' she went on saucily.

'But then I'm not a man,' Paula shot back.

As they climbed out she noted they were both dressed in sheepskins and jodhpurs. So who had been riding the horse? She got out of the car, stretched, glanced in at the back of the Land-Rover. It was crammed with cool bags, coils of rope and a ship's compass. She was wondering whether there was a pair of studded climbing boots hidden under the heap.

Both new arrivals wore gleaming leather riding boots. Gaunt leaned over into the back, grasped hold of a whip. He straightened up, saw Newman coming.

'I'll take the crop. And who have we here? The famous foreign correspondent. Read your book, Newman. Can even remember the title. *Kruger: The Computer Which Failed*. Rattling good stuff. And an international bestseller. Must have made you a mint.'

'It did reasonably well,' Newman said.

He didn't mention that he'd made a fortune out of the book – enough to make him financially independent for life. Jennie grabbed Gaunt by the arm.

'Don't forget the parking ticket. They check the cars here regularly.'

'What are you waiting for, then?' Gaunt asked in his most imperious manner. 'You know where the machine is.'

'I'll come with you,' Paula said.

She hadn't taken to Jennie up to that moment, but Gaunt's treatment of his girl friend aroused her ire. She asked the question as Jennie fed the machine with coins.

'Why do you put up with him?'

'Oh, he's utterly impossible,' Jennie replied. 'Then he turns on the charm and is utterly irresistible. You must

85

have found out,' she continued as they walked back to the Land-Rover, 'that men are not perfect, to say the least.'

'He's pretty damned imperfect, I'd have said.' Paula looked at Jennie as she went on: 'Incidentally, have you two been taking the fresh air this morning – roving round on the moor?'

Was it her imagination or had Jennie's expression frozen for several seconds? Were these two putting on a big act? Jennie lifted her hand to push back a wave of golden hair from her face and glanced sideways at Paula. She made a throwaway gesture with both hands.

'Floating round the back streets of Padstow. His lordship is trying to kid me he'll buy me a flat here. I don't believe a word of it. What's he on about now?'

'Come on!' Gaunt barked. 'I've just invited our friends to a drink. The Old Custom House. Best bar in town.'

'I can't wait,' Jennie said savagely as she attached the ticket. 'Now you can drink all day.'

'Makes me sound like a real boozer,' Gaunt roared. 'One of the great leg-pullers, my Jennie.'

'Your Jennie,' she said sweetly, 'would like to pull a leg off you. And this time you can buy the drinks for a change.'

'She's a joker, a real joker.' Gaunt slapped her on the rump. 'Likes to make out I'm mean and God knows what else. I like a woman I can cross swords with.'

'If I had a sword I'd stick it in you . . .'

Gaunt had gone, waving his arm in a dramatic gesture for everyone to follow him. Cardon joined him inside the entrance on the South Quay side. Newman paused until Paula and Jennie had entered. Beyond the doorway Jennie waited for Newman, looped her arm round his.

'Let's get to know each other better.' She gave him a wicked smile. 'I think you and I would make a wonderful team.'

86

'If you say so,' Newman replied neutrally.

She doesn't waste any bloody time, Paula thought, reverting to her original opinion of Jennie. Paula examined the bar with interest. An inviting place, it had an oak-beamed ceiling, a long bar to her right, and the main area in front of the counter had plenty of tables with comfortable chairs. To her left there was an elevated split-level section behind a wooden railing. Two steps led up to the entrance to the upper level.

The walls were cream-washed stone and the spacious room was illuminated by wall sconces with milky glass shades shaped like bells. A number of customers were already drinking and the atmosphere was warm and welcoming.

'What are you drinking, Paula?' boomed Gaunt. 'And you, Philip,' he said, turning to Cardon. 'And our distinguished foreign correspondent,' he went on booming. 'I suppose you'd like something too, Jennie,' he added as an afterthought. 'This is my round.'

'A gin and tonic,' Jennie snapped. 'If it won't break the bank.'

Her expression suggested she was amazed – that this was the first time Gaunt had stood a round of drinks. Newman frowned at the fair-haired girl behind the counter. He knew she was about to say, 'Your usual, sir?' He did not want Gaunt to know he was staying at the Old Custom House. Quick-witted, the girl kept silent.

'I'll have a Scotch. No water,' Newman decided.

'Make that a double!' Gaunt ordered.

'Very good, Squire...'

That was the first hint Paula had that Gaunt was a well-known customer. She had to admit he cut an impressive figure. Doffing his deerstalker, he turned, spun it across the rail where it landed in a green button-backed armchair in front of a blazing log fire.

He swept off the sheepskin coat he had been wearing

and underneath was clad in a check hacking jacket. Very much the country gentleman, Paula thought. He handed her the gin and tonic she had ordered and Paula passed it to Jennie. He frowned, shrugged his broad shoulders, collected another one, handed the second glass to Paula.

'Thanks,' Jennie whispered to Paula. 'He's in one of his roguish moods. I'd have been left to the last. Cheers!'

'Now, this way, ladies,' Gaunt commanded when they all had their drinks. He grinned impishly at Newman. 'You chaps come too – if you must. But I assure you I can cope with two exceedingly attractive females by myself . . .'

Before Newman could reply Gaunt had marched up the steps, bellowed out cheerful greetings to people at several tables, stood by the armchair where his hat rested and pointed.

'Jennie, you take that chair. Paula, my dear, come and sit by me . . .'

The instructions continued but Jennie outmanoeuvred him. Grabbing Newman by the arm again she led him to one of the green leather couches for two. Gaunt clapped his hand to his high forehead in mock frustration.

'Can't get people organized. I had it all planned so you'd enjoy yourselves. I'm pretty good at assessing who will get on with who.'

'The cool bags are still in the Land-Rover,' Jennie reminded him. 'Shouldn't they be put aboard? And I'm not carting them.'

Gaunt's expression changed. He looked furious. 'Haven't you realized it's like the Arctic out there? They'll be all right for the moment.'

'Aboard?' Paula chipped in. 'You mean aboard your super cabin cruiser, *Mayflower III*? Going somewhere in her?'

Gaunt looked ready to explode. 'Who told you that?' he barked at her. 'About my vessel?'

'One of the locals.' Paula gazed steadily back at him. 'I couldn't even identify him now.'

'That's the trouble with a place like Padstow.' Gaunt had lowered his voice. 'So parochial, so incestuous – they know all your business. I couldn't afford to own a vessel like that,' he went on more breezily. 'I just lease her for short trips. Down to Plymouth or up to Watchet.'

Paula nodded, not believing him. She stared at a shelf above the front of the bar. It was crammed with old suitcases, attaché cases and several ancient trunks. All pre-Second World War. She glanced towards the door.

Tweed was standing there. He gestured for her to join him.

'Excuse me,' said Paula. 'Back in a minute . . .'

'I'm going to phone Howard again,' Tweed told Paula as she joined him outside in the bitter cold. 'I'd like you to hear how he reacts. And there's someone else I want to try and contact afterwards . . . Later, tell me how you got on at Five Lanes. Too much happening at the moment . . .'

Squeezed up against Tweed inside the phone box Paula waited while he dialled the Surrey mansion. She had one ear close to the receiver. The operator put Tweed straight through to Howard. His first words were not reassuring.

'Tweed, I've never known a situation like this. I just don't know what the hell is going on.'

'Tell me why you say that,' Tweed suggested quietly.

'I've been trying to get through to the PM ever since we last talked. No dice. Always before he's taken my calls immediately – even in the middle of a Cabinet meeting.'

'Exactly what happens when you call Downing Street?'

'I get that bloody private secretary. Excuse my swearing, but this is crazy. The secretary always says he's busy, in the House or away. Anywhere except at

89

Downing Street. He said I should cease all operations until I do hear from the PM. Ruddy sauce!'

'And have you – ceased all operations with our people abroad?'

'I damned well have done nothing of the sort. Tweed, I feel like a prisoner, shut up here in this mansion.'

'You are a prisoner – but a safe one so long as you do not venture out,' Tweed warned.

'Have you any leads?' Howard asked desperately. 'You and your team are the only ones on the outside.'

'I might have. Just leave everything to me. Soon I'll be very active. Stay calm . . .'

Tweed stared at Paula after he'd put down the receiver. 'What do you think?'

'Scared. Who has the power to manipulate the PM to this extent?'

'I'm going to make that other call. To Jim Corcoran, our friendly Chief of Security at London Airport. That is, if he is still friendly. I have his private number at the airport.'

He dialled a number and it rang and rang. When it was answered the speaker sounded irritable.

'Corcoran. Who is it?'

'Hello, Jim, this is Tweed. I need your help.'

'That could be difficult. Under the circumstances.' He sounded cautious. 'What is it?'

'What circumstances? Come on, you owe me more than a few.'

'True, Tweed, true.' Corcoran sounded warmer. He paused. 'What can I do for you?'

'Three days ago someone called Joel Dyson – I'll spell out that name . . . may have flown to Zurich. I need confirmation if he did. You could find out by checking the passenger manifests. I can be—'

'Check the passenger manifests! Have you any idea just how long that would take?'

'I was going on to say I can be precise. Three days ago, I

90

said. Sometime in the evening. By Swissair.'

'That's better. I'm not promising anything. I have to use another phone . . .'

'I'll hold on,' Tweed repeated. 'I'm a long way off and it would be difficult to call you back.'

'Hang on, then . . .'

Paula, who had listened in, looked at Tweed, puzzled. He shook his head so she wouldn't speak. He put more coins in the slot. Corcoran was back within minutes.

'I've got it. A Joel Dyson travelled first class to Zurich three days ago. Aboard Flight SR 805. Departed Heathrow 2350 hours, ETA Zurich 0225 hours, local time.'

'I'm grateful. One more favour. This call was never made. You haven't heard from me – whoever puts pressure on you.'

'You know, I have a terrible memory sometimes. Tweed, are you OK?'

'No bones broken, not a scratch on me. I was born lucky.'

'Just make sure you *stay* lucky,' Corcoran said in a grave voice.

10

'I don't understand,' Paula said after they had left the phone box. 'Why these enquiries about Joel Dyson?'

'Let's walk about for a few minutes. There are things I should have told you.'

'Bob and Philip will start wondering what's happened to me . . .'

The words were hardly out of her mouth when Newman

came out of the bar, staring round. Paula waved to him, gave a thumbs-up signal. Newman grinned, relieved to find she was with Tweed. He waved to them and went back into the bar.

Paula led Tweed to the brink of the inner harbour. She pointed to the *Mayflower III*.

'Believe it or not, that belongs to Gaunt. When I mentioned the fact to him in the bar he looked annoyed that I knew, then said he only leased it. I didn't believe him.'

'Interesting. That's a millionaire's vessel.'

'Could Gaunt be a millionaire? He's always talking as though he's at the end of his tether financially.'

'Millionaires often do that. Talk as though they can't afford to spend a penny or a cent. Which gives me an idea I should have thought of. I'll call Monica down at the Surrey mansion and get her to run a check on our Squire Gaunt. Now, Joel Dyson . . .'

Paula led him across the car park as Tweed told her what Newman had reported over the phone from Baker Street Station after the explosion. He gave her all the details of Dyson's rushed visit to Park Crescent, about the film and the tape he had left.

As they walked over the white metal bridge above the barrier holding back the level of the water inside the inner harbour, she realized it wasn't really a lock gate. More like a mobile dam which could be opened and closed.

'I once met Joel Dyson,' she said when Tweed had completed his explanation. 'Bob took me into a pub in London for a drink and Dyson was there. A small man with pouched lips and shifty eyes which didn't miss a thing. He speaks with a well-educated English accent – Bob said afterwards he is British. But then he can suddenly mimic being an American and you'd really think he was a Yank.'

'Nasty piece of work, from what I hear,' Tweed remarked.

'Why did you think Dyson might have flown to Zurich?'

'Because Newman told me about Dyson taking compromising photos of Julius Amberg with another woman – Julius was married – and the fact that he persuaded Dyson Amberg could one day be a powerful friend. Dyson then handed the pics to Amberg. I imagine Dyson sacrificed a big fee from *Der Spiegel* or an American tabloid.'

'So?'

'Dyson made a big song-and-dance to Newman and Monica that he was handing them copies of the film and the tape, keeping the originals for himself. What safer place to hide those originals than in a Swiss bank vault? Specially, at Amberg's Zurcher Kredit Bank.'

'Why narrow his flight to Swissair? Other airlines fly to Zurich.'

'Dyson is an experienced globe-trotter. He'd feel safer aboard a Swiss plane. Especially travelling first class. And their security is first rate.'

'You're right. Incidentally, I was studying Jennie Blade. At the manor when we first saw her I guessed her age at twenty-eight. Now I think she's in her mid-thirties – and very experienced. She intrigues me, does our Jennie. Maybe I'd better get back to the bar or they'll think me rude.'

Paula pointed to the coastal path to the cove where the ferry left for Rock at low tide, then they turned back. Just in time to see Gaunt trooping out of the bar, leading the procession with Newman and Cardon behind him and Jennie bringing up the rear.

'Typical,' Paula said. 'Gaunt treats her like a lapdog. Thank Heaven she can bite back.'

Even as she spoke Jennie, taking long strides, caught up with Gaunt, chattered away to him and then pointed towards Tweed and Paula. She waved and Paula returned the wave as the party approached them.

'You know what you ought to do now, Tweed,' Gaunt boomed out across the car park. 'Take the ferry to Rock.

93

From over there you get the most terrific view of Padstow –
and if you enjoy climbing that's the place for you.'

'We'll consider it,' Tweed replied.

'What do you think of the rowboat?' Jennie asked
gleefully, pointing to the *Mayflower III*.

'Rowboat?' Gaunt roared. 'That's one of the most
powerful cabin cruisers in the world.

'He's sensitive about his toy,' Jennie told Paula.

'All aboard that's comin' aboard,' Gaunt bellowed.

He shinned down a short ladder attached to the harbour
wall, jumped on to the deck, spread both arms wide.

'Isn't she a beauty? I keep her in perfect trim.'

'Like hell you do!' Jennie burst out. She gestured to the
brass rails gleaming in the sun like gold. 'I've spent days
cleaning up this old tub.'

'I think the ferry is a good idea,' Tweed said.

Anything to avoid getting trapped aboard the *Mayflower*. Lord knew where Gaunt would decide to sail them
to once the tide returned – maybe down the estuary and
way out into the Atlantic.

'Have to take the coastal path to the cove, then,' Gaunt
shouted. 'Now it's low tide. Have a good trip . . .'

As Tweed approached the steps leading to the path with
Newman and Paula he saw Butler and Nield appear out of
nowhere. They had accompanied Tweed from the Metropole and had then melted away when he was joined by
Paula.

The group of six was climbing the steep path beyond the
steps when Paula noticed Cardon was still holding the
canvas bag looped over his shoulder from a strap. He had
held it close to his side all the time they had spent in the bar
at the Old Custom House.

'Philip, what goodies have you got inside that bag?' she
asked, walking alongside him.

94

'This and that. Might come in handy. You never know. Remembering what's already happened in peaceful Cornwall. The body count is now ten. Eight at the manor. Celia Yeo. And last night Tweed told me about Buchanan's call to him yesterday. So the real postman was found with his throat cut near Five Lanes. A very hospitable part of the world, Cornwall.'

Ten, Paula thought grimly. *Ten* bodies now – including poor Celia Yeo lying at the foot of High Tor. She must tell Tweed about their 'outing' as soon as she had him on his own.

In the brilliant sunshine they went on climbing out of sight of the town at the bottom of a green slope to their left. The sea to their right was masked by a thick hedge lower down. Paula kept thinking of the estuary as 'the sea' – it didn't seem like a river.

A signpost bearing the legend TO FERRY pointed to a side path descending the side of the hill. The path led to a flight of wide stone steps dropping steeply to a small cove surrounded with abyss-like rock walls. Not realizing it was the clear air, Tweed estimated it was only a two-minute crossing to Rock.

At the bottom of the steps they found themselves inside a tiny cove, hemmed in from the world by sheer granite walls. Paula glanced back as she picked her way to the water's edge over a scatter of ankle-breaking rocks. Under the cliffs at their base were dark deep caves disappearing into black gloom inside their granite alcoves. She didn't like this cove. She found the atmosphere eerie and they were the only people waiting for the approaching ferry.

Tweed raised his binoculars to his eyes, focusing on a tall thin old house halfway up the slope on the Rock shore. There was a series of flashes originating from an upper window.

'Someone across there is sending a signal,' he said grimly.

'It's just the sunlight reflecting off some glass,' Newman said.

'It was a brief Morse code signal with a lamp,' Tweed insisted. 'A series of long and short flashes. I'll tell you why I know later . . .'

The ferry had arrived. Paula wondered how on earth they were expected to board it. The ferry was a small craft capable of carrying only a dozen passengers. The wheel-house was a box-like structure close to the prow – hardly more than twice the size of the phone box Tweed had used outside the Old Custom House. There were only two elderly passengers coming over from Rock.

The boat aimed for the shore prow-first. One of the two tough-looking crew jumped ashore, hauled a plank out of the ferry, balanced it to provide a dry crossing platform to the shore. As the two passengers walked separately and gingerly along the plank the man ashore held one of their hands.

Tweed was the first to board the small vessel. Ignoring the extended helping hand, he climbed the plank nimbly, stepped into the craft. Passengers sat in the open on wooden plank seats with their backs to the gunwales.

Paula sat next to Tweed and studied him. He looked very tense. She knew he hated boats and water and he hadn't taken one of his Dramamines which neutralized sea-sickness.

'Are you all right?' she asked as the boat backed off from the shore.

'We could be in great danger,' Tweed warned Cardon and Newman who sat close to him.

'It's being on the water,' Paula soothed him. 'But it's only a short crossing. A couple of minutes.'

'At least five or more,' Cardon told her.

He unfastened the capacious canvas bag looped over his shoulder. As they proceeded down the narrow channel between sandbank and cliffs he slipped a hand inside and kept it there. Paula wondered what he was holding. A gun?

The two crew were squeezed inside the wheel-house and the skipper stared straight ahead, gripping the wheel. They reached the end of the sandbank and shortly afterwards the skipper swung his wheel. Paula realized there was open water now between them and the beach near Rock. Where do we land? she wondered.

'Quite a view,' Newman commented a minute later.

They had moved out towards Rock into the middle of the estuary. To the north they could see the open Atlantic, beyond two capes. In the exact centre of the oceanic expanse out at sea a huge brutal rock reared up shaped like a volcano. In places the sea glittered dazzlingly where the sun reflected off it. A sharp cold breeze rippled the blue surface.

'Soon be there,' Paula reassured Tweed.

'I hope so,' said Newman, his tone serious.

He leaned back to see past the wheel-house. Coming in from the ocean a large powerboat had suddenly appeared. It was rocketing towards them, its prow high above the water, curving in a wide arc towards them, leaving behind a great white wake stretching out towards the Atlantic. Newman stiffened, slid his hand inside his windcheater, then withdrew his hand empty. He'd never hit a target moving at that speed. They all heard the skipper's words, a mix of anger and anxiety, as he spoke to his mate.

'Bloody maniac. Never seen that boat before . . .'

Paula stiffened, then felt Tweed's hand on her wrist, squeezing it. She looked at him. He sat perfectly still, all signs of tension gone. She thought she detected an expression of satisfaction, but that was impossible. Tweed glanced across at Butler opposite him as the huge projectile thundered down closer on them.

Butler nodded to Cardon. She glanced at Philip. He was nodding back to Butler, the briefest of motions. Newman was staring inside the wheel-house at the skipper. His hands gripped the wheel tightly. He swung it a little to the left – to port – which appeared to be the wrong manoeuvre. It seemed he had panicked, was making a futile attempt to head back for the shore they had left from – taking them straight into the path of the advancing powerboat, which Paula now saw was huge.

Tweed took out Newman's binoculars, which he had put in his own pocket. Cardon, who had been switching his gaze swiftly from the wheel-house to the powerboat, reached across, took the glasses from Tweed's hands. Like Newman, he had summed up the skipper as a man who did not easily lose his nerve.

Cardon focused the field-glasses on the powerboat, which had changed course, was now slantwise to them. Through the lenses he saw the sole occupant, a figure at the wheel. A bizarre figure wearing a skin-diver's helmet and goggles. No chance of ever identifying who was guiding the powerboat. Cardon shoved the glasses back in Tweed's lap with his left hand. Both of his hands dived inside the canvas satchel as Paula watched him.

The roar of the powerboat was deafening as it swept even closer. Paula clenched her fingers tight inside her gloves. They were going to be smashed to matchwood, capsized into water which would be icy in February. Nield calmly inserted a cigarette between his lips without lighting it.

'The skipper knows what he's doing,' Tweed told Paula, his mouth close to her ear.

'You could have fooled me,' she snapped back.

In the brief time before a shattering collision took place the skipper suddenly swung his wheel hard over to starboard – away from the powerboat's course. It was tricky timing. The huge prow of the monster seemed to Paula to loom over them like something out of the film *Jaws*. One of her hands was now clamped round the plank beneath her, waiting for the frightful impact.

There were inches between the two vessels as the power-boat skimmed past them on the port side. And as it did so Cardon lobbed the grenade he had withdrawn the pin from. It landed in the well behind the hooded figure. Cardon immediately began counting silently, mouthing the numbers clearly as he stared at Paula.

'One . . .

'Two . . .

'Three . . .

'Four . . .'

On 'Four' something made Paula swivel round to the stern of the ferry which was now rocking madly under the impact of the wash from the powerboat. Tweed was already staring with the others in the same direction.

The explosion was thunderous. One second the power-boat was swinging round in a half-circle, ready to come back towards its target. The next second, as the detonation rang out, it split in two – the prow shooting skywards. Paula stared as a gigantic column of water like the geyser in Yellowstone Park soared up, taking with it dark objects which were debris from the shattered wreck.

The water boiled briefly where the powerboat had died, then it became calm with the surface ruffled only by ripples. Tweed was confident neither of the crew had seen Cardon lob the grenade, so intent had they been on steering the ferry clear of disaster at the last moment. The skipper handed over the wheel to his mate and his first words as he came out of the wheel-house confirmed Tweed's assumption.

'Sorry for that, folks. We've 'ad similar fools in the past. Think it's fun to scare the 'ell out of my passengers. But I don't know what that was. And then 'is petrol blew. That's 'appened before, too. Young idiots buys these expensive fast boats – must be fast for 'em – and then 'asn't the money to keep up any maintenance. I'm givin' you all your money back . . .'

'You most certainly are doing nothing of the sort,' Tweed said forcefully. 'Only one pound each for the return trip to Rock – and you saved our lives by your expert seamanship.'

'Anything that keeps you 'appy.' The skipper frowned. 'Never seen quite so big an explosion when petrol tank goes. Still, was a big boat. Now, we're landin' in a moment . . .'

11

They landed from the ferry by the same method – walking down the plank while the mate stood alongside, ready to give anyone who needed it a hand. Paula had no hesitation in reaching out for her hand to be grasped – her legs felt like jelly after their recent experience.

'See that stick with the flag stuck in beach?' called out the skipper. 'When you want to come back wait wherever it's been moved to. Tide will start to come in in the next hour . . .'

Tweed had walked down the plank, again ignoring the hand offered. His feet immediately sank into the sand which had recently been covered with water. Ploughing his way up to a ramp leading off the beach was like walking on a giant sponge. Paula and Newman caught him up as the other three men followed at a distance, spreading out, their eyes everywhere.

'You look smug,' Paula accused Tweed.

'Sorry. Just satisfied that my instinct was right.'

'What instinct?' Newman demanded.

'That the enemy had now tracked us to Padstow.'

'Anything to back that up?' Newman continued. 'You're always so keen on data to back up a theory.'

'Last night I couldn't sleep. As you know, my bedroom window gives a panoramic view of the estuary and this shore. You remember, Bob, you lent me your binoculars.'

'You saw something, then?'

'Oh, yes, I saw something.' Tweed chuckled, outwardly unaffected that they had just escaped sudden death. 'I saw something. Switching off the lights, I pulled back the curtains. Soon I saw a lamp flashing on and off over here. Red, then green, then red. Morse code – but the message was in cipher, if you understand me. A stream of meaningless letters, so I couldn't read what they were sending. But I could guess.'

'And you guessed what?' Paula pressed.

'That the sender in Rock was informing someone in Padstow that we have arrived at the Metropole. That was the first stage of targeting us.'

'And the second stage?'

'That was the lamp flashing which I noticed from the cove while we waited for the ferry. It was probably signalling to that powerboat cruising out at sea just beyond the estuary – that we'd be aboard the ferry.'

'Sounds thin,' Newman objected. 'It presupposes someone was watching the ferry for hours. We might never have come here.'

'So maybe they were watching the inner harbour through binoculars from Rock. These people leave nothing to chance. After we left perhaps a certain pennant was hoisted up the mast of that cabin cruiser, *Mayflower III*. Remember who suggested we take that ferry?'

'Gaunt!' Newman grated out the name. 'He waits until he's persuaded us to cross to Rock and then hoists the signal which tells whoever is waiting over here, wherever that might be.'

101

'Oh, last night through your binoculars I pinpointed the source where the lamp was flashing from.'

The shore of Rock was deserted and there was an atmosphere of being cut off from the world which Paula found disturbing. Tweed led the way off the soggy beach up a ramp which started out as concrete and then became wooden ribbed. He turned left, away from the few buildings which were Rock. They entered a desolate quarry which was apparently used as a car park during the season. Not a single vehicle was parked in the grim amphitheatre enclosed by granite walls.

'Don't point or look at it obviously,' Tweed warned. 'I saw the lamp flashing last night from that strange house perched on its own above us. From the first-floor window on the right.'

Paula glanced round as though taking in the view. Strange was hardly the word for the house. Weird, she said to herself. Isolated well up the steep slope it had a Victorian appearance but gave the impression half of it had been sliced off and taken away at some distant time.

Tall and thin, built of the universal grey stone, it had a single high gable with a turret below it at one corner. The building had a derelict appearance and Paula thought she'd never seen a more sinister house. Like something out of Hitchcock's *Psycho*.

'We'll climb up and have a look at it,' Tweed said as Butler joined them under the lee of the granite wall.

'What's the objective?' he asked tersely.

'That tall house above us. We're going to have a look at it.'

'I'll tell Cardon and Nield. We'll spread out. I'm going to approach it from the rear, which means a little alpine climbing . . .'

Tweed headed for a small flight of crude steps leading up out of the quarry to a winding footpath. He climbed so quickly that Paula and Newman had to move to keep up with

102

him. Newman tucked his Smith & Wesson inside his belt.

'What an awful area,' Paula commented when they reached a point halfway to the house.

The steep slope had an air of desolation and to her right was a dense wood of miserable firs hanging over Rock. The trunks were stunted, bent at an angle away from the sea, their branches twisted into ugly shapes like deformed arms. Now they were higher up a wind, blowing in off the ocean, whipped against them. No wonder the trees were so crippled. Beyond the path was scrubby grass and the undergrowth had a shaggy look, hammered over the years by ferocious winds.

'What a glorious view,' Newman said, pausing.

The wind was stronger, the Atlantic had come into sight. As they stood together the wind was battering like a thousand flails. Surf-tipped rollers were roaring in to the outer reaches of the estuary, breaking against the base of the eastern cape, hurling skywards great clouds of white spray. More rollers advanced up the estuary.

Tweed averted his eyes, looked across the estuary to the far side. The grey mass of Padstow sheered up like a gigantic fortress wall. The Metropole was well elevated and he realized why he had seen so clearly the lamp flashing from the house above them.

'Let's keep moving,' he urged.

The narrow path snaked from side to side in its gully, which made walking difficult. They were near the tall thin house which, close up, had an even more derelict appearance. Three steps led up to the front door inside a porch. No garden, no fence – the property was open to the wilderness. Then Tweed saw how it could be reached by car. A wide sandy track led downhill, went round a bend, vanished.

Butler suddenly appeared from the rear of the building. He was pocketing the compact tool-kit which he always carried.

'No one here,' he reported. 'No furniture inside, no carpets on the floor.'

'I'd like to have seen inside the place,' Tweed remarked.

'Follow me, then. Someone left a window unfastened at the back,' he said with a straight face.

Cardon appeared on a hillock in a commanding position above the house, gave a brief wave. Nield stood up from behind a dense patch of undergrowth closer to the house.

'They've established outposts to watch over us,' Newman commented as they followed Butler round the back.

Paula stared at the sash window which was open at the bottom. There were jemmy marks close to the catch on the inside which was turned to the open position. She spoke to Butler in a tone of mock severity.

'Breaking and entering? That's against the law, Harry.'

'So someone got here before us,' Butler retorted, grinning.

Tweed crouched to step over the ledge and ease himself inside. Butler, followed by Paula, was by his side in seconds. He put a finger to his lips, whispered.

'It *appears* to be unoccupied,' he warned.

Paula, with Newman by *her* side, studied the ancient floorboards, the window ledges and the mantelpieces with a housewife's practised eye. Undisturbed dust everywhere. She paused before entering the narrow hall while Tweed, followed by Newman and Butler, ran lightly up the bare wooden staircase.

In the hall the floorboards were perfectly clean, dust-free. Paula frowned as she mounted the staircase slowly. Every tread was equally clean and a familiar smell was assailing her nostrils. Pleasant, distinctive.

Tweed had entered the front bedroom at the left-hand side of the house. He took out of his coat pocket Newman's binoculars, stood in front of the clear glass of the window, focused them. His own windows in the suite at the Metropole seemed amazingly close.

'This,' he said, 'is where someone used a lamp to send a signal last night.'

'And have you noticed the floorboards?' Paula enquired from behind him.

'No, I . . .'

'Men are so unobservant,' she teased him. 'The room we came in by at the back had a musty smell and was covered in dust. Look at these floorboards – they've been scrubbed, probably during the past twenty-four hours. Was the door closed here?'

'Yes, it was.'

'Which is why the smell of the cleaner used – liquid Flash – is so strong in here. But you can smell it on the stairs and in the hall.'

'What's the idea of cleaning up the place so well?' asked Butler.

'Maybe to eliminate footprints,' Newman said, looking at Paula. 'Footprints with studded soles. Climbing boots.'

'If you say so,' replied Butler, mystified. He turned to Tweed. 'Want some evidence that you're still a good detective? Follow me.'

'In a minute.' Tweed was stooping over a corner of the window ledge. 'I'm doing a Sherlock Holmes. There's an intact roll of cigar ash here, a slight burn where the cigar rested while the smoker operated the lamp. Paula, give me one of those sample bags.'

Paula unzipped a section inside her shoulder-bag where she always carried several self-sealing polythene wallets. Tweed had taken out a penknife, used his other hand to take the wallet from Paula, used the knife to coax the ash off the edge and inside the bag, which he sealed and handed to her.

'There are experts who can identify ash. Now who have we seen recently who smokes cigars?'

'You want to see my evidence?' Butler broke in. 'Then follow me . . .'

He led them down the stairs, returned into the back room where they had entered, climbed out of the window and walked to a lean-to shed next to the rear wall of the house. A large new padlock hung loose and dangling from an iron ring.

'I suppose you found it just like that?' Paula asked.

Butler grinned again, took a ring of skeleton keys from his pocket, jangled them. He edged the heavy wooden door open with his foot, stood back and gestured for them to enter, handing a small torch to Tweed. Paula wondered what else Butler might have in the capacious pockets of his made-to-order coat.

'Satisfying to find you were right,' Tweed commented as Paula joined him.

He was aiming his torch beam at a large brass signalling lamp perched on top of a heavy wooden box. Bending down, he examined the lamp without touching it, stood upright again.

'It has a red filter which can be slid across the lamp. And a green one. Hence the signal flashes I saw from my suite.'

'So all we need to find out is who owns this dump,' Paula replied.

Tweed and Paula had had enough of the gully path. With Newman, they started down the sandy track which showed the ruts of a vehicle's recent passage.

'A four-wheel drive job, like a Land-Rover,' Newman said.

Before leaving the house with no name, Butler had donned surgical gloves, had fastened the padlock on the lean-to shed, then closed the entry window. He vanished from the trio's view along with Cardon and Nield.

'They're enjoying practising the fieldcraft they've been trained in,' Tweed commented.

He knew the three men were close by but didn't hear one

sound of their progress down the bleak heathland. He pointed to the channel of water which remained. Waves were tossing up and down.

'One thing I'm not going to enjoy is the ferry trip back to Padstow.'

'It may have calmed down by the time we return,' Paula suggested, not believing a word she said. 'And in summertime this place must be where the boaty types come.'

In the narrow channel of water a number of craft moored to buoys were wrapped in blue plastic to protect them against the elements. More were beached on the vast sandbank stretching clear across the estuary. Several boats were slowly circling the area where the powerboat had exploded. Paula still found the disappearance of the river extraordinary.

'It's as though there's a huge plug further out which they pull out and water just vanishes down it,' she remarked. She looked at Tweed. 'Was our journey here of any use?'

'Definitely. It's providing me with more pieces of the vague jigsaw I'm building up in my mind.'

The track fell more steeply and they saw the road leading to the quarry car park over to their right. Outside a bungalow a smartly dressed woman was shaking a blanket. Tweed stopped.

'Excuse me, have you any idea who owns that house at the top of this track?'

'A man called Gaunt. He lives somewhere way out on Bodmin Moor.'

'I might be interested in the property,' Tweed lied amiably. 'It appeared to be empty. I suppose he never comes near the place, this Mr Gaunt?'

'Someone does. Just occasionally. They did only last night. I had the TV on but I heard some kind of vehicle driving up there after dark.'

'Thank you for the information.'

'Wouldn't consider buying that old ruin,' the woman

warned. 'We bought this place in summer. Never do that. We did – and we'd sell up and get out tomorrow if we could. It's spooky. Rock is only an old hotel further along the road and a few terrace houses. Nowhere to buy everyday necessities. I have to cross in that beastly old ferry to Padstow. Keep away from here.'

'You said spooky,' Paula reminded her.

'Every now and then lights appear in that house up there you've just been to see. I don't mean the room lights. More like someone prowling round with a torch. Gives me the creeps.'

'Well, thank you for your advice. It has not fallen on deaf ears,' Tweed assured her.

He waited until they had reached the bottom of the track. Paula looked along the lonely road which led to the rest of Rock.

'A waste of time,' Tweed said. 'She described it perfectly. Bob and I explored it when we were once at the Metropole for a day and a night. What are you looking for?'

Paula was delving deep inside her bag. With a triumphal air she brought out a small press-pack of white tablets.

'Look. Dramamine! And just down the road there's a shop which sells soft drinks, according to that madly flapping flag . . .'

They sat inside a glassed-in enclosure overlooking the estuary. Tweed swallowed a tablet washed down with orange juice and Paula checked her watch, timing thirty minutes. The water was churning now like a cauldron. Since the woman who had served them was cleaning the counter close behind they sat in silence for some time. Then Newman heard the engine of the approaching machine.

'Let me have my glasses,' he told Tweed.

The grey chopper, flying low, came in from the direction of the Atlantic. In the lenses Newman saw two men at the controls – both with their heads covered in helmets and wearing goggles. Very similar to the figure which had been behind the wheel of the powerboat. The woman behind the counter disappeared through a doorway, slammed it shut. They were alone, so could talk.

'You'll say I'm paranoid,' Newman commented, 'but I think that chopper is searching for us.'

'Which would be alarming,' Tweed said quietly. 'Because it would mean someone has an excellent communication system. The crew of the chopper are either checking to see the wreckage of the ferry . . .'

'Or,' Paula interjected, stiffening to quell a shiver, 'they know we survived and, as Bob suggested, they are searching for us.'

'Looks like the latter,' Newman agreed. 'The ferry is just going back to Padstow, it's in mid-river.'

They sat in silence again as the chopper swept low over the outgoing ferry, circled it, then flew inland over Rock. Paula found herself sitting very still, although it would be impossible for the helicopter crew to see inside the café.

'The copilot was also using binoculars,' Newman told them.

He had hardly spoken when they heard the machine above their heads, a reverberating roar. Newman stood up, peered out of the window to his right. They could now hear it hovering. Newman sat down again and a minute later the machine reappeared, flying over the estuary, heading out towards the Atlantic, its engine sound fading. Paula let out her breath.

'It checked that old house we explored,' Newman reported.

'Then it *was* looking for us,' Paula said grimly. 'How the hell do they know so much? I feel like a bug under a microscope, our every move foreseen, monitored. It's uncanny, nerve-wracking.'

'They've also committed a major tactical error by

coming out into the open,' Tweed responded. 'I can see the ferry starting to come back so we'd better make our way to the landing point on the beach – wherever that may be now. The tide is starting to come in.'

They had barely stepped down on to the road when Butler, Cardon and Nield materialized from the rough ground behind the café. They were brushing themselves down when they reached the road.

'Did that chopper see you?' rapped out Newman.

'Silly question,' Butler rapped back, then changed his tune. 'Sorry. No, it didn't. We were flat on our backs under dead bracken and undergrowth. We saw it, heard it coming, but they didn't spot us.'

'Messy up there,' the normally immaculate Nield grumbled. He was wearing a smart business suit. 'Incidentally the joker next to the pilot had field-glasses. He particularly scanned the old house up the slope you went into.'

'We know that already,' Tweed told him.

There was a bounce in his walk as he headed for the gap in the hedge and made his way down the ramp on to the beach. The stick with the flag showing the landing point was closer to the ramp than when they had disembarked. Was that a day ago? Paula wondered. It seemed so. And why was Tweed so pleased with their diabolical trip to Rock?

12

'How dramatic!' Paula exclaimed.

As the ferry pitched and tossed and dusk began to fall the sea was surging in like a small tidal wave. The Atlantic was inundating the sandbanks which were shrinking in size

110

even as she watched them. She was surprised – relieved – when the ferry arrived close to the Padstow shore and moved on past the bleak cove where they had boarded it.

'We're going to land at the harbour now the water has risen high enough,' Newman told her.

The narrow channel they had left behind on the outward trip was far wider. They arrived at the foot of a flight of steps leading up the outer side of the pier. Tweed stepped ashore on the bottom stone step, where he stayed to help Paula.

'Careful,' he warned. 'The first flight only has a rail on the inner side against the wall . . .'

She clung to it as she followed him up. Glancing to her left, she looked away quickly. With no rail on that side there was a sheer drop into the river. Higher up there was a rail on both sides which made her feel more comfortable. She stepped on to the pier, took two paces forward, stopped, stared.

'They've opened the lock gate to the inner harbour.'

'That's because the river level is now the same as the water inside the harbour,' Tweed explained as he cleaned his glasses with his handkerchief.

'But it's gone!'

'What has?' Tweed asked, putting on his glasses again.

'The *Mayflower*.'

'She sailed soon as the gate was opened,' a seaman leaning against the wall told Paula. 'Don't expect we'll see her awhile.'

'Why do you say that?' she asked.

'Amount of provisions they took aboard her. So many cool bags. Fridge an' freezer must be stacked to gunwales.'

'Who was aboard when she moved out?'

'Squire Gaunt was at the helm . . .'

'Anyone else aboard?'

'Couldn't say . . .'

The seaman moved away as though he felt he'd already

111

said too much. The others had joined Tweed and Paula. Because the gate was open and no bridge spanned the gap they had to walk round all the quays encircling the harbour.

'That does surprise me,' Paula said. 'Gaunt leaving at such short notice and never mentioning it in the bar.'

'Doesn't surprise me at all,' Tweed replied. 'But I have no doubt we shall see Squire Gaunt again.'

Tweed said he wanted to make a strictly private call to Howard and went into the phone box. Paula walked into the bar with Newman and Cardon. Butler and Nield remained outside, taking up positions where they had the box under close observation.

Tweed dialled the Surrey mansion first. Howard came to the phone quickly.

'Have you made any progress? Any solid news?' he pressed anxiously.

'I can tell you that where we are – out in the wilds – we're being watched night and day. And I expect you are too . . .'

'*Who* is behind all this?' Howard asked vehemently. 'I tried the PM again. No luck. He's abandoned us.'

'What about Crombie? Are you still in touch with him?'

'Yes, bless him. He phones me with regular reports. There's still a mountain of rubble to remove. No sign of that safe you mentioned yet.'

'They've overlooked Crombie,' Tweed said with grim satisfaction. 'Try and throw an iron cordon round someone and a loophole is always left. Now, listen to me, Howard. I want you to phone Crombie, tell him when he uncovers that safe to let you know at once and keep it hidden. The moment you hear he has found it send that armoured car disguised as a security truck to collect it and take it down to you. Understood?'

'I'll call him as soon as we've finished talking. We are all feeling marooned here, Tweed. I tried to reach the PM three times today. Blocked off every time. He's abandoned us,' he repeated.

'Face up to it, Howard. He's done just that . . .'

Tweed's next call was to Jim Corcoran at London Airport. Again he had to coax the Chief Security Officer to do what he asked him. Eventually, he agreed. Tweed thanked him, told him in due course he'd realize he had done the right thing.

His third call, the briefest, was to Newquay Airport. He made certain arrangements on the basis of the data the girl receptionist gave him, then mopped his forehead, walked out of the box and into the bar. But he felt better. Very shortly they would be on the move.

Inside the bar, which was quiet, Tweed joined Newman, Paula and Cardon who were occupying the secluded corner on the upper level in front of the fire. When Newman asked him what he was drinking he said mineral water.

'Did you phone Howard?' Paula asked. 'I thought so. What sort of a mood is he in?'

'Feeling trapped. He's had no contact with the PM. He can't get through to him.'

'That's how I feel,' Paula said. 'Trapped.'

'Cheer up. And have your bag packed for an early departure tomorrow morning. You'll have to ditch the Browning before we leave. I must warn the others. No weapons.'

'I'll dump mine in the sea. But where are we going? Is anywhere safe any more?'

'One place is. Which is where we're going. It's time to smoke out whoever is after us. I'm leading them into a trap. Thank you,' he said as Newman put a glass before him. He drank greedily. All the recent activity had dehydrated him.

113

'We've been trying to work out who is behind all these attempts to wipe us out,' Newman began. 'The answer could be summed up in the name of one individual: Gaunt.'

'An assumption so far,' Tweed pointed out. 'Evidence?'

'Gaunt leased his manor for varying periods to Julius Amberg. Whoever unleashed that massacre knew the banker would be there. Who could have told them? Gaunt. We were nearly killed by that powerboat. Who knew we were taking that particular ferry to Rock? Gaunt. Who was absent from Tresillian Manor when Celia Yeo was hurled from the summit of High Tor? Gaunt – and Jennie.'

'Possibly.' Tweed drank more water. 'Are you suggesting he has the organization to arrange for that massive car bomb to be parked outside our building? He doesn't even know where SIS headquarters are – were.'

'That is a difficult one to answer,' Newman admitted. 'Incidentally, Butler and Nield followed you in here at separate intervals. Butler is sitting in a corner behind you where he can survey the whole bar. Nield is chatting up the barmaid . . .'

Leaning against the counter, Pete Nield was joking with the fair-haired girl. He asked her a question when he felt he had established an easy relationship.

'I hear that Squire Gaunt is off on his travels again in that floating palace of his. He could cross the Atlantic in that huge cabin cruiser.'

'Oh, I don't think he's done that. He flies to America. You see, he likes to go off in her by himself to Europe.'

'A trip to jolly old Paris?' Nield suggested.

'Maybe. But he's been cruising up the Rhine. I heard that when he was in here one night and he'd had rather a lot to drink.'

'A nice chap, though,' Nield probed.

114

The girl paused polishing a glass. 'That depends on his mood, between you and me. Sometimes he is and then again he can cut you dead.'

'I hear he lives in a lovely manor on Bodmin Moor. Must be peaceful out there.'

'Too lonely for me. I'd get the creeps . . .'

The very courteous and able manager of the Metropole met them in the hall as they returned. He spoke in a low voice to Tweed.

'I thought you might like to know two Americans have been enquiring about you, sir. Wanted to know how long you were staying. I said I'd no idea.'

'Are they staying here?' Newman asked quickly.

'No. But they're in the bar at the moment.'

'Think I'll pop in and take a look at them . . .'

Newman headed for the bar as the others waited for the lift. Two tall heavily built men were standing by the bar counter with drinks in front of them. Both wore loud check sports jackets and denims and had American style trench coats folded over their arms. Newman ordered a Scotch. The larger of the two men was standing next to Newman, had dense black hair, thick brows which almost met across the bridge of his broken nose.

'Your Scotch, Mr Newman,' said the barman, recognizing his customer. 'Thank you, sir,' he said as Newman paid.

'Newman? Robert Newman, the nosy foreign correspondent?' the big American enquired in a bullying tone.

'I'm retired,' Newman replied, refusing to be provoked. 'So no longer nosy, as you put it.'

'Old habits die hard,' the American said aggressively.

His elbow toppled his own drink. Liquid spilt over the counter and the barman hastily mopped up.

'Buddy,' the American went on, 'that was my whisky

you just knocked over. So what are you going to do about it?'

'Buy you another,' Newman continued amiably. 'Give this gentleman a fresh drink, please,' he said to the barman and put more money on the counter.

'They said you were something else again at one time,' the American sneered. 'Good thing you retired – seems like you lost your guts.'

'Your friend has just collapsed.'

As the American jerked his head to his left where his companion stood looking puzzled, Newman grabbed his drink, walked out of the bar and up the stairs. The enemy was moving in at very close quarters.

'I'm calling a council of war, Paula. In my suite. If you have just stepped out of the bath, five minutes from now will do.'

Paula put down the phone in her room on the second floor. Tweed had sounded imperative, calm, determined. She had not just stepped out of the bath. She went back to the window, her lights off, watching in the dark the final incoming surge of the tide. In the moonlight the edges of the remaining sandbanks looked like filleted fish. Even as she watched they were submerged. The water now stretched from shore to shore and Porthilly Cove, which had been a huge sand beach, was filled with water.

It was frightening, she thought, as she descended the stairs – the unstoppable force of the sea. She made a similar remark to Tweed as she entered his suite while Newman closed and locked the door.

'And that's what we're up against,' Tweed said, 'an unstoppable force. Power in its most extreme and ruthless form.'

His audience remained silent. They were all there – Cardon, Butler and Nield, seated while Tweed stood in the

116

middle of the large room, the curtains closed behind him. He looked at Newman.

'Tell them about your encounter in the bar downstairs.'

They listened while Newman related tersely what had happened in the bar. He was inclined to play down the confrontation. Paula was surprised he had kept his temper and said so.

'His reaction was perfect,' Tweed told her. 'They were trying to start a fight, probably challenge him to come outside with them. Supposing they had knives?'

'Why would two Americans pick on Bob?' she persisted.

'The enemy is closing in on us. It's the moment I have been waiting for. We are going to break out. My crazy idea as to who was behind all this murder and destruction could be right.'

'And the enemy's identity?' Paula pressed on.

'Work it out for yourself. You have the same data I have. List what has happened. From the beginning.'

'There was that horrible massacre at Tresillian Manor – when I was nearly a victim,' she reminded him.

'Chief target – besides ourselves?' Tweed rapped out.

'Julius Amberg, Swiss banker from Zurich.'

'Now, go back a few days to my office in Park Crescent. When Bob and Monica had an unexpected visitor.'

'Well, he left them a film and a tape recording. Copies, he said. He took the originals with him.'

'You've missed something,' Tweed snapped. 'Newman gave us a detailed description of that visit by Joel Dyson. What was inside his case?'

'Oh, I remember. Several lots of American clothes . . .'

'Which strongly suggests he had just flown in from the States. Dyson spent most of his time operating over there although he's British. Found there were much more profitable pickings on the other side of the Atlantic. Go on. Next event.'

'That massive bomb parked outside Park Crescent which destroyed the whole building.'

'Just another bomb?' Tweed enquired.

'No. You told us Commander Crombie had said they'd found relics of the trigger device – that it wasn't the IRA. A more sophisticated device than he'd ever seen.'

'And,' Tweed reminded her, 'how many people know where SIS headquarters were located? What sort of profession? What sort of organization could arrange for the massacre at the manor which almost coincided with the bomb outrage in London?'

'A pretty big one.'

'An international one,' Tweed added.

'I still don't think the massacre and the London bomb are linked,' Paula said obstinately. 'There wasn't time.'

'What happened next?' Tweed continued.

'Celia Yeo, the servant girl I feel sure had signalled the arrival of Amberg's guests, was thrown off High Tor.'

'And then?'

'We arrived here. Gaunt turns up with Jennie Blade. While we're crossing to Rock – at Gaunt's suggestion – that powerboat tries to run us down. We check the house with no name and find the signalling lamp used to send coded messages you spotted from the cove. Then we find out the house with no name belongs to Gaunt. Finally, that helicopter appears to search for us.'

'Not finally yet,' Tweed observed. 'What happens when we get back to the hotel this evening?'

'Oh, those two Americans who've been asking for you try to incite Bob into a free-for-all.'

'Now go back a year or two. To Zurich.'

'I'm not with you . . .'

'Tweed,' Newman intervened, 'is referring to when I persuaded Joel Dyson to hand to Julius Amberg the compromising photos he'd taken of the banker – instead of selling them to the press.'

118

'I'd forgotten that for the moment,' Paula admitted. 'I do remember that Jim Corcoran at London Airport found out that Dyson flew to Zurich after he'd left the film and tape copies at Park Crescent. And he'd just been in America.'

'It begins to link up, doesn't it? Tweed summarized.

'Does it?' Paula frowned. 'I must be thick.'

'Not at all,' Tweed reassured her. 'It's simply that if I'm right the truth is so awesome, *of such magnitude*, it is difficult to grasp. We are in real peril here – so we are leaving tonight. Before dinner. We tell reception we've been called away on urgent business. Philip, Pete, Harry – pay your bills separately, including your rooms for tonight.'

'I'd better go pack. Won't take me long,' Paula said. 'But where are we going?'

'There's a small pub hotel at a place called St Mawgan out in the country near Newquay, further west. Newman and I stayed there overnight once when we were down here. I'll phone them from that infernal phone box. I'm beginning to feel I live inside that box.'

Newman jumped up, a newspaper tucked under his arm. 'I am off to pack my things and check out of the Old Custom House. I'll wait for you by the phone box.' He waved the paper. 'Still nothing in the press about the massacre on Bodmin Moor, which I find sinister. News is all about the States and President March not yet agreeing to back the PM over the crises in Europe and the Middle East. Without American co-operation we can't take strong measures, can't take any measures . . .'

'Hurry, everyone,' Tweed urged. 'We want to get out of Padstow alive.'

119

13

President Bradford March sat sprawled in his swivel chair behind the antique desk in the Oval Office. His stance was, to say the least, inelegant. The chair was pushed well back from the desk and his stockinged feet rested on the surface, crossed at the ankles. He was looking out of the tall Georgian windows at Washington's Pennsylvania Avenue. The view was fuzzy due to the grey drizzle still falling. He turned back to face the only other occupant of the room, a woman.

'Shit, Sara, I'm goin' to have to kick ass to get those jerks in Europe movin' – Norton hasn't reported for two days.'

'He does have a difficult assignment, Brad,' she reminded him.

'Which is why I appointed him head of Unit One. Time he wrapped up the whole job in my book.'

Unlike most presidents – who were often six feet tall or over – Bradford March was a stocky man of medium height with a lot of black hair and thick black brows. Fifty-five years old, his aggressive chin was running to jowls, black as his hair. He shaved twice a day, when he felt like it. Above his short thick nose his ice-cold eyes moved restlessly.

He wore crumpled blue denims and a creased check shirt, open two buttons below the neck, exposing the dense hair on his barrel chest. He belched loudly, slapped his hard rounded stomach.

'That's good beer. Fix me another. Then call Norton. I'm going to kick ass.'

'Is that wise, Brad?'

Sara, March's personal assistant, the only person privy to his secrets, was a hard-faced woman of forty with long dark hair, a prominent nose and a wide thin-lipped mouth. She had been with him since the early days of his career – all the way from when he had sneaked in to become senator of a Southern state by a handful of votes. A handful delivered by a power broker after Sara had handed over to him one hundred thousand dollars in used currency.

Tall and slim, always dressed in black, she was the only person – apart from his wife – permitted to call him Brad. March's wife, Betty, had drifted away from him although she still lived in the White House. Sara was the one who kept a watchful eye on her.

'Time for Betty to have a lollipop, Brad,' she would say.

'Jesus Christ! Do I have to? Again.'

'We don't want her walking, do we? A sable stole will settle her for a while.'

'OK. If you can find the cash.'

'Brad, I can always find the cash. I just twist someone's arm, somebody who owes us a favour. Plenty of them around . . .'

March sat facing the north wall occupied by an elaborate marble fireplace. Sara came back with a bottle of beer from the fridge, uncapped. Knowing what he wanted she wiped the top and neck of the bottle with a crisp white napkin. March took the bottle from her, upended it and drank.

'That's better,' he said, placing the bottle on the desk and wiping his mouth with the back of his hairy hand. 'You know what? Some faggot on the staff here – I posted him to the Aleutians – wanted me to see a speech therapist.' He opened his mouth and bellowed with laughter. 'A speech therapist! You know how I barnstormed my way into the White House? Because I talk like the folks down in the street. It's called empathy – whatever the hell that is. Get Norton on the private phone.'

Sara was used to these sudden switches in subject. She

121

stood with her arms folded, frowning at him. He looked up, spat out the question.

'You got something on your mind?'

'Brad, what is it Norton's looking for? Besides certain people?'

'Certain people being Cord Dillon and Barton Ives. Is my ass covered with Dillon runnin' out? Deputy Director of the CIA. Questions will be asked when the press wakes up, finds he's gone missing.'

'Your ass is covered. I've spread the rumour he's been ill, has gone abroad for a long vacation.'

'Long vacation?' March grinned to himself. When Norton found Dillon his vacation would be permanent. No point in letting Sara know how rough he could play. 'What's getting to you?' he snapped.

'This Unit One. I think Senator Wingfield has caught a whiff of its existence.'

'That aristocratic old creep? Just because he happens to be Chairman of the Senate Foreign Relations Committee. Maybe his ancestors were one of the Pilgrim Fathers. He looks like one.'

'He carries a lot of clout, Brad. And Unit One is strictly an illegal organization. Trouble is, some members of Unit One are still here, not in Europe.'

'You're smart.' March grinned again. 'Real smart. So we may send the rest to Europe to Norton as reinforcements. Nothing left here then for old Wingfield to get a whiff of. I'll think about that.'

'That would be best. As you say, nothing left for him to get a hold on.'

'It's like tapes and documents,' March went on, folding his hands behind his thick neck. 'Never record anything on tape – reading about Nixon taught me that. Nothing goes down on paper. That way, no evidence. We go on keeping everything verbal.' He winked.

'Best way,' Sara agreed. 'It's worked like a dream so far.

122

Is the British Prime Minister co-operating?'

'The Brits do what I tell them to do. Norton is operating in London like he was in Louisiana. No interference. Their Prime Minister has no balls. He has two volcanoes smoking on his stoop – Russia and the Mid-East. He daren't move without my backing, which I'm withholding.'

'Sitting in his shoes I wouldn't either,' Sara commented. 'How do you handle the guy?'

'Oh, I borrow a tactic our wily Secretary of State uses if he wants to stall . . .' March was referring to the American equivalent of the British Foreign Secretary. 'I tell him I have the problem under consideration.'

'This FBI agent, Barton Ives, who has also disappeared – how does he fit into the picture? Operated in the South, didn't he – when you were a senator?'

'He could get in my way.' A crafty expression appeared on March's face, his eyes half-closed like a hyena poised to strike. 'You can leave him to Norton.'

'Pardon me for treading in the wrong territory.' Sara smiled. She knew she'd made a mistake. 'Brad, I don't tread on sensitive ground – could be a minefield.'

'Sara Maranoff,' the President said slowly, 'you could get blown to small pieces doin' just that – walking into a minefield.' His expression changed, became amiable as a family man. 'That was a clever idea of yours – suggesting I tell the Prime Minister we have people over there tracking a gang of terrorists planning to assassinate me. He shut his trap fast when I fed him that one. You're a real smart lady.'

Sara, arms still folded, bobbed her head in acknowledgement of the compliment, but she wasn't fooled. March had used that trick on her before – first hammering her for an indiscretion, then following that up with a tribute to her loyalty. Bradford March might have come from the sticks but he had a native cunning when it came to manipulating people. Wisely, she changed the subject.

'Can I ask you something else? Has Norton found the

two pieces of equipment he's endeavouring to locate? I don't know what they are but I do know they worry you.'

March's expression became brooding. 'No, he hasn't. But he will. His job's on the line and he knows it. Sara, maybe we should put a tail on Senator Wingfield? Don't trust him as far as I can spit.'

'Don't do it,' Sara warned. 'He'll know. Then he'll guess there's something to conceal. He could start digging up dirt about Unit One. Let him rest in peace.'

'Which is where I wish he was. In the cemetery. Now, try and get me Norton on the private line. Then go take a shower or something . . .'

Which was another precaution March had learned from reading up the history of previous occupants of the White House. Never completely trust the one closest to you – man or woman. In a crisis it was the loyal friend who stabbed you in the back. Today's friends – tomorrow's enemies.

Bradford March was not psychic, but on that cold drizzly February morning a meeting of three men was being held not a world away from the Oval Office. The meeting took place in one of the luxurious mansions in Chevy Chase, the most sought after – and exclusive – residential district near Washington.

The small group was seated round a Chippendale table in the study of Senator Charles Wingfield. Even though it was daytime the curtains were drawn closed in the large room at the rear of the house. Illumination came from the glass chandelier suspended above the table.

The Senator, a white-haired vigorous man of sixty and Chairman of the Foreign Relations Committee, looked at his guests as they began sipping the excellent coffee he served.

The short plum-faced guest, in his fifties, was the most

powerful banker in the States. Alongside him sat a man known as an elder statesman. The latter was of medium height, bulky build, clad in an immaculate suit and he wore horn-rimmed glasses. Behind the lenses strange penetrating and shrewd eyes watched the other two men. The Senator opened the meeting, going straight to the point.

'I'm getting more and more worried about the President's behaviour. There are two crises brewing up in Europe and both could damage our vital interests.'

'And March is doing nothing to support Europe,' the statesman snapped. 'All he can think of is his "America First, Last and All the Time".'

'Which was the slogan which won him the election,' the banker pointed out.

'You can interpret "America First" as the best reason for our intervening in Europe, for supporting the British in this situation,' the statesman replied waspishly. 'God knows enough history has proved our front line is on the European continent. The Veep has more grasp of foreign affairs in his little finger than March has in his ugly ape-like head.'

By Veep he was referring to the Vice-President, Jeb Calloway. March had chosen Calloway as his running mate because he was from Philadelphia and was popular in the north-east and the so-called 'rust' states of Michigan, etc.

'Calloway is a very different man,' Wingfield agreed. 'He's a cultured man with a global view. But he's still the Veep.'

'Nothing more than a decoration with no say in policy,' the banker reminded them. 'So what can be done?'

'Politics is the art of the possible,' the Senator said in a soothing tone. 'March has done nothing yet we can openly criticize him for. He's quick on his feet and a

125

master of the Washington ball-game. Gentlemen, all we can do is wait.'

'You did say you'd heard rumours that March has secretly organized his own private paramilitary force,' recalled the statesman.

'Rumours. Nothing I can get my teeth into. Washington abounds in rumours. The private army thing may be a trap March has set. We go public about what is nothing but a rumour, he proves we're off the wall, and any influence we possess is destroyed.'

'I may make a statement criticizing his inaction over foreign policy,' the statesman insisted. 'The position is we *have* no foreign policy. It might stir Calloway into urging immediate action.'

'I still advocate silence,' Senator Wingfield replied.

In certain circles, limited to a very few old Washington hands, they were known as the Three Wise Men. Wingfield was very strong on the strategy of their remaining in the shadows.

They talked for a little while longer. The banker could hold himself in check no longer. He burst out with unusual vehemence.

'The President has done nothing to reduce our soaring deficit. America is going bankrupt. The way he's increasing our debt, we're heading for a crisis right here.'

'He's very popular still,' the Senator warned. 'I would advise both of you to make no public statements pending our next meeting.' He looked at his watch. 'And I am due at the Senate in thirty minutes . . .'

Courteously he ushered them into the hall, shook them by the hand, but was careful not to be present when the front door was opened. The statesman and the banker left the mansion separately – with five minutes between their departures. Outside a chauffeured limousine waited in the drive when each man hurried out of the front entrance.

Back in his study Wingfield decided he would make a

126

few very discreet enquiries. The problem was always to find an ear where the mouth would stay shut afterwards. Calm and dignified during the meeting, inwardly the Senator was a very disturbed man.

14

It was dark as they waited close to Padstow harbour. Newman sat with Paula alongside him in his Mercedes. Cardon had taken over the wheel of the Escort. Butler and Nield had taken the Sierra – but at that moment they were both outside, watching the phone box with Tweed inside it.

A storm had blown up, the sea was in a rage. Paula got out of the Merc., leaned in to speak to Newman.

'I'm going to get a closer look. It's really wild tonight.'

'I'll come with you,' Newman said, jumping out of his seat.

They walked near the edge of South Quay, but not too close. The gale nearly blew them off their feet. Fascinated, Paula watched the boats in the outer harbour swaying and tossing. Huge waves rolled in, crashed against the rear wall, exploded in a burst of surf and spume rising way up above the wall. One smaller craft looked as though it was going to be upended at any moment.

Newman grasped her arm to prevent her getting any nearer to the brink. She glanced over her shoulder where the interior light shone down on the occupant of the telephone box.

Tweed had dialled the Surrey mansion, was put through very quickly to Monica. He spoke rapidly.

'Short of time. Monica, I want you to prepare a profile

127

on a man called Gaunt. Lives at Tresillian Manor on Bodmin Moor. You won't hear from me for some time, but don't worry.'

'What the hell is going on?'

It was the first time he'd ever heard her swear. Even on the phone he could sense her tension – a tension which probably pervaded the whole mansion.

'No idea yet,' he answered. 'Now, put me on to Howard . . .'

'Tweed, are you all right?' were Howard's first words.

'Yes. We're moving on. Had a word with the PM yet?'

'No, we're completely cut off from the outside world – which is an eerie feeling. I did get one thing out of that fool of a private secretary when I threatened to go up to Downing Street. He said I wouldn't be admitted, that there's a major terrorist hunt in progress. I can't imagine what he's talking about.'

Then you haven't got much imagination, Tweed thought. He had a pad and a pen at the ready.

'Can you give me Commander Crombie's private number? I may need to contact him.' He scribbled down figures of a phone number in London. 'Thanks. Now listen, Howard, you may not hear from me again for a while. Don't worry about it. I'll be in a safe place with my team.'

'Well, I hope you know what you're doing. Where is this safe place?'

'Sorry, I'm leaving no forwarding address. Must go . . .'

'Wait! I've just remembered. Had a call from Cord Dillon. Take down this number . . . Got it? He must be in Switzerland. He wants you to call him urgently. Gave me different times. Half a sec. Just checked my watch. You could get him now, allowing for the time difference. There are only fifteen-minute periods during the times he gave me.'

'I'd better get off this line, then . . .'

'But I need to know where I can get in touch with you.'

'No forwarding address . . .'

Tweed put down the phone, fished in his pocket. He needed more coins. The wind nearly hurled him back inside the box as he emerged. Battling against the gale he beckoned to Butler and Nield as Paula and Newman came back to the Merc. Tweed climbed into the back, called out brusquely.

'I need all the change you've got to make a long-distance call. Hurry it up . . .'

'Not another call?' Paula exclaimed. 'Maybe we'd better set up a coffee and sandwich bar for you inside that box,' she teased.

'It's not funny. Just give me the change. Cord Dillon is waiting for me to ring. Sounds like a fugitive, from the way Howard reported it. The Deputy Director of the CIA – something is terribly wrong . . .'

Armed with a large collection of coins Tweed returned to the box. The first number Howard had passed to him was 010.41. Switzerland. Followed by 1. Zurich. Followed by the rest of the numbers. The operator put him through quickly and he began listening to the ringing sound. He checked his watch. He was damned close to the end of the fifteen-minute period.

'Who is this calling?'

Dillon's abrasive American voice. No doubt about it.

'Tweed here. I got your message from Howard . . .'

'Where are you calling from? I can't hang about here much longer . . .'

'Public phone box . . .'

'Like me. In Shopville. Just listen. Joel Dyson is here. Still alive. Least he was when I spotted him, then lost the guy. So is Special Agent Barton Ives, FBI. Again I go and lose him. At least he's here.'

'You're staying at . . .'

'The place you suggested. No names. Don't see how

they can tap every goddamn phone in this country, but you just never know.'

'Cord . . .'

'I said just listen. I'm filling you in on the situation. Too many Americans here who don't look like tourists. I guess they're after Dyson. Ives, too.'

'Tell me about this Barton Ives . . .'

'Not over the phone. Maybe we can meet some place some day. If I'm still walking around . . .'

'Cord. You may see me sooner than you think. Keep under good cover . . .'

'What is good cover in this situation? Got to go. Hang in there, Tweed . . .'

There was a click. Tweed sighed, pushed open the door as another gale-force gust tried to slam it shut on him. He walked back to the Merc. with his head bowed, followed by Butler and Nield, and dived inside the back. The wind closed the door for him. Paula twisted round in the front passenger seat.

'It's quite a night. You should see what's happening in the harbour.'

'Which is exactly what I shouldn't see. Bob, get moving. You've found St Mawgan, Paula?'

'I can take us straight there.'

'That will be a miracle.'

Paula didn't reply. Tweed was tauter than a guitar string.

Newman drove along the A389 once he was clear of Padstow. Cardon followed in the Escort and the Sierra, with Butler at the wheel and Nield beside him, brought up the rear. The wind beat against the side of the Merc., bent over hedges as though intent on tearing them up by the roots.

'We're heading for Wadebridge,' Tweed called out.

'We could have taken a side road and come out on the A39 much further west.'

'Who is the bloody navigator?' Paula snapped. She'd had enough of Tweed's brusqueness. 'I'm keeping us on A-roads. On a night like this we don't want to be driving on windy B-roads. Not until we have to later.'

'She's right,' Newman said. 'I'm driving and this is a big car to take down narrow country roads on a night like this.'

'Sorry, Paula,' said Tweed, who realized he'd been sharp with her. 'I'll leave the two of you to get us there.'

Tweed was enduring a mixture of emotions – impatience to reach their ultimate destination and anxiety about the safety of Cord Dillon.

'What about accommodation for the night?' Paula queried after a while. 'Did you manage to fix up rooms for the night at St Mawgan?'

'Yes. The Falcon Inn only has four rooms but we will cope somehow.'

'One for you,' Newman said, 'one for Paula. I'll share with Cardon and Butler and Nield won't mind sharing the other. It's a nice place, the Falcon, Paula, and just about the most difficult place on earth to find.'

'The latter being the main reason why you chose it?' Paula asked Tweed over her shoulder.

'Partly,' he said and relapsed into silence.

Paula guided them to the right on to the A39, another good wide road, and they drove on through the night, meeting no other traffic, the wind still hammering the car. Later she guided them off the A39 with a fresh right turn on to the Newquay road, the A3059. She soon warned Newman they had to keep a lookout for a side road. It was Tweed who spotted the turning.

'Right here,' he called out. 'We're getting close now to where we turn off yet again . . .'

Paula was conscious they were getting into very remote

country. They drove down a steep narrow winding hill and Tweed warned Newman to crawl. He then completed answering Paula's question.

'St Mawgan is close to what is called Newquay Airport. We are booked to catch the 11.05 flight to Heathrow. It arrives at 12.15 p.m. During one of my visits to that phone box I called this airport, booked our seats in our own names.'

'Was that wise?' Paula ventured.

'It was deliberate. I am leaving a trail for the enemy to follow. I want him out in the open, where I can see him, identify him – and deal with him,' Tweed concluded grimly.

At St Mawgan it was nine o'clock at night. In Washington it was four in the afternoon as Jeb Calloway, Vice President, paced slowly round his office while his aide waited for him to speak.

'I'm secretly in touch with someone in Europe to find out what the hell is going on, Sam,' Calloway said eventually. 'The difficulty was to find someone I could totally trust, but I think I found the man.'

Calloway, forty-five years old, was six feet tall and heavily built. Clean-shaven, with fair hair, he was dressed immaculately in a blue Brooks Brothers business suit. Strong-featured, he had a long nose, grey eyes and a determined mouth and well-shaped jaw.

'That could be dangerous, sir,' Sam suggested. 'You've sent this emissary to Europe on a secret mission without the President's knowledge?'

'He was there already. He contacted me. I've also had a talk with a top gun in the establishment. He also approached me. He's as worried as I am about the mounting world crisis. And March doesn't give a damn.'

'Isn't this possibly a catastrophic move?' Sam persisted.

'If Brad March ever finds out he'll close all doors to you.'

Calloway smiled wryly, a smile which had made him very popular. It was the smile of a man of integrity and conviction. He waved a large hand as he went on.

'All doors are closed to me now. March doesn't tell me a thing that matters. And I've heard a whisper that he's assembled a secret paramilitary force, his own Praetorian Guard – like a Julius Caesar.'

'Whispers! Sounds like a load of crap. March wouldn't do that – it's against the Constitution.'

'Brad isn't too hot on obeying the Constitution – if some overt move helps him to increase his power.'

'Who are you in contact with in Europe?' Sam asked.

Sam was a short plump man of fifty-eight. He'd had experience of serving under more than one president, knew the pitfalls of the Washington power game. Calloway mentioned a name. Sam looked dubious.

'Wouldn't play poker with that guy. I heard he had to flee to Europe overnight. Some mysterious investigation his new boss in Memphis chopped. That guy is trouble.'

'I'm still keeping in touch. Rare type, Sam – an honest man.'

The Falcon Inn at St Mawgan was a compact building of old grey stone. It stood on the edge of the lane at the very bottom of the steep winding hill. Newman drove the Merc. slowly past it, turned right down a narrow lane alongside the inn.

'The car park is a little way from the Falcon,' he explained to Paula. 'Hidden well away behind it.'

His headlights swept over a small village shop, swung to the right. They shone down an even narrower track with ramps.

'This is a pretty lonely spot,' Paula commented.

They had reached a dead end, a forest-shrouded bowl

133

which was the car park. No other vehicles were parked. Behind them Cardon followed in the Escort while Butler and Nield brought up the rear end of their small cavalcade in the Sierra. Newman had switched off his engine but he left on the headlights so Tweed and Paula, climbing out of the car, could see. Paula adjusted her shoulder-bag as she stood in the bitter cold, staring round at the bowl overhung with dense trees rising up slopes.

'Don't like this,' she said. 'It's creepy. And anyone could tamper with the cars while we're asleep in the Falcon.'

'You have a point there,' Tweed agreed. He looked at Butler, Nield and Cardon who had joined them. 'I think we ought to organize a roster among us so someone is always here to guard the cars.'

'You and Paula can get your beauty sleep,' Newman decided. 'The four of us will take it in turn through the night to sit in the Merc.'

'I've got a better idea,' suggested Butler. 'The four of us split into twos. I take the Sierra back, park it out front of the inn. That way we have the back and the front under surveillance.'

'Agreed,' said Tweed. 'Now let's go and see what we can get for dinner . . .'

It was the middle of the night when Butler, slumped behind the wheel of the Sierra parked outside the Falcon, heard a car approaching down the steep hill. He sat up, took a bottle of beer he'd kept for the purpose, swilled some round in his mouth, spat it out of the window he'd opened.

Newman was taking his duty stretch in the Merc. in the park behind the inn where he could also keep an eye on the Escort. In the wing mirror Butler saw the headlights of the oncoming car dip. When it stopped close to him he saw it was a cream Chevrolet. He recognized the driver as soon as he stepped out and came over.

134

It was the big American with dark brows which almost met across his boxer's nose. The American who'd tried to pick a quarrel with Newman in the bar at the Metropole in Padstow. Butler had seen the Yank as he slipped past the bar entrance on his way with the others to the elevator. But the Yank had *not* seen him.

'You been here long, buddy?' the American asked.

'Hours. What's it to you? I had a skinful back in the inn and I'm not risking getting caught by a patrol car. So *you* have a problem, mister?'

'Maybe my approach was wrong.'

'So, we've got that settled. You lost?'

'You know the area?'

The American was eyeing Butler carefully. He leaned inside the window. Butler chose that moment to manufacture a large belch. Beer fumes assailed the American's nostrils. His brutal face showed distaste.

'I asked you a question.'

'I know the area. And I asked you a question, mate.'

'You been here long?' the American persisted.

'I told you. Something wrong with your memory?' Butler snapped.

'Sorry. Wrong approach again. It's a friggin' cold night. I'm looking for a Mercedes 280E. Blue colour. Seen a car like that around here?'

'No.'

'Sure?' the American persisted further.

'There you go again. Asking the question I've answered. And you still haven't answered mine. You lost or something?'

'My pal and I – the one in the Merc. – were going to meet with each other. I've lost the note he gave me of the name of the hick place he said he'd wait.'

'I was right, mate,' Butler jeered. 'You are lost.'

'How do I get out of this dump?'

'This is a very small and attractive village. You piss off

135

out of it by driving straight on. Get it?'

The American gave him a savage look, walked back to his Chevrolet, clashed the gears and gunned the motor as he drove off, not giving a damn how many people he woke in the middle of the night.

'And you just missed getting a bullet in your gullet,' Butler said aloud.

He holstered the Walther he'd been holding in his lap under his windcheater. Checking his watch, he saw it was 3 a.m. Nield would be coming to take his turn while Cardon relieved Newman at any moment. He grabbed for his Walther again as a slim figure appeared next to his window. It was Nield.

'Time for your beauty sleep, Harry. Had a restful doze?'

Newquay Airport – several miles outside Newquay itself – was one of the bleakest departure points Paula had ever seen. Perched on a lonely plateau in the middle of nowhere, it was little more than a grassy field crossed by concrete runways. An eight-foot wire fence surrounded it and 'reception' was little more than a single-storey shed. They had found a place they could leave the cars and Tweed had reassured the attendant.

'It's a business trip and we might not be back for some time. All right to leave our cars?'

'At your own risk, guv'nor . . .'

Newman asked the girl behind the counter the question after they had checked in with their luggage when Tweed had collected and paid for the tickets.

'Yesterday a helicopter buzzed us as Padstow, nearly sank the boat we were in,' he lied smoothly. 'Does anyone ever hire choppers from here?'

'It happens occasionally, sir. Yesterday? I heard two Americans hired a machine for a few hours. It caused a bit of gossip – one of them had a British pilot's licence, which is unusual. And your flight is ready for departure . . .'

Newman exploded after they had all trudged across to the waiting machine with their luggage. It was a sizeable plane but he pointed at the nose.

'Look at those things!'

'They're propellers,' Tweed said quietly, knowing Newman disliked prop aircraft. 'It will fly, you know.'

'Yes, but will it get there? And we seem to be the only passengers for the 11.05 flight . . .'

The Brymon Airways aircraft was in mid-air before Paula looked down on the grey landscape. She was seated next to Tweed who stared ahead grimly.

'A penny for your thoughts. You've been very quiet since Harry Butler told us at breakfast about the reappearance of the American brute.'

'I'm worried and relieved at the same time,' Tweed admitted. 'Staggered that one of them should turn up at an out of the way place like St Mawgan. You realize what that means?'

'No, but you might tell me. I expect you will anyway.'

'For one to arrive in St Mawgan they must have an army of them combing Cornwall for us.'

'That's the worry. What's the relief?'

'That I guessed right early on in this sequence of macabre and mass-murder campaigns against us. To operate on such a scale calls for an organization of enormous magnitude. With all this firepower against us the ultimate enemy can only be one source.'

'You're not going to tell me what it is, are you? Before you say it, I'm sure you need more data to be absolutely sure. But where are we going now? London could be a death-trap.'

'It would be exactly that,' Tweed agreed. 'Which is why we're flying on to the one safe haven.'

'I suppose I shouldn't ask where?' Paula remarked.

'Switzerland. Where we have a powerful friend.'

15

'Norton is on the private line, Brad,' said Sara Maranoff.

'OK. Put him through. Time that street bum got results.'

'Brad, Norton is the best we've got. Hold yourself in. I also have Ms Hamilton waiting to see you.'

Sara knew what Ms Hamilton was about. She glanced round the Oval Office, checked that there were plenty of cushions on the large couch stood against one wall. She waved her index finger at him, warning him to cool it with Norton.

The President often omitted to shave until the end of the morning. His jaw and upper lip would be covered with a black stubble. But this morning he was freshly shaved, wore a smart blue suit with a crisp clean shirt and a tie. Ms Hamilton, Sara thought. Had to be at his best for *her*.

'I'll leave you to take your call,' she said.

Alone, March pushed back his chair, planted his feet on the desk top, crossed his ankles. He picked up the phone kept in a drawer.

'That you?' he barked.

'Norton here. I need those reinforcements . . .'

'They're aboard United flight 918 flying non-stop to London. Over the Atlantic as I speak with you. That's all the rest of Unit One we had in reserve here. Marvin Mencken is in charge.'

'That barracuda . . .'

'He's the best . . .' March remembered Sara's warning.

'I mean the best next to you. Now where are we with this goddamn problem? Where is Joel Dyson? Where is *Special Agent*' – his tone was savagely sarcastic – 'Barton Ives? Give.'

'In Zurich . . .'

'You've traced those bastards? Well, well. Miracles still happen. They're six feet under the ground now?'

'Not exactly. Not yet . . .'

'Don't give me no smoke, Norton. You sittin' on your thumbs out there? What the hell is the position?'

'We know both men are in Zurich. They've been seen but they disappeared again. Temporarily . . .'

'Temporarily is too long. What about the CIA shyster – Cord Dillon?'

'No sign of him yet, but we'll track him. An operation like this doesn't happen overnight.'

'I want all three of them put away for good. Norton, your head is on the block. There's always Mencken . . .'

March slammed down the phone, inserted a thick finger inside his neckband, loosened it. The phone rang again as he stood up to go to the door. He snatched it up.

'Yes?'

'Norton here. We got disconnected. I'm handling this my way. I'll be meeting Mencken's flight at London Airport. I'm flying to Zurich to take personal charge. How many reinforcements are aboard that flight? I need specific information.' A brief pause. 'Mr President.'

'Forty men. With what you've got you should be able to check everyone in Switzerland.'

'I said I'd handle this my way . . .'

The line went dead. March stared at the phone. Norton had had the balls to hang up on him. He remembered what Sara had said. Norton is the best. So maybe he was.

He checked his appearance in a mirror, went to the door, opened it, beaming his famous smile. The elegant blonde woman waiting on a seat outside returned the smile, walked in, he closed and locked the door. Taking her by the arm he led her to the couch, turned her round, lowered her gently.

'You've got too many clothes on, Glen. I'll start by undoing this top button . . .'

Swissair flight SR 803 had departed from London on schedule, taking off for Zurich at 13.50 hours. Tweed and his team were aboard in first class and had that section to themselves. One of the advantages of flying in February.

The Brymon Airways flight from Newquay Airport had arrived on time at London at 12.15 p.m. Tweed had collected and paid for the tickets by calling on Jim Corcoran. He had then had a tough conversation with Chief Inspector Roy Buchanan when he phoned him at the Yard.

'Where are you?' Buchanan had snapped.

'My whereabouts are not important. I see there has been not a single report of the massacre at Tresillian Manor in the press. Nine corpses and the press isn't interested? I suspect a "D" notice has been issued to the press. What excuse was used this time? A matter of national security?'

'This is a major anti-terrorist operation, Tweed. Which is all you're getting out of me. And there were ten corpses. A Tresillian Manor servant girl called Celia Yeo was found at the foot of High Tor. An anonymous caller alerted me. You wouldn't know anything about it, I suppose?'

Buchanan's tone dripped sarcasm. Tweed made him stick to the point.

'A major anti-terrorist operation? You really swallowed that? So they've got at you too . . .'

'My patience has run out with you, Tweed. I want you here at the Yard yesterday.'

'You're a man of integrity,' Tweed said quietly. 'You know you should be investigating a case of mass murder.

And not by terrorists. Don't take it out on me because they've fenced you in.'

'I said I expect you here at the Yard at the earliest possible moment. Needless to say, you don't leave the country.'

'You're still evading the main issue. Check up on the mass murder in Cornwall. Check on who set up fake roadblocks one night recently. Get a description from anyone who was stopped by them. Make sure you ask what nationality they were . . .'

'Are you telling me how to do my job?'

'I'm simply suggesting you actually *do* your job. Have to go. Goodbye . . .'

Sitting next to Paula in mid-air he had relayed his conversation with Buchanan to her. He made his comments after he told her how he had ended the call.

'The significance of that verbal duel was what Buchanan *didn't* say.'

'What was that?'

'He didn't deny he'd been told to pigeon-hole the case. I expect he was ordered to by the Commissioner. After the Commissioner had taken a call from Downing Street. They have thrown a tight net round the whole horrific business.'

'But why? I'm getting scared the way Howard can't contact the PM.'

'Someone with immense power has thrown out a smoke-screen. By labelling these violent events as the work of a major terrorist organization it gives the people at the top a perfect excuse for their inexcusable actions. I know I've just contradicted myself, but you grasp what I'm getting at.'

'Except I can't grasp who could have such an evil influence over our Prime Minister.'

'Read the papers – the international news. That's where one of the keys lies. Now I want to give a message to the pilot to be radioed ahead of us.'

141

'Can I see it?' Paula asked, her curiosity aroused.

While Tweed was writing on a small pad he'd taken from his pocket Paula glanced beyond him from her window seat at Newman and Cardon who were seated opposite across the aisle. Newman grinned at her, gave a thumbs-up signal. Tweed and Paula occupied the front seats where there was plenty of leg room. Immediately behind them sat Butler and Nield who had refused drinks and remained very alert.

Tweed finished writing, showed her the message, put it in an envelope, sealed it and called to the stewardess.

'Could you please hand this to the wireless operator? It's very urgent.'

'Certainly, sir . . .'

Paula sat frowning. She asked her question as the plane flew on over dense clouds which looked just like the Alps, shining in the brilliant sun. At that moment the aircraft was barely midway between London and Zurich.

'I thought you said Switzerland would be a haven of safety?'

'It won't be,' Tweed said with a face like stone. 'Not for the opposition once I locate them.'

The radio message, addressed to Tweed's old friend, Arthur Beck, Chief of Federal Police, had been terse and to the point.

Urgently request full protection six people aboard flight SR 803. ETA Kloten Airport, Zurich, 1625 hours your time. Tweed.

The plane had begun its descent to Kloten when Paula saw out of the opposite window a breathtaking panorama of a great range of snowbound mountains. Massive in their continuity, she realized she was staring at the Bernese Oberland, the most spectacular mountains in all Europe.

She continued gazing at them. They reminded her of

142

some enormous tidal wave about to engulf the entire continent. The descent increased in angle, the view vanished. Beyond her own window there was nothing to see but a curtain of clouds drifting past, growing denser as they dropped lower and lower.

Suddenly the clouds cleared and the lights of Switzerland were coming up to meet her. The stewardess returned again, whispered to Tweed.

'We've had instructions from Zurich Control that you and your party will leave the plane first after landing.'

'I'm glad you added "after landing",' Tweed joked.

Paula sensed his sudden change of mood – Tweed was looking forward to the opportunity to take action. She felt her own spirits rise. For days she had lived in a state of suppressed terror. She stared eagerly out of the window again.

They were landing – she could see the forest of evergreens which surrounded Kloten Airport. The Swiss pilot brought the machine down so smoothly the wheels barely kissed the concrete runway. As they emerged Paula saw a familiar figure waiting just beyond the metal platform leading from plane to airport building. The Chief of the Federal Police. He took hold of her in both arms and hugged her.

'Welcome to Switzerland, Paula.'

'I'm here too,' said Tweed, amused because he knew Beck was very fond of Paula.

Arthur Beck, in his forties, was slim and plump-cheeked. His most arresting features were his alert grey eyes beneath dark brows and his strong nose above a trim moustache. Of medium height, he moved his hands and feet quickly, his complexion was ruddy and he wore a smart grey suit, a blue striped shirt and a blue tie. Tweed quickly introduced him to Philip Cardon: Beck had met the others before and knew Bob Newman well. He led the way, talking rapidly to Tweed and Paula in perfect English.

'We're bypassing Passport Control and Customs. I have limos outside waiting to take you wherever you want to go.'

'The Hotel Schweizerhof opposite the Hauptbahnhof. It will be our official residence but we won't actually be staying there. We'll be at the Hotel Gotthard just behind the Schweizerhof,' said Tweed.

'You are taking great precautions, my friend,' commented Beck. 'This must be a very serious affair.'

'A matter of life and death – for all of us. I'll tell you what's happened while we're driving into Zurich.'

'Our bags,' Paula intervened. 'They'll be delivered to the carousel . . .'

'We travelled first class and were the only passengers,' Tweed said quickly.

'Easy.' Beck grinned. He spoke to an aide in plain clothes who had walked alongside them. As the man dashed off he explained. 'I've told him to collect all the first-class luggage off the carousel. He'll bring it to the cars . . .'

They were escorted via a devious route which bypassed Passport Control and Customs. Striding across the concourse, Beck guided them to a convoy of three waiting stretched Mercedes, all black in colour. Near by uniformed motorcyclist police waited, straddling their machines. Beck gestured towards them as he opened the door of the first car.

'Outriders. Our escort. After receiving your message I decided to take no chances. I drop you outside the Schweizerhof?'

'Yes, please,' said Tweed. 'Later we make our way on foot one by one to the Gotthard. I've booked rooms in both hotels . . .'

It was a twenty-minute drive from the airport into the centre of Zurich. Beck sat next to Tweed in the rear of the limo while Paula was seated alongside Tweed. The driver wore civilian clothes, as did the tough-looking individual in the front passenger seat.

Newman, Butler, Nield and Cardon occupied seats in the limo behind them and the third car was full of more men in plain clothes. The outriders on motorcycles led the way into the Swiss city while two more brought up the rear.

Beck listened in silence as Tweed told him concisely everything that had happened to them – including the bombing of SIS headquarters in London and the events in Cornwall. Frequently the Swiss glanced back through the rear window. At one moment he interrupted Tweed for the first time.

'Excuse me, I have to radio a message to the rear car. We were followed from the airport by an Impala – significant, possibly, that it is an American car . . .'

Picking up the microphone slung from the side of the car he spoke in Switzer-Deutsch, the dialect understood only by the Swiss. Tucking the microphone back on its hook, he explained after again glancing through the rear window, 'I ordered interception. The third car has just stopped that Impala. They'll think up some fictitious traffic regulations the driver's broken to delay him. And all these cars are bulletproof. Your story, Tweed, is very strange, but of course I believe you. It might interest you to know there are too many Americans arriving in Switzerland – especially in Zurich.'

'Too many?' Paula leaned forward. 'How do you know that?'

Beck smiled cynically. 'Oh, we do know what is going on in our country. In late February you might expect a few businessmen, even the odd wealthy tourist from the States. But these men – and we don't like the look of them – all carry diplomatic passports. From my headquarters in Berne I've already phoned their embassy and complained that they're exceeding their complement of diplomatic staff. The Ambassador, an old friend – and one of the few

President March has not replaced by some of his cronies and backers – was embarrassed. I found it significant. He told me these men were soon to be routed to other embassies in Europe. Both of us knew he was not telling the truth.'

'So Zurich could be dangerous?' Paula suggested.

'Yes, it could.' He smiled again. 'But not as dangerous as Britain, from what Tweed has told me. How are you going to proceed, Tweed? Or is that top secret?'

'Not at all. I want to locate three men. Joel Dyson – I think it may have all started with him. Then Special Agent Barton Ives and Cord Dillon. One of them has to tell me what the blazes is happening.'

'I do find' – Beck paused to ruminate – 'the most unexpected of those three people to be running is this Barton Ives. FBI – why should someone be after his blood?'

'That mystifies me too,' Tweed admitted.

'A pity you don't know what this Norton looks like,' Beck commented.

'I gather no one knows that. Which I find sinister . . .'

Tweed, carrying his bag, led the way into the Schweizerhof, where he had stayed on previous visits. The same concierge greeted him warmly. As they went up in the lift after registering, Tweed told Paula to come and see him urgently when she'd left her bag in her room.

'I have room 217,' he reminded her as he left the elevator.

She was tapping on his door within three minutes of his arriving in the large corner room overlooking the main station at the front. The side windows looked down on the famous Bahnhofstrasse – the street of great banks and some of the most luxurious shops in the world. He went out of the spacious living-cum-bedroom into the lobby to let Paula in.

'I'm afraid I've got rather a lot for you to do,' he said.

'Fire away!'

'All of us must leave in our rooms here convincing evidence that this *is* where we are staying. Toothbrushes, toothpaste, shaving kit, et cetera in the bathrooms . . .'

'The ones we're using now would be most convincing . . .'

'Agreed. Plus about half our clothes in the wardrobes. Now that means I want you to . . .'

'Go out and buy six toothbrushes, six tubes of paste, five electric shavers, more make-up for myself,' she interjected.

'Why more make-up?'

'Because you expect to find some in a room occupied by a woman. While I'm buying I'll have to collect a load of large carrier bags. Presumably we need those to sneak out of here to the Gotthard with the clothes we take. I foresee one other problem.'

'Which is?' Tweed enquired.

'We would look suspicious turning up at the Gotthard without suitcases. I know – two of the men wait with new suitcases we buy in the men's lavatory down in Shopville.' Paula peered out of the side window at the escalator leading down into the underground shopping centre. 'Two more of us, say Bob and Philip, can take the carriers with the clothes into the lavatory and they can be put inside the cases in cubicles.'

'I don't know why I bother planning things like this out,' Tweed said, raising his hands in mock frustration. 'Not when I have you with me.'

'I'll be away for a while on my shopping expedition,' she warned. 'It would look funny if I bought six of everything at one shop.'

'I'm not letting you go alone,' Tweed said firmly. 'I'm calling Butler to accompany you as bodyguard.'

'Harry is a perfect choice. And he can help to carry

my purchases. What about the suitcases?'

'I'll phone Newman and Cardon. They can buy the suitcases and call me back when they've done the job. Then they can get coffee at Sprüngli and call me again. By then you and Harry should have done your shopping. I'll fix a precise time for Pete Nield and myself to meet you, collect the carriers and make the switch in Shopville. Have you got enough Swiss money?'

'You gave me sufficient at London Airport to go out and buy an outfit Elizabeth Taylor would be happy to wear. Come to think of it, I rather fancy a Chanel suit,' she teased him and left the room.

Tweed summoned Newman and Cardon and gave them their instructions. As they left, the phone rang. Tweed frowned, lifted the receiver cautiously.

'Yes. Who is it?'

'Beck here,' the familiar voice opened. 'I have bad news. Remember that Impala my men stopped on the way from the airport? They found him just ending a conversation on a mobile phone. He undoubtedly warned his chief that a competitor had arrived.' Beck was phrasing his message carefully, knowing it was passing through a hotel switchboard. 'You might have company from the opposition earlier than you expected. Keep in touch. I'm staying in Zurich.'

'Thank you.'

Tweed put down the phone with a sense of foreboding.

16

The move to the Hotel Gotthard, only a short distance behind the Schweizerhof, had been completed by eight in the evening. Tweed arrived in his room, threw back the lid of his case, went down to the bar. He ordered a glass of champagne, paid for it and began exploring the hotel.

With the glass in his hand he appeared to be looking for someone. He tipped some of the contents into a plant pot and continued checking on the few people who sat in the lounge area. No one suspicious anywhere, no sound of an American voice.

Strolling slowly along he passed a man sitting in a chair reading a paper. A slim individual, smartly dressed, he glanced up, folded his paper, followed Tweed to a quiet area near the cheaper restaurant fronting on the Bahnhofstrasse.

'Excuse me, sir. Have you a light?'

Tweed tensed, turned round slowly. The slim man was clean-shaven, his dark hair slicked back over his head. About thirty years old, he held a cigarette in his hand. Tweed continued staring at him as he reached for the lighter he carried for other people's cigarettes.

As he ignited it the man leaned forward, holding one hand to shield the flame although there wasn't a current of air in the place. The man took his time getting his cigarette lit and it was then Tweed saw the open folder held in the palm of the extended hand, the printing inside below a photo of himself.

Federal Police. P. Schmidt. A visiting card had been

attached in the lower half with Sellotape. *With the compliments of Arthur Beck.*

'Thank you, sir,' the slim man said. 'It's very quiet here. February, I expect . . .'

Tweed went back up in the lift with mixed feelings. It was very good of Beck to post one of his men inside the hotel. But it also indicated that Beck was worried about their safety.

He inserted the key into his door, opened it, reached for the switch to illuminate the room before entering it. On the carpeted floor was a long white envelope which had been slipped under the door.

Tweed closed and locked the door. Using a penknife, he slit open the envelope carefully. There was one sheet of folded paper inside. No address at the top and a brief hand-written message.

Call me from a safe phone at this number . . . Between 8 p.m. and 8.15 p.m. this evening. Dillon

He was startled. Dillon must either be staying in the hotel, as he had suggested he should – or he had observed their arrival. Tweed checked his watch. 8.08 p.m. He had seven minutes to reach an outside phone. Picking up the phone he dialled Butler's room number.

'Tweed here. Harry, we have to go out. Very fast . . .'

'I'm on my way . . .'

Tweed had his overcoat on when Butler arrived wearing a padded windcheater. He opened the front, whipped a 7.65-mm. Walther automatic out of a hip holster, grinned and replaced the weapon. Tweed waited until they were hurrying on foot up the Bahnhofstrasse in a bitterly cold night before he asked the question.

'Where the hell did you get that? We ditched all weapons on our way to Newquay Airport.'

'By courtesy of Chief of Police Beck. You didn't see

the canvas hold-all he handed to Paula after you'd left the car outside the Schweizerhof?'

'No, I damn well didn't.'

'It contained Walthers for Pete Nield and me, a .32 Browning automatic for Paula and a Smith & Wesson for Newman. Plus ammo for all the guns. Paula guessed what was in the hold-all, passed it to Newman before she followed you inside. There were also special certificates to carry a firearm, signed by Beck, for each of us.'

For Butler it was a long speech. By the time he had ended it they had arrived at the down escalator into Shopville. Tweed's only reply was a grunt. He liked people to keep him informed but it *had* been a rush, moving to the Gotthard.

At that time of night the underground complex was quiet and few people were about. Tweed deliberately didn't glance inside the phone cubicles which were occupied. If one contained Cord Dillon he wasn't risking drawing attention to him.

'I won't be long,' he told Butler as he entered an empty cubicle.

He dialled the Zurich number, standing sideways. Butler was taking an apparent interest in a closed vegetable shop opposite.

'Who is it?' Dillon's voice asked brusquely.

'Tweed here. Got your message . . .'

'Just listen. Special Agent Barton Ives is in town. He will try to contact you if it's safe . . .'

'Why did he leave the States? I need some data . . .'

'He was investigating a chain of serial murders in Tennessee, Mississippi, Louisiana, Alabama, Georgia and Florida. All of them women. Raped, murdered . . .'

'So why would he need to flee to Europe?'

'Ask him. Got to go now. Zurich is swarming with Norton's gunmen. I have a hunch Norton will be here soon, may be already. Then the earthquake rocks Zurich.'

151

'Cord, how on earth do these serial murders link up with what's going on . . .'

'Not over the phone. Ask Barton. Stay under cover. I'm doing just that . . .'

'Since we don't know what Norton looks like it doesn't help to know we may be enjoying his company . . .'

'No one enjoys that. They just end up dead. Got to go . . .'

Again the line was cut before Tweed could ask him a vital question. The abrupt termination of the call worried Tweed as he walked back to the Gotthard with Butler. Dillon was a tough character and he'd never known him be scared of anyone before. This Norton must be quite something.

Norton was waiting at London Airport when United flight 918 landed from Washington. He stood among a small crowd of people who were waiting to greet arrivals. Alongside him stood a porter holding a large heavy envelope Norton had given him together with a £20 tip.

Marvin Mencken appeared first followed by four of his men. A tall well-built man, Mencken had a cadaverous face and behind his back he was nicknamed 'the Skeleton'. Wearing a dark blue trench coat and carrying his bag, his narrow foxy eyes swept the concourse as he paused.

'That's him,' Norton told the porter. 'The one in a dark blue trench coat.'

The porter, who had been given very precise instructions, hurried forward. Sidling his way between people he stopped in front of Mencken, presented him with the envelope.

'I've been asked to hand you this.'

'Who by?' Mencken flashed back, his eyes darting round the concourse as he took the envelope. 'Point him out to me.'

'Not part of my instructions, sir . . .'

'Look, you bum . . .' Mencken had dropped his bag, his hand grasped the porter by the shirt collar. 'You're goin' to point him out to me. Then you get fifty dollars. Play dumb and I'll tear your throat out.'

The porter, scared stiff, gulped. Indignation overtook fear. This was his airport. Reaching up, he dug his finger-nails deep into the back of the hand holding him. Mencken let go, was about to tread hard on one of the porter's feet when his victim spoke.

'Any more of this and I'm calling Security. I can see the Chief over there.'

'Get lost,' Mencken snarled.

He couldn't afford trouble here – especially if Norton was watching him. He ripped open the envelope. Inside were forty one-way Swissair tickets to Zurich, a wad of banknotes, high Swiss denominations, and a typed instruction.

Board the flight with your friends. At Zurich you receive fresh orders.

The instruction ended with a flourishing 'N' written in ink. Norton. Mencken gritted his teeth. Sara Maranoff had told him in her curt way that he was second in command to Norton. Which was something he didn't appreciate. Especially as he had no idea what Norton looked like. Always just an abrasive voice on the phone.

Mencken had divided his group of forty men into sec-tions of five, each with a leader. He began to distribute five tickets to each section leader, gave them the instruction for arrival in Zurich.

'You hang around the carousel at Kloten. I may give you orders then. Or I may wait till we hit the concourse. Just depends the mood I'm in. Well, look at the time – move ass . . .'

* * *

153

'I've made an appointment to see Walter Amberg at the Zürcher Kredit Bank in Talstrasse,' Tweed announced.

They were all having an excellent breakfast at a long table in La Soupière. This was the high-class dining-room on the first floor of the Schweizerhof. Having slept at the Gotthard they had wandered round to the Schweizerhof in pairs. It confirmed the impression they were staying at the hotel.

At Tweed's suggestion, the previous evening at nine o'clock Newman and Butler, carrying keys to all their six rooms, had paid a brief visit to the Schweizerhof. Each had taken three rooms, had then pulled back the covers, kicked off their shoes and rolled in the beds, rumpling sheets and pillows. This further confirmed the impression to the management that they were sleeping there.

'Walter is the twin of poor Julius,' Paula recalled in a whisper.

'The identical twin. Seen together you couldn't tell them apart,' Tweed agreed. 'The Swiss do have a sense of humour. Julius and Walter used to wear exactly the same outfits – so often their own staff got them mixed up.'

'And does Walter know about Julius's murder?' Paula asked in the same low voice.

'No. Which is unfortunate. No one – even Buchanan – had thought of asking who should be informed. I think the Chief Inspector was too appalled by the scale of the massacre. I shall have to break the news to Walter. Would you like to come with me?'

'Yes, please,' said Paula. 'Had Julius a wife?'

'He had, but I don't know her address. I did think of trying to get hold of it – but it's hardly the type of news you want to tell people over the phone.'

'A Swiss wife?' queried Paula, her curiosity aroused.

'No, English as a matter of fact. Much younger than her husband was. I think her name is Eve. Walter will have to undertake that unpleasant task. Walter is Chairman –

Julius was Chief Executive, the man who really ran the bank and its various branch offices.'

'Is Walter up to it?' asked Newman. 'To taking over and running the organization?'

'No idea.' Tweed polished off his bacon and eggs, pushed his plate back. 'You know, Paula, among all the things which have happened one stands out, puzzles me.'

'And that is?'

'Why, after shooting down Julius Amberg at Tresillian Manor, did the assassin throw acid all over his face? Not for revenge – we're not dealing with that kind of enemy. So why the acid?'

17

Norton travelled on the same flight to Zurich as Mencken and his large team. But whereas the forty men who were reinforcements occupied economy seats Norton was in the first-class section.

He wore an English suit and spoke with an English accent without a trace of his native American. When he had boarded the plane at London Airport he had chosen the aisle seat next to an elegantly dressed Swiss woman. He was careful that nothing in his manner suggested he was trying to pick her up.

'May I sit here, if you don't mind?' he had enquired courteously. 'There is more leg room and I have business papers I must study before we arrive.'

'The seat is vacant,' she replied after glancing briefly at him.

The plane took off and Norton extracted a folder of

papers with statistics about computers. He didn't understand any of it but if Mencken peered into First Class it would seem they were a couple travelling together.

Holding his briefcase, he moved quickly when the plane landed at Kloten. By the time Marvin Mencken arrived at the carousel a uniformed porter was waiting for him. He handed him a large envelope.

'I was asked to give this to you, sir. Your baggage will arrive very shortly.'

Remembering his experience at London Airport Mencken made no attempt to question the porter who was walking away. He glanced round at the passengers – not a chance of identifying Norton, assuming he was near the carousel, which he doubted. Mencken opened the envelope. Another sheet with no address and detailed instructions.

Distribute your men among the following four hotels – two groups should occupy the first hotel listed. Golden Bay Tours have booked accommodation. I will call you at your hotel telling you where to pick up special equipment. Hotels – Baur-en-Ville, Eden au Lac, Dolder Grand, Baur au Lac.

The sheet was again signed in ink with the flourishing 'N'. Mencken swore to himself at the familiar abrupt commanding tone of the instruction. He began strolling among the passengers, giving each section leader the name of his hotel. As he did so the luggage started moving along the carousel.

'Special equipment' – Mencken knew that referred to guns and explosives.

Newman had decided to accompany Tweed and Paula to meet Walter Amberg at the bank headquarters in Talstrasse, which ran parallel to Bahnhofstrasse. Paula was intrigued and a little nervous. She couldn't get out of her head 'snapshot' pictures of Julius Amberg before the attack – and how he had looked with his face destroyed by acid. Now she was going to meet the identical twin . . .

Prepared as she was, it came as a shock when a Swiss personal assistant showed them into a large office and a man came forward, hand extended, to greet them.

'Welcome back to Zurich, Tweed. Always good to see you.'

Small and portly, in his fifties, he also wore his black hair without a parting, slicked back from his high forehead. Under thick brows his blue eyes were shrewd, his face clean-shaven and plump. Inwardly, Paula gasped. She was staring at a mirror image of the banker she had met at Tresillian Manor. He even wore the same dark suit with a red silk display handkerchief protruding from his breast pocket.

Tweed introduced Paula, who gathered that Newman had met the banker before. Amberg escorted them to comfortable chairs round a long polished antique board-room table.

'I'm sure you would all like coffee,' he suggested and gave the order over an intercom. 'I understand you have met Julius down in Cornwall,' he went on, addressing Tweed as he sat down with Paula on his right and Tweed and Newman facing him. 'I haven't heard from him – not unusual since Julius often told me little about his affairs. I trust all went well.'

Tweed took a deep breath. He had not looked forward to this moment.

'I'm afraid I have bad news for you about Julius.'

'He's ill?' Amberg looked surprised. 'He's hardly ever ill. Always says he hasn't the time.'

'The news is worse than that, much worse,' Tweed warned.

'You can't mean he's . . . dead?'

'I mean just that . . .'

157

Tweed began to give a terse account of the events which had taken place in Cornwall. Amberg listened, his face blank of emotion, but Paula noticed his lips had tightened as the gruesome tale unfolded. The Swiss listened with his hands steepled, fingertips of each hand touching – a mannerism she had noticed at the dining table in Tresillian Manor.

'It's a grim tragedy,' Tweed concluded, 'and we have no idea who made the fatal attack – or why. I was hoping you might have some inkling.'

'As I told you, Julius handled his own affairs. Which makes it difficult for me to help. I don't – didn't – even know why he was going to Cornwall to meet you.'

'Have you ever heard of a man called Joel Dyson?' Tweed enquired.

'Yes. Not an individual I took to – I'm sorry, is he a friend of yours?'

'He most certainly isn't. Do go on.'

'This Dyson arrived recently with a suitcase and asked to see Julius. He was quite aggressive and I was surprised when my brother agreed to see him.' Amberg looked at Newman. 'I understand you once did Julius a great favour which involved this individual.'

'It was nothing,' Newman said, dismissing the incident.

'Dyson seemed frightened on his second visit here,' the banker continued. 'After seeing my brother he asked to be let out by the rear door. Later Julius told me Dyson had handed him a film and a tape recording for safe keeping. I haven't seen Dyson since.'

'Where were the film and the tape stored?' Tweed asked casually.

'In the vault, of course. Then Julius had them transferred to the vault in our Basle branch. I've no idea why.' He clapped a hand to his forehead. 'Oh, God, I had forgotten about Eve. Since this is the first I've heard of this dreadful news she may not know. Eve is his estranged English wife.'

'Estranged?' Tweed enquired delicately.

'Yes. Julius had his final quarrel with Eve just before he flew to London on his way to Cornwall. They had not been getting on well for some time. Foreign wives . . .' He tilted his head towards Paula. 'Please do excuse my phraseology. Foreign wives,' he continued, 'are often a disaster when they marry Swiss men. Julius told me just before he left for London they had agreed on a separation, that he never wanted to see her again. But someone must tell her . . .'

Amberg trailed off, looked all at sea. The shock of what happened is beginning to sink in, Paula thought. It was Tweed who intervened.

'If you would like to give me her address, Walter, I will go and see her myself. I was at Tresillian Manor shortly after the tragedy occurred.'

'As her brother-in-law I suppose I should, but . . .'

'Give me her address, if she's still in Switzerland,' Tweed urged.

'She's here in Zurich.' Amberg extracted a white card from a box, wrote down the address and phone number, handed it to Tweed. 'She lives in the villa Julius has – had – in the Dolder area. He was moving into an apartment when he came back. I'm very grateful to you.'

'One more thing.' Tweed had stood up after draining the excellent coffee his assistant had brought in earlier. 'I expect you know whether Julius had viewed the film, listened to the tape Joel Dyson delivered before having them sent to Basle?'

'No idea. Why was Dyson so frightened when he brought them to us?' Amberg asked.

'Oh, that's simple. There are assassins here looking for him – to kill him. At least ten people have so far been murdered over this business. Maybe you should have a guard, Walter.'

'This *is* Switzerland,' the banker said indignantly.

* * *

159

'Something's very wrong about the sequence of events,' Tweed said as they left the building and headed for Bahnhofstrasse.

Butler and Nield appeared out of nowhere as they walked along. Newman was walking on the inside nearest the shops with Paula between him and Tweed on the outside. Butler strolled slowly past Tweed, staring ahead as he spoke out of the corner of his mouth.

'You've been followed. Chap in ski gear. Peaked cap with tinted visor . . .'

He continued on ahead of them while Nield remained behind the trio. Paula stopped for a moment, apparently to glance into a shop window. In the reflection from the brilliant sun she saw the man in a ski outfit walking ahead of Nield. She resumed her conversation as they approached Bahnhofstrasse.

'What is wrong about the sequence of events Walter described to us?'

'Dyson arrives with film and tape. Who could resist the temptation to watch, to listen? This coincides with Julius leaving his wife, Eve. It further coincides with his urgent call to me to meet him, followed by his flight to Tresillian Manor. Plus the fact he transferred film and tape to the bank vault in Basle. Dyson asked to be let out by the back exit. The only reason for that is he suspected he'd been followed, which he probably told Amberg. Even if he didn't, Amberg would guess the reason.'

'Why do you think Julius left his wife so suddenly?'

'I can only guess. But I know he had a mistress in Geneva. Normal lifestyle for *some* Swiss bankers. Live in one city, have your mistress in another, visit her at the weekend on a fictitious business trip. Maybe Eve found out – being English she might not have appreciated old Swiss bankers' customs. That's why I want to see her. I'm hungry. Let's have a coffee and cake at Sprüngli before we start checking . . .'

*　　*　　*

160

The tea room at the famous Sprüngli was on the first floor, overlooking Bahnhofstrasse. It gave Paula an eerie feeling when she recalled the package the 'postman' at Tresillian Manor had delivered before murdering eight people – a box of chocolates from Sprüngli.

'Excuse me a moment,' Newman said.

They ordered coffee from the waitress as Newman peered out of the window down into the boulevard-like street. He joined them as they went to the counter to select a cake, waited until they were seated again.

'We still have company. Ski-man with his tinted visor is leaning against a tree on the far side where he can watch the entrance to this place. No sign of Pete Nield or Butler.'

'There wouldn't be, but they'll be out there,' said Paula as she dug her fork into a cream pastry. 'This is super.' She glanced round the long room where wooden-topped tables were carefully arranged, at the hygienic counter they had visited for their cakes. 'I think this is where the Zurich *grandes dames* meet each other to natter about the latest gossip. Bet there's plenty of that if they have bankers for husbands.'

'Why should they be bankers' wives?' Newman asked.

'Just look at them. Dripping with pearls, three or four solid gold bangles round their wrists. Dripping with wealth.' She looked at Tweed. 'What's next on the programme – and why did we register in our own names at the Gotthard?'

'To smoke out the enemy,' Tweed said, his expression determined. 'This is the battlefield. When we leave here we'll go to police headquarters, hope to find Beck there. Philip Cardon wants a weapon. Then we'll take a taxi up to that villa in the Dolder area in the hope I can talk to Eve Amberg. That could be interesting . . .'

*   *   *

161

Sara Maranoff walked into the Oval Office, closed the door, locked it. She ran a finger over her lips as she tried to assess her boss's mood. Bradford March was twisted sideways in his chair, staring out of the windows, his thick lips pressed together. A black stubble covered his jaw and she didn't like the look of his expression. She took a deep breath as he turned to glare at her.

'Bad news won't wait, Brad. I just took a call from Zurich – whoever it was cleverly insisted on speaking to me. You may be glad about that.'

'More bad news I can do without. Get to it. Norton telling us he hasn't achieved one friggin' thing?'

'Norton is holding on the line, but this call came from a no-name guy. Said he had a couple of items you might not want him to go public with – not how he phrased it but that's what he meant. He's demanding twenty million dollars for them – whatever they may be. Could be a crank . . .'

She was watching March's reaction closely. The President leaned forward, folded his hairy-backed thick fingers, rested them on the desk. He had a look of thunder and she was careful to keep quiet.

'You traced the number he was calling from?' snapped March.

'Tried to. He wasn't on the line long enough. All they could get was a Zurich call. Is there something I should know, Brad?'

'You should put Norton through *now* . . .'

'Norton here, Chief. I've taken personal control of the operation on the spot. I'm in Zurich. I've traced Tweed and company, got the bastard in my sights.'

'Handle that your own way.' March's tone became tough. 'This is an order. Track down Dyson, Ives and Dillon. Take them out. Got it? No more friggin' around. Just do it . . .'

He slammed down the phone, stood up and began

prowling. Wearing an open-necked shirt which exposed his hairy chest he was also clad in jeans and sneakers – the outfit he wore when mixing with the 'common folk'.

'What about this crank?' Sara pressed. 'We ignore him if he calls again?'

'He calls again, say we'll pay. Ask him where the money is to be deposited. Then call Norton, tell him the location. He's to surround it with an army of concealed and armed men. Tell him to make up a bundle which looks like it contains banknotes as bait. Just do it – and it isn't anything you need to know about.'

Tweed had left Sprüngli with Newman and Paula and they were walking up Bahnhofstrasse *en route* to police headquarters. Despite the brilliant glare of the sun it was bitterly cold and there were few people about. A small crowd stood waiting for a tram.

They heard one rumbling from behind them and had just reached the crowd when the Ski-man brushed close to Tweed. Newman had gripped his Smith & Wesson and behind the skier Butler held his Walther concealed in his hand. The Ski-man had white hair projecting from under the back of his cap. Tweed laid a restraining hand on Newman's arm.

'It's all right . . .'

'Tweed' – the Ski-man spoke rapidly in an American accent – 'one thing I forgot. My office safe at Langley was raided – they have photos of yourself and Paula . . .'

He leapt aboard the tram just as the automatic doors were closing. Newman and Paula stared at Tweed.

'That was Cord Dillon,' he told them. 'Wearing a white wig. Well disguised. And now we know the worst. Paula and I are recognizable to the opposition. Bob, stay close to Paula.'

'And I'm staying close to you,' Butler told him. 'I was

163

expecting Dillon to produce a knife. If he had done he'd have got a bullet through the spine.'

'Don't think badly of him. He's on his own and running. He just did us a big favour. Now for Beck and then Eve Amberg . . .'

Amberg's estranged wife lived in a large old grey villa perched high up above the city. As they'd climbed higher and higher a panoramic view of Lake Zurich and the city had appeared below. The three-storey villa stood back from the road behind tall railings rising up from a low stone wall. A short distance behind their taxi a black Mercedes slowed, parked by the kerb.

Behind the wheel, Butler, who had hired the car, looked at Nield seated alongside him. He checked his rear-view mirror again.

'No sign of a tail, Pete. So I suppose we just wait.'

'Someone in the BMW parked in front of the villa. A girl, I think. Tweed and Co. are approaching her . . .'

After paying off the cab driver, Tweed, with Paula and Newman, was approaching the wrought-iron gates when Tweed stared at the BMW. He paused, spoke half under his breath.

'I don't believe it. I think a word with her would be a good idea before we go barging in.'

The girl sitting in the front passenger seat by herself wore a pale blue woollen helmet but it didn't conceal the wave of golden hair falling to her shoulders. She wore sun-glasses and turned as Tweed bent down to speak to her. Paula was stunned. It was Jennie Blade, last seen in Padstow.

'You're a long way from Cornwall,' Tweed greeted her genially. 'You flew to Zurich?'

164

'Bloody hell, no. Look, it's freezing out there. Bob, come and sit beside me. Tweed, you and Paula climb in the back. It's warm as toast in here. Then we can talk.'

She flashed Newman a warm smile as he settled in the front passenger seat. She had the heaters going full blast and the warmth hit them. Jennie twisted round to talk to Tweed.

'We sailed here in the flaming *Mayflower*. Across the North Sea, up the Rhine and berthed at Basle. Then by train to here. I was thrown all over the place during the sea crossing. His lordship is mad keen on sailing.'

'His lordship? Gaunt, you mean?' Tweed queried. 'Where is he now?'

'At this moment? He's inside that villa. Enjoying himself.' She gazed fixedly at Tweed. 'Could you and I meet for a drink this evening? I'll tell you the story of my life.' She grinned wickedly. 'You'll find it a rather lurid tale.'

'Certainly,' Tweed agreed promptly. 'Six o'clock at the Hummer Bar in the Gotthard? You'll find the main entrance in Bahnhofstrasse a stone's throw from the Bahnhofplatz.'

'I'll look forward to that.'

'What did you mean when you said Gaunt was enjoying himself inside that villa?'

'Oh, didn't you know? Eve Amberg is one of his girl friends.'

18

Tweed hauled on the long chain bell-pull inside the massive porch of the villa. Turning round, he waved to Jennie Blade, who waved back. Newman stared at the door.

'Is this a good time to call?' Paula asked. 'What on earth are Gaunt and Jennie of all people doing in Zurich?'

'That's what I hope to find out . . .'

He broke off as the massive door was unlocked, unchained and swung inward by a maidservant in uniform. A Swiss girl, Paula thought when she heard her speak in English.

'Is Madame expecting you?' She studied the card Tweed had given her. 'You are an insurance salesman?'

'Hardly. I'm Chief Claims Investigator. Just take the card to your mistress and tell her we've travelled here all the way from Cornwall to see her.'

'I suppose she has to get dressed quickly,' Paula said in a low voice.

'Not necessarily,' Tweed replied.

In less than a minute the door was opened again, the maid informed them that Madame would see them now. The hall was very large and something about the atmosphere repelled Paula. The old woodblock floor was highly polished and a large over-ornate grandfather clock against one wall ticked ponderously. Leading them to the rear of the hall, the maid opened a door, stood aside. Tweed, sensing Paula's reluctance, marched straight into a vast living room with windows overlooking a neglected back garden which was a tangle of undergrowth and stunted evergreens.

'Mr Tweed? I believe you have met Mr Gaunt. I don't know about your friends . . .'

'They all know me. Naturally,' boomed Gaunt. 'We've had drinks together in the local pub. Right, Tweed? You following me around? Want to know what I'm up to, I expect. Eh? Let me introduce you all. This is Madame Eve Amberg, wife of the late lamented Julius Amberg.'

'Not all that lamented, Mr Tweed. Do sit down, all of you. Gregory is just leaving.'

166

Eve Amberg was an attractive woman in her mid-thirties. She had long titian hair and looked as though she had just returned from an expensive hairdresser. She had greenish eyes, strong features, a full mouth and a shapely chin. Her complexion had the marble-like glow Paula knew came from careful and lengthy make-up. She wore a bolero jacket over a green dress which emphasized her shapely figure. Her long legs were crossed elegantly. She had an aura of a strong personality and her voice was soft and appealing.

She patted the empty seat beside her on a couch inviting Tweed to sit next to her. The vacant cushion showed no sign of recent occupation. Gaunt was standing under an elaborate chandelier, clad in a houndstooth jacket and cavalry twill trousers with a blue silk cravat under his jaw. Very much the country gent, Paula thought.

'Eve, I really must go. I regret the reason for coming to see you.' He looked at Tweed before leaving. 'I now leave you to the tender mercies of Eve. Survive her charms if you can . . .'

Newman, seated next to Paula on another large couch, detected a note of irony in the remark. Eve chuckled good-humouredly, called out to him as he reached the door.

'You really are a horrible man, Gregory – leaving my new guests with the impression that I'm a monster.'

'But she is, she is,' Gaunt shot over his shoulder and closed the door behind him.

'I gather, Mrs Amberg, that you have heard the tragic news about your husband,' Tweed began. 'I was actually at Tresillian Manor shortly after the massacre had taken place.'

'Don't think I am a monster, Mr Tweed.' Eve stretched out a bare arm below her short-sleeved dress along the couch behind him. 'Julius and I had parted company for good before he left for England. But the manner in which

167

he died has shocked me. I can tell you that – the Squire has a tendency to despise women who can't stand up to a shock.'

'You are thinking of going back to England?' Tweed asked.

'Not bloody likely.' She reached for a cigarette out of a pearl-encrusted box, lit it with a gold lighter. 'Not yet. During the final blazing row Julius let slip he was expecting to make a fortune within days. Think I'm mercenary if you like, but I'm entitled to something after enduring his way of life for two years.'

'His way of life?' Tweed probed.

'Some bankers have their girl friends in other cities – are discreet. Not Julius. He visited a high-class call-girl on his doorstep. She has an apartment in Rennweg – in the middle of Zurich, for God's sake.'

'You know her name?'

'Yes. I had him followed by a detective. Helen Frey is her name. Rennweg 590. An apartment on the first floor. A bit too close for comfort. My comfort.' Her expression clouded over. 'I still think it's beastly the way he died. Damned weird, too.'

'Have you any idea where this fortune he spoke of was coming from?'

'No real idea at all. He speculated successfully on a large scale buying and selling foreign currencies. It might be that – although I gathered it was some new and unique deal. God knows how the bank will fare under the guidance of Walter.'

'He wasn't as competent as Julius?' Tweed ventured.

'I can never make him out. He's devious, gives the impression he's just chairman to preside over meetings. Sometimes I wonder about Walter.' Her arm touched Tweed's neck, her voice very soft. 'Did Julius suffer before he died? Gaunt gave a perfectly horrific description, but he's not known for his subtlety. He thinks *finesse* is a French pastry. Do smoke if you want to, Mr Newman. I

168

saw your hand reaching towards your pocket. May I call you Bob?'

'Please do.'

Paula had taken an instant dislike to Eve Amberg at first sight. Now she was changing her mind about her: she was only human after all, had shown genuine distress at the manner of her husband's death. Newman reached down for a crystal glass ashtray on the lower shelf of a small table.

Inside it was a crushed cigar stub. Gaunt must have spent some time with Eve to have smoked a whole cigar. Which reminded him of the cigar ash sample which Paula and Tweed had left at police headquarters for analysis – the sample Tweed had collected off the window-ledge in the no-name house at Rock in Cornwall. Eve jumped up, brought him another ashtray.

'That one is messy.'

She returned to her place on the couch beside Tweed. She was smoking her own cigarette in a long ivory holder and waved it to make a point. Her other hand clasped Tweed's and squeezed it.

'It really was very sweet of you to come here to tell me about Julius's tragic death. It just happened Gregory Gaunt got here first. I'm grateful to you. Now I am wondering whether po-faced Walter knows. Hardly ever see him but I'll have to call him.'

'I've saved you the trouble,' Tweed informed her. 'We visited him at the Zurcher Kredit . . .'

'Ah! And rather than come to see me himself he agreed you should perform the horrid task. Typical of him. But Walter and I are practically strangers.'

You catch on quick, Paula thought. You have got all your marbles. Julius was a fool to play around with other women. They chatted for a little longer, then Tweed said they must go. Eve accompanied them to the door, her arm looped through Newman's.

'Please do come and see me again before you leave

Zurich. Promise.' She looked at Paula. 'That invitation does include you, Paula. I'm sorry that I haven't paid you the attention a perfect hostess should have done.'

'Think nothing of it,' Paula assured her. 'This really is the most difficult time for you.'

'The maid said you came by taxi,' Eve recalled suddenly. 'There aren't any as high up as this. I'll phone for one. Be here in no time . . .'

As the taxi was driving them away from the villa Tweed glanced back through the rear window. The BMW was still parked further up the hill and there were two people inside. He had told the cab driver to drop them on the Limmat quai, close to the Rudolf bridge.

The sun was still shining out of a clear blue sky as he led the way across the Rudolf-Brun-Brücke. Looking back to the Altstadt – the Old Town on that side of the river – Paula drank in the ancient stone buildings, the green spires of churches which had once been gleaming copper. Butler's black Mercedes was just turning on to the bridge.

'We're going first to police headquarters again,' Tweed told them. 'Let's hope Beck is in this time.'

'Talk of the devil,' Paula said as they turned right up a steep incline. 'There is Philip – staring at police head-quarters.'

'You must be psychic,' Tweed told Cardon as he joined them. 'Where have you been?'

'Exploring Zurich, sniffing the atmosphere. You might be interested that the city is crawling with Americans who appear to be drifting round to no purpose. I stress the word "appear". All of them men and all carrying handguns. In this weather in a tight overcoat – topcoat as they call it – a holster is a giveaway.'

'Significant,' Tweed commented, and left it at that.

* * *

Arthur Beck, whose Federal HQ was in Berne, had an office in the solid four-storey building which is Zurich Police HQ. His large first-floor room overlooked the Limmat and the university perched high up on the opposite bank. He greeted Tweed and his three companions gravely and smiled briefly at Newman.

Paula sensed Beck's change of mood as he squeezed her arm, escorted her to a chair at a table. Cardon sat beside her. Newman and Tweed were seated as Beck took his place at the head of the table. The atmosphere was tense. Beck unlocked a drawer, took out a certificate signed by himself, a Walther with ammo, pushed everything across to Cardon including a hip holster.

'I fear you are all in great danger,' Beck began. 'And I have to warn you I cannot guarantee your protection. You have been followed by armed men since you left the Gotthard this morning. Your unknown adversary appears to be employing American gunmen – many dressed in Swiss clothes. They work in teams which alternate frequently. Only a very smart detective observed that you were followed again when you left the Zurcher Kredit Bank. I was informed because my people carry walkie-talkies. I took action.'

'What was that?' Tweed asked quietly.

'When you took a taxi to somewhere across the Limmat a car attempted to tail you. One of my patrol cars blocked this car. You had disappeared by the time the car was free to proceed.'

'Thank you for that,' Tweed said.

'Even so, I cannot guarantee your protection,' Beck repeated. 'The situation is exceptional.'

'Exceptional in what way?' Tweed enquired. Lord, he thought, are we back to square one? Is it possible that this huge organization we are up against can reach out and taint the Chief of Swiss Federal Police? Beck's next words in response to his question told him how wrong he

171

had been to doubt the Swiss.

'No fewer than forty more Americans – all carrying diplomatic passports – have arrived via Kloten. I do not have the manpower to track them – bearing in mind those who arrived earlier.'

'If they are carrying guns . . .' Paula began.

'I understand your thinking. But they have diplomatic immunity. We cannot arrest or search any of them. It is against international law.'

'You are powerless,' Tweed commented.

'There is a further difficulty. Last night in Munich an American diplomat was shot down, murdered. A woman got in the way of the assassin who shouted and threatened her with his gun. She reported that the killer spoke with a strong American accent before he escaped. So for the moment all American so-called diplomats in Europe have an added excuse for carrying a gun.'

'You're suggesting the Munich diplomat was murdered to provide this excuse?' Newman asked.

'I think these are very ruthless people we are dealing with. Yes, that is what I was suggesting. It conjures up nightmares, does it not?'

There was a heavy silence after Beck's words. Paula sat stunned. Newman looked thoughtful. Cardon, after checking the Walther, slid it inside the hip holster he had strapped on. He looked at Tweed and grinned, quite at ease with the situation.

'This calls for a Swiss protest to Washington,' Tweed said eventually. 'All these pseudo-diplomats flooding in.'

'Which is exactly what I have done,' Beck said in a very different tone. 'You think I remain passive regarding this invasion of our territory? I have already phoned Anderson, the American ambassador in Berne. You would like to guess what he said to me?'

172

'No. What did he say?'

'The same old phoney story as when I contacted him last time. The March administration is recalling diplomats from all over Europe. These men are supposed to be the replacements. Anderson, a friend of mine, sounded most embarrassed. He has already protested to Washington.'

'So that road is closed. But it tells me something.'

'But I am a fox.' Beck smiled at Paula. 'Today I fly to Berne to confront Anderson with evidence. I shall be taking with me one of the new arrivals' so-called diplomatic passports. My experts tell me it is forged.'

'I'd better not ask you how you got hold of the passport,' Tweed remarked.

'Oh, he dropped it in the street after leaving the Hotel Baur-en-Ville. By chance one of my men picked it up when the owner had disappeared.'

Newman grinned and Tweed smiled. They had guessed that Beck's man who was there 'by chance' had picked the American's pocket. Yes, Beck was a fox, Tweed said to himself. He stood up to leave.

'Sit down for a moment more,' Beck urged. 'Since that episode I had a call from another visitor at the Baur-en-Ville – an individual I suspect could be the leader of the new contingent. A Mr Marvin Mencken.'

'And what did this Mencken want?' Tweed asked.

'To report the loss of the diplomatic passport. He said his assistant had had his pocket picked, that I should know which petty thieves patronized Bahnhofstrasse and would I trace the criminal and return the passport within the next twenty-four hours. A very unpleasant man, this Mencken. One of my men, disguised as a street photographer, tried to take his picture and he smashed the camera.' He paused. 'The photo is a good one.'

'But you said the camera was smashed,' Paula reminded him.

'I said just that. But the first man in civilian clothes was a

173

decoy. While his camera was being smashed a backup man took another picture. You might like copies . . .'

Opening a drawer, Beck took out an envelope and extracted four glossy prints. Paula studied her copy. The slim man's face came out clearly, a foxy face twisted into an expression of cold fury.

'A savage-looking brute,' she commented.

'Not the sort of chap you'd invite to your London club,' Newman remarked ironically.

'Keep those pictures,' Beck advised as his guests prepared to leave. 'They might save your lives . . .'

'Who is it?' Norton answered the phone in his usual abrasive tone.

'Marvin here . . .'

'Get to it, Mencken. Any news? There should be by now, for Christ's sake.'

'It's Tweed. He's just returned from a visit to Amberg's wife, Eve. I had the news ten minutes ago . . .'

'Why the hell didn't you report earlier, then? Tweed? I want him taken out – before he reaches Dyson, Dillon or Ives. Especially Ives . . .'

'Tweed's at Zurich police headquarters now . . .'

'Then organize it. I want him carried away in a box before tonight. Just do it . . .'

Outside police HQ a black Mercedes was parked. Butler sat behind the wheel. A short distance away Pete Nield stood, taking a great interest in the River Limmat.

'Our next port of call is Helen Frey's apartment at Rennweg 590,' Tweed told Paula and Newman. 'It's only a short distance on foot.'

'Our next port of call is lunch,' Paula said firmly. 'My stomach is rumbling.'

Tweed agreed reluctantly. He seemed to be able to go for hours without food once he'd picked up a scent. Newman said he was starving too.

'The Baur-en-Ville is close,' Tweed said. 'We'll get a quick meal there.'

'I'll trail along behind you,' remarked Cardon, who had heard every word.

'Then first go over and tell Butler to take Nield back to the Gotthard for something to eat . . .'

The Baur-en-Ville's lunch bar is entered by climbing curved steps just off Bahnhofstrasse. Newman led the way as the automatic doors slid back. He scanned the few customers as he walked inside. The bar is a split-level room with a curved bar on the ground level. At the back steps lead up to the second tier which is separated from the lower level by a low wooden wall topped with a gleaming brass rail.

Newman walked up the steps, chose one of the blue leather banquettes with its back to the wall. Illumination came from lights recessed in the ceiling. Paula thought the atmosphere was luxurious and welcoming. While she sat with Tweed on the banquette Newman went back down to the bar for a pack of cigarettes.

Tweed was studying the menu when Paula nudged him. He looked up.

'That man who has just come in from the hotel entrance and stopped at the bar. The tone of this place has dropped to zero.'

At that moment, Mencken, standing at the bar, glanced up at the second tier. His cadaverous face froze for a second in an expression of vicious hardness, his foxy eyes bored into Paula's. She slowly switched her gaze as though interested in the other customers. Tweed noted the soulless blank eyes as he also looked round the bar.

Seated at a small table by the door, Cardon's right hand had slid inside his windcheater, was gripping the butt of his

Walther. Mencken appeared to change his mind and walked rapidly back into the hotel. He had not noticed Newman.

Later, Tweed ate his club sandwich of smoked turkey, egg and bacon with great gusto. His manner was buoyant.

'It's starting – what I hoped for. The enemy is crawling out from under the rocks. Remember Cord Dillon warned us photos of myself and you, Paula, had been taken from his safe in Langley? That walking skeleton recognized us,' he said with great satisfaction.

'What a perfectly horrible thug,' Paula commented. 'And while I remember it, why are we visiting Helen Frey? I've always wanted to see a call-girl's apartment, particularly a high-class one. It will add to my experience.'

'Helen Frey may have vital information,' Tweed explained. 'During one of his visits Julius Amberg may have indulged in pillow talk . . .'

Only one person noticed something unusual as they entered Bahnhofstrasse. Philip Cardon, strolling well back from them, observed a cripple in a battery-operated wheelchair emerge from an alley-way. The wheelchair kept pace behind Tweed and his companions.

19

Rennweg was a narrow street of shops which led off Bahnhofstrasse at a slanting angle. No. 590 had a closed door with a metal grille speakphone beside it. Tweed pressed a button below the grille, wondering what he was going to say to a professional call-girl. Best to improvise on the spur of the moment.

'*Ja?*' a soft feminine voice answered in German.

'Helen Frey?' he asked.

'*Ja.*'

'I only speak English. I'm a friend of Julius Amberg, the banker. Zurcher Kredit, Talstrasse. I was given your name.'

'You sound OK,' the voice replied in English. 'Come up – push the door when the buzzer goes . . .'

Tweed leaned against the door and it swung inward, revealed a straight staircase. Followed by Paula and Newman, he mounted the stairs quickly. A door opened at the top landing and Paula stared at one of the most attractive women she had ever seen.

A natural blonde, Helen Frey had a long face, a shapely nose and full lips, emphasized with red lipstick. She gazed back at Paula, turned her attention to Tweed and spoke in English again.

'What the hell is this? I don't do foursomes.'

She was closing the heavy door. Tweed used shock tactics. He rammed his foot between the door and the frame. The girl, twenty-eight or so, Paula guessed, wore a smart blue figure-hugging suit. Her other hand appeared, holding a wide flick knife. There was a loud click as the blade shot out.

'Julius Amberg is dead, murdered in England,' Tweed said quickly. 'I'm concerned about a lot of money. This is my assistant, Paula, and my adviser, Newman. A lot of money,' he repeated.

She studied Paula again, then Newman, who stared back with no particular expression. Tweed folded his arms, a pacific gesture, and kept his foot in the door. She nodded as though answering a question she had asked herself.

'You'd better come in, then.'

'I'd feel happier if you put away that knife,' Tweed told her. 'All we want is a discussion. I am willing to pay a

177

reasonable fee. I appreciate your time is valuable,' he ended without a trace of sarcasm.

'I did say you could come in.' She held up the knife and there was another click. The blade shot back inside its sheath. 'Feel more comfortable now, Mr . . .?'

'Tweed. Now we're all introduced.'

Discreetly, Paula glanced curiously round the large sitting-room. The main colour motif was pink, which normally would have seemed over-ornate, but instead the effect was welcoming. Curtains drawn over the window protected the room from the outside world.

It was illuminated by soft pink wall-sconce lampshades. The deep-pile carpet was off-white and against one wall stood a vast couch – large enough to take two reclining people. Comfortable armchairs were scattered about the carpet and an antique desk occupied one corner near the curtains. A huge wall mirror faced the couch.

Presumably some men liked to watch what they were doing while others didn't – a long brass rod ran full length along the top of the mirror flanked by pink curtains, held in place with tie-backs. A silver champagne bucket perched on a metal tripod stood at one end of the couch.

Helen Frey walked slowly over to the couch, sat down, waved her hand towards the chairs.

'Well, make yourselves at home, everyone. And tell me what this is all about. You're sure Julius is dead? He was my most profitable client.'

'Oh, he's very dead, I assure you,' Tweed said with rare brutality. 'I myself saw his blood-soaked body. A machine-gun makes an awful mess fired at point-blank range.'

'I can hardly believe it,' Helen said.

'You'd better believe it,' Newman told her.

'It must be a shock to you,' Paula intervened. 'I also saw poor Julius, Miss Frey. It gave me one hell of a shock.'

'Call me Helen, everyone. You seem decent people. But

I'm wondering what your interest is in the tragedy. You've shaken me.'

Tweed changed tactics. He had assumed Helen Frey would be as hard as nails, but Paula's more sympathetic approach had altered Helen's attitude.

'You could call me an investigator,' he began. 'Julius was a friend of mine and I'm trying to find out who murdered him. If I can find out why this hideous crime was committed I'll be closer to the murderer. Was Julius expecting to make a great deal of money in the near future?'

Helen sat very erect on the couch, her long legs crossed. She reached for a silver cigarette box on a table, offered it to her guests.

'Thank you, but I prefer my own,' Newman said, producing his pack. 'My friends don't smoke. This is a lovely room you have.'

He stood up and lit Helen's cigarette. She was concentrating on Tweed as Newman then wandered round, looked at a portrait of Helen, moved a few paces apparently to look at a framed landscape above the desk. A diary lay open at the day's date, reminding him that they were at the beginning of March. What caught his attention was Helen's next appointment.

4.30 p.m. Emil Voser.

'Was Julius expecting to make a great deal of money in the near future?' Helen said, repeating Tweed's question after she'd taken several deep drags on the cigarette, blown smoke rings into the air. 'Yes, he was.'

'May I ask how you know that?' Tweed asked gently.

'You may.' She gave him a bewitching smile. 'It was on the day before he left for Cornwall.' She phrased her next remark delicately. 'He was here with me. He'd lost a big sum investing in foreign currencies. But he said he would more than make up the loss and end up with a fortune.'

'Did he give you any idea where this fortune was coming from?'

'He said fate had handed him a gigantic royal flush. I remember his exact words – they were so graphic. Julius was an enthusiastic card player.'

'May I also ask what his mood was like when he was here for . . .' Tweed trailed off.

She smiled wanly, took another drag on the cigarette, blew another perfect smoke ring.

'You were going to say when he was here for the last time. And you are right, Tweed. That *was* the last time I saw him alive. His mood? It was rather strange – a mixture of excitement and . . .'

'Fear?' Paula suggested.

'Yes! That was it. He was very nervy as though what he had in mind was dangerous. I even told him not to take too great a risk.'

'And how did he react to that?' Tweed enquired.

'He said that making a lot of money always involved taking a risk. He added that also it was too late for him to change his mind, so he was going ahead to push the deal.'

'Thank you for being so frank, Helen. Now, I owe you a fee for your time. Business is business.'

'I normally charge one thousand Swiss francs.'

Tweed was reaching for his wallet when Helen thrust out a hand to stop him. Her tone of voice had an appealing quality which touched Paula.

'I don't want your money, Tweed. I'm convinced you are telling the truth – that you are determined to track down the monster who murdered Julius. A woman in my profession becomes an expert in knowing when men are lying. Regard it as my contribution to bringing the swine who killed him to justice.'

'If you insist . . .'

'But I do.' She stood up to unfasten the two deadlocks on her door. 'By the way, as you leave the opposite door on the landing may open. It will be Klara. We are in the same business but good friends. She is often curious about my clients.'

Tentatively, she held out her hand to Paula. Without one moment's hesitation Paula grasped it warmly and stared into Helen's steady blue eyes. She felt that they were, when all was said and done, sisters under the skin.

Newman walked out on to the landing first to make sure it was safe. The door opposite opened and a tall brunette peered out. She wore a housecoat loosely tied and grinned wickedly at Newman.

'I'm Klara,' she said as Helen closed her door. 'Have you the energy left to come and play with me?'

'A tempting proposal.' Newman smiled at her. 'There are two things against the idea. I've just had a very large lunch recently. And I'm late for an appointment which could be profitable.'

'Come back later, then. Spend a little of the profits on me. You and I could make music together.'

'I'm sure of it,' Newman agreed. 'I may see you later,' he lied.

'You should have accepted her invitation,' Paula teased him as they got to the bottom of the stairs. 'I liked Helen, but I think Klara could be great fun too . . .'

Rennweg was quiet as they stepped back into the street. Opposite Helen Frey's doorway was a small café. Inside, close to the window, Cardon sat with a soft drink in front of him. He stroked a hand across his forehead to signal he had seen them.

'I want to call Eve Amberg,' Tweed said. 'I need a public phone box.'

'There's one near Bahnhofstrasse,' Paula told him. 'I

remember seeing it on our way here . . .'

As the three of them walked off Cardon waited for a few minutes inside the café. He had seen the cripple in the wheelchair taking an unusual interest in shop windows near Frey's doorway. The invalid man wore a peaked shabby cap like those once sported by German students. His face was muffled in a woollen scarf, but it had slipped for a moment and Cardon had a good look at his face.

The nose curved downwards over his upper lip, reminding Cardon of an evil parrot. In his forties, Cardon had estimated. A worn rug covered his lap and his hands, on the controls, remained concealed underneath it. The wheelchair now began to follow Tweed and his companions. Cardon walked slowly after it.

Tweed entered the phone cubicle, looked up Eve Amberg's number in the directory. He inserted coins, dialled and she answered quickly.

'Amberg. Who is calling?'

'Tweed here, Eve. Sorry to bother you again but there are one or two personal questions I didn't ask when we met.'

'Ask away. It's a relief to talk to someone English. I come from Cornwall. I'm reverting to my maiden name – Eve Royston. Now, the stage is yours.'

'Would you mind confirming how close it was to Julius's departure for England that you separated?'

'Two days before,' she said crisply. 'I'd challenged him earlier about his visits to Helen Frey. She may be a call-girl but I sensed their relationship was close. He then phoned me, as I said, two days before he flew to Britain. Said he wanted a separation and a divorce in good time. We had a helluva row over the phone. I told him I'd already decided to walk, so his suggestion was a bit late in the day.'

'You mean you never saw him again before he left? All this was over the phone?'

'It was,' she said emphatically. 'Something else I did not

182

appreciate. He might have come to see me.'

'May I also ask how you first knew about Helen Frey?'

'Like something out of a cheap play. He was careless. Came home with traces of lipstick on his collar and he smelt of the wrong perfume. Despite smoking, I have a good sense of smell. I didn't say anything. I phoned the best private detective in Zurich to follow him. A bit sordid, but I was desperate to know the truth. He – the detective – followed him three times to Frey's place in Rennweg. That was it.'

'Would you be willing to give me this detective's name, address and phone number?'

'Of course. Name is Theo Strebel. He has a small apartment in the Altstadt – on this side of the Limmat. Here are the details . . .'

Tweed had his notebook and pen ready, scribbled down the information. Outside the phone cubicle Newman was leaning against a wall as though waiting to use the phone. Paula appeared to be window-shopping.

'Thank you, Eve,' Tweed said. 'I'm most grateful.'

'Did you want to interview Strebel? If so, ten in the morning is the best time. He's going through his post. Would you like me to call him, introduce you, arrange a time?'

'That would be helpful. Ten in the morning tomorrow would be fine. And thank you again . . .'

Tweed emerged and continued walking with Newman and Paula into Bahnhofstrasse. Behind them the wheel-chair began moving again.

Tweed told them about his conversation with Eve. Paula guessed why he wanted to talk to Strebel, but asked him, to see if she'd guessed right.

'He's a detective – a good one, Eve said. I want to see whether he took any photos of Julius entering Helen's place.'

'Why?' Paula persisted.

'Just an idea I have. Helen said Julius was in a strange mood.'

'But she explained that,' Paula recalled.

'So she did,' Tweed agreed, and Paula knew he wasn't going to tell her any more. In Bahnhofstrasse commuters on their way home were clustered in a crowd round a tram stop twenty yards or so away. Cardon came up behind them.

'Freeze. Don't move . . .'

They obeyed his instruction instantly. Newman saw out of the corner of his eye that Cardon was gazing at something. He looked in that direction. A man in a wheelchair was backing it inside a side-street where there was a small modern white church Paula admired. When the wheelchair was alongside the street's far wall it stopped moving.

The man huddled inside the chair whipped back his lap rug. He showed startling agility. His right hand, holding something, was hoisted high, like a bowler in a cricket match about to throw the ball. A cylindrical object sailed through the air in an arc, descending to land at Tweed's feet. Cardon's left hand, clawed, caught the object before it landed on the pavement. In a blur of movement he lobbed it back. It landed in the lap of the man in the wheelchair. The 'cripple' jerked upright, had one foot on the street, when there was a loud explosion.

The man who had hurled the grenade disintegrated. The relics of his body were smashed against the white wall where a red lake appeared. The wheelchair became a shambles. One wheel rolled up Bahnhofstrasse, leaving a trail of dark red blood in its wake. Paula saw a severed hand lying in the street.

As the commuters jerked their heads round Newman suddenly dropped into a crouch, his Smith & Wesson gripped in both hands. Behind them, five feet or so away, a man in a belted raincoat had opened a violin case, extracted a snub-nosed Uzi machine-pistol. The muzzle was aimed at Tweed as Newman fired three times in rapid succession. The sound of the shots was masked by the screeching stop of an approaching tram – the driver had seen the lake of blood spilling into the road. The man holding the Uzi was hurled back against a plate-glass window with such force it fractured as he sagged to the ground.

'Scatter!' Tweed ordered. 'Meet up at the Gotthard . . .'

20

Paula sat on the edge of the bed in Tweed's room at the Gotthard. Her feet were pressed hard on the floor to prevent them from trembling. She was suffering from delayed shock brought on by the events in Bahnhofstrasse. Also in the room, seated in chairs, were Newman and Cardon. Paula's mood was not helped by Tweed's – she sensed he was puzzled by something. His first words didn't help her to detect what was bothering him.

'Let's sum up what happened. While we were in the bar at the Baur-en-Ville that villainous-looking type – I'm going to nickname him the Skull – spotted Paula and myself and then hurried back into the hotel.'

'I don't see what you're getting at,' Paula said, forcing herself to speak in a calm voice.

'Have patience. We didn't spend long over lunch but when we left to walk to Helen Frey's place in Rennweg the fake cripple was waiting for us, presumably already armed with his grenade. The speed with which the Skull and his associates move is incredible. Professionals of the top rank, I fear.'

'I still don't really see what you're driving at.'

'Communications. I feel sure the wheelchair man also had a mobile phone under the lap rug which concealed his grenade. He could have used that phone without Cardon seeing him. I'm worried about Helen Frey.'

'What on earth for?' Newman intervened.

'Because the cripple must have used the phone to report we were nearing that tram-stop. Hence that man with the Uzi you dealt with was waiting for us.'

'I see that,' Paula agreed, 'but why this anxiety about Helen Frey?'

'The cripple could have reported our visit to her to the Skull. She could be in danger. Time for me to call her.'

'She has a 4.30 p.m. appointment with an Emil Voser,' Newman recalled. 'I noticed it in her desk diary. So she may be busy.'

'Then she'll indicate that on the phone.'

While Tweed was checking Frey's number in the directory Paula began talking to Cardon. She kept her voice down as Tweed dialled the number.

'Philip, I still can't understand how you were able to catch that grenade in time and lob it back. Or, Bob, how you spotted the second assassin.'

'Easy.' Cardon grinned. 'First I'm good at cricket as a bowler. But mainly it was Butler's training me on a course down at the Send manor in Surrey. In the grounds he'd throw me a live grenade with the pin out – I had to lob it over the other side of a brick wall before it detonated. He tested me first with a cricket ball. Just one of the many contingency attack situations he trained me in. So, easy.'

'You make it sound so simple,' Paula remarked, her hands pressed against the bed. 'What about you, Bob?'

'Oh, I'm getting the measure of this mob. Organized up to the hilt. It occurred to me the grenade thrower might well have back-up, so I checked all round, saw this character with a violin case. Rather old-fashioned technique – a method used by Chicago gangsters at one time, carrying a sub-machine-gun in a violin case.'

He stopped talking as Tweed put down the phone. His expression was serious. He began to put on his overcoat.

'I don't like it. I called Frey's number. No reply for a number of rings, then the phone was lifted, no one spoke, the phone was put down again. I just asked to speak to Helen Frey, gave no name. We're going back to Rennweg. I'm really worried now . . .'

It was dark as they approached Rennweg 590 for the second time. Again Paula and Newman walked with Tweed while Cardon trailed behind them. On opposite sides of the street Butler and Nield strolled along, pausing to gaze into shops. The café opposite the entrance to No. 590 was still open and Cardon slipped inside it.

Tweed was about to press the speakphone button when he stiffened. The door was not closed properly – its automatic lock had failed to work. Glancing up and down the street, he pushed gently and the door swung inward. No light on the staircase. Odd. He stepped inside, produced a pencil torch, shielded it with his hand so it gave just enough illumination to see the stair treads.

'I'd better go up first,' Newman whispered, the Smith & Wesson in his hand.

He squeezed past Tweed who gave him the flash. Their rubber-soled shoes made no sound as they slowly mounted the staircase. Paula, who had quietly closed the front door, brought up the rear. The atmosphere of the dark staircase was eerie: she felt as though the walls were closing in on her. The closed front door shut out all sounds from the outside world. A stair tread creaked loudly as Newman stepped on it. He climbed higher, shone the torch back to illuminate the giveaway tread. Tweed and Paula stepped over it.

Arriving at the landing, Newman first pressed gently against Klara's door. It held firm. He walked over to Helen's door, saw that it was open half an inch or so. Someone had left in a hurry – so why hadn't she secured it afterwards?

With his gun still in his right hand, he used his left to push the door wider open, waited, listened. He had switched off the torch. He was listening for sounds of breathing, any sound. Nothing. He switched on the torch again, shone it slowly round, then held it motionless. With a swift movement he shone it towards the window: the curtains were still closed. He spoke over his shoulder.

'Paula, I wouldn't come in if I were you.'

That was just the sort of remark which made her determined to go inside. She followed Tweed, who took two steps inside and stopped. She saw him reach inside his jacket pocket under his raincoat, produce a pair of surgical gloves and put them on his hands. She extracted her own pair from her shoulder-bag. Newman stood very still inside the room, his torch beam held steady. He had pushed the door open with his knuckles. No fingerprints.

Tweed reached for the wall switch he'd noticed on their earlier visit, pressed it down. The pink wall-sconce lights came on and Paula saw what Newman had been staring at.

'Oh, no!'

Helen Frey, clad only in underclothes, lay sprawled back in an armchair. The front of her white slip was drenched with dark red blood. Her head flopped against the back of the chair at an unnatural angle. A savage crescent moon, blood red, circled her throat. She had been garrotted.

Tweed went close to the armchair followed by Paula. He guessed that a strong sharp wire had been used. The head had been almost severed from the body. She looked hideous with her lipsticked mouth open and her tongue

188

protruding. The weird angle of the head was now explained. Very little remained to attach it to the body.

'Emil Voser. 4.30 p.m.,' said Paula, recalling Newman telling them about the desk diary.

'Which is probably not his real name,' Tweed commented, his eyes scanning the apartment. 'I don't think that we ought to linger here. What is it, Paula?'

She was crouched near the side of the chair. She used her index finger to point and Tweed crouched beside her. On the carpet lay a blood-stained pearl, pierced at either end as though it belonged to a string.

'Bring it with us,' Tweed ordered.

'Which means we are tampering with evidence.'

'Which means exactly that,' Tweed agreed. 'But we know more about these people than anyone.'

Paula was already extracting a Cellophane specimen wallet from her shoulder-bag. She fumbled in her bag again and her right hand came out holding a pair of tweezers. She used them to tease the pearl, split along one side, into the wallet and sealed it. With a pen she wrote on the attached tab the date and *Rennweg 590*, and slipped the wallet inside her bag. She was sniffing the air as she stood up. She began prowling round the apartment.

'Can't you smell the faint whiff?' she said to Tweed. 'I caught it as soon as we came in – someone has been smoking a cigar. Got you . . .'

From a low table concealed by the arm of the couch Paula lifted up a large glass ashtray. Inside nestled an intact roll of cigar ash. Extracting another wallet, she carefully tipped the roll of ash into the second wallet. Sealing it, she wrote only *Cigar ash specimen No. 2*, and put this wallet into her bag.

'I missed that. Good work,' Tweed told her.

Newman was standing by the desk near the curtained window. He was staring down at the open desk diary.

'She had no other appointments today. Only this Voser.'

189

'We'll go now,' Tweed decided. 'I'll leave the door, half an inch open as we found it. Move silently – mind that creaking stair. We don't want to attract Klara's attention . . .'

They stepped into a quiet street, Tweed leaving last to pull the door almost closed, his hands now wearing leather gloves. Again Cardon signalled to them from the window in the café. This time Newman went inside, then turned to beckon Tweed and Paula to follow him. Tweed understood his motive when he saw Klara sitting by herself at a side table with a cup of coffee in front of her.

'I'm going to talk to Klara,' Newman said. 'She might have information.'

'Good idea,' Tweed agreed after a moment's hesitation.

'So you've come back again for a frolic?' Klara greeted Newman.

Tweed smiled as they sat at her table. He ordered coffee from the waitress for himself and Newman after Paula shook her head. Her stomach was queasy. Like Tweed, she kept quiet while Newman and Klara talked.

'I'm afraid I haven't,' Newman began. 'Maybe you ought to put that cup down. I have some rather shocking news for you. Just about as shocking as you can get.'

'I've got strong nerves,' Klara told him, her expression serious. 'You need them in my business. Some of the men who come to see you.'

'That's really the tragedy in Helen Frey's case.'

'Tragedy?' Klara looked down as she slowly drummed the pink-varnished nails of her right hand on the table. She looked up again direct at Newman. 'I'm tough – so don't treat me like a kid. Just tell me what's happened to Helen.'

'We came back a few minutes ago to ask her some questions we'd overlooked earlier. The front door was open, her door was open a bit. We found her inside. Murdered.'

'Oh, hell. I was always telling her to be more careful.

Which is why – if I hadn't a client – I used to open my door a crack when one of the stairs creaked. Not to be nosy, believe me. Just to try and look after her. I hope it wasn't a pervert. Did she suffer?'

'I'd say it was pretty quick. He slashed her throat open. It's not a nice sight. Did you by any chance see her four thirty appointment arrive this afternoon?'

'Yes, I did.'

'But there's no light on the staircase. In daytime the fanlight at the top gives enough illumination to see your way, but now . . .'

'There's a time switch, lasts one minute. If you know where to find it you can switch it on from just inside the front door. Then Helen and I have switches inside our apartments we can operate. When he came upstairs she'd obviously operated her time switch.'

'So you can describe him?'

'Well, yes and no. I only open my door a crack so her client won't spot me. I'd say he was taller than you are. His feet seemed to hurt him a bit the way he was walking slowly and carefully.'

'Slim?'

'No. Pretty fat, I'd say. His black overcoat was tight across his waist and the buttons looked as though they could fly off at any moment.'

'Colour of hair?'

'No idea. He also wore a black broad-brimmed hat pulled well down. Couldn't see his hair.'

'Describe his face.'

'That's difficult too. He had a pair of those wrapround tinted glasses which covered a lot of his face. And a white silk scarf which covered more of it. I do know his feet hurt him.'

'What about his age?' Newman pressed. 'Thirty, forty, older?'

'I honestly couldn't tell. I judge a man's age by the way

191

he moves – but coming up unfamiliar stairs with tender feet throws any body language.'

'Would you recognize him again if you saw him?'

'Only if he was dressed exactly as he was when he came up those stairs.'

'Then you'd really just be identifying the clothes,' Newman pointed out.

'I suppose you're right.'

'Sitting here, did you see him leave, get a better view?'

'No, I didn't. But just before you came in I was chatting with a girl friend. I didn't even see the three of you go back inside.'

'You're English, aren't you?' Newman suddenly shot at her.

'Yes, I am,' Klara said after a pause. 'So was Helen – her real name is – was – Helen Dane from Cornwall. We teamed up to come out here, hoping we'd have a novelty value for Swiss men. And we do. But they prefer you to have a common Swiss name. Don't ask me why. And don't ask my real name.'

'What's your Swiss surname, then? Klara who?'

'I'm not telling you that either. I'm clearing out of my apartment within the hour. Do the police know about Helen yet?' Klara asked.

'No, they don't. I'd just as soon you didn't mention our visits.'

'You can count on that,' she assured him. 'First, I simply couldn't stay in a building where poor Helen was murdered. Second, what clients are going to come back to me here? Rennweg 590 will become notorious once the press get hold of the story. That girl friend I was chatting to is about to vacate her apartment to take up a job in Geneva. I'm also not giving you the address.'

'Fair enough.'

Klara looked at Paula. 'Would you do me a great

favour? Come back with me to my apartment while I pack?
Please.'

Paula looked at Tweed. He checked his watch. His six
o'clock appointment with Jennie Blade at the Hummer
Bar was coming up soon. Klara sensed his problem – time.
She gazed at Paula.

'I'm the world's quickest packer. One suitcase and in five
minutes we'll be in the street again.'

Tweed, reluctantly, nodded agreement to Paula. Newman warned Klara as she stood up, door key in her hand:
'When you're going to this new address I'd take a taxi. You
know Zurich well? Good. Think of two fake destinations.
Then get a third taxi to take you where you're going.'

'Good idea. Thanks . . .'

Tweed checked his watch again as the two women left
the café. He doubted Klara's statement that she could pack
in five minutes. Paula could but how many other women
achieved that speed?

'Her description of Voser was pretty distinctive,' Newman commented. 'A tall fat man with tender feet.'

'I found two aspects of her description intriguing,'
Tweed remarked.

'Which two aspects?'

'I want to chew them over in my mind,' Tweed told him
cryptically. 'I did notice Klara is very tall.'

Newman gave up trying to penetrate the subtle recesses
of Tweed's mind. He sat watching the closed door
opposite.

Tweed had time to call Monica after he arrived back at the
Gotthard. Klara had been as good as her word – she had
packed the suitcase and emerged back on Rennweg with
Paula in five minutes. Newman saw her safely into a taxi
before they hurried back to the Gotthard . . .

'Monica, Tweed here. Are you alone? I do not want to

get in touch with Howard now. I'm speaking from my hotel.'

'All's quiet down here in Surrey . . .' Monica was wording what she said carefully. Anyone could be listening in. 'I have the details of the Gaunt concern. The top man is a millionaire. He likes to spread it round that he has no idea where the next penny is coming from. He owns the manor – no mortgage – a property in Rock with no name and has considerable assets in Switzerland. No details about them, of course. He was once a captain in the SAS. Had to resign – too independent-minded. A bit of an adventurer, like the old buccaneers. Popular with women. Has had a lot of girl friends. That's it.'

'Thank you. Now, two women have applied to me for jobs. I need to have detailed references. Ready to take down their names? Good. Jennie Blade. And Eve Amberg – maiden name Royston. I'll spell that last name. Got it? I suggest concentration on the Padstow area. I must go now. I'll call you in the near future. Take care . . .'

Paula was intrigued as Tweed put down the phone. Waiting while he loosened his collar, she asked her question.

'Why especially do you want to know about those two women?'

'Both of them have connections with Cornwall. Which is where it all started.'

21

Walking briskly into the Oval Office Sara Maranoff knew the moment she saw the President that he was expecting a visit from his latest girl friend, Ms Hamilton. Bradford

March was freshly shaven, wore a smart grey suit, had a bottle of champagne in the ice bucket.

'Senator Wingfield has asked to come and see you.'

'That friggin' wooden Indian? Stall the bastard. Tell him I'm up to my neck in paperwork for a new bill. Oh, I didn't tell you, Ms Hamilton is calling on me in half an hour. See I'm not disturbed while we talk.'

'Sure, boss.' Sara's expression suggested it was news to her. And she liked the word 'talk'. He wouldn't waste time talking to her. 'Norton is on the line,' she went on. 'Sounds to be in a hurry.'

'Does he? I'm in a hurry – for him to finish the jobs he was sent out to do. Put him on the line . . .'

'Norton here. We're closing in on Tweed. Nearly got him today . . .'

'*Nearly!* You mean the pest is hospitalized?'

'Not exactly. I've thought up a new angle to fix him for all time. Thought you'd like a bulletin . . .'

'Oh, you're issuing bulletins now, are you?' Livid, March leaned across the desk, shouting down the phone. 'For bulletin I read bullshit. The only bulletin I want from you is that Tweed, Dyson, Ives and Dillon are all gone to join the fathers they never had. How is Mencken working out?'

'He takes orders . . .'

'More calls like this and *you* will be taking orders from *him* . . .'

He crashed down the phone and Sara shuddered inwardly. If Brad went on like that he was going to shatter the instrument. It would be expensive replacing that special private phone. Sara was money-conscious. She tried another tack.

'I just heard you've recalled Ambassador Anderson from Switzerland. That you're sending out Mike Gallagher in his place.'

'I congratulate you on your source of information,' March said sarcastically.

'Anderson is an experienced diplomat. Gallagher is raw, a rough diamond. He could cause trouble, the language he uses.'

'Gallagher is a man I trust. Anderson has been interfering with things that don't goddamn concern him. He is out. *Out!*'

'Gallagher hasn't left the States yet. You could change your mind. I would if I were you . . .'

'But you're *not* me!' March roared at her. 'When you're sitting in this chair you can decide who goes where. And Gallagher contributed plenty to my election campaign.'

She sighed. Normally she could handle Brad, but there were times when he acted like a maddened bull. This was one of them. Time to change his mood. A reference to Ms Hamilton, bringing her back into his thoughts, should do the trick.

'Another bottle of champagne – to oil the works?' she suggested.

March glared at her and Sara realized her tactic had misfired. He pointed a short stubby finger across the room.

'The door is there. Walk. Preferably through it without opening it . . .'

'Thank you, Sara,' said Senator Wingfield. 'Don't worry about it. I know you tried.'

He put down the phone in the room at his Chevy Chase residence where the Three Wise Men were gathered. The banker and the elder statesman, nursing their drinks at the round table, watched the Senator as he joined them. Wingfield shook his head regretfully.

'I'm sorry, gentlemen. The President refuses to see me at the Oval Office. Some nonsense about paperwork piling up. It's a ploy to avoid meeting me. He probably guessed the subject I was going to raise.'

'Gallagher,' snapped the statesman. 'From my own experience I know the Berne embassy isn't a plum job. But Berne is a good listening post. How can he contemplate appointing a man who may come under investigation by a Senate sub-committee – for corruption in obtaining government contracts?' He lapsed into unusual vulgarity. 'When the shit hits the fan, when the press gets a whiff of it – which they will – the US government is going to be a laughing-stock all over the world.'

'You may be right,' Wingfield agreed.

'He is right!' the banker burst out. 'On top of that he is spending money on programmes like there's no tomorrow. Face up to it, March has become a menace.'

'Thank God Jeb Calloway is waiting in the wings,' said the statesman.

'Don't let's get excited,' Wingfield urged. 'Timing is everything in politics. We'll wait and see how it all pans out . . .'

Jeb Calloway paced his office, his six-foot frame taking long strides while his closest aide, Sam, watched him. Calloway sat down suddenly, pounded his clenched fist on the table where Sam sat.

'The rumours are growing about this private army March has organized. Ever heard of Unit One, Sam?'

'Maybe the odd whisper.'

'You have?' Calloway looked surprised, annoyed. 'Is that the name of the secret paramilitary force Brad March is rumoured to have built up?'

'Brad,' Sam remarked, watching the Vice-President closely, 'is wily, throws out smokescreens, spreads rumours. Best forget all about this thing, even if it did exist.'

'You seem to know one helluva lot. Most Americans

here in Washington have never heard of it.'

'Jeb, I'm not "most Americans". I've been on the Hill for quite a few years. Stay cool. What about that guy you contacted secretly?'

'He's already been in place for some time,' Calloway snapped. 'I heard a rumour that forty more invisible men were being flown to London aboard a United flight.'

'What source fed you that dangerous info., Jeb?' enquired Sam quietly.

'I don't name informants.'

'OK, clam up. We're just talking.'

'When I heard that,' Calloway rattled on, 'I called someone I know inside the American Embassy in London. He was at London Airport when the flight landed. They transferred to a Swissair flight for Zurich. So-called diplomats.'

'And the guy you have in place – to quote your own words. Where might he be?'

'In Zurich, of course,' Calloway said with a smile of self-satisfaction.

Sam lit a cigarette. Calloway pursed his lips. He didn't allow smoking in his office, but Sam was a law unto himself. Sam eyed Calloway shrewdly. He was wondering how he could persuade him to stop playing the power game.

'Better watch your step, Jeb,' he advised. 'All this intrigue you're tangled in. If Brad gets just one hint of what you're up to your ass will end in a sling.'

'I know what I'm doing. I need to know what's going on.'

Sure you do, Sam thought, but what *are* you doing?

The phone message which had come through while Tweed was talking to Monica was slipped under his door by a member of the Gotthard's staff. Tweed opened the envelope, read the typed sheet inside and half-closed his eyes. Paula knew something had happened which was making him think furiously. He handed it to her.

'Read it, then show it to Bob and Philip.'

I am sorry I have to cancel our date for tonight. Something urgent cropped up. Can we meet same place same time tomorrow instead. Again, apologies. Love. Jennie Blade.

'She does leave it till the last minute,' Paula remarked as she handed it to Newman, who scanned it, passing it on to Cardon.

'The last minute is the significant factor.' Tweed went on talking before she could react. 'One key to this whole grim business is Newman's friend, Joel Dyson. I suspect everything started with him . . .'

'Acquaintance, not friend,' Newman said sharply.

'Just listen, I hadn't finished. Paula was always good at art, drawing portraits. Do you think, Bob, you could describe Dyson to Paula while she makes a sketch, an identikit picture?'

'I could try,' Newman agreed.

'I can use some of the good notepaper in that hotel folder,' Paula suggested. 'Pity I haven't a piece of charcoal. I'd get a much better result with that . . .'

'This do?' Cardon produced a short stick of charcoal. 'I use it to darken my eyebrows when I'm changing my appearance.'

'Now I can get to work. You seem to carry everything on you . . .'

Newman sat on the arm of the chair Paula occupied, began to give her a description and she made bold strokes on her paper with the charcoal. 'Nose a bit longer,' he said at a later stage.

While they were working on the identikit sketch Tweed took out his notebook, started writing down names and linking them. Cardon watched over his shoulder, fascinated.

Joel Dyson – Julius Amberg – Gaunt – Jennie Blade – Eve Amberg (Royston) – Amberg – Helen Frey – Klara – Theo Strebel, Eve's detective – Gaunt? – Norton. Cornwall: Gaunt – Eve Amberg – Helen Frey. Washington: Dillon – Barton Ives, Special Agent FBI – Norton.

'It's beginning to link up,' Tweed remarked.

'Darned if I can see how,' Cardon commented.

'You might – if you bear in mind most of them are not what they seem.'

'You've lost me . . .'

'Bob says this is Joel Dyson,' Paula said, bringing her third sketch.

'The very image of the little creep,' Newman said, joining them.

'Good,' Tweed told Paula. 'You've done very well. Now tomorrow we need six small photocopies of that sketch.'

'I noticed there was a photocopying firm in Rennweg,' she recalled. 'I'll go there and get six reduced in size copies.'

'Why reduced?' Cardon asked her.

'Because the result will be clearer if you reduce it. If you enlarged it the detail would begin to disappear.'

'And,' Tweed told Cardon, 'I want every one of us to have a copy. I'm convinced Dyson is still in Zurich. This way whoever encounters him – if anyone does – will recognize him instantly. Paula, could you make a second copy of that sketch?'

'I'm sure I can. Why?'

'Joel Dyson is on the run. My guess is he's running for dear life. So he may well try to disguise himself. He's had time to take the obvious precaution – to grow a small moustache. Can you add that to the second sketch? Then

200

get the Rennweg printer to run off six copies of each version?'

'It will only take minutes,' she said.

'And I'll accompany her,' Newman announced. 'Dillon told us before he leapt aboard that tram that the opposition has photos of Tweed – and of Paula.'

'Don't leave her side for a moment,' Tweed ordered.

Cardon had just left the room after saying he was going to have a quick bath when the phone rang. Tweed raised his brows, glanced at Newman, let it ring several times before he answered.

'Yes, who is it?'

'Tweed?' a hoarse voice said. 'Cord here. I've got a bad cold, goddamnit . . .'

'You do sound awful . . .'

'Tweed, do you want to meet Barton Ives or is this a bad time? I can send him along to the Gotthard now.'

'Do it,' Tweed agreed and then the connection was broken.

He put down the phone slowly. 'At long last we are about to meet Barton Ives, unless he changes his mind. He's also running for his life. We mustn't overwhelm him with too many people.'

He reached for the phone, called Cardon, Butler and Nield in their rooms. He gave each the same instruction.

'From now on don't come to my room or approach me. Your first priority is still our protection – but stay in the background . . .'

They waited thirty minutes and no one arrived. Tweed was still studying his list of people whom he had linked together. He checked his watch, folded the sheet he had torn from his notebook, slipped it into his wallet and stood up.

'You don't think he's coming after all?' Paula suggested.

'I was doubtful from the beginning. He's survived so far by staying in deep cover. It takes a great effort of will to emerge into the open in that sort of situation. I'm hungry. They serve marvellous food in the Hummer Bar restaurant. We'll go down, the three of us, and eat . . .'

Tweed was locking his door as Newman strolled slowly down the corridor. He stretched a hand across his face, a mannerism Paula had noted when he was puzzled by something.

She brought up the rear as Tweed followed Newman. It was very quiet in the corridor as they headed for the lift. A man was walking towards them with a deliberate tread. As he passed Newman Paula automatically noticed that he was of medium height and athletic build. He had a large head, was clean-shaven and his dark hair was cut short. His eyes, under thick brows, were blue and penetrating. He reached out a hand as Tweed was passing him, grasped his arm.

Paula's hand was inside her shoulder-bag, gripping the butt of her .32 Browning in a flash. Newman had swung round, had taken three swift strides and pressed the muzzle of his Smith & Wesson into the stranger's spine.

'You wanted something?' Newman snapped.

'Hold it, fellas,' he whispered. He stretched out both hands and his square-tipped fingers touched the walls. 'Cord said it would be OK. I'm Special Agent Barton Ives, FBI.'

22

Tweed unlocked the door, Paula backed into his room, gun pointed at the American, and Newman nudged him inside with the Smith & Wesson muzzle. As Tweed followed them, locking the door again, Newman slipped his revolver into his holster, began to feel the captive all over for concealed weapons.

'I'm loaded,' Ives told him. 'Under the left armpit.'

Newman hauled out the weapon. The American also favoured a .38 Smith & Wesson. Paula noted that all his clothes, a business suit under his open trench coat, were of Swiss make. With his neatly trimmed short hair he reminded her of a tough teddy bear.

'I'll need to see some identification,' Tweed told him.

'Can I reach into my breast pocket? You folks sure don't take any chances. That's good . . .'

'He's clean now,' Newman said, checking the revolver and slipping it inside his large jacket pocket.

Ives produced a folder, handed it to Tweed, looked at Paula and grinned wearily.

'I could do with a glass of water, if that's permitted.'

She poured him mineral water, handed him the glass. He swallowed the contents with one gulp, sighed with relief. Tweed examined the folder carefully, checked the photo, the details printed behind the plastic cover.

'You do appear to be Special Agent Barton Ives,' he said, handing back the folder. 'Welcome to Zurich. And sit down.'

'You make it sound like I just arrived,' the American commented as he sat in an armchair and crossed his legs. 'Fact is I've been here a while, never staying in one place for more than a night. That gets kinda tiring, I can tell you. Cord sends his regards.'

'Do you mean you've been moving round Switzerland or just inside Zurich?' Tweed enquired, still standing up.

'Zurich and some of the hick places just out of town. I was real worried about this Swiss system which means you've gotta register at a hotel, give them your details.'

'So you were compelled to register under your own name?'

'You think I fled from the States with a bundle of phoney identities?' Ives asked aggressively. He leaned forward. 'I had to run like hell to stay alive, packed one bag and boarded the first flight.'

'How did you recognize me in the hall?' Tweed pressed on. 'There are hardly any photos of me in existence.'

'That was Cord. He described you from your hair down to your toetips. Only way I agreed to take the chance, to come and see you. Cord was very pushy about me seeing you, Tweed.'

Tweed sat down. He took off his glasses and cleaned them with his handkerchief. He took his time and Ives, sitting erect, clasped his hands in his lap, waiting patiently. Apart from his Swiss outfit, he was Paula's idea of an FBI agent. Wary, watchful and controlled. Tweed put on his glasses, studied Ives for a moment before he spoke again.

'You said you fled from the States, that you had to run like hell to stay alive. Why? And who was pursuing you?'

Ives looked pointedly at Paula. He switched his gaze to Newman behind him who still held his gun in his hand.

'I can't answer those questions unless we're alone. I know the guy is Robert Newman – seen enough of his pics at one time in papers over pieces he wrote and he hasn't changed.'

'Did Cord advise you to take that attitude?' Tweed asked.

'No, I'm taking the attitude.' Aggressive again. Paula thought she understood: Ives had been staying under cover for some time. This was his first excursion into the open. Despite his outward air of self-control he was probably a bit trigger happy. 'What I have to tell you is confidential, top secret – you name it.'

'Both Paula and Bob are trusted members of my team. You talk in front of them or you just go away somewhere . . .'

'Cord said you were tough.' Ives waved his hands in a gesture of resignation. 'God help you if any of this strays beyond this room.'

'Is that a threat?' Tweed enquired mildly.

'No, it's stating the situation. You'd become targets for people who never miss.'

'They do sometimes,' Tweed observed. 'I'm still waiting. Would you like some coffee? There's plenty left in the pot.'

'I'd be grateful for that.' Ives looked at Paula. 'Very grateful. My mouth feels like the Sahara . . .'

Tweed waited again while Paula poured a cup. Ives refused sugar or milk. He took the cup and saucer from her and gulped half the contents down.

'That's better, a whole lot better.' He seemed to relax for the first time since he'd entered the room. 'Well, here goes. I was born and raised in New York, but I was stationed in Tennessee in the South. I was investigating the disappearance of huge sums of money. We thought at first someone was laundering drug money, but now I think the money went into a political fund . . .'

'Are you talking about bank robberies?' Tweed asked.

'Hell, no. Creative accounting. I'd interview a key witness, get a tape recording of what was said, then the witness would disappear off the face of the earth. I never did find where the bodies were buried.'

'Bodies? Plural?'

'Ten. Including three women.'

'That's mass murder,' Tweed said slowly. He paused. 'But why would the FBI be called in if the crimes were all committed in Tennessee?'

'They weren't. They crossed state lines. That's when the FBI is called in. I'm sure you know that. The trail led me from Tennessee to Mississippi, Louisiana, Oklahoma, New Mexico and Arizona.'

'That's a lot of territory. Earlier you said you thought at first *someone* was laundering drug money. Who did you mean?'

Ives took a deep breath, sighed. Again he looked at

205

Paula and Newman who were hanging on every word.

'I'm talking about Jeb Calloway, now Vice President of the United States.'

There was a hush in the room. Tweed walked across to the closed curtains, opened them a little, peered out. It had begun to drizzle and the street had a sweaty look. He went back to his chair, sat down and stared at Barton Ives.

'Are you sure about this?' he asked.

'Positive,' Ives snapped.

'I understood Calloway came from the Philadelphia area in the north-east.'

'He does.' Ives smiled bitterly. 'Which was why Bradford March, who is a Southerner, had him on the ticket for the election as running mate. Calloway was able to deliver New York, Pennsylvania and other key states.'

'So what was Calloway's connection with the Southern states where you carried out your investigation?'

'Quite a few years ago Calloway moved his electronics outfit to Phoenix, Arizona. It was the trend. The climate in Arizona was unpolluted, the unions hadn't the tight grip they exercised in the North. The money-laundering operation was controlled from that outfit in Phoenix.'

'And you say this money ended up . . .'

'In Bradford March's war chest to fight the election. I doubt he knew it was stolen money. What politician enquires too closely the origin of desperately needed funds for a presidential election?'

'And the ten witnesses who disappeared?'

'Were murdered,' Ives corrected. 'Any one of them could have testified to the illegality of the operation. Most of them were married, had families. I even had a witness who saw a woman I'd interviewed dragged into a car late at night. Neither was ever seen again. I was closing in on

Calloway when the election took place. That was when I found myself dodging bullets.'

'You mean that literally?'

'I do,' Ives assured him. 'I'd driven back to Memphis to report my findings to my chief, Murcall. I found Murcall had been replaced by a guy I didn't know called Foley. He told me to close my investigation. Orders from Washington. That was just after the election . . .'

'You mentioned bullets,' Tweed reminded him.

'Goddamnit! Let me finish my story. It was night. On my way home to my apartment from FBI HQ a red Caddy was following me. In a quiet street it drew alongside. I ducked just in time – they machine-gunned my car. When I got to my apartment a guy slipped into the elevator with me. I shoved my gun into his side, searched him, found he had an automatic. He tried to grab it and I hit him on the head. That was when I packed and took off for the airport.'

'And flew here?' Tweed enquired. 'Why?'

'Switzerland seemed a safe place, but they followed me. Don't ask me how. I'm pretty good at spotting tails. But Calloway has plenty of money. He's used it to hire a lot of people to come after me—'

Ives broke off as the phone rang. Tweed jumped up, answered it.

'Sorry to bother you,' Butler's voice said quickly. 'But I think you'd better come to my room pretty damn fast.'

'I'll come down and collect it.' Tweed turned to face the others. 'There's someone arrived downstairs I must see. But they'd better not see you, Ives. I may be a little while.'

'I'd like to visit the bathroom,' Ives said.

'Certainly,' Newman agreed. 'But I'm coming with you – for protection after what you've told us . . .'

Tweed waited until the door had closed and he was alone with Paula.

'That was Butler,' he whispered. 'Could be bad news. I want you to have your Browning in your hand the whole time I'm away. Anyone knocks on the door after I've gone – don't answer it. When I get back I'll rap on the door like this . . .' He beat a short tattoo on the top of a desk.

'Is it closing in on us?' Paula asked calmly. 'Maybe since we have Barton Ives.'

'It could be, I fear . . .'

Afterwards, Tweed was never sure what instinct had made him grab hold of his raincoat before he hurried to Butler's room. He knocked on the door, which was opened a few inches. Butler peered out, swung the door wide open and closed and locked it the moment Tweed was inside. In his right hand he held his Walther.

The room was in darkness. Tweed remained quite still as Butler touched his arm.

'I'll guide you over to the window. Then I'll open the curtains a fraction. You won't like what you see . . .'

Arriving at the window, Butler pulled open the curtains a few inches. Tweed peered down into Bahnhofstrasse. It was still drizzling, a fine veil which blurred the street lamps. Tweed counted four men standing in the rain and all wore American-style trench coats.

'I see them,' he said grimly.

'There are more,' Butler warned him. 'Pete spotted them first from his window. We count ten men leaning against tree trunks, walls, just inside shop doorways. We are surrounded.'

'So we are.' Tweed mused in the dark. 'We do have in our room a fugitive from the States they've attempted to kill at least twice.'

'I'd like to do something about this,' Butler said. 'We are surrounded,' he repeated.

'Perhaps not. Get your coat on, Harry. I have a phone call to make. From Shopville.'

208

'They'll see you come out. They could be waiting for *you*.'

'We may not be as surrounded as you think. Ready? Good. There's an exit they may well not know about. A single door leading direct into the Hummer Bar – well away from the main entrance . . .'

Tweed was proved right. No one waited in the deserted side-street beyond the door leading from the Hummer Bar. They descended into Shopville, Tweed walked into the first empty phone cubicle, dialled Beck's private number at his Berne HQ. The Swiss answered the phone at once.

'Beck . . .'

'Arthur, Tweed here . . .'

'There has been a lot of violence in Zurich since I left—'

'I know,' Tweed interrupted him. 'Talk about that later – an emergency has arisen . . .'

'Details?' Beck demanded.

'The Gotthard, where we are staying, is practically besieged by ten Americans standing in the drizzle. Wearing belted trench coats, leaning against trees, walls. It may be because someone new has arrived, but I'm not sure about that.'

'They saw you leave?'

'No, they've missed the side-door exit from the Hummer Bar. I'm talking from a Shopville phone.'

'Bloody nerve!' Beck prided himself on his command of the English language. 'I've had enough of them. Fortunately Zurich police HQ is close to the Gotthard. They'll find themselves moved pretty damned quick, and their so-called diplomatic passports won't help them. That's it? Right. I'm calling Zurich now . . .'

Tweed and Butler returned the way they had come, entering the hotel via the Hummer Bar. They heard the sound of police car sirens before they'd closed the side door. Tweed thanked Butler, went up to his room. When Newman opened the door Ives was standing at the window, peering through a crack in the curtain. Paula sat a distance away, gun in her hand.

'That's sorted out,' Tweed announced. 'So we'll all have a decent meal in the Hummer Bar restaurant . . .'

A patrol car full of uniformed police stopped in a side street just off Bahnhofstrasse. A lieutenant, followed by his men, ran into Bahnhofstrasse, paused, glanced round. The lieutenant unbuttoned the flap of his holster before he approached a tall, heavily built man wearing a coat and a slouch hat, brim pulled well down against the persistent drizzle. Uniformed police from other patrol cars were flooding into the street.

'You can't stand loitering here,' the police officer told the man. 'We've had a complaint from a Swiss woman – she's frightened to walk along here.'

'Don't ruffle the feathers, buddy,' the man replied with a pronounced American accent. 'I'm a diplomat. You can't touch me.'

He reached inside his pocket, the officer whipped out his gun.

'No call to get nervy,' the American continued. 'I'm showing you my passport.'

The officer flipped open the folder, closed it, handed it back.

'We're not convinced those are genuine. Where are you staying?'

'Baur-en-Ville. Now look here, buddy . . .'

'Then get back inside your hotel now. And don't come out again tonight.'

'Christ! You can't do this . . .'

'The Baur-en-Ville. Now! Or I'll haul you off in that

210

police van over there and you can spend the night in a cell. Arrested as a suspect character . . .'

The American swore foully, pulled up his collar, walked off in the direction of the hotel. Other Americans, similarly accosted, were leaving, trudging off through the drizzle which had given the street a surface like a band of wet blue leather. All was quiet in minutes.

In the restaurant Paula sat opposite Ives. She thought he looked more like a teddy bear than ever with his ice-blue button eyes, his closely trimmed brown hair. He looked up from his menu and smiled, the most charming smile. So why did she feel disturbed?

Tweed sat beside her with Newman opposite him. They had a table by the wall with no one near them. Tweed was studying his menu when he asked Ives the question.

'I heard a rumour that while you were in Memphis you had another job, investigating a spate of serial murders in different states.'

Ives hesitated for a fraction of a second. Paula was watching him, felt he was unsure whether to reveal dangerous information.

'Hell,' Ives addressed Tweed, 'that was one of my failures. I spent months on that grim case, got nowhere. Serial murderers are the most difficult to catch. Murcall, my old boss, switched me to checking Calloway, the embezzlements.'

'Which was not one of your failures,' Tweed observed, 'even though you were later removed from that case.'

He ordered the same as Paula had chosen, *filet de fera* with boiled potatoes, a fresh salad and mineral water to drink. Ives plumped for lobsters – this was a lobster bar and the German word for lobster was *Hummer*. Newman once again ordered his favourite dish which he had lived off at main meals since they arrived – *émincé de veau* with *rösti* potatoes. He drank white wine while Ives ordered half a bottle of Beaujolais. When the waiter had gone Tweed continued asking questions, gazing at Ives.

'Why would Calloway want you killed since you had no evidence strong enough, no witnesses left alive to confront him with in an American court of law?'

'Calloway,' Ives responded promptly, 'is a success in both business and politics. He made it by taking no chances, leaving no loose ends. I'm a loose end.'

Paula sensed Ives was tense. Whenever a new customer entered the restaurant he glanced quickly over his shoulder. Newman was unusually silent. Only Tweed seemed completely relaxed as he glanced slowly round the restaurant.

The dining-room was oblong, divided from the bar with sheets of frosted glass which had Edwardian couples etched on its surface. The main colour motif of the room was red. The ceiling was divided into large crimson panels, the walls were covered with carmine velvet. The small table lamps which provided the main illumination had crimson shades and the tablecloths were pink.

Paula thought it was a daring decor which could so easily have been chichi. But it worked: the whole atmosphere of the Hummer Bar suggested a warm and welcoming intimacy. She felt relaxed – except for an aura of tension which seemed to originate from Barton Ives. She thought she now understood it – Ives probably hadn't relaxed for a second since leaving the States. Now he was finding it difficult to adjust to the pleasant and secure surroundings. Other tables were full but the restaurant wasn't noisy. Just a gentle chatter and the occasional chuckle of pure enjoyment.

'I wonder who those guys were standing about outside in the rain,' Ives said suddenly.

'Doesn't matter now,' Tweed told him. 'They've all gone, I heard. Chased away by the police.'

212

'The police?'

'That was what I heard at reception.'

'You think those characters knew I'd arrived here?'

'I very much doubt it,' Tweed reassured him. 'I expect they were looking for me. Oh, by the way, have you taken a room here in your own name?'

'Had to, didn't I?' Ives flared up. 'I told you – I'm not carrying any phoney papers.'

'I check details,' Tweed told him quietly. 'Our job is to protect you. How is Dillon? And how did you happen to meet him here in Zurich?'

'Jesus Christ! One question at a time.' Ives quietened down. 'Cord is restless, jumps at his own shadow. I met him by accident in Sprüngli. He didn't immediately know who I was when I sat opposite him. I was wearing tinted glasses. Damned near fell off his chair when he realized it was me.'

'How did you two first meet?' Tweed went on. 'The Deputy Director of the CIA doesn't normally have contact with the FBI. The CIA isn't supposed to operate inside the United States.'

'But they do when it suits them. I found the head man of a sabotage ring Cord was looking for. He was always grateful for that.'

'He would be . . .'

Their meal arrived and no one spoke as they consumed the excellent food. Paula, who ate quickly, as usual finished first. She watched Ives handling his lavish helping of lobster. When they had all finished Ives reached into his pocket.

'Goddamnit, I've left my cigarettes in my room. Won't be long.'

Newman offered his pack of Silk Cut.

'Thanks,' Ives said, 'but I only smoke Lucky Strike . . .'

'Seems very edgy,' Newman commented after Ives had gone.

'You can understand it – after what he's been through,' Paula countered. 'Who wouldn't be?'

'We'll wait for coffee until he gets back,' Tweed said and checked his watch.

Ten minutes later Tweed suddenly stood up. He put his hand on Paula's shoulder to keep her in her chair.

'Bob, I want to make an urgent call. Your room is much closer than mine. Could I borrow your key?'

He was absent for longer than Paula had expected. When he came back into the restaurant he asked the waiter for the bill, scribbled his room number and signature. Hurrying to the table, he remained standing, leaning forward and keeping his voice down.

'Did Ives return?'

'No, he didn't,' Paula said, alarmed. 'Is something the matter?'

'You could say that. I've phoned police headquarters – luckily Beck had flown in from Berne to check the situation after my first phone call. He's on his way over with a team of specialists.'

'Specialists?' Newman queried. 'What kind?'

'His top man with a machine-pistol. And a chemist with his equipment. Plus a bomb squad team.'

'What on earth for . . .' Paula began.

'Beck is in the entrance now,' Newman told Tweed.

They walked over to where the Swiss police chief waited, fresh as paint in his business suit, calm in a crisis.

'I have this Barton Ives' room number from reception and a master key,' Beck said as he ushered them out of the restaurant.

'I could be wrong about this,' Tweed warned.

'Never known your instinct to be wrong yet. I have armed guards at either end of the corridor where his room is. And I'd like to have your room key for the chemist and the bomb squad. Thank you . . .'

Mystified, Paula and Newman stood with Tweed and

214

Beck as the lift ascended. Beck stepped out first, looked in both directions, waved for them to follow him out. He was striding ahead of them when Newman asked Tweed what the devil was going on.

'For one thing, my room lock has been tampered with since we came down to dinner. I was careful not to turn the key, let alone go inside. Also the so-called Barton Ives had the wrong answers to quite a few questions.'

'So called?' Paula repeated.

She got no reply. They had come close to the room taken by Ives. Beck's hand gestured for them to keep well back. Standing against the wall opposite the closed door was a uniformed policeman. He wore a flak jacket and was aiming a sub-machine-gun at the door. Two other men, pistols in hand, were flattened against the wall on either side of the door. A fourth man stood close by, holding a short wide-barrelled gun. Tear-gas. Beck was on red alert.

Taking out his own pistol, Beck leaned past one of the men against the wall, rapped on the door with the muzzle.

'Police. Open up. A team of armed men are outside.'

He waited. A long silence. Eventually Beck pressed an ear to the door, listened. Stepping back, he tossed the master key to the other man pressed against the wall. Paula saw the man with the machine-gun stiffen. The policeman with the key quietly inserted it in the lock, turned it, took hold of the handle, glanced at the man with the flak jacket, who nodded.

The door was hurled wide open. Flak Jacket literally dived into the room, sprawled on the carpet, swinging the muzzle of his weapon in a wide arc. He called over his shoulder to Beck, who had stepped in behind him, his gun ready.

'Empty, Chief . . .'

'Check the bathroom. Same approach . . .'

A minute later they realized the bathroom was also empty. Beck looked at Tweed.

'The bird has flown. So you were right. Now for your room. You all stay here, standing where Stefan sprawled. You don't touch anything. You don't drink anything.' He pointed to a half-empty bottle of mineral water. 'You don't use the bathroom . . .'

A policeman with his pistol in his hand stood outside the room while they waited. Newman asked the question in a low tone.

'Look, Tweed, what is this all about?'

'I am certain we've just dined with a man Dillon warned me against for fear of our lives. A man called Norton.'

23

Beck reappeared after about ten minutes. He waved for them to follow him. As they left the room two policemen wearing protective clothing, one carrying a tool-kit box, arrived, slipped inside the room.

'Bomb squad boys,' Beck remarked. 'Your room is clean – as regards explosives . . .'

When they entered Tweed's room a small gnome-like figure in civilian clothes was waiting for them. On a table a compact leather case was open and inside lay a collection of instruments. The only one Paula recognized was a calibrated dropper – like an eye dropper. A small container made of thick glass with a screw top stood next to the case. Inside it was half full with a crimsom liquid. Beck introduced the gnome.

'This is our chemical specialist, Dr Brand.'

'After what I found, Beck,' the gnome said, 'you might be interested to take them into the bathroom.'

Tweed stood with Beck just inside the bathroom doorway. Paula peered over Tweed's shoulder.

'Now have a good look round,' Beck suggested to Tweed. 'You're exceptionally observant. Notice anything not the way you left it before dinner?'

Tweed stared slowly round. His eyes lingered on items from his spongebag he'd placed on a glass shelf over the basin. He shook his head.

'It appears to be the same. I can't see anything unusual.'

'When do you use the mouthwash?' Beck enquired, pointing to a bottle.

'First thing every morning. It freshens me up for the day.'

'In that case,' Beck said cheerfully, 'you had only a few hours to live. Come back into the bedroom.' He looked at the gnome. 'My friend here uses the mouthwash every morning when he gets up.'

'I gargle with it,' Tweed added.

'Then maybe you would sniff this,' Dr Brand suggested and unscrewed the cap on the small thick glass container. He held it a moment before handing it to Tweed. 'Be very careful. It contains a small quantity of the mouthwash and a certain solvent I tested it with.'

Tweed raised the container, took a cautious sniff. Paula saw his facial muscles stiffen for a second. He handed it back to Brand, who immediately screwed on the cap.

'A faint aroma of bitter almonds,' Tweed said slowly.

'That's right,' Brand said agreeably. 'Prussic acid. I calculate you'd have gargled for two seconds. I placed the mouthwash bottle back exactly as I found it after I tested it.'

'So did someone else,' Beck said grimly, 'after he used a pick lock to get into your room.'

'Prussic acid. Oh, my God,' Paula said half to herself.

217

She had a sudden vivid picture of Amberg at Tresillian Manor in Cornwall, his face destroyed with acid.

Beck and his team had left as Tweed sat with Newman and Paula in the bedroom. Before leaving he'd reported to Tweed that not a single fingerprint had been found in the room occupied by the man who'd registered as Barton Ives.

'Probably wore surgical gloves before he even entered the room,' he commented. 'And all the glasses and cutlery he used at dinner has been washed. His case also has disappeared. It's as though he'd never been here. And Brand has taken the mouthwash bottle with him. Take care . . .'

Newman had ordered a double Scotch from room service when they were alone while Paula decided she needed a glass of white wine. Tweed stayed with mineral water.

'God! That has shaken me,' Paula said. 'How on earth did you spot that it wasn't Barton Ives?'

'An accumulation of things,' Tweed told them. 'First the phone call from a hoarse-voiced man asking if Barton Ives could come. He opened up with "Cord here" – something like that. Unlike many Americans, Dillon is very formal, always introduces himself by his surname. Not conclusive.'

'Why phone at all?' Paula asked.

'To make sure the real Barton Ives hadn't already come to see us. After he'd arrived he kept referring to Dillon as Cord, which increased my suspicion. From his own made-up story about how they met, he was only an acquaintance. Still not conclusive . . .'

'So what was – conclusive?' Paula persisted.

'An accumulation of implausible things, as I just said. The real giveaway was no reference on his part to pursuing the serial murderer – and that information came from Dillon, so has to be true. Then I bring up the subject over dinner – and he dismisses it in two or three sentences! A gory long-drawn-out case like that. Then there was the story he'd thought up as to why he *had* fled the States. Why should Calloway send over an army to kill "Ives" when he'd admitted he had no evidence that would be accepted in court? A rubbish story. Then at dinner he kept checking every customer who entered the restaurant.'

'What was the significance of that?' Paula enquired.

'Link it with his nervousness about the men who'd been watching the hotel . . .'

'Yes,' Newman intervened, 'he was obsessed with them. While you were away he kept peering out to see if they had gone away.'

'No,' Tweed contradicted. 'To make sure *they were still there!*'

'Don't follow that,' Paula commented, frowning.

'You're usually quicker,' he gently chided her. 'The men outside were Norton's. Placed there in case the real Barton Ives arrived and tried to enter the hotel. That would have been a disaster for Norton, impersonating Ives. His men were there to take care of the real Ives for good if he showed up.'

'So when you came back from phoning Beck . . .' Paula began.

'*My* story,' Tweed interjected. 'Yes, it was my remark – invented – that reception had told me the police had removed the watchers which told Norton he was in trouble. Again, the real Ives could have walked in on us. Hence his exit to his room, supposedly for cigarettes.'

'And to your room,' she reminded him.

'Well, that's why he came here – to kill me. But for Beck bringing Dr Brand he'd have succeeded. I find the method he chose interesting.'

'Not the word I'd have used,' she remarked. 'But using acid does make me wonder if Norton was the fake postman who committed the massacre at Tresillian Manor.'

'I was going to say interesting because it's a measure of the ruthlessness of the man – and his determination. He was worried stiff Ives himself might turn up but he still went ahead and tried to murder me.'

'What is the programme for tomorrow?' Newman asked impatiently.

'I have a ten o'clock appointment with that detective of Eve Amberg's, Theo Strebel,' Tweed reminded him. 'I'm hoping he'll lead me to wherever Klara, Helen Frey's friend, has moved to. I want to talk to her again. I have an idea she knows more than she realizes. Then in the evening it's drinks with Gaunt's girl friend, Jennie Blade, at 6 p.m. downstairs in the Hummer Bar.'

'I wonder how Squire Gaunt fits into all this,' Paula mused.

'He was in Cornwall at the time of the massacre,' Tweed reminded her. 'He could be a key figure.'

While it was dark and drizzling in Zurich, it was still daylight in Washington. 'A kinda daylight,' March reflected as he gazed out of the window. It was snowing heavily. The traffic down on Pennsylvania Avenue was already getting snarled up. He pressed a button on his intercom.

'Sara, get hold of the shit-kicker who's supposed to send out snow ploughs. I want them on Pennsylvania Avenue in ten minutes. When the machines get moving let the press know I gave the order.'

'Good thinking, boss . . .'

'Sure is. Let the folks know their President is lookin' after them.'

'There's a call, long distance, on your private phone. The caller won't give a name. Said you might be interested in a couple of items you were searching for . . .'

'Put them through. And put a trace on the call . . .'

'They're leery, boss. They rang off, said they'd call again shortly. I'll try a trace . . . Hold it, I think they're back on the line . . .'

'Who is this?' March barked when the connection was made.

'No names. Got a pad and pen? Good . . .' The voice was husky. 'I have a film and a tape recording for sale. The price is still twenty million dollars . . .'

'A courier is on the way to Zurich with the pay-off. I need first to be sure . . .'

'You need to shut your trap . . .'

March's mouth became ugly. You didn't talk to the President of the United States that way.

The voice went on: 'I know you're trying to trace this call. Write this down. The three possible rendezvous for the exchange – money for film and tape. On the Zurichberg, Orelli-strasse by the hotel. I'll spell it . . . Next possible place, airfield at Hausen am Albis. Here's that spelling . . . Third is Regensburg, outside Zurich . . . I'll be in touch again with specific details . . .'

The connection was broken. March was puzzled by the voice. Husky, yes. Growly, yes – very growly. But twice it had become high-pitched, sounded like a woman. Sara came on the internal line a few minutes later.

'No luck, boss. Trace took us to Zurich in Switzerland. Couldn't get the number in Zurich . . .'

'Hell! Don't know why we bought that trace equipment . . .'

March slammed down the phone. He'd pass this info. over to Norton when he next came through.

In Zurich the woman who had called March smiled at the man who had listened. She had disguised her voice by speaking from the bottom of her throat.

'March would never recognize your voice even if he ever

221

met you,' the man said, wrapping his arm round her.

'I *growled*. That's the trick. Twenty million dollars. That should enable us to live in style.'

'You were great. What about going to bed to celebrate?'

'Why did I think you had that in mind?'

The following morning Tweed had breakfast with Paula and Newman in the first-floor dining-room, La Soupière, at the Hotel Schweizerhof. Butler, Cardon and Nield sat by themselves at separate tables. The previous evening Butler and Nield had visited the hotel, entered all six rooms and rumpled the bedclothes.

'Since Norton knows we're staying at the Gotthard,' Paula suggested, 'is there any point in us remaining there?'

'None at all,' Tweed agreed. 'Which is why we're moving our things back here after breakfast. I've already paid our bill at the Gotthard, told Harry, Pete and Philip to do the same thing.'

'What is the next move?' Newman asked. 'I'd like to get to grips with Norton and Co.'

'If he *is* the real enemy,' Tweed remarked. 'Nothing is certain. I'm now convinced few of the people we've met here – and in Cornwall – are what they seem.'

'That's reassuring,' Paula said ironically. 'Anyone in particular you're after?'

'I need more data before I can plan an elaborate trap. Elaborate because someone is masterminding a complex plot. I only realized that after we arrived here.'

He was keeping his thoughts all to himself once again, Paula said to herself. She tried another tack.

'Well, we're staying in Zurich, then.'

'No, we aren't,' Tweed told her. 'Tomorrow we catch an express train from the Hauptbahnhof to Basle.'

'Why Basle?'

'I phoned the Zurcher Kredit before breakfast to speak

to Amberg. Luckily I got Amberg's personal assistant. She told me he had left suddenly for Basle in a great rush.'

'I remember – Zurcher Kredit has a branch in Basle. But why are we following him there?' Paula asked.

'Maybe you've forgotten. Amberg told us Julius had moved the film and tape Dyson delivered to the bank vault in Basle.' He checked his watch. 'I'll have to leave soon for my appointment with Theo Strebel.'

'Well, at least we know now what Norton looks like – the man who up to last night no one had ever seen.'

'I wouldn't count on that,' Tweed replied.

Inside the apartment he had rented, Norton returned to the bathroom. Thirty minutes earlier he had rubbed grey colourant into his normally light brown hair. Now he rinsed off the surplus with water and examined the result in the mirror.

His appearance was changing already. He'd forget his weekly visit to a barber, and let his hair grow longer. It grew very rapidly. Satisfied with its progress, he put on his jacket, checked the time.

Timing was everything. He had his whole day planned out with the precision of a general preparing for a major battle. He was whistling a tune as he left the apartment.

Tweed was accompanied by Paula when he climbed ancient stone steps inside the old building in the Altstadt which housed Strebel's office. Newman followed a few paces behind, waited in the corridor as Tweed opened a door with a frosted-glass window in the upper half. Etched into the glass was a simple legend. THEO STREBEL. No indication of his profession.

They walked into an empty ante-room. A solid oak door in the opposite wall with a glass spyhole. Paula was suddenly nervous – the atmosphere on the old stone staircase had been eerie, the smell of a musty building barely occupied for years had assailed her nostrils.

Here the atmosphere was even more sinister. A heavy silence filled the room which was furnished only with an old empty desk. She was sure no one had occupied the room for ages. She slipped her hand inside her shoulder-bag, gripped her Browning automatic.

'Announce yourselves. Your names, please.'

The disembodied voice seemed to come out of nowhere. Tweed pointed to an ancient cone-shaped speaker fixed to a corner high up. The voice had spoken in English.

'Is that you, Mr Strebel?' demanded Tweed.

'I said announce yourselves. Your names and business.'

'I have an appointment with Theo Strebel. For 10 a.m. Eve Amberg said she would phone you. My assistant, a woman, is with me.'

'Tell her to say something,' the disembodied voice commanded. 'Anything. Apples are green.'

'Only when they are not normally ripe,' Paula called back.

'Enter.'

There was a sound like the buzzer Helen Frey had operated on the front door in Rennweg. Tweed pushed at the heavy door and, reluctantly, it swung inward.

'Good morning, Mr Tweed. Don't just stand there. My greetings to you, Fraulein.'

A very fat man dressed in a black suit sat behind a desk. His hair was dark and brushed back over his high forehead without a parting. Below a short pugnacious nose he sported a trim dark moustache. The door closed automatically behind them as they walked inside the office. Paula heard the lock click shut, felt trapped.

'You are Mr Tweed. You fit Mrs Amberg's description. Do sit down, both of you. Now, what exactly can I do for my latest client?'

224

'You are Theo Strebel?'

'The great detective himself. No impersonations here.'

As Paula followed Tweed's example, seating herself in the other hard-backed chair facing the Swiss, she found she rather liked Strebel. He radiated energy and the good humour often associated with fat men. He leaned both elbows on the desk, clasped his surprisingly small hands under his jowly chin and smiled.

'The ball is in your court, Mr Tweed.'

'I am trying to locate the new address of a brunette who lived in the apartment opposite Helen Frey . . .'

'Whose ghastly murder is written about at length in the newspaper. So?'

'I have just said what I wish you to find out. Where Helen Frey's friend went to. I only know her first name. Klara.'

'And have you any clue as to her profession? Clues are my lifeblood, Mr Tweed.'

'She was a high-class call-girl. Like Helen Frey.'

'I appreciate the description. Everyone has to earn a living. That profession can be highly dangerous – as the latest news indicates. They are entitled to charge the high fees they do for their services. Danger money, Mr Tweed.'

'I need to locate her urgently.'

'First things first. Would you be so kind as to show me some identification? Your description may fit, but I am known as the most careful man in all Zurich.'

Tweed could have produced his driving licence. Weighing up Strebel, he produced instead his Special Branch folder, a document forged in the Engine Room basement at Park Crescent – when it had existed. Strebel raised his thick eyebrows as he studied the folder, looked at Tweed while he handed back the document.

'Special Branch? I am honoured,' he said gravely. 'You are a new experience for me.'

'I realize I have no jurisdiction here,' Tweed commented quickly.

'I was not about to make that remark.' He clasped hands under his jaw again. 'Unprecedented movements of certain people are taking place in Zurich. I get a hint of why you are here. There could be danger for me.'

'Why do you say that?' Tweed asked.

'That I cannot tell you.'

'Mr Strebel, I know you watched Rennweg 590. Could you tell me who called on Helen Frey recently – apart from Julius Amberg?'

'Ah! Julius . . .' The Swiss paused. 'I cannot reveal information confidential to clients of mine.'

'This is now a murder case – a particularly horrible one.'

'True, Mr Tweed. True. Let us say I observed someone from your country entering that door and leave it at that.'

'You won't even give me a hint?'

'I have already done that, Mr Tweed.'

'Thank you. Now I still need to locate Klara urgently.'

'That could take some time. Zurich is an intricate city. It has two Altstadts – the one you are now in and then another equally complex area on the other side of the River Limmat.'

'I haven't got the time, Strebel.'

'Obtaining information quickly is more expensive. My fee would be one thousand Swiss francs.'

Tweed produced his wallet. Extracting a 1,000 Swiss franc note, he laid it on the desk, his hand still resting on top of it. Strebel gave him his warm smile and included Paula in his hospitality. He was reaching into a drawer when Paula spoke for the first time.

'I've never seen such a tidy office. Not a single filing cabinet, no cupboards – just yourself and your desk.'

'Also my head.' He smiled at her again as he placed a notepad on his desk. He wrote something on the top sheet with care in a neat legible script. 'My files are stored in a bank vault. I respect my clients' confidences. Also I carry a secret filing cabinet in my head.' Strebel tore off the sheet, folded it, handed it across the desk to Tweed.

'That is the new address of Klara. She is in this Altstadt. Not five minutes' walk from the front door to this building.'

Tweed smiled, pushed the banknote across the desk. The Swiss picked it up, inserted it carefully inside a slim wallet.

'So,' Paula teased him, 'you knew all the time?'

'In my profession I charge for providing the information a client requires. Mr Tweed is paying for what I know.'

'I've said this before, Paula,' Tweed reminded her. 'It is not always what you know, it's where to find it.'

'Were you once a police detective?' Strebel asked.

A perceptive man, Tweed thought. It was the first time he'd ever been asked the question in that form.

'I was with the Murder Squad at Scotland Yard once,' he said.

'And he was the youngest superintendent the Yard had ever had up to that time,' Paula told Strebel.

'No need to go into details,' Tweed snapped.

'I can well believe it,' Strebel told Paula. 'Mr Tweed, maybe before you leave Zurich you would join me for a drink. We could exchange experiences – I mean from when you were at the Yard,' he added hastily.

'It would be my pleasure.'

Strebel accompanied them to the door after pressing a button underneath his desk. He shook hands formally with both of them and when Paula glanced back as they reached the outer door he smiled again, bowed his head.

'What a nice man,' Paula said as Tweed closed the outer door. 'I always picture private detectives as nasty little men in shabby raincoats.'

'I suspect Strebel was once a member of the Swiss police. He may well know Beck.'

Newman was waiting for them at the end of the dark corridor. He spoke to Tweed immediately.

'Someone started to come in downstairs, opened the door. I think they saw me and changed their minds. Didn't get a glimpse of who it was.'

'People calling on private investigators are often shy of being seen. We've got Klara's new address . . .'

Outside on the uneven pavement which, like the buildings, looked as though it had been there for centuries, Paula consulted her map. She looked to the end of the deserted square from the edge where they stood. The square was surrounded with six-storey buildings as old as time.

'Klara is living at the far side of the square. No. 10.'

The entrance hall was similar to the one they had just left. As they entered a door opened on the ground floor. A hook-nosed woman with beady eyes and dressed in a black dress peered at them.

'You want the girl who's just moved in upstairs?' Her thin lips curled. 'Some people don't care how they make their money. Mixed doubles this time, is it?'

She slammed the door before Tweed could retort. Newman led the way up the old iron-railed stone staircase. Close to the only door on this landing he stopped. Tweed and Paula stared past him. The door was open a few inches.

Newman had his Smith & Wesson in his hand as he moved silently to the door, paused to listen, pushed the door open wider with his left hand, took a step inside, froze. He called over his shoulder.

'Paula, for God's sake don't come in here . . .'

24

It was a replay of the grim tragedy in Helen Frey's apartment. Klara, fully dressed, lay back in an armchair, her head flopped at an unnatural angle. A dark crimson sickle gash curved round her throat, disappearing round the back of her neck.

'He's been here,' Paula said quietly.

Despite Newman's warning she had followed Tweed into the apartment. She pulled on her surgical gloves as Tweed walked slowly round the back of the chair. Again the head was almost severed from the neck. Someone favoured garrotting.

Paula stood sniffing the air. She frowned, began prowling round the apartment, careful not to disturb anything.

'What is it?' Tweed asked Paula sharply.

'Cigar smoke . . .' She continued walking slowly, weaving her way among armchairs, passing a large couch. 'Got you,' she called out.

She was extracting a specimen wallet from her shoulder-bag when Newman stood alongside her. On top of a small piecrust table, hidden by the arm of the couch, stood an ashtray. Inside it rested a thick roll of cigar ash. Tweed joined them as she lifted the container with her gloved hand, skilfully tipped the ash roll inside the wallet. Sealing it, she wrote the date, the second of March, and a name. *Klara*.

'She had a customer at nine thirty a.m. according to her desk diary,' Newman said.

He took them over to a table where a new diary lay open.

9.30 a.m. *E*dwin *A*llenspach. Tweed and Paula stared down at the entry.

'Strange she underlined the initials of each name,' Paula remarked.

'Could have been any reason,' Newman reacted dismissively. 'Maybe it was a new client and she was reminding herself to check up on him.' He glanced at Paula. 'Or maybe he had certain tastes she catered to,' he suggested, phrasing it carefully.

'You mean kinky,' Paula suggested. 'Somehow I don't think Klara went in for that sort of thing. And nine thirty in the morning seems rather early for . . . although I suppose some men . . .'

She trailed off as she saw Newman watching her. She grimaced at him.

'You know what I mean.'

'I wonder whether either of you are right,' said Tweed.

He was still gazing at the entry. He made no attempt to explain what had crossed his mind. Standing in the centre of the apartment he scanned it swiftly, taking in everything.

'Again no sign that the place has been ransacked, searched in any way.' Paula realized he was talking to himself as he continued: 'So, whoever is the murderer came for that specific purpose. Murder. He's systematically exterminating everyone who might provide vital information.'

'Maybe it's just become a habit with him,' Newman said, attempting to lighten the traumatic atmosphere with a little black humour. 'Could be a psychopath, I suppose.'

'I think not,' Tweed objected. 'But yes, systematically exterminating all potential witnesses,' he repeated.

'Well, the bastard's doing a damn good job,' Newman remarked.

230

Tweed was strolling round the apartment. Paula, watching him, saw him suddenly clap a hand to his forehead. He grunted. He stiffened.

'On our way out, I'll try out my German again on Old Nosy downstairs. I did understand the dirty remark she made. She may have seen him arrive or leave. She has the mind of a concierge who can't abide not knowing what people are doing. I also suspect she's greedy.'

'We must report this crime,' Newman said. 'I know we skipped out of Helen Frey's place . . .'

'It was important we didn't get tangled up in an inquiry, slowed down. But this I was going to report,' Tweed agreed. 'Something else is worrying me though. We'll report it to the police shortly.'

As they made their way back down the stone stairs the door on the ground floor opened and Old Nosy stood in her doorway, arms akimbo. Both Paula and Newman also understood German.

'That was a quick one,' she sneered. 'Must have been easy money for that new girl.'

'I have a question to ask you,' Tweed said in German.

'Ask away. Don't promise you'll hear anything from me. Not as though I'm the local gossip.'

'I'm sure you're not,' Tweed said amiably. 'The new girl had someone who called on her before we arrived. Did you by chance see them? Could you give me a rough description?'

Between his fingers he held a hundred-franc note. She was eyeing it with great interest. She tossed her head.

'Information costs money in Switzerland.'

'Which is why I'm willing to pay – if I'm convinced you're not making it up.'

'Me make something up for money?' she blazed indignantly. 'Who do you think you're talking to?'

'Someone, apparently, who isn't interested in accepting a fee in good faith,' Tweed replied, his tone harsh.

'Didn't say that, did I?' She simpered and Paula felt nauseated. 'I didn't see them go up,' the woman said in a regretful tone. 'I was listening to my favourite radio programme. But I did hear them leaving. Tiptoeing down those steps pretty fast.'

'You saw who it was?' Tweed asked, mentally crossing his fingers.

'Only saw the back of the caller. As they was leaving, going out the front door.'

'Describe them for me as best you can,' Tweed coaxed.

'He had a black wide-brimmed hat on, pulled well down . . .'

'Colour of hair?'

'I just told you – he had the hat pulled well down. So how could I see the hair? One thing I can tell you is his height. I always notice how tall someone is. About as tall as her.' She nodded towards Paula, looking her up and down. Paula's gaze remained steady as she stared back at the ferret-like eyes. 'Wore a long black·overcoat and a thick woollen scarf.'

'A fat man?' Tweed enquired.

'No. He was tall and fairly slim. Had a funny walk.'

'Funny in what way?'

'Took quick short steps. Like a pansy.'

'Did he move like a pansy then?' Tweed pressed.

'No, I don't think he did. Didn't mince, if that's what you mean. I only got a glimpse as the door was closing.'

'A thick neck?' Tweed probed.

'No idea. How could I? He was wearing this thick woollen scarf. I just told you that.'

'So you did,' said Tweed, who was checking her powers of observation. 'Was he carrying anything?'

'Not in his hands. But he had something pretty heavy in his coat pocket. Weighed it down, it did.'

'Thank you,' said Tweed and handed her the banknote. 'I congratulate you on your powers of observation.'

'Something funny has happened up in her apartment?' she asked, her eyes gleaming at the prospect.

'According to you something funny is always happening in that apartment.'

Tweed left the building before she could think up some vicious retort. He began walking rapidly across the square, returning to the side they had come from. His legs, despite his shorter stature, moved like pistons and Newman had trouble keeping up with him. Paula was running when they reached the entrance to Theo Strebel's building.

'What is wrong?' Paula asked.

'Nothing, I hope. But I am very much afraid . . .'

Newman managed to get alongside Tweed as he took two steps a time up the staircase to the first floor. On the landing Tweed stopped suddenly, pointed. The door with frosted glass in the upper half leading to the ante-room was open several inches. Behind them, Paula froze briefly. Doors partly open were beginning to fill her with terror.

She grabbed for her Browning as Newman, Smith & Wesson in his hand, used his other hand to hold Tweed back. Paula caught up with them.

'Strebel is so careful about security,' she whispered.

'Exactly,' Tweed responded in a grim tone.

'You're not armed,' Newman reminded Tweed. 'We'll go ahead, check the lie of the land.'

Paula had slipped off her gloves, held the Browning in both hands as she followed Newman into the ante-room. It had the same long-uninhabited feel she had sensed last time. But there was one difference. The heavy oak door to Strebel's office was open several inches.

Tweed had followed closely on their heels. He stood for a moment, fists clenched out of sight in his trench coat pockets. Newman, on the hinge side of the door, reached out his left hand, pushed it hard. It swung open slowly,

233

noiselessly on its well-oiled hinges. There was a terrible silence pervading the atmosphere, a lack of life. Paula, awaiting a signal from Newman, was pressed against the wall on the other side of the door.

Tweed, standing very still, watched the door expose more and more of the room beyond. There was something theatrical about its movement. Then he had a clear view of the interior of the room.

Without hesitation, Tweed marched straight inside. Newman, inwardly cursing what he regarded as foolhardiness, jumped in after him, stopped. Paula, Browning aimed for instant firing, stood in the open doorway, slowly lowered the angle of her gun until the muzzle pointed at the floor.

'Dear God, no!' she exclaimed in anguish. 'Not again.'

'Yes, again,' Tweed said in a voice which held no emotion. 'Exactly what I expected. Except for the method of execution . . .'

Theo Strebel lay back in his chair behind the large desk. His jacket was open, revealing his white shirt front. A large red rose shape decorated the white shirt to the right. Over the heart. A red rose which blossomed and spread slowly as Paula watched, almost hypnotized.

Tweed walked swiftly round the desk. He felt the carotid artery, shook his head.

'He's dead,' he said simply. 'Shot through the heart. One bullet, I suspect. And I blame myself. I was so looking forward to having that drink with him. Some people – a rare few – make an instant impact on you – he was one of that rare breed. Such a bloody waste.'

Paula had seldom heard Tweed swear. And he had spoken with a ferocity that startled her.

'Where's the flaming phone?' Tweed demanded.

'Why, for Heaven's sake, blame yourself?' she enquired.

'Because the murderer arrived while we were talking to

234

Theo Strebel.' He looked at Newman. 'You gave me the hint and a faint alarm bell rang. I was fool enough to ignore it.'

'What hint?' Newman, puzzled, asked.

'When we were leaving here before you said someone started to come in through the front door. You thought they'd seen you and changed their minds. That was the murderer. He'd just committed one and was on his way here to kill Strebel.'

'Committed one?' queried Paula.

'Yes. The garrotting of Klara. I only realized Strebel was probably in great danger when I said aloud that the murderer was exterminating everyone who might provide information. I shouldn't have delayed our departure by questioning that awful woman. But on the other hand she did say something very significant, and Strebel was by then probably already dead.'

'What was very significant?' Paula asked.

'So where *is* the phone? I must call Beck . . .'

It was Paula who found out where Strebel hid his phone. Wearing her surgical gloves, she began opening drawers in his desk. Hauling open a deep drawer at the bottom, she lifted out a telephone. She dialled police headquarters, then handed the instrument to Tweed who was wearing gloves. He asked for the Swiss police chief, giving his name.

'Tweed here, Arthur . . .'

'I have news for you,' the familiar voice broke in. 'I have at long last received the expert's report on that cigar ash specimen you gave me. Whoever smoked the cigar has expensive tastes. It is a Havana.'

'Thank you, I have another specimen for you to check – but that can wait. There have been two more murders . . .'

'Two more?' Beck's tone was ironical. 'You know then about the killing of a certain Helen Frey?'

'Yes, we can talk about that when we meet. One victim is

Klara, the girl who had the apartment opposite Helen Frey's. The other is a private detective. I'm speaking from his office now. A Theo Strebel . . .'

'Strebel! Oh, no, not Theo. He worked in the police force just before I got the top job. I wouldn't have thought anyone could have murdered Theo. You said you were at his office?'

'Yes. The address is—'

'I know it. I'm on my way there now . . .'

25

Paula sat in the front passenger seat next to Butler as he drove them up the steep hill to Eve Amberg's villa. Nield was in the back. The two men had discreetly followed Tweed to the Altstadt address when he had first visited Theo Strebel.

Before Beck arrived at Strebel's office, Tweed had given Paula careful instructions as to the information he wanted her to obtain from Eve Amberg. He had warned her not to mention the murders of Klara and Strebel, had then taken her down into the street to find a taxi. Relieved to see Butler and Nield, he had left her in their safe hands while he waited with Newman for Beck.

'Shouldn't you have phoned her first to make sure she is in?' Butler suggested as he pulled up in front of the wrought-iron gates.

'I did think of that but Tweed was anxious for me to get clear before Beck arrived.'

'Makes sense – under the circumstances,' Nield remarked.

On the way Paula had told them about the two murders. They had listened in silence as she put them concisely in the picture.

'A pretty grisly experience,' Butler had commented when she had finished. 'The murder count is climbing. Tweed could be next if he's not careful.'

'Bob stayed with him. Tweed will be all right. Now, if you don't mind, I'll go in by myself. I shouldn't be long . . .'

Tweed had made that point – that she should talk to Eve on her own.

'She may tell you more on a woman-to-woman basis . . .'

Pushing open one gate, Paula walked past an Audi parked in the drive, bonnet pointed towards the garage, caught a whiff of petrol in the fresh clear morning air. She hauled on the ancient chain bell-pull and the door was opened almost at once by Eve Amberg.

The Englishwoman wore denims, a padded windcheater and a knitted blue woollen cap. Her titian hair cascaded down her back. She gave Paula a warm smile, invited her inside, took her into the living room.

'I was just going shopping. Hateful task but it has to be done. Just before I left a Swiss woman friend called on the phone. She's nice but once she gets talking her mouth is glued to the phone. Goes on and on. Would you like some coffee? It's bitterly cold out there.'

'No, thank you just the same. Am I throwing your whole schedule out of gear? I tried to phone but the line was engaged,' she lied to cover up what might appear to be lack of manners.

'Not at all.' Eve pulled off her woollen cap, took her guest's coat, laid it neatly over a chair and sat down facing Paula. 'It's a relief for me to talk to someone English. The shopping can damn well wait.'

'Tweed is still trying to find out who committed those terrible murders – the ones at Tresillian Manor and now Helen Frey. We went to see her yesterday.'

'What happened to her was horrific. I read about it in the paper. What was she like? I am still wondering what Julius saw in her.'

'I thought she was rather ordinary,' Paula said tactfully. 'You mentioned to Tweed you knew Cornwall. He wondered what part of it you come from?'

'Launceston, just beyond where Bodmin Moor ends. That's how I know Gaunt.'

'And he came all this way to tell you about Julius? A nice gesture. Tweed is intrigued by Gaunt.'

'I don't wonder. He has such a strong personality. No, he didn't come just for that. He has business interests in Zurich. Don't ask me what they are. I'm hopeless when it comes to money. That's why the fact that Walter now controls the bank is a worry. What money I have is in that bank.'

'Walter is still in Zurich?'

Eve produced her ivory holder, inserted a cigarette, lit it. She waved the holder.

'I imagine so. Haven't heard a word from him, let alone seen him. Strange man.'

So she didn't realize Walter was now in Basle, Paula thought. He obviously doesn't let his sister-in-law know a thing.

'Lucky – from your point of view – that you didn't think of going to Cornwall with Julius,' Paula suggested.

'I can't make up my mind about that. He might still be alive if I'd gone.'

'I think that's highly unlikely – considering what took place. *I* was there – and only escaped with my life by pure chance.'

'Frightening,' Eve said. 'You lead a charmed life. I expect I shall go back to Launceston when this is all over.'

'They didn't try to get you back to attend to the funeral arrangements?'

Eve took a deep drag on her cigarette, blew out smoke. Again she brandished the holder.

'It was all settled by phone. Julius always said if anything happened to him he wanted to be buried in Cornwall. He loved the place, hoped to retire there. I suppose in a macabre way he got his wish. I didn't go – it would have been too upsetting. I'll visit his grave when I do go back.'

The phone began ringing. Eve made a moue, crossed the room with brisk steps. She picked up the phone, her back to Paula.

'Yes, who is it?'

She listened, then replied, her voice high-pitched.

'Not now. It's not convenient. I'll get back to you this afternoon. At least, as soon as I can. Goodbye.'

She waved the holder a third time as she sat down again. Paula thought she detected a trace of annoyance in Eve's manner.

'That was Gaunt,' Eve said. 'Wanted to come and see how I was getting on. Very considerate, but you can have too much of a good thing.'

'Sorry, I'm not with you.'

'Just between you and me, he's a nice man. But I find him overbearing at times. Wants to order your life for you.'

'Where did you first meet him?'

'In Padstow, where I was born. That was when I was long grown up. Quite a while after I'd left Roedean School and started to live a normal life. You won't believe this, but I was Head Girl for a short time – and hated every minute of it. Felt like a fish in an aquarium. I bought a house outside Launceston when my father died – I'd had enough of Padstow. The summer, the best time, was ruined with ghastly trippers.'

'I've taken up a lot of your time. I think I'd better go, let you get on with that lovely shopping.'

239

'Excuse my attire. Don't like women who frolic about in denims. You see a lot of that in Padstow these days. But they're practical for shopping.'

Paula was standing up to go when she turned round as Eve prepared to see her to the front door.

'One more thing Tweed wanted to know, if it's not too personal. He gathered Julius decided on his trip to Bodmin Moor at short notice. So he must have phoned Gaunt to see if Tresillian Manor was available for him. It really was very short notice for Gaunt to clear out to his cottage at Five Lanes. How did Gaunt react?'

'Said Julius could have the manor for as long as he liked, that he needed the money.'

She opened the front door and came out into the porch as Paula thanked her. Eve looked at the parked Audi.

'I'm glad to see that. It's just been returned from our service garage after a maintenance check. Something about the brakes. Arrived just before you did.'

'In time for your shopping. Again, many thanks . . .'

Butler waited until he had turned the black Mercedes in the road and was heading back for Zurich, before he asked Paula: 'Did you get what Tweed wanted?'

'No idea. I won't have until I've reported our conversation to him. You never know what he's really after.'

Tweed arrived back in the late afternoon from police headquarters with Newman. He went straight to Paula's room and Butler left them alone.

'Tell me,' Tweed requested.

Paula began to speak by rote. She spoke with her eyes closed, seeing and hearing all that had happened from the moment she had left the car and walked up the drive to Eve Amberg's villa.

Meticulously, she recalled every detail – the Audi in the drive, Eve answering the door quickly, dressed to go out

240

shopping. Her clothes, her manner, every word she had said. Tweed sat in a chair facing her, recording every word Paula said.

'That's it,' she eventually told him.

'Word for word?'

'That's what you asked for. That's what you got.'

'What was her mood after she'd taken that phone call?' he asked.

'I told you. Annoyed. Irked. A bit put out.'

'Gaunt. Gaunt. Always Gaunt,' he repeated.

'No point in asking what you're after?' she suggested.

'A link, between Cornwall, Zurich – and Washington.'

'Norton here . . .'

President Bradford March lounged in his chair, his feet clad in sneakers perched on his desk. He wore jeans and an open-necked shirt exposing the hair on his broad chest. A leather belt encircled his waist in an attempt to hold in his ample belly.

'Norton here,' the abrasive voice repeated. 'I got the code-word on my answerphone to call you . . .'

'So squat on the butt and listen. The courier with the big bucks is on his way. He hits Zurich airport tomorrow certain. Aboard Swissair flight SR 805, ETA Zurich 4.25 p.m. He takes a cab to Hotel Baur-en-Ville. That right? Where Mencken is shacked up?'

'I don't want Mencken in on this . . .'

'Shut your trap. I said listen. OK? Great. You'll make it yet. Courier's name is Louis Sheen. Got it? He'll carry a suitcase, brown in colour. When he arrives at this Baur place 5.30 p.m. Zurich time, he goes to reception, tells them at the top of his voice that he's Louis Sheen, that they have a reservation, which they won't have. You contact him immediately with the code-words Lincoln Memorial. Got that? Then you take him to a safe place, wait for instructions from the creep who calls me.'

'I'm not showing my face . . .'

'Your problem. The creep demanding the dough pho-ned, gave three possible exchange points. Note them – I'll spell them out . . . OK? Something else – Sheen will be handcuffed to that suitcase. It stays that way until you meet the bastard who tries to collect. The case has combination locks. Only Sheen knows the numbers which open it. Try opening that case without operating the combination, a small thermite bomb inside explodes, burns the contents to crap.'

'I ought to know that combination,' Norton demanded.

'All those big bucks? You're a joke, Norton. One more thing – you kill the guy who comes to collect . . .'

In Zurich Norton was surprised when the line went dead. He'd never have thought March could have dreamed up such a diabolical trap as the thermite bomb.

At the Schweizerhof, after talking to Paula, Tweed was in a rush to keep his appointment with Jennie Blade. He asked Newman to phone the Zurcher Kredit to make sure Walter Amberg was still in Basle.

Newman recognized the voice of the girl who answered the phone. She was the attractive personal assistant who had shown them into the banker's office.

'Bob Newman here. I was with Mr Tweed when he called on your boss . . .'

'I remember you well, Mr Newman. How are you? How can I help?' she enquired.

'Well, I just wanted to check that Mr Amberg is still at the Basle branch, that he will be there tomorrow.'

'Oh, he will be. He'll be in Basle for several days. You can count on it. And you are the second person within the hour who has asked that question.'

'Who else did? Or shouldn't I ask?'

'Oh, that's all right, Mr Newman. He didn't leave a name. I'm new here, don't yet know all the clients. The man who called had a husky growly voice. Not very polite.'

'A lot of people aren't. I really am very much obliged to you. Thanks a lot.'

Newman wondered who 'growly voice' could be, made a mental note to tell Tweed.

Newman sat in the dimly lit bar leading off the lobby, drinking a glass of white wine. He was recalling the tough interview with Beck after the Swiss police chief had arrived at Theo Strebel's office.

'I'm not easily shocked, as you know,' he told Tweed as he viewed Strebel's corpse. 'But before he left us to set up a private investigator business – you can make more money that way – he solved a baffling murder case I couldn't crack. He was a great detective and it's a great loss.'

Beck kept his voice down. The office was swarming with the forensic and fingerprint teams. The police doctor had just left after officially pronouncing Strebel dead.

They had then hurried over to Klara's apartment. Newman had come with them and was not disappointed when Old Nosy poked her vulture-like nose out of the door.

'Is there some trouble upstairs?' she asked.

'Stay in your apartment,' Beck ordered. 'I'll want to talk to you later.'

'And who do you think you are?'

'Police.' Beck flashed his folder under the nose. 'I said stay until I get round to you . . .

'Local Eye-at-the-Keyhole,' he remarked as he strode up the stairs. 'There's one in every district . . .'

The doctor had visited Klara's apartment first and by the closed door to the ante-room stood a uniformed policeman. He saluted Beck, opened the door and they went inside.

Beck stared at the garrotted woman. He pursed his lips, turned to Tweed.

'I see now why the doctor said it was a bit nasty here. Never known him make a comment like that before and he's seen everything.'

Beck leaned against a wall. He folded his arms as he stared first at Tweed, then at Newman.

'Yesterday there was a small blood bath in Bahnhofstrasse. Have you seen the papers? No? Well they report a cripple in one of those battery-operated wheelchairs blew himself to pieces with a grenade. At about the same moment an American was shot dead – holding a machine-pistol. Now would you by chance know anything about these events?'

Tweed explained exactly what had happened – that he'd been up to his neck in trying to track down who was behind the murders. Beck nodded without comment as Tweed continued, then concluded: 'I'm sorry I didn't contact you earlier.'

'And I'm damned sorry too you didn't. I do like to know what is happening on my patch, as I think they say in Britain. And my patch is the whole of Switzerland – which includes Zurich.'

'I have apologized,' Tweed said quietly. 'How close are you to discovering what is happening, to solving the murders of this poor woman, Klara, and Theo Strebel?'

'I've only just arrived,' Beck pointed out. 'You mean you have some idea of who the murderer is?'

'The pieces of a huge international jigsaw – stretching all the way from Washington via Cornwall to here – *are* beginning to fall into place. I'm a long way from seeing the whole picture, but I'm getting there. Your further co-operation would be much appreciated.'

'Oh, you have that. Unreservedly. You're continuing your investigation in Zurich?'

'Not for much longer. Tomorrow we leave for Basle.'

'May I ask why?'

'You just did,' Tweed told him tersely. 'Walter Amberg is reported to have gone to Basle. I need to talk to him again.'

'Thank you. I think I can hear the technical teams arriving. Let's get out of here. If you could come to police headquarters I can take statements from both of you. It will take time, I fear. Oh, while we are still alone, I have had installed 'at Customs at Zurich, Geneva and Basle airports a special new machine. It checks the contents of cases without the arrivals knowing. A Swiss invention.'

'You mean an X-ray machine?' Newman asked.

'Much better than that. It photographs all the contents of a closed case. I want to see what any new American arrivals are bringing in to this country . . .'

Louis Sheen, from Washington, arrived at Kloten Airport. He waved his diplomatic passport and prepared to walk past Customs.

'Excuse me, sir,' the Customs officer behind the counter said. 'Please place your case on the counter.'

Sheen was tall and slim, his face long and pale, and he wore rimless glasses. He put down the case, waved the passport again, spoke in a nasal drawl.

'This is a diplomatic passport. Something wrong with your friggin' eyesight? You can't examine my bag.'

The Customs officer nodded to one of his subordinates who stood on the same side of the counter as the American. The Swiss picked up the case, placed it in a certain position on the counter, which was etched with a curious mosaic design.

'Goddamnit! You can't open that case,' Sheen shouted. 'It would be a breach of diplomatic etiquette.'

'Who said anything about opening the case, sir?' asked

the Customs officer. 'Could I have a closer look at that passport?'

'Your friggin' Passport guys saw it.'

'And now I would like to see it. This will only take a moment.' The officer opened the passport, walked a few steps along the counter, flipped open the pages. He handed it back, put his hand on the case as Sheen reached for it.

'Just leave it there for a moment longer. I have to check this passport number. It will only take a moment.'

'Friggin' Swiss bureaucracy,' Sheen stormed.

'It takes up a lot of our time too.'

The officer smiled, disappeared through a doorway behind him. The technician who had photographed the case through a hole in the patterned wall showed the officer the photo which was already developed. After one glance, the officer nodded to a plain-clothes policeman standing in the small room. The policeman nodded back.

When Sheen, fuming, was ushered on his way – fuming because he'd had to hold his left hand with the handcuff chain on top of the case – he was followed. Sheen was sweating as he sank into a cab.

It will take time, I fear. Beck had proved to be right. He'd had an excellent lunch brought in for Newman and Tweed at police headquarters. Each dictated a statement of considerable length and then both statements had to be typed out. By the time they had signed them the lunch had arrived. It was early afternoon. Tweed decided they might as well eat it and Beck joined them, chatting about past experiences.

It was late afternoon when a tired Tweed reached the Schweizerhof and listened in her room to Paula's account of her visit to Eve Amberg.

When she had finished, he thanked her and left for the Hummer Bar. It was dark as he walked down the side street to the direct entrance to the bar. Behind him on either side of the street Butler and Nield strolled along as though taking the night air.

Tweed pressed the bell which opened the door. He took a deep breath before walking inside to meet Jennie Blade. What would the girl he'd first met that grim afternoon outside Tresillian Manor have to tell him, he wondered.

26

Norton checked his changing appearance in the bathroom mirror before he left the apartment. After the second application of the colourant his hair was starting to look very grey. The half-moon glasses perched on his nose gave him a professorial look. He carried a large file full of business statistics which he had no interest in.

Checking his watch, he left the apartment to arrive in good time at the Baur-en-Ville before Louis Sheen turned up. The cab he flagged down swiftly transported him to Parade-platz. A short walk across Bahnhofstrasse and he was inside the Baur-en-Ville.

He entered the hotel, made certain arrangements with a messenger boy, then sat in a chair where he could see reception. The boy stood a distance away and watched Norton. It was precisely 5.30 p.m. when Louis Sheen walked in with the brown suitcase attached to his left wrist with a handcuff chain.

Norton was ice cold as he watched over the top of his file. The reception area was crowded with soberly dressed Swiss men greeting each other. Norton knew they were bankers. He had phoned the hotel earlier, pretending to ask for a room.

'I'm sorry, sir,' the girl had told him. 'We have no rooms at all available. There's a convention of bankers from all over Switzerland . . .'

Sheen went up to the reception counter, perched on it the suitcase to rest his hand. His voice was loud and overbearing when a receptionist turned to him.

'Louis Sheen, Philadelphia. I have a room reserved for several nights.'

'Certainly, sir.' The receptionist checked his records. 'Did you say Sheen, sir? I fear there is no reservation.'

Norton put down the file in his lap. It was the signal the generously tipped messenger boy had been waiting for.

Norton also noticed a man in a Swiss suit who wandered in within thirty seconds of Sheen's arrival. He stared as the man checked his watch, picked up a magazine, remained standing. It appeared he was waiting for someone – but he hadn't glanced round the reception area. Norton pursed his lips. Sheen had been followed from the airport.

'Now look here,' Sheen continued at the top of his voice, 'Louis Sheen, Philadelphia. I phoned the booking—'

He broke off as someone touched his right arm. Glancing down he saw a uniformed messenger boy.

'Mr Sheen?' the boy asked.

'Maybe. Why?'

'I have a message for him. Are you Mr Sheen?'

'I am. Give it to me . . .'

He turned away from the counter, ripped open the envelope. A white sheet of paper without a printed address at the top was inside. The message was brief.

Take a cab at once to the address given below. Walk out now and get a cab. Lincoln Memorial.

Underneath the address the message was signed with a flourishing 'N'. Sheen had been warned this was how

Norton always signed his instructions. He resisted the temptation to look around at the people assembled in the reception area.

Norton waited as Sheen left the hotel entrance leading to a side street. The man in the Swiss suit strolled after Sheen. Something would have to be done about him, Norton decided. He left by the same entrance in time to see the Swiss climb in behind the wheel of a BMW. His own limo, ordered in advance, was parked by the kerb. He climbed in the back as Sheen entered a cab.

'That cab is the target,' he ordered the driver, one of Mencken's subordinates. 'Don't lose it. Just don't make it obvious we are following it – we have company. The white BMW. It will follow our target. You follow the BMW. One more thing you will not do. Just listen. Do *not* look at me in your rear-view mirror. See me and you're dead. Now, for Chrissakes, get moving . . .'

Jennie's golden hair glowed in the subdued lighting of the Hummer Bar. She sat on a bar stool and Tweed had to admit to himself she looked stunning.

She wore a deep purple suit, the jacket open to reveal a low-cut white blouse. Round her neck was a string of pearls which disappeared in the dip between her breasts. On the stool beside her lay a folded pale lilac coat.

She swung round off her stool to greet him. Her short skirt exposed her long legs. She kissed him on the cheek and a faint waft of perfume drifted in the air.

'I hope I haven't kept you waiting,' Tweed remarked as they hoisted themselves on to the stools.

'Not for one second. I like a man who is prompt. And I arrived early. You look very fresh and eager.' Her blue eyes were animated and she was giving him her full attention.

'I don't feel all that fresh,' Tweed confessed. 'I've been on the go all day.'

'Time to relax then.' She squeezed his arm. 'Sorry I didn't make it last night. But from my point of view that gave me this evening to look forward to.'

She was openly flirting. Tweed decided to hit her hard when the time came with his first question. He suggested champagne. He rarely drank but he wanted her in a co-operative mood – she might tell him more that way.

'Lovely,' she said. 'My favourite tipple. You'll join me?'

Tweed ordered two glasses of champagne from the waiting barman. Glancing along to the end of the bar he saw Philip Cardon sitting on a stool, nursing a drink as he read a paperback.

Jennie gazed in the same direction as Cardon looked up from his paperback. She waved to him, then shook her golden mane as though to say, 'No good. You were pipped to the post.'

'Cheers!' said Tweed and they clinked glasses.

Jennie drank half the contents of her glass while Tweed downed his in two long gulps. Before leaving Paula he had drunk a lot of water, hoping it would keep him sober. Jennie finished off her drink.

'Another?' Tweed urged. 'You'll join me?'

'Sky's the limit.'

She grinned appreciatively at his using her own words back at her. They consumed most of the refills before Tweed threw the question without warning.

'When did you first know Julius Amberg was coming to stay at Tresillian Manor?'

'But I didn't.' She looked at him, her eyes wide open with innocence. 'Not until we were leaving for the cottage at Five Lanes an hour or so before he arrived.'

'Then why did you think you were leaving at all?'

'The Squire said he had some friends coming he rented the manor to from time to time.'

'Did you ever talk to one of his servants, a girl called Celia Yeo? She was found dead at the foot of High Tor –

which is not far from Five Lanes. Someone pushed her over the abyss.'

'How perfectly horrible.' She played with the stem of her empty glass. 'Tweed, you're some kind of investigator. You know something? I'm beginning to get the idea you're investigating me.'

'What I am investigating,' Tweed said grimly, 'is a series of murders . . .'

'You mean those poor people at Tresillian Manor?'

'Within the past twenty-four hours three more people have been murdered here in Zurich – one man and two women,' Tweed said grimly.

'You're frightening, Tweed. How does any of this concern me?'

'Where is Gaunt?' he asked.

'He's on his way to Basle . . .'

'By plane?'

'No, he's driving the hired BMW there . . .'

'Why is he going to Basle?' Tweed demanded.

'On some sort of business. How the hell would I know? I don't know anything about his affairs.'

'Don't get worked up,' he said quietly.

'Why the bloody hell shouldn't I?' Jennie blazed. 'I'm being interrogated like a suspect.'

'It's Gaunt I'm interested in, not you,' he said mildly. 'How long have you known him? Now don't jump down my throat. I am trying to find out why those poor people were brutally massacred.'

'I've known Squire Gaunt just over two weeks. Really, I think I should go.'

'Stay a little longer – help me to find out who is behind these hideous murders . . .'

Louis Sheen was startled to find after he had shown the cab driver the address on the sheet of paper that they were driving back along the route to the airport. The BMW with the Swiss driver followed them carefully, keeping one vehicle between himself and the cab. Behind him Norton's driver adopted the same tactic.

Within ten minutes the cab turned off the main road and pulled up outside a modern apartment block. Sheen paid him, climbed out carefully, manoeuvring the suitcase clamped to his wrist. Norton watched him go inside the building, then gave his driver fresh instructions.

'There's a phone box a few hundred yards beyond where we are now. I have to make a call. Drop me outside it, then wait for me. Keep your eyes staring ahead . . .'

Norton had seen the BMW park out of sight behind a big truck which stood stationary. He realized that from this point the Swiss could keep the exit to the apartment block under surveillance. As his own car stopped he jumped out, ran to the phone box, inserted coins, dialled the Baur-en-Ville, asked for Marvin Mencken.

'Yes, who is this?' Mencken's distinctive drawl asked.

'It's me. I arranged for you to check on a competitor.'

He was referring to Tweed, but was careful not to mention him by name.

'We know his exact whereabouts now,' Mencken snapped.

'And?'

'Well, it *is* all arranged,' Mencken said irritably.

'You pick him up and escort him to the meeting?'

The word escort meant *exterminate*.

'We're all set up for when he pokes his nose into the side-street. Don't worry any more about the competition. He'll co-operate. End of problem.'

'Make damned sure it is. The end . . .'

Norton slammed down the phone, went back to his car. It was all beginning to come together. Amberg had flown to Basle – so the film and the tape must have been transferred to the Zurcher Kredit Bank branch in that city.

252

He would fly that evening aboard flight SR 980, departing Zurich 7.15 p.m., arriving Basle 7.45 p.m. Sheen would find the message waiting for him in the apartment with the air ticket to board the same flight, to take a cab on arrival at Basle Airport to the Hotel Drei Könige. Norton, under a different name, would be staying at the same hotel.

Earlier he had given Mencken instructions over the phone to lead a team of men who would also fly to Basle. They would stay at the Hilton. While he waited for Sheen to emerge another cab had already drawn up outside the apartment block. Norton glanced at the parked BMW. He had no doubt the Swiss inside it would follow Sheen to Basle. There Norton himself would personally take care of the nuisance.

Yes, everything was coming together. And within the hour Tweed, who was proving to be a potential menace, would be dead. Norton felt the adrenalin surging inside him at the prospect of final action.

'Have you ever met Eve Amberg?' asked Tweed, casting about for a significant link between Cornwall and Zurich.

'I'm pretty sure I saw that woman in Padstow,' Jennie recalled as she sipped her third glass of champagne.

'I wasn't aware you knew her. If I'm right how would you recognize her?' Tweed queried.

'When Gaunt was leaving her villa the other day – not the day when you came up to me in the BMW – I saw her very clearly saying goodbye to Gaunt at the front gate.'

'But surely that was after you'd seen her in Padstow?'

'That's right. I have a photographic memory for faces.'

'So when did you see Eve Amberg in Padstow? I suppose you couldn't recall the exact day?'

'The day her husband arrived at Tresillian Manor just before the massacre. I was with Gaunt, having a quick drink at the Old Custom House early in the day. He went outside to look at his wretched boat – I followed him after finishing my drink. I saw Eve when she was hurrying away from South Quay.'

'And you're positive it was Eve Amberg?' Tweed pressed.

'I'm damned sure it was that woman. Damned sure.'

Tweed wondered why he thought she could be lying. Was it the double reference to 'that woman'? Also, if true, what she had said placed Jennie in Padstow at the time.

'I must go now,' she said. 'To a party.' She had checked her watch. 'It's been lovely talking to you. Do let's do it again . . .'

He helped her on with the lilac coat but she said she'd carry her scarf which had lain underneath the coat. As they moved towards the door Cardon was already opening it, disappearing outside. Tweed opened the door, let Jennie go out first. She dropped her scarf as he joined her and the ice-cold atmosphere of night hit them.

A cream Mercedes parked at the top of the street began to move towards them. The rear window was open. From inside the barrel of a gun projected. Cardon, standing against the wall, cannoned into Tweed. As he was falling to the ground Tweed deliberately collided against Jennie, who was still crouched low to retrieve her scarf. A hail of bullets thudded against the wall, sending chips of masonry flying in all directions.

Cardon, holding his Walther in both hands, fired three shots. More shots were fired by Butler and Nield who stood on either side of the street. The Mercedes sped off, weaving from side to side, reached an intersection, disappeared. Unhurt, Tweed helped Jennie to her feet. She was shivering and shaking, but also unhurt. She looked at Tweed.

'What happened, for God's sake?'

'Someone tried to kill me. Are you all right?'

'I'm OK.'

'Still want to go to your party?'

She was brushing grit off her coat. She opened it to check her suit, closed and re-buttoned it.

'Yes,' she decided. 'I'll recover faster at a party.'

'You're coming with us,' Cardon intervened.

He grasped her firmly by the arm. His expression was grim. Tweed spoke as he tightened his grip when she tried to free herself.

'Let her go, Philip,' he ordered. 'Here's a cab. Flag it down for Jennie . . .'

'She signalled to that car that you were coming out,' raged Cardon as the cab drove off. 'She dropped her scarf and that car started moving.'

'Possibly,' Tweed agreed. He looked at Butler and Nield who had joined them. 'Jennie may be a very skilful liar. *May* be,' he emphasized. 'Back to the Schweizerhof.'

'A brief council of war, everyone,' Tweed announced.

He had summoned Paula and Newman to his room. Cardon, Butler and Nield had come up with him. Cardon had tersely told Newman and Paula what had happened.

'Let's not dwell on it,' Tweed said briskly. 'They missed. Thanks to Philip, Harry and Pete I'm still very much alive. We are leaving for Basle first thing tomorrow. The key to everything, I'm now convinced, lies in the mysterious film and the tape Dyson left at the Zurcher Kredit. Those items are now in the vault of the Basle branch. Amberg is in Basle. I want to see him again. It's time we watched that film, listened to the tape.'

'Hadn't you better report that assassination attempt to Beck?' Paula suggested. 'He's going to get very annoyed if we don't tell him something else.'

Tweed phoned police headquarters. He was put straight through to Beck who worked all hours. Briefly Tweed explained, leaving out any reference to Jennie Blade.

255

'A patrol car has already found your cream Mercedes,' Beck informed him. 'Abandoned near the Quai-Brücke down by the lake. The bullet holes in the windscreen and windows attracted their attention. There was blood on the rear seat. Do you have to take such risks?'

'Zurich seems to be the battlefield. So perhaps you'll be relieved to hear I'm flying to Basle tomorrow.'

'There will be plain-clothes men watching you all the time. Good night. Stay in your hotel until you're leaving . . .'

Tweed put down the phone. He looked at Newman.

'Bob, I doubt if that girl at the Zurcher Kredit you seem to get on with is still there, but try. I'd like to be quite sure Amberg is still in Basle . . .'

Newman dialled the number of the Zurcher Kredit. The same girl answered immediately. The Swiss worked late.

'Bob Newman here again. Sorry to keep bothering you.'

'That's all right. I'm catching up on finding things out. I am new here, after all.'

'I wanted to double-check that Mr Amberg is still in Basle. In case I have to call him in the morning at an early hour.'

'Yes, he's definitely there. Will be for a few days. And someone else wanted to know – besides the man with the growly voice who phoned earlier. This time before I told the new caller I asked for a name and looked at the client file. He is a client of the bank. I think he wanted to see Mr Amberg urgently.'

'Could you possibly give me that name?' Newman coaxed.

'I suppose I shouldn't, but you're always so polite, unlike a lot of the clients.'

'So the name was?'

'Joel Dyson.'

256

27

The express train from Zurich to Basle thundered across northern Switzerland. Tweed sat in a first-class compartment with his case on the seat beside him while Paula sat opposite. Across the central aisle Newman occupied the seat next to the aisle while Cardon sat in the next two seats by himself. Cardon was in a corner, facing Tweed so he had a good view of him diagonally.

'We are not flying to Basle,' Tweed had announced in his hotel room before they left. 'Philip has been over to the Hauptbahnhof and bought return tickets for all of us to Basle.'

'Why the train?' Paula had asked.

'Because it's quicker for a start. Driving out to the airport, waiting to board a flight, taking a cab from Basle Airport, which is half an hour's journey – it all takes longer. Also, we can slip away more easily with the station just across the way.'

'But you told Beck you were flying there,' she reminded him.

'So I did.' He had smiled. 'I don't want to be hemmed in by his protectors. In any case, I have my own. I'll call him from the hotel in Basle . . .'

Paula sat looking round the sparsely populated compartment, alternately gazing out of the window. So far there were few mountains on this trip. They were travelling through industrial Switzerland, where many factories stood close to the railway line.

Out of the corner of her eye she saw someone

approaching their compartment. She glanced in the direction of the automatic door. A tall monk had entered. He wore a dark robe, his waist spanned with a rope girdle. A hood was pulled over his head and he had a pair of hornrimmed glasses perched on his nose. She slid her hand inside her shoulder bag, gripped the butt of the Browning.

The train was swaying round a bend as the monk, carrying a case in his left hand, made his slow progress towards them. Newman had seen Paula's reaction. He glanced quickly in a mirror, saw the monk coming, slipped his hand inside his jacket, rested his hand on the Smith & Wesson.

Tweed, apparently absorbed in writing names on a pad, linking them with different permutations, sensed the tension. He glanced up as the monk arrived alongside him. At that moment the express lurched again as it roared round a curve.

The monk's case hit Tweed's, toppled it over on the seat. Tweed stared at the face under the hood. Cord Dillon.

The uniformed conductor who had checked their tickets a few minutes earlier left another first-class compartment which had been empty. Not many people travelling at this time of year. It was early March.

Out of a lavatory where the door had been open a few inches a tall heavily built man stepped into the deserted corridor. At this point no other passengers were visible.

'Ticket, sir,' the conductor requested.

'Sure, buddy. Got it here somewhere . . .'

The American glanced in both directions. No other passengers in sight. The train swayed again. The conductor, accustomed to the movement, stood quite still, feet splayed.

The American, as tall as the conductor, appeared to lose his balance. He lurched against the conductor. The flick knife concealed behind him appeared, was rammed swiftly up through the open jacket and between the ribs of the conductor. As he grunted, sagged, the American grabbed him and hauled the body inside the lavatory, used an elbow to close the door. He lowered the body on to the seat, locked the door. Checking the neck pulse he felt nothing.

Swiftly he began the awkward task of removing the conductor's uniform – jacket, trousers and peaked cap. As he stripped off his own suit, folded it roughly, shoved it inside a plastic carrier, the eyes of his victim stared at him.

Tucking the carrier behind the seat, the American took out a penknife. He opened the door a few inches, saw no one. From the outside he used the penknife to move the small notice which indicated that the lavatory was occupied.

Straightening his cap, he checked his watch. Only a few minutes left before the train stopped at Baden. Mencken had a car with a driver waiting there to take him back to Zurich. He checked the Luger tucked inside his shoulder holster to make sure he could whip it out quickly from under the jacket, felt the handle of the second flick knife tucked inside his belt. The jacket, buttoned up, was a little tight across the midriff, but who notices a conductor? Holding the instrument used to clip tickets in his left hand he made his way back to the first-class compartment where Tweed was sitting. He'd be able to kill him and any guards in seconds . . .

Three things happened at once as the 'monk' toppled Tweed's suitcase. Newman rammed his revolver into Cord Dillon's back. Paula's Browning appeared in her hand. Tweed held up a hand to indicate all was well.

'My apologies,' Dillon whispered to Tweed, relieved when the gun muzzle was withdrawn from his back. 'The train lurched . . .'

As he spoke he dropped a card with writing on it in Tweed's lap. The message was terse, clear.

Barton Ives is aboard the train. Where can he meet you? Not on this train.

'No need to apologize,' Tweed said in a low tone. 'You can both contact me at Hotel Drei Könige – the Three Kings – in Basle. Sooner speak to you first.'

'Thank you, sir,' said Dillon.

He proceeded on through the compartment, carrying his bag. The last Tweed saw of him was when he disappeared beyond the compartment door. Paula leaned forward.

'What was all that about? I nearly shot him.'

'That was Cord Dillon. He did take a chance, but he's on the run still, obviously. On the train that outfit is a perfect disguise.' He folded the card, tucked it inside his wallet without showing it. 'He had an urgent message for me. We could take a mighty leap forward at Basle.'

'How in Heaven's name did he know you were on the train?'

'Because he's a trained observer, one of the best in the world. I can only guess – I imagine he saw us leaving the Gotthard for the Schweizerhof. He could have been up all night watching the hotel exit from the station across the Bahnhofplatz. That station never goes to sleep.'

'Tweed,' Paula persisted, speaking loud enough for Newman to hear her, 'there must be danger aboard this train. For Dillon to go to such lengths. If he saw us waiting at Zurich to board the express the opposition could also have seen us.'

'I doubt that. I didn't tell you I'd phoned Swissair and booked reservations for us on a flight to Basle. In our own names. They'll be watching the airport . . .'

He stopped speaking. Paula wasn't listening to him. In a mirror she was watching a uniformed conductor about

260

to enter their compartment. She started fussing with her hair in the mirror to give a plausible reason for staring in that direction.

'Tickets, please . . .'

Paula shifted swiftly into the empty seat beside her so Newman could also hear her. She leaned forward.

'We've already had our tickets checked by one conductor. This is a *different* man . . .'

Paula had travelled on many Swiss trains. She knew that the conductors had remarkable memories. They would instantly spot a fresh passenger who had boarded *en route*, ask him for his ticket. But they *never* asked the same passenger twice.

The only people in the compartment were Tweed and his five companions. The conductor could see that from the moment he had entered. And yet he had said . . .

'Tickets, please . . .'

The conductor clipped Cardon's ticket a second time. He was walking slowly as he approached Tweed and Paula. His right hand slipped inside his tight jacket, which slowed down his lightning movement. The Luger was half out from behind the cloth when Newman jumped up. He grabbed the barrel of the gun, forced it to point at the ceiling of the car. The American was strong as an ox. He began to press the barrel down to aim it at Tweed.

Butler, seated at the other end of the compartment, hurtled forward. His bunched right hand hit the assassin a savage punch in the kidneys. The assassin sagged, butted Harry Butler in the chest. Butler grunted, stayed standing where he was, gasping for air.

Paula was on her feet, holding the Browning by the barrel, awaiting her chance to smash the butt against the attacker's head. Cardon came up behind him, tried to kick his legs from under him, but it was a confused struggle, everyone close together. Newman's fingernails, hard as a chisel, dug deep into the American's gun hand. He loosened his grip and Paula caught the weapon in mid-air.

'Get the bastard out of the compartment,' Newman panted.

Nield was standing at the far end of the compartment where he had sat near Butler. He was watching to make sure no one was coming. An extra body flailing into the turmoil would be one too many.

In the violent struggle in the aisle the conductor's cap the assassin had worn fell off. Paula bent down, picked it up off the floor. Newman now had worked his way behind the American, had an arm round his throat. Butler bent down, grasped both legs by the ankles, crossed them and elevated. The thrashing assassin was now held between Butler and Newman who carried him out of the compartment.

The struggle became more violent outside the compartment as they carted the American towards the platform joining two coaches. The assassin twisted his head, his teeth were closing over Newman's hand. Newman let go, jumped back, hauled out his Smith & Wesson. He had no intention of firing it – even above the rumble of the swaying express's wheels it would be heard. Butler held on to the ankles and Newman cannoned against Cardon, whose back hammered into a lavatory door. Not completely locked, the door gave way and Cardon fell inside the confined space.

'It's occupied . . .' Newman started warning him.

'It bloody well is,' Cardon agreed. 'Take a look but don't move the door any more . . .'

Newman glanced round the door. A tall man in shirt and underclothes sat on the seat. A knife handle projected from the shirt, the blade was inside the body. From its position Newman realized it had penetrated the heart. The conductor . . .

In the corridor the attacker had broken free from Butler. He was on his feet faster than Newman would have believed possible. The flick knife in his hand was aimed at Butler's abdomen. As he lunged forward Newman moved. He brought down the barrel of his revolver with all his strength on the assassin's skull. The knife point was within an inch of Butler's abdomen when the barrel bounced back off the skull. For one incredible moment the assassin remained standing and Newman raised the revolver for a second blow. Then the assassin fell backwards into the lavatory.

Newman caught him round the waist. Cardon had sidled out of the lavatory to give assistance. Newman was heaving the assassin's inert body back into the lavatory when he saw Butler stooping to pick up the flick knife which had dropped from their adversary's hand.

'Don't touch that!' he shouted.

'You want this?'

Paula had appeared, holding the conductor's cap. Through the gap on the hinged side of the door she had seen what was sprawled on the seat.

'Yes. Give it to me,' Newman snapped.

He had fitted the body of the assassin into the corner facing his victim and under the washbasin. A brief check of the carotid artery told him the man was dead as his victim. He rammed the cap on to the corpse's head, kicked the knife inside the lavatory.

'Fingerprints,' he told Paula and the other two. 'It has to have his fingerprints on that knife. Now to shut this damned door . . .'

Using a handkerchief round his fingers, he closed the door. He then took a slim gold pen out of his pocket. Working with a steady hand, he eased shut the slide which indicated the lavatory was occupied. He'd made a better job of it than the assassin had earlier. Paula, delving in her shoulder bag, handed him a wad of tissues.

'Your gun,' she said. 'Blood on the barrel.'

Newman had automatically clung on to it while he had

wrestled the body inside the lavatory. He thanked her, quickly cleaned the barrel. Paula held out more tissues she had flattened out.

'Drop the messy ones here. I'll get rid of the lot in a litter bin at Basle . . .'

Nield was standing by the entrance door to the compartment, his right hand inside his jacket. Paula told Butler to wait a minute. She then refastened two buttons on Newman's shirt which had come undone in the struggle. She straightened his tie, told him to comb his hair, then gave Butler similar attention.

'What about me, Paula?' Cardon asked, looking doleful to lighten the atmosphere.

'You can look after yourself, Cry-Baby,' she told him, hoping she was keeping the tremble out of her voice.

Tweed sat very upright in his seat, staring at them as they came back. Newman sat in his old seat and Paula perched herself facing Tweed. His expression was grave as he asked the question.

'What about the real conductor?'

'He's dead,' Newman said simply. 'The assassin killed him to get his uniform.'

'I see. Was he married, do you think?'

'Don't know. No sign of it,' Newman lied.

Tweed was too quiet. Both Paula and Newman realized he was very upset because he knew he was the target the conductor had died for. And Newman had seen that the conductor *was* married. A gold band had adorned the third finger of his hand hanging down by the side of the lavatory.

'It's a bit scary,' Paula suggested. 'The way they're following us like wolves, know exactly where we are. Whoever "they" may be.'

'The mastermind behind all this,' Tweed said quietly, 'is going to pay a heavy price for the loss of life. I'll see to that personally . . .'

264

28

Basle – where Switzerland meets France and Germany. The moment Tweed alighted from the express he found a phone box, called Beck in Zurich. To his surprise they told him Beck was already in Basle. He phoned police headquarters in that city.

'Beck speaking . . .'

'More bad trouble I'm afraid, Arthur. Aboard the express from Zurich . . .'

Tersely he told Beck what had happened, that the bodies were inside the lavatory of the fourth coach from the rear, that the express was scheduled to wait twenty minutes before proceeding north into Germany.

'Hold on,' Beck interjected.

He returned to the phone three minutes later. His tone was crisp, calm.

'Patrol cars and an ambulance are already on the way to the Bahnhof. I phoned the station superintendent. That express won't leave until they've done their job. Which hotel are you staying at?'

'Drei Könige. I'm speaking from the station . . .'

'Go straight to your hotel. Do not leave it under any circumstances until I get there, which may not be for some time. The killers have tracked you. Once again. Drastic action must be taken. *Stay in your hotel . . .*'

Tweed arrived at the Drei Könige with Paula and Newman. As planned, Butler, Nield and Cardon would come later one by one, as though they didn't know each other. The concierge greeted Tweed warmly.

265

'So good to have you back with us, Mr Tweed,' he said in his perfect English. 'We have three nice rooms for you, all overlooking the Rhine . . .'

As Tweed registered, a man wearing a Swiss business suit with half-moon glasses perched on his nose sat in the large lounge area adjoining reception. He was reading a local newspaper, his eyes hooded with disbelief as he saw Tweed enter. His grey hair was shaggy and he raised the paper a little higher to conceal his presence. Norton was recovering from the shock of seeing Tweed still alive.

Paula went along to Tweed's room. She had showered and changed into her blue suit in fifteen minutes. Tweed opened the door a few inches, then swung it open wide and ushered her inside with a sweeping gesture. He immediately relocked the door. Paula looked round the double room.

'What a super room. Mine's like this. And it has a magnificent view of the Rhine.'

She ran to the window. It was a brilliantly sunny day and very cold. The hotel was perched on the very edge of the Rhine which was about a hundred yards wide even as high upriver as Basle. On the far bank a number of ancient houses with steep pointed roofs lined the river.

'Look,' she called out, 'a barge train.'

Tweed joined her and they watched a stubby tug hauling downriver a string of huge barges. They were container craft and the German flag flew from each stern.

'I've got the same view,' she enthused. 'Oh, dear, I suppose I shouldn't feel so buoyant after the horror on the express. That poor conductor . . .'

'He was dead before we knew anything was happening.' Tweed put his arm round her. 'So we couldn't have saved him. Now we go after the people responsible for the atrocity. But first, interested in lunch?'

'Ravenous.'

To reach the lift they moved along a railed walk which surrounded a well looking down on to the floor below. Not a very high rail, Paula observed. Newman arrived from his room as they entered the lift and squeezed inside with them. Stepping out into the lobby the first person they saw was Eve Amberg.

'It's a small world, to coin a cliché,' Eve greeted them. 'My, it's cold outside.'

'I love it,' Newman said cheerfully. 'I can work and think better in this weather.'

'Bully for you.' Eve turned her attention to Tweed after nodding to Paula. 'I'm just going in to lunch.' She smiled at him warmly.

'By yourself?' Tweed enquired.

'As it happens, yes.'

'Why not join me for lunch, then?'

'How nice of you.' She glanced at Paula and Newman. 'But you have your friends.'

'Oh, that's all right,' Paula said quickly. 'Bob and I have something to work out. Do it better on our own.'

Eve was again looking as smart as paint, reminding Paula of their first meeting, as opposed to when she had caught Eve leaving the villa on a shopping trip. She wore a soft green tailored jacket, a mini skirt and a cream blouse with a high neckline. Must have cost a bomb, that outfit, Paula estimated.

As they followed Tweed and Eve towards the dining room Paula looked round the large lounge area. Out of the corner of her eye she'd seen someone sitting there when they arrived. The grey-haired man had gone.

They entered the dining room – oblong with windows to their right giving a view across a canopied platform extending over the Rhine. Tweed pointed towards it as a waiter showed them to a window table.

'That's what they call the Ry-Deck. In summer you eat

out there and it's like being aboard an ocean liner.'

'I know,' Eve agreed. 'Julius brought me here when he was visiting Basle.' She sat down. 'What a coincidence – the two of us arriving at the same time at the same hotel.'

'Not really, if you are visiting Basle. This is the most prestigious hotel, as I'm sure you know. Goes back ages and the food and service are excellent.'

Like the entrance hall and the lounge area, the walls were covered with old panelling and the comfortable atmosphere suggested somewhere which had existed for ever.

'There are buildings just along here by the river which have amazing dates of origin,' Tweed remarked as he studied the menu. 'Incidentally, why are you in Basle, if I may ask?'

'You may,' she teased him, squeezing his hand. 'I came to have a serious talk with Walter, to pin him down – about money, of course. My money. I phoned the bank and the pest has flown to France.'

'Really?' Tweed concealed his anxiety. 'Any idea where in France?'

'Oh, I can tell you exactly. Walter owns a place up in the Vosges mountains. Very remote. The Château Noir. Easiest way to get there is to take the train to Colmar, a picturesque town only half an hour from Basle Bahnhof. Then you hire a car to drive you up into the mountains. I'm going to catch him up if I have to follow him all over Europe.'

'Would you like a drink? Wine? White, then how about Sancerre?'

'Love it.'

'Would you excuse me for a few minutes?' Tweed asked when the wine had arrived. 'I have to phone London – should have done it before I came down to lunch . . .'

He left Eve sipping her wine appreciatively. Newman and Paula sat together at a table some distance away.

Seated alone at a table which gave a view of the whole room was Harry Butler. At two other tables, also by themselves, sat Pete Nield and Philip Cardon.

In his room Tweed checked the number of the Zurcher Kredit in the directory, dialled the number. A woman with a severe voice answered his call.

'Mr Amberg is away at the moment. No, I have no idea when he will return.'

'I am a client,' Tweed persisted. 'Mr Amberg was going to collect two items which belong to me from the bank vault. Do you know if he did visit the vault . . .'

'I really have no idea. If you will leave your name . . .'

Tweed put down the phone, waited a moment, dialled police headquarters, asked for Beck. He explained what he wanted. Beck said he'd contact the Zurcher Kredit and call him back. Five minutes later the phone rang and Beck was on the line again.

'I put pressure on the old dragon who took my call, told her I was investigating three murders which took place on Swiss soil. Amberg did collect something from the vault before he left . . .'

'For his château up in the Vosges behind Colmar,' Tweed interjected.

'Don't go into France,' Beck warned. 'I can try to protect you here but France could be even more dangerous. The train incident has been dealt with. I'll need some more statements.'

'You'll get them before we leave.'

'For France? *Don't do it*, for God's sake. I'm carrying out a sweep through Basle. They obviously know you're here. Take care . . .'

Tweed was leaving the room when the phone rang again. He locked the door, ran to answer it, sure it would stop just as he reached it.

'Yes?' he said.

'There's someone on the phone for you, Mr Tweed,' the

269

operator told him. 'He won't give a name but says it's very urgent.'

'Put him on.'

'Dillon here. We have to take a decision—'

'Operator!' Tweed interrupted suddenly. 'This is a bad connection. I can't hear the caller . . .'

He waited. For the hotel operator to answer. For the click which would betray the fact she had been listening in. Nothing.

'Sorry, Dillon. It's all right. Go ahead.'

'Barton is in town. But so is the opposition. Believe me. Barton won't come to see you in Basle.'

'Cord, first give me a description of him. Detailed, if you please. I need to be able to recognize him.'

There was a pause. Tweed was taking no more chances – not after the fake Barton Ives, whom he was convinced had been Norton, had turned up at the Gotthard. Dillon spoke tersely.

'Six feet tall, slim build, wiry, black hair, now has a small black moustache, a small scar over his right eye – where a scumbag caught him with a knife. Speaks very deliberately. Economical in movement. Except in a crisis. Then he moves like a rocket taking off from Cape Canaveral. That enough? It had better be.'

'Enough. Today or tomorrow latest we move to the Hotel Bristol, Colmar, in Alsace. A thirty-minute train ride. He contacts me there. And so do you. In person. I'll meet you both in Colmar – together or separately. I don't give a damn. The alternative? Forget it.'

'Look, Tweed, when you're on the run . . .'

'By now I know at least as much as you do – maybe more – about being on the run. Time to stop running, to face the swine who don't care what methods they use. Ives *must* see me in Colmar. So *must* you. I have to go now . . .'

Tweed, his mood cold as ice, put down the phone. He had meant it. No more being driven from place to place by the opposition. Time to lay a huge trap for them. Probably in the Vosges mountains.

Tweed apologized to Eve as he rejoined her. She was smoking, waved her ivory cigarette holder.

'Please, say no more. I've been enjoying myself now I'm away from Zurich. Awful thing to say, but I'll always associate that city with Julius. Does that sound too too dreadful?'

Tweed noticed she must have drunk about three glasses of the Sancerre during his absence. Some of these women had heads like rocks. She showed no sign of being even slightly inebriated. He refilled her glass.

'No, it doesn't. If he gave you a bad time. The lines to London were busy. Hence my neglecting you.'

'Nonsense. As regards Julius, all those women. Ah, here is the waiter . . .'

They both ordered grilled sole. Tweed remembered from a previous visit that sole was particularly good at the Drei Könige. When they were alone again Eve leaned towards him, her greenish eyes holding his.

'You've changed since you made that call. You're like a pulsating dynamo now. Like a man about to do battle. I can sense the change.'

Tweed became aware that he was sitting very erect in his chair, that as he spoke he'd been making vigorous gestures. It was uncanny the way Eve had hit the nail on the head. He felt rejuvenated at the prospect of meeting Barton Ives, a man he was convinced knew a great deal about why the world was exploding about them.

He chatted to Eve about Switzerland in general until the main course arrived. They ate in silence, devouring the excellent fish. He began probing again when they had ordered their dessert. But first he refilled her glass. So far he had consumed one glass of wine and a lot of mineral water.

271

'How did you get here? By car?'

'Lord, no! The traffic is terrible. I flew from Zurich. It's only a half-hour flight. For some stupid reason I got to the airport at the last minute, boarded the plane and it took off.' She toyed with her half-empty glass. 'Are you still investigating the horrible murder of that woman – what was her name? Helen Frey.'

'I have other fish to fry – pardon the unintended pun. Could there be a link with her murder and the fact that she . . . knew Julius?'

'Why on earth should there be?'

'Just a thought. When are you leaving for Colmar?'

'Haven't made up my mind.'

'Where is Squire Gaunt at this moment?'

'No idea.' She emptied her glass. 'He comes and goes. I'm not his keeper – if I can put it that way.' She played with his sleeve. 'He's just an acquaintance – if you were thinking something else.'

'Never crossed my mind,' Tweed lied.

The orange mousse with Grand Marnier they had chosen was as mouth-watering as their grilled sole. Tweed was puzzled. Eve seemed so poised and interested in him. When she had finished her mousse she carefully wiped her full lips with a tissue and swung round in her chair to face him. Her jacket was open and the movement drew attention to her well-shaped breasts protruding against the white blouse. She plucked at his sleeve again.

'Why don't we have coffee upstairs in my room? It will be quieter there. And I would like to hear how you got on with Julius. He was, after all, my husband. Please excuse me for a moment. The powder room . . .'

As she left the restaurant Tweed glanced across at the table where Paula sat with Newman. Paula was watching him with a half-smile, roguish. She beckoned to him, got up to meet him.

'Something fascinating you must see. There's a really

272

weird ferry which keeps crossing the Rhine.' She led him to an end window. 'It's like a gondola. Bob says it's controlled by a wire running from the ferry to a cable which spans the river. There it is . . .'

In some ways the very small ferry did resemble a gondola. The stern half was roofed over with the for'ard part open to the elements. A strong current was running as it made its slow way across from the opposite bank. The craft was swaying in a brisk breeze and inwardly Tweed winced. His mind flashed back to the ferry from Padstow to Rock, the large powerboat which had attempted to overturn them, Cardon lobbing his grenade. They watched it until it reached the side.

It carried a single passenger. A large man with his back to them. He wore a deerstalker.

'A curious contraption, that ferry,' Tweed commented.

'Your lady friend awaits,' Paula mocked him.

'I've just had a message that I have to go somewhere,' Tweed explained to Eve as they left the dining-room.

She looked at her watch, glanced at the reception clock.

'My watch is fifteen minutes slow. No wonder I nearly missed my flight at Zurich. There you go. A Swiss watch. It must have been slow for days . . .' She hesitated. Tweed thought she'd been going to say more, had changed her mind. 'Oh . . .' she said.

She was staring at the revolving entrance doors. A man in a deerstalker had just entered the lobby from outside.

'Ah! So we meet again,' a familiar voice boomed. 'What about drinks in the bar? My round . . .'

Squire Gaunt had arrived.

Marvin Mencken, his expression unpleasant – because he had failed again – hurried out of the Hilton Hotel in Basle to call Norton from a phone box in the station. He only

273

had a number – a Basle phone number. Norton never gave him an address, the cunning bastard.

A bitter east wind blew through the large Bahnhof as he found the nearest phone. He took a deep breath, dialled.

'Who is it?' the abrasive voice at the other end demanded.

'Mencken here. The large team which flew with me from Zurich is in place. We've hired transport . . .'

'And botched up everything on the train. I saw them unloading the useless cargo. You really must get your act together this time,' Norton said in a dangerously soft tone.

'Sure thing . . .'

'There don't seem to be any sure things. Listen. Tweed is at the Drei Könige down by the river. The profile of him says he likes fresh air, taking a walk. So this time you eliminate the competition. Or your head is on the block. Shut up and listen, damn you! This is what you do . . .'

This conversation, which involved the killing of Tweed, took place while the target was finishing lunch at the Drei Könige.

'Thank you,' Tweed said to Gaunt, 'but we have an urgent appointment.' He looked round at Paula and Newman who came closer, then lowered his voice to speak to Eve. 'I appreciate your invitation to join you for coffee. But seeing the time when you looked at your watch made me realize I was behind schedule. Another time?'

'Yes, please,' Eve said in a whisper. She ran a hand through her hair slowly, her eyes half-closed as she stared at him. 'I get so lonely.'

'I do understand. There is always another time,' Tweed assured her.

Paula and Newman collected their coats from the concierge who then helped Tweed put on his heavy overcoat. As they went outside and Tweed turned right Paula asked her question.

'What appointment? Or was she moving in too close for comfort?'

'An appointment with a walk so I can think. We could be close to discovering something important – even the key to the mystery.'

As they walked uphill and along the deserted street called Blumenrain Tweed told them about his conversation with Cord Dillon. They passed a short side-street which, Newman pointed out, led to the landing point for the strange little ferry shuttling back and forth across the Rhine. Another narrow street of ancient buildings continued on parallel to the river. Totentanz. Tweed stopped briefly in the piercing wind to look at the different dates. 1215. 1195. 1175.

'One of the oldest cities in Europe,' he commented.

'It's early Middle Ages,' Paula added.

The wind dropped suddenly and it became very silent and still. Paula's mood changed to one of premonition. The narrow street was still deserted – they were the only people walking in the silence.

The ancient stone houses were tall and slim, all joined together to form an endless wall. Each house had a heavy wooden door flush with the wall and she had the feeling no one lived there. The old pavement was very narrow, so narrow they moved in single file.

Tweed, hands deep inside his coat pockets, shoulders hunched against the cold, was in front. Paula followed on his heels while Newman brought up the rear. It was like a city abandoned by the inhabitants who had fled from the plague. Creepy.

The sun had vanished. The sky was a low ceiling of grey clouds which suggested snow. It did nothing to dispel

Paula's premonition of imminent doom. Do pull yourself together, she thought. At that moment she heard the car coming ahead of them, the first vehicle they'd seen since starting out on their walk. It's the time of day, she reassured herself – mid-afternoon in March and most people inside offices at work . . .

Tweed had stopped, put out a hand to grasp her arm as he searched desperately for a protective alcove to thrust her into. Newman had no time to whip out his Smith & Wesson. Racing towards them on the opposite side of the street was a large grey Volvo. The driver wore a helmet and goggles. Newman had a glimpse of other men inside the car as it swerved across towards them, mounted their pavement, hurtled forward like a torpedo.

Nowhere to run. They were hemmed in by the wall of houses. It was going to mow them down, drive on over their bodies. Tweed grasped Paula round the waist, prepared to try and throw her out of the way across the street. He doubted whether he'd manage it. The Volvo was almost on top of them. The driver wearing the sinister goggles accelerated. They were dead.

The white Mercedes appeared out of nowhere, rocketing down the street from the same direction the Volvo had appeared. It drew alongside the Volvo. The driver swung his wheel over, his brakes screeched as he stopped just before he hit the wall.

The Volvo, unable to stop, slammed into the side of the Mercedes. Four uniformed policemen, guns in their hands, left the Mercedes as it rocked under the impact. As three of them leapt to the doors of the Volvo, guns aimed, the fourth man waved as he grinned at Tweed, waved again for him to go away.

"Back to the Drei Könige,' Tweed said, his arm round Paula, who was shaking like a leaf in the wind.

29

In a state of shock, no one spoke until the Drei Könige
came into sight. Tweed was the first to recover. He glanced
at Paula. The colour had returned to her face. They could
talk now.

'That was Beck who saved us,' he said. 'He told me he
was carrying out a sweep of the whole city.'

'But it was sheer luck that unmarked police car turned
up in the nick of time,' Newman objected.

'Organized luck. Don't stare at him,' Tweed warned,
'but see that man standing near the bridge over the Rhine?
Note he's carrying a walkie-talkie by his side, that from
where he's standing he would see us leaving the hotel. He
was standing there when we started out on our walk.
Obviously he radioed to Beck at HQ. So now the question
is – who signalled to the opposition that we were staying
here, maybe even reported when we were leaving for the
stroll?'

Pushing his way through the revolving door, he noticed
the concierge had gone off duty. A girl he had not seen
before was on duty behind the counter. He leaned on the
counter as he asked for the key, waited until she handed it
to him.

'You have an English friend of mine staying here – or
you will have. Has he arrived yet? A Mr Gregory Gaunt?'

'Oh yes, sir. Mr Gaunt checked in early this morning.
Do you want me to see if he's in his room now?'

'Don't bother him, thank you. I'm going up to have a
rest. I'll surprise him at dinner.'

'So Gaunt has been here for quite several hours,' Tweed remarked as they entered the elevator.

It was three o'clock in the afternoon in Basle when Tweed narrowly escaped with his life.

In Washington it was nine o'clock in the morning. Bradford March had a black stubble all over his jaw and upper lip. Which told Sara Maranoff that neither Ms Hamilton nor any other attractive woman would be visiting the President in the Oval Office today.

When she had bad news she always tried to tell March in the morning. He was fresher then and less inclined to react viciously. Standing by the window, March glanced at her, scratched with his thumbnail at his stubble. He had guessed from her expression that something he didn't want to hear was coming.

'Go on, spit it out, Sara,' he snapped.

'Tom Harmer, who contributed a sizeable proportion of the big bucks you sent to Europe by courier, has been on the phone.'

'So Tom wants what?' he demanded.

'The money he gave you back. Apparently a large loan he took out has been called in. Needs the money back inside fourteen days.'

'Does he now.' March hitched up his pants and smiled unpleasantly. 'You've got those photos of Tom screwing that bimbo – use one of them. Tom's wife would find them interesting souvenirs on her coming wedding anniversary.'

'You mean send one to her? Brad, that will get you no place.'

'Slept badly last night, did you? Wake up, Sara. I mean you send a copy – choose a good one yourself – to his office marked for his confidential and personal attention. Soon as it's arrived call him. Ask him how he likes his picture. Then tell him the money he gave was a contribution to party funds, can't be sent back.'

'I think he's desperate, Brad. He has to repay that loan or he's in deep trouble.'

'That's his problem. Handle it the way I told you.'

Sara, her black hair perfectly coiffured, wore a plain grey dress belted at the waist. As long as she looked neat she never bothered much about clothes. March's 'hatchet' woman from his early days of obscurity in the South, she tried to watch every angle to protect her boss. She bit on the end of her pen, decided to take the plunge.

'I hear a team of Unit One has returned from Europe, a large team. At your request to Norton, I presume.'

'So what?' March demanded impatiently.

'I didn't know they were taking over the duties of the Secret Service. You never consulted me.'

It was a tradition that the President's safety was in the sole hands of the Secret Service. They sent men ahead to any destination the President was flying to, checking out the lie of the land in advance, with full powers to override the local police. They were professionals to their fingertips.

'That's right,' March said off-handedly. 'As from today those Secret Service types are out. They seem to think they can run my life. Unit One takes over from them. And you're right again – I didn't consult you.'

'I don't like it . . .'

'Don't recall asking you to like it. That's the way it's going to be. Unit One types are tougher than the Secret Service. My own ruthless boys. I want men I can trust around me.'

'They haven't the experience of the Secret Service,' she persisted.

'They shoot on sight. They don't monkey around. I like their attitude. And I tell *them* what to do.'

'I think it's a mistake . . .'

279

'You're due for a break.' March leaned against a wall, ankles crossed, hands shoved inside his baggy trouser pockets. 'Go climb Mount Rushmore. Drop off it.'

Sara gave up, said nothing. There was a time when he'd listened to her. All of the time. The phone rang. The private line. She answered it, put her hand over the mouthpiece.

'Norton on the line.'

He raised his thick eyebrows, walked slowly towards her, grinned. He stroked her strong-boned face with his index finger. He grinned at her again.

'I know I'm an old grouch. Pals again? Don't know what I'd do without you. Let's hope Norton's cleaned up.'

He took the phone and waited until she'd left the office. Sara's head was spinning. One moment she could kill him, then he turned on the charm and she knew she'd go on being his right arm.

'President March here,' he said in a cold voice. 'You've got the two items I'm waiting for?'

'Not yet, but I'm close . . .' Norton began.

'Close to Mencken taking over from you. Norton, how many of the four targets have you hit?'

'Taking twenty men away from me back to Washington hasn't helped . . .'

'Bullshit. You still have over thirty under your control. What do you need? The friggin' Army? Norton!' March shouted. 'This is final. You have ten days to bring me those two items. In case your memory is failing, you'll recognize the film in the first few seconds when you see who is on it. You then switch it off. On the tape you will hear a hysterical girl screaming because she's seen fire. She's in no danger but as a kid she had to run out of a burning building. Soon as you hear screaming you switch off the tape. Bring them both to me. Got it now?'

'Nothing wrong with my memory, Mr President . . .'

'So maybe you lack guts. Now you listen and listen good.

You have ten days to take out that Brit Tweed, Ives, Joel Dyson and Cord Dillon. To remove them from the face of the earth. It's March 3. That ten days includes today. That's your deadline. I stress the word "dead" . . .'

March put down the phone, took out a handkerchief, mopped his brow and his thick neck. He was sweating like a bull. Within twenty-four hours of handing over to him the film and tape Norton would suffer an accident. A fatal one.

'We may well be close to the moment of decision,' Tweed said. 'Tomorrow we take the train to Colmar and go up into the Vosges. We'll have an advantage there we've lacked so far.'

He had phoned Beck, had thanked him for saving their lives. He'd had to take a gentle lecture from the Swiss about the risk of leaving the hotel. In his bedroom he was outlining his plan of action to Newman and Paula.

'What advantage?' Paula queried.

'So far it's been like street fighting – we've been in cities, not sure where the opposition would strike at us next. Out in the open we'll see them coming – in the mountains.'

'When we go up to see Amberg at the Château Noir?' Newman suggested.

Earlier, Tweed had told them of his conversation over lunch with Eve. He had recalled the information she had given him about Amberg leaving for France. Newman was dubious when Tweed confirmed that was their destination.

'Here we have Beck's protection,' he pointed out. 'The moment we cross into France we're on our own. There appears to be a huge apparatus operating against us. Have you any idea who is controlling it? If it's the film and the tape Dyson brought here, what could be on it to cause all these deaths?'

'I've no idea. That's why I'm going to see Amberg. I'm convinced he's taken the film and the tape with him.

Maybe he's been threatened – so he's using possession of the film and the tape to stay alive. That's one thing.'

'What's another?' Newman asked.

'I'm determined to watch that film, to listen to that tape. I've phoned Monica and she's been in touch with Crombie, who's supervising clearing the rubble at Park Crescent.'

'Why?' Paula queried.

'Because he's still digging for my safe – which has the copies of the film and the tape inside it. No sign of it yet.'

'I'd also like to know what Cardon has been up to,' Newman remarked. 'We hardly saw him in Zurich.'

'Then let him tell you. I'll get him along here now.'

Tweed grabbed the phone, dialled Cardon's room number, asked him to come at once. He looked at Newman when he put down the receiver.

'You want to know. Ask him yourself . . .'

Tweed stood staring out of the window while they waited. An incredibly huge oil tanker was moving upriver. Along its deck was a network of pipes and warning notices. Newman let in Cardon when he knocked on the door.

'The floor is yours,' Tweed said, moving around restlessly.

'Philip,' Newman began, 'we're interested in what you spent your time doing in Zurich.'

'Using the photocopy of Joel Dyson Paula helped to produce. Criss-crossing Zurich hour after hour. Looking for Dyson.' Cardon grinned. 'Then I found him.'

'You did!' Paula exclaimed. 'Where? Why didn't you grab him? He can probably tell us all we desperately need to know.'

'Hold your horses.' Cardon smiled at her. 'I spotted him getting into a cab in Bahnhofstrasse. Couldn't grab him when the cab was moving, could I?'

'You lost him, then?'

'I said hold your horses,' Cardon went on patiently. 'I took another cab, followed him to Kloten Airport. Lots of people about – a plane had just come in. Plus security men. Again, couldn't just walk up and stick a gun in his ribs.'

'I suppose not,' Paula agreed. 'What happened next?'

'The only thing that could happen. I watched him check in. I was close behind him. He had one case. He really has a foxy-looking face.'

'He's a creep!' Newman snapped.

'Do get on with it,' Paula urged, knowing Cardon was playing with her.

'He'd worked it so he just had time to catch his flight. Without a ticket – and no time to get one – I couldn't follow him through Passport Control and Customs. Guess what his destination was.'

'The planet Mars,' Paula said in exasperation.

'Not quite as far as that. His destination was Basle. He's somewhere in this city.'

Paula looked stunned. Newman suggested a course of action immediately.

'Let's trawl Basle like we did Zurich. Philip came up trumps there eventually. We all have photocopies of the sketch of Dyson.'

'No,' said Tweed. 'Beck told us to stay in the hotel. We ignored his advice – at least, I did. The result? I came within a hair's breadth of getting us all killed. Basle, like Zurich, is a big city. Within a few hours – tomorrow morning – we leave for Colmar. I'm not risking anyone's life again in this city.'

'What about the weapons we're carrying?' Cardon queried. 'Won't Beck want them back?'

'Significantly, knowing we will be venturing into France, he hasn't mentioned them. And Arthur Beck never forgets a thing.'

'But we'll be crossing a frontier,' Paula reminded him.

'Bob, you remember when we once went to Colmar? It's

the most curious set-up at the station here. You walk direct from the Swiss Bahnhof into the French station. If we catch a train at eleven in the morning there should be no one manning either control point. There wasn't before.'

'Supposing the control points are manned this time? No way to guard against that,' Paula insisted.

'Yes, there is,' Tweed explained. 'I'm carrying nothing. I go through first, you lag behind. If you see me stopped, turn back. We'll think of something else.'

'I wonder where Joel Dyson is now,' Paula mused.

'What I'd like to know is who murdered Helen Frey, Klara and that detective, Theo Strebel,' Newman commented.

'I think I've worked that out – from information one of you provided me,' Tweed replied.

Bankverein, the tram-stop midway between the Rhine and the railway station, is where most of the Basle banks are situated. The Zurcher Kredit was one of them. The hippie sitting on the pavement near the bank's entrance had his legs sprawled out in front of him. He wore a shabby old Swiss hat, the brim pulled down over his forehead. His worn dark overcoat was buttoned up to the neck against the cold. His stained corduroy trousers were too long and draped over his ancient Swiss climbing boots. By his side Joel Dyson had a large canvas bag.

Dyson had rubbed dirt into his plump face and a torn scarf concealed his receding chin. Several Swiss who passed by glanced at him curiously, but Dyson knew the American watcher on the other side of the street would find nothing strange in his presence.

Dyson was waiting his opportunity to slip into the bank without the American seeing him enter. He had worked out the moment – providing a customer went inside the bank at that moment. The guard inside the bank would then escort the customer out of sight of the lobby and take him or her to whoever they were visiting.

Dyson knew it would take split-second timing, but he'd learned to move fast taking compromising photographs of celebrities. He gripped the canvas bag tightly by its wooden handle as a woman dressed in black approached. Three small green trams – toys compared with the modern blue giants of Zurich – trundled up from the direction of the Rhine close together. This could be the right moment.

The woman in black entered the bank, the guard spoke to her, escorted her out of sight. The trams masked him from the American. Dyson leapt up, pushed open the door into the empty lobby, then moved even faster.

Unbuttoning his disreputable overcoat, he tore it off, revealing a smart blue business jacket. Slipping out of his trousers, he exposed the blue suit trousers. Hauling off the boots, he opened the canvas bag, took out a pair of smart slip-ons, tucked his feet inside them. Pulling off the hat he bundled the boots and old clothes inside the canvas bag, closed it. Smoothing his hair with a comb and wiping his face with a cloth he had dampened earlier, he held a visiting card in his hand when the guard returned. He presented the card without saying a word. The guard examined it, turned it over to look at the writing on the back. He read the message in German carefully.

Please give every assistance to this gentleman. He is a most valued client.

On the front side was printed *Walter Amberg, Zurcher Kredit*. The printing was embossed. Dyson had asked Julius's brother for his card when he had deposited the film and the tape with Julius. On his recent visit to Zurich he had entered several bars before he struck up a conversation with a Swiss by buying him several drinks. He had then asked him to write this message in German on the card, saying he was playing a joke on a Swiss friend.

Dyson was an expert at bluffing his way into offices and houses where he wasn't known. The guard said something to him in German.

'Sorry,' Dyson said, 'I only speak English.'

'I think you should see Mrs Kahn,' the guard suggested in English.

'I think that was the name of the lady I was given . . .'

Mrs Kahn was a dark-haired lady of uncertain age wearing gold-rimmed glasses. She studied the card after asking him to sit down. Then she said she would be back in a minute. She closed the door to another room carefully after leaving.

Dyson grinned to himself. He knew exactly what she was doing. She was phoning Zurich to check on him. Dyson had deposited a small sum of money when he had handed over the film and the tape for safekeeping. He had realized that if you were a client – no matter how small or large the account – you had joined the club.

While he was alone he took out his handkerchief, wet it with his tongue, rubbed vigorously at his cheek. He had already cleaned off most of the dirt in the lobby but he was anxious to make a good impression. A man of substance was the phrase. A pukka member of the club. Mrs Kahn returned, sat behind her desk.

'What can I do for you, Mr Dyson?'

'I have to get in touch with Mr Amberg. He is keeping something valuable for me. He said I should ask for him when I needed to collect the valuables. The matter is rather urgent.'

'Mr Amberg is in France.'

'I know.' He smiled briefly. 'I've left the address he gave me at my London apartment. I'm a bachelor so there's no one there I can call to look it up for me.'

'He's in Alsace . . .'

'I can remember that. Foreign addresses go out of my head.'

'It is not too far. The Château Noir in the Vosges. You can take the train to Colmar.'

'I travel by car. I've driven there before. To Colmar.'

'It's difficult to find, Mr Dyson. Up in the mountains. I suggest you purchase a road map. When you get to Colmar there is a hotel outside the railway station. The Hotel Bristol. Show them the map and they will guide you.'

'I am much obliged, Mrs Kahn.'

'It is my pleasure. The guard will show you out . . .'

That was inconvenient. He had hoped to change back into his hippie clothes in the lobby before emerging from the bank. The guard appeared, escorted him to the main front door, opened it, nodded to him.

Dyson stepped out into a freezing cold afternoon. The interior of the bank had been cosily warm. He walked a few paces down the street, watching the American who still stood on the opposite side of the street. A gun barrel was rammed into his back from inside a trench coat.

'Where is Amberg, Mr Dyson? A correct answer means I may not pull the trigger.'

'At the Château Noir. France. Up in the Vosges mountains. Near Colmar.'

Dyson was scared stiff, but he was a survivor. So close now to a huge fortune. He wasn't going to risk a bullet in the back at this stage. The man with the American voice behind him might be testing him.

'So let's you and I go for walkies,' the voice continued. 'There's a short cut through an alley . . .'

He stopped speaking. Dyson had spotted a police car patrolling slowly along the street. He shoved both hands in the air, way above his head. Everything happened in a flash. The patrol car stopped, the gun was removed from his back, he heard the sound of feet running as a policeman, gun in hand, came up to him.

'He held me up with a gun, wanted my passport and money.'

Dyson glanced over his shoulder. No sign of the American.

'He didn't get anything. You arrived . . .'

The policeman had nodded, was now running with long strides towards where several streets radiated. He disappeared round a corner. Dyson sighed with relief, picked up the canvas bag he'd dropped, walked quickly away.

He'd already hired a silver Mercedes. Within the hour he'd be driving across the frontier, heading for Colmar.

Talking to the President, each time Norton started out by giving the phone number of his latest perch. The President had no idea what city the first numbers identified – Sara found that out after he'd closed the call.

Norton, his 'grey' hair now getting shaggy, was sitting in the Basle apartment he'd commandeered. It was normally occupied by a diplomat from the Berne Embassy. The Ambassador, Anderson, hadn't liked it when Norton had told him to throw out the present occupant.

He'd had no option but to agree to Norton's demand when the man with untidy grey hair and wearing half-moon glasses had waved his Presidential aide pass at him.

Anderson had also told him that he was clearing his desk, going home. A man called Gallagher was taking his post. Norton had smiled to himself – Anderson, an old-school diplomat, must have rubbed March up the wrong way. The phone rang.

'Mencken here. We've located Amberg. The Château Noir in France. Near a place called Colmar. The château is up in the Vosges mountains . . .'

'Move the whole unit to Colmar. Where will you be staying? The Hotel Bristol. Got it. It's a short drive from here. I'll be there. What about the courier with the dough?'

'Locked in a hotel room. You know which hotel. I have the key.'

288

'Take him with you – with the money. Whoever has what I'm after will try a fresh exchange. Get moving . . .'

Norton began packing his clothes in the single case he moved around with. Small enough to take aboard a plane. Save hanging about at the friggin' carousel. The phone rang again.

'Yes, who is it?'

'The guy who's given you ten days to clean up,' March barked. 'I know now you're in Basle. What gives? You had three different places to cover in the Zurich area to exchange the money for the film and tape.'

'It was a bust. I had them covered. No one turned up. Someone is playing smart. Using kidnappers' technique. Send you to one place – three in this case – then they don't turn up. Trying to break our nerve. You'll get a fresh call, new rendezvous. I'm just moving to the Hotel Bristol in Colmar, France. Give you the phone number when I get there. We're going to score. All four targets wiped out, plus grabbing your film and tape . . .'

'Norton, you've no idea how encouraging I find what you just said,' March replied with vicious sarcasm. 'You read me? And how are you going to play it this time – before March 13?'

'They'll be in mountain country. I'll use the mountains to get them. By ambush . . .'

For the first time Norton was the one who slammed down the phone.

PART TWO

The Terror

30

Norton was the first to arrive in Colmar. Clad in a black astrakhan coat and a fur hat, he looked like a Russian professor as he peered through his half-moon glasses at the receptionist of the Hotel Bristol.

What was it about the new arrival that made the girl behind the counter shiver inwardly? He stood motionless and the eyes behind the lenses which stared at her seemed dead, devoid of all human feeling.

'I want to book a double room for five days,' Norton told her. 'I have business elsewhere so I may not be here every night. I will pay in advance for the five days . . .'

He registered in the name of Ben Thalmann, paid in French francs, then produced the Michelin map of the Vosges area he had purchased in Basle. He had left that city within twenty minutes of speaking to President March.

'I have to visit the Château Noir, the residence of a Mr Amberg, a Swiss. Can you show me how to reach this château by driving there?'

'You'll have to hurry, sir,' she replied in her excellent English. 'It gets dark early and there is snow on the mountains. The roads will be icy . . .'

'Just show me . . .'

She stopped talking, studied the map, marked a route up the N83 to Kaysersberg and then high up into the Vosges mountains along the N415. It became complicated and she carefully drew her pen along a side road. She was repeating her warnings about the hazards when Norton interrupted her brusquely.

'Can I use that phone to make a private call?'

'Certainly, sir . . .'

Discreetly, she opened a door behind her and closed it. The truth was she was only too anxious to escape from the presence of that black figure. Norton smiled as he dialled the number of the Drei Könige. He had sensed the fear the girl had felt and it gave him a kick. He asked the hotel operator for Tweed. There was a brief pause.

'Who is speaking?' a man's voice enquired.

'Barton Ives,' Norton said through the silk handkerchief he had stuffed in the mouthpiece. 'Who is that?'

'Tweed here. Where are you, Ives . . .?'

Norton put down the phone. Tweed was still in Basle. At last he had arrived ahead of the enemy. Which would give him time to prepare the death-trap. And it was interesting that Tweed expected to meet Barton Ives. Clean up the whole lot out here in the wilds of Alsace.

Norton hurried outside and got behind the wheel of the blue Renault he'd hired in Basle. He had never stayed at the Drei Könige – he had simply had an early lunch and sat in the lobby area afterwards. In time to see Tweed and his friends arrive.

Using the same approach, he wouldn't be staying at the Hotel Bristol. He had picked up a brochure in the railway station opposite the hotel, a brochure which gave the names of several small hotels in the Old Town. One of those hotels would be his base.

He drove rapidly across the flatlands beyond Colmar. It was a cold sunny afternoon, the air fresh as wine. But this was wine territory – grids of vineyards stretched away on either side as he came close to the foothills.

He drove more slowly through the medieval town of Kaysersberg, little more than a large village. Norton did not notice its picturesqueness. He did notice a narrow stone bridge spanning a small river in the centre.

An excellent place to plant a bomb under the bridge,

detonated by remote control. Mencken, who still had to reach Colmar, was an expert with explosives. Driving from Basle to Colmar, Norton had observed a stone quarry, a shed with the warning sign in French, *Danger – Explosives*. He had marked this location on his map.

He drove on beyond Kaysersberg into the foothills. Looming above them was the long chain of the snow-bound Vosges mountains. Norton had taken the precaution of hiring a car with snow tyres. The road began to twist and climb, up, up, up . . .

There was no other traffic and dense stands of firs began to close in on both sides. The road surface was icy, treacherous, then covered with snow. The temperature nose-dived. The firs were blanketed with frozen snow, the branches pressed down under the weight. It was like Siberia.

Norton smiled to himself. This was ideal territory for what he had in mind. At numerous places the topography lent itself to lethal ambushes. He foresaw that Tweed and his minions would disappear from the face of the earth until spring came – only spring would reveal the frozen vehicles, the rotting bones of their occupants.

On the other side of the road the mountain slope fell away into a sheer abyss. Norton had a view of a deep ravine plunging into the depths. The territory was getting better and better. He had no doubt Tweed would be driving up to see Amberg at the Château Noir.

He drove on up the steep winding ascent, alert for hidden ice under the snow. By his side the map the girl at the Bristol had marked lay open. He glanced at it frequently. Soon he'd be coming to the turn-off on to the side road leading to Lac Noir.

The intense cold was penetrating his coat. He turned up the heaters full on. His breath steamed up his glasses. He took them off – they were merely a disguise. Still only rare signs of human habitation – the odd whitewashed old house with its ancient pantile roof crusted with snow. Norton could stand the cold, but this was something else again.

He passed through a small village called Orbey, which was on his route. No sign of a soul. Everyone huddled inside, he imagined. By now he had turned off the N415 and studied the map more frequently. Driving along a narrow road he suddenly arrived at Lac Noir and gasped.

Once, still with the FBI, Norton had operated in Europe for the State Department on secret missions – which under American law were forbidden and were extremely illegal. Norton was familiar with the Continent, but he had never seen anything like this.

On the far side of the lonely silent lake rose a sheer granite wall, towering above him. At its summit was perched a castle with turrets and lights in some of the windows. He was staring up at the Château Noir. On an impulse, he decided to visit the elusive Mr Amberg.

Norton drove up a steep spiralling road which, again, the girl at the Bristol had marked for him on the map. Arriving at the summit, he saw the castle's high point was a massive keep.

Most people would have been overawed by the grandeur of the edifice. To Norton it was just the type of a monster of a building they'd erected in medieval times. A high wall surrounded the château and Norton scanned it swiftly before leaving his car and approaching on foot the tall wrought-iron gates which closed a gap in the wall.

He pressed the button below a speakphone with a metal grille embedded in the left-hand pillar. He'd have to hurry this up: he wanted to be out of the mountains before dusk descended on those hideous roads. A voice said something in German.

'I don't speak German,' Norton replied, muffling his American accent.

'Then kindly identify yourself,' the precise voice said in English.

'Tweed. Tweed . . .'

'Please be so good as to enter.'

There was the sound of a buzzer. Norton pushed at both gates. The left-hand one opened. He took out a matchbook, inserted it in the lock. He suspected the gates opened and closed automatically from controls inside the château. It was a trick he'd used before. And sure enough, as he walked across the paved courtyard and glanced back, the gate was closing.

As he hurried up the wide flight of stone steps leading to a massive porch he took out the Luger from his shoulder holster, held it by his side. The great wooden door swung inwards, a small portly man with black hair brushed back from his high forehead stood inside the entrance. He wore a black business suit and surprise, then alarm, appeared in his shrewd blue eyes.

'You're not Tweed.'

He was starting to swing the door shut when Norton showed him the Luger. He lapsed into his normal voice.

'Mr Amberg? Don't lie. I've a nervous trigger finger.'

'Yes, but . . .'

'Let's talk inside. You could catch a cold. You have two items I'm in the market for. You can make a lot of money, Mr Amberg. Let's negotiate.'

While he spoke Amberg backed inside and Norton followed still holding the Luger. He had the impression of a vast hall which was dimly lit by wall sconces.

'I have no idea of what you are talking about, *Mr Tweed.*'

Norton was puzzled by the emphasis the banker put on the name. His words echoed round the enormous hall. Norton, watching Amberg closely, was vaguely aware that a wide staircase climbed out of the hall to his left, climbed a considerable height. He also thought there was the silhouette of someone on the staircase.

The next moment Amberg took a handkerchief out of his pocket as though about to blow his nose. There was a click, an object landed at Norton's feet. Amberg was backing away. Grey vapour enveloped Norton and his vision swam. Swiftly holstering the Luger – Norton was no longer able to see clearly – he held his breath and grabbed for a handkerchief with his left hand. The tear-gas had reached his eyes just before he clamped the handkerchief over them. Amberg had covered his own face with his handkerchief.

Norton, able to see – but with blurred vision – turned round and headed back to the door. Removing the handkerchief, he turned the lock on the door and hauled the heavy slab open. Staggering out on to the porch, he grasped the round black iron handle, pulled the door shut, took in a deep breath.

Stumbling towards the gate, his vision was better with the cold air clearing his eyes. He'd only taken a small quantity of the stuff, mostly in his left eye. The match-book had prevented the gate locking. In a hurry to get away, he still paused to retrieve the matchbook – he might want to use the same trick when he returned to the Château Noir.

He stood by his car, sucking in great breaths of the mountain air, then slid behind the wheel, closed the door quietly, turned on the ignition. The girl at the Bristol had marked an alternative route back via the D417 down the Col de la Schlucht. He'd go back that way.

He turned the car round, determined to check the second route Tweed might use to visit the Château Noir. His left eye was still watering as he drove carefully, expertly negotiating the bends in the road.

Norton was livid – and furious with himself. He had broken his golden rule – never act on impulse, always check out the target in advance, then send in the soldiers.

He had given in to the temptation to do the job on his own. Never again . . .

His great regret was that he'd not had the remotest idea what the figure which had stood on the stairs looked like. Who the hell could that have been, the figure which had fired the gas pistol? One thing was for sure – he was returning to the Château Noir with Mencken's complete team. Norton had observed a lot during his brief humiliation. There was a wire – presumably electrified – spanning the top of the wall which surrounded the stone monstrosity.

Norton had also noticed a stone-flagged path leading behind the château in the direction of the towering keep. One man on top of that with a machine-pistol could command all the exits and entrances.

He had turned on to the D417 a while back, a much more main highway. He reached a point where a large building carried the legend LA SCHLUCHT 1139. He was 1139 metres high, over three thousand feet. Norton drove on and it was then he encountered a hideous and endless spiral of hairpin bends.

At one point he stopped, marked the location on his map. To his left a sheer granite cliff rose vertically from the road. To his right the world dropped into another bottomless abyss. The cliff wall was covered with steel mesh to prevent it crumbling on to the road. A first-rate ambush point.

He was still well above the snow line as he drove on down and round icy spiral bends. Despite the risk he kept his foot on the accelerator – the light was fading. Dusk was beginning to fall over the Vosges.

Norton kept moving, meeting no traffic. He dropped below the snow line and rammed his foot down further. The lights were on in Colmar as he entered the town. He stopped outside the station, went inside to ask how to get to the Old Town, saw a huge wall map of Colmar.

He soon realized that the Old Town where the small hotels were situated was called Little Venice. Amazing how many Venices there were in Europe. The next thing to do when he'd found a room was to call the Bristol, ask to speak to a Mr Tweed. He felt sure that was where he'd hit the sack. When Tweed came on the line – if he did – he'd put down the receiver. That should twitch at his nerves. Mr Tweed didn't know it, but they'd bury him in Alsace.

31

'I expect the Vosges to be an area of maximum danger,' Tweed announced to the gathering in his bedroom at the Drei Könige.

Newman and Paula shared a couch, Butler and Nield sat in armchairs and Marler adopted his usual stance, leaning against a wall and smoking a king-size cigarette.

Marler, a member of the SIS and the deadliest marksman in Europe, had been summoned to fly from London to Basle when Tweed had phoned Monica. Of medium height and light build, he had fair hair, was in his early thirties and wore a smart check sports jacket and razor-creased slacks. He spoke in an upper crust drawl and was always crossing swords with Newman.

'Is this intuition on your part?' Marler asked. 'Or have you solid data to base your warning on?'

'Does it make any difference?' Newman snapped.

These two men were hardly mutual friends. But if it came to a firefight each knew they could rely on the other to the hilt.

'Yes, it does, old man,' Marler replied patronizingly. 'Is there any solid data?' he asked Tweed.

Since his arrival Tweed had brought Marler up to date on everything that had happened. Marler, with his fresh eye, might notice something significant they had missed.

'There is some data,' Tweed told them. 'Beck phoned me and reported that a man whose description sounds very like Joel Dyson's was held up outside the Zurcher Kredit here.'

'Held up?' Paula queried.

'Yes. An American shoved a gun into Dyson's back as he left the Zurcher Kredit. Fortunately a patrol car turned up, the American with the gun fled, and if it was Dyson he'd asked a Mrs Kahn at the bank where Amberg was. Beck never overlooks a thing – he phoned the bank, spoke to Mrs Kahn. She confirmed what Eve Amberg told me – that the banker is at the Château Noir.'

'You said *if* it was Dyson,' Paula commented. 'Not like you to accept an identification without proof.'

'Which is why,' Tweed told her, 'I sent Cardon to show the photocopy of your sketch of Dyson to Mrs Kahn . . .'

There was a knock on the locked door. Newman opened it and Cardon strolled in. He winked at Paula who made a moue.

'It was Dyson who called at that bank here in Basle,' Cardon addressed Tweed. He handed back the envelope containing the photocopy. 'She recognized him at once from the sketch. Beck is helpful – he had a detective waiting there to escort me into Mrs Kahn's office. She didn't hesitate to talk to me.'

'All of which confirms my warning about danger waiting for us in the Vosges. That American who held up Dyson and then escaped probably asked him where Amberg was. We shall have company – unwelcome company – in Alsace.'

The phone rang. Paula picked it up, listened, said she

would tell him, put down the receiver and looked at Tweed with an amused smile.

'You already have company waiting for you in the lounge. More welcome company. Jennie Blade is anxious to talk to you.'

'She didn't mention Gaunt?' Tweed asked, frowning.

'Not a word.'

'When I spoke to Monica she told me she'd added to her profile on Mr Gaunt. At one time he was an officer in Military Intelligence. Intriguing . . .'

Jennie Blade sat upright in an armchair. She was dressed in ski pants tucked into smart leather ankle boots and a blue silk polo-necked sweater which hugged her figure. Folded neatly on a nearby chair was a fur-lined jacket.

When Tweed stepped out of the lift she was smoothing down her blonde mane with one hand, checking her appearance in a compact mirror with the other. The moment she saw Tweed she snapped the mirror shut, put the compact inside a Gucci handbag with a shoulder strap.

'Long time no see,' she greeted him.

She tilted her head, held up her right cheek. He bent down and kissed it, perched himself on the arm of her chair. It was an unusual place for him to sit but he sensed she was putting herself out to be seductive. Her long legs were crossed.

'Not so long since we had a drink in the Hummer Bar in Zurich. Where is Gaunt?' Tweed asked.

'Oh, the Squire? God knows. He's a pain in the prover-bial. Disappears for hours, days. He told me he'd seen you here. I have the strong impression you're a very reliable man – by which I mean a man a woman can rely on.'

'Depends on the woman, the circumstances.'

'And I thought you liked me.'

She twisted round – as she had on the stool in the Hummer Bar – clasped her strong slim hands and rested her forearms on his leg. She gazed up at him pleadingly.

'Let's say I do like you,' Tweed suggested. 'What comes next?'

'I'm frightened. I'm being followed by someone. They appear when I'm least expecting it. As I'm leaving a shop just before closing time when it's dark outside. When I'm getting my keys out to enter the apartment Gaunt has near Bankverein. It takes a lot to scare me but I admit I'm really worried about this shadow man.'

'Describe him.'

She took hold of his right hand. Holding it between both of hers she continued gazing up at him.

'I said describe him,' Tweed repeated in a hard voice.

'Wears a black wide-brimmed hat, tilted down over his face. About five foot six tall. I might be wrong about his height. He also wears a long black overcoat and a woollen scarf.'

Without showing it, Tweed was taken aback. Jennie had just given almost exactly the same description of the man seen leaving Klara's apartment in Rennweg after she had been garrotted. Her words were almost precisely those used by Old Nosy who occupied the ground-floor apartment in the Altstadt building where Klara had been murdered.

'You are talking about Basle?' he checked. 'This man is following you here in Basle?'

'Yes. The Shadow Man.' She shivered. 'It's getting on my nerves. Which is ridiculous considering the jobs I've had.'

'What jobs might those be?' he asked gently.

'I had a training as an accountant. Found it frantically boring. Then I got a big job with a huge firm in New York. They checked up on the financial stability of firms

303

all over the world for a fabulous fee. Also on prominent individuals. I had to bluff my way into offices and private apartments to check on the lifestyle of certain individuals. That's how I saved quite a packet. I left them when one target threatened me with a gun. Felt my luck was running out. I came back to Britain, to London.'

She was interlacing her fingers with Tweed's as she spoke. He thanked Heaven that Paula wasn't there to see him. She'd pull his leg unmercifully.

'And then you met Gaunt?' he suggested.

All the time she told him the story of her life she was gazing at him, her glowing eyes almost hypnotizing him. Watch it, he warned himself.

'No, Gaunt came later,' she went on. 'Back in London I got a job with a private investigation agency. That lasted six months and was sordid work, but it led me to Gaunt.' She paused.

'Go on, I'm still listening.'

'You make a good audience. My last job at the agency was to check up on Walter Amberg.'

Again Tweed was taken aback. Again he maintained a poker-faced expression, but stared back at her to try and penetrate her character. Her voice was soft and soothing, which added to the hypnotic effect. Gaunt was mad not to grab her. For the first time since his wife had left him years ago for a Greek millionaire Tweed wondered about throwing overboard his solitary life. He pulled himself up sharply. This was a job he was working on, the most dangerous he'd ever encountered.

'Who asked the agency to check on Walter?' he enquired.

'Julius Amberg. He came to the London office once with Gaunt – which is how I met Gaunt.'

'When you were checking up on Walter Amberg what aspect were you looking for? Did you come to Switzerland?'

304

'Yes to the second question. As to what I had to check on, Julius was very precise. Had Walter an expensive apartment in another city? Now what else was there?' She played with the string of pearls looped over her sweater with her free hand. 'I remember. Was he keeping a mistress? If so, was she expensively dressed and had she her own car? Had Walter any other cars which he kept in other cities? Stuff like that. I drew a blank – except for his visits to a girl in Basle. I never reported that because I'd had enough. There was another reason. Gaunt asked me to come and live with him. I love Cornwall, the sea and the cliffs.'

'I'm going to ask you some more questions. I want you to answer them quickly. Your jobs must have made you unusually observant. First question, describe the face of the Shadow Man.'

'Can't. Never saw it.'

'How did he walk, move?'

'Body language. Can't say. He was always motionless.'

'But you saw him several times.'

'I did. Looked up, saw him, paid for what I'd bought. Then he'd gone.'

'Outside the Bankverein apartment, finding your keys?'

'He stood at a corner. When I looked again he was gone.'

'You're saying you never actually saw him move?'

'Never.'

'Ever see him in Zurich?'

'No. Always here in Basle.'

'How many times have you seen him?'

'Five. Six. No more.'

'Within what space of time?'

'Couple of days.'

'Is his surveillance on you getting more frequent?'

'Yes, it is, Tweed. What the hell am I going to do?'

305

'You're staying at the Bankverein apartment with Gaunt?'

'Yes. He's not always there. As I told you.'

'You're going back there now. I'll get a taxi for you. Stay inside until Gaunt returns. Tell him about the Shadow Man.'

'You have to be joking. He'd say it was a figment of my imagination.'

'I'll get that taxi . . .'

The concierge, who had just returned on duty, phoned and a taxi arrived in five minutes. Tweed accompanied Jennie outside into the icy cold – it seemed even more Siberian. She kissed him on the cheek before leaping inside.

'We must see each other again,' were her last words.

Tweed remained standing outside on the pavement for a short time. He wanted to be sure no one was following Jennie. He was also beginning to think she was telling the truth. Her story about the Shadow Man bothered him. He was turning to go inside when a white BMW appeared, pulled up in front of the hotel with a jerk and screeching brakes.

Gaunt jumped out. He handed the car keys to a porter who had come out through the revolving doors.

'Park my car for me. I'm staying here. Gaunt is the name.' He clapped Tweed on the shoulder. 'What a splendid welcome. You guessed I was coming! Brrr! It's cold out here. Forward march to the bar. The drinks are on me . . .

'Two double Scotches,' he told the barman when they were comfortably seated in an otherwise deserted bar. 'And hurry them up. Need some internal central heating, my good man.'

'No Scotch for me,' Tweed said firmly. 'Mineral water.'

'Can't cope with alcohol, eh? A man of your experience. Shame on you, sir.'

'You ought to take more care of Jennie,' Tweed told him bluntly. 'She's scared out of her wits – someone is following her, someone I don't like the sound of.'

He waited while Gaunt doled out money to the barman and added a meagre tip. Gaunt raised his glass.

'Here's to survival of the fittest. Down the hatch.'

'I said Jennie is being followed by an unknown man. He's tracking her, prior to something pretty unpleasant happening, I fear.'

'Stuff and nonsense! She gets these fancies. She's an attractive-looking filly. Of course men notice her, try to get to know her.'

'Gaunt!' Tweed hammered his glass down on the tabletop. 'Keep quiet and listen. In Zurich a girl called Klara was foully murdered – her head was damned near severed from her neck. Garrotted. Someone saw the murderer leaving. Their brief description fits the man following Jennie. Don't you care a fig?'

He watched Gaunt closely. His visitor had worn a camel-hair coat which now lay thrown across a chair. He was clad in a check sports jacket, a cravat with a design of horses' heads, corduroy trousers and hand-made leather shoes. His sandy hair was windblown. His grey eyes above a strong nose stared back at Tweed. His mood had suddenly become serious and his firm mouth was tightly closed. Tweed thought he glimpsed the ex-Military Intelligence officer.

'Think I read something about that murder in the paper. Before I left Zurich. Can there really be a link-up between that murder and this man who is supposed to be following Jennie?'

'Who *is* following Jennie.'

'How do you know all this?' Gaunt asked brusquely. 'Has Jennie phoned you?'

307

'She's been here. Was telling me about it not five minutes before you turned up. Hadn't you better get back to your apartment near Bankverein? Make sure she's all right? *Now*, I suggest,' Tweed said emphatically.

'She'll be safe.' Gaunt stared hard at Tweed. 'We leave early tomorrow morning for Colmar in Alsace. We'll be out of Basle by daybreak.'

'Why Colmar?' Tweed asked quietly.

'Because that's where Amberg's gone to. Place called the Château Noir. Up in the Vosges. I've just come from a brief visit to Mrs Kahn, his assistant at the Zurcher Kredit here in Basle. Had to put a bit of pressure on her to get that information. Thought maybe you'd like to know. Amberg must know something about his twin brother's last visit to Tresillian Manor. No one kills a guest in my house and gets away with it. I'm going now. Remember what I said. Survival of the fittest.'

Gaunt stood up, shoved his arms into his coat, walked out. Tweed sat thinking before returning to his room. Gaunt didn't strike him as a man who ladled out information without a purpose. And had there been a hint of a threat in his last remark?

32

'Norton here,' the American reported when he was connected with the President. He gave him the phone number of the Hotel Bristol. 'When you want to contact me get Sara to leave a coded message. I'll come back to you as soon as I can . . .'

'Like hell you will. I need the number I can reach you at pronto. There's been a development.'

'That's my best offer,' Norton snapped.

'OK, if that's the way it has to be,' March agreed in a deceptively amiable tone. 'Now pin your ears back. I've had a fresh message from the man with the growly voice. About the exchange. The big bucks for the film and the tape. Where are you? Basle?'

'No, Colmar, France. On the edge of the Vosges mountains.'

'Ever heard of a dump called Kaysersberg? I'll spell that to you . . .'

'No need. I was driving through it an hour ago.'

'Really? Department of Sinister Coincidence.'

'I don't get that . . . Mr President.'

'Say it was a joke. There's some crappy hotel in this Kaysersberg. L'Arbre Vert. I'll spell that. Sara says it means the Green Tree . . .'

'No need to spell it out. I noticed it, passing through.'

'You take a room there. Under the name of Tweed . . .'

'You can't mean it.'

'Growly Voice says you do. You wait for a call. You have the big bucks where you can lay your hands on them? The call may come tomorrow morning. It's up to you to get the film, the tape – and Growly Voice. In a box. Laid out nice and neat. You're running out of days. I said you had a deadline. Time is flying. I'm counting on you, Norton . . .'

'You can rely on me, Mr President . . .'

He was speaking into the air. March had gone off the line. Norton swore to himself as he left the phone cubicle in Colmar railway station. He'd deliberately given the Bristol number – where he'd never spend a night. He could call for messages. No way was he going to give the number of his small hotel at the edge of a stream in Little Venice.

309

He climbed in behind the wheel of his parked blue Renault. Switching on the ignition, he turned up the heaters. He didn't like the arrangement March had agreed one little bit. Registering as Tweed, goddamnit! Why? The blackmailer with the film and the tape had to be someone who knew Tweed, knew he was in the area.

Norton would make a list of everyone his unit had reported as having been seen with Tweed. One of those names on that list had to be Growly Voice.

When Bradford March had put down the phone he clasped his hands behind his bull neck and stared at the marble fireplace on the opposite wall without seeing it. He was in a vicious rage.

The blackmailer was playing games with him – with Norton, too. This constant switching of locations from one Swiss city to another – and now he'd moved the whole operation to France. Norton, persuaded to 'resign' from the FBI because the Director hadn't liked his tough, ruthless ways, was being led around by the nose. Growly Voice was running circles round him.

March looked up as Sara entered the Oval Office. He didn't like her expression.

'Very bad news, boss. Just heard about it.'

'Heard about what?'

'Harmer. Who gave you that large sum of money, then said he needed it back to pay off a bank loan. I guess he sure did.'

'What the hell are you talking about? Give, Sara.'

'Harmer committed suicide a few hours ago. Took a load of sleeping pills, then drank a lot of bourbon.'

'So.' March spread his hands, exposing their hairy backs. 'Problem solved.'

'If you say so.'

'Are you hinting he left a note?'

'For his wife, yes, he did.'

March leaned forward. 'C'mon. We'd better find out what he said in that note.'

'I know. I rang his wife to offer *my* sympathies. I also said you were shocked and sent *your* deepest sympathies.'

'Great. Don't have to write my own dialogue with you to do it for me. Just a moment. What did the note say?'

'The usual thing. He was so sorry, he loved her dearly, but the pressure of his responsibilities had proved too big a burden. She read it out to me over the phone before she broke down in a flood of tears.'

'Bye-bye Mr Harmer. It happens. All is well.'

'I hope so. I do hope so, Brad. For your sake.'

The Three Wise Men were assembled in Senator Wingfield's study. Again the curtains were closed, concealing the grounds of the estate. The lights were on. The banker and the elder statesman had been called urgently to the Chevy Chase mansion by Wingfield, who looked grim. He stared round the table at his guests.

'I am sorry to summon you here at such short notice, but the situation inside the Oval Office is not improving.'

'I heard about Harmer's suicide,' the banker commented. 'That's a big loss to the party. He not only contributed generously himself – more important still, he was a genius at fund-raising.'

'Let's face it,' said the elder statesman, gazing at the Senator through his horn-rimmed glasses, 'politics is a mobile situation. Harmer must have managed his affairs badly. He's replaceable.'

'I have a personal letter from Harmer,' Wingfield informed them. There was an edge to his cultured accent. 'I know the real reason why Harmer took his life. Read that . . .'

He tossed a folded sheet of high-quality notepaper on

the table. The statesman read it first before handing it on to the banker.

Dear Charles: By the time you read this I'll have gone to a better place. I hope. Bradford March asked me to loan him fifteen million dollars. Don't know what this large sum was for. I did so. When I wanted it back to repay a bank loan on demand he refused to speak to me. Sara Maranoff phoned his message. The money was no longer available. Go to hell was the real message. Maybe I'm going there. Someone has to stop the President. Only The Three Wise Men have the clout.

'What could March have wanted that money for?' queried the banker.

'We'll probably never know,' the statesman told him. 'I hold the same view. It's not enough – for impeachment.'

'That letter could be passed to the *Washington Post*,' the banker suggested.

'Definitely not,' Wingfield said quietly. 'Ned, can't you imagine how March would play it? He'd get handwriting experts to prove it was a forgery. Then he'd rave on about a conspiracy – about how the three of us were trying to be the power behind the throne. Give him his due, he's a powerful orator. He'd destroy us. It's not enough for us to make a move.'

'Then what the hell is?' burst out the banker.

'Cool it,' the elder statesman advised. 'Politics is the art of the possible. I worked on that basis when I held the position I did under a previous president.'

'There's the business about him dismissing the Secret Service,' the banker continued, his anger unquenched. 'I understand he has a bunch of his own thugs guarding him now. Unit One, or some such outfit.'

'Which is the paramilitary force I told you about at an earlier meeting,' Senator Wingfield said quietly.

'It's against all tradition,' protested the banker.

312

'Bradford March is breaking a lot of traditions, Ned,' Wingfield reminded him. 'Which is another popular move in the present mood of the American electorate. We can only wait.'

'For what?' demanded the banker.

'For something far worse, Ned. Pray to God it doesn't surface . . .'

The tall figure of Jeb Calloway created distorted shadows on the walls of his office as he paced restlessly. Sam, his closest aide and friend, watched him, undid the jacket button constraining his ample stomach.

'Heard from your mystery man in Europe yet, Jeb?' he asked.

'Not a word. I think he's on the run.'

'Which means someone is running after him. Which means someone over there knows he exists. You're playing with fire. This gets back to March and he'll smear you for good. He's an expert. Part of how he got where he is. Trampling over other people's bodies. That's politics. March is the original cobra at the game.'

'There's no way anyone can connect my informant with me. And there's a safe way he can contact me – if he's still alive.'

'I think you should forget him, Jeb,' Sam warned.

'No. I have a duty. To the American people.'

Tweed was proved right when he passed through the Swiss, then the French, frontier controls at Basle station. The counters were deserted, the shutters closed; no one was on duty.

He boarded the Strasbourg express with Paula and found an empty first-class compartment. The whole train was nearly empty close to eleven in the morning. Behind them

313

Newman followed, the two Walthers belonging to Nield and Butler tucked inside his belt at the back. Cardon brought up the rear. At eleven precisely the express moved off.

'That conversation you had with Jennie Blade which you told me about,' began Paula, facing Tweed in a corner window seat. 'I've given it a lot of thought.'

'And your conclusion?'

'Jennie worries me. Has anyone except her seen this mysterious Shadow Man with the wide-brimmed hat? Has Gaunt?'

'It was the one question I forgot to ask him,' Tweed admitted. 'Although he didn't seem to take it seriously. Why?'

'Because if no one else has seen this Shadow Man how can we be sure he exists?'

'You've forgotten something,' Tweed reminded her. 'Old Nosy in Zurich gave us exactly the same description of a man who'd left the building shortly after Klara was garrotted.'

'Maybe Jennie was close by in the Altstadt when we were there. Saw a man like that leaving that building.'

'You're stretching supposition to breaking point.'

'Jennie *was* in Zurich at the time. We know that.'

'True.' Tweed sounded unconvinced.

'You know something?' Paula leaned forward. 'When a woman persists with trying to persuade a man of something he can eventually come to believe her.'

'Like you're persisting now,' he told her. 'Sowing a few doubts in my mind.'

'Who do you think is behind all these brutal murders?' Paula asked, changing the subject. 'Have you any idea yet?'

'A very good idea. Go back to the beginning. Blowing up our headquarters in Park Crescent with a huge bomb. The timer for the bomb – a more sophisticated device than Crombie had ever seen. The fact that there are so many Americans swarming over Switzerland – all holding diplomatic passports. The fact that when Joel Dyson arrived at Park Crescent to hand over copies of the film and the tape Monica saw inside his suitcase American clothes – which suggests he'd just arrived from the States. The fact that our PM seems to be in the palm of the American President. All that has happened suggests limitless sums of money, a huge hostile organization. All that adds up to *power* – great power. Work it out for yourself. It's frightening.'

'You don't sound frightened,' she observed.

'*I* am not. I'm indignant, determined. The garrotting of Helen Frey and Klara was bad enough – although sometimes it's a risk of their trade. But Theo Strebel was a nice chap, didn't deserve to be shot. And that's curious and significant – two women garrotted, a man shot by someone he *knew*.'

'How do you know that?'

'Think of the precautions he took when we arrived – how we had to say who we were before he'd admit us.'

'I don't see the significance,' Paula confessed.

On a seat across the aisle Newman sat listening. He'd removed the two Walther automatics from behind his back. They now rested inside the pockets of the trench coat folded beside him.

Their owners, Butler and Nield, had hired cars in Basle for future use in the Vosges. It would have been risky taking firearms by car past a frontier post. They were now racing along the A35 autoroute to Colmar where they'd wait for Tweed and his team at the Hotel Bristol.

Cardon was seated in his usual strategic position at one end of the long compartment. Armed with his Walther, he could see any stranger approaching from either direction. He appeared to be asleep but his eyes never left the back of Tweed's head.

The express had stopped at St Louis, later at Mulhouse. Then it raced along to the distant stop of Colmar. Paula gazed out of the window to the west on the stretch from Mulhouse to Colmar. The Vosges were coming into view in the distance.

The sun was shining brilliantly again and the range, snowbound to midway down its slopes, showed up clearly. They'd be driving up into those mountains soon. Why did she find them sinister on this lovely morning? They swooped up and down in great saddlebacks with here and there a prominent summit. They looked so dreadfully lonely, Paula thought, so remote from the villages amid vineyards on the lower slopes.

As the express raced on north she reflected on the strangeness of this beautiful province. Its odd mix of French and German which appeared in the names of towns on a map she'd studied. Bollwiller. Ste-Croix-en-Plaine. Munster. Ribeauville.

In 1871 Bismarck's Prussia had annexed Alsace-Lorraine. At the end of the First World War France had taken Alsace-Lorraine back. She was still staring out of the window. Many of the houses had steep-pitched rooves like flat chutes, which suggested winter could be severe, with heavy snow.

She glanced at Tweed and he was humming to himself, which was a rare habit. Why was he so pleased?

'What are you thinking of?' she asked him.

'That with a bit of luck soon I shall meet the two men who, I'm convinced, hold the key to this whole horrific business.'

'And you're keeping their names to yourself?'

'Joel Dyson – who knows Amberg is at the Château Noir. Who is, I'm sure, so anxious to get back the originals of his film and tape.'

'The second man?'

316

'Probably the most important of all. Barton Ives, Special Agent of the FBI . . .'

'These are the ideal ambush points,' Norton said. 'All up in the Vosges. You should wipe out the whole of Tweed's team at one blow.'

Norton was meeting Marvin Mencken for the first time, because he had to make sure Mencken didn't make a mistake. But even at this face-to-face meeting Mencken realized Norton had been clever. Close together as they were, he couldn't see Norton's face.

They were sitting inside a small café in Little Venice, deep inside Colmar. Norton had searched the area to discover this place before phoning Mencken. The café was divided into two sections, separated by a heavy lace curtain. Tables on either side were close to each other.

One side was for customers who required food. Norton had arrived early, consumed an omelette and salad and a huge quantity of French bread. He needed plenty of food to fuel his exceptional energy. He had finished the meal before Mencken arrived, had waved away the waiter.

'Later . . .'

The windows facing the narrow street were also hung with heavy lace curtains. Mencken, as instructed, went into the bar entrance, ordered a glass of white wine and took it to the table next to Norton's beyond the curtain. As he sat down, facing the curtain, the only other customer had twisted round in his chair as though greeting a friend.

Yes, Mencken thought, Norton had been clever. The face he looked at was distorted by the lace curtain. Norton wore a French beret he'd purchased and his grey hair was tucked under it. He also wore a windcheater and a scarf which covered his chin. Perched on his nose was a pair of pebble glasses. The eyes which stared at Mencken

317

were huge, intimidating. The map was held so Mencken could see it clearly, pressed against the curtain.

'Each cross marked on this map locates the ambush points,' Norton continued. 'See this one in Kaysersberg.'

'I've studied my own map. That place is a short drive from Colmar . . .'

'Just listen. The cross marks a bridge. If they go that way into the Vosges you could mine that bridge with explosives, detonate them by remote control.'

'OK,' Mencken said impatiently. 'I visited hardware and electrical shops before I drove here from Basle. I have the equipment I can use to make a timer system; crude, but it will work.'

'There's a stone quarry I've marked here – on the way to Colmar from Basle. It has a shed with explosives inside . . .'

'OK, I don't miss much. I spotted it on my way here. It'll be like breaking into a piggy bank . . .'

'Kindly *listen*! Tweed and his team may arrive in this area at any moment – he moves very fast. So your first priority is to grab those explosives . . .'

'Which was my priority one anyway . . .'

'This cross, if you're listening, marks a cliff by the roadside. It looked pretty unstable and faces an abyss. Maybe you could create an avalanche when they . . .'

'OK. I like that . . .'

'This position – again high up above the snowline – is where you could catch them in a crossfire. You're not making notes.'

'Yes, I am.' Mencken tapped his forehead. 'Up here. I've a mind like a computer – one that works. Next?'

Norton gazed at Mencken from his side of the curtain. His view was also distorted – and the pebble glasses increased the effect. Mencken's face looked very skeletal with its hard pointed jaw line and prominent cheekbones. A man who would not hesitate to carry out any

318

cold-blooded execution. Which suited Norton. But he still didn't trust him. In the slate-grey eyes which stared back he detected overweening ambition. You wouldn't miss a single chance to take over from me, he thought. So the answer was to be very tough with Marvin Mencken, a natural killer.

For several minutes he listed other areas in the Vosges marked by crosses. With his hands covered with silk-lined gloves, he eventually passed the map through to Mencken under the curtain. Mencken found the use of gloves interesting. It suggested Norton's fingerprints were on record in the States – maybe under a different name. Ex-CIA, FBI? Or a criminal history?

He snatched the map from under the curtain, put it in his pocket. He'd had a bellyful of Norton – explaining everything as though he was new to this type of work. Plus the fact that there was something patronizing in the other man's attitude. But Norton wasn't finished yet.

'Stay where you are. It's not just Tweed and his team we need to eliminate. I'm confident Joel Dyson will appear in this area . . .'

'Because *my* man spotted him outside the Zurcher Kredit in Basle, made him squawk . . .'

'And then let him escape alive,' rasped Norton. 'Not a great success, Mencken. Don't interrupt me again. Just concentrate on what I say. Joel Dyson must be eliminated. Equally important, that Special Agent FBI, Barton Ives, must be too. We need all of them wiped off the face of the earth.'

Mencken leaned forward. His nose was touching the curtain.

'I'll terminate the lot. It will be a blood bath.'

'Don't forget they could drive to the Château Noir by either route,' Norton reminded him.

'It will be a blood bath,' Mencken repeated.

33

Marler, typically, had told Tweed before leaving Basle that he'd hire his own car, make his own way to Colmar.

'I may not reach the Hotel Bristol until late in the evening,' he had warned.

Tweed, knowing Marler liked to operate on his own, had agreed immediately.

'See you at the Bristol then,' Marler ended jauntily.

Hiring an Audi, he had driven to Mulhouse. There, instead of continuing north along the autoroute to Colmar, he had turned west, heading for the Ballon d'Alsace in the southern region of the Vosges. He had reached the French glider airfield and had a long chat in his fluent French with the controller.

Marler, after training in Britain, was an expert in flying gliders. He had examined a machine, climbing into the confined cockpit. The controller had leaned against the side as Marler haggled over the price. He would want the glider for several days.

'Incidentally, you've seen my licence, but accidents happen. How much if I smash it up?'

'Sir, that would cost you a lot of money.'

'How much?'

The controller had told him and Marler had nodded. He knew Tweed had the funds to fork out if necessary. The deposit paid, Marler drove off, returning by the route he'd come until he joined the autoroute north near Mulhouse.

Keeping just inside the speed limit, he raced along the

autoroute, bypassing Colmar, continuing north to the great river port of Strasbourg on the Rhine. Arriving there, he was driving much more sedately. Marler knew Europe as well as Newman, and he thought the ancient city unique.

The old city is perched on an island and spanned by many bridges. Marler parked his Audi outside and walked the rest of the way, crossing one of the bridges, glancing up to admire the medieval architecture. This was history, the Free City where once Protestant refugees had fled from French Catholic oppression. Which probably explained why it housed so many craftsmen in different fields. It was one of these craftsmen Marler was visiting. A gunsmith – who provided on the quiet the greatest range of weapons of any secret armaments supplier on the Continent.

Near the immense mass of the looming cathedral, Marler turned down a narrow stone-flagged alley. Suddenly he entered a world of silence, all sounds of traffic and human bustle gone.

He mounted a flight of worn stone steps to a landing on the first floor. Facing him was a massive studded wooden door with a Judas window. The only modern item in sight was a metal-grilled speakphone with a button alongside it. No indication as to who lived there.

'Who is it?' a quiet voice asked in French.

'Marler. You know me, Grandjouan. We've done business before.'

The Judas window opened, eyes peered out at him through a pair of gold-rimmed spectacles perched on a hooked nose. Marler waited while chains were removed, bolts pulled back, locks unfastened. The place was a fortress. The door swung open.

'Marler, indeed. So long since we last met. Come and join me for a glass of wine.'

Grandjouan was a hunchback with tiny feet. Marler

was careful not to stare at his deformity. When his host had closed the door, chained and relocked it, they shook hands.

'I hadn't time to press the button, you old rascal,' Marler remarked. 'So how did you know someone had arrived?'

'One of my state secrets.' Grandjouan chuckled throatily. 'Now the wine . . .'

'Not for me, thank you so much. I have a long way to drive when we've completed our business.'

'Such a pity. I have the most excellent Riesling.'

'Well, just a small glass.'

Grandjouan had a clean-shaven weathered face. Impossible even to guess his age. He had a nice smile and his eyes twinkled behind the spectacles as he handed Marler the glass.

'*Santé!*'

'*Santé!*' Marler repeated. 'This is very good.'

'I told you so. Now, as always you are a man in a hurry. So down to business.'

'I want an Armalite rifle, dismantled, with plenty of ammo. Twelve hand-grenades. A tear-gas pistol with a supply of shells. A Luger, again with ammo. All without any history.'

'Of course.' Grandjouan sipped again at his wine. 'I believe you are going to start a small war?'

'It could be something like that.'

Marler had carried from the car a cricket bag which contained a bat and several balls. He had put it on a table when he accepted the glass. Grandjouan looked at it, shook his head, covered with thinning grey hair.

'You proposed to carry these items away in that? Yes? I can do better. The container will come free, my friend.' He opened a cupboard, produced a cello case. 'Much better. It will take the load, which your cricket bag will not. Also we like some camouflage, in case you are stopped by the police.'

Grandjouan wore an old leather jacket with a woollen blue shirt underneath, open at the neck. His trousers were old but clean corduroy. Marler looked round his lair as his host ferreted about.

The walls were lined with huge old wooden chests and cupboards. When Grandjouan opened one cupboard it was stacked to the gunwales. Heaven help any policeman who came to search this place. Illumination came from a large oval window in the slanting roof. Heating was provided by several oil heaters. The only reasonably modern item of furniture was the massive old fridge from which Grandjouan had taken the bottle of Riesling. The place reminded Marler of a hermit's cave.

Grandjouan returned holding a black beret in one hand, a folder of leather tucked under his other arm. He handed Marler the beret.

'You are English. Obvious – very – from the clothes you're wearing.'

Which was true. On the Continent Marler was always taken for what they imagined the typical Englishman to be, a member of the idle upper classes. His drawling way of speaking reinforced the impression. It had thrown more than one adversary off guard.

Under the British warm, which he had placed on an armchair, he wore a houndstooth sports jacket, heavy grey slacks, a blue cravat below his strong jaw. He looked at the beret.

'Why this?'

'You are posing as a musician with that cello case. The beret on an Englishman dressed as you are suggests the artistic temperament.'

'God forbid!'

'Wear it. And here in this folder are some sheets of music. Spread one or two on the car seat beside you. They will strengthen the impression that you are a musician.'

Marler glanced at the sheets. He paused at one sheet –

'*La Jeune Fille aux Cheveux de Lin*', 'The Girl with the Flaxen Hair'. Unconsciously he began to hum the tune to himself. Grandjouan performed a little dance of delight.

'Excellent, my friend! You have thought yourself into the part . . .'

Grandjouan himself packed the twelve grenades, the tear-gas shells in the cello case after wrapping each item in thick tissue-paper. He performed the same routine with the tear-gas pistol, the Luger and ammo. Then he took a box he had extracted from beneath one of the floorboards which was hinged invisibly. Inside was the Armalite, dismantled.

'I'll assemble that if I may,' Marler suggested.

Grandjouan watched with approval the speed at which Marler put the separate parts together. He attached the magnifying night scope, squinted through it at the skylight, pressed the trigger of the unloaded gun.

'It feels good . . .'

With equal rapidity he dismantled it and Grandjouan picked up the pieces, again wrapping them in the tissue-paper. He fitted them inside the cello case, added ammo. Then he took a large piece of black velvet, spread it over the case's contents. From another deep drawer in an ancient chest he took out a long slim object inside a silk sleeve. He pointed to the end projecting before laying it on top of the velvet.

'More camouflage. The bow for your imaginary cello – with the end showing.'

He closed the case, snapped down the latch. Grandjouan had been right – everything had fitted in snugly, filling the case. Marler picked it up, tested the weight as the hunchback beamed, spoke again. Marler was wearing the beret.

'Perfect,' enthused Grandjouan. 'I used the tissue-paper so there was no danger of any rattle.'

324

'Talking of danger, why did you say I might be stopped by the police? Oh, let's first settle up.'

Marler made no attempt to haggle over the price. Producing a wad of French thousand-franc notes he counted out the correct amount on a table. He was reaching for the cello case and his cricket bag when Grandjouan explained.

'Yes, you could well be stopped by the police. I have an ear to the grapevine. Paris has received a message that a team of terrorists is crossing into Alsace.'

'Where from?' Marler asked sharply.

'From Switzerland.'

'I see. I'll be careful.'

He shook hands, thanked the hunchback for his service. As Grandjouan closed the door behind him he paused to pull up the collar of his coat. Standing on the platform at the top of the stone steps he glanced down. Inset into the stone was a square piece of rubber. Of course! A pressure pad. That was how the wily old hunchback had known someone had arrived before he had pressed the bell.

Marler was very alert as he walked back inside the alley, pausing at the exit to glance out. No sign of a patrol car. It was, of course, Beck who had warned Paris – warned them about the Americans.

A little unfortunate from Tweed's point of view – that the Haut-Rhin, where Colmar was located, would be swarming with *flics* on the lookout. On the other hand the news confirmed that the Americans had followed them close on their heels. Maybe it was only just beginning.

In mid-afternoon at the Château Noir the banker, Amberg, stared at his uninvited guest, listening, saying nothing. Gaunt had arrived in his hired white BMW without phoning first to make sure it would be convenient

325

for him to call. Now his voice boomed in the Great Hall.

'I was a close friend of your late lamented brother, Julius. I am a close friend of your sister-in-law, Eve. I feel I have a responsibility to track down whoever murdered Julius so brutally. After all, my dear chap, the tragedy did take place in my house in Cornwall, Tresillian Manor.'

'I see,' Amberg replied and was silent again.

Gaunt sat in one of the very large black leather button-backed armchairs scattered about the vast space. The chair would have dwarfed most men, but not Gaunt. His stature with his leonine head seemed to dominate the room.

Swallowed up in another armchair close to a crackling log fire, Jennie Blade warmed her hands. If you were any distance from it the place was freezing. The Great Hall merited its name. About sixty feet square, it had granite walls and miserable illumination from wall sconces. She doubted whether the bulbs inside them were more than forty watts.

The walls sheered up to a height of thirty feet or so. Scattered here and there, as though rationed, small rugs lay on the stone-flagged floor. The entrance hall was grim enough, but this so-called living-room was pure purgatory, Jennie said to herself. There was hardly any furniture except for the chairs and two large, bulbous – and repellent – sideboards standing against a wall. Gaunt was ploughing on, as though unaware of the lukewarm reception.

'The question I have to find an answer to is *why* he was murdered, Amberg. I had a chat with him when he arrived. He told me he had fled Switzerland because he was scared stiff. Apparently a Joel Dyson had deposited with him at the Zurich headquarters a film and a tape. Is that so?'

'That is correct,' Amberg replied and again lapsed into silence.

Gaunt leaned forward. Jennie had the impression that he was studying the banker carefully. His voice became a rumble, his manner like that of an interrogator.

'You saw what was on the film, you heard the tape?'

'No. Dyson handed them to Julius.'

'And did he watch the film, listen to the tape?'

'I don't know.'

'Where are they now?'

'They have gone missing.'

'What!' Gaunt exploded. 'Look, Julius told me he had first stored them in a vault at the Zurcher Kredit in Zurich. He then had them transferred to a less obvious place of safety. The bank vault in Basle.'

'I know. He told me.'

'So how the hell can they be missing?' Gaunt demanded. 'I always thought Swiss banks were like fortresses, that they kept the most meticulous records of every single transaction. Now you tell me they are missing.'

'Mr Gaunt, if you can't speak more quietly I may have to ask you to leave.'

'Plenty of room for my voice in this mausoleum. You haven't answered the question.'

Amberg, perhaps to compensate for his lack of height, sat in a low-backed hard chair perched on a dais behind an old desk Jennie thought could have come from a second-hand stall in the Portobello Road. To break the tension, to get a little more warmth, she reached into a basket, took out two logs, placed them on the fire. Amberg frowned at her.

'Those logs are very expensive.'

'Oh, pardon me.'

Stuff you, she thought. Everything here is rationed. The logs, the rugs, the words Amberg allowed to escape his lips. She stood up, straightened the jodhpurs she'd worn against the cold, thrust her hands inside her pockets

327

to ward off the chill, wandered past the dais.

At the far end of the hall, down a wide flight of stone steps, was an indoor terrace. A huge picture window gave a panoramic view across the lower slopes of the sunlit Vosges. The glare of the sun off the snow was intense. The air was so clear Jennie could see in the distance another range of mountains. The Black Forest. In Germany beyond the Rhine.

She happened to glance down and sucked in her breath. Beyond the picture window the ground fell away into a sheer precipice. At the bottom was a sinister black lake, shrouded from the sun by the Vosges. Behind her the conversation continued. Assuming 'conversation' now meant one man talking to another.

'I have no idea why they went missing,' Amberg replied. 'It was Julius who supervised the transfer.'

'I thought you were Chairman of the bank,' Gaunt threw at the Swiss.

'That is correct. Day to day business was handled by Julius.'

'Are you saying you have no idea what happened to two items given into the bank's safekeeping?'

'That is correct.'

'Put that remark on a record so you can play it,' Gaunt snapped.

As he stood up, his expression grim, Jennie decided to intervene. Amberg had also stood up, small, portly, dressed in a black business suit. He turned to her in surprise, as though he'd forgotten her presence. Jennie realized the intensity of his concentration on his duel with Gaunt.

'How on earth do you manage to run this enormous place?' she enquired. 'Surely you need servants?'

'True. They don't live in. Too much of an invasion of privacy, which I value highly. The peasants from the local villages provide all the manpower needed.' His blue eyes twinkled. 'Of course, I have to pay them more in summer, but that's understandable. They can make a living tending the vineyards. I own a vineyard myself. Next time you come and see me you can sample some of my wine. I think you will like it. But your friend appears anxious to leave.'

Jennie had been staring straight into his shrewd blue eyes for every second he spoke. The transformation in his personality astounded her. Then she thought of the probable explanation. He was a man who preferred the company of women – and Gaunt had gone at him like a bull at a gate. She glanced at the Squire. He stood like a man carved out of stone. Furious that he'd got nowhere with the banker.

Amberg escorted them into the entrance hall. As she was stepping out of the château Amberg held out his hand, shook hers warmly.

'Don't forget my invitation to taste the wine . . .'

His expression changed suddenly as he looked at Gaunt. It reminded her of the expression the Swiss had adopted during the 'conversation'. Like a slab of ice.

'Goodbye, Mr Gaunt.'

'And it hasn't been a pleasure,' Gaunt roared at the top of his voice.

34

'Trouble. Here it comes,' Marler said to himself.

He was driving along the autoroute towards Colmar in mid-afternoon and it was still light. He was in the middle of nowhere, tilled fields stretching away on both sides, when he heard the police siren, saw the patrol car racing up to him in his rear-view mirror. Slowing down, he stopped.

As he lowered his window icy air flowed inside. He was humming the tune of '*La Jeune Fille aux Cheveux de Lin*' when the patrol car parked a few yards ahead of him. Before leaving Strasbourg he had pushed back the front passenger seat to its furthest extent and perched the cello case with its base on the floor and the rest of it angled against the seat. Several sheets of music were spread on the seat itself.

A tall lean-faced uniformed policeman got out of the patrol car. Leaving his companion behind the wheel, he wandered back to Marler. The flap of his pistol holster was unbuttoned.

'Papers!' he demanded.

Marler had his passport and driving licence ready and handed them over. The *flic* perused both documents carefully, returned them to Marler. He peered inside.

'You are on holiday?' he asked in French.

'No, I'm a musician,' Marler replied in the same language. 'I'm working.'

'Where are you driving to?'

'Berne in Switzerland. To perform in a concert.'

Marler hoped there *was* a concert hall in the Swiss capital. But he doubted whether the *flic* knew either. He was saying as little as possible, using the minimum of words to answer. The police were always suspicious of voluble travellers. The *flic* stared at the cello case.

'Your concert is today?' he asked truculently.

'No, tomorrow. I'll put up somewhere for the night to get some rest. I need to be fresh for the concert.'

Marler's mind, racing, was considering every angle. It was not impossible he'd bump into this same *flic* when he reached Colmar. Walking round the front of the car, the policeman opened the door to the front passenger seat, leaned in, opened the clasp, lifted the lid of the cello case. He stared down at the long slim silk sleeve with the end of a bow projecting.

Marler said nothing. He was careful to display no sign of impatience, nervousness. No drumming of his fingers on the wheel. The *flic* peered into the back of the Audi.

'What are you carrying inside that bag?'

'It's cricket. One of our national games. Inside is what we play the game with – a bat and a ball.'

The policeman frowned, reached in, unzipped the bag, stared at its contents. He shrugged, re-zipped the bag. The English had peculiar tastes. Marler realized he'd made one of those glaring mistakes the most careful people sometimes make. Who played cricket in winter in this part of the world?

Slamming the back door shut as he had done the front, the policeman shrugged again at the strangeness of the English. Without another word he walked back to his vehicle, climbed inside. The patrol car took off like a rocket.

'And that experience is enough for one day,' Marler said to himself as he closed the lid of the cello case and resumed driving.

For Jennie the drive back from the Château Noir to Colmar was a nightmare. Gaunt was moving over snow-covered roads which might conceal ice underneath, racing round hairpin bends on the edge of precipices. Once he skidded close to an endless drop. With great skill he came out of it, proceeded down another steep slope. Jennie had her hands clasped tightly inside her gloves.

'We didn't get much out of Amberg, did we?' she remarked. 'Very Swiss. Although most Swiss I've met have been so polite and helpful.'

'Shut up! I'm driving.'

She knew Gaunt fairly well now, his volatile moods. As they swerved round another bend she studied his profile. No tension, no sign that the BMW could slide at any moment into a fatal skid. She suddenly grasped that only half his mind was on driving the car.

A superb driver, he was controlling the car automatically. Half his mind was miles away, pondering something which bothered him. What could it be that he was mentally gnawing at like a dog with a bone?

A yellow tractor was emerging from a snow-covered field a score of yards or so ahead of them. If it occupied the road ahead of them it would be difficult to overtake. Gaunt rammed his foot down on the accelerator, pressed his hand on the horn, blaring out across the mountains non-stop. God! He was going to try and get in front of it!

Jennie closed her eyes, waited for the shattering collision, couldn't bear not to see what was happening, opened them again. She gritted her teeth. Racing down the curving road, the BMW increased speed. The tractor driver seemed to take no notice. Its yellow hulk loomed over Jennie as the car sped past, almost skimming the side of the machine. She let out her breath.

'Silly devil,' Gaunt commented offhandedly. 'Should have waited. My right of way.'

'Only your right of way if the other chap gives it to you,' she reminded him.

'What was that you said?' He glanced at her briefly.

He hadn't heard a word she had spoken. Now she knew she was right – he was driving on automatic pilot. *Most* of his mind was miles away. Where?

She went over in *her* mind all that had been said while they were at the Château Noir. Was it frustration that was affecting Gaunt? Frustration at hearing that the film and the tape had gone missing?

Then it hit her. Did Gaunt *know* what was on the film, the tape? During an early stage of his verbal exchanges with Amberg she recalled one thing Gaunt had said. When Julius had arrived at Tresillian Manor Gaunt had had a chat with him. Had Julius told Gaunt then what he had seen on the film, what he had heard on the tape? It was possible, maybe even likely.

Suddenly as they approached Colmar a dense mist crept in from the fields, entering the town. Gaunt switched on his fog lights. He was crawling now as they came close to the Hotel Bristol, were passing a shopping parade. She put a hand on his arm.

'Greg, could you drop me here. There are lights on in the shops, they're still open. I want to buy something from the chemist.'

'Here do you?'

He pulled in by the kerb. She opened the door, swung out her long legs. As she turned to close the door and looked at him he seemed to be finally aware of her existence.

'Bristol's just down the way. You'll know where to find me. In the bar. Of course . . .'

The rear of the BMW was swallowed up in the mist which had now become a fog. Glancing in the mirror, Gaunt's last sight of her was a vague silhouette standing by the kerb.

At the Bristol Tweed had chosen the Brasserie for a belated lunch. After their arrival he'd spent a long time alone in his bedroom studying a map of the Vosges, checking the different routes to the Château Noir.

There was a more upmarket restaurant at the hotel, entered from the reservation lobby. The waiter who met Tweed as he led Paula and Newman wore formal black jacket and trousers. His manner, as he attempted to guide them to a table, was that he was conferring an honour on them.

'I'm looking for the Brasserie,' Tweed told him in English.

'Really, sir?' The waiter's tone conveyed that he'd misjudged the quality of the client. 'Through that door, then turn left and left again.'

'This is more like it,' Tweed remarked. 'More homely. That other place you could wait an hour for the first course with a lot of chichi nonsense, removing the covers from the plate and all that rubbish.'

Paula agreed the atmosphere was more welcoming. And in contrast to the restaurant, where the guests had sat like waxworks, the few customers here were locals having an aperitif, eating a main meal.

In the main dining area a waitress led them to, the panelled walls were painted a bright ochre. The cloths on the table were a cheerful pink, Paula noted with approval. The Brasserie faced the railway station across a wide road. Tweed had chosen well.

'I think I'll have a glass of wine,' Tweed announced to her surprise when they were seated. 'We're in Riesling country. A beautiful wine.'

The waitresses, bustling about, wore white blouses, black skirts and short white aprons. Tweed ordered a bottle of Riesling when the others agreed enthusiastically.

'This is when you say it's a good year,' Newman chaffed him, when a bottle of 1989 vintage arrived.

'Let's hope it is. I've no idea. Have you heard of the Château Noir?' he asked the waitress in French.

'Yes. Up in the mountains above the Black Lake. A bad place. It is fated.'

'Why do you say that?'

'Its strange history, sir. It was built by an American millionaire years ago. Built of granite from plans of a medieval fortress. It cost many millions of francs. He committed suicide.'

'Who did?' Tweed asked.

'The American millionaire. He jumped from the château into the Black Lake. No one knows why. It remained empty for years. Who would buy such a place?'

'I heard that someone did. A Swiss banker.'

'Of course. He bought it for a song. Mr Julius Amberg from Zurich. Maybe he was not superstitious. He did not think he would become dead before his time. Good luck to him. He is a nice man.'

Paula was watching Tweed, wondering whether he was going to tell her that Amberg was no longer alive. Tweed simply looked interested, asked the waitress another question.

'You said he is a nice man. You have met him?'

'Many times. When he comes to Colmar he always comes in here – to the Brasserie. For an aperitif, for a main meal.' She lowered her voice. 'He said the restaurant is for snobs, that the food here is much better and you get it quickly. I must go now . . .'

'Has Mr Amberg been here recently?' Tweed asked before she could rush off.

'No, not for some time. Yet when it was clear this afternoon just before dusk we saw lights in the château. Maybe a ghost walks there. You have decided what you would like to eat? I can come back.'

'The veal escalope *panée* for me, with sauté potatoes.'

Tweed looked at Paula. 'What do you fancy?'

'The same for me, please,' Paula said, looking at the waitress.

'Make that three,' Newman requested.

The waitress darted away. Paula, who was facing the rear of the Brasserie, stared at a huge mural painted in oils above the door leading to the kitchen. It depicted a small lake sunk in the grim heights of the Vosges. Tweed followed her gaze.

'I wonder if that's Lac Noir,' she mused. 'If so, it looks pretty forbidding. And what a strange story she told us

335

about Château Noir. Obviously Walter Amberg doesn't patronize the Brasserie.'

'Walter,' Newman commented, 'from what I've seen of him, would patronize the restaurant, silver-plate covers and all that jazz.'

'From what we've gathered,' Tweed pointed out, 'Amberg has only been at the château for two or three days. It was interesting to hear that the place *is* occupied. The lights the waitress mentioned.'

'We are going up there to beard him in his den, aren't we?' Paula enquired.

'It's one reason why we came here. Incidentally, I don't want to spoil your meal, but I think the opposition has already arrived. As we walked through the restaurant I noticed six men sitting at a quiet table in a corner. I also caught a snatch of conversation – with an American accent. They're not pleasant-looking characters.'

'But why here, for Pete's sake?' Paula asked.

'In Zurich there is a whole number of first-class hotels. In Basle there are only two, the Drei Könige and the Hilton – if you prefer that. Here the only major hotel is the Bristol. It's logical some of them would choose to stay here. They may even have detected its strategic position.'

'Strategic in what way?' Paula wanted to know.

'If their objective is also the Château Noir then we are on the right side of the town. From here we can drive straight into the outskirts across the railway and up into the Vosges. We practically bypass Colmar.'

'There's a heavy fog drifting in,' Newman remarked.

Twisting round in her seat, Paula looked at the windows fronting on the street and hung with net curtains. For customers coming in off the street there were double doors leading into the Brasserie.

Newman was right. As she watched the fog seemed to grow denser every minute. The blurred headlights of crawling cars appeared, disappeared in the milky haze.

And the temperature had dropped swiftly. A man came in through the entrance and briefly a current of ice-cold air drifted into the Brasserie.

A waiter, wearing a white shirt, black trousers and a long apron tied round his waist, went to push the door shut quickly. Outside stooped silhouettes of people hurrying home as fast as they dared passed beyond the windows.

'I like this wine,' Tweed said, finishing off his glass. 'It really is a very good Riesling.'

Out of the corner of her eye Paula saw Newman refilling his glass. She turned round, picked up a bottle of Perrier the waitress had brought, topped up Tweed's water glass.

'You'll end up floating,' she teased him.

'Riesling is my favourite wine. It helps me to think. I'm going to order another bottle.'

'Any excuse is better than none,' she teased him.

She twisted round again. The ghostly tableau of cars and people beyond the window fascinated her. Then she stiffened. A woman had hauled open the door, came inside looking frightened to death. Jennie Blade. She spotted Tweed, ran to his table. 'I've been followed again,' she burst out. 'By the man with the wide-brimmed hat.'

Her blonde hair glistened with fog vapour. Her eyes were wild. Tweed stood up, walked round the table, pulled out a chair for her which faced his. Returning to his seat he sat down, gazed at her as he spoke.

'When did this happen?'

'Just now. He damn near caught up with me. Thank God this place was so close. The same man – following me with his bloody wide-brimmed black hat, turned down so I couldn't see his face. I'm scared to death, Tweed.'

337

35

'I need a drink,' said Jennie as she took off her coat, draped it over the back of a nearby chair. 'Brandy.'

'No spirits at the moment,' Tweed advised. 'You are in a state of shock. Try a glass of this Riesling.'

Paula reached across to another empty table, picked up a glass, placed it in front of their guest. Tweed was glad he'd placed Jennie facing him as he poured the wine – she was not looking at Paula, whose expression was full of doubt.

'Can you tell me exactly what happened?' Tweed suggested.

Jennie drank half the contents of her glass, put it down, then almost immediately raised it again, drained it. Tweed refilled it.

'Why were you outside in this fog?' he coaxed.

'I'd been with Gaunt in the BMW. We'd just returned from the Château Noir. I asked the Squire to drop me by the shopping parade so I could go into a chemist. It was when I came out that it happened.'

'Go on, you are doing fine,' Tweed encouraged her.

'I came out of the shop and it was eerie. I hadn't realized how dense the fog had become. He was standing with his back to me, holding up something in his left hand. The same black wide-brimmed hat, turned down as I told you so I couldn't see his face. The same long black overcoat. I began to walk towards the Bristol, towards here. I heard him coming after me. I panicked, began to run. Behind me he was moving much faster.'

'How do you know that?' Paula enquired. 'Did you look back?'

'God, no! I was too scared. But there was no other sound in the fog – just the clack of his shoes catching me up. The clacking sound hit the pavement at longer intervals – so I knew he'd increased the length of his stride.'

'Very shrewd of you,' Tweed commented. He sipped at his coffee which the waitress had brought just before their frightened guest appeared. 'Especially as you were so scared.'

'Then I saw the Brasserie. I dived in here, saw you. What a relief.'

'Drink some more wine.' Tweed waited until she had swallowed half her second glass. He topped it up. 'What happened to your pursuer?'

'I've no idea. At least he didn't follow me in here. But then I'd have been all right.' She smiled wanly for the first time. 'You were here.'

'Are you feeling better?' Tweed reached across, took hold of her right hand resting on the table, squeezed it reassuringly. 'You are safe, among friends.'

Newman had remained silent, leaving it to Tweed. He noticed that in the warmth of the Brasserie the vapour drops had melted on Jennie's golden hair, giving her a somewhat bedraggled look. She was still incredibly attractive.

'Would you like something to eat?' Tweed asked her.

'Just some bread. My stomach can't face anything else.'

She took a piece of French bread, piled on it some of the butter Newman had ordered, chewed ravenously, then reached for a second hunk.

'That's better,' she announced a minute later. 'Pardon my table manners. I haven't eaten for hours.'

'You said you'd just returned from the Château Noir with Gaunt in his BMW,' Tweed began. 'Would you mind telling me what took place? You met Amberg?'

339

'Yes. That was an experience for Gaunt . . .'

She started to tell Tweed in detail everything that had taken place. She recalled almost every word of the conversation between the two men. Gaunt's expression, Amberg's lack of it. Then at the end the warmth of Amberg when he talked to her, the theory she had come up with that the Swiss preferred the company of women. Her descriptions were graphic.

Paula glanced at Tweed. He was leaning forward, totally absorbed by what Jennie was saying. Paula sensed that Tweed was *seeing* the scene which had been enacted in the Château Noir, so strong was his imagination. Newman was also gazing fixedly at their guest. As an ex-foreign correspondent maybe his mind was also inside the Château Noir.

'So,' Jennie concluded, 'after the hideous drive back when I thought we'd end up dead, Gaunt – at my request – dropped me outside the shops.'

There was a long silence. Tweed was still staring at her as she drank more wine, watching him over the rim of her glass. He eventually leaned back in his chair.

'You have remarkable powers of observation. So many see but do not *observe* what they see.'

'Coming from you I'm taking that as a great compliment.'

'Just a statement of fact.'

'I think I've taken up enough of your time – and I could do with a hot shower.' She stood up, looked at Paula and Newman. 'I do hope I haven't spoilt your meal – and thank you for putting up with my maunderings.' She looked at Tweed. 'If we could have a quiet talk sometime at your convenience?'

'I'm in Room 419. It has a sitting area. Come and see me any time you feel like it. So I know it's you beat a little tattoo on the door. Like this.'

He drummed his fingers briefly on the table. Jennie

340

repeated the rhythm. Newman also stood up, collected her coat.

'You don't want to go out into the fog again to find the main entrance. There's a short cut through the restaurant. I'll see you safely to your room.'

'That's very kind of you.' She gave him her warmest smile. 'I do still feel a bit shaky.'

Paula waited until they had disappeared. Then she turned to Tweed.

'I don't believe one word she said.'

Tweed sipped some more wine before replying. He put down his glass.

'That really is first-rate Riesling.'

'Translation, you don't agree. You think I'm being catty. Maybe I am.'

'Not like you, so that I don't agree with. Give me your reasons.'

'It's stretching the imagination to breaking point. In Basle she gives you the same story. The famous Shadow Man. We are quite a distance from Basle. Now the Shadow Man turns up here on the edge of the Vosges in Alsace. I don't go for it.'

'Have you forgotten?' he enquired gently. 'An impartial witness in Zurich – Old Nosy – described the Shadow Man leaving the building in the Altstadt where Klara was murdered.'

'But we thought of an explanation for that. Jennie was in the square out of sight, saw him leaving the building – which gave her the idea.'

'What motive could she have for inventing this menace? Also, how could she have known we were in this brasserie?'

'Made it up on the spur of the moment when she came in that door from the fog. No flies on our Jennie. She's got mental reflexes as quick as lightning. I will give her that.'

'Possible. Yes, you could be right. And her motive?'

'She's after the film and the tape. I'm beginning to think they must be very valuable to someone.'

Tweed nodded his agreement. Paula's theory had disturbed him. Women were so often more perceptive than men about their own sex. Paula had produced a very plausible theory.

'Then why the charade – rushing in here as though scared stiff?' he questioned.

'She'd seen you were in here – maybe we didn't see her starting to come in by the short cut. She then goes back into the fog, puts on her act? Why? To get closer to you. She thinks you'll lead her to the film and tape.'

'I can't fault your reasoning,' he admitted.

'Another thing,' Paula went on. 'When she was relating her experience at the Château Noir – and I admit I was a little jealous of how well she did it. Supposed to be my forte, that. Sorry, I'm off the track. When she relayed what happened at the château, I think something she reported as said – or happened – struck you with great force.'

'It did. I don't want to talk about it until I've had time to mull it over.'

'Bob is taking a long time.' She grinned wryly. 'Maybe he not only saw her safely to her room, but inside it. He's smitten with her.'

'You've underestimated him,' Tweed told her. 'I've seen him do this before – pretend to have fallen for some attractive girl. And all the time he's asking himself, "What's she after?"'

'Shush! Here he is. And with more feminine company . . .'

Eve Amberg was laughing at something Newman had said as they approached Tweed's table. She had one hand looped inside his arm and used the other to brush away a lock of her titian hair from her face. Paula studied her outfit.

She wore a dark green jersey suit and a low-cut cream blouse. Bet that cost a mint, thought Paula. Newman, who was clearly enjoying himself, made a pantomime of introducing her. Sweeping one arm low, he used the other hand to pull out a chair.

'Look at the jewel I found hiding upstairs,' he joked.

'Hello, Paula,' Eve greeted her, bent and kissed her on the cheek. 'And a big hello to you,' she went on, turning to Tweed, administering a lingering kiss on his left cheek. 'Bob caught me coming out of my room, thank God. I'm an abandoned woman.'

'Sounds exciting,' Tweed chimed in, continuing the game. 'You look like a glass of this excellent Riesling.'

'And he says that!' Eve addressed Paula. 'After I spent half an hour on my make-up. Isn't he just too awful?'

'We can't take him anywhere,' Paula joked back.

'Wish me success.'

Eve raised the glass Tweed had filled, tasted the wine, looked mischievously at Newman.

'At least the man knows his wine. This is delicious. I may be after more.'

'Why abandoned?' Tweed asked.

'The Squire. Again. He drives me here with his latest girl friend, Jennie Blade. Then he ups and offs with her to some unknown destination. For the whole afternoon. Seriously, Tweed, it's good to see you again.'

'Likewise.' Tweed paused. 'What success do we wish you?'

'It's Walter again. Walter Amberg, my dear disliked brother-in-law. I phoned him from here. I was going to take a taxi. The Squire can drop dead, mooning over his Jennie. So what reception do I get when I call Walter? Not this afternoon. Out of the question. Have guests.

343

Some time when he's not so busy. Guests? I didn't believe a word of it. He's avoiding me. I'll catch him off guard – drive up there without phoning first.'

'Why the reluctance on his part?' enquired Tweed.

'Same reason as I told you before. He doesn't want to hand over my money. But he will, he will, I promise you. Face to face, he's putty in my hands, the little creep.'

'And Gaunt?'

'God knows where he is.' She glanced to her left when someone entered the Brasserie. 'Speak of the devil, here he is. After a drink, of course.'

Gaunt, still clad in his sports jacket and corduroy trousers, had stormed in via the short cut from the hotel. As he arrived his voice boomed out, causing the few locals sitting at other tables to stare.

'I want a double Scotch, *garçon*!' he roared in English. '*Tout le suite*. Over at that table.' He looked at Tweed and Newman, turned back to the waiter he'd shouted at. 'No, make that three double Scotches. And get a move on, I'm parched.'

The young waiter, who had smiled every time he passed their table, glared at Gaunt. Newman called out in a loud but polite voice.

'No, waiter, please. Only one double Scotch. Thank you.'

Gaunt marched up to their table. He stood for a moment, surveying the glasses.

'Drinking local plonk? That's just for pansies. A Scotch would put some guts into you.'

Eve was furious. Her greenish eyes gleamed with a venom Paula would never have suspected she was capable of. Her full lips, treated with scarlet lipstick, tightened as Gaunt hauled up a chair, joined them.

'Greg,' she raged, 'you will apologize immediately for using that term about my friends. Or go to hell.'

'I apologize immediately,' Gaunt mimicked as he sat

down. 'No offence meant,' he said in a more reasonable tone. 'I take the word back. Unpardonable of me – but I've had a helluva drive up and down the Vosges this afternoon.'

You've also had a skinful already before you came in here, Newman thought. Whisky fumes drifted across the table. But Eve wasn't finished yet. She leaned towards Gaunt.

'And, you ignorant hulk, it's *tout de suite*. You can't even insult a waiter in correct French.'

'Sorry, sorry, sorry.' Gaunt sounded sincere this time. 'You're quite right, Eve. Again, my apologies to everyone. Had a strange experience this afternoon. Threw me off my balance. That doesn't often happen.'

His mood had changed suddenly. He had spoken the last three sentences in a sober, almost grim tone. Tweed frowned, then spoke to him.

'Care to tell us about it? Get it out of your system?'

'Do you mind if I don't for the moment? Sorry, but I need to mull it over.'

Paula stared at Gaunt in astonishment. He had used almost precisely the same words Tweed had spoken earlier. Moreover, it sounded as though, like Tweed, he was referring to the Château Noir.

Gaunt looked up as the waiter placed his drink before him. He had his wallet out in a flash, added a generous tip as he stared at the waiter.

'Thank you very much. Your service is really excellent.' He looked round the table. 'Jennie disappeared. I can't find her anywhere.'

'She was sitting at this table a while ago,' Tweed informed him. 'You dropped her off in the fog, apparently.'

'At her own request,' Gaunt barked back defensively.

'She then left us to go to her room to take a shower,' Tweed continued, ignoring Gaunt's rudeness.

345

'But I hammered on her door before I came in here. There was no reply. Her door was locked. I pressed my ear to it, couldn't hear a shower running. In any case, she'd have wrapped something round her and come to see who it was. Like most women' – he glanced at Paula and Eve – 'present company excepted. Like many women she's always curious. I'd stake my reputation she's not in her room.'

'What reputation is that?' Eve snapped at him.

Tweed rose from the table. Newman and Paula stood up almost at the same time. They'd had enough of Gaunt. Tweed nodded to Eve and Gaunt, led the way out by the short cut and through the restaurant. Paula noticed there were several groups of Americans at different tables, none of whom she liked the look of. Tweed was hurrying into the reception area which had a minute sitting area off to one side. Philip Cardon sat reading a paperback. No one was present behind the reception counter.

'I had an early lunch,' Cardon explained. 'Since then I've sat here keeping an eye open. No less than fifteen Americans have arrived, booked in. Most are stuffing their stomachs in that restaurant.'

'Have you seen Jennie Blade?'

'No.'

So Gaunt was right, Tweed thought grimly. Jennie had disappeared.

36

Tweed stood quite still in the lobby. The only people in the place besides himself were Paula, Newman and Cardon. They all kept quiet – they knew Tweed was thinking furiously. He turned round once to gaze at the deserted reception area, the closed door behind it. He turned back to Cardon.

'Philip,' he said in a low voice, 'you counted fifteen Americans arriving. Did they see you?'

'Of course not.' Cardon was incredulous at the idea. He raised his book to above eye level, completely concealing his face. 'Can you see me?'

'No. Where are Butler and Nield?'

'Here.' Cardon handed Tweed a piece of paper with the names of the two men, their room numbers. 'Like me they had an early meal. They're up in their rooms now.' He checked his watch. 'Harry is due down to relieve me in five minutes. We worked out a roster to keep an eye on who comes and goes out of this place.'

'I see. They're both on the first floor? Good. Now, I want you to think hard. Did some of the Americans arrive here recently?'

'Yes, they did. They turned up in batches.'

'So at times there was a lot of movement here in this lobby. You were concentrating on concealing yourself – at the same time as you checked people arriving. You might have seen a woman with long blonde hair without really registering the fact.' Tweed gave a brief description of how Jennie had been dressed. 'Think hard. Did a woman like that walk *out* of the hotel?'

'Half a mo! – now I come to think of it a woman like that came out of the dining-room exit just as you did. Fifteen minutes ago – roughly. She entered the lift. That was the last I saw of her.'

'Did all the Americans go straight into the restaurant? All fifteen of them?'

'Yes, to start with. Come to think of it two of them, ugly-looking types, came out of the restaurant almost on the heels of Jennie Blade. They must have taken the lift immediately after she'd gone up.'

'Thank you. Stay here.' Tweed turned to Newman and Paula. 'We must hurry, but first I need to collect something.'

He lifted the flap at the end of the reception counter, slipped behind it, grabbed hold of the master key hanging from a hook apart from the other room keys. He ran across to the lift, went inside as soon as the doors opened and pressed the button for the first floor as soon as Paula and Newman were inside.

'What are you up to?' Paula asked.

'First we get hold of Butler and Nield, with their handguns. You may need yours. No shooting unless it's the only way . . .'

Paula was still puzzled until Tweed had collected Nield and Butler, had explained the situation.

'We'll check this floor first . . .'

Tweed began to walk up to each room door, pressing his ear close to the wooden panel. He had acute hearing and soon moved on to the next door. It was outside the third door he tried that he froze, ear pressed hard against the panel. Voices inside. One with an American accent.

'Look, do you smoke? You don't? Well, honey, you're going to when I press this lighted cigarette into your face, then lower down. What man will ever look at you again . . .'

348

'No, you bastards—'

The woman's voice was cut off with a scream. Tweed inserted the master key quietly, turned it noiselessly, took hold of the handle, glanced at Butler who stood with a Walther in his hand. Tweed nodded, turned the handle. Standing aside, he threw the door wide open.

Butler, Walther gripped in both hands, charged into the room in a crouch, prepared to drop to the floor, gun swinging in an arc. Behind him Newman followed with Nield. Tweed removed the key, stepped in after them, inserted the key back into the lock and turned it to the locked position.

Jennie was sprawled back in an armchair, ankles bound with rope, her wrists pinioned behind her. The blouse was pulled down, exposing her breasts. A cloth gag had slipped from her mouth. One tall lanky American was standing behind her, holding her head back with a hand round her throat. A shorter stocky American stood stooped over her, holding a lighted cigarette close to her cheek.

Butler was on his feet in a flash. He brought the muzzle of his Walther down hard on the stocky American's nose. His target screamed with pain, dropped the cigarette. Tweed picked it up off the carpet.

At the same moment Newman reached the lanky American who reacted more quickly. He'd let go of Jennie, his hand had slid inside his jacket. Newman's left arm coiled round his neck from behind, squeezed his Adam's apple. The hard nails of his right hand dug into the back of the American's. There was a grunt of agony, a Luger dropped to the floor. Nield kicked the American's feet from under him and he sagged, gasping for breath.

Tweed had picked up the Luger as the stocky man had one hand over his damaged nose while his other hand fumbled inside his jacket. Tweed rammed the muzzle of the Luger into his abdomen, shook his head. The fumbling hand emerged empty. Tweed used his left hand to explore under the thug's armpit, gripped the butt of a weapon in a shoulder holster, withdrew it. Another Luger.

Everything had happened in a matter of seconds. The stocky man began to swear, using filthy words. Paula hit him across the mouth with her Browning, breaking teeth. He spat out blood.

'Mind your language,' she told him. 'There are ladies present. Any more of that and you know something? *All* your teeth will go.'

The stocky man glared at her with hatred as he took out a handkerchief, emptied two teeth and blood into it. He saw the expression in her eyes and looked away hastily.

By now Butler and Nield had the lanky American sprawled on the floor, face down. Butler checked him for weapons, found nothing more. As Newman administered the same treatment to the stocky man Tweed and Paula tended to Jennie. Butler handed Paula his clasp knife. She used it to remove the ropes round the victim's ankles and wrists while Tweed untied the gag. He could see no signs of burns on her.

'I'm going to ask you a silly question,' Tweed said and smiled. 'How are you feeling?'

'OK.' Jennie rubbed each wrist in turn. 'The fat one is Eddie, the tall one Hank.' She stood up and Paula stood close, ready to grab her, but she seemed quite steady. 'Do me a favour,' she requested. 'Get Eddie on his feet, two of you hold his arms tight.'

Puzzled, Butler went over to help Newman when Tweed had nodded to them. They hauled Eddie upright, held him tight by each arm. Paula had pulled up Jennie's blouse so she was decent. Her feet were clad in walking shoes. She walked forward slowly until she was within a few feet of the stocky man.

'Eddie is the sadist. Eddie enjoys his work.'

She picked up the burning cigarette Tweed had perched

in the lip of a clean ashtray. Flicking off the end of the ash, she faced the stocky man.

'Eddie likes giving people a bad time, *revels* in it.'

'Look, lady . . .' Eddie began.

Jennie stabbed the burning cigarette towards his face and he flinched. Tweed frowned, came close to her and whispered.

'Don't burn him. It would take you down to his level. And I won't permit it.'

She shook her head to indicate that wasn't what she had in mind. Her eyes were blazing at the stocky man, who was sweating profusely.

'Spread your feet, Eddie,' Jennie ordered. 'Or you get this cigarette smeared down your face.'

Eddie, mystified and frightened at the same time, stretched out his feet. Jennie moved. Her right leg arched up with all her strength. Paula was startled by the muscular power she displayed, then recalled she was a horse rider. She kicked her target in the groin. He groaned, gulped, gasped, bent over. Released by Newman and Butler, Eddie crouched on the floor, hands clasped to where her foot had contacted him.

'I like to settle my accounts,' Jennie said. 'Can we get out of here?' she asked Tweed.

'Of course. Now . . .'

As soon as she was inside his room she sank into a chair and broke down, sobbing endlessly.

'I've got a message for you to take back to your boss,' Newman told Hank and Eddie. 'You never come back here again. If I ever see either of your faces one more time you'll never leave Alsace alive. Get out . . .'

Newman was controlling a pent-up fury. Butler opened the door of the room and Hank walked out, one hand nursing his injured Adam's apple. Eddie had trouble

351

making his exit. Stooped over, he duck-waddled into the corridor. Butler closed the door and with Nield they began a quick search of the room. The most valuable treasure they found was an Uzi sub-machine-gun with plenty of ammo. They took these items with them.

Paula had accompanied Tweed and Jennie to his room. It had plenty of space, was like a small suite with the sitting area just inside the door and sleeping quarters beyond. After consulting Jennie, Paula had nipped down to the Brasserie and asked for a mug of milky coffee with plenty of sugar.

There was no sign of Eve or Gaunt. He was pretty bloody hopeless at looking after a woman, Paula thought as she carried the mug to the room. She'd tell him so when she next met him.

'Hold the mug in both hands,' she coaxed Jennie.

It was a wise precaution. Jennie's hands were shaking but with a little help from Paula she drank some of the liquid. She looked up gratefully.

'Thank you so much. I felt so damned cold.'

'That's shock,' said Tweed quietly. He was standing as he watched her. 'It will wear off. Drink it all if you can.'

'The *bastards*!' Jennie burst out after she had emptied the mug.

Tweed knew then she was recovering rapidly. He had the impression she had not only considerable physical powers but also great mental resilience. He waited while Paula sat beside her on a chair she'd pulled close.

'I'm feeling much better,' Jennie announced suddenly. 'Thanks to both of you. I suppose I shouldn't have done what I did to that punk, Eddie.'

'I'd have scratched his eyes out,' Paula assured her.

'Feel up to my asking a few questions?' Tweed enquired.

'Fire away!'

'What information were they trying to extract from you?'

'They wanted to know about a film and a tape. Seemed to think I knew where they were after my visit to the Château Noir. I told them I didn't know what the hell they were talking about, that kidnapping was a capital offence in France if anything happened to the victim. I made that last bit up – but as they were Americans I didn't think they'd know much about Europe. When I kept that up – which is true – that I didn't know what they were talking about, they turned very nasty. I was so lucky you got there just in time.'

'Did they know you'd driven with Gaunt to the château?' Tweed asked gently.

'Oh, they knew all right. I didn't tell them.'

'Did they mention Amberg?'

'Not a word. Just kept on about their flaming film and tape.'

'I see . . .'

Tweed saw more than she realized. To know of Gaunt's visit to Amberg the opposition had to have the Château Noir under close surveillance. It was valuable information, but disturbing. It meant the American apparatus had had no trouble tracking Amberg from Zurich to Basle and then to the Vosges.

'Any more questions?' Jennie asked. 'Anything I could help you with?'

'I don't think so,' Tweed replied. 'But you have been very helpful.'

'You're the ones who've been helpful. I'm more grateful than I can tell you. And now, I'm feeling a bit tired. I think a lie-down for a while would help.'

'Flop on the left-hand bed,' Tweed suggested. 'I'll see there's always someone in this room to guard you. If you could take over for a start, Paula? Thank you. The bathroom is through that door.'

'Do you think they'll try something else?' whispered

Paula as she accompanied him to the door into the corridor.

'Bound to,' he whispered back. 'And next time it's likely to be something pretty diabolical – worse than what they were going to do to Jennie. These aren't just barbaric thugs. They're top professionals.'

'So you two made a real balls-up,' Mencken commented.

It was a deliberately cruel remark in view of the fact that Eddie sat on a bed in Mencken's room, still nursing the injured part of his anatomy. He glared at Mencken, then looked quickly away. Mencken's eyes had all the soul of a python's.

Hank stretched his lanky frame, standing against a wall. He didn't like the remark, he didn't like Mencken. Who did?

'We'd have got it out of her if Tweed's troops hadn't burst in on us,' he protested.

'Troops?' Mencken sneered. 'I could strangle Tweed with two fingers. What else had you to deal with? Newman, a tabloid gossip gone to seed. Some broad. And another amateur.' He took out a cigar, lit it slowly, blew smoke in Hank's face. 'You two are straight out of Mickey Mouse. My old mom could have done a better job.'

'Didn't know you ever had one,' blazed Hank.

He regretted the insult the moment the words had left his mouth. Mencken had leapt out of his chair as though propelled by a spring. His skeletal head was inches from Hank's as he held the burning cigar end so close Hank could feel its heat on his face. Mencken projected two long talon-like fingers into Hank's painful Adam's apple.

'You said what?' Mencken asked.

'Sorry, boss.' Hank gulped. 'Sure we made a balls-up. Sure we did. Next time we'll do better,' he croaked.

'If there *is* a next time.' Mencken removed his hand,

puffed at his cigar as he stood back a couple of feet, the smoke getting into Hank's eyes. The lanky American licked his lips.

'Something we never got time to tell you, boss. There was a third man came into that room. Thought you should know.'

'So now I know.' Mencken continued staring at him, puffing the cigar. 'For Chrissakes, you mishandled it from the start. One of you should have been enough to deal with the twist . . .' Which was his flattering reference to Jennie Blade. 'If the other had stood guard with the Uzi you could have cut down the lot – including Tweed. Then taken the twist to your car, driven into the foothills, screwed the information out of her, then phoned me. That is how I'd have handled it.'

'The noise that sub-machine-gun would have made—' Hank began.

'Would have woken up the hotel,' Mencken interrupted. 'So you moved straight out of the hotel as I suggested. You blow a lot of smoke, Hank. You and Eddie never sat with us in the diner. We'd have been OK. No more crap.'

Mencken had decided Eddie and Hank were expendable. They were known now to Tweed and his team. He'd terminate that problem once they got up into the mountains. The phone rang. Mencken walked towards it with a slow deliberate pace, picked up the receiver. It was Norton.

The shaggy grey-haired man with half-moon glasses perched on his nose had to use the phone from his room. He had registered at the small hotel, L'Arbre Vert – the Green Tree – in Kaysersberg, as Harvey Cheney. There were no public phone boxes in this village.

'Norton here. Time you gave me a progress report. Watch any confidential information about our competitors – we're on open lines.'

'I visited that place you noticed where the product is stored, obtained sufficient samples. Get me?' Mencken rasped.

Norton got him – he had broken into the explosives shed near the stone quarry, had walked off with an ample supply. Mencken had moved fast, but Norton had no intention of congratulating him.

'What about the construction of the bridge? Have you surveyed it?'

For 'construction' Mencken understood 'destruction' of the hump-backed bridge in the centre of Kaysersberg.

'A team has examined it. Some blasting operation will be necessary. Long-distance work. Everything is prepared. Goddamnit! I know my job.'

Norton ignored the irritable outburst. Explosives had been placed under the bridge, waiting for Tweed's team to drive over it. The explosion would be detonated by someone who needed a good view of the target.

'Since it's a remote-control operation we need to have an observer at a distance but close enough to see the result.'

Mencken sighed audibly. 'That also has been worked out. All that we planned is arranged. OK? OK?'

Norton sensed resentment about his authority. That had to be stamped on immediately. Mencken must be in no doubt as to who was running the show.

'Then,' Norton went on remorselessly, 'there's the section of rock which has to be cleared. Have you attended to *that*?'

'Jesus! Why don't you come and hold my hand,' snarled Mencken. 'Yes, the rock is ready to come down. Now, if that's everything . . .'

There was silence at the other end of the line. Mencken had just confirmed that the rock above the cliff looming over the road had been drilled, explosives inserted. He had sent up two men per team on a roster basis.

He had hired plenty of transport in Basle, had drawn

356

up a roster of men, giving them their objectives as soon as he had returned from the café in Little Venice after talking with Norton through the lace curtain.

'You'll have to do something about your manners,' Norton said eventually, very abrasive. 'Talk to me like that just once more and you're on the first plane back to the States. I'll take over the operation myself. Imagine what will be waiting for you when you leave the aircraft. I trust, Marvin,' the voice continued softly, 'you do have some imagination?'

Mencken froze. Fury gave way to fear. Yes, he knew what would be waiting for him. A limo with an open window and the muzzle of a gun aimed point blank.

'I'm trying to do my best for you. No one is going to let you down. Maybe I was a little bitchy. Everything is under control. It will be a breeze . . .'

'No, it won't, sonny boy. Get that into your thick skull. Our competitor, Tweed, is a barracuda. Don't you ever forget that. Sonny boy . . .'

The phone went dead. Mencken kept his face to the wall so his men couldn't see his expression, a mixture of fright and rage. He was careful not to slam down the phone. Glancing down at his cigar, he saw that a length of ash had dropped on to the floor. He ground it savagely into the new carpet. When Tweed was blown into a thousand pieces he'd be top gun. And when Joel Dyson and Special Agent Barton Ives raised their heads above the parapet he'd personally put the bullets into both of them. Then he'd take out Cord Dillon.

Norton wandered out of the small hotel into the dark and paused. Snow had begun to fall. He adjusted his fur hat, pulled up the collar of his astrakhan coat. It was bitingly cold, well below zero, he reckoned. He began to stroll back into Kaysersberg – the Green Tree was located on

357

the northern outskirts. No one else was in sight.

Norton had no eye for the beauty and character of the medieval village with its cobbled streets and leaning houses. Disneyland, he thought contemptuously.

A few minutes later he saw the bridge. He paused and studied it. Glancing up to his left he saw an ancient castle looming over the village – the perfect vantage point for the watcher who would control the detonation of the explosive under the bridge. Norton had a strong feeling this was the route Tweed would choose. He'd never even see the Château Noir. He turned back to the hotel. He was expecting a call from Bradford March. He had already informed Sara of his new phone number.

37

'We must prepare a battle plan for our expedition into the Vosges,' Tweed announced. 'Especially after what Philip has reported, which is alarming.'

He was standing in the sitting area of his bedroom. It was nearly midnight. When he had slipped down several hours before to put back the master key the hotel had been deserted.

Jennie had woken earlier, and said she wanted to go back to her own room for a shower. Nield had been selected to go with her to sit in the room on guard. Jennie had been secretly pleased with the choice. She rather liked the look of the slim Pete Nield with his trim moustache. He could be fun.

Paula sat on one of the beds, hands rested on the coverlet on either side, her legs crossed. Newman, Butler,

Cardon and Marler listened. The latter, adopting his usual stance, leaned against a wall, smoking a king-size. The others occupied various chairs.

Marler had arrived back recently, carrying his cello case, cricket bag and a suitcase. He had carefully placed his wares in a corner.

'You'd like some sustenance?' Tweed had asked him. 'We got the Brasserie to prepare sandwiches and coffee in a Thermos.'

'Thank you. Might indulge later. I stopped for a snack on the way back from Strasbourg,' Marler had replied.

'What alarming news did Philip bring?' Paula asked. 'I was in the bathroom when he came in.'

'Philip,' Tweed told them, 'was observing comings and goings from a discreet position off the lobby. He told me he'd seen at least six pairs of Americans leaving the hotel at intervals. He heard cars starting up and all of them were a long time before they returned, again at intervals. I find those movements ominous.'

'Why?' pressed Paula.

'Butler,' Tweed continued, 'took over from Philip. He also reported pairs of Americans returning late in the evening. They had snow on their boots.'

'Why ominous?' Paula persisted.

'First, because I'm convinced that Norton – the man who impersonated Ives, I'm sure, at the Gotthard – is the evil genius behind the huge apparatus brought over here from the States.'

'Evil genius?' drawled Marler. 'A bit strong that, isn't it?'

'Is it?' Tweed looked grim. 'I told you how convincingly he bluffed us when he turned up at the Gotthard. Then when he ran for it he left behind a present for me. Prussic acid in my mouthwash. And that trap he had organized in Bahnhofstrasse. The fake cripple with the grenade – backed up by a second man with a machine-pistol. Norton is a top pro. I'm not making the mistake of underestimating him.'

'And the second point?' Cardon enquired.

'Those Americans who have been away from the hotel this evening for hours. Some returning with snow on their boots. I think they've studied the routes up into the Vosges to the Château Noir.'

'I think so, too,' Newman agreed. 'And God knows what booby traps they've prepared for us – whichever of the routes we use.'

'So we must outmanoeuvre them,' Tweed went on. 'First we should list our resources. Yes, Harry,' he said, addressing Butler.

'Pete Nield and I brought in some useful transport. First, a Renault Espace V6, a spacious vehicle. I drove that and carried a couple of high-powered motorbikes inside it. Pete Nield hired a station wagon. We crossed the frontier into France without trouble. No one tried to search us. We could have taped our handguns under the chassis.'

'Anyone like to see my contribution?' enquired Marler.

Unfastening the cello case he had placed on the bed next to Paula, he raised the lid, removed the bow and then the black velvet cloth. Paula glanced at the contents, dropped off the bed, walked to the other bed and perched on it.

'If you don't mind,' she snapped at Marler. 'That little collection looks lethal.'

'Oh, very!' Marler assured her and grinned.

The men all gathered round the cello case. Cardon gave a yelp of delight.

'Grenades! Could I borrow six of those?'

'Which means I don't get them back,' Marler commented in mock annoyance. 'Help yourself.'

'I'll relieve you of the Luger,' Butler suggested. 'It makes a good back-up for a Walther.'

'Go ahead,' Marler told him. 'The Armalite is mine, of course. And I'm hanging on to the tear-gas pistol.'

'Like to see my contribution to the arsenal?' Newman suggested.

Fetching a canvas hold-all he'd dumped in a corner he unzipped it. When he produced the Uzi sub-machine-gun Paula stared.

'Are we thinking of starting a small war?' she asked.

'Which is just what the chap who supplied me with my toys said,' Marler recalled.

'We're well equipped,' Tweed decided. 'Put it all away. Now we must decide how we move into the mountains when the time comes. Which may be tomorrow. I have to talk to Amberg urgently – while he's still alive.'

'I could ride ahead of the cars on one of those motorbikes,' Cardon suggested. 'I can sniff danger a mile away.'

'Agreed,' said Tweed. 'Next suggestion . . .'

They spent less than half an hour working out the details of a convoy which would make its way up to the Château Noir. Cardon would be the advance scout on his motorcycle. He would travel ahead of the large Espace which Newman would drive, with Tweed and Paula as passengers.

Butler would ride the second motorcycle, was given a 'roving' duty to travel back and forth along the well-spaced-out convoy – well spaced to make a smaller target.

Nield would drive the station wagon, sometimes behind the Espace, sometimes ahead of it. A tactic which should confuse the opposition, if they were waiting for them.

That left Marler, who insisted on driving his red Mercedes. Tweed was doubtful of the wisdom of this, pointed out its colour could be spotted a long distance up in the mountains.

'I realize that,' Marler commented. 'But it moves like a bird. That's what I'll be driving.'

'Then we've worked out an action plan,' Tweed concluded. 'Time you all went to bed, got some sleep. Harry, do you mind relieving Pete Nield, who's watching over Jennie? Fix up with Bob when he'll take over guard duty from you . . .'

'All this sounds like an assault force attacking the Château Noir,' Paula said to Tweed as everyone except Marler left the room.

'It may be just that,' Tweed warned her. 'If Norton has already taken over the place before we arrive.'

'I won't be coming with you,' Marler told Tweed when Paula was the only other person still in the room.

Tweed listened as Marler told him about his visit to the glider airfield at the Ballon d'Alsace. Paula was appalled, thought that Marler's plan sounded like a suicide trip, said so.

'I'm touched that you should worry about my welfare.' He grinned. 'Don't worry. I had a Met forecast over the radio on my way back from Strasbourg. Wind direction is perfect. A southerly – blow me north. Tweed, you'll have a spy in the sky above the château. Cost you a bomb if I crash the bird landing.'

'We'll find the money, I suppose.'

'And the glider will act rather like a flying bomb – if Norton's thugs are crawling round in the area.'

'We go into the mountains tomorrow, then?' Paula asked.

'Yes,' Tweed replied. 'I've decided not to delay. Amberg may be in great danger. We'll go via Kaysersberg.'

'Jolly good.' Marler gave Paula a little salute. 'Get to bed now. I'll be up at crack of dawn. For *Der Tag*.'

*   *   *

Norton had returned to the Green Tree, satisfied that the bridge was a perfect ambush location – if Tweed chose the Kaysersberg route. He took off his fur hat and astrakhan coat in the entrance hall, shook off the snow, went up the staircase to his room.

As he inserted his key he heard the phone ringing inside. Once in the room, he slammed the door shut, locked it and hurried to the phone. He had no doubt it was the President calling yet again.

'A call for you,' the hotel operator informed him and he heard the click as she went off the line.

'Norton here.'

'Good evening to you, Mr Norton,' a hoarse growly voice said. 'You will know who has given me your number. Now please be so good as to listen carefully to my instructions. If you really want the film and the tape.'

'Who is this?' grated Norton.

'Are you deaf? I told you to listen. One more comment and I go off the line. Have you got that?'

'Yes,' Norton replied with great reluctance. He was used to giving orders, not receiving them.

'You will drive to Lac Noir in the Vosges tomorrow, arriving there at sixteen hundred hours. Since you are American that is four o'clock in the afternoon . . .'

'I damn well know that . . .'

'One more interruption and this call ceases. Someone in Washington would not be pleased with you. The *patron* of the Green Tree, where you are staying, will show you on a map how to reach Lac Noir. Tell him you want to arrive at four and he will tell you when you must start. Have you understood me so far?'

The growly voice purred with menace. Even Norton, who thought he had experienced everything, was disturbed. He was careful with his reply.

'Yes, I have understood you.'

'Lac Noir – the Black Lake – is a lonely place. It is also

easy to observe from many points. You will bring the money and you will come alone. I said *alone*. If you bring anyone else we will never meet. I will show you the film, play the first section of the tape. You will give me the money. The exchange will be completed.'

Norton instantly saw his chance to manipulate the arrangement to suit his own purpose. His tone was dominant and grim.

'OK so far. But hell, you think I have that kind of dough in my back pocket? Because I haven't. It's in a safe place under heavy guard. I might be able to bring it up to you by six in the evening. No earlier. In any case, I want proof you have the items I need. So now you'll listen to me – if you want that dough. Or, to use your own words, we'll never meet. Six o'clock,' he repeated emphatically.

'Washington isn't going to like this at all . . .'

At this point Norton knew he had Growly Voice on the defensive for the first time. He hadn't broken off the call. He hadn't refused the later time of six o'clock Norton had laid down. Keep up the pressure, Norton told himself, and barked into the phone: 'Screw Washington. You can tell them I said that. I am the guy in charge of this operation. I am on the spot. I know where the money is. You're dealing with me? Get it? Just me. I'll be at the Black Lake at six o'clock in the evening tomorrow. All on my ownsome. And since presumably you're a European, six o'clock is eighteen hundred hours. Good night . . .'

Norton slammed down the phone before the voice at the other end could respond. He lit a cigar, dwelling with satisfaction on how he'd turned the tables on Growly Voice. Four in the afternoon it was still daylight, but by six it was black as pitch. The blackmailer was going to get a very nasty surprise tomorrow. And the timing fitted in with eliminating Tweed and his team if they went up into the mountains – they were bound to choose daylight hours. The big bucks were safe, too. Maybe he could clean up the whole operation by this time tomorrow evening. He took another puff at his cigar, a choice Havana. Banned in the States – just because it came from Cuba.

Twenty million dollars is a lot of money to have suspended from a chain attached to your right-hand wrist. Louis Sheen still had the chain linking his wrist with the brown suitcase containing the fortune in US banknotes. From his room in the Basle Hilton he had been transported by car across the frontier to the Hôtel Bristol in Colmar.

His room, on the first floor, was probably the most heavily guarded area in Alsace-Lorraine. At all times three armed men occupied the room with him. Sheen was beginning to get fed up with room service. He peered at Mencken who had just been let into the room, glared at him through his rimless glasses.

'Look, Marvin, there are too many scumbags infesting this room. If I have to stay here a night longer I want them cleared out. You think I enjoy trying to sleep with this case as a bedmate? Because I don't.'

Mencken stroked a finger down the side of his long pointed jaw. Through half-closed eyes he studied Sheen with an expression which hardly radiated liking or sympathy. He spoke throatily as he made his casual suggestion.

'You've got the keys to unlock those steel cuffs hidden somewhere. Must have for when the time comes to hand over the billion dollars. So why not unlock the cuff on your wrist? No one can fool with trying to open the case. You're the only one who knows the code for those combination locks. Anyone who did try fooling around would end up igniting the thermite bomb inside – burning the money to a crisp, probably themselves, too.'

'I have my instructions,' Sheen snapped. 'And they

365

come from a far higher source than you'll ever meet, let alone reach.'

Sheen, wearing a grey Brooks Brothers suit, was an accountant by training. He felt himself superior in intellect and class to these people. It was just unfortunate he had to spend time in such bad company. This attitude was not lost on Mencken. He leaned his face close to Sheen, who sat on the bed, propped against pillows, the case next to him.

'I'm Marvin to a few good friends,' he informed Sheen. 'But you don't come into that category. So, in future it's Mr Mencken. I'm the boss. OK?'

'Makes no difference to me,' Sheen retorted in a bored tone. 'And the boss is Norton. He's the only one who can tell me to release what's inside this case.'

'You listen to me.' Mencken's expression had become ugly. 'These men are here to protect your worthless hide. They heard you call them scumbags – so if that door burst open and the Marines arrived, just how much enthusiasm do you think they'd have protecting you?'

'*You* were ordered to protect me. You must have a good idea how high up that order came from. And the amount in this case is not a billion. You know that. Now, go away and put these men outside in the corridor.'

Sheen's eyes gazed contemptuously at Mencken from behind the rimless glasses. Mencken shoved the fingers of both hands inside his belt. At last Sheen had given him an opening to hit back at the creep.

'Listen, buddy boy, you know this is a hotel, that we're keeping you under cover. So what the hell do you think it would look like if I put the three scumbags – wasn't that the word you used? – outside your door in the hotel corridor? I've got news for you, Sheen. You look after the dough, I'll look after everything else. Sleep well, buddy boy . . .'

Mencken left the room which was immediately locked

again from the inside. The secret order from Norton gave him a big kick. When the case had eventually been opened, the thermite bomb removed, at the first opportunity Mencken had personally to shoot Louis Sheen in the head and dispose of the body. He couldn't wait for that happy moment.

Prior to going to bed, Newman had gone into the Brasserie to buy a large bottle of mineral water. He often woke up in the middle of the night feeling parched. They were cleaning up in the Brasserie as he entered, sweeping floors, wiping the counter, polishing glasses. Newman was surprised to see Eve Amberg nursing a glass of champagne at a table. She raised her glass to him.

'What's the celebration in aid of?' he enquired, accepting her invitation to join her.

'Victory! I've pinned down Walter Amberg. He's agreed on the phone to see me at the Château Noir tomorrow morning. This time I won't leave till I get all the money which is mine. Hence the champers. Come on, Bob. Join me in my celebration.' She summoned a waiter, ordered a glass before Newman could protest. Worried, when the waiter had brought his glass, he tried to think of how to get her to delay her visit.

'Cheers, Bob!' Eve clinked his glass. 'Wish me luck up at the château.'

Even at this hour she was full of energy and the enthusiasm he found so infectious. She leaned her head on his shoulder, her long titian mane draped over his jacket, face turned sideways so her greenish eyes could study him. I could fall for this woman if I don't watch it, Newman told himself.

He was worried that if Eve went up into the mountains tomorrow she could easily drive into an area where the guns were firing. Because the guns *would* be firing –

Newman was convinced of this. Norton would exploit all the advantages of the mountain terrain to annihilate Tweed and his team. He'd already tried to wipe them out on a smaller scale in Zurich's Bahnhofstrasse, plus the memory of how he himself had just been saved by Beck's police car from being run down in Basle. Eve was stroking his hand when he spoke.

'Amberg has been very difficult with you recently – he's deliberately avoided you. Now he's agreed graciously to receive you into the presence, shouldn't you play hard to get? Throw him off balance – phone him tomorrow morning and say you'll be driving up to see him the following day.'

'You don't know Walter like I do. I appreciate what you suggested. With many men it would work. Not with Walter. He's more stubborn than a mule. Now I've pressured him into seeing me I must grab my chance. He may have decided to pay me off to get rid of me. You only get one chance with Walter—' She broke off and, her head still resting on Newman's shoulder, stared at the newcomer who had entered the Brasserie by the short cut. It was Tweed.

'We're celebrating!' Eve greeted Tweed buoyantly. 'Champers for you. Drink to my successful trip tomorrow.'

The waiter had already arrived with a fresh glass of champagne. Tweed waved it aside, asked for a glass of Riesling.

'Helps me to sleep,' he explained amiably to Eve. 'It's the only wine I really like – so being in Alsace I'm making the most of it. Thank you,' he said to the waiter, raised his glass, stared at Eve who was eyeing him sideways. 'So what are we celebrating at this late hour?'

Newman explained Eve's plans, emphasizing that he'd

tried to persuade her to wait for twenty-four hours. Tweed grasped at once Newman's motive in attempting to delay her visit. While listening to the explanation Eve stared fixedly at Tweed, her full lips moving slightly. It was a situation not unfamiliar to Tweed – an attractive woman who liked to flirt, who pretended to be interested in one man while she took aim at her real target. In this case, he suspected, himself.

To Newman's surprise Tweed made no attempt to back up his failed argument to stop Eve driving to the Château Noir tomorrow – almost today now. Sipping his Riesling, Tweed held Eve's inviting gaze and then took a view which infuriated Newman.

'I think you're right to keep the appointment with Amberg. It's taken long enough to track him down. What time are you to meet him?'

'Eleven in the morning. He even said he might provide lunch since there wasn't anywhere else to eat near the château. I accepted.'

'You were surprised when he suggested lunch?' enquired Tweed.

'Very. I've never taken to Walter and assumed it was a mutual feeling. I'm beginning to think maybe it could be pure shyness where women are concerned. Perhaps I'm due for a pleasant shock tomorrow.'

'Don't bank on it,' Newman told her sharply.

'What a pessimist Bob is.' Eve raised her head from his shoulder. Smoothing down her hair, she leaned over the table to where Tweed faced her, grasped his hand. 'Do you object to my driving up to see Walter in the morning?'

'Why should I? Because of the ice and snow the roads are very dangerous, I gather. And very low temperatures during the night won't help. But you must make up your own mind.'

'Then I shall be going, so I suppose I'd better get up to bed.'

Tweed noted she moved very steadily as she came round the end of the table, bent down, kissed him on the cheek. Her hair brushed the side of his face, giving him a tingling sensation.

'Thank you, Tweed. For your moral support.' She turned her gaze on Newman. 'As for you, Mr Pessimist, have a nice day – as the pathetic Americans are always saying.' She gave him a little wave, a wry smile and disappeared into the hotel.

'What the devil are you up to?' Newman burst out when they were alone. 'All hell is liable to break loose on those mountain slopes tomorrow . . .'

'I agree,' Tweed interjected amiably, then finished off his wine.

'Every conceivable weapon could be used against us,' Newman raved on, keeping his voice down. 'So why send Eve into a battlefield?'

'You'd managed to persuade her not to go then?'

'Well, not exactly . . .'

'Be frank. Didn't she refuse point blank to take any notice of your attempt to get her to change her mind?'

'Yes, she did,' Newman admitted.

'I sensed this as soon as I arrived. Eve is a woman of great character, of exceptional willpower. By agreeing with her, I made her sympathetic to me. There is a faint chance – no more – that when she recalls what I said about the dangerous roads she'll change her mind.'

'So why do I get the feeling you're conducting some very devious manoeuvre?' Newman demanded. 'And what time do you plan we reach the Château Noir?'

'Not long after eleven in the morning – when Eve Amberg has arrived there, if she makes the trip.'

38

Paula tapped on Tweed's door at seven the following morning. He called out for her to come in and she found him in the bathroom, shirt collar open as he stood before a mirror shaving.

'Should I come back later?' she suggested. 'You ought to be able to get ready in peace.'

'You've seen a man shaving before today. Sit down while I talk. I need a sounding-board about this whole business – going right back to the massacre at Tresillian Manor.'

'Fire away.' She perched on the edge of the unused bed. 'I'm listening with all my ears, as the French say, and we are in France.'

'So far I have assumed that the same people who blew up our Park Crescent HQ also perpetrated the hideous massacre at Gaunt's manor. You were always sceptical.'

'Yes, I know. Maybe I underestimated the enormous power of the apparatus we're up against.'

'I'm wondering now if *I* gave them a little too much credit for almost superhuman organization – synchronizing the two events.' He wiped soap off his face, cleaned his brush and razor. 'It *would* require truly superhuman planning – to blow up our HQ in London and then commit the massacre all within a few hours.' Tweed's tone sharpened as he put on his tie. 'I honestly don't now believe such timing was possible, that it happened that way. They wouldn't have the information in time – that Amberg was at the manor and that Joel Dyson had deposited copies of the film and the tape with us. Not enough time to organize both the massive car bomb and the massacre way down in Cornwall.'

Paula frowned as she snapped her compact shut after checking her appearance behind Tweed's back. She stared at him as he put on his jacket.

'What you are suggesting contradicts all our theories.'

'*My* wrong theories.' Tweed folded his arms on the back of an upholstered chair and stared down at her. 'It came to me in the middle of the night when I couldn't sleep. I've assumed I was trying to assemble the pieces of a single complex jigsaw. Now I'm sure that there are *two* jigsaws.'

'Help!' said Paula in mock confusion. 'I don't think I could cope with that. Two *separate* jigsaws?'

'No, it's far more diabolical than that. These two jigsaws interlock. To put it simply, one couldn't exist without the other.'

'Simply? If you say so.'

'Paula, it all started with Joel Dyson flying in from the States with a film and a tape. Whatever is recorded on those two items is so earth-shattering that an army of top professionals flies in after Dyson. Those pieces of the jigsaw fit. One jigsaw so far.'

'And these cold-blooded professionals – killers – are all American,' she pointed out.

'True. Ponder that and you might get a glimmer as to who is behind the apparatus controlled by Norton. I admit the idea is world-shaking. Want to guess who?'

'No idea. Go on.'

'Maybe we should have breakfast . . .' Tweed began.

'Let it wait a bit. I want to hear more,' Paula urged him on. 'I sense you've had a mental breakthrough.'

'Let's call the American apparatus Goliath. They track Dyson to Park Crescent, assume – correctly – that he's left the film and tape with us, although they don't know they're copies. Goliath organizes the massive car bomb to destroy the film and tape. Still with Jigsaw One.'

'What about Jigsaw Two?'

'I'm now convinced the massacre at Tresillian Manor was carried out by someone else. Let's borrow Jennie Blade's Shadow Man. He knows Dyson flew on to Zurich with the copies of the film and the tape—'

'Assumption,' Paula objected. 'How do you know that?'

'It's the only sequence of events which explains the new theory I've developed, which I'm sure is the right one. Do let me finish. Shadow Man has to be someone who knows the Ambergs – and therefore knew what Dyson had left with them. He has to be someone who knows the Ambergs,' he repeated, 'because he knew Amberg would be at Tresillian Manor on the day of the massacre. Those two items are worth a fortune – proved by the tremendous efforts the Americans are making to get them back, to eliminate anyone who might know about their existence. Am I going too fast?'

'No. I'm beginning to get ahead of you. Shadow Man wants to lay his hands on film and tape, wants the fortune they could bring him.'

'So, logically, he plans and carries out the massacre at Tresillian Manor. His real target was, of course, Amberg.'

'Why?' Paula enquired.

'Because he knows he can handle the more passive twin – Walter. He also knows he'd never get Julius to release them to him. Solution? Murder Julius. Which leaves the weak Walter to obtain the film and tape from. Hence the two interlocking jigsaws – and the fact that one couldn't exist without the other.'

'I do see what you mean now. Whatever happened in America created a chain reaction among a lot of people.'

'Which is why I insist the two jigsaws are linked like

identical twins.' Tweed gazed into the distance out of the window. The sun shone on steeply slanting rooftops. 'What we need to do is to get hold of that film, see what is on it, and listen to the tape. Which is what I'm going to demand from Amberg when we reach the Château Noir today. He must have hidden them somewhere, may even be carrying them around with him. Now, breakfast.'

'Just before we go down, we have a problem,' Paula warned. 'It's called Jennie Blade. Somehow she's found out we're going up into the Vosges this morning. She insists on coming with us. I argued but got nowhere. She's scared stiff of the Shadow Man.'

'Let Gaunt take care of her,' Tweed said, grasping the door handle. 'She's his girl friend.'

'Gaunt has driven off early this morning in his BMW. He had Eve with him. She didn't look too happy with him. I saw Gaunt heading off towards the Vosges and Eve had her chin up, staring fixedly away from him.'

'I can guess what that was about,' Tweed remarked and smiled wrily. 'Eve wanted to go up to see Amberg at the Château Noir on her own and Gaunt – dominating as ever – bullied her into going with him. He may have made a mistake. Eve can handle even Gaunt if push comes to shove. And we can't be lumbered on this trip with Jennie.'

'Better tell Jennie yourself. Oh, I waved off Marler when he drove away at dawn on his way to the Ballon d'Alsace.'

'Why were you up at that hour?'

Tweed had paused, still holding the door handle. He had not yet unlocked the door while he waited for her reply.

'Couldn't sleep,' Paula told him. 'Something someone said was important and I can't recall it. Got up in the middle of the night, had a shower, got dressed, went downstairs. Which is how I saw Marler before he left for that gliding school. I had an early breakfast, then saw Eve leaving with Gaunt. But I'll join you for more coffee. This is going to be a rough ride up into the Vosges, isn't it? I found all the Americans had checked out early.'

'Yes, it will be a very rough ride up to the heights of the Château Noir,' Tweed warned her.

Tweed and Paula did not breakfast alone in the Brasserie. They had hardly sat down and ordered continental breakfast when Jennie Blade appeared. Clad in ski pants tucked into ankle boots, a white woollen polo-necked sweater which emphasized her figure, and carrying a sheepskin, she sat down at their table, facing Tweed.

'May I join you?'

She gave him a ravishing smile and nodded to Paula who stared back at her without comment.

'You just did,' Tweed pointed out.

'I hope I'm not interrupting an intimate tête-à-tête,' she went on, glancing again at Paula.

'Hardly, at breakfast time,' Tweed replied drily.

'I hear you're driving up into the mountains today. You know' – she gave him her most beguiling smile – 'I couldn't sleep a wink last night – I couldn't get out of my mind my experience with that Shadow Man in the fog. So, please, please, take me with you. You could come back and find me dead.'

'Anything is possible,' Tweed agreed neutrally.

'Then that's settled, you'll take me up there with you – and with you by my side I'll feel perfectly safe, Tweed.'

'Paula is likely to be by my side.' He drank the coffee a waiter had appeared with as though by magic, which Paula had then poured. 'Space will be at a premium,' he said.

'What is the premium you would like me to pay?' Jennie shook her golden mane off her shoulder, gazing at

Tweed with an expression which made Paula grit her teeth. 'I will pay in any currency you specify,' she went on suggestively.

'How about Hungarian forints?' Paula snapped.

'I am asking Mr Tweed,' Jennie said politely, not looking in Paula's direction. 'Seriously, it was a horrible experience last night. And the Met forecast is for more fog this evening. That's when he appears – the Shadow Man. I won't be any trouble. I'll do exactly what you tell me to do – or not to do.' Her voice trembled. 'Please. Oh, please, Tweed. Let me come with you.'

'If I let you,' Tweed said grimly, 'you will obey orders from the word go.' He held up a hand. 'No more protestations. I've laid down the conditions. No more to say.'

Inwardly Paula swore as she savagely piled butter on her croissant. You wily, conniving little devil, she said to herself. What surprised her most was that Tweed had fallen for Jennie's feminine tactics. Or had he? She glanced at Tweed and he looked back without any expression.

Brilliant sunshine reflected off the snow which had descended on Colmar overnight. Tweed screwed up his eyes against the glare of the strong light as he walked alone outside the main entrance to the Bristol. He was waiting for Newman to drive the Espace from where it had been parked overnight.

Locals were hurrying to work. A girl slipped on a patch of invisible ice beneath the snow and Tweed saved her, grabbing her arm. She peered at him gratefully from beneath her hood. '*Merci!*' With her hair concealed under the hood, a scarf pulled up over her chin and drainpipe trousers protruding from under a long padded wind-cheater Tweed had briefly mistaken her for a man.

As he stood near the kerb a large man wearing a hood

with earmuffs and a long heavy trench coat brushed against him. Tweed stiffened as a strong hand gripped his arm.

'Now don't get alarmed, old chum. I've waited for ever for you to come out. Important development . . .'

The American twang was distinctive. Cord Dillon's voice. Tweed stood quite still, clapping his gloved hands together as though feeling the cold. He spoke without looking at the American, his lips hardly moving.

'From now on we must keep in close contact. You can phone me at the hotel after nine in the evening. What is the important development?'

'Special Agent Barton Ives is near by. Wants to talk with you. The recognition signal will be a Union Jack, your national flag.'

'Describe him to me again, briefly . . .'

'About my height. Much slimmer build. Thick black hair. Now clean-shaven. Aged thirty-seven. Strong Anglo-Saxon features. Ice-blue eyes. He'll find you when it's OK. This place is crawling with watchers – hostile.'

'Ives will be taking a chance unless he's careful,' Tweed warned.

'He's careful. He's FBI. Was. Be in touch . . .'

Tweed was still clapping his gloves together in a slow rhythm as Newman arrived with the Espace, punctuating his thoughts. Was one of the two key men in this crisis – Barton Ives and Joel Dyson – really going to contact him? If so how? He wished he'd told Dillon they were on their way into the mountains. Paula walked briskly out of the hotel. It was no surprise that close on her heels Jennie Blade, clad in sheepskin, hurried up to the vehicle.

Tweed wondered if Jennie would have been so eager to join them if she'd known what was facing them during the long climb into the even more heavily snowbound mountains.

39

'We're being followed already,' Newman commented as he drove the grey Espace along the snow-covered road across the plain below the foothills rising in the near distance.

'The big cream Citroën, you mean?' Tweed suggested.

'That's the bastard.' Newman glanced over his shoulder to where Jennie sat. 'Excuse my French but if you had any idea this would be a holiday outing you're in for a very big surprise.'

The Renault Espace V6 was a spacious vehicle which could easily seat six people in three rows. Its large curved snout reminded Paula, seated next to Tweed, of a shark. Tweed occupied the middle seat with Newman on his left. In the row behind them Jennie, huddled in her sheepskin, was curled up like a cat on her seat.

Butler, clad in leathers with a large helmet, had passed them riding a Harley-Davidson and was leading the convoy as it drew closer to Kaysersberg. A distance behind them Nield drove the station wagon with his Walther tucked under a cushion on the front passenger seat.

Philip Cardon, astride his own motorcycle, roared past them, then slowed as his eyes kept swivelling from side to side. The Citroën shadowing them had so far kept well back from Nield's station wagon.

'Why should anyone follow us?' called out Jennie.

'Presumably to see where we're going,' Paula snapped without bothering to turn her head.

'Why would they want to do that?' Jennie persisted.

'So when we skid they can see in time the dangerous stretches of the road,' Paula snapped again. 'Could we possibly have a little quiet so the driver can concentrate? Also I'm checking a map. We're coming into Kaysersberg very shortly,' she warned Newman. 'I can see the old buildings on the outskirts.'

'I'm not worried at all about us skidding,' Jennie went on. 'Bob is a marvellous driver. You should have more confidence in him.'

Paula's eyes blazed as she checked the map again. So far as she was concerned Jennie Blade was spare luggage which could be dumped by the roadside at any time. Tweed, seeing her expression, was secretly amused. He was also suspicious.

Jennie's air of naïvety was just a little too innocent and he was certain she was baiting Paula. Cardon returned on his motorcycle, made a gesture for them to slow down. Newman responded immediately, saw Cardon perform a highly skilled U-turn in the snow, then come racing back, speeding up as he overtook them.

'We shall soon be inside Kaysersberg,' Paula warned again. 'Which probably means we'll have to crawl.'

'Presenting a slow-moving target,' Newman commented.

The ancient buildings of the medieval gem closed round them on both sides as Newman reduced speed to little more than walking pace. Paula stared with admiration at the antique buildings, many with wooden cross-beams buried in the plaster walls and slanting at crazy angles.

'This is wonderful,' she enthused. 'It reeks of character, of the Middle Ages. And look at that hump-backed bridge . . .'

Standing by himself in an alley-way midway inside Kaysersberg, the man wearing a fur hat and an astrakhan coat held a mobile phone to his ear. The aerial was extended as he peered at the bridge through his half-moon glasses and listened to the report from another mobile phone inside the cream Citroën.

'Our main competitor is aboard the grey Espace,' the driver reported. 'Plus a man and two women.'

'Maintain your present position,' Norton ordered. 'Keep well back. I'm talking about survival . . .'

He slid the aerial back inside the phone. Once the Espace started to cross that bridge it was the end of Tweed. One mission accomplished. Château Noir next.

'Brake!' Tweed ordered. 'Stop this vehicle at once.'

Newman obeyed immediately, sat behind the wheel with the engine ticking over. Cardon was approaching on his motorcycle. Newman was mystified by Tweed's sudden command.

'What is this in aid of? The pause?' he enquired.

'Something about that bridge I don't like. If I were planning an ambush – and ruthlessly, didn't care tuppence about innocent civilian casualties – that bridge would be the death-trap.'

'I think we may have a problem,' Cardon said, speaking through the open window, straddled on his machine. 'I suggest you don't proceed any further until Butler and I have spied out the lie of the land. OK?'

'What triggered off this mood of caution?' Tweed asked.

'There's an old castle perched up just behind these old houses. Anyone located on top has a perfect view of the bridge and any vehicle crossing it. Harry and I saw at least one man at the summit of the keep – with what looked like a rifle in his hands. I'm going to check under the bridge, Harry takes the castle. Sit tight.'

'Look! A lovely cat . . .'

Before Tweed could stop her Paula had opened the door, jumped out and was walking briskly behind Cardon who was approaching the bridge on foot, leaving his motorbike leaning against the Espace. There was a large fat cat on the parapet of the bridge and Tweed knew she was fond of cats. But he also noticed she had undone the flap of her shoulder-bag next to her hip. Inside was an easily accessible pocket which had been specially designed to take her .32 Browning.

Tweed watched as Paula, clad in a padded windcheater and ski pants tucked into leather boots with rubber soles, strode confidently on to the bridge. Any watcher was unlikely to suspect her of being anything but a ski-season tourist.

She picked up the heavily furred cat which was coffee-coloured with white 'stockings' and a white chest. She glanced around as it purred at her attentions and saw the swiftly moving figure of Harry Butler disappearing below the looming castle. Cardon had referred to a 'keep' and this was a great round tower rearing up above the rest of the edifice. She nipped one of the ears of the cat which protested, prepared to leap out of her arms. She aimed it over the edge of the parapet on to the snow-covered bank at the edge of the frozen stream.

Cardon, seeing the opportunity she'd provided, lowered himself over the stone wall as though in pursuit of the animal. Agilely, Paula dropped over the wall, followed him under the bridge. The cat perched on a snowbound rock at the far end of the arch, glaring at them. Cardon raised a warning hand.

Paula followed the direction of his pointing finger. An explosives expert, Cardon recognized lethal hardware. Attached by ropes to ancient iron rings in the centre of the arch was suspended a large metal plate supporting a large number of what appeared to Paula to be Roman-candle type fireworks.

'Dynamite sticks,' Cardon commented. 'That collection adds up to one big bomb, powerful enough to blast the stone bridge and any vehicle on it sky-high.'

'It can hardly work by pressure of a vehicle crossing the bridge,' Paula mused. She was scared stiff and kept talking to conceal her reaction. 'Otherwise a farm wagon could have set it off at any time.'

'Correct,' Cardon agreed. 'A bit diabolical this one. See that grey cable running from the bomb to the other end of the arch near where the cat is? Butler, who has a nasty mind, scraped away snow from the base of one of the old buildings near the climb to the castle. He found more of that cable. The snow kept people indoors last night, now it's concealing the cable this morning.'

'Where does the cable end? Can we cut it?'

'My guess is that if we did it would blow us sky-high. It runs to the top of the castle keep – where someone watching can press the button at the right moment.'

Butler took long careful strides through the snow as he reached the heavy wooden door leading into the castle rearing up above him. The snow was a giveaway – other footprints had preceded his to this same doorway.

He turned the iron ring-handle slowly, making not a sound as he pushed the door inwards inch by inch. For a sturdily built man Butler could move with deadly silence. He held the Luger in his right hand as he padded inside, closed the door with the same care behind him.

Waiting while he listened, while his eyes accustomed themselves to the dim light, he heard nothing. Ahead of him a stone staircase climbed alongside the outer wall of the castle. He used a large handkerchief to clean snow off the soles of his shoes. If it came to a showdown he did not want his feet slipping from under him. He began to mount the staircase, following a trail of snow patches which he guessed the man above him had left behind off his own soles when he'd made the same ascent.

Butler came to a point where an archway led off the main staircase to another narrower staircase which curved up constantly. He guessed that this led up round the sides of the looming turret to the high roof where he'd glimpsed a man with a weapon. Again Butler knew he was heading in the right direction – a fresh tell-tale trail of snow patches smeared the well-worn stone steps, steps smoothed down by footfalls over the centuries.

A draught of even colder fresh air warned him he was near the exit at the summit. It was freezing cold on the spiral staircase and the snow patches had frozen solid. He took a firmer grip on the Luger as he edged round a corner and saw an archway framing the clear blue sky beyond. He had to get there in time – he knew Cardon would be investigating what the opposition had planted underneath the bridge.

'You really should get the hell out of here, Paula,' Cardon warned. 'I make one false move deactivating this bomb and we both end up playing harps in the sky.'

'You mean two and a quarter of us,' Paula joked to hide her fear. 'Don't forget Puss. He would take a fancy to me at this moment.'

The cat had come running back to her, had reached up with its forepaws on her right leg. She'd picked it up and tickled it under its ear while Cardon made his preliminary examination with a pencil torch. Philip, she thought, always seemed to carry a complete tool-kit with him.

'Can't I help you in some way?' she pressed.

'Well . . .'

He was reluctant to agree, but he knew it would be safer if he had an extra pair of hands. No, he decided, scare her well away from this potential tomb before he

383

started experimenting. He gestured with the secateurs he'd taken from a small cloth hold-all.

'Look, Paula, this is the score. I count six sticks of dynamite – probably stolen from a stone quarry. Plenty of them with explosives stores in the Vosges. Now – to neutralize, make them inert sticks of nothing – I have to cut six cables attached to six detonators. It's a crude but effectively improvised bomb. So I cut each of the green cables . . .'

'Not the red ones?' The cat was still purring as she tickled it under the ear. 'I always thought red was for danger.'

'That is the crude trick they played.' Cardon turned his pink healthy face towards Paula and grinned. 'I've checked this thingumajig carefully. To render it harmless I've got to snip through six *green* cables. That was their idea of a boobytrap. Assuming, of course, I know what I'm doing. You know what an explosives expert will tell you? That you can never rely on explosives reacting as they're supposed to. Still want to risk hanging about here?'

'What can I do to help?'

'It's your funeral – mine too. See this canvas bag I brought from the bike? As I snip a cable I'll take hold of a stick of dynamite and hand it to you. Then you lay it carefully in the bottom of the bag. Put the next jigger alongside it.'

'What are we waiting for?' Paula enquired as she placed the cat in the snow.

'I don't like it,' Tweed said from his seat in the Espace. 'Philip has found something under that bridge – and Paula is down there with him. I'm going to see what's going on.'

Newman grasped him by the arm, forced him down back into his seat.

'You're going nowhere at all. What's the matter with you? Lost your capacity for waiting? You've always been hot on that aspect of our work. How many times have you told members of your team who were getting impatient that they must learn to wait?'

'I suppose you're right.'

'I know I am,' Newman said firmly. 'We may be under observation. Two people under the bridge is enough. Just hope there's no big bang.'

Butler stood three steps below the archway leading out on to the flat roof. He held the Luger gripped in both hands, aimed at the Norman arch. He was waiting to hear something that would tell him where the man – or men – who had climbed the tower before him were located.

The waiting was getting on his nerves. He couldn't forget the cable he'd found by scraping his foot along the base of the stone wall of a house near the castle. He couldn't forget that Cardon was probably now beneath the bridge, fooling around with God knew what devilish device.

The pressure was almost unbearable, the urge to dash out on to the roof, but he resisted the overwhelming temptation. Then, without warning, the back of a heavily built man clad in a windcheater and jeans appeared as he stood close to the edge of the low parapet. Butler realized he was staring at something through binoculars. He spoke to some unseen person. The twang was American.

'Gary, that friggin' Espace is still stuck a distance from the bridge. Looks like they could be staying there all day. Would the bomb reach them? Debris from the bridge? Great hunks of rock. Shall we give it a try?'

'Norton said to wait till it was on the bridge.'

'Gary, Norton is the friggin' Invisible Man. We can see the situation. And that girl who was fooling with that cat has gone to earth under the bridge. What say we give it a try? Hell, Norton is probably filling his belly in some upmarket restaurant in Strasbourg while we freeze.'

'If you say so, Mick. But it was you who . . .'

Butler jumped on to the platform. Mick, by the parapet, reacted with the speed of a pro, hauled out an automatic from inside his windcheater. He never had a chance to take aim as two bullets from Butler's 9-mm. Luger slammed into his chest. The force of the bullets toppled the thug over the edge. Butler never saw his arms and legs splay in his final fall into eternity. He had swung the Luger's muzzle to where Gary was crouched over a square box with a handle protruding a foot from the top. Gary's clawed hands descended, ready to grasp the handle, to depress the plunger.

Butler shot him twice in the left armpit. Gary jerked upright, blood streaming over his windcheater, staggering above the deadly box. Butler walked forward, used the muzzle of his weapon to shove the reeling American to the brink. He fell backwards and this time Butler saw what looked like a matchstick man plunging into the depths, both arms stretched out like a swimmer. He struck a projecting rock, was thrown off it by his own momentum and vanished into a tangle of deep undergrowth. No sign of Mick. He must have vanished into the same wilderness.

Butler slid the Luger back inside his hip holster, bent over the detonating mechanism. Cardon had trained him in explosives and Butler realized this was a crude improvised effort, reminiscent of photographs he'd seen of similar devices used in the First World War.

He took hold of the handle gently, twisted it slowly. It unscrewed anti-clockwise. He lifted the handle clear of the box, went to the edge of the parapet and threw the handle into the undergrowth which now concealed two bodies.

*   *   *

Paula had taken five of the six sticks of dynamite from Cardon and placed them carefully in the open canvas bag. The danger came from a most unexpected direction.

'Here you are. That's the last one. All OK,' Cardon said as he handed Paula the sixth stick of dynamite.

She had reached out her right hand, had grasped the stick, when the fat cat appeared out of nowhere, leapt up on to her left arm. It must have weighed almost nine pounds and threw her off balance.

She performed several reflex actions at once. Moving her right foot out, ramming it deep into the snow, she stood straddled in a desperate attempt to maintain her balance. Still gripping the dynamite stick in her right hand, she clutched at the great ball of fur and muscle with her left hand, hugging it to her breast. The cat dug its forepaws into the shoulder of her padded jacket, which at least relieved her of some of the weight. For Paula, the last straw was when it began to purr with pleasure.

'I could kill you,' she said in a deliberately affectionate tone which wouldn't disturb it.

'Stay just as you are,' Cardon said. 'I'm going to take the stick out of your hand. I'll tell you when to let go. Easy does it . . . Now, I've got it . . .'

Crouching down, he slid the last stick alongside the others, used a collection of chamois cloths he kept inside the bag to separate one stick from another. When he'd zipped the bag closed he looked up.

'I could throw this hunk into that frozen stream,' Paula told him.

The cat, still purring, had closed its eyes. It was going to sleep – unlike Norton who was standing in the main street of Kaysersberg, waiting expectantly.

Norton had been standing patiently outside the entrance to a small bar for over half an hour. He excelled in patience. He had pushed up his fur hat so that it was clear of his ears. His eyes showed no warmth, no particular expression as he waited for the sound of the explosion. He had stepped back from viewing the bridge. It was a sizeable bomb his men had placed under it during the ice-cold night when the streets were deserted.

He stiffened as he heard a vehicle approaching, moved back further out of sight into the entrance. The station wagon, driven by Nield, crawled past him, bumping over the cobbles. The Harley-Davidson, with Butler on the saddle, appeared, overtook Nield, headed west out of the village for the Vosges. Almost at once a grey Espace crawled past, also bumping over the old cobbles. It was moving so slowly Norton had a clear view of Tweed in one of the front passenger seats.

A second motorcycle ridden by Philip Cardon brought up the rear of the convoy. Norton waited until the sound of its engine had died away and the heavy silence of the snowbound morning descended again. Taking out his mobile phone, Norton contacted Mencken who was located high up in the mountains.

'Norton here. Our competitors are leaving Kaysersberg. Their director is a passenger in a grey Espace which is driven by a man and also is carrying two women. Two motorcycles and a station wagon are escorting them. So activate Phase Two. Immediately. Understood?'

'OK. Understood. So OK!' Mencken's rasping voice acknowledged.

Norton slid back the aerial inside his instrument, walked down to a side street where his hired blue Renault was parked. The next stage was to drive towards the Château Noir. Long before he reached it Tweed would be eliminated. Norton didn't waste a moment's thought as to why the bomb had not exploded. A faulty detonator? It didn't matter. Mencken was waiting for his target. Norton was indeed a man who excelled in patience.

40

'There will be fresh attempts to ambush us,' Tweed warned as they left Kaysersberg behind and the road spiralled up.

'What made you really suspect that bridge?' Newman asked.

'Sixth sense. Reverse thinking, if you like.'

'What's that?' Paula asked.

'Knowing the route between Colmar and the Château Noir the average man would assume the real danger would lie high up in the remote regions of the Vosges . . .'

'But you're not the average man,' Jennie remarked, leaning her arms on the back of Tweed's seat. 'Do go on.'

That's right, dear, Paula was thinking cynically, lay on the flattery with a trowel.

'Reverse thinking,' Tweed explained, ignoring the interruption, 'is like looking through the wrong end of a telescope. Turn everything round, and learn from any precedent where you can. We have one – demonstrating Norton's callousness when it comes to loss of innocent human life. The attack on us in the Bahnhofstrasse – where the second killer had a machine-pistol and was about to use it until Bob shot him. Spraying a weapon like that in a crowded city street could easily have caused fatal casualties to bystanders. So blowing up a bridge in Kaysersberg which could have killed several locals bothered Norton not one jot.'

'This is going to be a dangerous journey, then,' Jennie suggested.

'Well, you were warned before you joined us,' rapped out Paula.

'Oh, I'm not frightened. That man on top of that rock was watching us through something,' she went on. 'I saw the sun flashing off glass, maybe binoculars.'

'Are you sure it wasn't imagination?' queried Paula.

'Check it,' Tweed ordered Newman. 'Jennie may well have seen something . . .'

Despite its snow tyres, the Espace was rocking as it passed over hardened ruts. Newman slowed to a stop on a steep incline, lowered his window. Arctic-like air flowed into the vehicle. Paula could now see the massive bluffs and high knife-edge ridges of the Vosges very clearly in the glaring sunlight. Cardon appeared at Newman's window, paused astride his machine.

'Something suspicious ahead of us,' Newman began.

'On the top of that ridge,' Jennie said, leaning forward, aiming her extended arm and index finger like a gun. 'I *know* I saw at least one man.'

'Keep the Espace parked here,' Cardon said as Butler returned and pulled up astride his own machine. 'We'll investigate.' He looked at Paula. 'Those dynamite sticks we collected may come in useful. I've got them in my panniers.' He pointed to the containers slung from either side of his machine. 'See you . . .'

'He's got grenades,' Tweed commented.

'Saving them for a rainy day,' Paula suggested.

After a brief conversation between Cardon and Butler the two men sped off up the curving ascent, bouncing over the ruts. Newman took out a pair of binoculars and scanned the ridge Jennie had pointed at. No sign of anyone, so maybe Paula had been right in suggesting it was Jennie's imagination.

Carrying out the plan they had improvised, Butler and Cardon each played a separate role. Butler continued riding at reduced speed up the road, acting as bait. Behind him Cardon had turned his machine off the road and sped under the lee of the ridge which made him invisible to any watcher on the heights. Before leaving the Espace he had tucked one stick of dynamite, folded inside his scarf, behind his belt. The ground was rough, treacherous, the snow concealing rocks and dips, and he prayed the vibration would not disturb the dynamite. Should have used a grenade instead. Too late to worry about that now.

Cardon was aiming to mount the ridge at its northern extremity where he was likely to have a sweeping view over the entire terrain. He just hoped he'd reach that position before Butler rode up the section of the spiral road which passed under the ridge. He gritted his teeth as the machine bucked like a wild bronco, kept his balance, saw he was close to the end of the ridge. Then up, up, up!

Newman sat very erect in his seat, binoculars screwed close to his eyes. Butler was now approaching the point where he'd be most vulnerable – *if* Jennie had seen someone up on the ridge.

Cardon had vanished from sight. Newman guessed he was driving his machine to the limit over very rough terrain. He wished to Heaven he was with them, helping out.

Tweed had steeled himself to remain calm, passive. Every instinct made him want to snatch the binoculars from Newman. *To see for himself!* Beside him he felt

Paula shift her position and guessed the tension was mounting for everyone inside the Espace. Then he felt Jennie's gloved knuckles pressing into his shoulder. His tone of voice was off-hand when he spoke.

'Not much going on up there, Bob?'

'I'm not sure. I thought I saw something.'

'Tell us what you think your something was,' Tweed requested, his manner still deliberately low-key.

'Movement on the ridge,' Newman said tersely.

'Can you be a little more specific?'

'Thought I saw two men, but it was only a quick glimpse.'

'Keep looking. Let us know if there are any fresh developments, please.'

Newman had closed his window earlier and now the heaters were beginning to build up a more bearable atmosphere inside the Espace. The two men and the two women sat like waxwork figures, not moving as they stared up the ascent to the ridge which reminded Tweed of the back of some prehistoric beast. But the growing warmth did nothing to reduce the rising tension inside the vehicle.

'Harry Butler is nearly at the real danger point,' Paula observed quietly.

She was right, Tweed thought grimly. Butler was approaching a location where to his left the road stood at the edge of a sheer abyss. Worse still, to his right the eastern tip of the ridge was a gradual and shallow slope from the summit to the road – exposing him fully to any firepower which might be aimed at him from above.

'Oh, God!' Paula exclaimed. 'No . . .!'

'Two men, both armed with machine-pistols, point-blank range,' Newman reported in a dull tone.

Butler must have sensed danger. Through his glasses Newman saw him bring his machine to a sudden halt. He was staring up to the summit of the slope as both men took aim with their weapons. Cardon appeared out of nowhere from behind the ridge, stopped his machine so suddenly the back wheel jumped off the ground. He was about thirty feet from the American killers. Distracted for a moment, they turned round as Cardon hoisted his arm like a cricket bowler about to throw the ball. A missile sped through the air, landed almost at the feet of the two potential assassins.

The dynamite exploded with a thumping roar they heard inside the closed Espace. A fountain of rock hurtled skywards, mingled with the blood-stained remnants of his targets. The mangled debris moved in an arc, fell straight down on to the road a few yards in front of where Butler had paused. The upper half of one American, severed at the trunk, littered the road. Butler walked his machine forward, used the wheel to nose the relic over the edge into the abyss.

On the ridge Cardon had ridden his machine the short distance to where he could look down on the road. Butler gazed at him, gave the thumbs-up sign, which Cardon returned. Perched on the summit Cardon couldn't resist the gesture. Staring towards where the Espace waited, he beckoned them on with a grand wave. *Advance!*

'Let's get moving,' Tweed said in a businesslike manner. 'I want to be at the Château Noir as close to eleven as we can. And Pete Nield behind us is champing at the bit in his station wagon. I *must* talk to Amberg.'

Higher up amid the snows of the Vosges there was another more distant watcher who had observed everything. Seated in a green Renault – the colour merging well with surrounding evergreens – Mencken had positioned himself on a platform which provided an almost uninterrupted view of route N415. He now had the undesirable obligation to report to Norton.

'Don't apologize to the creep,' he told himself.

He dialled Norton on his mobile phone, watching the progress of the convoy towards him far below. They were well organized – he'd give them that, the bloody Brits.

'Norton here,' the familiar voice answered after a lot of atmospherics.

'Mencken. Phase Two of the experiment was a complete bust. I do mean complete,' he continued, piling it on. 'There are two more players out of the game.'

'Plenty more from where they came from,' Norton responded with his usual considerate regard for human life. 'I am now sure our competitors, who are coming up via Route Two, will return via Route One. There the possibilities for the neutralization of the opposition are more promising. You will now assemble the team for the château.'

'Understood,' confirmed Mencken.

'And I hope you also understand that our competitors must never reach Colmar again. That would disturb me. More to the point, you would find it disturbing . . .'

Mencken swore as he realized Norton was no longer in touch on the phone. His language was an attempt to ignore the fear he felt from Norton's last words. They had implied a lethal threat to Mencken in the event of failure.

Seated behind the wheel of his Renault, Norton drove on up into the mountains after giving his orders to Mencken. He was beginning to have his first doubts as to whether Marvin Mencken was the man for the job. He'd decide about that later.

Norton's next priority was the coming assault on the Château Noir. It was just possible that Amberg had the film and the tape with him in his castle. That would solve the whole problem.

But Norton was not banking on this. He had his six in

the evening rendezvous with Growly Voice at Lac Noir. Here he had a problem. He'd been instructed to come alone – and to continue to conceal his appearance he would have to go to this isolated spot by himself. It was not a prospect he relished – meeting someone whose identity was as secret as his own. He hoped it was a rendezvous he'd never have to keep.

Finally, Norton thought, ticking off priorities, Tweed and his team would be eliminated before nightfall. Phoning Mencken in Colmar, he had coded the way into the Vosges via Kaysersberg as Route Two – N415. The more southerly way into the mountains – D417 – had been coded as Route One. Which was where Tweed would perish.

41

Paula gazed in wonderment at the Ice Age world they had entered at this high altitude. Massive snow-covered bluffs loomed far above them as Newman guided the Espace higher and higher up a diabolical spiral. Suspended from overhanging crags were immense spears of ice like stalactites. They were now near enough to the summit to have lost the sun, driving in cold menacing shadow on the side road Newman had turned along.

She shivered inwardly as she peered up at the immensity of snow and ice hovering above them. She had the feeling it might all topple on them at any moment, burying them under a sea of snow and ice for ever.

'Don't think the sun ever reaches here,' Tweed commented.

'I think it's getting creepy,' Jennie replied.

'You ain't seen nothing yet,' Newman joked. 'Look what is coming up. Ladies and gentlemen, our guided tour of the Vosges has just reached Lac Noir. The infamous Black Lake.'

'Time we stretched our legs, limbered up,' Tweed suggested. 'We're close to the château and want to arrive fresh.'

'Oh, my God! What a horror,' Paula burst out as she stepped out after Tweed.

Newman had switched off the engine and a terrible silence descended on them. The Espace had been stopped close to a low stone wall. Beyond it the waters of Lac Noir stretched away – waters black as pitch and still as a pit of tar, which Paula thought it resembled. Worse still, the small lake ended at the base of a black granite cliff facing them – a cliff which rose vertical and sheer in the bleak shadows. Paula looked slowly up the wall of the cliff and felt dizzy when she saw the iron-hard line of the summit, the hideous medieval-like castle which stood perched way above them on the high brink. It was the intense stillness as much as the Siberian cold which paralysed her mind as she gazed at the monstrous edifice, the fantasy brought into existence by some crazy American millionaire Heaven knew how long ago. There were lights in the château windows – there would have to be on this grim shadowed side.

'A bit bleak round here,' Tweed commented.

'Bloody terrifying,' replied Jennie who had climbed out after the others.

'That's a bit of an exaggeration,' Tweed said, aware the atmosphere was affecting morale. 'Bob, I want to get up to the château at the earliest possible moment – to see Amberg . . .'

The drive up the narrow precipitous road overhanging the southern end of the lake was a nightmare. Newman had his headlights on as he drove up and round hairpin bends with fearsome drops into the black water now far below.

'Some Grand Tour of the Vosges,' Paula said bitingly.

'At least it's a unique experience,' Jennie responded as she peered out of the window down the endless drop.

'One way of looking at it,' Paula snapped.

'One positive way of looking at it,' Jennie corrected her.

'Are you trying to pick a verbal fight with me?' Paula demanded, twisting round in her seat to glare at the other woman.

'Why should I want to do that?' Jennie flashed back, her eyes blazing. 'And I do have my uses – in case it has slipped what passes for your mind, I spotted those men on the ridge. Butler could be dead by now if I had not warned Tweed.'

'All right. You were a help, a big help. You saw something I missed and should have seen.'

Paula was startled. Jennie could be a hellcat, had looked at Paula as though she could have strangled her. Tweed wasn't prepared to be distracted by a female dispute as the moment approached when he would confront Amberg.

'If both of you would keep quiet maybe I could think. So not another word. Bob, we must be close now.'

'We'll reach the summit within five minutes,' reported Paula, who despite her altercation with Jennie had kept a close eye on the map. 'From there it appears to be no distance at all to the château.'

Tweed looked ahead at a moment when the snake of a road was inclined at an angle of forty-five degrees. Butler, who was still preceding them on his motorcycle, paused briefly, waved Newman on, continued the ascent on his machine.

Glancing back over his shoulder the view made Tweed

397

feel dizzy. Inclined at this precipitous angle he was staring down direct on to the deathly stillness of Black Lake – so far below now he almost suffered an attack of vertigo.

'Don't look back,' he warned Paula and Jennie. 'That's an order.'

Behind the Espace Nield was driving the station wagon up the ascent with Cardon bringing up the rear on his motorcycle. The system of the two outriders racing back and forth past the vehicles which had been employed earlier was now impossible. Any attempt by Cardon to overtake the station wagon and then the Espace would undoubtedly have ended with his machine falling over the brink and plunging hundreds of feet into the still waters of Black Lake.

'I think we've reached the top,' Paula called out, unable to suppress the relief she felt.

Butler had again paused, twisting round in his saddle to give the 'V' for victory sign. The road levelled out, Paula risked a quick glimpse back, saw only a projecting rock bluff which masked any view of the lake or the panorama beyond. She swung her head to face front.

'We're home and dry! There's the Château Noir. A grim-looking brute, but it's heaven to be back on the level. Home and dry,' she repeated.

'Not my idea of home,' Tweed commented. 'Just look at the place.'

Paula gazed at the high granite wall surrounding the great castle, at the huge square stone keep rising up even higher than any other part of the grim structure. Newman had stopped the Espace close under the lee of the wall, close to but out of sight of the tall wrought-iron gates which barred the entrance.

Nield parked his station wagon behind the Espace, got out to speak to Tweed, and was joined by Butler and

Cardon. Tweed had jumped out of the Espace and stood stretching the stiffness out of his arms and legs. It had been a somewhat tense journey, he reflected.

'How do we handle it?' asked Newman as Paula and Jennie followed him out into the bitter air.

'Tactfully – until we get inside,' Tweed replied.

Paula gazed round, relieved also to be able to exercise her limbs which had become tense with fear and anxiety. At least on this side of the château they were in the full blaze of the sun shining down out of a clear blue sky. But still there was the brooding silence of the high Vosges and she stamped her boots in the iron-hard snow to stop herself shivering. Cardon pointed to a wire elevated above the top of the wall which ran out of sight.

'Electrified,' he commented. 'I hope Amberg doesn't rely on that for security – I could neutralize it inside five minutes.'

Tweed addressed Nield, Butler and Cardon after checking his watch.

'I'm going to insist that Amberg allows you inside with your transport. As soon as you're parked check the layout of the whole set-up from the outside. Look for weak points where an attack might be launched. Plan a defence of the whole castle.'

'You're expecting an assault?' Newman queried.

'Norton's objective right from the beginning has been to get hold of the mysterious film and tape. He'll think – as I do – that Amberg has them in his safekeeping. So yes, an assault is possible – even probable. Now let's hope Amberg is at home . . .'

Tweed left the others hidden behind the wall. Marching up to the closed gates, he operated the speakphone he'd seen embedded in the left-hand gate pillar, pressing the button below the metal grille. He had to press it again before a disembodied voice he recognized spoke.

'Who are you?' the voice demanded in German.

'This is Tweed outside,' he said, speaking in English. 'I must talk to you urgently.'

'Someone else called here yesterday, said he was Tweed. He was an imposter, an American. How do I know you are the genuine Tweed?'

Paula, who was watching Tweed closely, saw a very strange expression cross his face. If she hadn't known him so well she'd have sworn it was bewilderment, but Tweed was never bewildered.

'All right,' Tweed continued, 'you want proof of my identity. You had an identical twin brother, Julius. He was murdered in a wholesale massacre at Tresillian Manor in Cornwall. Just before he left Switzerland on that fatal trip he was separated from his wife, Eve, who is English. I visited her at her villa on the heights above the Limmat in Zurich. I met you, Walter, a few days ago before you left Zurich for Basle. Bob Newman was with me. Look, surely that's enough, for God's sake!' he ended with deliberate exasperation.

'I am sorry, Tweed. I do hope you realize I have to take precautions. Actually, you have said more than enough for me to recognize your distinctive voice. When the buzzer sounds the gates will open . . .'

'One more point,' Tweed interjected. 'I have Newman and Paula Grey with me. I also have three guards – members of my organization. I want them to enter the courtyard I can see through the gates as protection.'

'I agree. Listen for the buzzer.'

Paula had again been watching Tweed closely. He had bent his ear close to the metal grille while Amberg spoke and when he straightened up he was frowning. He looked at Paula and his expression became blank. Raising his hand he gestured for them all to move into the stone-flagged courtyard as the automatically operated gates swung inwards. Paula joined him as they walked swiftly towards the large stone porch which appeared to be the main entrance.

'Has something disturbed you?' she asked.

He pointed towards the right-hand corner of the huge stone façade which reared above them. Parked almost out of sight was a white BMW.

'Looks very much like Gaunt's,' Paula commented.

'I think we'll find it is Gaunt's . . .'

Amberg himself, again neatly dressed in a black business suit, opened the heavy door to let Tweed, Paula and Newman inside. Paula blinked at the vastness of the entrance hall, at the poor illumination provided by the sconces on the walls. Amberg stroked a hand across his well-brushed hair after closing and locking the door.

'Will you please excuse me for a few minutes? I can hear the phone going and I'm expecting an important call. Eve has come for a business discussion. Gaunt, who brought her, will take you to her. A little pleasant company in my absence . . .'

Gaunt, who greeted them as though their arrival was the most natural event, led them through a series of stone passages and up and down flights of ancient stone steps. As he led the way he called back to them as though he owned the place.

'Remarkable place, this château. Of course the Yankee who had it built on the basis of old plans was mad as a hatter. But he was Yankee to the core. Show you some of the bathrooms later. Now, ladies and gentlemen, we are about to enter the largest bathroom of all,' he boomed.

His voice echoed back along the labyrinth of passages they had walked through. Paula was dying to tell him to cut down on the decibels. Gaunt had paused before a pair of large double doors shaped like a Norman arch. With a grandiloquent gesture, he opened both of them,

401

gestured for them to enter. Tweed nodded to Paula to go ahead in front of him. She did so and stopped abruptly, suppressing a gasp of astonishment.

She was gazing at a vast swimming pool, entirely constructed of marble. Enclosed under an arched roof, the marble covered all the surrounding surfaces. A figure was swimming in the pool, racing up and down the full length with powerful breast-strokes.

Eve Amberg had tucked her titian hair inside a black cap and was clad in a one-piece black bathing costume. She waved to Paula as she reached one end, paused at the foot of a ladder, called out to her.

'Welcome to Valhalla! Be with you in a minute. I have to complete thirty lengths. Make yourselves comfortable in those chairs . . .'

Then she was off again. As Tweed and Newman walked over to comfortable chairs round a table, Paula watched Eve. The Englishwoman was an incredibly strong swimmer. Her long limbs glided through the greenish water, her slim arms moved like pistons. Thirty lengths! I couldn't do that, Paula thought, and I'm a few years younger than she is. As she wandered towards the table Eve reached the ladder, paused, shinned up it, stood on the edge of the pool, reached for a large towel. Drying her shoulders, she stripped off her cap and her mane cascaded down her back.

'You look stunning,' Paula commented as she sat down at the table.

'Thank you, Paula. After that, I do feel good.'

Eve had a flair for clothes, Paula mused. With her titian hair the black one-piece costume was a perfect choice. Gaunt, who had stood by the side of the pool, watching her with his arms folded, joined the others at the table. There was a whole array of glasses, bottles and one decanter.

402

'I'm mine host,' Gaunt announced. 'Amberg was involved with yet another phone call when we arrived, showed us the way to this palace of pleasures. Talking of pleasure, who's for a double Scotch to get things going?'

'I'll have a glass of Riesling,' Eve called out. 'Tweed, maybe you'd pour me a glass – providing you pour one for yourself. It's good Riesling.'

'Certainly,' Tweed replied. 'You brought a swimming costume with you?' he suggested conversationally as he poured two glasses.

'I did. This pool is heated. I used to swim here when poor Julius brought me here from time to time. Hate the rest of the place. Like a blasted mausoleum. But the pool is terrific.'

She had towelled herself all over, brought another dry towel to sit on. She stood very erect while she answered Tweed's question.

'I'll go change into something decent in a few minutes, but if you don't mind me like this I'm gasping for some wine.'

'I don't mind you like that at all,' Newman told her and smiled. 'Feel free to join us.'

'I suppose you're both here on a social visit,' Tweed suggested after raising his glass to Eve.

'You know jolly well I'm not,' she rebuked him, following it up with a winning smile. 'Business is business.'

'And you, Gaunt?' Tweed enquired, turning in his seat to the large figure occupying the seat next to him.

'I'm here to find out who used my manor as a blood bath . . .' Gaunt had lowered his tone so only Tweed could hear. 'I'm not leaving until Amberg has put on his picture show, with talkies.'

'He's admitted he has those items here?' Tweed queried in a whisper.

Newman, sensing the two men wanted to talk in

secrecy, was joking in a loud voice, causing Paula and Eve to become near-hysterical.

'Not exactly,' Gaunt confessed in the same grim tone. 'He can be very evasive, very Swiss in the least complimentary sense.'

'Then I'll have to talk to him. By myself. Now would be a good moment if I knew where to find him.'

'Show you the way.' Gaunt stood up, bent down as he added the remark, 'Suspect you and I are on the same side in this one.'

I wonder, Tweed thought, but he smiled agreement as he stood up. Gaunt explained to the others that they had a bit of business to discuss with Amberg, hoped they'd excuse their absence.

'Take all day as far as I'm concerned,' Newman assured him breezily. 'I'm more than happy chatting with two interesting women . . .'

Gaunt left Tweed in the strange quarters Amberg used as his office, the vast room with the raised dais and behind it the huge picture window with a panoramic view down over the Vosges, across the flat plain to the distant hump which was the Black Forest in Germany.

Still standing, Tweed studied the small, portly Swiss with his black hair slicked back over his high forehead – no parting – and the thick brows above the shrewd blue eyes. Did he always wear this depressing black suit? Tweed asked himself.

'Please sit down,' Amberg invited, indicating the low chair placed beneath the dais.

'Thank you. I'm sure you won't mind if I join you,' Tweed said at his most amiable.

Picking up the chair, he stepped up on to the dais, walked round the large desk, planted the chair next to Amberg's and sat down, facing him.

'What is the problem?' Amberg asked in a peevish tone. 'I haven't a lot of time.'

'You have all the time in the world,' Tweed assured him, 'but first I want to view the film, listen to the tape – the two items Joel Dyson left with you for safekeeping.'

'I don't understand what you're talking about,' snapped the Swiss, and he pursed his thin lips.

'I'm talking about murder on a grand scale. Mass murder at Tresillian Manor in Cornwall.' Tweed's manner was no longer amiable. 'I'm talking about the murders of Helen Frey, her friend Klara and the private investigator, Theo Strebel. All of which took place on your home patch – in Zurich.' He paused. Amberg stared back at him with a blank expression, but Tweed thought he detected a hint of alarm in those blank eyes. 'Theo Strebel was an ex-member of the Zurich Homicide force, a close friend of Arthur Beck who, as you know, is Chief of the Swiss Federal Police at the Taubenhalde in Berne. Beck also happens to be a close friend of mine. So produce the film and the tape or Beck will be waiting for you the moment you return to Zurich. Which is it to be?'

Unusually, Tweed had fired all his guns in one massive verbal barrage. The effect was electrifying.

'It is a question of ethics,' Amberg began in a feeble tone. 'Joel Dyson gave us those items to keep for him.'

'Forget the ethics. Didn't you know? Dyson may be dead. He hasn't been seen alive since he visited your bank in Talstrasse. Another fact which will interest Beck.'

'I do have a small cinema at a lower level,' Amberg said.

'And the film and the tape?'

'They are in a safe here. I'll get them now. Also we have a recorder to play the tape on.'

'Good. I want to synchronize the film with the sounds on the tape. And Gaunt also would like to be present. At long last we are getting somewhere.'

42

Like a general planning a major battle, Mencken stood up in the front of the Land-Rover he had driven up into the Vosges. He had hired the vehicle before leaving Basle, anticipating driving over some rough country.

From where he'd parked the four-wheel drive – on the edge of a small copse of evergreens – he could look down on the Château Noir, scanning the interior courtyard with binoculars. In the back two of his men sat carrying machine-pistols.

'We launch the attack precisely at noon. So synchronize your watches,' Mencken ordered. 'It is now exactly fifteen minutes to noon. Repeat the instructions I gave you. Word for word or I'll break your necks.'

'At noon,' Eddie began, reciting by rote, 'I blow open those gates to let the cars burst into that yard with the troops they'll be carrying.'

'Hank?' Mencken prodded.

Eddie and Hank were the two men who had been on the verge of torturing Jennie Blade when Tweed and his men had stormed into her bedroom at the Hôtel Bristol. Both men were still on Mencken's list for liquidation, but maybe someone else would do the job for him in the coming assault.

'At one minute to noon,' reported the tall lean Hank, 'I neutralize that electric wire running atop the outer wall. The telescopic ladders are in position—'

'OK,' Mencken interrupted him. He elevated the aerial on his walkie-talkie. 'Calling Blue, Green, Yellow,

Orange, Brown. Are you in position? Check back in the sequence I called you . . .'

'So that's it,' Mencken commented when the last team leader had confirmed. 'Everything really depends on Johnny,' he remarked, speaking half to himself. 'He's an expert at scaling heights. With a rope and grappling iron he'll get to the top of that tower – I guess they call it the keep. Armed with machine-pistols he'll dominate all entrances and exits to the château. He'll be way above everyone. And if Newman and his amateurs get in your way, kill 'em. OK.'

Mencken twisted round, stared down at his henchmen. 'So what are you waiting for? Take up your positions – this is going to be an easy run. Who can stop us? I'll be inside roughing up Amberg by a quarter after noon.' He glanced up at the clear blue sky as Eddie and Hank hastily jumped out of the Land-Rover. 'What a perfect day for a slaughter . . .'

Earlier, Marler had arrived at the Ballon d'Alsace high up in the southern Vosges. The controller of the gliding school, Masson, a large genial Frenchman, was apologetic.

'My own team has been laid low with this accursed flu. I felt I could not let you down – especially after the large deposit you paid me.'

'So you didn't let me down? What is the problem?' Marler enquired genially in French.

'Problem solved. I contacted a Swiss friend who also runs a gliding outfit. He has sent a Swiss pilot with his own machine to take you into the heavens.'

Marler had wondered why a Piper Tomahawk, a single-propeller plane with Swiss markings, was waiting on the runway. Behind it, attached to the Tomahawk's fuselage, stretched along the runway was the tow-rope linking it with the glider which Marler would be flying a long way north.

'I got the Met report on my bedroom radio,' Marler told Masson. 'But although it sounded good the data you get is what counts.'

'For a flight to the north? To the Col de la Schlucht, sir? The wind direction is perfect. At the moment, I must emphasize. The weather' – Masson shrugged – 'it can change its mind faster than the most temperamental woman. But this I am sure you know. It is quite a trip you plan to make. Now, the Swiss pilot is waiting . . .'

Marler chose a moment when he was alone with the Swiss to give him instructions which differed from those he had suggested to Masson the previous day. He wanted the pilot to tow him considerably further north – closer to the Col du Bonhomme, and closer to the Château Noir, an objective he did not mention.

It was cold as Marler settled himself inside the cockpit of the glider, adjusted his helmet and goggles. Alone – for Masson had returned to the single-storey admin. cabin – Marler unzipped his canvas hold-all, swiftly assembled and loaded the Armalite. Then he loaded the tear-gas pistol and tucked both weapons by his side in the confined space of his little world. Round his neck he had slung a pair of field-glasses.

He tested with his feet the pedals controlling the glider, especially the rudder which guided the plane once it was turned loose. Satisfied he had done all he could, he raised a hand, dropped it, signalling to the Swiss pilot of the Tomahawk that he was ready.

The pilot already had his engine tuned up. The revs increased, Marler saw the Tomahawk begin its take-off down the runway, the tow-rope linking him to the mother plane stiffened, elevated above the runway. The glider moved forward after a brief jerk.

Less than a minute later the Tomahawk was airborne

and so was the glider. Marler glanced at his watch. If he had timed it properly he would arrive over the Château Noir just before noon.

While Tweed had been talking to Amberg in his strange working quarters, pressurizing the Swiss banker, Newman had stayed by the indoor pool with Paula and Eve. From the beginning, Jennie, who had accompanied them inside the château, had sat in a chair near the entrance, well away from the pool.

Seated with her legs crossed, an elbow perched on them, she had supported her chin with her right hand while she appeared to be observing Eve closely as she completed her lengths in the pool, and later when she sat with Newman, Paula and Gaunt. Newman had called out for Jennie to join them but she had smiled and shaken her head. He offered her a drink.

'Orange juice, no ice, would suit me very well, thank you.'

'Jennie seems a bit stand-offish,' Paula remarked to Newman in a low tone, standing up and joining him as though stretching her legs. He paused, the drink he was carrying to Jennie in his hand, replied also in a whisper.

'My impression is something important struck her and she's mulling it over. Let her be.'

'Struck her?' Paula persisted. 'What do you mean?'

'At some point since we arrived at the château and Amberg let us in. Let it rest. I'll make sure Jennie's not feeling out of it when I give her this drink.'

'Remember to come back sometime,' Paula chaffed him. 'She is very attractive.'

'Paula!' Gaunt roared at the top of his voice. 'Paula, I need your company. I always work on the principle that a man should have two devastatingly sensual women so he can play one off against the other. Eve is seducing me with her gorgeous eyes.'

409

And not just with her eyes, Paula thought when she saw how Eve had arranged her legs as she sat in full view of Gaunt. It was shortly after this that Tweed appeared briefly and spoke to Gaunt.

'Amberg has something to show you in the cinema. Can you find it? At a lower level, Amberg said.'

'Enjoy the picture show. I suppose it's pornographic as we're not invited. Let's time you.' Eve looked at her waterproof Blancpain. 'In ten minutes from now it will be noon. Tell Walter I shall want lunch . . .'

Tweed was not surprised to be shown with Gaunt into a large luxurious cinema by Amberg. There was row upon row of comfortable seats and the floor slanted downwards towards a large screen.

'I have set up the tape on a recorder,' Amberg informed them in his fussy manner. 'I will operate the projector to show the film. Make yourselves comfortable. It is air-conditioned, of course.'

'Of course!' Gaunt whispered to Tweed as they walked together towards a middle row. 'That Yankee millionaire who built this horror wasn't short of a dollar. Damned place reminds me of pictures I've seen in magazines of a pre-Second World War Odeon.'

'I'll take an aisle seat,' Tweed said, glancing back to where Amberg had retreated to a large projector mounted on a high dais.

'At least we didn't have to buy a ticket,' Gaunt continued as he settled in a seat next to Tweed. 'Which is a surprise – considering Amberg's love of money.'

'This should be what we have come all this way to see.'

'What happened to Newman?' Gaunt enquired. 'He disappeared on our way down here.'

'Probably gone to the loo.'

Tweed was lying. Newman had taken Tweed aside and told him he was going outside.

'I think I'd better see how Butler, Nield and Cardon are getting on with checking the defences.'

Tweed had nodded agreement. He'd also noticed Newman was carrying the hold-all he had kept close to himself ever since they had arrived inside the château. The hold-all contained the Uzi sub-machine-gun Newman had taken off the two American thugs who had kidnapped Jennie at the Bristol.

'Time, gentlemen, for the big picture,' Amberg called out with unaccustomed humour.

The lights were switched down. Tweed and Gaunt sat in near darkness. Taking off his glasses, Tweed cleaned them on his handkerchief, put them on again, looked back once more to where the vague silhouette of Amberg was crouched over his projector.

'How on earth does he keep this place clean without any servants?' Tweed mused.

'He brings in peasants off the lower slopes,' Gaunt told him. 'Pays them a pittance but in cash. This is France. The tax man never sees a franc of their earnings, which makes it all worthwhile – for the peasants and for Amberg.'

A glaring light flashed on to the screen, white with odd streaks of black. Tweed leaned forward intently. In the heavy silence he could hear the tape recorder revolving, spewing out atmospherics. No voices yet.

The light continued to blaze at them. No picture yet. Tweed checked the running time by the illuminated hands of his watch. Almost noon.

The light continued glaring non-stop. The tape recorder went on spewing out atmospherics. Tweed stirred restlessly. It was about time they saw something in the way of images. He suspected Gaunt was equally irked. Gaunt took out a cigar, lit it, blew the smoke away from Tweed, who now had a grim expression.

411

The strong light vibrated for a while longer, accompanied by the recorder's atmospherics. Without warning the light was turned off. Gaunt blinked, but Tweed had earlier taken the precaution of staring at the floor to keep his vision. The screen went blank. Tweed jumped up, made his way along the aisle to where Amberg stood.

'It's blank,' the banker said in a bewildered tone of voice. 'There's nothing on the film, nothing on the tape . . .'

'That's because you've substituted an unused film for the real one,' Tweed said in a ferocious hiss. 'Same with the tape. Where have you hidden the real ones?'

Then he heard the distant rattle of a machine-pistol and froze. None of his team possessed one. Newman had the Uzi sub-machine-gun, but Tweed could hear the difference. The Château Noir was under attack by Norton's murderous professionals.

When Newman had left the château by a rear exit, armed with the Uzi and his Smith & Wesson, his objective had been to take the high ground – to get inside the keep and reach its flat roof.

Close to the keep's wall, which sheered above him, he had reached a closed door inside an alcove when he saw Butler waving frantically to him. With the Luger in his right hand, Butler was crouched inside and close to the open doors of the old building used as a garage. He appeared to be warning Newman for God's sake to keep under cover.

Newman then spotted Nield and Cardon pressed against the side wall of the building. What the devil was going on? He suddenly saw a strong rope, knotted at intervals, hanging down the side of the tower. A climber's rope.

He glanced upwards in the nick of time. Way above

412

him on the roof a man was peering down, aiming a machine-pistol at him. Newman jumped back inside the alcove as a fusillade of bullets hammered down on the cobbles only feet from where he had been standing. They were trapped.

43

Marler's glider had been released from its tow-line some time before by the Swiss pilot, who had waved and flown away towards the Ballon d'Alsace. It was a beautiful sunny day and below him Marler saw the savage summits and snowbound ravines of the Vosges drifting past.

He had crossed route D417 and the formidable endless hairpin bends of the Col de la Schlucht. He was approaching the Château Noir. On the lower slopes of the map-like landscape spread out beneath him he saw the tiny figure of a man guiding a snowplough. The driver waved to the pilot of the glider. Marler briefly waved back.

He was concentrating on operating the controls. Since he was deliberately losing altitude he was wary of down-draughts, sudden gusts of air which could suck him down without warning. Then he saw it. The massive pile of the pseudo-medieval castle which was the Château Noir. As he removed his goggles he was surprised by its vast size.

He checked the time by his watch. Noon. As the glider continued to lose height he raised his binoculars, pressed them to his eyes. He frowned as he detected a Land-Rover half-hidden inside a copse of evergreens. Only one man – behind the wheel – but the vehicle probably was positioned to give the driver a clear view down inside the château wall. Not one of ours, he thought.

Marler continued to swivel his binoculars, focusing them now on the château which was coming closer every second. He stiffened as he saw Butler crouched, as though hiding, inside the entrance to a building. Then he saw Newman at the base of the keep, saw a burly figure in a sheepskin on the flat roof of the tower, peering over as he aimed a machine-pistol. Newman jumped back out of sight as the heavy silence of the Vosges was fractured by the rattle of a hail of bullets.

'You really shouldn't have done that, old man,' Marler said to himself, addressing the man on the roof of the keep. He pressed the foot pedals gently. 'Time for a really smooth glide. This will only take seconds . . .'

He heard a muffled explosion. Out of the corner of his eye he saw the wrought-iron gates guarding the entrance collapse. He did not allow his attention to be diverted from the task in hand as he reached for the Armalite.

On the roof of the keep the burly man in a sheepskin was peering over the edge, his machine-pistol reloaded, ready for a fresh burst, when his target reappeared. Confined inside the garage, Butler had fired three shots from his Luger but the range from where he crouched to the summit of the tower was too great.

Praying that the glider would continue on its level course for a few more seconds, Marler took careful aim. With his eye glued to the sniperscope attached to his rifle, he saw the cross-hairs covering the upper back of the burly thug on top of the keep. Holding his breath, Marler pressed the trigger.

His target jerked upright in a convulsive movement. The machine-pistol left his hands, dropped to the cobbles far below. He staggered, then fell forward, following his lost weapon, screaming in terror as he plunged down the

414

side of the keep. His body hit the cobbles with a bone-breaking thud close to the alcove where Newman sheltered. The corpse lay inert.

Up to this dramatic incident the odds had been heavily in favour of Mencken's assault force. From this moment they swung decisively the other way.

Newman noticed that the heavy studded wooden door leading inside the keep was not completely closed. It was simply stuck. He hammered his shoulder against the obstacle. It seemed to give a little. He took a deep breath and thrust against it with all his strength. It burst open, flying inwards so suddenly he nearly lost his balance.

Diving inside, gripping the Uzi in both hands, he saw a flight of stone steps, worn down in their centres, leading upwards, curving out of sight round a corner. He began to run up them non-stop, unaware of what was happening at the front of the château.

At the first rattle of machine-pistol fire Tweed had reacted instantly. Grabbing Amberg by the arm, he forced him to the cinema exit, up the flight of stairs leading into the main hall. Gaunt, hauling a .455 Colt automatic from the shoulder holster under his thick sports jacket, took giant strides, close on their heels.

Entering the hall, Tweed saw Paula, Jennie and Eve – now wearing winter clothes – appear from the direction of the swimming pool. With his free arm he waved them back, a commanding gesture.

'Return to the pool at once. Don't argue. Do as I tell you. There is great danger.'

Eve and Jennie rushed back into the labyrinth of passages but Paula stayed her ground. From the special pocket inside her shoulder bag she had whipped out her .32 Browning.

'I'm staying here with you,' she snapped at Tweed. 'You are not armed.'

'I am,' Gaunt assured her aggressively.

'We may need someone who can shoot straight,' she told him.

'What the hell—' Gaunt began.

He never completed his sentence. Tweed, still dragging a reluctant Amberg, had headed for the main door. Outside he could hear the sound of some large machine approaching. Reaching the door he peered through the tall Norman window with leaded lights at one side of the door. The view was not reassuring. Norton – or his henchman – who had organized the attack knew what he was doing.

The clanking grinding machine proceeding across the cobbled courtyard towards the door was a huge orange bulldozer, its massive grab elevated several feet – ready to batter down the heavy door and open the way for the final assault. Tweed compelled Amberg to glance through the window. The Swiss shuddered, tried to get away, but Tweed had a firm grip on his arm.

'I must go to the swimming pool as well,' Amberg protested. 'There is a rear exit. I am a banker . . .'

'Surely you want to witness the defence of your own home,' Tweed said grimly, determined to break his nerve. 'You will stay with us in any case.'

'I might be able to shoot the driver,' suggested Gaunt who had also peered through the window.

'Not a chance, not yet,' Tweed snapped. 'And behind his cab the driver has several armed men clinging on aboard the bulldozer. We must wait until it appears in the gap after it has smashed down the double doors. Then shoot. We might jam the machine in the doorway, although I don't issue any guarantees. So, we stand back and wait . . .'

The one thing which irked Tweed was that he had no

idea what his team outside the château were doing – assuming they were still alive.

Having disposed of the gunman who had pinned down all Tweed's men, Marler immediately turned his attention to what was going on at the entrance. His glider was still airborne but he knew he must soon land or crash – maybe both. What was happening was taking place in seconds.

He had fired the Armalite from a distance, but now the glider was cruising very close to the château, would be above the courtyard at any moment. Afterwards, if he survived, Marler hoped to land on the summit of the ridge close to where the Land-Rover had been parked.

Then he saw the orange bulldozer advancing, the clutch of armed men hanging on behind the driver's cabin. The machine was a deadly menace. Marler took a dangerous chance, lost more height, and was now gripping the tear-gas pistol with a spare shell in his other hand. The wings seemed to almost skim the roof of the keep, although the machine was higher. Marler looked down.

The bulldozer had covered two-thirds of the distance between the ruined gates and the porch entrance to the château. His arm rested firmly on the edge of the fuselage of the glider as he pressed the trigger. The tear-gas shell was aimed for the glass window in front of the driver's cabin, smashed it to pieces, exploded inside the cabin. Marler had reloaded, fired again at the rear of the machine where the armed men were hanging on.

The outcome was devastating. Overcome with the fumes the driver lost all control. The bulldozer swung through an arc of a hundred and eighty degrees. In his panic the driver pressed his foot on the wrong pedal. The machine rocketed over the cobbles at speed, spilling its passengers, who were disabled by the second tear-gas shell. The bulldozer thundered towards the outer wall, hurtled into it with tremendous impact, crushing the cabin and the driver inside it.

At that moment a Citroën drove in through the gateway, crammed with armed men. Cardon, Nield and Butler had emerged from under cover. The Citroën driver, startled by the disaster to the bulldozer, skidded to a fatal halt. Cardon carefully lobbed a grenade. It landed under the petrol tank of the Citroën. Before any of its passengers could get out the petrol tank exploded. There was a fountain of flame and Newman saw its occupants incinerated in the ferocious heat.

He had reached the top of the keep and was crouched behind the low wall. As several of the men who had dropped off the bulldozer produced weapons, rubbing their eyes, he fired a long burst from the Uzi. A 9-mm. weapon, it fired at the rate of six hundred rounds a minute. He rammed in a fresh magazine, continued firing.

Butler saw a man perched on the top of the wall, guessed he had cut the electrified wire. He aimed his Luger, fired twice. His target shot out both arms as though about to swim, dived head first down on to the cobbled courtyard.

Marler's glider continued on course, away from the château, heading for the ridge as he struggled to maintain a few more feet of height. He braced himself for a crash landing. The ridge rushed towards him, the nose of the glider lifted briefly of its own accord. It was this accident of luck which saved Marler from the machine upending. It scraped along the rocky ground, came to a stop.

No more than thirty feet away Marler saw that the Land-Rover was still stationed at the edge of the copse with its driver behind the wheel. He snatched up the Armalite as the vehicle began to move, fired at random. Mencken, who had witnessed the débâcle, shuddered as his windscreen was shattered, all the glass blown away from the frame, but the bullet had missed him. He drove

418

off at speed, heading for the vital ambush area on route D417.

Half a mile away, well clear of the action, Norton sat in his Renault at a road intersection. He lowered his field-glasses. This time he was not feeling too philosophical about the next stage of the struggle. What could he tell President Bradford March? At that moment he had no idea – and he had lost a lot of trained men.

44

'That is what we have saved you from . . .'

Tweed almost thundered the words as he stood in the snow, still gripping Amberg's arm. They had walked out of the front door and beyond the porch to survey a scene of carnage.

Blood disfigured the white of the snow, the bodies of Mencken's assault group lay in grotesque attitudes. Paula stood on his other side, the Browning still in her hand, ready for use. Gaunt had brought up the rear.

As they stood in the bitter cold Butler, who had medical training, completed checking each body to see if anyone was still alive. He stood up from the last corpse and shook his head. A station wagon full of Mencken's troops had followed the Citroën into the yard. The occupants, all armed, had been despatched by Newman with his Uzi as they had emerged.

Butler, Cardon and Nield, with Newman's help, were now carrying the bodies and laying them inside the station wagon. Amberg was shivering with fear. Tweed gripped his arm more tightly.

'All this havoc has been caused by the accursed film and the tape. I've lost track of how many have died – many of them innocent of any crime. My patience is exhausted, Amberg. You will produce the real film and tape or I will contact Beck, Chief of the Federal Police at the Taubenhalde in Berne. You will be charged as an accessory to mass murder, so make up your mind now. I repeat,' he continued in the same grim tone, 'I've run out of patience with you.'

'As a banker I felt I should keep my word to Joel Dyson who deposited . . .'

'Forget Dyson. Your own life is in great danger. Can you at long last grasp that? Look at those corpses – those men came to kill you. For the last time, where have you hidden the film, the tape?'

'At my bank in Ouchy on the shores of Lake Geneva,' Amberg gulped, using his free hand to wipe beads of sweat off his high forehead. 'It belonged to Julius but it was registered in a different name. It was the only place no one could connect with us.'

'So they are still in Switzerland,' Tweed commented more quietly.

'Yes. After this terrible experience perhaps we should return at once to my country. To Ouchy, I mean,' he added quickly.

'You will travel with us.' Tweed made no attempt to reassure the Swiss. 'I must warn you we shall face other attacks on our way back to Colmar. Whether we arrive there alive is in the lap of the gods.'

He looked at Paula. 'Where are Jennie and Eve? They are safe, I assume?'

'Safe as houses – safer than this castle was,' Paula replied. 'When you first came out here I nipped back to the swimming pool. They were both sitting down at the table, drinking hot coffee from a percolator.'

'To steady their nerves?'

420

'In the case of Jennie, yes. Eve is made of sterner stuff. She had an automatic rifle across her lap – she'd brought it from somewhere. She made the remark that if any thugs arrived at the pool she'd take some of them with her. Tough as old hickory,' Paula ended in an admiring tone.

'She is a very strong-minded woman,' Amberg agreed in a regretful tone. 'I expect she will want to come with us. A little business matter which can only be settled in Ouchy.'

'Why?' Tweed demanded. 'Have you transferred all the assets to the shores of Lake Geneva?'

He was suspicious. Ouchy faced the shore of France and there was a regular boat service from there to Evian.

'Merely a matter of banking policy,' Amberg replied. 'Is there a safe way down to Colmar?'

'No,' Tweed informed him. 'It will be a journey of pure terror . . .'

Norton had recovered swiftly from the shock of the fiasco of the assault on the château. Sitting in his Renault, he used his mobile phone to contact Mencken. It took him several minutes to establish a link free of atmospherics.

'I'm on route D417,' Mencken said, talking quickly before he could be questioned. 'I'm sure they will come this way heading back to Colmar. After what they faced on their journey up by the other route. All the roads west are blocked by snow.'

'You'd goddamn better be right,' Norton rasped. 'What happened at the château? You only sent in two cars and you had five.'

'I kept Yellow, Orange and Brown in reserve. They'll be needed to finish the job on route D417 . . .'

'You could have overwhelmed them if you'd kept to your original instructions.'

'I don't think so,' Mencken rapped back in a burst of

fury. 'It was that friggin' glider which took us by surprise . . .'

'Crap!' Norton shouted down the phone. 'It should have been shot down . . .'

'That's what I like,' Mencken snapped. 'Armchair strategists who stay a safe distance from the action. I'm closing this conversation. The new ambushes have to be checked . . .'

'Mencken! You talk to me like that just once more . . .'

Norton swore foully when he realized no one was listening at the other end. He sucked in a deep breath of cold air to calm down. There was an important job waiting for him – at six in the evening he was due to meet Growly Voice at the Lac Noir rendezvous. It could be that inside a few hours he'd have both the film and the tape. He'd then drive to Strasbourg, catch an Air Inter flight to Paris where he would board Concorde for Washington.

'Here is Marler, the man who saved the day,' announced Newman. 'I sent Nield out to find him.'

Tweed was waiting impatiently inside a huge living-room which led to Amberg's bedroom. Newman had earlier briefed Tweed on the arrival of the glider. Paula ran forward and hugged the new arrival.

'Thank you,' Tweed said simply. 'You saved our bacon – and our skins.'

'Really, it was dead easy,' Marler drawled. He lit a king-size. 'Pure luck I floated in when I did. What's next on the agenda? I see they've tidied up the courtyard.'

'The station wagon with the bodies is parked inside the garage building at the back as you suggested,' Newman confirmed. 'What about the French authorities?'

'We'll wait until we get to Basle,' Tweed decided. 'I'll call my old friend Chief Inspector René Lasalle in Paris.

Otherwise we could be delayed in France for ages with red tape, statements, all that hogwash—'

He broke off as he heard Eve's voice calling out to Amberg in the bedroom. She was helping him to pack.

'Two clean shirts here, Walter. They'll see you through until we reach Ouchy.'

'Shouldn't I have more?' Amberg's voice asked querulously.

'Two are enough,' Eve responded firmly. 'We have to get a move on. Now, these documents . . .'

'Put them in the zip-up folder.' Amberg's tone was decisive. 'Don't alter the sequence. They're important.'

Paula had winked at Tweed when she heard Eve again running the show as she had done a few minutes earlier. Tweed, who had glanced at his watch a moment before, frowned and stared at Paula without seeing her.

Marler had amused himself by asking Jennie to show him the indoor swimming pool. He returned with her, stubbed out his cigarette in a crystal glass ashtray. Jennie was gazing at him with more than normal interest as she played with the string of pearls round her neck. Marler reached out to touch them.

'Those are quite beautiful . . .'

'*Don't touch!*' She coloured as Marler withdrew his hand, raised an eyebrow. 'Sorry I snapped at you. It's just that I'm superstitious about anyone else handling them.'

Paula noticed that Tweed, despite his impatience to be on their way, wasn't missing even the most trivial incident. He frowned again briefly, glancing at the pearls and then at her expression. Eve strode out of the bedroom at that moment, carrying a large Louis Vuitton case. Behind her ambled the banker, looking unhappy.

'I'm not sure I've packed enough.'

'You haven't packed anything. I have,' Eve reminded him. She slapped her hand against the case she'd perched on a table. 'Enough in there to get you to Cape Town. We are only going to Ouchy. And I can see Tweed is in a hurry. In case you've forgotten it, Walter, from now on Tweed is your protector. He may even get us to Colmar and points south alive.'

'Don't joke about things like that,' Amberg protested. 'It's bad luck.'

'Someone else is superstitious,' Jennie remarked. 'I'm not the only crackpot round here. Am I riding in the same chariot I was transported up here aboard? Hope so. Bob and Tweed got me here in one piece. Oh dear. You are shaking your head, Tweed.'

'One thing I forgot to tell you, Tweed,' Marler broke in. 'The glider is a complete write-off. I warned you. Cost you a bomb.'

'Don't worry about that. Jennie has raised the question of transport. I've discussed that with Newman and we've made some changes in the sequence of the convoy. Object, to confuse the opposition.'

'I insist I'm driving back down those mountains in the BMW,' Gaunt barked out. 'Feel comfortable behind the wheel of that car. Eve, are you joining me? If not . . .' He turned to Jennie. 'You'll be most welcome as a passenger. And I'm a good chap as escort – with my trusty Colt.'

Gaunt appeared to be adopting a jovial manner to lighten the atmosphere. Watching him, Paula couldn't decide whether he was just a show-off, full of his own importance, or a formidable personality.

'I'd like to ride back with Tweed,' Eve said, gazing at him. 'If that's all right with you.'

'Newman will head the convoy, driving the station wagon this time,' Tweed explained. 'He has the advantage of being armed with the Uzi, a deadly weapon. Marler will travel next to him. He has the advantage of carrying his Armalite and the tear-gas pistol. The station wagon becomes the spearhead of the convoy.'

'What about the Espace?' Paula asked.

'That will follow behind the station wagon and I will be driving it with you alongside me. Cardon, armed with grenades, will travel in the row behind us. That leaves Butler and Nield, who will ride the motorcycles. But this time the convoy will maintain its sequence come hell or high water – with Butler as outrider in front of the station wagon all the time and Nield bringing up the rear. Eve sits next to Cardon in the Espace.'

'Hold on!' Gaunt boomed out, raising a hand. 'I'm with this party in case you've forgotten.'

'Which I hadn't,' Tweed shot back. 'You're car number three, following my Espace, with Nield behind you. And Philip,' he said, addressing Cardon, 'I know that inside your hold-all you have a collection of walkie-talkies. Give one to Marler, one to Paula, who has sharp eyes, one to Butler, one to Nield, and one to Jennie, who proved on the way up she also has sharp eyes.'

Cardon unfastened his hold-all and had distributed the walkie-talkies in less than a minute, including a clear instruction to Jennie as to how to operate it. Holding the instrument, Jennie looked at Eve with a mocking expression. She spoke to her in a whisper.

'You're lucky, darling. Nothing to do except make up to Tweed. They call it spare luggage.'

'Not too spare, dear.' Eve reached behind a couch, came up holding an automatic rifle in both hands, the muzzle pointed at the ceiling, Tweed noted with approval. 'And I'm a crack shot,' Eve went on, also in a whisper.

'Modesty really has become an old-fashioned virtue,' Jennie flashed back. 'I'll look after Greg for you.'

Tweed's acute hearing had picked up the catty exchange. He put his hands round the shoulders of both women.

'I am relying on both of you to back up the team when it comes to a crisis. Both of you have my full confidence.'

425

'What about me?' asked Amberg, who had remained silent and still while he listened to the arrangement of the convoy. 'I do have a Mercedes in the garage . . .'

'Leave it there,' Tweed told him. He'd purposely not mentioned the banker earlier, exerting a little more psychological pressure. 'You will be sitting in the Espace, in the second row of seats between Eve and Cardon.'

'Will you be carrying that rifle?' Amberg demanded, staring at the weapon Eve was holding.

'Bet your life I will,' she told him cheerfully. 'So when we're attacked, keep your head down. Now, what are we waiting for, everybody?'

'I'm waiting for you all to get a move on,' Tweed said brusquely.

'Amberg,' Newman snapped, 'you'd better hurry out to the garage and lock it up. Has anyone else a key to this place?'

'Yes. The woman who acts as housekeeper in my absence and lets in the other servants.'

'Wouldn't want them poking around in that garage, considering what it contains besides your car.'

'No, of course not . . .'

The convoy was drawn up in the deep snow in the courtyard and everyone was aboard their allotted vehicles when an ashen-faced Amberg, huddled in a fur coat, returned. Only Newman stood outside the Espace. He gestured for the Swiss to get aboard.

'I saw that car – and what was inside,' Amberg remarked. 'The garage is like a charnel house.'

'And may I remind you,' Newman said brutally, 'that all those men came here to kill us? Get in your seat and shut up.'

'This could be a memorable journey,' commented Eve as the banker climbed in beside her, the rifle across her lap. 'Who knows? We might even survive it . . .'

45

'Ives, whichever route Tweed and his team use to come back down off the mountains they have to pass this point,' said Cord Dillon. Seated inside his car, his window open, Dillon had the hood of his coat pulled well down over his head.

He was speaking to a man astride a motorcycle parked next to the open window. At the front of his machine a Union Jack fluttered in the icy breeze, attached to the top of the extended radio aerial.

Barton Ives, Special Agent of the FBI, was even more muffled up. Wearing a helmet and goggles, the lower part of his face was masked with a thick woollen scarf. He had lifted it above his firm mouth to converse with Dillon.

'Tweed knows the Union Jack is partial proof of your identity,' Dillon went on. 'But he'll need more than that . . .'

'I have my papers . . .'

'He'll need more than those,' Dillon warned. 'So he has your description. When you contact him show him your face and hair immediately. He has a tough bunch with him who don't hesitate to shoot any suspect character.'

'I'll tell him my story as soon as I get the guy on his own. Trouble is,' Ives went on, 'he'll never believe it. Too goddamn earth-shaking.'

'It's all of that,' Dillon agreed. 'Didn't believe it myself when you first told me. It's quiet here but we'd better not be seen together any longer.'

'That gas station over there,' Ives commented. 'It has a

coffee shop. I'll buy myself a drink, sit at a window table. I'll have a good view of the road from there.'

'OK,' Dillon agreed, reaching for the brake. 'But make contact before Tweed and his team hit the heavy traffic. I saw him go up in a Renault Espace, with a Renault station wagon and two motorcycle outriders as escort. The Espace is a grey colour. On your own now, Ives. So stay lucky . . .'

The convoy's journey down through the Vosges had been uneventful so far. That is discounting the fact that an icy breeze combined with a fall in temperature had made the twisting road like an endless skating rink. Inside the Espace, even with the heaters turned up full blast, Paula felt the chill penetrating her gloves, her clothes.

Several times Tweed, behind the wheel of the Espace, had felt the insidious slide of a skid. On one occasion he had a cliff wall to his left, a bottomless abyss to his right. He had driven with the skid, which had taken the front right-hand wheel within centimetres of the drop.

'Oh, my God!' Amberg cried out, jerking upright.

'Shut up, like Newman told you to,' snapped Paula.

She glanced at Eve, saw her hands had tightened on the rifle. Paula's own hands had stiffened inside her gloves. Eve turned on Amberg.

'Walter,' she said in a cold voice, 'I'm beginning to suspect you are the real target. After all, whoever those people were, they attacked the Château Noir. So you could be the one who is putting our lives at risk. That being so, kindly shut your face. I hope you are understanding my message, Walter.'

Cardon turned slowly sideways and nudged the banker before he spoke.

'Do keep quiet, old chap. The driver needs all his concentration. Ready for the next skid.'

Tweed heard all this with a corner of his mind as he stared ahead at the next bend, trying to detect whether there was more ice under the treacherous covering of snow on the steep downward spiral.

Ahead of them, Newman, behind the wheel of the station wagon with Marler next to him, had negotiated two skids and had been driving slowly. Now he reduced his speed to a crawl. It was only a few minutes later that the road levelled out, widened on a small plateau. He signalled that he was stopping.

Tweed pulled up behind him after signalling to Gaunt who was following them in the BMW with Jennie huddled in a sheepskin next to him. Newman had alighted and Tweed, his arms aching with tension, was glad to join him in the snow as Paula and Cardon followed him. Marler then stepped out, the Armalite gripped in his right hand. Newman pointed to a large sign in front of a large single-storey wooden building which appeared deserted. Paula read it.

LA SCHLUCHT 1139.

'I don't believe it,' she said. 'We're still over three thousand feet up in the Vosges. I assume that height is in metres.'

'You assume correctly,' Tweed responded, banging his gloves together to get the circulation back into both his hands. 'In summer I imagine that place is open for refreshments. This is what is called a panoramic viewing point on maps – something like that.'

'A panorama it is,' Paula agreed.

To the north and south stretched the Ice Age world of the peaks and crevasses of the Vosges, the white summits reminding Paula of shark-like teeth. They had emerged from the zone of shadow and everywhere the sunlit snow sparkled like a million diamonds.

The cold was intense and Paula, like Eve and Jennie,

who had run down from the BMW, began stamping her booted feet, which felt like blocks of ice. Gaunt came striding up as Tweed conferred with Newman, Marler and Cardon.

'I don't like it,' Tweed warned. 'So far there has been no sign of the opposition, no attempt to stop us. Yet! Something pretty nasty has to be waiting for us beyond here.'

'Oh, I don't know about that,' said Gaunt, who had taken no part in the defence of the château. 'My bet is they shot their bolt, back up there, whoever they were. Let's press on, regardless. Get back to Colmar and the Brasserie before dark. I can feel a drink comin' on.'

Paula stared at him blankly. Jennie raised her eyebrows to heaven. Tweed ignored him, hauled out his walkie-talkie, called Butler.

The two outriders, Butler and Nield, posted at the front and rear, had stopped their machines without coming to join the conference.

'Butler,' Tweed said, 'keep your eyes skinned for anything unusual. I don't like the peace we have enjoyed so far.'

'Agreed. Neither do I,' Butler responded.

Nield also agreed when Tweed contacted him, made a similar reply to Butler's.

'Let's get moving,' Tweed ordered. 'Proceed with extreme caution . . .'

Beyond the Col de la Schlucht the road descended at a precipitous angle round a series of hellish hairpin bends. During their brief stop Paula had been struck by the sinister silence which had fallen over the Vosges. A heavy silence which you could almost hear. She sat upright, staring ahead.

The mountain began to rise up sheer to their left. To

the right the abyss became a white chasm with no sign of where it reached bottom. Beside Newman, in the station wagon, Marler had laid his tear-gas pistol in his lap, was craning his neck to check the heights. It was Butler who issued the early warning.

'Everyone slow to a crawl. Be prepared to stop the moment I tell you. Two men on top of the big cliff ahead.'

'Message received,' Tweed replied, holding the wheel with one hand briefly along a short straight stretch.

He had finished speaking when, thirty seconds later, he heard Nield calling him. An urgent note in his tone.

'We're being followed. Bloody great truck. Nestlé. A half-mile behind me and coming like the clappers.'

In the distance, just short of yet another bend, Butler had propped his machine against the rock wall, had begun to climb up a ravine. Marler told Newman to stop, jumped out, Armalite in his left hand, tear-gas pistol in his right. Keeping close to the rock wall, he ran down the icy road like a marathon entrant, reached the ravine and shinned up it close behind Butler.

Paula had focused her binoculars on the rock wall near the bend. She pursed her lips before she spoke.

'That's a huge granite cliff sheering up vertically from the road by the bend. Obviously unstable. I'm sure it's covered with a curtain of steel mesh.'

Tweed nodded as he stopped the Espace. Paula's news was disturbing. They had something possibly very danger-ous ahead of them – and coming up fast behind them was this huge Nestlé truck Nield had spotted. Tweed didn't think the two incidents were a coincidence. They were caught in a pincer movement of potential destruction. It all had the signature of Norton written across it.

'I'd better go and give them back-up,' Paula suggested.

Tweed swung round in his seat, grasped her arm. He shook his head.

'Stay here. Marler and Butler will be more than a

match for two thugs. I just hope they clear the way before that truck coming up behind us arrives. It's going to try and push us all off the road into eternity.'

'If I run back now past the BMW I could probably shoot that truck driver,' Eve suggested.

'Stay put. No one moves,' Tweed ordered.

'Are we just going to sit here?' Amberg demanded.

'We are going to do just that.'

'Surely someone can do something,' Amberg persisted.

'Two men are doing something,' Tweed replied in the same flat tone. 'You can do something – keep quiet.'

Tweed had experienced similar reactions before. In a crisis people couldn't just wait. To soothe their nerves they needed action – anything which involved movement. So often it was safest to wait – once counter-measures had been taken. And they had been.

Butler and Marler, using their gloved hands, had hauled themselves up to the top of the ravine. Butler peered over the rim of a rock. Then he crouched down again and looked at Marler below him over his shoulder.

'Tricky,' he reported. 'Two thugs about thirty feet away. Top of the cliff is flat. Boulders scattered in groups across it.'

'I could take them with the Armalite.'

'Not that simple,' Butler objected. 'They have set up explosives to bring down the cliff on the road . . .'

'How do you know?' Marler whispered impatiently.

'Because I can see another of those old-fashioned plunger devices like the one on top of the tower at Kaysersberg. Hang on, you weren't there. They're both near the handle that only needs pressing to bring down that cliff. I'm sure of it. And on the road they've got the Nestlé truck coming after them . . .' Butler had heard Nield's message just before switching off his walkie-talkie

432

and knew they were desperately short of time before the truck arrived.

'We have to lure those thugs away from that plunger handle,' he told Marler. 'Question is, how the hell do we do that?'

The stocky American driving the truck was grinning wolfishly to himself. He had caught a glimpse of the stalled convoy and was closing the gap rapidly. He wore a woollen cap pulled down over his low forehead and talked to himself for company.

'Won't be long now. I'll ram the lot of you over the edge down into that abyss. You'll end up dead meat. Maybe spring before what's left of you is found. Old bones . . .'

With two accomplices he had earlier hijacked the big vehicle as the original driver crossed the Vosges. They had cut his throat and thrown the body into one of the crevasses in the ice. But not before the American now driving had pulled off the victim's woollen cap. He felt the cold.

The truck was loaded to the roof with supplies, adding to the enormous weight of the juggernaut. The weight was now helping the driver to keep going, holding the surface of the snow-covered road well.

'Another five minutes,' he said to himself. 'Then it will be all over for you poor schmucks . . .'

Marler had eased himself up the ravine alongside Butler. He peered over the rim of the boulder, looked at the side of the ravine where they had pressed away snow during their ascent. With his gloved hand he began digging and clawing at a small piece of protruding rock while Butler held his tear-gas pistol. The rock came loose, Marler tested its weight in his hand and nodded.

'Give me back the pistol,' he said. 'With luck this will get

433

them well clear of the explosive box. You take the one with the sheepskin, I'll sort out the thug with the windcheater, if it works.'

'It has to,' Butler said, glancing at his watch.

Marler hoisted himself higher up, being careful to hide himself behind the boulder. Sheepskin was standing with binoculars pressed to his eyes, obviously wondering why the convoy had stopped moving. Windcheater hovered dangerously close to the plunger handle.

About thirty feet away from where the thugs waited, well inland from the brink of the cliff, was a scatter of very large boulders massed close together. Marler raised his arm, aimed for the centre of the scatter, threw the rock.

'Hey, Don, what the friggin' hell was that?' called out Sheepskin, dropping his binoculars looped round his neck with a strap.

'Came from over there, Jess,' Windcheater replied. He pointed to the scatter of boulders. 'We'd better take a look. They could've sent up someone. Get ready to take him out . . .'

Gripping machine-pistols, both Americans advanced alongside each other, their gaze fixed on the boulders. Marler smiled to himself as he half-crouched, half-stood behind the boulder. He used it to rest both arms to steady his aim. Very stupid to walk next to each other. He pressed the trigger.

The shell struck a boulder just in front of the two thugs, burst, flooded the air with tear-gas. Earlier Marler had noted the icy breeze at la Schlucht was no longer blowing. Marler and Butler moved like greyhounds as the Americans coughed, spluttered, staggered, held a hand to their eyes, still clutching the machine-pistols.

Despite the pain of the tear-gas both thugs were staggering at surprising speed back towards the plunger. Marler realized that a lot of the deadly vapour had exploded away from the targets. They were nerve-wrackingly close to the plunger when Marler reached Don, whose vision was obscured. He saw only silhouettes.

Marler had dropped his pistol, was holding his Armalite with the barrel across his chest, gripped at both ends. He drove it with a ferocious thrust against Don, forcing him backwards, preventing him from making any use of his own weapon. At the last moment Don realized he was on the edge of the brink.

'No! For Chrissakes . . .'

Marler, careful where he placed his own feet, gave one final savage shove. The American fell back into space. In a bizarre gesture he hurled his weapon away from himself. Marler caught it with one hand in mid-air. With a high-pitched yell of pure terror the American plunged down. At this point the lip of the cliff protruded well over the road below. The piercing yell continued echoing round the Vosges as the somersaulting body, arms flailing, missed the road and plunged on down, down, down into the abyss.

At almost the same moment Butler hammered the barrel of his Luger down on to the hand of Jess, forcing him to drop the weapon. He then struck his adversary across the face, left, right, left. The onslaught drove Jess back and back. He was close to the edge when Butler brought the barrel down on his skull with all his force. Jess collapsed out of sight, following his fellow American into the chasm.

Marler and Butler had worked as a perfect team, keeping to the original plan, each tackling the thug closest to him. Butler was breathing heavily as Marler ran back to retrieve his tear-gas pistol. When he returned Butler had recovered his breath, was operating his walkie-talkie.

'Tweed. Cliff laced with explosives. Later we can get down the shallow slope south of the cliff, join you on the road. Get Cardon to grab my machine if he can. Pete can

435

be bait for the truck. We'll take it from there . . .'

'Agreed,' Tweed's voice answered tersely.

There was very little time left. He gave Nield brief instructions. Nield acknowledged. Tweed signalled to Newman to move on, told Cardon the plan, started the Espace moving, warned Gaunt via Jennie over her walkie-talkie to get moving, keep close . . .

At the summit Butler pointed out to Marler several places where holes had been drilled in the unstable cliff, explosives inserted. Dynamite, he thought. Marler took up a position at the brink, looked down. It was lucky he had never suffered from vertigo. The drop beyond the road was dizzying. From this point he could see the movement of the convoy and – more important still – the position further back where Pete Nield sat astride his motorcycle, calmly waiting for the arrival of the juggernaut. Live bait. He'd have to time it to a fraction of a second.

The driver of the Nestlé truck was chewing gum. Whatever he was doing – driving, talking, waiting to kill a target – he was always chewing gum. The truck swayed a little despite its great weight as the front wheels passed over ice, but the vehicle held on to the surface as though glued to it.

He had had the heaters turned up full blast for quite a while, the windows of the cab firmly closed, and the atmosphere inside was a nauseating mixture of sweat, oil and heat. The driver was unaware of this. He was about to open the window briefly to spit out gum, prior to inserting a fresh stick in his thin-lipped mouth, when he rounded a corner and saw Nield seated on his machine, a stream of exhaust like steam ejecting from the pipe.

The driver grinned wolfishly again, rammed his foot down on the accelerator. Nield took off like a bird, keeping close to the wall of rock as he appeared to fly across the snow. Chewing Gum was startled, annoyed at the lightning take-off. He rammed his foot down further.

'You're the salad, pal,' he said to himself. 'Then we can get on with the main course.'

He was particularly looking forward to tipping the Espace over the edge. That was going to give him a real kick. He burned rubber as Nield disappeared round the corner of the massive cliff overhanging the road. This was fun, Chewing Gum thought.

The corner was sharper than he'd anticipated. He braked to take it. That was when he heard a rumbling sound. He frowned, glanced up, then stared in horror. Above him as he leaned forward, gazing up through the windscreen, he saw a vast black curtain descending on him. Huge boulders crashed on to the road ahead of him and bounced off the edge.

He was no longer chewing gum. His teeth were clamped together in sheer fright. Something hit the top of his cab, denting the roof. A small boulder rolled off and down into the white hell below. The windscreen was suddenly blotted out as shale fell, piled up on the hood. He was driving blind.

'Jesus! No . . . o . . .!'

He screamed. The wheel no longer responded to the frantic turn of his clawed hands. A sound like thunder roared out as thousands of tons of granite fell on the juggernaut like a giant sledgehammer. He felt the truck tipping over towards the brink. Through the side window he saw the chasm coming up to meet him. The juggernaut was pushed off the road, began turning like an immense cartwheel as it dropped into the depths. Chewing Gum's head, his mind, was spinning out of control. The truck gathered speed, plunged on down into the three-hundred-foot ravine. It hit ice-covered rocks, burst into flames which sizzled as the snow quenched them and the juggernaut died.

46

On the summit of the cliff Marler and Butler had operated again as a skilled team. Butler had waited by the plunger while Marler ran further along the brink away from the convoy. He had stopped at a point where he could look down on the winding road and see it clearly.

Holding his right arm upright, Marler watched the roof of Newman's station wagon pass below him, followed by the grey Espace and Gaunt's BMW. He had waited until he saw Nield on his motorcycle, speeding past. The moment Nield was well clear of the cliff he had dropped his hand and run like hell away from the brink to the centre of the plateau. That was the moment when Butler pressed down on the plunger with all his strength.

His job accomplished, he began running back to join Marler. Butler felt the ground trembling under his feet and wondered whether he was going to make it. Reaching the scatter of boulders where Marler waited he looked back and sucked in his breath.

The two Americans had misjudged placing the plunger mechanism. Butler stared in awe as a fissure zig-zagged across the plateau, as half the plateau crumbled away, taking the mechanism with it. The roar was deafening. Clouds of rock dust appeared from under the snow. Choking, both men ran for the shallow slope, Marler gripping his Armalite and tear-gas pistol.

The crash and rumble of the avalanche continued as they ran, slithered down the long slope to where the convoy was stationary, waiting for them. Cardon greeted them as they arrived on the road, calling out to Butler.

'We manhandled your machine into the back of the Espace. Paula helped me. We had only seconds.'

'I'll get it out, then,' Butler decided. 'Take up my old position at the head of the convoy.'

'Congratulations, both of you,' Tweed said tersely when he had jumped down to meet them. 'Marler, get back into the station wagon. Tell Newman to get moving. I want us out of the mountains before dark. And again, everyone keep a sharp lookout for more welcomes from the enemy.'

'I'll go ahead of Newman as before,' repeated Butler.

With Cardon's help he had been hauling his machine out of the back of the Espace. Amberg was twisted round in his seat, staring fixedly. Butler gave him a brief wave, whispered to Cardon.

'The Swiss looks stiff as a poker. Obviously not used to these day trips . . .'

Mounted on his machine, he started it and sped off as Gaunt came striding down from his BMW.

'What the devil was all that about?' he barked.

'Avalanche,' Tweed told him. 'You get them in this part of the world in winter. Get back to your car. We're on our way . . .'

Soon the convoy was driving down an even more murderous series of spiral twists and turns which went on and on. Dusk was descending and great stands of fir trees closed in on either side, immense branches weighed down with thick coatings of frozen snow. Paula shivered at the sight of them – it reminded her of films of Siberia she had seen.

The forest moved in to the edges of the road, creating tunnels which she found claustrophobic. Inside the Espace the temperature was dropping despite the fact that Tweed had the heaters turned full on.

They emerged from the tunnels as they reached lower levels and lights inside houses appeared as they passed hamlets tucked into bends and located inside ravines. Their headlights swept over small houses with red-tiled rooves showing in patches close to chimneys: heat from a stove inside had temporarily melted a little snow. First-floor balconies looked as though they'd soon sag under the accumulated snow they supported.

They passed through the small town of Munster, bumping over cobbled streets, slowing down as they approached the outskirts of Colmar. They had just passed a petrol station with a small café attached when a motor-cyclist drew alongside the Espace out of nowhere. Eve, who had remained calm and quiet during the drama of the falling cliff, raised her rifle. Paula was already aiming her Browning as Tweed slowed down, saw them.

'Put down those weapons, for God's sake, both of you!' he shouted.

He stopped the Espace as the motorcyclist, a Union Jack whipping from its aerial, pulled up. Tweed left the engine running and looked over his shoulder before he opened the door.

'Paula, keep him covered with your gun, but don't fire unless he produces a weapon.'

He opened the door and the tall motorcyclist stood in the road, the machine leant against him, both hands raised above his head.

'You're Tweed. I've been waiting here hours for you. I'm Barton Ives, Special Agent FBI . . .'

'How did you know I would be coming this way?' demanded Tweed.

'Cord Dillon said you had to pass this spot when you came down from the mountains. That was in the after-noon. I have papers . . .'

'Be very careful what you take out of your pocket,' warned Paula as the stranger reached inside his leather jacket.

He slowly produced a folder, handed it up to Tweed, who examined it by the courtesy light. With the front door open the temperature inside the Espace dropped even further.

Newman appeared behind the stranger. He pressed the tip of his Smith & Wesson into his back.

'This is a gun,' he warned.

'Yeah. I guessed it was. You guys are wise to take all precautions. But aren't we exposed, standing out here?'

'Not really,' Newman told him.

Marler had left the station wagon, was now positioned at the side of the café next to the petrol station. He had loosened the belt round his fur-lined windcheater so he could thrust the tear-gas belt inside it. He was holding the Armalite, his eyes scanning the whole area. Butler, who had returned on his motorcycle, had taken up a position on the opposite side of the road.

Tweed had examined the folder, which seemed genuine, had compared the photograph with Ives' appearance. The American had removed his helmet, had pulled down the scarf from his face. What convinced Tweed of the man's identity was that he fitted the descriptions Dillon had given him. At long last he was meeting the real Barton Ives.

'Get in,' Tweed ordered, 'sit next to me, keep your hands in your lap. There are people behind you with guns and itching trigger fingers. Bob, put his machine in the back of the Espace . . .'

Tweed's careful check had taken no more than a minute. He signalled to Marler and Butler that they were moving on. He waited until Newman had returned to the station wagon and Ives whispered to him.

'I need to be alone with you. I've one helluva story to

tell you. My guess is you've no idea what you're up against. Doubt if you'll believe a word I say. It's all incredible, but true.'

'Not now,' Tweed replied. 'We're in a hurry to leave France to cross the border into Switzerland – travelling non-stop this evening. Norton hasn't given up yet – of that I'm sure.'

'You can bet on it,' agreed Ives.

Paula was impressed with the FBI agent's appearance and manner. In his late thirties, she estimated, he was tall, had thick dark hair, his strong-featured face with a firm jaw was clean-shaven. Despite his long ordeal of staying under cover, moving constantly from place to place in fear of his life, he showed no signs of strain. His voice was quiet, controlled, almost matter-of-fact.

'We're going to have to hurry to do that,' Ives observed. 'To reach Switzerland tonight.'

'It's just a matter of organization,' Tweed commented as he continued to drive the Espace close to the station wagon.

The rendezvous point where they had picked up Barton Ives had been well chosen. An oasis of quiet, there had been no one else about. Now, only minutes later, they were caught up in Colmar's rush-hour traffic. The convoy had closed up and Gaunt's BMW was on Tweed's tail, a little too close for his liking, but that was Gaunt.

'How shall we manage it?' Paula called out.

'I'll go out the way we came in. By train to Basle. I want you to come with me, and you too, Eve. Philip,' he called over his shoulder to Cardon, 'you'll also be with us as bodyguard, together with Butler and Nield. Ives, you come with us aboard the train.'

Tweed had no intention of letting the elusive American out of his sight after waiting so long to contact him.

'Anything you say,' Ives agreed cheerfully.

'What about the Espace, the station wagon and the

weapons?' asked Paula, her mind racing ahead to the next problem.

'I'm changing tactics from the way we came in,' Tweed said with a surge of vigour in his voice which made Paula feel tired. He glanced briefly back at her at a red traffic light and his eyes gleamed with purpose and drive. This, Paula thought, is where we really take off.

They were nosing their way closer to the Bristol as Tweed explained further.

'I'm assuming our friend, the Swiss police chief, Beck, will be on the alert at the frontier. The French frontier control will still be on the look-out for terrorists *entering* France – not the other way round. If Newman and Marler meet trouble Bob will immediately ask to be put in contact with Beck.'

'What about the Uzi Bob is carrying?' Paula pressed.

'All the weapons will be hidden, attached under the chassis of the station wagon and the Espace – including the Uzi. That is the sort of trouble Newman may run into. We shall need those weapons for a final showdown, I'm convinced of that.'

'And we stay in Basle overnight?' Paula asked.

'No! We keep on moving. We arrange to meet Newman and Marler with their transport at Basle Bahnhof. From there we drive on non-stop south-west into French-speaking Switzerland. From Basle to Neuchatel, on past the lake to Yverdon, then due south to Ouchy on the shores of Lake Geneva. Amberg, you did say that is where you have hidden the items I want to see and hear?'

'I did,' the banker replied tersely. 'But we have to stop at my branch in Basle for a few minutes – so I can collect a safe deposit key.'

'Make sure it is only a few minutes. Two of my men will accompany you into the bank. Paula, when we reach the main station in Basle phone up two hotels in Ouchy – the Hôtel d'Angleterre to book rooms for Butler and Nield,

443

then the Hôtel Château d'Ouchy to book rooms for the rest of us, including Amberg.'

'I prefer to stay at—' Amberg began.

'Your preferences went out of the window when we watched a blank screen at the Château Noir,' Tweed snapped. 'You stay with us – all the way.'

'So,' Paula mused, 'we'll be ahead of the opposition for once, may never see them again.'

'That,' commented Eve, stretching her arms above her head, 'will be a dream.'

'And if you believe that,' Tweed warned, 'considering the huge organization we're up against, you are dreaming . . .'

On the heights of the Vosges Norton, just managing to stop himself from freezing into a block of ice by keeping the engine running, the heaters turned full up, had earlier received a static-ridden report on progress from Mencken.

Progress! Norton would probably have strangled Mencken had his subordinate been close enough. Bleakly and bluntly Mencken had told his chief about the failure of the major ambush planned on D417.

'You say the Nestlé truck was crushed, sent over when the cliff came down?' Norton asked incredulously.

'It was lousy luck . . .' Mencken began, glad that he was miles away from Norton and close to Munster.

'Luck? *Crap!*' Norton shouted. 'Don't give me no smoke. What happened to Phase Two?'

'The huge log pile we were going to roll down on them was frozen solid. So was the earth-moving machine we'd planned to use . . .'

'And Tweed's convoy is where now?' Norton rarely lost his iron self-control and now had a tight grip on himself as he planned the next move. 'Also where are the cars

444

Yellow, Orange and Brown – the vital reserve? I am assuming you know,' he added sarcastically.

'Cars Orange and Brown got frozen up. I had to call back Yellow to jump-start them. It all took time. I sent the three of them back down route N415 and through Kaysersberg. I hoped to intercept Tweed, but my guess is they were too late. They couldn't go back down the other route – we'd have been caught by the cliff fall.'

'We were,' Norton reminded him. 'Stay where you are until I contact you again. I've got a job to do – since I want it done OK, I'm handling it myself. Keep the reserve in Colmar until I get back to you . . .'

Norton, due to arrive at Lac Noir at 6 p.m. to keep the appointment with Growly Voice, deliberately reached the rendezvous early at 5.45 p.m. Switching off his headlights, he left the engine running to avoid freezing to death.

Night had fallen and the temperature had fallen with it – to below zero. He lowered the window a few inches, his right hand gripping an HP35 Browning automatic in his lap. His headlights had illuminated a low stone wall with the black waters of the silent lake beyond it.

Very little rattled Norton's nerve but the total lack of sound, the incredible silence and tomb-like atmosphere was unsettling. Where the hell was Growly Voice?

There was no sign of another vehicle, of any human habitation, of any human being. Using his left hand he switched on a powerful torch beam, used it to slowly scan the top of the wall. It was then he saw the wooden box perched on the parapet.

He slid out of the car fast, closing the door quickly so he wasn't illuminated by the courtesy light. For a long minute he stood listening. The icy cold seeped through his astrakhan coat. He approached the box slowly. About a foot long and a foot deep, it was old and the lid was closed. He had an unpleasant suspicion this was a booby-trap. No, that didn't make sense. Growly Voice wanted the big bucks.

The huge sum of money was still under guard in the care of Louis Sheen at a room inside the Hotel Bristol. Earlier Norton had been amused at the thought of Sheen staying tied with handcuffs to the suitcase. The only time he released himself from his burden was when he went to the bathroom or took a shower. Even then he took the suitcase with him.

Norton studied the old box. He was still suspicious. No sign of wires in the torch-light beam. Using the tip of his Browning, he gently lifted the lid until he could see inside. It appeared to be empty. Sucking in a deep breath of icy air, he raised the lid wide open, stared, swore in Marine Corps language.

A sheet of paper was lying at the bottom. Words had been crudely written on it by someone using a felt-tip pen. The infuriating message was clear enough.

Mr Norton. Welcome. If you really want the two items you are interested in bring the money. Proceed now to Ouchy, Switzerland, Lake Geneva. A room has been reserved for you at the Château d'Ouchy. Occupy it this evening. You will hear from me. Do not delay a minute. This time, do bring the money. This is your last chance.

Norton hurled the box into the still black waters of the lake. By the light of his torch beam he watched it sink. He returned to his car, closed the door, the window, and pulled out from the glove compartment a collection of maps until he found one of Switzerland.

It took him a while to trace his finger along the shore of Lake Geneva until he located Ouchy. He picked up his mobile phone. By some miracle Mencken answered at once and the connection was loud and clear.

'Ouchy, Switzerland . . .' Norton spelt the name of the

446

port. 'Move the entire reserve to this goddamned hick place tonight. Spread them out among as many little hotels as you can find. Call me at eleven tonight but don't come near the Château d'Ouchy. OK? What the hell do I care how you make it? Get on it, street bum . . .'

For the moment Norton was no longer concerned with Tweed. His mind was concentrated on getting hold of the film and the tape – and that meant reaching Ouchy fast. Disinclined to linger by the sinister lake – he had glanced up once and in the moonlight had seen the fateful château perched like a menace above him.

He drove on as fast as he dared until he reached the N415 which would take him back to Kaysersberg. There he'd make a brief call at the Green Tree, collect his few things, pay the bill. At a lonely spot he pulled in off the road on to a snow-covered verge, kept the engine running.

Taking out his collection of maps, he studied them and decided to take the autoroute to Basle. From there he'd drive on through the night until he reached Ouchy. As he put away the maps he decided he'd better later call in at the Hotel Bristol to check that all his remaining team had left. A careful man with detail, Norton was a fanatic for checking out everything.

Marvin Mencken had taken a few decisions of his own. After receiving orders from Norton, he used his mobile phone to contact car Yellow and arranged to meet the men in that car in Munster.

The leader of this team was Jason, a professional gunman from New Jersey. With a face like a bulldog and the determination of the animal, he was probably the most ruthless American below the ranks of Norton and Mencken.

Unlike Norton, Mencken was still very much concerned with the fact that Tweed still survived. It was an insult to his

447

professional integrity. Reaching Munster, he parked his car close to Yellow, got out into the bitter night and walked to give special orders to this reserve team. Cars Orange and Brown were already on their way south to Switzerland. Mencken had warned them over his mobile phone first to collect their bags from the Bristol, to pay their bills. In his own cunning way Mencken rivalled Norton in attention to detail.

'Jason,' he began without ceremony, talking through the open window, 'later you grease your butts and move like the wind to this dump, Ouchy. I've marked it on this spare map. OK? It had better be. Put your men up in a small hotel. Avoid the Château d'Ouchy – I've written that name down on the edge of the map.'

'You said later. We've got a job to do first?'

Jason spoke in a hoarse tone – he was a three-pack a day smoker. His large head and face were faintly illuminated by a nearby street lamp. With his piggy eyes, his pug nose and his lower teeth protruding slightly above his bottom lip, even Mencken thought he looked horrific.

'You've got three other men,' Mencken continued. 'I want you to drive straight to the Bristol. Make yourselves inconspicuous – and keep a lookout for Tweed and his mob.'

'We lose that guy for ever – and the rest of his team?' Jason suggested hopefully.

'You do just that. I'll be following you, get there later. Do a nice quiet job. Afterwards maybe you can prop them up in their beds in their rooms. Give the night maid a nice surprise,' Mencken suggested with his macabre sense of humour.

47

'To the Brasserie!' Tweed called out as they approached closer to the Hôtel Bristol. 'And a glass of Riesling!'

It was an attempt to cheer up his passengers. He sensed that reaction was setting in after the events of the day.

'Anyone would think you hadn't eaten or drunk a thing since leaving Colmar,' Paula chided him.

In fact they had taken refreshment 'on the hoof'. Before leaving the Bristol in the morning Paula had collected a large quantity of *sandwich au jambon* – ham inside French bread. She had also had six Thermoses, purchased in Basle, filled with coffee and another one with cold milk. In addition she had brought twelve litre-bottles of mineral water.

They had eaten and slaked their thirst during the first stage of their descent from the château, and later after the cataclysmic collapse of the cliff. At the same time, Paula reflected, they had had no more than snacks and she too was feeling peckish.

'Are we safe now?' Amberg suddenly demanded in a commanding voice.

'No,' Tweed told him. 'We are only safe when we have our hands on the film and the tape. So really,' he went on in an offhand manner, 'it's entirely up to you, Amberg.'

'They won't know we're going to Ouchy,' the banker suggested.

'Don't count on that either,' Tweed replied, determined to keep the Swiss rattled.

'Do stop fussing, Walter,' Eve broke in with one of her

rare interventions. Her manner was calm, her voice fresh. Paula admired her stamina. 'Walter,' Eve continued, 'if you're nervous don't eat or drink anything at dinner. You might get indigestion. You wouldn't like that, Walter,' she ended, her voice dripping with sarcasm.

Amberg relapsed into silence after casting her a venomous look which Paula noticed. The traffic was now very heavy and, following Newman, Tweed was inching the Espace next to the kerb along the wide pavement outside the shops facing the railway station.

He braked as Newman stopped the station wagon ahead. It occurred to Tweed that it was along this same pavement at a later hour that Jennie Blade had encountered the Shadow Man. What had been her description of the sinister figure? A man wearing a long black overcoat and a wide-brimmed hat which completely concealed his face. Had she been telling the truth? he wondered. Newman appeared at his open window.

'I suggest you all get out here and walk straight into the Brasserie where there are other people. Marler is parking the station wagon a short distance away. I'll take over the wheel of the Espace. Paula, could you run back to the BMW which is pulled up a few yards behind? I want you to escort Jennie into the Brasserie. But first tell Gaunt to follow me in the Espace. And *tell* Gaunt – I don't want any argument.'

'Butler and Nield?' Tweed queried.

'Told over my walkie-talkie to follow the convoy. Now, I want to get behind that wheel fast . . .'

Tweed dropped into the road and hurried to the pavement followed by Paula, Eve, Amberg and Cardon, who had a firm hand on the arm of the Swiss. Newman, Tweed ruminated, was now capable of taking control of the whole operation if anything happened to him.

Eve caught up with him, linked her arm inside his, her rifle concealed under her long trench coat. Paula ran back to where Gaunt had begun to honk his horn non-stop, just when they didn't want to be noticed. Jennie lowered her window when she saw Paula coming. Paula stopped, her tone icy as she addressed Gaunt.

'Stop making that noise at once. Jennie, get out and I will take you inside the Brasserie.'

As Jennie opened the door, moving quickly, Gaunt leaned forward. He glared at Paula.

'Just who do you think you're addressing?' he demanded in a lofty tone.

'You, you stupid arrogant bastard!' she blazed. 'You're putting people's lives in danger. To hell with your own, but get that tin can moving pronto.'

Gaunt was so taken aback, he obeyed. As Paula slammed the door shut he nodded to her, began moving forward, following Newman who was disappearing round the corner in the Espace. Paula took Jennie by the arm, glanced at the mob of people pushing and shoving up against each other while they hurried across to the station. Gaunt had just beaten the lights before they turned red.

Rush hour with a vengeance. Everyone looked sick of doing a day's boring work, sick of trudging through the slush, sick of the penetrating cold. Paula found the normality of all this strangely reassuring after their nightmare trip into the Vosges.

A wave of warmth met them as they pushed open the doors into the well-heated Brasserie. Tweed was already seated at a table in the dining area closest to the hotel with Eve beside him. Cardon sat at the end of the long table where he could survey the whole restaurant.

'A glass of Riesling for everyone who likes the idea,' Tweed announced. 'I think we need a stimulant before we go to our rooms and freshen up before dinner.'

Well, at least we're safe in here, Paula was thinking as she sat next to Cardon and Jennie chose the chair next to

451

hers. Paula agreed enthusiastically to some Riesling and glanced round the restaurant. A handful of locals having a drink on their way home. Then she frowned.

At a table by himself, not ten feet away, sat one of the most repulsive men she'd ever seen, a man who looked just like a bulldog.

Norton drove very slowly when he reached Kaysersberg. The snow was piled up in the ancient narrow streets. This was some country. Hadn't they ever heard of snow-ploughs? He parked the Renault in a side-street some distance from the Green Tree. The less the proprietor of the small hotel knew about him the better.

He met no one as he trudged back through the snow. The old buildings, lit by wrought-iron lamps, had oak beams sunk into the plaster walls. The plaster had a different colour for each building – bright scarlet, deep ochre, flaming orange. Kaysersberg was beautiful, but Norton noticed none of it. Whole lot ought to be pulled down, replaced by modern buildings with plenty of plate-glass.

He walked into the entrance hall of the Green Tree, ignoring the iron scraper outside, littering the carpet with snow. The woman behind the desk called out to him.

'A phone call for you. The same person each time, I think. Called six times. Left a message.'

Norton nodded, took the folded piece of paper. He waited until he'd taken off his fur hat and coat in his small room, then read the message.

Call urgently. Repeat, urgently. Sara.

'Hell. Go jump off a building. A high one,' Norton said out loud.

He checked his watch. It would be 2 p.m. in Washington. He'd half a mind to ignore the message. Sitting on the bed, he decided he'd better make the call. Probably he'd get such a lousy connection it would be pointless.

In a grim mood, he started the laborious business of trying to get through to Washington. The connection wasn't lousy, it was perfect, goddamnit. Sara answered.

'He's pretty anxious to talk with you. I'd go easy if I were you . . .'

'You're not me,' Norton snapped.

'Please yourself.' Sara's tone was calm, indifferent. 'I am putting you on the line. Don't ever say I didn't warn you . . .'

Norton, who had exceptional stamina, was in an ugly mood. It had been a tough day. All attempts to exterminate Tweed had failed. And he hadn't laid his hands on the film or the tape. He wasn't going to bow and scrape.

'Norton?' President Bradford March's tone was aggressive. 'What crap are you feedin' me this time? Give.'

'I know now where what you want is. I'm leaving for some dump called Ouchy in Switzerland. That's where they are. I'll give you my new number after I've got there. Later this evening, European time. We're almost there.'

'I don't give two shits for "almost",' March shouted. 'I should have sent a bell-boy to do this job. Someone is playing you like a fish on a line.'

Which was true, Norton had realized. Growly Voice *had* adopted the technique used by kidnappers. Always sending him on to a new destination to wear him down. The aptness of the President's comment did not improve his temper.

'Just you listen to me for once,' he rapped back. 'I'm the guy on the spot. I know the angles now. Get off my back. Hear me? You listenin' in that snazzy office?'

March had not reached the Oval Office by losing self-control in a crisis. His explosions of abuse were always calculated. Leaning back in his chair, March perched his feet on his desk, crossed his ankles while he thought.

'You still there?' Norton demanded abrasively.

'Sure I am,' March replied quietly. 'Is Mencken still around?' he asked casually.

It was Norton's turn to pause. The one possibility which bothered him was that he might be replaced by that scumbag, Mencken. He decided to hold back nothing. March mimicked in a controlled voice Norton's earlier question.

'You still there?'

'Yeah. Let's hope the line holds. You'd better realize we've taken heavy casualties . . .'

'So this Tweed is smarter than we thought?' commented the President in the same quiet tone.

'He just got lucky.' Norton was leading March away from the subject of Marvin Mencken. 'We've taken some heavy casualties,' he repeated.

'So you can't make the omelette without breakin' a few eggs,' March responded in a bored tone.

'I was going to say we could do with more manpower.'

'Would Mencken need more manpower? You didn't tell me – is Mencken still around?'

'Yes.'

'I can't spare more manpower. I need what I have left here in Washington. Certain guys have to be clamped down on. You said earlier Tweed got lucky,' March recalled, building up to bait Norton some more. 'I'd say he got smart as he's still around.' A pause. 'I don't hear no denial of that. I gave you a time limit, Norton. Time's almost up. I want the film, the tape. I want Tweed, Joel Dyson, Cord Dillon and Barton Ives dumped. For ever. Get on it . . .'

The connection to Washington had gone. Norton slowly put down the receiver and didn't even bother to swear. Ouchy was going to be a blood bath.

* * *

Inside his study at his Chevy Chase house Senator Wingfield looked round at his two guests seated at the round table with a cold expression. His guests, the banker and the elder statesman, watched him closely, realizing there had been a very serious development.

The Senator had summoned them to attend a meeting of the Three Wise Men urgently at short notice. It was not this factor which caused them to sense the atmosphere of tension inside the comfortable room. Wingfield normally had the appearance of a benevolent father figure. He rarely showed any emotion and it was the grimness of his aristocratic features which held their attention.

'Gentlemen,' Wingfield began, 'I have just received this highly confidential communication from the Vice President. Jeb Calloway has received the report I have inside this folder by special delivery from Europe. It makes incredible reading – I just hope its author is insane.'

'But do you think he is? Insane?' the statesman enquired.

'If he isn't – and I have a horrible idea he's as sane as any man round this table – our country faces the most serious crisis of this century.'

'You know who the report is from?' asked the banker.

'Yes. A special agent of the FBI. A man called Barton Ives.' He extracted the typed sheets from the folder, handed them to the banker. 'Judge for yourselves.'

'These documents allege this Barton Ives knows who is responsible for a number of particularly beastly serial murders in several Southern states,' the banker, who was a fast reader, commented in a shaky voice after a few minutes. 'Each involves the murder of a woman by cutting her throat – after rape had been committed, according to the medical examiner's report in the state concerned. All the murders have remained unsolved, even though they took place several years ago. It's beyond belief.'

'What is?' demanded the statesman as the banker handed him the documents.

'The man he names as the perpetrator of these vile crimes. Not only was the throat of each victim cut with a serrated knife – a kitchen knife is suggested – but similar sadistic mutilations were found on each corpse.'

'Who is this Barton Ives?' the statesman persisted before examining the documents. 'I seem to have heard the name.'

'A very senior agent of the FBI,' Wingfield said reluctantly. 'I made discreet enquiries before I called you. Ives was in charge of the investigation linking all six murders. He was about to prepare a comprehensive report when his superior at the Memphis office was posted to Seattle. The new man ordered Ives to discontinue the investigation and destroy the files. He was sent to Memphis on direct orders from Washington. Ives alleges he had to flee to Europe to save his life. My enquiries back up this strange sequence of events.'

There was a heavy silence as the statesman skimmed through the reports. He held each page at the edges between his fingertips, leaving no prints of his own. Dropping the last sheet back inside the folder, he used his elbow to push the folder back to Wingfield across the polished table.

'There is mention of a thumbprint being found on the side of a Lincoln Continental belonging to the sixth raped and murdered woman,' he pointed out. 'Barton Ives says he has that thumbprint and it still exists on the car. So where the hell is the car?'

'I enquired about that,' Wingfield told him. 'Before he left Memphis on his flight to Europe Ives hid the car somewhere. Difficult to achieve – considering the size of the car – but Ives has a wealth of experience. You see, he says he is the only one who knows its location.'

'Well,' said the statesman, 'we've had every kind of corrupt president, quite apart from Watergate. Presidents with mistresses – common enough. Some with illegitimate children. Others who've walked into the Oval Office with little more than the clothes they stood up in. By the time they stepped down from the presidency they were millionaires. So, I suppose one day – in this age of exceptional violence – we should have expected something like this.'

'*If* it's true, he can't stay untouched in the Oval Office,' the Senator said with great force.

'But you haven't enough evidence there to do anything,' the statesman objected.

'So I need this Barton Ives in this room so we can grill him. I think I'll have a word with the Veep.'

'Is Barton Ives Jeb Calloway's man?' enquired the banker.

'I didn't say that, did I?' Wingfield replied cautiously.

'And how would you handle it if all this grim business concerning six serial murders proved true?' demanded the statesman in his direct way. 'Impeachment?'

'We can't have the nation's name dragged through the mud. That's the only certainty I know now,' the Senator replied. 'As to how we'd handle it – I suggest we adjourn this meeting, tell no one of our suspicions, and await events . . .'

Bradford March was drinking beer out of an upended bottle when Sara answered his summons. She waited while he wiped the back of a hairy hand across his mouth.

'I hear strong rumours that the Holy Trinity are meeting more frequently,' he remarked. 'Don't like it.'

This was the President's irreverent way of referring to the Three Wise Men. He pouched his lips, stared at Sara. She realized he expected a reaction.

'So we do something about it? Is that what you're saying? If so, how do we hack it? We could be dealing with a load of dynamite. Those three may be old dinosaurs but they sure as hell carry plenty of clout. Back off, Brad.'

'Sometimes, Sara, your advice is good, very good.' March leaned back in his chair, nursing the beer bottle. 'And sometimes it's lousy, real lousy. This is one of those times.'

'It's your' – she had been going to say 'funeral' but hastily changed the word – 'decision. Just tell me.'

'I want three guys from Unit One – each in his own car – to follow the senator, the statesman and the banker night and day. Draw up a duty roster so they get relieved, stay fresh, on the job. I want daily reports of every person the Holy Trinity bums contact.' His head tilted up, he stared at her hard. 'Why not get started now?'

Sara moved fast on her new mission. Inside an hour the three chosen watchers from Unit One were stationed near Senator Wingfield's house in Chevy Chase. Sara had just heard rumours of a meeting taking place there.

The watchers arrived exactly thirty minutes too late. The two limousines had already called at the house, had picked up and driven away their illustrious passengers.

48

Seated by himself at a table in the Brasserie, Jason, the American with a head and a face like a bulldog, wore his padded windcheater despite the warmth of the restaurant. He had to – in the shoulder holster under his left armpit nestled a Luger.

As he sat drinking beer and piling omelette into his wide mouth he congratulated himself on his luck. His main target – selected by Mencken himself – was sitting facing him with a couple of good-looking chicks and a harmless young guy who couldn't be a day over thirty.

Between shovelling mouthfuls of omelette into his maw he took another look at Paula and Jennie. The target – Tweed – was a pushover, he'd decided. At that moment his eyes met Tweed's. The Englishman gazed back at him with a penetrating stare and Jason hastily glanced away. The eyes worried him – but no one shot with their eyes.

Jason glanced towards the exit leading to the street and decided he'd make the distance in seconds. After putting a couple of bullets into Tweed – which would guarantee his next destination would be the local cemetery.

Accompanied by Newman, Barton Ives walked in from the hotel. Tweed's admiration of the FBI man increased as he looked at his appearance. Ives was wearing one of those deep medical collars of foam material used to support the head and restrict its movements. With his jaw tilted up and a dark beret concealing his trim black hair his appearance was transformed. He sat next to Tweed and spoke in an urgent whisper.

'The sooner we can talk with each other alone the better. What I've got to tell you concerns the present occupant of the White House . . .'

'Later,' Tweed whispered back. 'Arrangements are being changed. I've had second thoughts. You'll travel with me by train to Switzerland and Newman will come with us. Don't look at that rough character facing me at a table opposite . . .'

At that moment Butler and Nield walked into the Brasserie by the short cut from the hotel. Tweed watched the two men as they suddenly paused.

'Don't much like the look of that chap sitting by himself and facing Tweed,' Nield commented.

459

'Reminds me of a pit-bull terrier,' replied Butler, who didn't know much about dogs.

'He must be roasting in that heavy windcheater. Funny he hasn't taken it off.'

'Maybe that bulge under his left armpit is the reason. I could swear he's carrying a gun,' Butler remarked. 'And he's a Yank – the sort Norton would employ. Look at the way he shovels food into his mouth with a fork. No table manners. I think he's trouble.'

'I wouldn't dispute that,' agreed Nield. 'I think maybe we ought to keep a close eye on Brother Pit-Bull. Let's outflank him. Rattle him. With a bit of luck he'll push off outside and we can follow him . . .'

As Tweed watched, the two men separated. Jason had already noticed their arrival, the pause while they stared in his direction. He began to feel less confident.

Nield made a lot of noise as he pulled out a wooden chair from a table behind Jason, scraping it across the tiled floor. Butler chose a more distant table, at a diagonal angle to the American's thick neck. To see either of the new arrivals Jason had to twist round in his seat in two different directions – making it obvious what he was doing.

Tweed had surreptitiously watched the manoeuvre of Butler and Nield with a mixed feeling of amusement and relief. The arrival of Barton Ives, despite his effective disguise, worried him. It was a very public place. Ives spoke to him from behind the menu he was studying.

'I had spotted him. A professional gunman. A Norton recruit would be my guess. Cold as ice. Except he's now hot and bothered, as I believe you Brits say. Literally – sweat is running off his forehead. Those two guys who came in are yours? Thought so. I like their tactics . . .'

Jason had decided – rightly so – that it would be suicide to draw his Luger. He called for the bill, paid the waiter, left half his beer in the glass, stood up and walked casually to the exit leading to the street. Outside rush hour had vanished like water down a plug-hole and the pavement was deserted now night had fallen.

'After you, sir . . .'

Jason paused at the open door, a door held open by Nield who had reached it first the moment Jason began to move. The American suffered a rare moment of indecision. If he said he'd changed his mind and started back into the restaurant, where would that get him? The only alternative was to proceed on into the deserted street – a course of action Jason felt uneasy about.

'OK, buddy . . .'

He stared at Nield who was smiling pleasantly while holding the door open with his left hand. Jason walked out.

Nield followed him immediately, moving as silently as a cat close up behind his quarry. Jason felt something hard and cylindrical pushed hard against his spine. He froze.

'This is a Walther 7.65-mm. automatic and the magazine holds eight rounds,' Nield informed him in a conversational tone. 'I'm prepared to pull the trigger until the mag is emptied. Turn slowly to your right, walk twelve paces, again slowly, then stop. Start counting now.'

'This a friggin' hold-up?' Jason blustered.

'Don't ask questions. Just do what I told you to . . .'

As Jason began counting paces Butler appeared alongside him, keeping in step. The American glanced sideways and didn't like the expression on Butler's face. After twelve paces he stopped. Nield pressed the Walther harder into his spine to remind him of its presence. There was no one else about as Butler stood in front of Jason, reached inside his windcheater with his gloved hand, hauled out a Luger.

'You said something about a hold-up,' Butler remarked. 'Is that the trade you practise?'

'I need protection . . .' Jason began.

'Shut up!' snapped Nield.

Near where they stood two chairs were propped against a wall. In more clement weather tables and chairs were spread out on the pavement for customers to sit at while they enjoyed a drink. Shoving the Luger behind his belt inside his jacket, Butler moved swiftly. He arranged the chairs together so they could be sat on. He went back to where Jason stood with a puzzled expression.

'Turn round and face my partner,' Butler ordered.

As the American turned away from him Butler brought down the barrel of the Luger on Jason's skull. The American was sagging when both Butler and Nield grabbed hold of his inert body, dragged him to the chairs, sat him down, arranged him so he leaned against the back of them.

Nield produced a half bottle of wine he'd brought from the Brasserie. Uncorking it, he spilt a liberal amount down Jason's chin and over his windcheater. Butler had checked his neck pulse, which beat steadily, before they walked back inside the Brasserie. He had also shoved the Luger back inside the shoulder holster.

The one thing both men omitted to notice was a Renault parked in the shadows, apparently empty.

Marvin Mencken, his seat pushed as far back as it would go, had concealed himself when he saw the three men emerging from the Brasserie. In a state of shock, he instinctively hid himself. Once again an apparently foolproof plan had gone wrong. Mencken had told Jason he'd wait outside to pick him up, drive the hell out of Colmar once he'd killed Tweed.

His expression was malevolent and evil as he climbed out of the Renault he had commandeered from one of his surviving teams. In return, he had given them the Land-Rover with a shattered windscreen. Listening, he heard

462

only silence. At this hour even the streets were clear of traffic.

Bending over Jason, he checked the carotid artery, felt its steady beat. His expression became matter-of-fact as he pulled on a pair of gloves. Like Butler, he reached inside Jason's windcheater, hauled out the Luger. Unlike Butler, who had used only enough force to render Jason unconscious for some time, Mencken checked again to make sure he was alone.

He then raised the barrel of the Luger high above his shoulder, brought it down on Jason's skull with such vicious force it rebounded off the skull. Again Mencken checked the carotid artery. Nothing. Jason was dead meat. He'd failed in his task – and there was the added chance the police would find the corpse. Thrusting the Luger back inside the holster, Mencken was about to topple the sagging corpse on to the pavement when he heard a car approaching. He dived back inside the Renault, dipped his head out of sight. The car moved on into the night. Mencken straightened up, adjusted his seat, started the engine and drove off. Bound for this Ouchy dump on the shores of Lake Geneva.

'Do let me in on the secret,' Gaunt's voice boomed out as he joined Tweed's table unasked. 'What's our next port of call on this Cook's tour? Ouchy and points south? Eve is dying of curiosity.'

'Eve is doing nothing of the sort,' Eve Amberg rapped back at Gaunt, obviously well tanked up on alcohol. 'You're the one devoured with curiosity.' She looked at Tweed. 'Then he pretends I'm the one after all sorts of strange and weird information.'

Paula pricked up her ears. Eve sounded convincing. Why would Gaunt adopt this devious ploy?

'I've ordered the largest omelette in the world,' Gaunt

went on as his bulk sagged into a chair at the table. 'I trust, Eve, you'll be keeping me company in the BMW. Can't travel without some feminine companionship.'

'Your trust is misplaced,' she shot back at him. 'I'm travelling back by train with Tweed.'

'I suppose you'd accept me as a substitute companion?' Jennie suggested.

'Damn right I will,' boomed Gaunt. 'Jennie and I are on the same waveband.'

Paula glanced at Jennie and then at Gaunt. She had the impression Gaunt had known Eve would refuse, had known Jennie would offer to come with him. Paula had begun to sense that Gaunt and Jennie were working hand in glove without making it obvious.

Gaunt's relationship with the two women intrigued her. At first she'd thought it was Eve who was close to the Squire. Now it appeared Gaunt had used that as a cover for his closeness to Jennie and Eve had consistently distanced herself from him. Why?

Eve had joined Tweed for dinner soon after the incident of the man with a face like a dog. They were finishing the meal, drinking coffee and Tweed was draining his glass of Riesling while Gaunt wolfed down his huge omelette. At that moment Butler, who had strolled out of the exit on to the street for the second time, came hurrying back. He laid a hand on his chief's shoulder.

'Excuse me,' Tweed said, standing up. 'Arrangements to make!' He looked at Newman. 'Take care of the bill for me, Bob.' He guessed that some kind of emergency had just arisen from Butler's action.

Tweed was leaving the Brasserie by the short cut into the hotel when Butler, close behind him, gave a little jerk of his head to Nield who was lingering over coffee at a table by himself.

Having paid the bill earlier, Nield left the table and strolled casually after them. At Tweed's table Gaunt was holding everyone's attention with some outrageous story – except for Newman, who saw Nield leaving.

Passing through the main restaurant – now empty – Tweed led the way into the reception hall and into a small sitting area in a large alcove. There was no one behind the reception counter as the others joined him.

'A crisis?' Tweed enquired in a mild tone.

'A major one,' Butler reported, keeping his voice down as Nield sat in a third chair. 'That gunman we dealt with outside the Brasserie is dead.'

'So what happened?'

'Pete and I sorted him out. I knocked him unconscious with his own Luger, left the gun with him after we'd parked him on a couple of chairs.'

'I poured wine down his jaw and over his windcheater,' Nield added. 'No one wants anything to do with a drunk sleeping it off.'

'You definitely left him unconscious?' Tweed probed.

'Fact one,' Butler began, 'I checked his neck pulse. It was normal. Fact two, there was no blood from the blow I gave him. Now there's blood all down the side of his face – and a second blow has split his skull. Dead as a doornail.'

'Then we leave here fast.' Tweed took out a notebook, checked train times Paula had obtained earlier. 'An express for Basle leaves here in thirty minutes. I'll be aboard – with Paula, Eve, Amberg, Barton Ives, Newman and Philip Cardon. You both know what to do, where to meet us.'

'I drive the Espace to Basle, Pete drives the station wagon,' Butler replied. 'We park near Basle Bahnhof and wait for you to arrive in the station's first-class restaurant.'

'I have phoned Beck,' Tweed told them. 'He has the registration numbers of both vehicles and has given orders to the Swiss border guards to let you through. So you can tape the weapons underneath the chassis of both cars without worry. Now, speed is the order of the day.'

He had stood up, checked his watch. They had to get out of France before the corpse outside was discovered. In the Brasserie there were locals who had nothing better to do than to notice what was going on. He hurried back into the Brasserie to collect the others. It would be a race against time – to cross the frontier before a *flic* decided to check the body.

They boarded the express with two minutes to spare. At that hour and time of year they found an empty first-class coach. Tweed sat with Barton Ives. Cardon, who had left the table in the Brasserie to guard Amberg before the meal started – the banker had been locked in Tweed's room – sat next to the Swiss further along the coach.

Newman occupied a seat on his own, which gave him a good view of both entrances to the coach. Paula sat chatting with Eve in seats out of hearing of any conversation between Tweed and Ives. Earlier, Tweed had given instructions that he wanted to travel alone with Ives.

Much earlier still, Marler had left Colmar, driving his red Mercedes down the autoroute. His instructions from Tweed had been clear and decisive.

'We are approaching a major crisis – a climax to this whole business might be a better phrase. I'm assuming that in some way Norton will have discovered that Ouchy is our destination. He's discovered everything else we planned to do.'

'I'll drive like the wind – strictly within speed limits, of course,' Marler drawled. 'And when I reach Ouchy?'

'In your own individual way – you can pass for a Frenchman and Ouchy is in French-speaking Switzerland – you check all the hotels which are open at this time of the year. You're looking for recently arrived Americans.

466

When I say "recently", I mean today. When I arrive you should know the location of the opposition, if they have arrived. We are going over on to the offensive.'

'It's Switzerland,' Marler said thoughtfully, 'so gunshots are liable to bring the local police running. If a shop is still open when I reach Basle I'll buy some Swiss Army knives. Useful little tools, Swiss Army knives – for silent kills.'

'In this situation you have a free hand. Come to think of it, you usually have one anyway.'

'You did use the word offensive,' Marler reminded Tweed.

The express took about forty minutes to reach Basle from Colmar. During the journey Barton Ives began talking, hoping to Heaven that Tweed would believe him.

'Several years ago, Mr Tweed, I was stationed at FBI headquarters in Memphis, Tennessee. I'd been promoted to senior agent, responsible only to Humphries, the local director. There was a hideous murder in that state soon after I'd settled there. An attractive woman driving a Cadillac across lonely country was somehow persuaded to stop her car after dark. I'd gotten to know the local medical examiner – what you call a pathologist. He told me the details of the autopsy. Got a strong stomach, Mr Tweed?'

'Reasonably so. Try me.'

'The woman – from a wealthy family – had been savagely raped. Then her throat had been cut. The instrument used was a knife with a serrated blade. Most probably a kitchen knife, the ME said. She had then been sadistically mutilated in a way which suggested the murderer was a psychopath. Quite horrendous. After viewing the body I can tell you I didn't eat much that evening. The mutilation puzzled the ME. He told me it was exactly how he'd commence an autopsy.'

'Someone with medical knowledge?' Tweed queried.

'The ME didn't think so. But he thought the sadist who'd inflicted the wounds may once have witnessed an autopsy being performed. That was the first case.'

'You were investigating it?' Tweed asked, puzzled.

'No. The local police handled the case, never even came up with a suspect. As I think you've realized, the FBI only enters the scene when a criminal crosses a state line. I came into the picture when the second rape and murder occurred six months later.'

'Why were you able to do so then?'

'The second victim – again a wealthy woman driving home in the dark – was attacked in another Southern state. I heard about it, checked the details – the same gory procedure had been carried out as in the first case. That strongly suggested the same rapist and killer was in business again – and he'd crossed a state line. Which brought in the FBI and I was given the investigation.'

'Was any evidence left behind in either case?' Tweed enquired.

Tweed was recalling cases he had solved years before – in the days when he had held a high rank while working for the Murder Squad at Scotland Yard. So often chance had fingered the guilty party.

'Not yet.' Ives sighed. 'It was a frustrating time. Then after six months I heard the details of the third case. This time in a different Southern state. By now we were thinking in terms of a serial killer. So the data from case three was fed to me almost at once. After the autopsy. Again the victim was a wealthy woman driving home in the dark by herself in an expensive car across a lonely area. After viewing the corpse – like the others, she had been physically attractive – I began to think, to ask questions of myself.'

'What sort of person would these women stop for in the middle of nowhere in the dark?' Tweed suggested quietly.

'Yes.' Ives sounded surprised. 'That was my main

question. I saw you once at a security conference in Washington and friends who knew you said you were good. Very good . . .'

Tweed said nothing. He noticed that Paula was gazing into the night and he looked in the same direction. In the moonlight the snowbound summits and saddlebacks of the Vosges showed up clearly. There were pinpoints of light in remote villages. From her expression he guessed that Paula was contrasting the beauty of the scene with the terror they had experienced among the spiralling roads, the Siberian cold and icy ravines. Ives was talking again as the express began to lose speed.

'Then there were three more similar cases – so similar it was uncanny. In three more different Southern states. He never struck in Tennessee again. Always a wealthy woman by herself and driving across a lonely area in the dark. And he used the same hideous technique in every case. He was a serial killer – six cases.'

'And never a clue?' Tweed probed. 'Remarkable. They usually slip up once.'

'He did. In the last case. He left a clear thumbprint under the handle of the car which stopped, a Lincoln Continental. I'd heard rumours that Humphries, my old chief, was going to be recalled, replaced by someone new from Washington. Some sixth sense made me hide the Lincoln Continental in an old barn in the wilderness. It's still there, I'm sure. And I've got a replica of that thumbprint . . .'

Newman had stood up, was leaning against the end of his seat, his windcheater unzipped so he could swiftly grab hold of his Smith & Wesson. The express was approaching Basle Bahnhof. If anyone was going to make an attempt on Tweed it would be soon – as soon as they could jump out of the train at the station after they'd pulled the trigger. Tweed knew exactly what he was doing. He stood up to put on his coat as he spoke to Ives.

'Have to continue this conversation a little later,' he suggested. 'Cardon is strolling towards us. He'll be guarding you. And maybe you'd watch over Amberg.'

'We should be OK now we've returned to Switzerland.'

'Just how OK were you when you were dodging from one hotel to another in Zurich?' Tweed reminded him.

Tweed and Newman left the express together, walking side by side. Close behind them Paula followed with Eve Amberg. Cardon brought up the rear, a step behind Barton Ives, who escorted the Swiss banker.

French Customs and Passport Control were deserted. As they passed through the Swiss checkpoints Tweed's fears were doubly confirmed. Standing in civilian clothes behind uniformed Passport officers he saw Arthur Beck. The Swiss police chief took no notice of him. As they walked on, heading for the first-class restaurant, Harry Butler appeared. He fell into step on the other side of Tweed.

'I'm amazed you made it here so quickly,' Tweed commented. 'Mind you, the express did stop a while for no reason soon after we left Colmar.'

'We put our feet down,' Butler said tersely. 'Auto-routes help. Do you really want to go into the first-class dining-room? Pete Nield is waiting there – he's watching a member of the opposition who followed us. Head like a skull. Saw him giving orders back at the Bristol . . .'

49

Leaving Colmar on his way to Basle in the Renault, Marvin Mencken had been lucky. Butler and Nield, however, had been unlucky.

After killing his subordinate – who had failed in his mission to liquidate Tweed – Mencken had headed for the autoroute. He had only moved a short distance from the Bristol when he saw a gas station. At that same moment his engine coughed and spluttered.

Pulling into the petrol station, Mencken asked a mechanic to check his ignition when his tank was refilled. He was about to drive on when he saw two familiar vehicles pass – a grey Espace and a station wagon. Mencken grinned, followed them.

'You know we have a tail,' Nield warned Butler over his walkie-talkie as they proceeded along the autoroute.

'The Renault,' Butler replied. 'Can't do a damn thing about it. We've been told to get into Switzerland at the earliest possible moment. Just keep driving. Leave the problem until later . . .'

Reaching Basle Bahnhof, they parked their cars, walked into the first-class restaurant as two separate individuals, sat at different tables, ordered coffee. A skeletal-faced character in a trench coat walked in after them, chose a table by the wall some distance away, ordered a drink.

'I could score one off Norton,' Mencken said to himself. 'They could be waiting for the rest of their gang . . .'

He wasn't in the least worried that he was delaying his

arrival in Ouchy. Plenty of his men were on their way to the Swiss resort. Mencken had, with his usual efficiency, arranged for Louis Sheen, the courier with the suitcase containing a huge fortune, to be driven under guard to Ouchy. That, apparently, was where the vital exchange would take place. He frowned when, some time later, Butler stood up and wandered out of the place.

Pete Nield had remained sitting at his own table. Mencken glanced at the slim man with the trim moustache who was, apparently, watching a blonde girl at a distant table.

Mencken decided his opponents had made a mistake. He'd wait until he could get Moustache on his own in a less public place. Mencken had no doubt he could make Moustache spill his guts.

'When you saw this American giving orders,' Tweed said to Butler as he continued walking slowly towards the restaurant, 'did you get the impression he carried a lot of authority?'

'One of Norton's top brass, would be my guess. I saw where he's parked his Renault just outside,' Butler added.

'First, point him out to me from the entrance. Second, you then take Ives, Paula, Eve, Amberg and Cardon to the Espace. Third, you fix our American friend's Renault.'

'What are you going to do?' asked Butler, alarmed.

'It's time Bob and I had a word with the opposition face to face . . .'

Tweed had decided it was time to stop running. He'd said in Colmar they were going on to the offensive. This seemed like a good moment to start. Butler indicated Mencken to Tweed from the door, although Tweed now recognized him instantly – the same man had walked into the bar at the Baur-en-Ville in Zurich, had stared up at Paula and himself before retreating back into the hotel. At that moment the American was watching Nield.

Hands deep inside his trench coat pockets, Tweed headed straight for Mencken's table with Newman beside him. He took out one hand, pulled back a chair at the table for four, sat facing the skeletal-faced man, who stiffened. Newman sat alongside Mencken, used his left hand to stop the American pushing his chair back from the table. His right hand was slipped inside his wind-cheater, gripping his Smith & Wesson.

'Relax,' Newman advised him. 'Take it easy, as you never stop saying in New York.'

'What's New York got to do with anything?' Mencken sneered.

He reached inside his own trench coat. Newman's right hand closed over his wrist.

'Be careful what you take out,' he advised again.

'Your nerves all shot to hell?' Mencken sneered again.

He withdrew his hand slowly. It was holding a pack of Marlboro and a lighter. Lighting a cigarette, he blew the smoke in Tweed's direction. Tweed waved it away before he spoke.

'Maybe my friend should have said Washington,' he remarked.

'Don't give *me* no smoke,' Mencken snapped, his manner nervy at the reference to Washington.

'I hope you don't mind our joining you,' Tweed went on, 'but you've been keeping us company for a long time. Maybe you would tell me why?'

'What the shit does that mean?'

'Manners,' Newman interjected. 'You ought to wash out your mouth more often. It means you've been stumbling over us all the way from Zurich. My friend would like to know why. He just asked you.'

'I don't have to talk to you guys, whoever you are . . .'

473

'I wouldn't think about leaving.' The suggestion had come from Nield who was now sitting at the next table, his chair twisted round so he faced the American. 'Ever felt the walls closing in on you?' he enquired.

'This is a free country. We're in Switzerland.'

Mencken's aggressive manner was fading. Minutes ago he had been confident he would get Nield on his own. Now he was the one on his own. He cursed the fact that he'd sent all his men rushing down to Ouchy. He suddenly realized that the blonde girl had left the restaurant, that it was empty except for himself and his interrogators. Even the staff seemed to have vanished. The time of the year – March – and the time of day.

'Is America such a free country these days?' Tweed asked him. 'Considering the people in power? Talking about power, how is my old acquaintance, Mr Norton?'

'Look . . .' Mencken was talking fast as though making a desperate attempt to convince Tweed he didn't know what he was talking about. 'Look, I'm an executive of a company selling machine tools. Business is lousy . . .'

'You sell a lot of machine tools in the Vosges mountains?' Newman demanded.

'If you guys don't get off my back I'm going to want some police . . .'

The strain was showing in Mencken's shifting eyes, in the way he smoked his cigarette, being very careful to keep smoke away from Tweed, in the way his shoulders kept jerking under his trench coat. Marvin Mencken was coming apart at the seams.

'You can have the police,' Newman assured him. 'Right out of the top drawer. The Chief of Federal Police happens to be here in this station. Want me to go and fetch him? Just say the word.'

'Look, you guys, I didn't expect this. I've had a long day. Nothing but pressure.' He turned to Newman. 'You know? That's what gets to you when you're away from

474

home. Pressure. What's all this stuff about, anyway?'

'Maybe we could start with your name?' Tweed suggested.

'Sure. Why not? I'm Marvin Mencken . . .'

'What company do you work for?' Tweed pressed on.

'An outfit based in the Middle West. I guess you mixed me with someone else. Right?'

'Not right.' Tweed shook his head, his attitude still cool, almost offhand. 'You could spend Lord knows how many years in a Swiss gaol. Not comfortable places, Swiss gaols. Over here they believe in punishment for criminal offences.'

'What criminal offence?' Mencken stubbed out his cigarette, immediately lit a fresh one. 'Like I said, you're all mixed up . . .'

'The bomb thrown in Bahnhofstrasse by the pseudo-cripple,' Tweed went on remorselessly. 'The Chief of Police, Beck, is handling that case himself. A hard man.'

'Don't know nothin' about a bomb,' Mencken protested.

He was sweating. Beads of moisture had formed on his low forehead. Newman passed him a handkerchief.

'Use this. Clean yourself up.'

Mencken took the handkerchief. Afraid to show fear, to take out his own handkerchief, he mopped himself dry, returned the handkerchief.

'See the state you guys have got me into? What is this? The third degree? I don't have to take this . . .'

'Then there was the mass murder down in Cornwall, England. Eight people just shot down in cold blood by a masked gunman.'

'Mass murder? In England?' Mencken had jerked himself upright. 'You guys *are* crazy. Cornwall, you said? So where's that? I ain't never been to the place. This is screwy. You *have* got the wrong guy.'

Tweed had been watching the American closely,

listening to him intently. For the first time there was vehemence in his tone, the vehemence of a man telling the truth.

Nield had been keeping one eye on the entrance to the restaurant. Now he saw Butler appear briefly, giving a thumbs-up signal. He had dealt with Mencken's Renault. Nield nodded twice to Tweed as Butler disappeared. Tweed sighed, checked his watch, pushed back his chair, stood up, both hands in his pockets as he addressed Mencken.

'I advise you to catch a flight from the airport here in the morning to Zurich. From there you can board a non-stop flight to Washington. You might just get clear of Norton.'

'Washington? I told you – I'm from the Middle West. Why this Washington thing? And Norton, Norton, Norton. Who the hell is he?'

Mencken was talking to himself. Tweed had walked away, leaving the restaurant. Newman followed, leaving Nield behind to watch the American. When they had disappeared Nield also stood up, leaned down, patted Mencken on the shoulder.

'I wouldn't leave for ten minutes. If you do there are police outside who'll arrest you. They'll take a great interest in that gun you're packing under your armpit. Do yourself a big favour. Start counting now . . .'

'I think I achieved my aim,' Tweed said to Newman as they walked towards the station exit.

'Which was?'

'To shake Master Mencken to the core – to rattle his cage. Above all, to persuade him to underestimate me. He'll report the encounter to Norton sooner or later. I want them off guard for the final confrontation . . .'

Butler escorted them to the Espace. Barton Ives had

476

done exactly what Tweed had quietly suggested to him as they earlier conversed briefly before leaving the train. He'd escorted Amberg to the Espace, parked just outside the station. The two men were sitting near the rear while Ives, alert as ever, watched Tweed and his companions approaching.

Paula, assuming that Tweed would again be driving, sat by herself in the front passenger seat. In a row further back Eve sat on the other side of Amberg, flanking the banker with Ives. Was she also suspecting that the Swiss was going to try and run off if he got the opportunity?

Tweed climbed in behind the wheel while Newman boarded the Espace at the rear. Closing the door, Tweed suddenly stood up, made his way swiftly to where Amberg sat in grim silence. He tapped the banker on the knee.

'You said the key to the security box in Ouchy is kept at your branch in Bankverein. I'm driving there now. You will, accompanied by Newman, open the bank, go in, collect the key, come straight back to the Espace. You understand me clearly?'

'At this time of night there are alarms . . .' the banker began.

'Which you know how to deactivate so they won't wake up half Basle. Don't play games with me, Amberg. I'm no longer in the mood for them.' He looked at Newman. 'Where is Philip Cardon?'

'Just about to come aboard. He insisted on maintaining a watch hidden in the entrance to that hotel over there. He told me he'd wait outside just before we entered the restaurant. Cardon is smart . . .'

As Tweed settled himself behind the wheel again, started the engine, he glanced all round. In the depths of winter no one lingered outside the station. A tram, ochre-coloured and smaller than its Zurich counterpart, trundled in to a nearby stop. No one aboard except the driver. No passengers waiting to board it. The empty tram seemed to Paula to symbolize the deserted desolate atmosphere of Basle in March after dark. She had purposely said nothing to Tweed, sensing his concentration on his secret thoughts. He saw Butler and Nield hurrying towards the parked station wagon, waited until they were inside the vehicle and moved off. To the Zürcher Kredit Bank.

Tweed followed the tramline along a deserted street which curved and sloped steadily downwards – towards the distant Rhine and the Drei Könige where they had stayed. Was it a million years ago? There was no other traffic and Paula found the street, hemmed in on both sides by tall, solid stone buildings, eerie and unsettling. In his wing-mirror Tweed saw the station wagon transporting Butler and Nield following him.

'Should be round the next corner if I remember rightly,' Tweed commented, sensing Paula's unease.

'They go to bed early in Basle,' she remarked.

'Not a lot to stay up for, is there?' Tweed replied.

'Stop the car! There are lights in my bank. Someone has broken in . . .'

Amberg's voice, calling out in surprisingly commanding and vigorous tone. Tweed signalled, pulled in to the kerb. Unfastening his belt, he twisted round in his seat, staring at the banker and Eve, who had laid a restraining hand on his arm.

'There is a woman who works for you at the bank . . .' Tweed began.

'It can't be her, I tell you,' Amberg rapped back with an air of authority. 'Karin would have gone home hours ago. Always at the same time to her apartment near by.'

'And always by the same route?' Tweed suggested.

'Yes. It's the quickest way for her to get home. Even when she's going shopping she goes home first to collect her basket . . .'

'Always at the same time and by the same route?' Tweed repeated.

'Yes. I've already told you that . . .'

So even Swiss security can be fallible, Tweed thought grimly. The deadly scenario was so obvious. Someone had followed Karin home after checking her routine. They had probably forced her at gunpoint to return after dark with the keys to the bank. They'd been clever enough to foresee the alarm system, to force her to deactivate it. Now they were inside and doubtless she knew about the key to the vital safe deposit. Tweed thought he now knew why Mencken had lingered in the restaurant at the station – waiting for his thugs to do this job.

'I'd better go inside, see what's happening.'

Newman had left the Espace, was now outside Tweed's open window. His right hand by his side held the Smith & Wesson.

'Take Butler and Nield with you,' Tweed ordered. 'They may have a number of armed men inside.'

'So I'll go with them too,' said Cardon, who had materialized beside Newman.

'I'm coming,' said Paula, her Browning already in her hand.

'You're staying to guard me,' Tweed told her.

Paula bit her lip, opened her mouth, closed it without saying anything. Tweed had cleverly checkmated her. Newman had to hold on to Amberg's arm to compel him to accompany the team.

'I wonder what hell is going to break loose inside that building,' Paula remarked aloud.

'I'll take the lead,' Newman told the others. 'I don't like the look of this. They've forgotten to close the door properly . . .'

All the lights were on the first floor. The entrance hall

was a cavern of darkness. Newman paused, held the others back with his left hand while his eyes became accustomed to the dark. He'd have liked to use his pencil flash, but they might have left a lookout at the top of the wide curving staircase. It had a wrought-iron rail and the hall floor was solid marble. Some Swiss banks liked to show clients they had come to the right place.

'Can't hear a thing,' Cardon whispered in his ear. 'It is too quiet. Maybe they've come and gone . . .'

'Assume an army is waiting up there,' Newman whispered back.

Holding on to the rail to help guide himself, he began to mount the steps. His rubber-soled shoes made no sound as he continued higher and higher – the first-floor landing was a surprising distance above the ground floor. Then he heard a voice.

'Come on, my dear, we haven't got all night. Before I spoil your face for ever open the bloody safe . . .'

The voice had spoken English with an upper-crust accent. Blurred by distance, Newman thought of Gaunt, who, when he had caught up with Butler at Basle Station, had said he was driving straight on to Ouchy. A brief remark of Butler's which hadn't really registered. Until now . . .

'No! Don't! Please! I'll do it . . .'

A woman's voice also talking English, a woman's voice expressing the last extremes of panic. Newman moved, ran up the last few steps with Cardon at his heels and the others close behind. He ran across the landing to an open doorway framing light, rushed in, crouching low, gun in front of him, then stopped in sheer surprise.

A man was holding a knife close to a woman's throat as she bent in front of a large safe, operating a combination lock. A small slim man with a plump face and pouched lips. In his thirties, he had a receding chin and a sneering smile as he watched the terrified woman opening the safe.

There was a click and she heaved the massive door open.

'Drop the knife,' Newman ordered. 'There are four of us.'

'Stand back or I'll cut her throat,' the slim man screeched.

Newman smiled, walked forward, placed the muzzle of his Smith & Wesson carefully against the side of the man's head. He pressed the metal close to the skull.

'You won't cut anything,' Newman said in a quiet voice. 'Because if you did in the next second half your head would be plastered over that wall. So stop playing silly games. *Drop it!*' he roared. 'Or you're dead.'

The knife clattered to the floor. Cardon noticed that the hand which had held the knife was trembling like a leaf in the wind. The woman's assailant stared at Newman as though seeing a ghost.

'Who the heck is this creep?' Cardon asked impatiently.

'Meet Mr Joel Dyson, notorious member of the paparazzi mob. Someone outside wants to meet you badly, Joel.'

PART THREE

The Power

50

In Washington it was late afternoon, the lights were on, blurred in a steady snowfall. President Bradford March was pacing the Oval Office restlessly when Sara came in.

'What is it now?' he snapped. 'More trouble? And when do I get a report on the treachery of the Holy Trinity?'

'It may be good news,' she replied in a soothing tone. 'Norton is on the line.'

'Leave me while I talk to the bastard . . .'

March took a deep breath as he sank into his chair and picked up the phone. He was in a foul mood.

'Norton here. I've reached Neuchâtel . . .'

'Have you? Great. Where is the friggin' place?'

'In Switzerland. French-speaking Switzerland . . .'

'Cohabiting with the Frogs now, are we? You haven't got a woman with you, have you? Because if you have I'll hear about it from Mencken and . . .'

'I'm alone and in a hurry. Are you going to listen for a change or shall I put down the receiver?'

'Norton . . .' March's tone became dangerously soft. 'If you ever threaten me again Mencken takes over instanter. Get to it.'

'I'm close to Ouchy – where the exchange will take place. The money for the two items you need. The place is ringed with my troops. I may clean up the whole job before the night is out . . .'

'You'd better. You're running out of time. Remember? I gave you a deadline. Of course, if you obtain what I'm after without paying over the big bucks there'd be a nice fat bonus waiting for you.'

'Any point in asking how much?' Norton enquired.

'Thought you were in a hurry to get to this Owchy. OK. You asked. Fifty big ones,' March said, clutching a figure out of the air.

'I'll be in touch. My new number at the Hôtel Château d'Ouchy is . . .'

'Got it. Get on your horse . . .'

In the Neuchâtel hotel where he'd paid for a room for the night so he could use the phone, Norton put down the receiver. At least this time he'd beaten March to the punch in contacting him and giving him his new phone number.

He went downstairs, pulling on his coat, told the receptionist he'd be back for dinner later, went out into the arctic night to drive on to Ouchy.

In Washington March was pulling at his stubby nose with his thumb and forefinger. A bonus? The only bonus Norton would get when he returned would be a bullet in the back of the neck.

March never took a chance he didn't have to. He was working on the assumption that – despite orders – Norton would take a peek at the film, would listen to the tape when he laid his hands on them. That risk could only be eliminated by eliminating Norton. Maybe things were now looking good. He opened a bottle of beer, drank from it and wondered about the Holy Trinity.

Senator Wingfield was alone in his study with the curtains closed against the night. He was also drinking but his beverage was Brazilian coffee from a Royal Doulton service arranged on a silver tray. He was studying a typed message which had come special delivery from Europe. No indication on the sheet of paper of the whereabouts of the sender – except the stamps were Swiss.

'That's right, Calloway,' he said to himself, referring to the Vice President. 'When the bullets start to fly keep your head down.'

The experienced Senator was cynically amused that this communication had come direct to him. He could imagine the brief phone conversation Jeb Calloway had had with his FBI contact.

'Barton, from now on I guess it would be best if any further communication was sent direct to Wingfield . . .'

The message was very direct – and highly dangerous if it got into the wrong hands. The Oval Office, for example. Events appeared to be moving to a climax and the Senator knew he was going to have to devote thought as to how to handle a potentially explosive situation. The ball was now in his court.

Have positive evidence as to identity of six-serial murderer in the South. Expect soon to have conclusive data. Will then communicate with you again – in person if at all possible. Barton Ives.

'Meet Joel Dyson,' Newman said, introducing his captive to Tweed, who had climbed down from the Espace. 'At long last,' he added.

Cardon, who always seemed equipped with everything, had produced a pair of handcuffs inside the Zurcher Kredit Bank. Dyson's hands were now pinioned behind his back and Butler, who was holding him by one arm, had shown him his Walther. The slim little man, his hair dishevelled, stared at Tweed.

'I'm going to complain to the British consul. I'm still a British citizen.'

'I have a better idea,' Tweed suggested. 'We can hand you over to the American Embassy in Berne. I'm sure there's a man very high up in Washington who would be happy to meet you.'

'Blimey, guv, for Gawd's sake don't do that. Like handing a Christian to the lions,' he pleaded in his best cockney mimickry.

'Some Christian,' Newman commented. His voice hardened. 'Don't play silly games with my chief. He means what he says.'

'God, no! I'm begging you . . .'

Dyson's nerve had broken suddenly. Tweed looked down at the man who had sunk to his knees, his body shaking with terror. He pursed his lips with distaste, nodded to Butler.

'Take him to the station wagon. Keep him quiet while we drive to Ouchy. I'll question him later.'

Dyson opened his mouth to scream. Newman clamped a gloved hand over the mouth before it could utter a sound. Nield twisted his handkerchief into a gag, inserted it inside Dyson's mouth, tied it at the back of his neck. Butler and Nield carried him away to the station wagon. Tweed and Paula listened as Newman gave a brief account of what had happened inside the bank.

'Karin, Amberg's kidnapped assistant, is in better shape than you'd expect,' Newman reported. 'She insisted on staying back to make coffee for herself and the guard Dyson coshed when he first arrived with Karin. You're looking impatient,' he ended.

'I think we ought to get out of Basle like bats out of hell,' Tweed ordered. 'The sooner we reach Ouchy the happier I'll be.'

'Who was that funny little man your people carted away?'

The voice called out from the back of the Espace – Eve Amberg's.

'A minor member of the opposition,' Tweed called back quickly.

'Eve does like to know what's going on,' Paula commented. 'Unlike Amberg, who seems to have thrown in his hand.'

A door slammed. Newman and Cardon were aboard. Cardon took up his old position next to the Swiss banker while Newman sat behind Paula. Tweed replied as he started the Espace moving, heading out of Basle, 'Amberg is sitting there with a grim expression. Typical that he hasn't enquired if Karin is all right. But he always was the cold fish of the two brothers as I recall. Let me concentrate on driving,' Tweed said brusquely.

Paula glanced at him. What he really meant was – let me concentrate on thinking this thing out.

They were well south of the city, driving with the Jura mountains rearing up to their right, when Tweed began talking to Paula in a voice which wouldn't carry to his passengers in the rear.

'I was right in my theory about two different jigsaws interlocking, that one wouldn't exist without the other. Two quite different styles of murder have been committed, which suggests two different groups are involved.'

'Two different styles of murder? That's a graphic phrase,' she remarked. 'Explanation, please.'

'The blowing up of our headquarters at Park Crescent, the bomb thrown at me in Zurich, the planned demolition by explosives of the Kaysersberg bridge, the second use of demolition by explosives of that cliff up in the Vosges. All those are what I'd call organization acts, requiring the services of a large and powerful apparatus. In short, Norton and the Americans. That is one distinctive style of attempted murder.'

Tweed accelerated a little more. There was no other traffic on the road below the mountains. He was anxious to reach Ouchy, to question Joel Dyson, to compel

Amberg to produce the film and the tape, and to hear the rest of Barton Ives' story. Paula glanced back and saw Ives, seated next to Newman, staring out into the night with a far-away look.

'You said *two* different styles of murder,' she reminded Tweed. 'What about the second style?'

'Highly individual. One person, disguised as the postman, arrived at the manor, knifed the butler, walked into the kitchen, sprayed the staff with tear-gas, then marched into the dining-room with a machine-gun and mowed down the seven people sitting there. Cold-blooded, audacious.'

'Not Norton, you mean?'

'A different style from Norton. Then take the hideous garrotting of the call girl Helen Frey and her friend Klara. I think the killer had a wire garrotte disguised as a string of pearls – hence the single blood-stained pearl found in Frey's apartment.'

'How do you think it was managed with such horrific skill?'

'Oh, not difficult. You offer to loop the pearls round Frey's neck so she can see how she looks in them. What woman could resist such an offer? Same technique with Klara.'

'A man,' Paula said thoughtfully. 'Maybe he even offered to give them the pearls. That *would* be irresistible.'

'Again an individual murder – as opposed to Norton's mass killing attempts.'

'But what about that nice detective, Theo Strebel? He was shot,' she reminded him.

'You'd hardly play the murderous trick with the pearl garrotte on a man, would you? But I'm sure he was shot by someone he knew, who put him off his guard. Again an individual murder. Don't forget the Shadow Man with the wide-brimmed hat who stalked Jennie Blade.'

490

'Butter wouldn't melt in Jennie's mouth. That type of woman always makes me suspicious.'

'It couldn't be simply that you dislike her?' Tweed probed.

'Men can be very naïve about attractive women,' Paula persisted. 'Especially when a woman like her gazes at a man adoringly. And much earlier Jennie remarked she'd seen Eve in Padstow about the time of the massacre. I think she was lying, but it could be a significant lie.'

'In what way?' Tweed enquired.

'It suggests that *Jennie* herself could have been in Padstow at the time of the massacre.'

'You could be right, I suppose.'

'And,' Paula went on, in full flood, 'I only caught a glimpse of the fake postman who killed all those people, riding along the drive up to the mansion.'

'Which suggests something to you? Remember Jennie has a mane of golden hair.'

'There again men don't know enough about women. Jennie could have piled up her hair on top of her head. That fake postman wore a uniform cap which could conceal the hair. It was a cold day so I didn't think it odd that the figure on the cycle wore a cap – it was a *very* cold day.'

'I still find it difficult to believe,' Tweed commented.

'And now she's gone off with Gaunt, who, according to Butler, was in the devil of a hurry to get to Ouchy in his BMW.'

'If you add Gaunt to the equation you do make out a very strong case,' Tweed admitted. 'I have an idea we'll break this mystery open in two bites. First the film and the tape will tell us the Washington angle – solving Norton's frantic efforts to stop us. Later we may have to return to Padstow to pin down who was responsible for the massacre. To say nothing of the murders of Frey, Klara and Theo Strebel.'

'You think you know who is guilty of those murders, don't you?' Paula challenged him.

'I've known for some time. The key is Jennie Blade's references to the so-called Shadow Man appearing in Colmar.'

When Marvin Mencken left the restaurant in Basle Bahnhof – he had carefully waited for fifteen minutes to be on the safe side – he hurried to where his Renault was parked. He was about to climb behind the wheel when he noticed his front right tyre was flat.

He swore aloud, then began the time-wasting task of changing it for his spare tyre. He had no way of knowing it was sabotage. While Tweed was confronting him inside the restaurant Butler had used a simple method of disabling the car.

Crouching down by the front tyre as though lacing up his trainer, he had taken out a ballpoint pen, unscrewed the cap, inserted the end of his pen and pressed down the valve, holding it there until all the air had escaped. He had then replaced the cap.

Mencken worked frantically in the vain hope of arriving in Ouchy before Norton. Sweating with the effort, despite the bitter cold, he eventually got behind the wheel and started the car. The delay meant that when Norton reached his destination there was no one to tell him where his troops were located in different hotels.

The Hôtel Château d'Ouchy was one of the weirdest, most intriguing hotels Paula had ever seen. Tweed had driven the Espace down a steep hill, had turned on to a level road and as the moon came out from behind a cloud Paula had her first view of Lake Geneva, the largest of all the Swiss lakes. The water was calm, without a ripple, stretching away towards distant France on the southern shore.

Butler overtook them in the station wagon as Tweed paused, crawling ahead to sniff out any sign of danger. As Tweed waited Paula peered up at the Château d'Ouchy. Illuminated by external arc lights, it was built of fawn-coloured stone and its steep, red-tiled roofs were decorated with a black, almost sinister zigzag design. At the corners steepled turrets reared up and it looked very old.

'Looks as ancient as history,' she commented.

'Used to be a castle in the twelfth century,' Tweed told her, 'before ages later it was rebuilt and converted into a hotel. At least it's quiet down here.'

Paula thought that was an understatement, recalling the furious hustle and fast tempo of Zurich. Across the road from the hotel was an oyster-shaped harbour encircled with eerie green street lamps, their light reflected in the harbour water. Boats cocooned for winter in blue plastic covers were moored to buoys.

But it was the stillness which most struck her – the waterfront was deserted, there was no other traffic, no one else in sight. To their left beyond the road they had driven along was a line of small hotels and cafés, all apparently closed. Tweed had lowered his window and refreshing air drifted inside – so different from the ice-cold of the Vosges. Marler appeared from nowhere alongside the window.

'OK to come ashore,' he drawled. He handed a sheet of paper to Tweed. 'That lists the hotels round here where Norton's men are stationed. The Château d'Ouchy, so far as I can tell, is clean . . .'

Tweed had parked the Espace in a courtyard alongside the hotel and next to Marler's red Mercedes. He entered reception with Paula, who spoke to the girl behind the counter, reminding her of the phoned reservations.

'And you said we could have dinner even if we arrived at a late hour.'

'The dining-room is at your service, but only when you are ready.'

'I think we'd like to go up to our rooms to freshen up first,' Tweed told her.

He had seen Ives coming in, accompanied by Amberg and Cardon. Behind them followed Butler and Nield flanking a defeated-looking Joel Dyson. He ordered Butler to take turns with Nield in guarding Dyson in his room, that the photographer was only to be given sandwiches and mineral water, then he asked Paula and Newman to accompany him with Ives to his room after registering. There was no time to waste. Lord knew what the morning would bring.

'What sort of person would those six wealthy women who were then brutally raped and murdered stop for – driving in the middle of nowhere in the dark?'

Tweed deliberately repeated the key question he had put to Barton Ives aboard the train from Colmar to Basle. He had previously recalled, for the sake of Paula and Newman, in abbreviated form the story Ives had told him. The FBI man sat up straight on the couch he occupied with Paula, facing Tweed and Newman who were sitting in chairs.

'Yes, that *was* the question I asked myself over and over again. Then, in the last two cases, there was someone else driving late on the fatal nights. They overtook the cars of the victims – and saw a brown Cadillac parked in a nearby field. I had a hunch, a sudden flash of inspiration, luck – call it what you will. I began checking the movements of a certain man to see whether by chance he was in the state concerned on any of the six fatal nights.'

Ives paused, lit a rare cigarette. Paula glanced round at the suite she had booked for Tweed. It had its own sitting area, spacious and comfortable, and beyond a row of arches, the bedroom. She concentrated again on Ives as he continued.

'The checking on this point wasn't too difficult. What was difficult was carrying out my enquiries without anyone knowing what I was doing. If I was right I knew my life could be in danger. Power carries a lot of clout.'

'So you were investigating a powerful man?' Paula suggested.

'Powerful and ruthless,' Ives agreed. 'To get where he had, to get where he is now. As I checked I began to get more excited – I was hitting more pay dirt than I'd ever really believed I would. The person I was after had made a political speech early in the evening in the same state in the first three cases. And the city where he'd made the speech wasn't all that far, in driving distance, from where a woman was raped and murdered later that same evening.'

'Circumstantial. But not conclusive,' Tweed commented.

'Wait!' Ives held up a hand, stubbed out the cigarette. 'I went on checking the last three cases. Certain that the same circumstances wouldn't apply. But, by God, they did. Senator X – as he then was – had again spoken in public in all three states hours before the last three women victims were attacked and died. A lot of speeches in six states, but then he was running for the highest—' Ives broke off briefly. 'I'll get to that in a minute.'

'What about this Senator's movements after he'd made his speeches?' Tweed asked. 'Were you able to check them?'

'That was my next task. Even more difficult to conceal. And he has a very shrewd hatchet woman who runs a whole network of informants. But over a period of time I did manage to do just that – to check his movements after he left the place where he'd made his speech, lifted his audience out of their seats – a real rabble rouser. He was known for wanting to be on his own after bringing the roof down. Always says he needs to recharge his batteries, go some place on his own, drink one bottle of beer. He did exactly that after all six speeches – on the nights when later within driving distance, I checked the times – a woman was raped, murdered.'

'So at least he has no alibi,' Tweed remarked.

'But he does have a brown Caddy he likes driving. And this I haven't ever told anyone so far. I explored round the area of the sixth victim, combed the grass for hours. I was about to call it zilch when I found this empty beer bottle, with a complete set of fingerprints. Some beer that the guy I was checking on likes. That bottle – inside a plastic bag – is in the boot of the Lincoln Continental I have hidden away in an old barn.'

'Again the evidence is circumstantial,' Tweed pointed out. 'No offence, but the trouble is a court would only have your word for where you found that bottle. Unless you can get the fingerprints of the man you were tracking. Of course, if they match . . .'

'Not so easy.' Ives lit a fresh cigarette. 'Not so easy,' he repeated. 'Not to obtain the fingerprints of ex-Senator Bradford March, now President of the United States.'

51

In Switzerland it was not difficult the following morning for Marler to obtain a film projector, a screen and the other equipment he needed on Tweed's instructions. He arrived back at the hotel at 8.30 a.m. to find Tweed having breakfast with Paula and Newman.

'I lay awake half the night,' Paula was saying. 'I still can't believe the President of the United States is guilty of such horrific crimes.'

'Read the history of previous occupants of the Oval Office,' suggested Barton Ives who had overheard her remark as he joined them. 'Under our crazy electoral system a really depraved guy was bound to get there one day. He has.'

'What do we do next?' Paula asked.

'You've got everything?' Tweed checked with Marler as he sat down.

'Everything.'

'Then our next trip is to take Amberg to his branch here, force him to produce the film and tape Dyson gave them in Zurich for safekeeping. Then we view the film inside the bank . . .'

Amberg was still under guard in his room with Cardon keeping him company. Their breakfast came up from room service. Joel Dyson was also trapped in his room with an extremely unsympathetic Butler acting as his guard.

'You know we were followed here all the way from Basle?' Newman warned his chief.

'Not to worry – it was an unmarked car but they would be Beck's men. After seeing us pass through the control at Basle Station when we arrived from Colmar he's not a man to let us out of his sight. Talk of the devil . . .'

Arthur Beck, wearing a smart grey suit, walked into the dining-room, which overlooked a small garden. He refused an offer of coffee, bent down to whisper to Tweed.

'I have brought a small army of men into Ouchy. We saw the Americans returning. So-called diplomats waiting for their postings. This is too much. I'm organizing a dragnet to check all the hotels.'

'I can save you time.' Tweed produced the list Marler had drawn up the previous evening. 'This lists where they all are. They will be armed.'

'So are my men.' Beck smiled wryly. 'Thank you for doing my job for me. May I ask how you tracked them down?'

'Marler, tell our friend about your researches.'

'Not difficult,' drawled Marler. 'I'd call at a hotel, tell the night clerk some American friends of mine had arrived, that I wanted to pay them some money I owed to them. Also I needed a room for the night and how much would it be? I had a handful of Swiss coins – which can be of reasonable value – and pushed them over the far edge of the counter. While he was scrabbling for them I checked his box of registration slips, memorized all names where the nationality was American. I then told the clerk I'd left my passport in my car, that I'd be back for the room I'd paid for. Then on to the next hotel. Quite easy.'

'And very skilled – to pull it off with Swiss hotel staff.' Beck glanced at the list. 'I should have this lot within the hour – for immediate deportation via Geneva Airport. Spoil their breakfasts . . .'

He had just disappeared when Gaunt trooped in with Jennie clinging to his arm. Marching straight up to

498

Tweed's large table, he sat down uninvited.

'Top of the morning to you,' he greeted them breezily. 'Lovely day. Sun shining on the mountains of the Haute-Savoie across the lake. A large English breakfast for two,' he commanded the waiter.

'I just want croissants,' Jennie said, her eyes glowing with annoyance. 'And I do like to be asked.'

'Nonsense! You must stoke up. Busy day ahead of us, eh, Tweed? Saw a bunch of American thugs filing into the Hôtel d'Angleterre just opposite last night. Have to keep a sharp lookout for spoilers.'

'We have an appointment,' Tweed wiped his mouth with his napkin. 'May see you later.'

He had hardly spoken when Eve Amberg appeared, asked if she could sit with them. Tweed gestured to an empty chair and Paula caught Jennie glaring at the new arrival. What was it between these two women? Eve wore a form-hugging purple sweater and black ski-pants tucked into knee-length leather boots. A striking outfit, Paula admitted to herself.

'Where is Walter?' Eve enquired as she selected a roll. 'Coffee for me,' she told the waiter. 'So where is Walter?' she repeated.

'He's exhausted,' Tweed lied. 'Sleeping in until about ten before he surfaces.'

'A poor fish,' Gaunt boomed. 'No energy . . .'

He was talking to a smaller audience. Tweed, followed by Paula and Newman, was leaving the restaurant. Walking briskly, he went up to Amberg's room, rapped on the door with the agreed signal, walked in with the others when Cardon opened it. Tweed was in his most aggressive mood when he addressed the banker, who was again neatly clad in his sombre black suit.

'Had your breakfast? Good. Time to get moving. To your bank. I want the film and the tape out of the vault five minutes after we arrive. We'll accompany you everywhere.

499

In case you feel like staging a protest, Beck, the Chief of Police, as you know, is here in Ouchy. He'd be very interested to talk to you about those murders in Zurich.'

'I had nothing to do . . .' Amberg began.

'Policemen never believe a word you say. We'll get moving now. By the back way into the car park. Avoid the dining-room that way. Three tough-looking American types are having breakfast. Don't want to meet them either, do you, Amberg?'

Marvin Mencken, who was staying at the d'Angleterre, had risen early and had a quick breakfast at another hotel. He liked to be up before any of his subordinates and he made a habit of not following a routine. He never ate where he was staying.

Returning from a brisk walk alongside the lake he saw two Audis pull up in front of the d'Angleterre. Men in plain clothes stepped out, walked towards the entrance with almost military precision, disappeared inside the hotel. Seconds later more cars pulled up outside two other hotels where his men were staying and uniformed police, holding automatic weapons, climbed out swiftly and moved inside.

'Jesus Christ!' Mencken said to himself.

Without hurrying, he crossed the road, reached his car parked behind a stretch of grass and trees. He got in behind the wheel, pulled out of his trench coat pocket a Swiss hat he'd bought in Basle, rammed it on his head and slid down out of sight as he started the engine.

Mencken waited until he saw the police bringing out his men, wrists handcuffed behind their backs. More cars with only a driver had arrived. His captured men were bundled inside the vehicles. Mencken had no worry that he would be betrayed – he'd been careful to ensure that none of these men knew he was driving a Renault.

500

As the convoys drove off he cruised slowly round the park towards the Château d'Ouchy. Norton had given him explicit instructions he was not to be contacted, not that Mencken had any idea what he looked like. But he had been told Norton would be using the name Dr Glen Fleming. He'd have to phone him, warn him quickly.

The Zurcher Kredit Bank was open for business when Tweed arrived in the Espace with Amberg alongside him. Paula, Newman, Ives and Butler were travelling with him. In the rear of the vehicle Marler sat with the projector and the rest of his equipment.

In the station wagon following close behind were Cardon, guarding Joel Dyson, and Pete Nield who was driving. Before leaving the Château d'Ouchy for the short drive to the bank Tweed had spoken to Dyson, making no bones about the position he was in.

'Cardon has a gun, won't hesitate to use it if you make one wrong move. But more likely, we'd put you aboard an aircraft for Washington at Cointrin Airport, Geneva.'

Watching the little man closely, Tweed had seen a flicker of triumph in Dyson's shifting eyes. Joel Dyson clearly knew Europe well, knew the lines of communication by air travel. There was no better way of subduing a man than by raising his hopes and then dashing them.

'Of course,' Tweed went on, 'there are no direct flights to Washington from Geneva. So Cardon would escort you aboard a flight from Cointrin to Zurich. Then you'd be put aboard the first non-stop flight for Washington. A phone call would be made so certain people would wait at Dulles Airport for you to disembark. Something wrong, Dyson? You've gone pale as a ghost . . .'

Amberg nodded to the guard at the entrance to the bank. As Marler came inside carrying his equipment the guard stopped him to examine what he was carrying.

501

'Do not worry, Jules,' Amberg called out over his shoulder. 'That gentleman is with me, as are the people behind him.'

Obeying Tweed's instructions, Amberg took everyone first to his private office, telling his secretary he must on no account be disturbed. Leaving the others inside the spacious room, Tweed accompanied Amberg with Newman and Paula to the vault where the Swiss opened his private box. Inside were two familiar-looking canisters. Was this really the end of their long journey, Tweed wondered as they returned to the private office.

In their absence Marler had drawn the curtains over the windows. After turning on the lights he had assembled the projector, had erected the viewing screen, had placed on the same desk the American tape recorder so he could synchronize viewing and listening.

He had removed a number of chairs from a boardroom table, arranging them in short rows like a makeshift cinema. He took the canisters from Amberg while Tweed personally made sure the door was securely locked.

Paula sat in the front row with Tweed next to her. Beyond Tweed sat Amberg with Barton Ives on his other side. In the row behind them sat a nervous Joel Dyson flanked by Newman and Cardon. The third row was occupied in the centre by Pete Nield, his Walther in his hand, and Butler. While Marler was fiddling with his machines Nield tapped Dyson on the shoulder with the muzzle of his Walther.

'Just to remind you you're never alone,' he informed the photographer genially.

'Ready to go,' Marler called out in a neutral tone as he switched out the lights.

A harsh white light appeared on the blank screen. Tweed could hear the tape reel whirring. Then, sharp as crystal, the images began to appear . . .

* * *

502

A one-storey log cabin in a forest clearing. A short, powerfully built man in a windcheater, open at the top, exposing his thick neck, struggling with a girl with long blonde hair. One hand gripped her hair, the other shoved her in the small of the back. She was screaming at the top of her voice and Paula gritted her teeth.

The man pushed her inside the log cabin, both faces were very visible before they disappeared into the cabin. The hard crack of the door being slammed shut. But they could still hear her screaming even with the shutters closed over the windows. Her screams stopped suddenly. Silence.

Now Paula could only hear the whirring of the machines behind her. Why did the silence seem even more awful than what they had seen so far? She was startled when the stocky man emerged by himself, closed the door, locked it, tossed the key on the roof. Why?

'Oh, my God, no!' she whispered to herself.

The answer to her question was horrifically clear. Smoke was drifting out from behind a shuttered window. Almost at once it burst into flames. The camera zoomed in for a close-up of the killer. A look of sadistic satisfaction. Sweat streamed off his face.

The camera now showed the man full length. He appeared to be staring straight at the lens. Snatching a gun from his belt, he moved closer. Paula flinched back in her seat. Her hand clenched as the whole cabin seared into a flaming inferno. The girl left inside would be incinerated.

The loud crackle and roar of the huge fire made the man pause, look briefly at the dying cabin. Gun in hand, the man turned again towards the camera, began advancing towards it, his famous face again so clear, identifiable . . .

The screen went blank, the white glare returned, vanished as Marler switched off the machines. The audience

503

sat as though frozen. The only sound was the click of Marler switching on lights. Paula blinked, glanced at Tweed, at Ives. It was difficult to decide which man looked grimmer.

It was Tweed who broke the silence. He leaned forward to speak to Ives across Amberg.

'Now you have your evidence. That was Bradford March, President of the United States.' He turned round, looked at Joel Dyson whose pouched lips were quivering.

'You took those pictures. Don't argue with me. I just want a simple answer. Who was the girl – the victim?'

'His secret girl friend. Cathy Willard, daughter of the San Francisco newspaper magnate.'

'So, well-heeled,' Ives commented.

'Oh, a very wealthy family. I heard later it was called an accident. She got herself shut in the cabin. The weather was cold, so she had a log fire' – Dyson was reverting to his normal loquacious self, Newman thought, as the story continued – 'a spark jumps out, sets fire to the rug and *whoosh!* the whole place goes up. Windows shuttered so she can't get out that way.'

'Sounds as though you wrote that version yourself,' Newman said cynically.

'No! But that's the way I heard they told it . . .'

'You have your evidence, Ives,' Tweed repeated, interrupting Dyson. 'It follows a similar pattern, doesn't it?'

'It does indeed. You see, March was a hick from the boondocks. It flattered his ego to make it with well-educated and wealthy women. Now you have your answer to the weird question – who would a wealthy woman driving in the dark across lonely country stop for? A man standing in the headlights of his brown Cadillac, a well-known Senator running for the White House, his mug plastered on billboards along every state highway. Maybe he pretended his car had broken down. They'd feel so safe with Senator Bradford March. It hit me suddenly that I'd found my serial killer – six women slaughtered. I have to take this film, this tape back to Washington.'

'They'll kill you thirty minutes after you leave the plane,' Newman warned.

'I have a powerful friend. He'll meet me at Dulles Airport with a large entourage, smuggle me into his house. Then it's up to him.'

'I think we'd better come with you,' Tweed said.

'I'm not coming,' Dyson protested.

'You'll be held in cold storage in Britain. After you've made a statement describing what you saw when you made the film.' Tweed's manner was harsh. 'A sworn statement made before a Swiss lawyer. That or come with us to Washington.'

'I'm not sure ethically I can release these items,' Amberg asserted.

'Ethically?' Tweed stared at the banker. 'You have to be joking. If you'd handed these over to me earlier think of how many lives would have been saved. Why did you hang on to them? You'd watched this film on your own much earlier, hadn't you?'

'Yes. When I saw what was on it I realized my own life was in danger . . .'

'So, ethically,' Tweed rasped, 'you kept quiet. If those are ethics I'll do without them. Amberg, from now on you had better shut up – if you want to stay alive. . . .'

52

The man with long shaggy grey hair peered over his half-moon glasses at the entrance to the Zurcher Kredit Bank. Norton was too smart to sit in the car he'd used to follow the Tweed group from the Château d'Ouchy. The rush-hour traffic had helped to mask his presence behind Nield's station wagon following the familiar Espace. He was standing in front of a book-shop, pretending to study a volume he had bought at random.

Norton, staying at the Château d'Ouchy, had watched Tweed having breakfast from his corner table, seated by himself. He was confident that the transformation in his appearance would save him from recognition – and so it had turned out.

Called to the phone, Norton had left his breakfast to take the call in his room.

'Mencken here,' the urgent voice had begun.

'I told you not to call except in case of a major crisis.'

'Which is what I'm dropping in your lap. All our troops have been rounded up, taken away in cars. Official . . .'

Which was Mencken's cautious way of saying 'police' over the phone.

'I'm glad everything is going so well. Thank you so much for calling . . .'

For Norton it was a panic situation, but Norton, ex-FBI, never panicked. He had created the core of Unit One when Senator Bradford March had offered him a large salary as his personal chief of security. It was Norton who had organized the attempts to kill Barton Ives before

Ives had fled to Europe. Norton had proceeded methodically.

He paid his hotel bill, put his bag in the hired Renault and returned to the dining-room. Five minutes later he watched Tweed and his companions leaving. Later he was ready to follow them in his Renault to the Zurcher Kredit Bank. Now he waited patiently, then saw Marler coming out with the same equipment he'd taken inside earlier – a long cylinder which could contain a viewing screen, a tape recorder, a canvas hold-all which was more tightly packed.

Pressed against the canvas was a circular shape about the size of a film canister. Turning over a page of his book, Norton shrewdly summed up the situation.

'If only I still had the troops . . .'

But he hadn't any troops left. They had all been taken by the police. Standing with the book in his hands Norton took a major decision. He couldn't report to March that he had failed – that would be committing suicide. Time to change sides again, to survive.

'That film March was raving to get his hands on must contain some deadly material. Otherwise why send such a large body of Unit One to Europe?' March was losing a battle – Norton's sixth sense, developed during his years as a top FBI agent, told him this.

He recalled a certain powerful senator he had once done a favour for, suppressing certain incriminating documents which would have ruined his career on the hill. Yes, it was time to contact Senator Wingfield, to offer him his services again. For a substantial fee . . .

Norton followed the Espace and the station wagon and was not surprised when the two vehicles entered the car park at the Château d'Ouchy. Parking his car near where the boats left for Evian in France, he walked back to the hotel. He strolled into reception just in time to hear Tweed giving instructions to the girl behind the counter.

'We shall be leaving today. Could you please make up the bill for myself and Miss Grey. No hurry. We'll be here for lunch . . .'

Which gave Norton time to clear up a loose end. Mencken. Norton was very careful about clearing up loose ends. He was not going to risk Mencken reaching Washington first – maybe even telling March how all the failures had been Norton's fault.

Returning to his car, he crammed a Swiss hat on his head, pulled it well down over his forehead. On the seat beside him, next to the mobile phone, rested a walking stick he had also purchased. Picking up the mobile phone he dialled Mencken's mobile phone number, hoping he was within range.

'Yes, who is it?' Mencken's voice demanded after a long wait.

'Norton. Where are you? We have to meet, urgently. To make future plans.'

'I'm halfway between Ouchy and Vevey. Away from the activity.'

'Very wise. Everything is quiet here now. But you are right – it would be wise to keep away from the town. As you drive along the lakeside road towards Vevey there is a point where the road turns away from the lake. By the edge of the lake there is a small wood near the path continuing along the lakeside. You noticed this? Good. I will meet you there in three-quarters of an hour. Best to make sure your car is hidden just off the path. And I did say it was urgent.'

'Understood,' Mencken replied tersely.

In his room at the Château d'Ouchy Tweed was giving his own urgent instructions to his whole team. Barton Ives

508

listened as he spoke briskly. Action this day, thought Paula.

'All of us – except Philip Cardon, who is guarding Joel Dyson in his room – are driving direct to Cointrin Airport, Geneva. From there we catch a flight to London. Which puts us on the spot to catch the afternoon Concorde flight to Washington non-stop.' Tweed looked at Ives. 'I do know Senator Wingfield, met him while attending a security conference in Washington, but are you certain you can trust him?'

'Wingfield,' Ives assured him, 'was born and raised a patriot. Not many of them about. That doesn't mean to say he has the track record of a saint – how else would he get to the position of great power he occupies?'

'You mean he can be ruthless?' Paula suggested.

'Maybe that's exactly what I do mean. But this horrific situation kinda suggests ruthless measures. I have phoned him,' he told Tweed. 'He's expecting me, with the evidence, but I omitted to tell him you'd be along too.'

'Thank God for that,' Newman said vehemently. 'Before we land at Dulles I want to radio ahead, hire several cars. I strongly urge that along with Butler, Nield and Marler, I go aboard Concorde as though I've nothing to do with you.'

'What danger could there be to you guys?' queried Ives.

'We have all seen that diabolical film which could wreck the entire government of the United States. I foresee that very strong measures will be taken to see that does not happen.' Newman looked at Tweed. 'This trip is going to take some organization . . .'

'All dealt with,' Paula interjected. 'Tweed told me some time ago to prepare for this contingency. Flights are booked, tickets waiting to be collected at airports. I'm wearing my skates, Bob.' She turned to Tweed. 'We take the film and the tape with us, then?'

'We do – to show Wingfield. Marler brings his equipment with him to save time. I want a quick in-and-out trip.'

'Preferably coming out alive,' Newman warned.

'What about Joel Dyson?' Paula interjected again. 'I've booked tickets on a separate flight from Geneva to London for Cardon and Dyson.'

'Where, after arriving, he will escort Dyson to a safe house. Where Howard is,' Tweed added.

'And what do I do with this?' enquired Marler, lifting up a second hold-all. 'With the weapons you've taken off us it's jolly heavy.'

As though on cue, there was a knock on the door. Newman jumped up, unlocked and opened it cautiously. He said, 'Wait a minute,' closed and relocked the door before he handed an envelope to Tweed.

'A Swiss in a business suit,' he reported.

Tweed opened the envelope, scanned the letter, nodded.

'It's from Arthur Beck. Among the men picked up was one with a suitcase containing twenty million dollars. He had experts open it and they defused a thermite bomb inside. That detective outside is to collect the weapons. We can hardly try to board an aircraft carrying them . . .'

'What about Gaunt, Eve and Jennie?' Newman asked when he had handed the hold-all to the Swiss and closed the door.

'I had a word with Gaunt before we came up,' Tweed went on. 'He's changed his mind about trying to identify who assassinated Amberg in Cornwall. Maintains it's now a hopeless task – at least that's what he said. He's driving back to Basle with Eve and Jennie. Remember, he berthed his yacht, cabin cruiser – call it what you will – the *Mayflower III* on the Rhine at Basle. He's sailing back to Padstow.'

'With Eve as well as Jennie?' Paula queried.

'So he said.'

510

'I find that curious, very strange,' she commented.

'So do I. But as soon as we get back from Washington that's where we're off to. Padstow. We still have to track down who committed mass murder at Tresillian Manor and why. To say nothing of who pushed that poor servant girl, Celia Yeo, off the top of High Tor . . .'

Marvin Mencken was excited as he sat behind the wheel of his Renault with the window open. As instructed, he had parked the car off the road inside a copse. Invisible to traffic passing along the road, it was close to the footpath running by the lakeside.

Mencken was excited because for the first time he was going to meet the mysterious Norton face to face. He had never liked taking orders from someone he'd not even recognize if he sat next to him in a diner.

Despite the sunshine it was a raw cold day. Mencken kept the engine ticking over so he could turn up the heaters full blast. When it became stuffy he had lowered the automatic window. He also took precautions – protruding from under a cushion on the passenger seat was the butt of a 9-mm. Luger.

He stiffened as he heard the click-clack of heels approaching, then relaxed when he realized it had to be a girl. He caught a glimpse of her as she passed along the footpath towards Vevey. A tall good-looking blonde. Mencken sighed. He had been so busy he hadn't had time to indulge in his favourite form of relaxation with a girl.

The elderly Swiss man with one of their funny hats trudged slowly along the promenade towards him. From under the hat a lot of untidy shaggy grey hair protruded. Perched on his nose was a pair of those weird glasses looking like a couple of half-moons.

The old character walked leaning on a stick, staring out at the lake. Probably came this same walk every day if the weather was OK. Bored as hell with life. Mencken promised himself a lot of fun before he ever got into that state. He put a cigarette in his mouth as the old man was turning on to the footpath. In the next second Norton rammed the muzzle of an HP35 Browning automatic against Mencken's chest through the open window, pulled the trigger. The sound of the shot was muffled by the thick scarf round Mencken's neck which fell over his chest. His head dropped forward.

Norton's gloved hand reached in through the window. He extracted the portion of the unlit cigarette Mencken's teeth had bitten through, dropped it into undergrowth. Opening the door, a wave of foetid heat swept into his face. He quickly shoved the body over sideways on to the floor, grabbed hold of the Luger, pressed the button to shut the automatic window, closed the door.

There was no one about, no traffic in sight when he first hurled the Luger way out into the lake and followed it by throwing the Browning in the same direction. A glance at the car before he left showed him that the windows were already steaming up, masking the view of the corpse even if someone peered in. He had already phoned Senator Wingfield and, with luck, he'd be aboard a flight for Washington before Mencken's body was even discovered. Yes, you must tie up loose ends.

53

Senator Wingfield had operated the projector screening the film himself. When he'd seen who starred in the horror of the burning log cabin he was glad he'd taken this precaution. His audience in the Chevy Chase study – the banker and the elder statesman – had sat in stunned silence through the viewing, listening to the girl's agonized screaming.

Wingfield switched on the lights, quickly packed film and tape away in the canisters. The banker reacted first in a hoarse voice.

'My God! I need a drink. Bourbon . . .'

Wingfield, a rare drinker, joined his companions with a stiff bourbon, seated again at the table. The statesman cleared his throat, spoke in a controlled tone.

'Well, now we know the worst. And if I had to dream up a nightmare scenario I couldn't have come up with anything to touch this.'

'And he's still adding to the deficit,' the banker reminded them, for something to say.

'He's also not taking any action to counter the threat from the East,' the statesman commented.

'Kids' stuff,' Wingfield snapped. 'Compared with what we have seen. I ran it through before you arrived. This is a national crisis. March can't be allowed to sit in the Oval Office any longer. I've taken the most difficult decision of my whole life.'

'Which is?' enquired the statesman.

'An ex-FBI man called Norton has arrived in

Washington. I knew him years ago. March has announced he's flying down South tomorrow. I've given Norton certain orders. A serial murderer in the White House – calls for drastic action.'

'How did you get hold of that terrible film?' asked the banker.

'Sent here by the very cautious special FBI agent Barton Ives. A messenger delivered it – together with a highly detailed report on the six serial murders never solved in certain Southern states. Damning evidence against Bradford March.'

'Why very cautious?' enquired the statesman with a quizzical expression since he'd guessed the answer.

'Because Ives is somewhere in Washington hiding. I doubt I'll ever track him down. And in his letter he says Tweed, a top security officer from Britain, will be calling on me. I remember Tweed – the kind of man you don't forget. He is the one who eventually obtained the film and tape.'

'What the hell are we going to do?' the banker asked in a desperate tone.

'I can't imagine you doing anything. Someone has to take the responsibility for initiating drastic action. Guess I'm elected. I'm using Norton. I met him secretly early this morning. He has his instructions. The President is due to fly south today from Andrews Air Force Base.'

'What does that mean?' the banker asked, showing a great degree of nervousness.

'Sure you want to know?' Wingfield fired back.

'The Senator is more than capable of handling the problem,' the statesman said emphatically. 'Remember how the John F. Kennedy situation was solved when his domestic policies were going wildly wrong.'

'I don't think I want to know any more about this,' said the banker, draining his glass. 'Time I got back to my desk . . .'

'What about this Norton?' the statesman queried when he was alone with Wingfield. 'He could know too much for your health.'

'I've thought about that too. We don't have to worry about Mr Norton. He's a top pro, bought and paid for to do the job. But I don't delude myself I've bought a tight mouth. Arrangements have been made. Just wait for this afternoon . . .'

In the Oval Office President Bradford March was checking his shave in a mirror – got to be smart when you're making speeches to the people. Sara came in without knocking. March grinned as he turned towards her.

'Tell me I look OK for the trip.'

'You look OK, but I think you ought to cancel this trip.' She was talking at machine-gun rate. 'I've heard plenty of rumours someone high up is gunning for you. Dallas all over again is the word . . .'

'Crap! Now I have Unit One pros guarding me. I've even got a Unit One crew to fly Air Force One from Andrews. Time I talked to the folks, whipped up the support with some of the most rabble-rousing stuff of my career.'

'Don't let anyone hear you call them rabble,' Sara warned.

'That's what they are.' He gave his famous grin. 'Look, I should know, that's where I came from. I know the crap that gets them throwing their hats in the air.'

'Listen to me.' Sara felt she had to make one more effort. 'Our watchers reported there was a meeting of the Three Wise Men an hour ago. At Wingfield's place again . . .'

'That old political hack . . .'

'This time both his guests arrived with an FBI guard –

515

who surrounded each man as he dashed from his limo into the house.'

'So they're running scared. Is *my* limo ready to take me to Andrews?'

Norton left the President's plane carrying a case which was supposed to contain explosive-detection equipment. As he descended the staircase he blinked in the strong sunlight. Dressed in an orange boiler suit zipped up to the neck – it carried a badge U1, Unit One – he made himself resist the temptation to hurry away from Air Force One.

He was the last maintenance man to leave the aircraft and a motorcade was approaching. The TV crews were already penned up by guards who were careful to let the technicians have a clear view of the aircraft's staircase March would walk up. The President was very publicity-conscious.

Underneath his boiler suit Norton wore a grey business suit. Earlier, arriving at the checkpoint, he had passed through without trouble – simply showing his Unit One card issued before he'd left for Europe weeks ago.

He had prowled the maintenance shed looking for a mechanic close to his build and height wearing one of the distinctive orange suits. Approaching him from behind, Norton had put him out of action by using a tyre iron on the back of his skull.

'Sleep well, baby,' he had whispered after taking off the boiler suit and stuffing the man inside a large waste bin.

In this way, and by again flourishing his Unit One card, he had boarded the plane, choosing a moment when most of the maintenance crew had left. Now, out of sight of the crowds, which were already roaring with

516

delight, he stripped off the boiler suit, stuffed it into the waste bin on top of its unconscious owner, smoothed out the creases of his grey suit and hurried out of the main entrance, again showing his card.

He had no hesitation in hurrying, wearing only a suit and no coat in the bitter raw cold which gripped Washington despite the sun. Again he heard the crowd roar, this time more prolonged. As he walked towards where he had parked his car Norton could picture the scene.

Bradford March climbing the steps of the mobile staircase slowly, pausing at the top. Then swinging round suddenly and hoisting both arms with clenched fists high in the air. Another louder roar from the crowd. Norton smiled to himself grimly as he climbed behind the wheel of his car and drove off. He parked his car a good half-mile away from the air base, positioning it so he could look towards Andrews.

Air Force One suddenly appeared, climbing steeply as it flew away from the parked car. Norton was peering out of the open window as he heard the scream of its jets, saw the diminishing silver dart ascend to five thousand feet.

He was wearing wrapround tinted glasses so he wasn't blinded by the sudden brilliant flash. There was a rolling boom as the plane disintegrated and tiny fragments of the fuselage spun out of a cloud of black smoke which had disfigured the duck-egg blue of the sky. Norton, who had kept his engine running, eased the car out of the side road and drove on to his house in Georgetown. While serving with the FBI he had been attached to the Explosives Division.

'Well, you haven't lost your touch,' he said aloud.

He used his remote-control device to open the door of the garage located under his house. Having parked the car, he came out, closed the door, mounted the steps to his front door. In the house opposite a woman looked out of her first-floor window, saw him climbing the steps. She was not surprised – her neighbour, security officer for some large international bank, often spent long periods away from home. She left the window to go downstairs.

Norton held his front door key in his hand when he got to the stoop. He inserted the key in the lock, frowned when it seemed difficult to turn. For once Norton's nose for danger deserted him – his mind was on what he had achieved out at Andrews. He turned the key and shards of the fragmenting front door pierced his body. The force of the explosion was so great it hurled his mangled body straight across the road. Peering down out of her shattered window, the woman opposite saw Norton's crumpled form lying on her own stoop.

54

Tweed never did keep his appointment to meet Senator Wingfield. He heard the news of the President's plane blowing up soon after take-off from a bell-boy in his hotel, saw it on television with Newman, Paula and Barton Ives in his hotel room.

'Time to leave America while we're still alive,' he said, using remote control to switch off the TV. 'You'd best come with us, Ives.'

'Reckon I had,' Ives agreed. 'They play rough over here – and I told you Wingfield was a patriot, a *ruthless* patriot. But can we make it? They could be coming for us now . . .'

'So we put into operation Plan Omega,' Tweed told

him. 'Worked out in advance for just this situation by Bob Newman and Paula – although we never anticipated a resort to assassination. Ives, you just stick with us and remember from now on your name is Chuck Kingsley when you check in at the airport.'

'Dulles?'

'No, not Dulles. That's a key part of Omega. I have to call Marler's room, let him know we're leaving within thirty minutes. No time to explain any more . . .'

They were driving by a devious route which could have taken them to Dulles Airport. Newman was at the wheel of the rented Lincoln, Tweed was beside him while Paula sat in the back next to Ives. They hadn't hit rush hour but there was traffic. Paula kept glancing back through the rear window.

'Those two black sedans which started tailing us as soon as we left the hotel are still there. With a lot of men inside I don't like the look of.'

'Can you see the three Chevrolets?' Tweed asked Newman.

'Yes, they're coming up behind us now, appeared out of side streets. Marler in the green Chevy, Butler in the white, Nield in the brown Chevy. Marler checked the map of the city with care, decided where they'd make their play. Any moment now those characters in their black sedans are in for a shock . . .'

The leading black sedan was driven by an ugly bald-headed thug, surprisingly nicknamed Baldy. He had three armed men as passengers and the twin sedan behind him carried four more armed men. As they arrived close to a complex intersection Baldy saw Newman suddenly turn right. He was about to follow when a green Chevrolet swung in front of him, stopped as its engine stalled. Baldy swore and braked so abruptly the sedan behind rammed him.

'Get off the friggin' road,' Baldy yelled as Marler got out of his car, strolled back to him.

'I say, old chap,' Marler drawled. 'Awfully sorry and all that. The old engine stalled, couldn't help stopping. These Yank chariots aren't much cop.'

'I said get off . . .'

Baldy broke off as a white Chevrolet stopped alongside and Butler got out, shaking his fist, shouting at the top of his voice.

'You want to learn to drive, buddy. Now we've missed the goddam lights . . .'

In his rear-view mirror Baldy saw a brown Chevrolet stopped behind the second sedan so his back-up couldn't move. What the hell was going on? Marler strolled back to his car while Butler continued shouting. After two attempts Marler let the engine start, waved his hand over his shoulder, drove on. Baldy rammed his foot down to catch the green lights, turned right, saw no sign of Newman's Lincoln.

'We'll catch the bastards at Dulles,' he informed his passengers. 'We know they booked aboard the London flight . . .'

Still working to the Omega Plan, Newman drove to a Hertz office near a cab rank. He was handing in the Lincoln when Marler, Butler and Nield arrived to hand in their rented cars. Two cabs took them to the railway station where they caught the Metroliner to New York.

'How did you work that one?' Ives asked Tweed as the train sped through the afternoon. 'We were dead ducks.'

'A small precaution. Paula has booked us in our own names on two flights out of Dulles Airport from Washington to London. Also in our own names she's booked us on two more flights from New York to London – in case they check. In fact, we'll be aboard a British Airways flight leaving Kennedy at 7p.m. Seats all booked in assumed names. We use our false passports made in the Engine Room – so that's why you're Chuck Kingsley.'

'What made you foresee we might be targets?'

'We know about the six serial murders. Above all, Wingfield knows we've seen the film which could destroy America's reputation. So all witnesses have to be eliminated. I realized that as soon as I heard Bradford March's plane had been blown up. It gave me the measure of Wingfield's ruthlessness – something I couldn't be sure of beforehand.'

'And those three different-coloured Chevies?'

'Newman sent a radio message renting them, plus the Lincoln. He specified the colours to make it easy for him to spot the cars if an emergency arose. It did.'

'What are you going to do?' Paula asked Ives.

'Stay in Europe, I guess. To stay alive. Rather like my new monicker, Chuck Kingsley. Think I'll keep it. And the way things are developing in the world I guess I'll build up a security agency. I'm sure you folks will be glad to get home, have a long rest.'

'We're going straight off the plane to a place called Padstow,' Tweed said. 'There was a mass murder down in Cornwall, Paula nearly got killed, and I know who committed that cold-blooded crime.'

55

A wild gale was raging as they walked slowly, leaning into the wind, along the road in Padstow leading from the Hotel Metropole to the centre of Padstow town. Paula clung to Newman's arm while ahead of them Tweed marched with a brisk step.

'Look, the Old Custom House,' Paula shouted to make herself heard. 'Where we used to have a drink. How marvellous to see it again, to be back in England.'

'I think that's where Tweed is heading for,' Newman replied. 'No, what's he up to now?'

Tweed had paused, gestured towards the inner harbour, entered the phone box he'd used on their previous visit. From inside he pointed towards the Old Custom House, mimicked a man drinking.

Huge waves were crashing against the outer wall, hitting the stone with a tremendous crash, hurling water and spray high into the air. Paula tugged at Newman's arm to make him stop at the point where Tweed had paused. Moored to a wall inside the inner harbour the *Mayflower III* rocked up and down, but was safe from the fury beyond the closed gate of the dam.

'Gaunt must have arrived back,' Paula shouted. 'Let's get inside out of this tumult. I wonder who Tweed is phoning . . .?'

Inside the box Tweed had dialled the number of police HQ in Launceston on the far side of the moor – a distance beyond it, in fact. Responding to his request, he was at once put through to Chief Inspector Roy Buchanan.

'Have you arranged what I asked you to at Tresillian Manor?' Tweed asked.

'Since you called me from London Airport I've been run off my feet organizing your mad – not to say macabre – idea.'

'You want the criminal who committed that hideous crime? It needs shock tactics to smoke this murderer out. Go to the manor at once. Keep out of sight and hide your cars. I'll be there with the suspects as soon as I've rounded them up.'

'I don't know why I've agreed to this insanity . . .'

'Because you've got nowhere solving the mass murder yourself . . .'

Hurrying with Newman into the shelter of the warm bar Paula stopped abruptly. The scene was pure *déjà-vu*.

Gaunt sat in one of the large leather armchairs on the elevated level facing the long bar. He was holding court, waving a large hand at his audience. Beside him sat Eve Amberg, wearing a white polo-necked sweater which did nothing to conceal her rounded breasts. She also wore a grey pleated skirt and grey pumps. A suede riding jacket was folded on the arm of her chair as she sipped her drink.

Facing her at a three-quarter angle to Paula was Jennie, listening while she fingered her pearls. A string of pearls? Why did they disturb Paula? The fourth member of the group, seated next to Jennie, was a surprise for Paula. Amberg sat very erect in his black business suit, his slick black hair gleaming. Didn't he ever wear anything else but black – and what was he doing in Padstow, Paula wondered.

'We had a whale of a trip down the Rhine in the *Mayflower*, Amberg,' Gaunt boomed. 'Kept going through the night. Advantage of being able to get by on four hours' sleep – I can. Eve took over the wheel when I needed a bit of kip. Make a good team, you and I, don't we, Eve?'

'Well, we got here in one piece,' she said unenthusiastically. 'Rounding Land's End in this gale wasn't frankly my idea of a whale of a time.'

'Nonsense! You revelled in every second of the voyage. Put a sparkle in your lovely eyes . . .'

'Isn't it illegal to sail on the Rhine at night?' asked Amberg.

Paula had the impression it was the first time the banker had spoken. He sat with his drink in front of him untouched.

'Oh, bureaucratic regulations,' Gaunt snorted contemptuously. 'Never get anywhere if you don't display

523

initiative. Not in this world run by those fat-cat commissioners in Brussels.' He looked at the door. 'I say! Look who's turned up. Your favourite boy friend, Eve.'

'Why don't you shut your trap?' she snapped.

Newman waved briefly, took Paula to the bar, ordered Scotch for himself, a glass of white wine for Paula. He perched on a stool, whispered to her as she sat next to him.

'I've no idea what Tweed is up to. Best to wait until he arrives.'

'I can't fathom the relationship of those three,' she said quietly. 'I mean Gaunt, Eve and Jennie. Something very odd is going on . . .'

Tweed walked in when they were sipping their drinks. He ordered mineral water, stood by the bar. He gave them the order as he picked up his drink.

'Let's join them over there. A few questions I'd like to ask. Paula, you did park the Land-Rover by the harbour earlier?'

'Out of sight, round the corner. As you suggested.'

'So, we're all back where we started from,' Tweed greeted Gaunt's group amiably. He sat perched on the arm of Eve's armchair, staring diagonally across at the banker. 'Except for you, Amberg. What brings you to this remote part of the world?'

'I have come to see where Julius died. I felt it was the least I could do. Then I wish to collect his body so it can be returned to Switzerland for decent burial.'

'You did say Julius?'

There was a sound of breaking glass. Jennie had knocked over her wine. She glanced across at the banker, who was ashen-faced, then spoke in a strangely remote voice to the bartender who had rushed across with a cloth to mop up the spilt liquid.

'I'm so sorry. That really was frightfully careless of me. Do be careful not to hurt yourself – there are pieces of broken glass you can hardly see.'

'Which is why I brought over this wash-leather. If you would just sit back and relax. Bring you another glass on the house . . .'

Paula was studying Tweed, expecting him to show sympathy to Jennie who was embarrassed by the accident. Instead, he sat very still, looking at each person seated round the table, as though assessing them one by one. Paula was conscious of a sudden change in the hitherto peaceful atmosphere. Now she sensed it was fraught with tension. If only she could identify the source. Tweed waited until the waiter had finished cleaning up, had brought a fresh glass and placed it in front of Jennie.

'I think I know why everyone's here,' he began, his manner and his tone authoritative. 'It's understandable that no one is anxious to go back to Tresillian Manor, considering the tragedy. That being so, the sooner we all do go there the better. It's called laying ghosts.'

'Bloody sauce!' Gaunt protested. 'In case you've forgotten, I happen to own the place.'

'But last night after you'd landed here in the harbour you took Eve and Jennie to the Metropole where you stayed the night. Bracing yourself for going back today. I can understand it,' he repeated.

'How on earth do you know all this?' asked Gaunt in a very subdued tone.

'I checked the hotel register, then had a word with the Harbour Master. Because it's your house you're the one most likely to be affected. No more protests. Drink up and let's get the show on the road.'

Paula glanced swiftly round the assembled company. She saw Jennie fingering her pearls, twisting her mouth, then, aware of Paula's scrutiny, she gave a cold smile. Eve sat calmly. Amberg had an expression which could have been bewilderment or controlled fury. Gaunt sat back in his chair, staring into the distance and she couldn't read his expression.

One thing she did know. By sheer force of personality Tweed had dominated them, persuaded them to do his bidding. He said one more thing before he beckoned to Newman and Paula and marched out of the bar.

'I insist that our Land-Rover leads the way. No attempt to overtake me, Gaunt. Let's get moving . . .'

The gale had reached a new pitch of frenzy on Bodmin Moor. Hunched over the wheel, with Paula by his side and Newman in a rear seat, Tweed drove the Land-Rover at high speed but within the limit, then slowed to turn off along the side road leading to Tresillian Manor.

Paula slid her hand inside her shoulder bag, gripped the .32 Browning in the special pocket. She had phoned Monica from Washington, and when they passed through Customs at London Airport Monica handed her the small cloth bag containing her gun.

'The gate's open,' she commented.

'That's Buchanan. I asked him to open it so we could not waste any time . . .'

He parked the Land-Rover at the foot of the long stone terrace in front of the house. They waited on the terrace for Gaunt to arrive in his BMW, Tweed met the car, held out his hand for the front door key.

'This is my house . . .' Gaunt began.

'The key. We're going in first.' Tweed looked at Jennie as she slowly stepped out of the car. 'You do want to know who killed them, don't you?'

'Why look at me?' she snapped back at him.

'Wait, everyone.' It was Eve, snug in her riding jacket, walking towards the stables at the side of the manor. She looked back at Gaunt. 'You said you'd look after Rusty, my beautiful mare.'

'Ned, a reliable chap, has come in every day, cleaned out her quarters, fed her, given her a trot over the moor.'

'I'll give you two minutes,' Tweed told her. 'We'll wait here on the terrace . . .'

Eve was as good as her word, returned in two minutes with a glowing smile for Gaunt.

'She's in beautiful condition, and so glad to see me.'

'We'll now all go inside,' Tweed announced.

Opening the heavy front door with the key, he strode inside the hall with the woodblock floor. With a firm tread he walked over to the closed dining-room door and looked back before he grasped the handle. Eve stood behind him, Jennie, looking grim, was close to her. Amberg came next, prodded forward by Newman.

Tweed flung open the door, strode quickly inside. The others followed and stopped dead in their tracks. A grotesque scene met their stunned gaze. Seven figures dressed in black men's suits were sprawled round the long table. Two were still seated, slumped across the table in pools of dark red blood. Four more, toppled out of their chairs, lay in more pools of blood on the floor. The ultimate macabre horror was at the head of the table – where Amberg had sat. This figure was bent over a broken-backed chair, its face eaten away by acid, skeletal bones like steel rods exposed, revealing the skull beneath the skin.

Epilogue

'The monster responsible for this obscene crime is in this room,' Tweed announced. 'She was seen in Padstow on the day of the mass murder – even though she was supposed to be in Zurich. Eight people – including the butler

527

– died. Add Helen Frey, Klara and Theo Strebel and she has coldly ended the lives of eleven human beings. Add Celia Yeo and the real postman . . .'

Jennie stifled a scream. Eve sucked in a deep breath and whipped a 6.35-mm. Beretta out of her jacket pocket. She aimed it point-blank at Tweed as Paula produced her Browning, pointed it at the widest target – Eve's chest.

'Pull that trigger,' Eve warned, 'and Tweed is dead. Very dead. Drop the bloody thing, you bitch.'

Her voice had changed, was a harsh growl, her eyes stared with a near-insane expression. Paula stood her ground as she snapped out a reply.

'Not that easy, Eve.' She lowered her aim. 'Shoot Tweed and you get bullets in your abdomen. It will take days for you to die in terrible agony.'

'Then we play it different, dear.' Eve's face seemed to be carved out of marble. 'I'm leaving this room. If anyone tries to stop me, Tweed is dead. If you all stay sensible – still – Tweed survives. Everyone except Tweed and Paula move away from the door . . .'

Newman grabbed Amberg, who seemed frozen with fear, by the arm and forced him further into the room. Gaunt and Jennie obeyed the order. Backing towards the open door, Eve kept her weapon, gripped in both hands, aimed at Tweed. Paula's Browning swivelled slowly, constantly aimed at its target.

Reaching the open door, Eve held the Beretta in one hand. With the other she slammed it shut as she stepped into the hall. As the door was closing she yelled out: 'First one who follows me is dead as a doornail . . .'

Paula was the first to react. She saw Eve dart past the windows of the dining-room, crouching low, heading for the stables. Running to the casement window, she flung it open and climbed outside. Instead of heading for the stables she ran to the Land-Rover, jumped into the seat behind the wheel. Tweed had left the key in the ignition. Men could be so careless.

She heard the clatter of hooves a second before switching on the engine. Newman was running towards her.

'Wait for me!'

'No time . . .!'

Paula shoved her Browning under the seat cushion beside her with one hand, driving in a semicircle with the other, driving towards the passage between manor and stables. She saw Eve on her horse, fleeing behind the manor, followed her. Beyond the stretch of rough grass extending away behind the manor Eve rode her horse through the gap in the firs on to the moor. Paula pressed her foot down, bracing her back against the seat, careering through the same gap . . .

Only a four-wheel-drive vehicle could have negotiated the rough rocky terrain of the ascending moor. Her target rode like the devil, titian hair streaming behind her in the fury of the gale. Grimly, Paula maintained her pursuit. This was personal: Eve had threatened to kill Tweed.

As Paula narrowed the gap between herself and the horsewoman, Eve turned several times in her saddle, fired the Beretta. Paula counted the rounds and knew when Eve's gun was empty. Not a single bullet had come close, not even penetrating her windscreen. Firing from a racing horse, Eve's self-control had finally cracked.

Paula suddenly realized Eve was heading for Five Lanes. She had a cottage there. High Tor loomed up ahead. As the cluster of whitewashed cottages came closer Paula saw a cream Jaguar parked outside one – Eve's hope of escape. She accelerated, came so close to the flying horse that Eve gave up all hope of using the Jaguar. Eve changed direction, plunged up a steep slope, heading for the summit of High Tor.

Paula drove up after her, had almost caught up with the flying horse when her right-hand front wheel mounted a boulder. She braked automatically as the vehicle tilted violently and she was hurled out to the left. She rolled like a parachutist landing, stopped, saw to her horror she was at the edge of the sheer abyss where the servant girl, Celia Yeo, had been hurled over.

Half-stunned by her fall, she saw the Land-Rover had righted itself, was standing four-square on its wheels. Then she saw Eve riding towards her, face twisted into an evil grimace of triumph. She was going to use the horse to kill Paula, its hooves hammering into her skull. On the verge of reining in her mare, the horse reacted with terror as it saw the drop. It reared up without warning. Paula stared as Eve left the saddle, was catapulted over the brink. She heard her long scream, saw her somersaulting body plunging down beyond the abyss, saw her head smash into a massive boulder, her arms jerk out sideways, then she was still, a broken corpse similar to that of Celia Yeo whom she had pushed over the same drop.

'The tableau in the dining-room was constructed of dummies with wigs,' Chief Inspector Buchanan explained as Paula drank sweetened tea. 'The blood was red oil-paint – nice and sticky. I enlisted the aid of a friend who worked at Madame Tussaud's Waxwork Museum before he retired. Most effective job.'

'But Amberg's face – or the dummy used to fake him. The face was also destroyed with acid.'

She looked round at all the people in the living-room at Tresillian Manor. Tweed, sitting close, with Newman near by. Amberg in a chair next to Newman, looking dazed. Jennie, gazing at the banker as though she couldn't believe what she saw.

'Yes, we used acid,' Buchanan went on. 'It exposed the metal struts inside so we painted them with red oil-paint.'

'It needed a powerful shock to crack Julius Amberg and

Eve,' Tweed explained, taking over. 'The tableau worked the oracle.'

'Julius Amberg? You mean Walter,' she said. 'Julius was killed in the massacre.'

'No, Walter was. That man sitting over there is Julius.'

'Identical twins,' Tweed went on. 'Julius has admitted the whole conspiracy while you were pursuing Eve. He viewed the film, listened to the tape Joel Dyson handed him for safe-keeping. He was frightened, but Eve, the driving force behind the whole thing, saw an opportunity to make a fortune – to blackmail Bradford March for twenty million dollars. Julius had been playing with the bank's money gambling in foreign currencies. He lost ten million. The other ten million was to keep them in luxury for the rest of their lives.'

'But where did Walter come in?' Paula asked.

'I said Julius was frightened – taking on the US President was a frightening thing. Eve came up with the solution. Walter, who knew nothing about the film, was persuaded to travel here, to impersonate Julius. They told him I was a specialist in securities, that I could tell Walter how to make a lot of money. But they also explained I only trusted Julius, who pretended to be ill. Walter was the scapegoat – they counted on the news of the fake Julius's death being broadcast as part of a sensational mass murder case. The guards who travelled with Walter were to ensure the secrecy of the meeting. With the news of Julius's death reaching President March they thought they'd be safe – that Joel Dyson would be the target.'

'What first made you suspicious?' she asked.

'Have some more tea,' Newman urged, refilling her cup.

After her grim experience on High Tor Paula had driven the Land-Rover back along the main road. Halfway to the manor she'd been met by police cars Buchanan had sent

531

out to find her, but she'd insisted on driving the rest of the way.

'Suspicious that the so-called Walter was Julius?' Tweed continued. 'First the acid – why destroy his face? To make true identification of the victim impossible. Then Eve kept going everywhere with Amberg. Her excuse – to get money out of him. A lawyer could have done the job. Also it would take strength to garrotte the two call-girls in Zurich – to the extent of nearly severing the head from the neck. At the swimming pool up at the Château Noir I noticed how fit and strong she was . . .'

'So she killed Helen Frey and Klara in that horrible way?'

'Yes. Eve was suspicious Julius had been seeking pleasure with other women. Hence her employing Theo Strebel, the detective, who tracked them down. Eve never took chances. She realized call-girls would know Julius better than any of his staff, might recognize him in Zurich.'

'I'd thought using the pearl garrotte meant a man,' Paula remarked.

'Eve visited each girl, offered her money not to see Julius again. Then showed them the pearls, said they were real and would they take them instead? She stepped behind them to fit the string round their throats, then pulled the wire supporting them with all her strength.'

'But what about Theo Strebel? He was shot.'

'She could hardly use the pearls on him. The significant factor was he knew Eve, so let her into his office without any inkling of danger. I also noticed that Eve had frequently used the name Walter – a little too often – to emphasize that it *was* Walter. An accumulation of small pointers made me focus on her.'

'And she was going to kill me,' Jennie said and shivered. 'She knew I had seen her in Padstow early on the morning of the massacre. She was the Shadow Man.'

'How do we know that?' Paula asked.

'Because,' Buchanan intervened, 'at Tweed's suggestion I came armed with a warrant to search her luggage at the Metropole. A phone call while you were chasing Eve – that *was* foolhardy – from my men in Padstow confirmed they'd found a large man's hat with a wide brim – and a cloak.'

'Hence the varying descriptions we got from different witnesses,' Tweed explained. 'Sometimes the Shadow Man was slim, sometimes well built. She used the cloak to change her appearance.'

'We also found the string of pearls in a secret compartment,' Buchanan added. 'There appears to be dried blood on the strong wire the pearls are looped on. Forensic will confirm, I'm sure.'

'So there *were* two interlocking jigsaws,' Paula commented.

'Yes, you've caught on,' said Tweed. 'The first was Joel Dyson taking that damning film of Bradford March killing his mistress then fleeing to Europe, handing one copy of film and tape to Monica, then flying on to Zurich to deposit the others with Julius. I've no doubt it was Dyson who intended to blackmail the President in due course, but Eve jumped in first. Without Dyson's actions there would have been no incriminating material. They triggered off the biggest man-hunt by March's thugs ever launched. The second jigsaw was Eve and Amberg taking over the role of blackmailers. One led to the other.'

'How do we know all this?'

Paula glanced round at the audience. Her gaze rested on Gaunt.

'Because,' Buchanan intervened again, 'after due warning that anything he said might be taken down and used as evidence, et cetera, Amberg admitted everything.'

533

'I shall be returning to Switzerland,' Julius said in his normal commanding tone.

'I don't think so,' Buchanan assured him. 'After the statement you made you will be charged as an accomplice to ten murders – all of which took place here. You ran the devil of a risk – taking on the President of the United States.'

'I was desperate. I was short of ten million of the bank's money. Maybe British prisons are less austere than Swiss.'

'I expect you're going to have a long opportunity to find that out,' Buchanan said unsympathetically.

'The tide's gone out. It's just a solid sandbank in the estuary,' said Paula.

'I hope you're packed,' said Tweed as they stood with Newman in Tweed's room at the Metropole. 'Incidentally, Cord Dillon is safely back behind his own desk in Langley – he's officially returned from a long leave. No one connects him with what happened. And I phoned Howard – while they rebuild our HQ we move into the communications centre further along Park Crescent. They say it will take eight months to rebuild – which means a year. The PM is talking to Howard each day, feels he got it all wrong.'

'He did,' Paula snapped.

'Better news from Washington,' Newman remarked. 'The newspapers report Jeb Calloway was sworn in as President the day we flew from New York. He's sending fresh troops to Europe to reinforce NATO. That should checkmate the crisis in the East. Middle East terrorists are rumoured to have put the bomb on March's plane.'

'That's Wingfield's propaganda machine gearing up,' Tweed commented cynically. 'There'll be conspiracy theories invented for ages just as there were after Kennedy's assassination. Let's get out of here as fast as we can.'

'Why the great hurry?' Paula enquired.

'The Squire – Gaunt – wanted us to have dinner with him at the Old Custom House. He feels a bit of an idiot the way Eve fooled him, used him as camouflage to distract attention from Walter, who was really Julius. And the PM has asked me to dinner at Downing Street, according to Howard.'

'You'll go, of course,' Paula teased him.

'Another bit of news Howard gave me. Commander Crombie's men, digging in the remains of the Park Crescent rubble, found my safe. It was moved along the Crescent to our communications centre. Monica said it was intact, opened it up, found the film and the tape in perfect condition. Oh, Bob, Dyson tricked you – said they were copies. What he delivered to you were the originals.'

'Well, I'll be damned!' Paula burst out. 'Everything we've gone through was unnecessary.'

'Was it?' Tweed queried. 'We've got rid of a psychopath who sat in the Oval Office. Would the PM have permitted that film and that tape to be sent to Washington? Never. March would have remained President. As it is, the film and the tape will remain classified material for the next thirty years. It was a classic case of Lord Acton's maxim. *Power tends to corrupt, and absolute power corrupts absolutely*.'